SAGA OF THE WINTER WITCH: BOOK ONE

NORTH STAR

AMELIA R. RIKSTAD

First paperback edition: December 1st, 2024

Interior Book Design by Amelia R. Rikstad
Cover Design Amelia R. Rikstad

Cover Illustration by Emily E. Jones
Illustrations on Pages 511 and 536 by Emily E. Jones
Emily's contact information:
Website: theartofemilye.com
Email: emilyeliseillustration@gmail.com
Instagram: @emily.e.draws
X: @EmilyE_Draws

Kringle Recipe by Erica Brown
of Sugar Struck Cookies
Instagram: @sugar_struck_cookies
Facebook: Sugar Struck

Files used to decorate this book by:
FreshCutsStudios

ByHanddrawntaste
DigiAndSVGDesigns4U
SVGInstantDOWNLOAD

Edited by Danielle Rikstad and Amelia Rikstad

ISBN: 9798218560294
Published by: Utopian Courier Press™

For more information, email:
theutopiancourier2020@gmail.com

BOOKS BY AMELIA R. RIKSTAD

Yours Truly, Della Coleman
Case One: The Grunch
Case Two: The Spirits

Saga of the Winter Witch
Book One: North Star

COMING SOON

SOTWW Book Two: Snowdrop

The Extraordinary Tale of the Man in the
Paisley Suit

YTDC: Case Three

For Papa

"THE WAR IS OVER. IT'S TIME TO GO HOME."

Dear Papa,

To be loved by a writer is to be immortalized in ink for eternity.

I have been keeping this secret for almost three years now. There were so many times I wanted to tell you about this world and these characters and all the little ways you've inspired me. I'm so glad I can finally do that.

When I sat down to write this book, I knew from the beginning it was a story of waking up every day and choosing family above all else. It was about two unlikely people—a finicky little Witch and a surly old werewolf—finding solace in one another. Ophelia needed a North Star, if you will. A protector. A guide. Someone to teach her about the world and how to weather it. Someone to lead her toward greatness. Someone who'd fight tooth and nail and make grave sacrifices just to see her make it out alive.

So I gave her a man modeled off my own North Star.

So much of myself is in Ophelia.

And so much of you is in Seamus.

I know you feel guilty for all the time you missed and all the sacrifices you made, but I want you to know how proud I am of all you've done for our country and how proud I am to call you my dad. You are the bravest man I know. I look up to you in so many ways.

Thank you for all you do for us.

The night I'm writing this, I sent you a silly little video that said, 'Do you think we're father-daughter in every universe?'

I hope this book proves we are.

Happy Birthday,
Millie

P.S. I'm sorry (not sorry) this book is so long.

CONTENTS

ALLE ÅRSTIDER

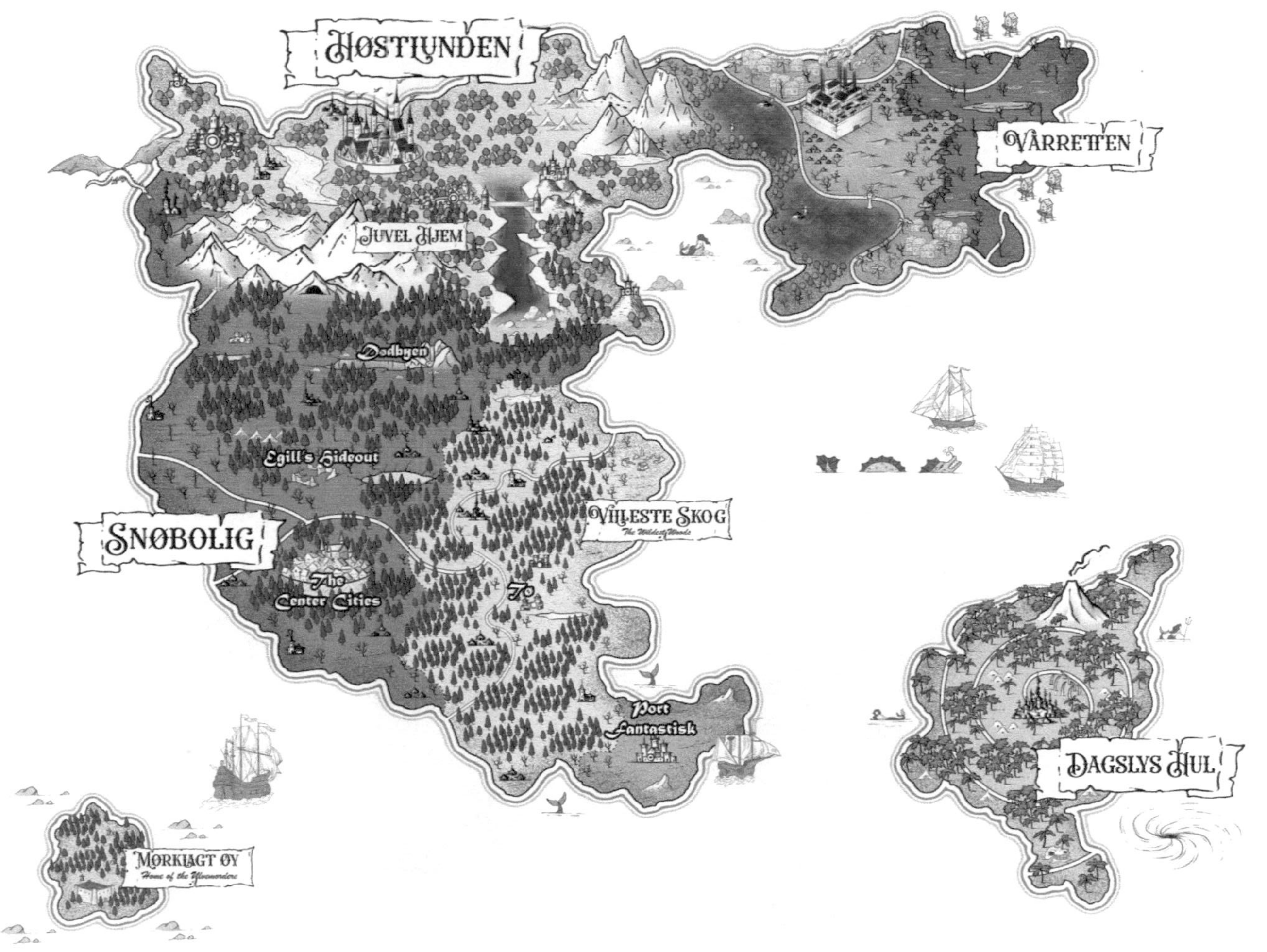

HØSTLUNDEN
VÅRRETTEN
JUVEL HJEM
Dødbyen
Egill's Hideout
SNØBOLIG
The Center Cities
VILLESTE SKOG
The Wildest Woods
Port Fantastisk
DAGSLYS HUL
MØRKLAGT ØY
Home of the Mironorders

1. Velkommen

CHAPTER ONE

VARULV

A trail of blood followed the wolf as it wove around densely packed evergreens, wondering where exactly it was.

Snow was still cascading all around it, but the flakes were lighter now. Most would see this as fortuitous, but the wolf had been hoping for a blizzard. A mere dusting of powder would not obscure the prints and crisp droplets of blood trailing behind him. It would not hide how his staggered paw prints eventually began to elongate—that the paws of a wolf had become frostbitten feet.

A blizzard would have.

Oh, how he wished there would've been a blizzard.

Then again, in his weakened state, a blizzard might have been the death of him.

The wolf, who was now a man, staggered through the forest, disoriented, hobbling along on two legs. He'd grown so used to four. Every shaking step sent searing pinpricks up his calves. He'd been running for days. If rest were an option, he would have found refuge miles back. However, a man on the run doesn't have the luxury of rest. There is only the fear of capture and how to evade it. Nothing else.

Even with the injuries he'd sustained, he could still hear *them* in the distance. He should've run faster in the beginning, but now, as his body tired, *they* were catching up to him. Every once in a while, he thought he could smell *their* putrid stink. However, after a panicked second, he realized the rancid smell was his own flesh on the verge of decay. There was little comfort in that.

His side ached worse than his legs as he pressed onward.

Using what little scraps of fabric still clinging to his body, he tried to staunch the flow of the ever-bleeding hole in his side. Some good that did. Footsteps would fade. Blood would linger. He grumbled to himself, tugging on his right earlobe out of anxious habit. The action made him wince. Words most would deem unsavory danced in his mind. It would take months for him to adjust to half his ear being gone and even longer to adjust to how the world had become muffled. Damn archers! He really hoped his ear was only clogged with dried blood, but just like the notion of rest, hope was a luxury scarcely available to him.

As such, a rush of hopelessness washed over him.

His senses were better as a wolf, but exhaustion had taken hold from maintaining that form for so long. Without respite, without food, it'd be suicide trying to shift again. He needed a safe place to heal, somewhere he could start a fire and cook himself a meal.

That is, if he could find a rabbit.

Or a deer.

Fish, perhaps? He'd always been partial to fish. Fishing in and of itself wasn't too bad, either.

His stomach growled.

The man slumped against the nearest tree, eyes drooping, limbs growing heavy, lungs burning from the cold. Had it grown colder the farther he'd ventured into this forest, or was death settling upon him? His shoulders sagged as he hid his face in bloodied hands, nothing but the sound of his wheezy panting to keep him company. This part of the woods was dead silent. It was as if the dirt beneath his feet sensed his presence and knew what was coming. It yearned for him, knowing one day he would be nothing but buried bones.

He winced again as he clamped a shaking hand over his right ear, relying solely on the ability of his left. Muffled voices echoed in the distance; close enough he could tell they were human—or at least *humanoid*—but not close enough to make out what they were saying. He removed his hand from his ear, wiping the blood off on what little remained of his pants. Steeling himself, he pushed off the tree, nearly collapsing from the effort it took.

He could not fight *them* like this.

The hopeless man—who was once a careless wolf and something worse before that—chewed his lip as he continued. Surely, he'd stumble across a village soon. Maybe he could hide amongst the townsfolk? Glancing down, he realized just how terrible he looked. There'd been no time to think before he'd transformed last. He'd been running nonstop for days, shifting in and out of wolf form since the last full moon. Tattered remnants of sullied clothing clung to him, torn by haphazard transformations and crossbow bolts that had barely missed him.

What a sight he must've been. A wolf in human clothes. You could've written fables about him.

Still, in this state, perhaps someone would pity him.

In a spur of momentary defiance, he stopped hoping for a blizzard and instead began praying for kindness. Kindness would be infinitely better than a blizzard. Kindness would bring him food and offer him room and board.

He hadn't prayed like this in ages. Why would the Stars even listen?

His stomach growled again, louder now. The hunger pains would be unbearable soon enough. He'd taken things like bread for granted. At this point, the man would be grateful for even a quarter of a stale or moldy roll.

His mind wandered just as his feet. He couldn't remember the last time he had eaten something. The constant growling of his stomach had nearly driven him insane. If he *did* stumble upon a village, he would gladly do whatever the villagers wished if it meant—

A faint buzzing met his ears.

Slowly, he tip-toed through the trees, following the sound. It almost sounded like music. Like the lilt of a harp accompanied by the hum of lightning. Or bees swarming a picnic as a fiddler plays a low, sad tune.

A voice from the left nearly made him jump out of his skin. Ducking behind a tree, he peered through the woods. Ahead, the evergreens thinned. He suspected there was a clearing just out of sight.

"There's no need to trample each other. I've brought more than enough to share," the voice said, it's tone sweet, almost motherly. Almost. "Settle down, everyone, please," it laughed. Definitely feminine. Though he could not tell for sure, he suspected the speaker to be on the younger side, unlike himself.

The man who was—and by technicality still is—a starving wolf stole a glance over his shoulder, then edged toward the voice.

Standing with her back to him was a figure in a dark tartan cloak. The man watched as tawny rabbits bounced excitedly around the young woman's legs. She knelt, setting a basket full of fresh vegetables beside her. With spindly fingers, she took out a few lettuce leaves, tearing them into smaller portions for the rabbits chittering around her. The man had never been so jealous. Damn rabbits, always toying with him. How were bunnies eating better than him? He hated rabbits. Good for nothing but their pelts and meat, they were.

Shutting his eyes, he drank in the smell of food just out of reach. Again, his stomach screamed for sustenance. Something murderous was building inside him. His wolf beckoned him. If he were to transform one last time, he could snag that woman's basket and a few rabbits. . .

No.

No, he would scare that young lady, and the wind would whisk away all hopes of sympathy.

He opened his eyes, debating how to announce his presence to her. Maybe he shouldn't. He looked—and felt—like a walking corpse. Then again, maybe seeing a traveler in this state would cause her to—

Rolling his eyes, he realized making a grab for a rabbit would be a thousand times easier than trying to plead his case to a stranger. Logic be damned.

Mustering whatever strength he had left, he rushed forward, skidding in the mud on his knees. As he slid by, he grabbed one of the rabbits then rolled forward until he was back on his feet. Running full speed, he made for the safety of the shadows and—

Fell flat on his face.

Rolling to the side, he sat up, the rabbit unharmed but terrified. He scanned the ground, looking for a root or rock to take his frustrations out on. Nothing. He must've tripped on his own staggering feet.

"May I help you?" the young woman asked, startling him. She stood with her back to him, taking something from her basket.

He froze, looking up at the unfazed woman. "I—I don't mean to trespass," he said as loudly as he could. His voice sounded odd in his ears. It was too deep, too raspy. Was this how it had always sounded?

The girl removed her hood and turned to him. A wooden mask made in the likeness of a fox obscured her features. Thin black material over the eye holes hid her eyes, but he swore he saw them move as she studied him. Ringlets of long ebony hair fell around her shoulders, the curls dotted with pine needles and snow.

"May I help you?" she repeated, tilting her head to the side as the remaining rabbits hid beneath the hem of her cloak.

She arranged her gloved hands neatly before her, crossing her ankles daintily. She reminded him of a noblewoman. Far too elegant a creature to feed rabbits in the middle of nowhere. Then again, the masked Skogens Søstre cultists were weird like that. The man's grip on the rabbit tightened until it screamed. Skogens Søstre felt a peculiar kinship toward animals. She wouldn't let him have this insignificant creature without a fight.

A verbal fight, that is. He couldn't imagine a Skogens Søstre to come out swinging, especially one that talked like a lady in waiting.

"Passing through, my lady. Might you point me in the direction of the nearest town? I've seemed to have lost my way. . ." The man had always tried to avoid lying through his pointy teeth. What a shame.

He swore the young woman narrowed her eyes. "Recently?"

The man reddened. "Obviously not," he laughed nervously. The rabbit squirmed.

The girl wrung her gloved hands as she took a step back. The rabbits scurried away behind her, all hopes of a substantial dinner disappearing with them. The one in his hands was barely a snack.

"I don't mean you any harm," the man said quickly, putting on his best smile. "I'm just. . . trying to find a place to rest my head for the evening."

"Did you plan on using that rabbit as a pillow, then?" the woman asked. There was a hint of laughter in her voice.

"If that makes you feel better, then yes."

". . . the nearest town is about twenty or so minutes in that direction," the young woman said cautiously, pointing to her right.

"Many thanks." Careful not to lose his grip on the rabbit, he stood and bowed, starting on his way.

He'd not made it more than a few steps before the girl spoke again.

"The village of Tø does not take kindly to wanderers. Such is the way of The Wilds," she said quietly, her feet shuffling nervously in the mud.

The man paused, squinting at her. "Thank you very much for the warning," he said gruffly, wishing to bid her farewell once and for all. "Carry on feeding your vermin."

She tilted her head again. The man had not thought such judgment could be conveyed in such a small movement. "I would, but you've scared them all away," she muttered, bending to pick up her basket. "All except one."

The man raised an eyebrow. "Then. . . go find them?" he said with a shrug, hugging his rabbit tightly.

"And disturb them in their burrows?" she scoffed. "Perish the thought. Plus—" she looked him up and down, a deepset pout on her lips, the only part of her face he could see, "—if you walk into town like that, you'll be lucky to get anything other than a noose."

The man froze, eyes widening. Whether he believed her or not, he didn't care to find out.

The girl smirked and bowed. "Welcome to The Wilds, dear traveler," she uttered in a tone that made his skin crawl.

With a swish of her cloak, snow kicking up behind her in a flurry, she waltzed off into the woods. Her ringlets of dark brown hair swirled behind her as if she were floating underwater. The buzzing began to soften as she walked. That was when he realized it was coming from her. He'd heard murmurs, clicks, and ticks in people before but never buzzing. Never music.

His wolf went still, calculating.

"Let that bunny go, and I'll feed you something better," the girl called over her shoulder.

There were stories about strange women in this forest. Some lured young ones to their deaths. Others stole the souls of men. And, though most of those stories were told to frighten or warn, the man and his wolf knew not one was a lie. He lived in a world where every story became reality one way or another.

No one was harmless.

Not even a young woman feeding rabbits.

As if she could read his mind, she paused her gentle gait. Without turning, she spoke in a soft yet exasperated voice that seemed to come from everywhere at once. "Well? I don't have all day. Places to be. Things to do." With that, she breezed away.

The man sighed heavily. He could very well be making the worst mistake of his life. However, he couldn't help but admit the young Skogens Søstre intrigued him. Curse him; that's probably how she'd killed all the other fools brave enough to grab one of her rabbits. She wrapped them up in a web of mystery and struck when they least expected. However, when he thought about it, following her was better than being captured or killed by *them*.

Maybe she was just as wary of him as he was of her. Even from a distance, he could hear her rapidly beating heart.

Plus, the girl smelled of baked goods.

No one evil smelled of sugar-coated pastries.

Daring a step forward, he gently put down the rabbit. Whatever it was, something told him this was a risk worth taking. The rabbit seemed to agree. It ran as fast as it could, never looking back.

Rabbits! It was always those Starsforsaken rabbits!

Grumbling to himself, the man hurried to catch up with the young lady, his aching body protesting every step. He hadn't realized how tired he was until now. They walked on in silence for a while, nothing but the sounds of their footsteps crunching in the snow to keep them company. The man welcomed the silence. Silence meant he was safe for the time being. No one had caught up to him.

He yawned, causing the girl to look sideways at him. Or,

at least, he *thought* she was looking at him. It was hard to tell with the mask.

The girl, it seemed, *wasn't* keen on silence. Her pounding heart skipped a beat now and then. She cleared her throat, peering over her shoulder at him. Even this close, he still couldn't distinguish the color of her eyes.

"You've made a wise decision, traveler," she said.

"We'll see," the man yawned.

The girl sighed heavily, turning to him, blocking his path. "We shall."

She held out her hand for him to shake, lips pursed thin. The buzzing he'd heard earlier grew louder, no longer elegant yet sorrowful music but a dangerous hammering crescendo. The girl's heartbeat entwined with the symphony, pounding away in her chest, the percussion to the string melody that was the buzzing.

She was frightened.

Gently, he shook her hand, forcing his numb face into a grateful smile.

The air around him chilled, catching his breath and stealing it away. The sparse snowfall around them grew dense, each flake like the point of a dagger against his skin.

Sharp, electric pain erupted in his chest, his vision swirling. The girl's grip on his hand loosened as his knees buckled. Before he knew what was happening, he was face down in the muddy snow, the world dimming, freezing air burning his lungs.

As everything went dark, he swore she whispered, "That's for my rabbits."

CHAPTER TWO

HEKS

The wind howled with fright as the Witch came to terms with what had happened. A giant polar bear followed her, a limp and lifeless man sprawled across its back. The bear had her own feelings regarding the whole situation, but she knew the Witch couldn't understand her. Not really. Instead, she listened to the Witch's incoherent muttering, hoping she'd get fed when they arrived back at the cottage.

Hands shaking, the Witch—who was really just a scared girl parading around as what most folks called a cultist— glanced over her shoulder at the bloodied man snoring atop her bear's back. Despite the rise and fall of his chest, he was nothing more than a corpse. The way his arms and legs hung over the side of the polar bear would've been comical had the Witch not been filled with such all-consuming fear.

The bear groaned as she fell in place beside her.

The Witch nodded as if she understood. She figured her furry companion thought this was a horrible idea, too. She knew she was putting herself in danger by taking him back to town. But she couldn't just leave him to die in the cold! He needed a healer. She just hoped this time, when she came waltzing into town with a bear, things would turn out differently.

So far so good, it seemed.

Every head turned in her direction as expected. The heathen had brought yet another dangerous creature into town. Two, no doubt! The Witch sighed, stroking her polar bear's head as they scuttled down the road. The townsfolks' eyes wandered to the man precariously balancing on the bear's back, looks of shock and fear lighting up their faces.

The Witch wondered what they thought.

In actuality, their opinions didn't matter. Not really. Some didn't want to admit it; others simply didn't know, but this domain was hers and hers alone. Every creature, even the humans who had made her life a living nightmare, was her responsibility—Wanderers who tried to steal rabbits included. The only problem was that bloodied travelers almost always meant trouble. What that trouble entailed was left to the Spirits to decide.

Thick snow fell upon her shaking shoulders as she and the bear hauled their cargo up the path to the healer's observatory. The bear squeezed inside after the Witch, grumbling to herself. The traveler was still sound asleep as the polar bear shook him onto the floor. The Witch thanked her with dried fish she'd kept in her pocket and sent her on her way. The bear was thankful, as always. She never expected anything in return, but the Witch always came through.

With the polar bear gone, the Witch was left alone in the old observatory. She glared at the man, studying his gaunt features. She didn't wish him any harm but wasn't sure he shared the same sentiment. There was a fire in his eyes she had seen many times before. But for him, it was as if the flames encompassed his whole soul, leaving no place for anything other than rage.

"Lochlan!" she called, not too loud, so as not to disturb the snoring man.

There was a shuffling sound behind her. A tapestry depicting constellations that no longer graced the sky moved to reveal a tall, spindly man in a long gray robe embroidered with those same constellations.

He took one look at the sight before him and rolled his eyes. "Oh. It's *you*," he yawned.

"I—I found him like this!" the Witch stuttered.

The healer raised a thin eyebrow, accentuating his pasty face's many lines. "Do not lie to me, child."

The girl curled in on herself, wringing her hands.

The elderly healer sighed. "What have you done now, child?"

"I was only feeding the rabbits, I promise," the Witch said quietly. "He stumbled into the clearing, I swear." The healer, as always, doubted her but didn't press further.

"Well, what's wrong with him? Fever? Boils? Or did—"

"I suspect a few broken bones, maybe an infection. Nothing you can't handle within a minute or two," she said quickly, waving away his unspoken assumption—an assumption that would've been correct.

The healer—Lochlan Gard, though few dared to utter his name—gave her a bored look. "Seeing as he is unconscious on my floor, I believe it may be worse than that," he said haughtily.

"Oh. . ." The Witch backed away slightly, grimacing. "That—That part might've been me. He attacked my rabbits. You have to understand th—"

"Such as I suspected." Lochlan crossed his arms tightly, nodding toward the many pillows dotting the floor. "Make him comfortable while I fetch dressing and ointments."

The Witch bowed deeply, avoiding his eyes though hers were still hidden behind her mask. Lochlan disappeared into his hidden office behind the musty old tapestry, mumbling about how he hated his job and this Starsforsaken town.

Looking back down at the man, hands on her hips, the Witch sighed heavily. Taking hold of his ice-cold feet, she struggled to drag him toward a pile of pillows, dropping him upon them like a heavy sack of flour. If only she hadn't sent away her polar bear so soon.

"Oh, yes, broken bones indeed," came Lochlan's sour voice.

Cheeks reddening, the Witch stepped aside, watching as he cleaned the man's wounds. She found herself lost in thought. Sometimes, she toyed with the idea that something was deeply wrong with her, that she was beyond crazy, borderline insane.

Oh, what had she done?

She knew this strange man desperately needed her kindness. He was bloodied, bruised, broken, and beaten. Helping him could be the difference between his life and death. So why did she regret coming to his aide?

"He's freezing. If his wounds don't kill him, hypothermia

just might. Stoke the fire," Lochlan said quietly.

The Witch bowed again, turning her attention to the dying fire a few feet away. Tossing a few dry logs upon it, she removed one of her gloves and snapped her fingers, sending down a spark to set the embers ablaze. Quietly, she returned to hovering over Lochlan. After replacing her glove, she stood with her hands folded neatly before her.

The traveler snored rather loudly, the sound mixing with the crackling fire. She couldn't help but think he looked rather uncomfortable where she'd dragged him. What was his story? What was his name? Was he going to be all right?

Lochlan, disillusioned by her questioning aura, smeared a potent-smelling tincture over what was left of the man's right ear in silence. He made to wrap the wound, but before he could, the traveler suddenly grabbed his wrist, eyes popping open.

The Witch's heart did somersaults. She pitied him. How terrifying it must be, waking up in a strange place with a masked young lady and scowling elderly man hovering over you.

"Be careful, sir," Lochlan said, his voice a raspy whisper. "Else, you'll bite the hand that heals you."

The traveler struggled to sit up, holding his head in his hands. He took a moment to collect himself as Lochlan stood, holding his arm protectively before the Witch. The man peeked at them through his fingers. Something unnerving passed behind his hazel eyes. The Witch got the feeling he'd decided what to do with them but couldn't quite act on the thought. Clamoring to his feet, he grumbled something she figured was rude. How charming.

"What did you do to me?" he asked, looking around wildly. He stumbled back, looking at himself as if he expect-ed to find a missing limb instead of freshly dressed wounds. His bushy brown eyebrows furrowed deeply over his eyes, his breaths coming in short bursts. He was panting like a scared dog.

The Witch—who, you'll remember, was really just a frightened young lady—had been so busy worrying about his past and her present that she'd forgotten he'd have questions. Questions she could not and *should* not answer.

"You collapsed," Lochlan said dryly as the girl made herself as small as possible.

The man squinted directly at her, looking her up and down with scrutinizing eyes. He worked his jaw, surveying his whereabouts quickly before turning back to her, seething anger filling his eyes. "Where am I?"

The girl had never been happier to hide behind her mask. She hoped the embarrassed blush of her cheeks stayed hidden behind the fox façade.

Thinking for a moment, hands trembling, she smoothed the wrinkles of her navy-blue tartan cloak. "I brought you to the town healer. I figured he'd be able to help you better than I could," she said eventually, hoping her voice didn't betray how terrified she was.

Slowly, the man's shoulders sagged, his face softening. Exhaustion washed away his anger. He yawned. "Thank you, my lady. That is quite kind."

She smiled softly, hiding behind Lochlan, putting space between herself and the strange man as if that would protect her. She knew Lochlan would happily take a bludgeoning if it meant protecting her. His reasonings may be twisted, but he'd take it nonetheless. Even so, he was so frail he wouldn't do much good as a human shield.

"I implore you, sir, to sit back down," Lochlan said, scrutinizing him the way the man had done the girl. "I am not finished with your wounds just yet."

The girl eyed him carefully. Every inch of visible skin was covered in cuts and bruises. There were three old scars across the right side of his face, matching the fresh wound on his ear. His hair was caked in dried blood and dripping wet with mud. The girl shivered. All she could think of were the undead creatures that all the poets seemed to be scared of.

The man gingerly touched one of the bandages around his arm. "That's quite all right. I've no money to pay for what you've already done."

Lochlan audibly rolled his eyes. "Suit yourself. Less work for me."

"Lochlan!" the girl hissed.

The traveler looked back and forth between them, his face full of curious trepidation. "Might you two point me in the direction of the closest inn?" He spoke almost drunkenly, eyes glazed over.

Lochlan blinked at him, his dry eyes sticking shut for a moment. "Sir, do you have any idea where you are? There are no inns in Tø."

Frustration took over curiosity. "Then point me in the direction of a town that *does* have an inn!" he snapped.

Lochlan turned to the girl, clicking his tongue in disappointment. "He's your stray. You deal with him." With that, he turned toward his office, muttering and mumbling again.

The girl stood straight, stiff with fear. "Apologies. He can be. . . frustrating."

"Really?" the man yawned, "hadn't noticed."

They stood in silence for a moment, staring at each other with equal parts confusion and dread.

Lochlan appeared again, several beakers of bubbling liquids in either hand. "You're still here?" The girl nodded, earning herself a rather nasty look. "If he's not going to pay or at least let me finish dressing his wounds, I want him gone. Good day to you both!" he shouted as he stomped down the hall, his beakers clinking like bells.

The girl swiveled on her heels, gesturing toward the door. "I can lead you into town if you'd prefer. Though we have no inn, I'm sure someone will let you stay the night," she said quickly.

"Oh, I wouldn't want to bother you, miss," he grumbled. "If I remember correctly, you have 'places to be, things to do.' I'd hate to keep you from any of your duties."

"I did say that, didn't I?" she whispered, more to herself than to him.

"You sure did," he sighed.

She scowled, wringing her hands. So, he remembered that, did he? Did he remember anything else? Say, the bolt of electricity colliding with his heart or what she'd said as he lost consciousness? Hopefully not.

"You know, if I'd not drug you here, the cold would've killed you," she said carefully, testing him.

The man laughed darkly. "Am I meant to thank you?"

"I suppose that'd be the polite thing to do."

The man rolled his eyes and shook his head. "Yeah, well,

whatever. I was fine on my own." He gave a curt nod, heading for the door. "I'll be on my way, thank you very much."

"Looking like that?" the girl scoffed. "At least let me get you something other than those rags to wear. I'm sure I can find something that'll fit you." She didn't let him respond, turning down the same hall Lochlan had floated down.

There was a room in the back of the observatory that housed items left behind by the dead. Families rarely wanted to take home the clothing their loved ones died in. The girl hurriedly sifted through drawers and cabinets until she found what she was looking for. A few moments later, she returned, carrying a neatly folded fern-green tunic and brown breeches.

"That healer—your grandfather? He won't mind?" Seeing how greedily he took the clothes, it was more of a courtesy question than a genuine concern. Though he tried to hide it, his teeth were chattering, his body trembling. If she were in his position, she'd want that tunic more than life itself.

It took her a moment to realize what he'd said. "These aren't exactly his to offer," she said, her voice colder than the snow outside. "The washroom is the first door down the hall. Call if you need warm water."

"Thank you," the man whispered as he staggered down the hall. Was that sincerity she'd heard in his voice?

Hands shaking, heart pounding so hard it rattled her bones, the girl waited for him to return. How dare Lochlan pin him on her. Sure, she was the one to. . . find. . . his near-corpse, but she shouldn't have to babysit this stubborn man! She'd gotten him to town as promised. What more did she owe him? Food? Had she said something about food?

"Thank you, my lady. These fit quite nicely," said the man from the hall. There was no gratefulness in his voice, just fatigue. That, or his earlier thanks *hadn't* been sincere.

The girl rolled her eyes, surveying him. The tunic was ill-fitting, the breeches loose, but he didn't seem to mind. It was a good start. Though, given the opportunity, the wind would surely freeze him to his core. Depending on how he treated her, the girl might hurry that along.

"Are you sure your grandfather won't mind that I've stolen his clothes?" he asked, pulling the tunic's collar away from his neck.

If only he knew.

"The healer is not my grandfather, and those clothes don't belong to him. A young man died of fever in them. As he will no longer be needing them, they're all yours," she said simply, emotionlessly.

The man only stared, not wincing like she thought he would. If anything, he looked bored.

"Don't worry, Lochlan held onto them for months. You won't be infected."

"You have a twisted sense of compassion, my lady," the man said, his words barely a whisper.

She curtsied. "Welcome to The Wilds."

He sighed, gesturing weakly around the room. "How far am I into them, exactly? I lost my map. Got turned around."

"Closer to the outskirts than you are to the coast. You're a lucky one, I must admit. The closer you are to the ports, the worse the people are. Some of them don't even act human," the girl explained, waiting for the fear she expected from him.

It never came. He was stiff as a board and as unreadable as an empty notebook.

"I've heard," was his reply.

She squinted at him accusingly, forgetting for a moment he couldn't see her expression. "You must be desperate coming here for refuge. It seems you have quite the story to tell."

He crossed his muscular arms over his chest, wincing as he shrugged. "A long one, at least."

A smirk tugged at her lips. "Let me guess: you're a thief who stole from the wrong person? Oh! I know! A nobleman whose convoy was attacked? You're the lone survivor?" the girl asked, her tone dark but not lacking a hint of whimsy.

"Naturally," the man shrugged.

"Or I suppose you could be. . . a criminal thrown to The Wilds as penance for your crimes. . . ?" she rambled on, leading him toward the door.

"And judging by your mask, you're a vagabond who worships foxes. Skogens Søstre will take in anyone, won't they?"

She eyed him cautiously, her smirk turning deadly. "I do not worship the foxes, dear traveler," she whispered, opening the door and allowing whistling wind to fill the observatory. "*They* worship *me*."

The change in his demeanor was small, but she swore she saw fright in his hazel eyes.

"I'm only joking," she laughed. Which was the lie? One may never know.

He didn't seem convinced, though he followed her out the door nonetheless.

The path leading back to Tø was quiet, spare for the chirps of birds and the chittering of squirrels. Nothing but shadows accompanied them.

"Was I right? That you're running from something?" the girl asked after a while.

The man's eyes trailed away from the road for a second. Before he even spoke, she knew he wouldn't answer her question.

"You never told me your name," he said instead.

"You never asked."

"Consider me asking."

"Ophelia."

He raised an eyebrow in her general direction. "Ophelia. . . ?"

"Just Ophelia," she said, shifting uncomfortably under his gaze.

A look of realization crossed his face. "Ahh. . . I see."

She couldn't help but smirk. "Precisely, dear wanderer."

He glared at her. "This whole 'traveler' and 'wanderer' thing really isn't working for me. I have a name, too, you know."

"And yet you never offered it."

He laughed to himself. "You never asked."

"Don't expect that I will."

"Do you always speak whatever crosses your mind, young one?" he sneered.

She nodded. "Only when I know it won't get me killed."

"You're putting a lot of faith in a stranger."

Her eyes swept over him with hidden pity. "Misplaced faith is my specialty. Besides, in your state, I do believe I'd be the dangerous one."

He rolled his eyes but seemed to agree. "It's Seamus. Seamus Norland," he offered, seemingly lost in thought.

"How interesting to meet you," Ophelia chose to say.

"Not nice?"

"Time will tell."

There was something off about this traveler, something she couldn't quite pin. She'd met a lot of strange men in the woods surrounding Tø, men who thought they could take advantage of a beautiful young lass, men who believed themselves higher than even the cosmos.

But this wandering soul? He was different. She didn't know how, but he was.

"You know," Ophelia said, "You don't have to tell me what happened to you, Mr. Norland. To be honest, I'm not entirely sure I want to know. But I must warn you: the people in town will weasel your story out of you one way or another. You'd do well to create a lie as we walk."

Seamus's eyes darkened. "Lies? I can do lies."

She didn't doubt that one bit.

"Well, then," he began, with a wry smile, "lead the way, wee one."

Ophelia paused and cocked her head to the side, just staring at him. Seamus wore his crooked smile like a mask. In that way, she guessed they were similar. Masks were used to hide one's identity. One's true intent. But what was *his* true intent? She hid behind a mask for protection, to stay alive. If he kept hiding behind his, it may just get him killed.

"I thought you had places to be, kid," he sighed, staring back at her with a puzzled look.

She shook herself from her thoughts, continuing on.

Above the path back to Tø, perched in the treetops, were owls. They chittered as the wolf and the Witch walked side by side, each skeptical of what was to come.

Ophelia glanced up at them. On any normal day, she could take an educated guess about what they were trying to tell her.

But today wasn't normal.

Not at all.

CHAPTER THREE

THE GOOD PEOPLE OF TØ

The man whose name was Seamus—the man who was once a wolf—followed the young lady whose name was Ophelia—the Witch who was really just a girl—as she led him to the mysterious village of Tø. He wondered how many times she'd taken this particular path. The snow had turned to mud beneath their feet, revealing several sets of footprints. No branches hung in their way. The trees must know this place was well-traveled. Stealing a glance back at the healer's place of practice, he couldn't help but grimace.

Seamus wondered what lay at the end of this path. What was the town like? How were the people? So far, he was unimpressed. Still, he'd been on the run for so long, reduced to nothing but a vagabond like he'd called Ophelia. He ached for a place to stay longer than a few days. Though *they* held more jurisdiction here than other places, The Wilds were still lawless by nature. His foolish side thought perhaps the safety he sought was at the end of this muddy road. Tø wouldn't be his forever home, not by a long shot, but it would do for now.

As the trees thinned and buildings began to jut up from the ground, the sky shifted to a magnificent shade of orange. Ophelia had been quiet the entirety of the trek. Seamus guessed she was lost in thought, like himself. What could possibly be going through her mind, he did not know.

"Who's in charge here?" he asked as he slowed to fall in step beside her.

Ophelia stayed quiet a moment longer, chewing her lower lip. "Our Earl and Countess live in the Center Cities. Despite the observatory, there is no Celestial Council. We have a sheriff, but he's a lousy one at best. Lochlan is about the only person who has any say over the people."

"Depressing," Seamus said before he could stop himself.

Ophelia nodded. "Very. Why do you ask?"

"Never mind, it's not important now," Seamus said.

Ophelia tilted her head in question as she led him through the tiny town of Tø. The edge of town mainly consisted of cattle pens and poultry houses. Nestled among cows and chickens were a few odd goats or pigs. The smell was horrid. The ground here was untrustworthy, turned to mush beneath hoof and foot. By how often Seamus nearly slipped in the mud, the girl probably guessed he was from the city. How lucky he was to experience the joys of cobblestone paving. Already, he was missing such luxuries. When they made it to the long row of dwellings the villagers called home, he wondered if he'd have better luck sleeping beneath the stars.

Land was cheap and abundant in The Wilds. Few truly wanted to live in a place like this. Folks like Seamus were a prime example of how people ended up stuck here. Even the original settlers were forced here under mysterious conditions. And though they thought they could turn this land into bustling cities, they quickly realized how foolish they'd been. Soon came the bears, the wolves, the trolls, the extreme conditions, sickness, and poverty. A village can't grow when the villagers keep getting killed.

"Regretting your decisions?" Ophelia asked as Seamus's foot got sucked down a particularly thick spot of what he prayed was mud.

It was only when he freed his foot that he responded. "Not yet," he sighed.

Ophelia tried to hide her smile as she turned down a narrow alleyway. The town center unfolded before them, their surroundings a miserable mosaic of gray, brown, and beige. Seamus continued to follow without question, scowling. Something told him he was in for a rather rude awakening stumbling upon Tø of all places.

Ophelia didn't seem to notice his foul mood as she explained where he could purchase clothing, shoes, and food. No weapons, unfortunately. Tø did not have a blacksmith. If he wished to buy weapons, he'd have to trek deeper into The Wilds or wait around for traveling merchants. There were, however, several butchers, all in competition with each other. Apparently, this town was known for its animal products.

All of this was terrible news. Seamus had an unusual effect on animals. Especially livestock. It's like they could smell the wolf on him. He'd hoped to offer his services as a smith. Now, what was he to do? Sell produce? Doubtful. The Province of Snøbolig, which included The Wilds, scarcely had fresh vegetables. How Ophelia had procured such things for rabbits was beyond him.

All this troubled Seamus greatly, but his mind kept wandering back to the matter of Miss Ophelia Without-A-Last-Name.

"Any questions?" she asked, cutting through his muddled thoughts.

"Not one. Thank you for the tour, my lady," Seamus said, bowing slightly.

"Of course! Happy to be of help," Ophelia smiled. She reached into her cloak and procured a small sachet of what sounded like coins. She emptied half the contents—about twenty pieces at least—and offered them to him.

"Oh. . . I. . . I couldn't," Seamus grimaced, curling her fingers back around the coins and shoving her hand away.

Ophelia's smile faded. "You have nothing but the clothes on your back, Mr. Norland. And those have only belonged to you for a matter of minutes."

Something told him that arguing with her would get him nowhere. Begrudgingly, he held out his hand. She smirked as if she'd tricked him into playing some wildly amusing game only she knew the rules to. Stories of faeries that stole names and firstborns flooded his mind.

"Use that on anything you may need," she said, crossing her hands behind her back and tilting her head again.

He tried to imagine what her face might look like beneath that mask. Was she scrutinizing him, or was she looking on with pity? Maybe a twisted mixture of both?

"I'll be waiting at a signpost at the edge of town before starfall. If you need anything, please come find me," she said with a smile and a curtsey before turning and sauntering away, a spring in her step.

Seamus shook his head as he counted his coins: twenty-five pieces, five silvers, twenty coppers. He was grateful, yes, but it wasn't much. In most towns, this would barely buy him a bed for the night. Yet it was half of what she had. Who knew how long it had taken her to earn it? He'd pay her back whenever he had the chance. If she wouldn't accept it, he'd leave a small stack of coins on her doorstep before disappearing into the night.

But what to spend this on now? One thing was certain: he had to find room and board. Whoever took him in would surely feed him, so he didn't need to think about food. Plus, he was warm enough in the dead man's clothes.

He looked down at his bare feet, wiggling his purply, frostbitten toes.

Shoes.

He needed shoes.

Socks, too.

The sky was turning purple-pink as he scoured the market for boots. When he finally found a stall selling leather goods, he felt himself perk up a little. Glistening in the sunset was a pair of knee-high brown boots with stark black lacings and scuffed-up metal buckles.

"Hallo!" said the woman running the stall.

He waved to her, pointing to the boots. "Price?"

She looked him over, starting with the long scars on his face and the mud on his neck, then down to the coins in his hand and ending with his barren feet. "More than you can afford, I'm afraid. Have you anything to trade?"

Seamus shook his head, dusting himself with dirt and pine needles that had been stuck in his matted locks for days on end. "Does it look like it?"

Her demeanor changed from friendly to. . . not. "Well, sir, then I believe I cannot help you." She turned away, sweeping her hair behind her shoulder.

Seamus frowned. "I can trade my services. I plan on staying in Tø for quite some time. I'll work in exchange for the boots." Lies. Though he had tried to avoid them, Seamus had always been good with lies.

The woman looked back at him, rolling her eyes. "Do you take me for stupid?"

"I—No. No, not at all."

"Ha det bra," she snapped.

"Yup, bye-bye," Seamus grumbled. He laughed darkly, deciding it was best to find another stall. Hopefully, there would be another leather worker with a better attitude and cheaper prices.

Bare feet numb to the sharp rocks under him, he walked on, the coins clinking in his hands as he went. So long had it been since he'd idly walked through a market. Though this one was small, the sun was setting, and the frigid night air was settling in around him, he couldn't help but feel content.

"I heard you were looking for work," whispered someone from behind.

Seamus spun to see a burly man leading a sorry-looking donkey down an alley. His eyes were set on Seamus's hand, which tightened around what little money he had. Seamus, in turn, let his eyes settle on the man's bloodied apron.

"Word travels fast around here, I see," Seamus said, stepping back. Any other day, and he'd be down for a brawl.

The man shrugged. "Seems like." He looked around as if to make sure no one was eavesdropping. "Listen, one of my 'farmhands'. . . *quit.* . . recently. Lookin' to fill the space with someone a little more. . . *capable.* All ya'd need to do is 'muck the stables' and 'feed the pigs.' Five coppers an hour." The grandiose show of air quotes made Seamus cringe.

"I'm not good with animals. Thanks for the offer, though," Seamus chuckled nervously, saluting him.

"You think anyone else around here will hire you?" the man said before he could turn away. He had a point.

Begrudgingly, his head hung low, Seamus said, "Fine. Five coppers an hour. When do I start?" 'Mucking the stables' and 'feeding the pigs' couldn't be half as bad as some of the things he'd done prior to meeting this *lovely* man.

The man shrugged. "I'll fetch you when I see fit. Where are you staying?"

"Haven't found a place just yet. Would you be willing to offer room and board?"

The man's face darkened. "Do I look like a charitable young man to you?"

Seamus squinted at him. He had to stop himself from saying, 'You don't look young at all.'

"The healer—Lochlan, I believe—and a young lady named Ophelia can vouch for me. They suggested I find somewhere to stay for a few days so my wounds can heal," Seamus explained.

The burly, aproned man stood stiff as a board, scowling, fear lighting up his eyes. "I see. Well, in that case. . . My offer is off the table. Have a nice night." With that, he yanked his donkey down the alley and disappeared.

"That's not weird at all," Seamus whispered before continuing.

There were, in fact, several other leather workers. After some negotiation, he was able to purchase a cheap pair of ankle boots with coins left to spare. No one seemed to need an extra hand, but he guessed that was only because of his current 'stranger status.' Seemed he really would be hard-pressed to find work. He hoped Ophelia knew of someone who would need him. He'd have to ask.

He stood under the signpost waiting for her now, his new boots tucked under his arm, his extra coins rattling inside them as he tapped his bare foot on the soggy ground. He'd forgotten to buy socks. He sighed, looking to the stars for reassurance.

They offered none, as per usual.

The girl had said to meet here before nightfall, so there he sat, waiting.

As the moon rose over the trees, Ophelia came waltzing down the path, carrying all manner of goods. Seamus could smell the raw beef from where he stood. His mouth watered.

"Was beginning to think you'd abandoned me," Seamus teased as they began their trek to somewhere he hoped had a fire.

"Sorry, I got sidetracked. Thank you for waiting." She curtsied. "Nice boots."

"Why thank you," Seamus said, bowing in return. "Need help carrying anything?"

"I've got it, but I appreciate the sentiment."

Seamus snickered to himself. "No problem."

He could just barely see her watching him out of the corner of her eye. "How was town?" she asked, a hint of anxiety in her otherwise neutral tone.

All he did was sigh.

Ophelia sighed. "I had a feeling that would be the way of things. No offense."

"None taken," he shrugged. "Was offered a job, but I made the mistake of dropping your name, so I'll have to keep searching."

"Tall guy with blood-stained clothes and an attitude? Most likely carting around a miserable donkey?"

"How'd you know?"

"About a month ago, I messed with his traps. He was trying to make extra coin on fox fur."

"And the high and mighty Fox Goddess just couldn't let that happen?"

"Of course not," she laughed.

"Well done, oh high and exalted one. That *mule* deserved whatever he got," he smiled. "To be clear, I don't mean the donkey."

Ophelia held her head high, a content smile on her purple-blue lips. Seamus admired the girl's spunk. She reminded him of someone he once knew.

Sadness surged through him at the thought.

That person was long gone.

"You're welcome to stay with me," she said absent-mindedly, her voice low, cutting through his wandering thoughts.

A home-cooked meal, a warm place to sleep, new boots—what more could a man want? "Are you sure?" Seamus couldn't believe his ears.

She nodded. "Just so you know, I don't mind the company. But there are rules." He had the feeling she was gazing at him with shifting eyes. Seamus gestured for her to continue. "Number one: the animals that visit me are friends, not food. You harm them, I'll be sure you're hanged. Number two: tidy up after yourself. And finally—" she paused and chewed her lip "—number three: questions about my mask are strictly prohibited."

He almost broke rule three after it'd been set, wanting to ask if that meant she wasn't a Skogens Søstre after all. "Simple enough. I think I'll manage."

Soon, the dirt path turned into methodically placed steppingstones. The sight before him was beautiful and peculiar and something else Seamus couldn't quite pin. The girl smiled at him over her shoulder as she hopped along the steppingstones. A gate covered in bows of pine and holly stood before a quaint cottage. At the cottage's door slept a reindeer. At the garden's gate, played bear cubs. Owls dotted the fence. And sure enough, foxes sat waiting for her to pat the tops of their heads as she opened the gate and let in a lone pine marten.

All those stories and warnings he'd heard as a child resurfaced yet again.

'They worship me' kept repeating in his head. Maybe she really was a deity.

"How interesting to meet you," Seamus breathed, feeling that strange little sentence fit her far better than it did him.

Ophelia turned to him, beckoning him through the gate. "Did you say something?"

He shook his head, stepping through carefully so as not to squash the pine marten beneath his lumbering feet. "Not at all."

The reindeer paid them no mind as she unlocked the front door. Warmth enveloped Seamus as she swept him inside. The low light of a fire greeted him. Cinnamon and anise filled his lungs, the smell wafting off the wood stove where a steaming kettle sat.

The pine marten scurried inside before Ophelia could close the door. It settled into sleep atop a ratty cushion as if the old pillow belonged to it.

Cardinals had made a nest atop a crooked bookshelf.

A raccoon was rummaging around in the cupboard.

A wolverine lay lazily on the back of the patchwork couch in front of the hearth.

Interesting indeed, thought Seamus. For the first time, he felt bad about the rabbit. Whether she really was a Skogens Søstre or not, she seemed to share their values. Animals were friends, not food. He'd have to remember that.

Ophelia busied herself preparing dinner while Seamus tried on his boots. He was pleased to find they fit perfectly. He'd be forever grateful for the extra coin.

Which reminded him. After a quick count of his change,

he held out seven coins as she chopped up a potato. "Had some left over," he explained, setting the change on the table with a satisfying clink.

Ophelia eyed him, obviously confused. "I gave it to you to spend, Mr. Norland."

"I figured you'd want the rest."

She sighed. "You'll find the need to spend it eventually. Keep it."

As he watched her work, the kitchen was filled with the scent of fresh vegetables and spice. Whatever stew she was brewing up smelled divine. His stomach growled, causing his cheeks to redden.

"Fine. But you can't stop me from paying you back before I leave."

Ophelia stopped mid-chop. She stared at the stack of potatoes collecting on the table, the jars of spices, and the shredded beef. He could finally make out her eyes through the mask. Glinting beneath the black mesh of the eye holes was a hint of silver. He tried to read her through scent, but the room was so full of deliciously intoxicating smells he couldn't.

"We will discuss this then. For now, we will have dinner," she said with an air of finality.

"Yes, my lady."

CHAPTER FOUR

ACTIONS AND CONSEQUENCES

Ophelia woke to an angry wolverine nipping at her ear. This young one was rather aloof and quiet, so if it felt the need to alert her like this, something was obviously wrong. She dressed quickly, tied on her mask, and then tip-toed into the den.

The wolverine hissed at Seamus, who was sprawled out on her old lounge. His snores reverberated through Ophelia's body and into the walls, irritating all the sleeping animals that had made the den their home. Ophelia was used to odd noises, so his snores hadn't kept her up, but she imagined her animal friends had had a rough night.

"He won't be staying long, I promise," she said to them, her voice hushed.

The wolverine growled, scurrying up onto the back of the lounge, glaring at her.

"Let him rest," she scolded, anticipating Seamus being woken by claws or teeth. She imagined if she could understand the sound the wolverine made, she would be very cross with it.

Smiling to herself, she turned her attention to breakfast. If there was one thing Ophelia knew for certain, trust was built on pastries and good company. She just hoped this wasn't the kind of company she'd regret entertaining.

Putting her worries aside, she got busy baking, dropping berries and oats for animals curious enough to watch. This quelled their displeasure enough that they forgot about Seamus's presence, or at the very least, chose to ignore him for the time being. Once she'd placed her confectionery treasure on the wood stove to bake, she went out into the cold to start her daily chores.

The animals were her first priority. Long ago, she'd found if she took care of them, they'd take care of her. So, as always, she topped off the troughs with grain, filled feeders with nuts and dried berries, and set out a bucket of fish for anyone who fancied themself a quick snack. With those tasks done, she left carrots by the doorstep and chicken eggs outside the alcoves where pine martens and skunks liked to hide.

The polar bear—she'd named her Eydis—came sauntering out of the woods, climbed over the fence, and made her way inside, shimmying as her rear got stuck in the narrow doorway. Ophelia giggled, following her. The air inside was sticky with a sickening-sweet smell. Eydis settled into her spot next to the stove, watching intently as Ophelia removed the pastry from the wood stove and set it on the rickety kitchen table.

Seamus stirred not long after. No matter how hard he tried to rub away the sleep, the dark circles under his eyes stayed. In Ophelia's expert opinion, it seemed he was beyond exhausted. He winced as he stood, his bones creaking and cracking, rivaling the crackle and pop of the fire.

"You should really let Lochlan take another look at your wounds. If money is your only concern, I'll happily pay," Ophelia said. She meant it, too, so long as he was all right.

"I could never ask that of you, Ophelia," he yawned, ruffling his untidy hair. He should bathe, too. A putrid stink followed him like the plague. "Thank y—" he swore, stumbling back into the lounge, covering his eyes with a shaking hand. "Is a *bear* lying there, or have I completely lost it?" His words blended together a little.

"That's Eydis. Don't worry, she won't hurt you. She— uh—*escaped* a passing circus a few years back." Ophelia's cheeks redden beneath her mask.

Seamus looked over his shoulder, dread painting him green. He looked back at Eydis, nodded, and then snuck around the lounge ever so carefully. His footsteps seemed wobbly. Ophelia guessed he was worse for wear than Lochlan had thought. Steadying himself on the edge of the table, he sniffed the air, letting the smells wafting off the wood stove envelope him.

"Is that. . . Is that kringle?" he whispered. The look in his eyes was almost childlike, excitement brightening his features. He was handsome when he didn't look like a walking corpse.

"Freshly made," Ophelia said softly, trying to steady her ever-shaking hands as she cut him a slice. She placed the slice on a chipped plate, sliding it his way. "It's a tad overdone. I was busy tending to the animals. Nearly forgot all—"

Seamus shoved the slice into his mouth. Ophelia had never seen someone eat like that before. Animals, yes. People? No. His eyes were wild with joy and gluttonous greed as he reached for a slice intended for herself. Hunched over the table like a madman, he made sure not to lose a single crumb.

"You may want to slow down. Else you'll choke."

"I wouldn't mind," said the ever-strange Seamus Norland through a gaping mouthful.

Ophelia stared at him for a while before pushing the rest of the kringle toward him. "I do believe you need this more than I do."

"Much obliged," Seamus said with a quick nod.

Ophelia watched him eat for some time, glad most of her bewildered face was covered. She'd never met someone quite like Seamus. He was odd, even by her standards.

"Any plans for the day?" she asked, clearing away the crumbs too far away for him to easily lick off the table.

Seamus had stuffed half the kringle down his throat and was well on his way to devouring the rest of it. She couldn't help but give him a disapproving scowl. He was all wit, sass, and arrogance. No common courtesy whatsoever.

He swallowed hard, wiping the crumbs and icing from his face. "Apologies. I haven't eaten anything since. . ." he paused, staring off into the distance, ". . . I'm actually not sure."

"Tragic," Ophelia sighed.

He raised an eyebrow, studying her mask and what little he could see of her face. "You know, for someone so gener-ous, you can be quite finicky," he said out of the corner of his mouth before popping another piece of kringle into it.

Ignoring him, she pressed on. "Plans?"

He thought momentarily, taking a second to breathe and swallow between bites. "You know, I think I may go speak with the healer again," he said, staring into space. "I don't intend on keeling over anytime soon."

"Thank Salvia," Ophelia whispered.

"Do you know of anyone who may need a helping hand? Anyone who would pay, no matter how small the fare?" Seamus asked, continuing his incessant chomping.

"I thought you were just passing through."

He gave her a bored look. "I really don't think I'm in any shape to travel. I think I'll have to stick around 'til I find my footing again." He hesitated before continuing, clearing his throat. "If that's all right with you, of course."

He stood, brushed the crumbs from his clothes, stretched, then walked over to the fire—avoiding Eydis, of course—shivering as he went.

"I'll have to consult the animals," Ophelia smiled.

He nodded in agreement. "Wouldn't want the bear murdering me in my sleep."

"You're better off worrying about Narfi," she laughed, pointing to the wolverine. "He already told you off for sleeping on his bed."

Seamus eyed the wolverine cautiously. "Noted."

Curling in on himself, he returned to the fire, soaking in the warmth. Ophelia's mind went back to how cold he looked last night. It was a miracle she hadn't found him frozen solid this morning. Sighing, Ophelia grabbed one of the furs off the old bench by her bookshelves. It was just as wobbly as her kitchen table, but it had served her well. Sometimes, it was a bed for injured critters. Other times, it was a reading nook. Resting beside the bench was a discarded backpack, something she knew Seamus would get more use out of it than she ever had. She turned, holding out her offerings.

Seamus, hands held over the woodstove, gave her a confused look. "What's all this?"

"Consider it a welcome gift."

He frowned. "What kind of pelt is this?"

"It belonged to an old brown bear I used to know," Ophelia explained cautiously, "But don't worry, he died of natural causes. Old age, see? The fur is almost gray. He was very wise," she said absentmindedly. Losing animal friends was always hard, but Ophelia knew their souls were at peace, knowing they still served her long after they'd died.

Seamus hesitated before taking the pelt, wrapping it around his shoulders, stroking it softly. His countenance saddened Ophelia. He seemed embarrassed yet deeply grateful, giving her a small smile as thanks. She wondered how long it'd been since he'd had such a luxury.

"If there is anything you need, please don't hesitate to ask."

Seamus's face reddened. "There is one thing. Do you have a spare pair of socks?" he grimaced.

"Lochlan has plenty. I will grab you a pair when we visit him."

"Thank you, my lady," Seamus said, bowing. "For everything."

She knew in her heart of hearts that his gratitude was genuine. It almost made up for his attack on the rabbits.

Almost.

CHAPTER FIVE

TINCTURES

With Seamus in tow, Ophelia said her good mornings to the townsfolk. Though she wasn't exactly popular with the general population, a few were cordial enough. There was even one she called a friend.

"God morgen, Phee!" a woman's voice rang from above. Ophelia looked up to see a crown of curly red hair dangling precariously off a nearby roof.

"God morgen, Saoirse! Please be careful up there!" she called back, waving.

Seamus squinted against the cold winter sun, watching Saoirse clean moss from the roof of her father's shop.

"Aren't I always?" Saoirse laughed.

Ophelia laughed nervously, leaning over to whisper, "She is *never* careful," to Seamus before continuing.

Seamus chuckled to himself, gazing wide-eyed at the intricate workings of Tø. Crystal and steam-powered energy was hard to find here in The Wilds, so everyone made do without it. There were oil lamps on each corner, their light a flicker of warmth in an otherwise freezing town. Ophelia loved watching the lamplighters bring the streets to life on the darkest nights. The main street was nothing more than densely packed earth sprinkled with hoof and footprints, harkening back to all the traders and merchants who had passed through earlier in the week. A dry fountain stood in the center of town, a glimmering brass bell sitting at its base.

"Pretty nice place. For The Wilds," Seamus mused.

Ophelia smiled brightly, nodding.

Seamus walked backward for a moment, scanning where they'd come from, then cast his eyes toward the sky, marveling at the clouds. If he'd come from one of the cities, Ophelia doubted he'd ever seen clear skies like this. From what she heard, steam-powered mechanics covered the Center Cities with a haze that blocked the sun.

"Have you given any thought to what fanciful story you're going to tell our 'pretty nice place?'" Ophelia asked after some time.

"Kept me up all night," he replied dryly.

Ophelia felt whatever he'd come up with would be quite comical, especially the part where she watched him try to convince the villagers of his tall tale. In her experience, he would require a miracle to convince them fully. Even in a town like Tø, where the crime rate was considerably lower than the rest of The Wilds, the people were antsy. Ophelia remembered the last time a strange traveler seeking refuge came in with the cold, remembered how they were 'welcomed.' She glanced at Seamus, who was still marveling at his surroundings. At least he had his charm going for him. That would go a long way around here.

"Yesterday is a blur. Was the healer's hut outside of town?" he asked.

"On the outskirts, framed by the woods."

"How poetic," he mumbled, though not unkindly.

The dwellings began to thin until they were on a path into the forest less traveled. Seamus was quiet again until he saw the headstones. Hundreds of them dotted the forest floor, shaded from view by the tall evergreens.

"I don't remember the tombstones," he said, sounding suspicious. "You sure this guy is a healer? He doesn't seem to be a very good one. . ."

Ophelia only shrugged, continuing down the path toward a large circular building made of white stone. Eight tall stained-glass windows were separated by pillars inlaid with golden constellations. The pillars held up a balcony where telescopes once resided. Now, only fallen tree branches and snow littered the lookout. The cracked glass dome was adorned with a golden eight-point star cradled in a spiral that spun slowly with the wind.

"I thought you said there wasn't a Celestial council,"

Seamus muttered, standing in awe before the grand Celestial Observatory. His memory really was foggy.

"Religion isn't really practiced here. Anyway, this is the only building big enough to house the sick, dead, or dying."

The grimace marring Seamus's face made Ophelia cackle. "Again, you positive this guy's a healer?" he asked.

Ophelia paused at the intricately carved door, eyes tracing the constellations and planets depicted. "Healer by title," she said, clearing her throat, "Undertaker by profession."

"There it is," Seamus sighed, "Well, let's get this over with."

Ophelia gave him an apologetic smile, throwing open the doors to reveal the modest sanctuary. In many ways, this place still resembled what it must have looked like to those worshipping the Celestial Pantheon eons ago.

Multi-colored light filtered through the stained-glass windows, depicting the Celestial Spirits, commonly referred to as Stars. Each was a different animal, their meanings unclear unless you'd read the Compendium. Next to the door were the Rabbit and the Bat, Spirits of Life and Death, respectively. The Cat, Raccoon, Albatross, Peacock, Horse, and Scorpion were also featured. Ophelia recognized their traits as magic, mystery, devotion, passion, restoration, and ruin. She'd read the Celestial Compendium front to back numerous times, never tiring of the parables penned by devoted followers from way back when.

Cushions were strewn across the floor, once allowing devotees to sit in reflection and prayer while charting the cosmos. The bookcases were filled with stories, parables, divinations, and ponderings, each tome practically untouched and caked in dust save for a few Ophelia-sized fingerprints. The massive telescope in the center of the sanctuary was in a similar state. Seamus looked as though he'd never set foot in a place of worship like this, but Ophelia had been here many times over the years. As of late, she'd been the only one utilizing the telescope. Though countless people passed through these doors yearly, she considered those relics hers and hers alone. Even Lochlan seemed to have discarded them.

"Beautiful, isn't it?" she breathed as Seamus traced the inscriptions on the telescope with his fingertips. Awestruck, he nodded.

The creaking of a door startled them. The old star map tapestry moved to reveal Lochlan in his heavy woolen robes. He held a pair of forceps in one hand and a soiled cloth in the other. Ophelia's lip curled in disgust, trying not to dwell on whatever he'd been up to.

"I've convinced him to let you patch him up a little better," she said, nodding toward Seamus.

Seamus eyed her as he slipped out from behind the telescope. Back straight, head high, and hands crossed neatly behind his back, he inclined his head toward Lochlan. "I apologize for my attitude yesterday. You caught me at a rather bad time. I have fallen into misfortune, sir. My convoy was attacked and raided. Only a few of us escaped, but we were unfortunately separated. Every possession I own was taken from me," he explained.

It seemed Seamus was quite the liar indeed.

And a story thief, Ophelia noted. Pity.

"I see," Lochlan said, stroking his long white beard in thought.

Lochlan Gard was a rather fickle man. Time moved, but he refused to move with it. He used to preach in this observatory before the rest of the town decided religion was no more than make-believe. That was when his hair was midnight black, not a dull white. Before he became an undertaker. Lochlan often said that all the dead bodies were the Stars' way of punishing this faithless town. But Ophelia often wondered if the Stars were punishing *him* instead. In her humble opinion, that outcome was more probable.

"I am looking into work around these parts. Would I be able to pay you back in the future?" Seamus asked, putting on his best smile.

Lochlan gazed at him with unblinking eyes. He was one of the skeptics Ophelia had tried to warn Seamus about.

"Convoy, you say? That implies nobility or importance," he said, his tone dark, "but, Mr. . . . ?"

"Norland."

"But, Mr. Norland, you do not seem to be a man of importance, let alone nobility. You aren't trying to swindle my—ehem—*this* town, are you?" Lochlan drawled on, eyes boring holes into Seamus's very soul.

"Perish the thought!" Seamus gasped, placing a hand over his heart with a dramatic flourish.

Definitely a story thief, Ophelia thought with a roll of her eyes.

Lochlan's shoulders fell as he shut his weary eyes. He thought for a moment, head cocked to the side, his foot tapping impatiently. "Might I speak with you in private?"

"Oh! Of course! I—" Seamus began.

"Not you!" Lochlan and Ophelia said rather sternly.

Seamus fumbled over his words for a moment, feigning a hurt look, before marching back over to the telescope, once again busying himself with the symbols.

Lochlan swept his hand through the air, gesturing to the tapestry as he made toward the hidden door Ophelia knew led to his office. She gave Seamus a sympathetic smile as she followed. Lochlan held the door for her, slamming it shut the moment she was inside the dimly lit room. The window here depicted the Scorpion poised for attack. Lochlan stood under it, glaring at her. The trees outside blocked the sunlight, casting him in shadow. Bones, loose papers, vials, jars, and medical instruments littered every surface. Crude drawings of human anatomy and plants were plastered to the walls, their corners curled and worn from old age. The smell of musty oranges permeated everything.

"Sun, give me strength," he mumbled, aggressively rubbing his temples. Ophelia stood by the door, watching as he paced back and forth, continuing to mumble spiritual platitudes.

"In my defense, I—"

"Dear child," Lochlan began, "You are on such thin ice as it is. Why did you think inviting this—this—this *vagrant* into town was a good idea?" He was still pacing as he spoke. Not once did he look at her.

"I did not *invite*. I *rescued*. He's injured," Ophelia whispered, eyes cast to the floor. ". . . Forcefully rescued, one could say."

"Until you convinced him otherwise, he was perfectly fine with his current state. If he was concerned for his health, you should have sent that blasted bear and him to the farthest infirmary west!" Lochlan seethed. "Should've directed him toward another unsuspecting village far better equipped to handle the likes of him!"

He might have been right, but Ophelia knew Seamus wouldn't have lasted another night in the woods. As Lochlan continued pacing, gathering tinctures and bandages as he went, Ophelia mustered the courage to speak her mind, something she rarely did when it came to him.

"He needs a place to stay, to heal. If we deny him that, then we are no better than whoever harmed him," she said quietly.

Lochlan laughed, halting his pacing. He spun, his dusty robes swirling around him, causing loose papers to fly off his desk. He glared at Ophelia for quite some time before leaning down to her eye level. Ophelia swallowed hard, recoiling from him.

"And who *did* harm him, hmm? Do you know, or have you bought into a lie or a half-truth? I'd have thought I taught you better," he snapped.

"Does it really matter? A person in need is a person in need."

In dismay, Lochlan threw his hands into the air. "Of course, it matters, Ophelia! You could be inviting a murderer into the fragile ecosystem of our home! It's like—like—like putting a bear cub in a pit of bunnies."

"My bears and bunnies get along quite nicely," Ophelia whispered. "Not everyone is evil, Lochlan," she said. She regretted her words even as they tumbled out of her mouth.

"If you care about him so much, child, he can stay in your lonely little hut," he sneered.

"We've already made arrangements for that," Ophelia smiled, hoping he would be proud of her for once.

"Oh, of course, you have!" Lochlan snapped. "Caring for another mutilated stray. Typical! That is what you do, isn't it? Inviting dangerous creatures into your home despite my warnings? I should've known."

"Well, yes, but this time—"

Lochlan took her face in one clammy hand, fingers sliding under her mask, jagged fingernails digging into her cheek. "This time. That time. What if he's a good person? What if he needs our help? What if, what if, what if?'" he said mockingly, bobbing his head back and forth. "No good ever comes from your wild fantasies and feeble hope. You really should know this by now, *dømte en!*" He squeezed her face with all his might before pushing her away, her head colliding with the wall behind her.

Dømte en.

Condemned one.

"I do not want him here long," Lochlan snapped. "Have I made myself clear, child?"

Ophelia nodded but refused to meet his eyes despite his ignorance. Shrinking in on herself, she pulled her cloak tight around her trembling body.

He straightened, brushing his hands off on his robes as if touching her had covered him in a layer of filth he'd never be able to wash away.

"Get out," Lochlan growled.

Ophelia crossed her hands beneath her cloak, gave a curtsy, then slipped back into the sanctuary to find Seamus. Lochlan did not follow.

"What was that about?" Seamus asked.

Ophelia nearly tripped over a cushion from the sight of him. His eye was glued to the eyepiece of the telescope. Ever so gently, he turned the focusing knob, a wry smile on his lips as he peered up at the sky.

Interesting.

"Lochlan agrees you should stay with me," Ophelia said, looking over her shoulder at the tapestry. Her hand absentmindedly went up to touch her mask, ensuring it was covering her most dangerous secret. She could still feel Lochlan's fingers on her face. When she looked back, Seamus was watching her with a questioning look. She cleared her throat, rocking back and forth on her heels. "I am the only one equipped to add another member to my household," she explained. It wasn't a lie. It was just an unspoken truth.

Seamus removed himself from the telescope, arms crossed over his chest, eyebrows furrowed deeply over his hazel eyes. He scrutinized her, eyes lingering on her exposed lips and chin.

"What happened to your face?" he asked, loosely gesturing toward her. "It's red."

Ophelia straightened. "Not sure."

Seamus's eyes slid over to the tapestry. She could tell he wanted to say something else, but the anger on his face suddenly gave way to the false aristocratic air he'd donned not moments ago.

"Mr. Norland," Lochlan said, his voice echoing through the sanctuary like the voice of a malevolent ghost. "If you prove to be an upstanding citizen, you will not have to pay for my services. We shall give you a few weeks," he explained, speaking through grit teeth. "If you care to stay longer than that, I would have to speak to our Earl and Countess."

Seamus's eyes lit up with something Ophelia could only explain as victory. "I'll be forever in—" he began.

"Thank you, Lochlan," Ophelia interjected.

"Manners, child," Lochlan said, his voice tight. "Fetch me some water and rags."

Ophelia bowed to them, grabbed a spare bucket, and exited the sanctuary through a door in the back. Behind the magnificent structure sat a stream. Quickly, she filled the bucket, the current doing most of the work. When she returned, she found the sanctuary filled with tense silence.

Seamus sat shirtless on one of the old cushions as Lochlan tended his wounds with jagged movements, tying the bandages too tight for Ophelia's liking. Seamus was in visible agony but said nothing. Ophelia felt sorry for him. Lochlan may be an incredible healer, but he wasn't a gentle creature, especially when his mood swings got the better of him.

"Quickly, child," Lochlan said over his shoulder, shooting her a disgusted look.

Ophelia quietly deposited the bucket of water and rags she'd taken from a hall closet at Lochlan's feet. She stood to the side and watched him work silently, noting how Seamus kept glancing at her with a strange look. She hoped Lochlan hadn't said anything odd in her short absence.

When he finally finished patching Seamus up, Lochlan sat back to observe his handiwork. "That should do you for now. I shall bring some medication to fight off any infection and pain soon enough."

"Takk, sir," Seamus said gruffly, all aristocratic elegance and kindness gone. He pulled his tunic back on, careful not to rip the bandages.

Lochlan thought for a moment, eyes locked on Ophelia. "Here in Tø, we help all those in need."

Ophelia's eye twitched beneath her mask. Seamus looked between the two of them, his expression unreadable.

"Mr. Norland, I do believe we should leave. I would like to introduce you to a friend of mine," Ophelia said, her voice unsteady.

Neither of them said goodbye to Lochlan.

On the way back into town, Seamus followed close behind. Every time she looked back at him, his eyes were on the observatory.

CHAPTER SIX

BUTCHER BLOCK

Seamus's blood boiled as Ophelia led him through town. Something about this *Lochlan* fellow rubbed him the wrong way. He reminded Seamus of people from his past—people he'd do well to forget. If his suspicions were correct, then Lochlan was bad news—very bad news. He hoped that was the last he'd see of him for a while.

How Ophelia could stomach him was beyond Seamus's comprehension.

Speaking of the mysterious Lady Ophelia, Seamus nearly plowed her over when she stopped abruptly and turned to smile up at him. Apparently, they'd arrived at their destination. A small, narrow shop loomed over them, the windows caked in mud, the brickwork crooked. To top it all off, the front door was adorned with a crude painting of a severed chicken head. Peering through a clear patch of the window, Seamus could see a tall, pudgy fellow waving for them to come in. The clinking of a bell filled the still air as Ophelia pushed open the door. Seamus pleaded with his stomach not to growl, the smell of raw meat hitting him full force.

"Hallo, Åsmund!" Ophelia smiled.

The man behind the counter gave her the brightest smile Seamus had ever seen, which was alarming given the bloodied cleaver he waved in greeting. The man may not have been that much taller than Seamus, but his broad form made him quite the imposing figure. Between the two of them, Ophelia looked about two inches tall.

"God morgen, Av'Skogen!" the man said. He thwacked his cleaver into the wooden counter, a piece of wood flying across the tiny shop and implanting itself in the wall beside Seamus.

'Av'Skogen?' Translated that meant 'Of the forest.' It wasn't necessarily an uncommon last name, but Ophelia had him convinced she'd been without one. If that were the case, it seemed more of an insult. He gave her a sideways glance, but she seemed unaffected.

"Morgen!" Ophelia said, giving a slight bow. Seamus noted how she looked everywhere but at the sausages hanging on the wall and the—

Seamus's stomach rebelled, growling as loud as possible.

Before this Åsmund fellow sat the thickest, juiciest, fat-filled cut of—he took in a long, satisfied breath—venison Seamus had ever seen. This butcher shop was intoxicating. His wolf was content just being in the presence of such glorious cuts of meat.

"What brings you in, Phee?" Åsmund asked in a deep, booming voice that did not match his body or the smile on his face.

"Åssi, I'd like to introduce you to my friend Seamus. He's in need of some work. Are you still looking for an assistant?"

"Why yes, I am! Good of you to remember!" Åsmund's excitement was palpable. A maroon blush sprouted over his russet skin.

Ophelia left him and Seamus to talk, saying she'd stayed in the butcher shop for far too long but hoped the two of them got along.

Åsmund chuckled to himself as the door swung shut behind her. "She gets squirrely around dead animals."

"I can only imagine," Seamus laughed, turning his attention to the array of meats surrounding him. Sausages, sirloins, fillets—you name it, Åsmund had it.

"I see you're not," Åsmund said, looking him up and down, a glint in his eyes.

Seamus was more than happy to be around raw meat all day. In fact, he'd go so far as to say he was ecstatic at the notion. Should he work here, any scraps Åsmund wouldn't use would surely mysteriously disappear, ending up as a snack for his insatiable wolf.

Without a moment's hesitation, Åsmund cut him a deal. "How's ten coppers a day and the promise of your choice of cut at the end of each week?"

"I could get used to that," Seamus smiled, holding out his hand for him to shake.

When Seamus had finished his first full day of work, he set out to scour the markets. Ophelia had forgotten to grab him a pair of socks—he didn't blame her after the odd exchange with *Lochlan*—so he embarked on the grueling journey to find himself a pair.

Stalls weathered by the harsh ever-winter of Snøbolig littered the town square, each selling a specialty it claimed no other could boast. Seamus quickly found the lies ran deep in that aspect. Banners frayed by the violent winds stood tall, their colors faded by the cold sun. The whole place reminded him of where *they* came from.

Strange.

He suddenly missed a place he hated wholeheartedly. Such a feeling made him nauseous. The sooner he left the market, the better; nostalgia was not a feeling Seamus fancied. Where others saw the past through a tinted scrying glass, he saw it for what it was—something to move on from and forget.

So why couldn't he?

Why did the past cling to him like a shadow?

Though difficult, he pushed these thoughts to the back of his mind. Seamus had never been one for philosophy. Such topics made his head spin. Maybe he was a simple man; maybe *they* had beaten the wonder out of him long ago. Whatever the reason, he did not wish to ponder further.

Socks.

All he needed to care about at this moment was socks.

Nice, warm, woolen socks.

Walking on, he took care to peruse each stall, ambling along like he hadn't a care in the world. Other than socks, of course. He very much so cared about socks.

Tø seemed well-rounded enough. At one stall, a young couple was selling wooden dinnerware and cutlery. At another, an elderly man sat alone, painting intricate floral patterns on little boxes. There were leather goods, books, and even trinkets from faraway lands. Interspersed between those frivolous goods were merchants offering dried fish, pastries, milk, and eggs.

But most importantly, there were copious amounts of knitwear.

Three elderly women sat behind a simple table full of scarves, cardigans, hats, gloves, and socks. So many socks. In every color and pattern. Seamus couldn't remember the last time he'd had a choice in his clothes. He'd never been one to care about his appearance, but he had surely taken for granted little things like that. Most of the clothes he'd had over the last few years were hastily stolen, ill-fitting, moth-eaten, and frayed.

His fingers traced the mountain of knitwear, the soft fibers reminding him of fur.

Whoever had knitted these—or crocheted, maybe? He didn't know the difference—was exceptionally talented. They must've spent years perfecting their craft, their dedication visible to even Seamus's untrained eyes. There were socks knitted with animals, socks with snowflakes, socks with stripes, dots, and zigzags. He'd never seen such things. Of course, all the wares were exquisitely crafted, but the socks! Oh, Stars, the socks!

Purple socks, blue socks, green socks.

Red, orange, yellow.

Neutrals.

They had everything! Every shade, every hue.

They surely had Seamus's favorite color.

Did he have a favorite color? He'd never worried about such things, even as a child. There was never any time for that. Yet here he stood, old enough to be halfway to the grave, thinking fuchsia was a lovely shade and that he'd quite like a pair of shocking pink socks. Or maybe he'd prefer moss green. Maybe both. Yes, both would do. He grabbed both pairs, holding them as if they were made of gold.

The ladies paid him no notice, deep in conversation.

"Trouble that one. I always said so. Don't know what he was thinking all those years ago," said one, her husky voice as arrogant as the expression on her face.

Two of the women nodded in unison. Seamus guessed they were sisters. Twins, perhaps.

"He wasn't thinking, I'd say," said one.

"Not at all," said the other.

"I'll tell you what he was thinking," began the first woman. She opened her mouth to continue, but her eyes fell on Seamus. With what was left of her teeth, she attempted a coy smile. "Well, hello, handsome. Are you finding everything all right?"

Seamus smiled brightly, giving a curt nod, trying not to stare at the gaping hole in her teeth. "How much?"

She shrugged. "I'll have to ask my daughter. All of these are hers." With some difficulty, she cleared her throat. "Ute!" she screamed at the top of her lungs.

Down a nearby alley came a loud crash, accompanied by stomping footsteps. Soon, a woman a few years younger than Seamus rounded the corner. Her blonde hair was pulled back into a bun, a knitted handkerchief tied around her forehead. He knew for sure it was knitted since she had a pair of knitting needles sticking out of her poke, a small external pocket resting at her hip.

"Yes, mama?" she asked, looking rather concerned.

"How much for the socks again, dearie?" the mother asked.

"Oh!" Ute said gleefully, her eyes falling on Seamus. "Four coppers a pair, sir."

"Ute!" scolded the twins.

"Ute. . ." sighed her mother, shaking her head. "He's a rather *handsome* fellow," she whispered behind a wrinkled hand covered in large age spots.

Ute rolled her eyes.

"Travelers discount," said one of the twins.

"Four for the *set*," said the other.

Seamus chuckled, smiling sympathetically at the visibly distressed knitter. He procured eight coppers from his trousers pocket, set them near her on the table, bowed, then turned and walked away.

"Was that *him*?" he heard one of the twins breathe.

"I do believe it was. He's very easy on the eyes, Ute. You know, you're not the only single woman around here. Snatch him up while you can, girl," said the mother.

"Just this morning, you were saying how evil and vile a creature had to be to hang around the *Dømte En*," Ute scoffed.

Seamus had learned early on that the ears of a wolf were not always a blessing. Some things were best left unheard.

Dømte En. Condemed One.

Ophelia.

That phrase was not spoken lightly. In a place without religion, what could she have possibly done to deserve a title like that?

Again, the tall tales from his childhood flooded his mind.

Ophelia of the Forest, whom the foxes worshipped and polar bears adored.

What had he gotten himself into?

Who was she really?

CHAPTER SEVEN

WOODCHIPS

Ophelia and Eydis sat playing with the grizzly cubs as the sun began to set. Ophelia felt an affinity for these cubs. Not once had she seen their mother. They were orphans like her. The only difference was that they had her and Eydis to care for them. Even the smallest forest creatures had taken to them, occasionally bringing offerings and leftover food. The cubs had a whole woodland looking after them. How lucky they must feel. And while the forest cared for her, too, Ophelia knew it didn't compare to the gentility of a mother and the protection of a father. A *human* mother and father.

"Do they stay all day?" came Seamus's gruff voice from the garden gate.

"Most of the time," Ophelia said.

Seamus looked on in awe as Eydis gently pawed at the cubs while Ophelia scratched the polar bear's head contently. "Don't you worry they'll hurt you?" he asked.

Eydis paused, narrowing her eyes in his direction before rolling onto her back and nudging Ophelia with her enormous paws.

"If that were ever to happen, I'm sure I would be deserving of such a fate," Ophelia said simply as she laid her head on Eydis's belly. She could lay like that forever, knowing she was safe in her companion's care.

Seamus raised a suspicious eyebrow but said nothing. With heavy footsteps, he walked up to the porch, eyeing the reindeer. It irked Ophelia that he didn't stop to stomp the mud from his boots before going inside. Eydis groaned, taking the words from Ophelia's tightly pursed lips.

"We must be kind," she whispered, "Mr. Norland is our guest." She gave Eydis a gentle squeeze before standing.

Eydis didn't seem convinced.

Brushing herself off and scraping the mud and snow from her pointy shoes, Ophelia went inside to find Seamus sitting at the kitchen table, pulling on a pair of moss-green socks adorned with swirling ferns. It was then that she remembered her earlier promise.

Her cheeks flushed beneath her mask. "I was meant to get you socks at Lochlan's."

Seamus only nodded, wriggling his toes in his new socks. There was a hint of a smirk on his lips.

"I can pay back whatever they cost," Ophelia whispered.

He turned to her, a contemplative air to his scowl. "No need," he said rather sternly.

With that, he returned his attention to his feet, adjusting the socks until they sat just right. Ophelia stood awkwardly in the doorway before kicking off her shoes and placing them neatly in their spot near the door. Seamus's had been discarded by the couch, a trail of mud behind them. Frowning, Ophelia grabbed them, walked back outside, and knocked them together until they were clean. Eydis snorted, her version of a laugh. Ophelia just rolled her eyes, waltzing back into the cottage to set Seamus's boots next to her own. One task done, one to go. Slightly disgruntled, she went to fetch a rag from the washroom. Once she returned, she quickly got to work cleaning up his careless prints, satisfied with the shine that particular patch of flooring now had. Standing, she turned toward the kitchen, embarrassed to see Seamus looking at her with dull disgust. She expected him to comment on her cleanliness, but again, he said nothing.

However, his silence spoke a thousand words.

"Shall I start on dinner?" Ophelia asked, rocking back and forth on the balls of her feet.

He shrugged, reaching into his satchel. From it, he procured a small leather roll, unfurling it to reveal carving tools that looked far too small for his hands. With a slight smile, he took each tool and held it to the light, inspecting the craftsmanship.

"What do you carve, Mr. Norland?" Ophelia asked, taking a loaf of bread from the cupboard.

"Whatever the wood wants to become," Seamus said simply.

"You can help yourself to any logs that speak to you," Ophelia offered, nodding toward the small stack by the wood stove. That stack usually sat untouched, the fireplace rarely lit. It was only on the coldest days, when all the animals took refuge inside the cottage, that she bothered to start a fire. With Seamus around, she figured she'd better keep it lit. Her skin prickled with sweat, making her feel almost feverish.

Seamus stared at the pile, a far-off look in his eyes. "We'll see."

Confused by his detached demeanor, Ophelia busied herself with cutting thin slices of the hearty bread and buttering them—two for her, three for him. Somewhere around here, she had a bit of dried meat that would pair quite nicely.

"Are you and Åssi getting along well?" she asked as she began opening every cupboard.

"Quite," Seamus said, though he didn't sound as enthusiastic as he had earlier.

Finding what she was looking for, Ophelia placed a brown paper packet on the table, carefully untying the twine that bound it. Seamus raised an eyebrow, watching intently as she rolled up the twine, saving it for later use.

"Is everything all right, Mr. Norland?" she asked softly, sitting across from him, foot tapping nervously beneath the table. Her hands twitched with anticipation.

Seamus took several strips of the meat and placed them between two buttered slices of bread. He ate thoughtfully for a moment, staring at her as if he could see through her mask.

"You said you didn't have a last name," he said after a while. That statement was accusatory. She didn't like it.

"I don't."

"Yet they call you Av'Skogen."

All Ophelia could do was nod. "I've noticed."

Seamus took another bite, an eyebrow raised. "I overheard some things this evening," he said nonchalantly.

Ophelia stiffened, folding her hands tightly on her lap, a

violent, worried shiver threatening to overtake her. "What sort of things?"

"Gossip mostly. . ." His voice trailed off as he gazed around the kitchen. "What do you think of Miss Ute and her mother?" he asked, watching her carefully.

"Ute is kind enough. Her mother, Tine, tends to keep to herself. Why?" Ophelia hoped her half-lie sounded convincing.

Ute was indeed kind, but she'd never really tried to befriend Ophelia. Like most of the town, she steered clear of Ophelia and her menagerie. While she didn't know Ophelia was a Witch, she did believe her to be a Skogens Søstre. That alone was enough for most to keep a distance. Tine, on the other hand, was a menace. She was always sticking her nose in everyone else's business, so she and the other women who followed Ute like hawks had something to talk about.

"Are they the kind of women one can trust?" Seamus asked, those hazel eyes still melting holes into Ophelia's fox-faced mask. "Their opinions, I mean. The truth of what they say."

She shook her head. He tilted his to the side. For a while, he just sat before her in silence, the candle between them reflecting a raging fire in his unblinking eyes. His thin lips were pulled into a frown, and his brows furrowed in their usual fashion—halfway between confused and angered.

The moment he looked away was so sudden it startled Ophelia.

"I think the only opinion that should matter is the one you have of yourself," Seamus began through a mouthful of the world's saddest sandwich. "Whether or not you think yourself a good person. Whether you wake up each day and try to live up to that notion."

"Do you think yourself a good person, Mr. Norland?" Ophelia asked quietly, worrying the hem of her sleeve.

"Doesn't everyone?"

"I think you're a good person," she replied. Deep down, somehow, she knew he was.

His laugh was like thorns on a rose, meant to ward off those careless enough to pluck something beautiful without a second thought. "Kid, you don't even know me," he said, standing. There was a stagger in his step as he made for the lounge.

That was the truth of it. Still, she knew he was.

Ophelia wondered if she would ever get to know him. He was meant to stay in her home until he felt fit to take on the world. In that time, would his carefully constructed mask ever crack? Ophelia couldn't say why she yearned to know him so deeply, but she would do all she could to weasel his very soul out of him if that's what it took to see beyond all the scars and the sarcastic smiles. That's what she did. What she'd done to everyone she'd ever met.

Yet no one had ever done the same for her.

Seamus picked up a thin log and snapped off a piece. Bark fell to the floor as he whittled away. Ophelia took her sorry excuse for dinner to the bench by the bookshelves, picking a tome whose spine was worn from being read one too many times.

"Do you have a favorite color?" Seamus asked, sounding tired.

Ophelia repeated the sentence in her mind, unsure of what she'd just heard. She looked up from her book, watching him carve away, the knife nearly nicking his thumb one too many times.

"I quite like periwinkle," she said after a while.

He nodded to himself. "I am fond of moss green, myself."

"That's a good one. I have paint in that color."

He smiled, leaning toward the light of the burning fire. "You like to paint?"

"Very much," she mumbled, unsure where this was going.

"Are you any good?" he asked.

"I'd say it's not up to me to decide, but the only opinion that matters is my own," Ophelia teased. "So yes, I think I am a very good painter—an all-around good artist if I do say so myself."

His eyes flicked up to her as he held up his handiwork for her to observe.

A fox.

A fox whose face oddly resembled her mask.

He tossed it to her, sitting back on the lounge, his tired eyes scanning his surroundings as if seeing them for the first time.

"It's beautiful, Seamus," Ophelia breathed, running her fingers along every curve.

He waved away her praises. "It's not finished just yet. When I'm done, you should paint it. I think a periwinkle fox would be quite interesting."

He packed away his carving tools, replacing them in his satchel. He yawned, pulling a heavy fur off the back of the lounge. Ophelia took this as him turning in for the night. She stood, blowing out the candles near her, placing the wooden fox atop the book she'd been reading.

"Goodnight, Mr. Norland," she said as he settled into his makeshift bed.

"God natt, Ophelia Without-A-Last-Name," he said groggily.

CHAPTER EIGHT

MARKET DAYS

Days passed, and a routine formed.

Seamus rose with the sun, accompanied by a crotchety wolverine who had managed to curl up on his lap overnight without him noticing. Once Ophelia tended to her menagerie, they'd eat a quick breakfast, and then he went off to work. On the way, he'd ask if anyone needed help around town, finding odd jobs that paid with extra goods instead of coins. Ophelia was over the moon the first day he'd brought back a wilted head of cabbage. She said her rabbits would be eating well, thanks to him. Begrudgingly, he'd handed it off, burying the hopes she would've made a stew with it.

When Seamus was done with work, he'd collect his payment and return to the cottage, stolen scraps hidden in his satchel for a late-night snack. Ophelia would be in the kitchen starting dinner or baking a heavenly confectionery. After dinner, she would sit in the corner and read or scribble away in the giant notebook she kept at her side. All the while, Seamus would whittle away at a log or two.

Once the moon had risen to its apex, Ophelia would blow out the candles and bid him goodnight. He'd stare at the ceiling for an hour or two, then wind up sitting in the moonlight, listening to the quiet hum of night. He listened for hints of danger, but the forest was always silent. The only sound came from Ophelia's owls. Without fail, they would accompany him each evening, their hoots like music. Ophelia had stated multiple times they didn't enjoy his company, but Seamus liked to pretend she was wrong.

In the three and a half weeks he'd been there, Tø had become home.

He should be grateful to have a place to call his, even if he had to share it with someone he didn't necessarily trust and barely knew.

It wasn't that there was anything objectively wrong with Ophelia. She was kind, overly caring, soft-spoken, and generous. But the way the town whispered about her gave him pause.

He didn't believe her capable of doing something horrendous enough to be constantly called a 'condemned one.' Still, as far as he knew, she was the only Skogens Søstre in the area. That was odd enough to make him question things. The Søstre usually traveled in large groups, caring for the forest and performing rituals to send their love to the Stars above. Seamus had not heard of someone encountering a solitary Søstre. Besides that, her choice of mask unnerved him. Why a fox? The Fox was the Spirit of Illusion. Why had she picked that trait of all to represent herself? Most chose to take up the face of something more. . . innocent? They took their religion very seriously, only removing their masks during certain parts of the year or, in some cases, not at all. Especially not in front of men. They were wild creatures, more animal than human, which was why they felt the creatures of the forest were kindred spirits.

One of those boxes Ophelia checked. Everything else was a contradiction.

Furthermore, what did they think of him if the town held her in such low regard? Tine had judged him by whispers, calling him vile and evil for being around her. Yet her opinion changed the moment she laid eyes upon him. That strange man with the bloodied apron had hated him the second he learned he was frolicking around with Ophelia. And Lochlan? Well, he seemed to have a deep loathing for everyone and everything. What a fun characteristic to find in a healer. As for the rest of the town, the only person who'd genuinely accepted him with open arms beside Ophelia was Åsmund.

So, despite his better judgment, he kept the girl at arm's length. He was cordial and friendly enough to get by, but he never offered anything that could be used against him or sully the remainder of his good name.

Ophelia talked of him selling his carvings at her stall on the weekends. Seamus declined.

Ophelia asked if she could accompany him to work in the mornings. Seamus declined.

Ophelia offered to introduce him to all her animal friends. Seamus declined.

He did all he could to avoid her. Her mere presence risked everything he was working so hard to build.

Yet he was drawn to her. Inexplicably so.

She gave away her good graces so freely, never treating him differently just because he declined her many offers. She put up with his aloofness, unperturbed. It saddened him knowing she was used to such treatment. Of course, there was also the way she cared for beings that could never repay her. That touched his wolf's heart, for sure. He also respected how she valued quiet contemplation and a good book.

She was strange, infuriating, and lovable all at the same time. He hated the mystery surrounding her.

But he didn't hate her or any of her quirks.

Not even a little.

Seamus woke to the pitter-patter of footsteps he'd begun to associate with Ophelia trying her best to be quiet. She was always up before him, tending to whatever the night had drug in. Almost always, it was the grizzly cubs, cold and hungry, pawing at the front door. Nodding to Eydis, who had the cubs sleeping on her back, he stretched, shaking the cold from his bones. The cottage was always freezing in the mornings. The fire never lasted through the night.

"God morgen, kid," he yawned, wrapping one of his blankets around his shoulders to ward off his shivers.

Ophelia waved absentmindedly to him as she stood tying bundles of fur in neat little rolls. For a girl whose only friends were animals, she sure did have a lot of pelts, antlers, teeth, and bones lying around.

"God morgen Mr. Norland! Breakfast?" he asked, peering over her shoulder as her constantly shaking hands struggled to tie a bow.

"You'll have to grab a muffin on your way out. I'm already running late," she said, untying and attempting to retie the bow for the third time in a row. Over the past few weeks, he'd noticed her constant shaking worsened when her nerves got the best of her. On market days, she rattled like a snake's tail.

"You know, if you need help, you could just ask," he said, shrugging, his blanket swishing around his ankles.

Giving him a bored look, she pushed the bundle toward him. He smirked, tying a perfect bow on the first try.

"Thank you," she mumbled, rolling a fluffy raccoon tail into a spiral.

Seamus bowed, spreading his blanket wide and crossing his ankles. If he could see her eyes, he figured she'd be rolling her eyes at him as he walked down the hall to the washroom.

At the beginning of the week, he'd purchased a new pair of trousers and a thicker tunic. Despite their drabness, he thought the smoke-gray tunic and brown pants suited him. The act of purchasing instead of stealing had lifted his spirits a fair amount, too.

When he returned to the kitchen, Seamus made a spectacle of himself, doing a little spin to show off his outfit. Ophelia chuckled to herself, pushing the raccoon tail toward him to tie.

"Are you sure you don't want to sell a few of your carvings at my stall? I really don't mind, Mr. Norland."

Seamus thought for a moment. He could use the extra coin, plus it'd make the kid ever-so happy. He sighed heavily, succumbing to her smile and cheery disposition. The cold followed her wherever she went, but he'd be lying if he said she didn't try to be eternally sunny.

"I have a few I could part with," he said with a shrug.

After he tied a few more bows, he grabbed a muffin from the pantry and walked over to the bench by the bookshelves. Lifting the ratty blanket that covered it, he slid out a small box with an array of carvings inside. Usually, he carved people, but lately, he'd been inspired by the constant variety of animals in Ophelia's garden. Carefully, he picked up the box and set it on the table next to her.

"Which ones?" he asked, picking up a stocky carving of an old man wearing a horned helm.

Ophelia scanned the box's contents before plucking a carving of a sleeping bear cub with a moon on its forehead from inside.

"I'll take the whole box and bring back whatever didn't sell."

"I appreciate that. I'll come see ya on my break," Seamus smiled, reaching forward to pat her on the shoulder. Grimacing, he hesitated, his hand hovering for a moment before he dropped it awkwardly at his side. "Well, I best be off."

He bid her farewell, and out the door he went.

The ground was even muddier after last night's heavy rain. A particularly wet patch nearly stole Seamus's boot. A cart and horse must have come through sometime this morning. The path leading into town had deep wheel treads. Walking in the tracks was easier since they weren't as sticky, but they were still extra slippery.

Tø was bustling this morning. Villagers were going about their lives, a sense of excitement in the air. Seamus couldn't blame them. It was the last day of work before the weekend. He was grateful Åsmund had allotted him a break. His past employers hadn't given him such an amenity.

Still, he knew what was coming this weekend. At the thought, he bristled. He would have preferred the work to distract himself instead of idling away in morbid anticipation.

"God morgen, Åssi!" Seamus called upon entering the old butcher. He traded his fur mantle for an apron, reading over the order list for the day.

"God morgen, Seamus! Running a wee late, aren't we?" Åsmund laughed, handing over a cleaver.

"Ja, slept in and had to help Ophelia pack up for the market."

"Did you see if she had any antlers left from the last carcass? Wife wants to make some new runes." Åsmund laughed. "Our eldest son has taken to divination."

"I'll ask when I see her later."

For a man like Seamus, friends were a rarity. Åsmund was the closest he'd been to having one in years. They talked about life and sometimes death as they did their bloody work. Åsmund listened quietly, letting Seamus ramble about how he had no idea how to busy himself without work. He'd hoped that'd give him the hint that he wanted to work overtime this weekend.

"I'm sure Ophelia will find a way to keep you busy. She's always got some sort of long-winded rant prepared," Åsmund said, a soft smirk on his lips. For a butcher, he was rather soft-spoken. Despite the boom of his voice, his tone was almost papery. This unnerved Seamus. Deeply.

"So I've noticed. Her philosophical talks could kill a man," Seamus laughed. "Yesterday, she was going on about the books she was reading. Comparing the author's notes to the—" he cleared his throat "—the fragility of life," he finished haughtily.

"She learned that from Lochlan," Åsmund said, wiping his hands on his apron so he could tie up his long dreadlocks with a spare piece of twine. "Speaking of, he stopped by and asked about you yesterday. Have you met him?"

"Briefly. What did he want?"

Åsmund shrugged. "Just wanted to know what I knew about you. If you'd divulged any of your *mysterious* past to me," he said, wriggling his fingers in a way he must have thought amusing.

"Interesting." Nothing good ever came from someone asking too many questions.

"You aren't in any sort of trouble, are you?"

Seamus grimaced. "Not currently. However, I do tend to stick my nose where it doesn't belong."

"Why doesn't that surprise me?" Åsmund asked, tying his long dreadlocks into a bun at the back of his head.

Seamus gave a half-hearted shrug. "Beats me."

Åsmund's laugh was like thunder. "Well, point of advice: Lochlan has a soft spot for the kid. He'd do anything to protect her; Stars know why. Stay on good terms with her, and you'll be on good terms with him."

Seamus paused his constant chop-chop-chopping to look up at him. "You're serious? When I met him, he seemed like he didn't care for anyone, much less her."

"If it weren't for him, Ophelia would very well be dead." Seamus didn't like the tone Åsmund used. "He found her as a baby, abandoned in the woods. He's cared for her her whole life, even gifting her his old cottage once she was old enough to care for herself. I know he's a bit odd, but he loves that kid in his own special way," Åsmund explained.

"Could have fooled me," Seamus mumbled.

Ophelia stumbled into town, arms piled high with furs and crates full of antlers, Seamus's carvings, and a few bones. She'd nearly dropped everything twice, but thanks to an over-eager child ready to help, she hadn't ruined any of the pelts just yet. The day was still young.

"Ophelia!" came Saoirse, her voice full of excitement. "Need help?"

"I would very much appreciate that!" Ophelia chuckled.

Her load lightened as Saoirse—her red hair like fire in the bright sun and anxious breeze—took half her furs and set them on the stall she'd set up the night before. She and Saoirse set to work creating an artful display.

Saoirse was one of Ophelia's closest friends and happened to be one of the few who knew her secret and didn't treat her differently because of it. Her friendship meant the world to Ophelia. They were almost sisters, in a way. In the eyes of the oblivious, they would be should Saoirse join the Skogen Søstre.

"Did you do these?" Saoirse asked, picking up a carving of a raven.

"Seamus did. He whittles in his free time."

"Beautiful! How much?"

"Five coppers for the small, twelve for the bigger ones."

Saoirse picked up two more carvings and handed over the appropriate payment. "My sisters will love these. Tell Seamus he does good work."

"Will do! Good luck today!" Ophelia called as Saoirse skipped away to her father's store.

Despite how the townsfolk kept their distance on any typical day, Ophelia was used to her stall being busy. No one could deny her talent for finding such high-quality pelts, antlers, and bones. Ophelia knew each and every creature in the surrounding woods. This meant she knew when one died and how to pay respects to them properly. It was strange, but she seemed to know which animals would want to live on, their fur or bones being made into something humans would care for instead of laying in the dirt for all eternity. Others would rather snub humans entirely. Either way, Ophelia respected their wishes. Eventually, the villagers did, too. One too many tears had been shed, so they delegated the job of procuring pelts to Ophelia. The only people above this rule were the hunters, though she wasn't keen on that. Of course, some tried to oppose this, but for the most part, everyone was happy to entertain this quirk of hers.

By lunch, Ophelia had sold half her furs and nearly all of Seamus's carvings. That was the thing about Tø. The people sought joy in everything, for the gray skies and frigid air often made it difficult to find. Art in all its forms was prized above all else. No price was too high, and no amount of time was too much to hone one's craft. In this way, Seamus's carvings had been a hit. Several people had fought over the larger statues, one even offering triple the price to secure a howling wolf as their own.

Seamus would be positively ecstatic.

"God ettermiddag, Ophelia," came Lochlan's slow drawl.

"Afternoon to you too," Ophelia said, straightening, hoping this visit wouldn't last long.

"I've heard your stray is settling in nicely," Lochlan sighed, stroking one of the leftover furs.

"O—Oh! Yes! He's quite popular with the townies. Åsmund had him over for dinner the other night. I—I do believe they've become fast friends," Ophelia stuttered.

"How interesting. He seemed rather surly to me." Lochlan wore a disgusted expression as he wiped his hands on his robes. "Do you have what I requested, child?"

Ophelia nodded, digging around in the pockets of her cloak for a small sachet of cowbane, a poisonous plant Lochlan was studying. His curiosity led him down many winding paths. He had friends in every corner of the world seeking his help. Lately, he'd been experimenting with poisons. Again.

"This'll do nicely. Thank you," he said, his eyes filled with a sick sort of wonder. "How is the stray treating you, child?"

"Good." Ophelia shrugged. She bit her tongue before reminding him of Seamus's name.

Lochlan looked her up and down, nodded, and then

walked away. She'd become used to being his errand girl, but lately, she'd grown tired of it. Still, it was better than the alternative. . .

Ophelia slouched on her stool, pulling out her sketchbook as the townies dispersed for lunch. Chances were she wouldn't make another sale until after they returned, which was fine by her. She had more than enough in her pocket for some new books. Saoirse had told her there was a new bookshop in one of the nearby towns she'd very much enjoy visiting. Plus, she could use some new graphite sticks. Hers were on their last leg.

She sat waiting for Seamus and sketched some of his carvings in her sketchbook. One of her favorites was still left, so she added it to her book before it was gone forever. Some children were playing around the old fountain that she jotted down, too. This sketchbook wasn't just a place to scribble away in; it was a compendium of memories. She'd gone through so many over the years, but this one was her favorite. It was giant, bigger than her head, about as thick as a small log. She'd been working on filling it for about a year now and was nowhere near finished. Oftentimes, she flipped through it when she was too tired to read.

"Well, how'd we do?" Seamus asked, waltzing up to her with an overflowing cup of cloudberries.

Ophelia took a handful of berries as she slid over the pouch of coins she'd set aside for him. "All of this is what you made on your carvings."

Seamus's eyes about popped out of his head. "That entire pouch?"

Ophelia nodded as she snacked on her handful of berries. "I did well, too. Expecting both of us will sell out after lunch."

"Incredible," Seamus breathed, slipping around the stall to sit on the table's edge. "Which reminds me, Åsmund wants to know if you have any antlers left."

"I have a few he could look through! You can bring them back with you if you'd like. Tell him it's on the house."

"Will do," Seamus smiled, saluting her.

Ophelia picked at her handful of berries, happy to just stare at him for a while. He was not what she'd expected in many ways. Having Seamus around was a nice change of pace, though she knew he would be leaving soon. With today's sales and Åsmund practically overpaying him, he had more than enough saved to get out of Tø. There was something, somewhere, he needed to return to.

Plus, she was ready to get home back and not have to wear her mask all day. She missed the freedom living alone had brought her. So did her animals, though Eydis and Narfi were finally warming up to him. Jury was still out on the owls, however. That bothered her, of course, but something else did, too. If she was ready for him to leave, why did the thought of him leaving make her so sad?

Even in the care of Lochlan, Ophelia had been alone for most of her life. She'd always been a burden to Lochlan, never a blessing, which was strange considering how he viewed her powers. The most she'd been to him was something to poke and prod at, something to cut open and figure out its workings. Sometimes, she wondered whether he even saw her as human. She certainly didn't see him that way.

Lochlan and Tø had strikes against them, but it was home. The story goes that she was on her deathbed as a baby. Had Lochlan not taken her in on a stormy night eighteen years ago, she'd not be here today. Had Tø not been the hidden gem it was, her secret could've been found out, and she would've been hanged or worse. This was the first and only place that had given her shelter from the storm that was her life. She was grateful for this home, and in a morbid sense, she was thankful to Lochlan, too.

But she was lonely.

So very, *very* lonely.

Lending the lounge to Seamus had eased the ache in her heart if only a little. Ophelia had grown to like caring for Seamus Norland, the wandering traveler. She knew he did not feel the same, but maybe with time, he would.

With these thoughts swirling in her head, Ophelia cleared her throat, wringing her hands. "I'm thinking of heading west to a town called Gulch tomorrow. Would you like to join me?" she asked, watching Seamus's face fill with curiosity. "It'll be about a full day's trip there and back on foot, but I'm sure I can find someone to lend us a horse or two."

There was no doubt in her mind that his answer would be no, so to say she was shocked by his hesitation was an understatement. He seemed to mull over her question, a thoughtful expression on his face as he finished his berries. Part of him wanted to say yes.

"Tomorrow, you say? Would it be possible to go on a different day?"

Ophelia nearly fell off her stool from astonishment. He was considering it! He really was! "O—Of course! Do you have plans tomorrow, then?"

He stared blankly at the ground for a moment, opening and closing his mouth several times. "Yes. I'm going to the lake for some light fishing. Planned on spending the whole day out there." He chewed his bottom lip, not meeting her eyes.

Ophelia frowned. He was hiding something.

"Will Åssi be going with you?" she asked carefully.

"Haven't asked yet," he said dryly.

Ophelia hated being lied to. So many people had mistaken her kindness for stupidity and weakness. Whatever Seamus was up to, she hoped it wasn't nefarious. The last thing she needed was another reason for Tø to look down on her. One more misstep and even her pelts and antlers wouldn't be enough to win partial favor.

CHAPTER NINE

PHASES

Ophelia slept horribly that night. Wind and freezing rain had battered the cottage, fueled by her rampant emotions.

All who knew her had determined her value by her kindness. They'd convinced her to believe that was all that mattered in life. She knew how far a small gesture could go, how the smallest act could change the trajectory of one's life. Kindness was a currency, in a way. Most hoarded it like gold. Ophelia, however, offered it freely to those who needed it, those who asked, and even those who didn't necessarily deserve it. She'd not experienced such things herself and never wanted anyone to feel the way she had all her life. However, the older she grew, the more she wondered if her kindness should have been spent a little wiser.

One thing was certain: good deeds added up. One day, she'd be repaid. That's how karma worked.

Or at least that's what she hoped.

That's how her books often described it.

Maybe it was wrong to think such things, but she couldn't help but wonder when all those acts of kindness would finally add up. Selfishly, she had hoped Seamus would be the tipping point.

Now, she was second-guessing herself yet again.

She kept thinking back to how uneasy she felt that day he staggered into the clearing and tried to steal a rabbit. There'd been a voice in her head screaming at her to run, but she'd ignored it, and now she had to lie in the bed she'd made. She still believed deep down he was a good man, but it unsettled her how the owls refused to warm up to him, how his eyes held a darkness that seemed to consume everything around him, and how his many walls seemed impenetrable.

It didn't help that something was so obviously brewing today.

Whatever happened, Ophelia knew she'd be the one to take the brunt of it all. Should that happen, she'd rather know now than later if Seamus was up to no good. If he were innocent and genuinely spent the day fishing, then she would have to be his alibi. If not, then there was a chance to plead her case.

As always, she and Seamus sat together at the table for breakfast in comfortable silence. She had her nose in a book, one she'd read a thousand times before. The spine was cracked, the pages torn, but she never tired of joining winged pirates on their many adventures across the lands. Meanwhile, Seamus was laying out hooks for his fishing rod. Åsmund must've lent him a spare. He seemed distracted, his hands hovering in the air for quite some time as he stared at the gleaming silver hooks.

"May I join you today?" Ophelia asked, offering him the last kringle—a buttery, icing-covered pastry filled to bursting with cheese—to sweeten the deal. She'd baked them the day before, glad she had nuts and fruit to stuff between the layers of dough.

Seamus gave her a skeptical look. "You fish?"

Ophelia's cheeks reddened beneath her mask. Sometimes she wondered if the cover spread across the wooden fox's face, too. ". . . No. . . Well, I mean, no one has ever taught me before."

He smirked, graciously taking the kringle. "Maybe another time, kid."

"I'll pack lunches! I swear I won't scare the fish or anything. In fact, you'll probably have better luck with me around."

After finishing off his breakfast, Seamus stood, taking their empty plates to the washbasin. "Next time," he insisted, this time a little gruffer.

Ophelia huffed, cupping her face in her hands as she watched Seamus clean their plates.

"However," he said, using his fork to point at her. "I will take you up on the lunch offer."

"Of course you would," she said under her breath.

"I heard that, my lady."

"You know, Mr. Norland—"

"Seamus," he corrected. "Just Seamus."

"*Seamus*," she enunciated, "I really don't like it when you call me that."

Before setting their plates down, he turned back to her, looking a little hurt. "Someone is in a foul mood this morning."

"Maybe all I need is a day on the lake," Ophelia murmured, hoping that might finally convince him.

Seamus inhaled deeply. "Unrelenting. That's what you are," he sighed. As he spoke, he gestured with the plates. "Listen. I've had a very long week. All I want is some peace and quiet."

"I can be quiet!" Ophelia pleaded. If she was unrelenting, he was just as stubborn.

"I seriously doubt that."

"I promise I can! Please let me go, Mr. Norland! I swear—"

"I said no!" Seamus snapped, his voice shaking the room.

Ophelia scrambled to her feet, nearly knocking over her chair. The shadows on his face and his bear-like stance made him look monstrous in the light filtering in through the lacy curtains behind him. He was panting heavily, eyes wild, clutching a plate as though he intended to throw it.

When he finally noticed Ophelia's fear, Seamus's face softened, his eyes drooping like he'd come out of a trance. The plates slipped from his hands, horror replacing rage.

His actions reminded her of someone she'd once trusted with her life.

She hated it.

"I'm—I didn't mean to—" he stuttered, stumbling into the table as he reached down to pick up the broken plate. Quickly, he swept up the mess, never so much as glancing her way.

Ophelia recoiled into the corner as he grabbed his fishing pole and hooks. Without a word, he stomped out the door, mumbling angrily under his breath. Half of her wanted him to turn around and apologize. Maybe she really was asking too much, or perhaps someone had said or done something that had gotten under his skin. Even if his sudden shift in mood was her fault, she hoped he regretted yelling at her.

Her other half wanted her to run out into the garden and apologize to the owls for ignoring their warnings, even though she knew they were rarely wrong.

Ophelia wanted so badly to believe Seamus was like her, that he'd been judged too harshly, thrown to The Wilds by no fault of his own. But he hadn't offered an explanation as to why he was here. Sometimes, she wondered if he deserved The Wilds as punishment.

Was he who he appeared to be?

Or was he one of the people her books warned about?

Seamus had intended to spend the day in peace. Now, however, he wasn't sure he would ever find peace again.

He had never been a worrier. But he had always been a protector. If someone was loyal to him, he was loyal to them. That kid had put a roof over his head—had vouched for him to stay in Tø. Even if she didn't know it, she was protecting him.

And how had he repaid her?

Snapped at her for no reason.

Declined every kindness.

Treated her like a maid.

He hated full moons. The moon's pull made every emotion more potent, but his anger and irritation doubled tenfold. He hadn't meant to yell at Ophelia, but her nagging had driven him over the edge.

The moon magnified his guilt, too. It nagged worse than she did as he made his way to the lake. As he cast his line and waited for the fish to bite, he tried to devise a sufficient apology.

"Ophelia," he said to himself, "I would like to apologize

for my temper. Sometimes, it gets the best of me. Please don't kick me out of the cottage."

Not good enough.

"Dearest Ophelia," he yawned, reeling in his line just to cast it again. "I am a horribly cranky old man whose life is meaningless. Forgive me?"

He thought for a moment, frowning.

"You're not a creep, Seamus," he sighed, "and you're not *that* old. . ."

Actions would speak louder than words.

If he wasn't completely drained tomorrow morning, he could convince her to keep their plans and go to that town she'd been talking about. Maybe there was something at a shop she had her eye on? Surely, he could dip into his savings for a book or whatever she was so excited about. Or maybe there was an event of some sort? A musician? He could buy tickets to the show, perhaps.

Of course, words *and* actions were his best bet.

Clearing his throat, he opened his mouth to try out another horrid apology. Though he thought long and hard, his mind was blank. That was another thing he hated about full moons. The closer it came to rising, the more wolf-like he became. His thoughts would slowly shift to silence, every sound setting him on edge. If Ophelia thought his temper was bad this morning, she was in for a rude awakening. By sunset, he'd be unrecognizable.

Which was precisely why he'd come to the lake.

He couldn't risk hurting someone. Most days, he could keep a grip on his wolf, but on days like today and nights like tonight, the moon's power was intoxicating, turning him into a rage-filled drunk. There wasn't a full moon he could fully remember, at least not in recent years. He could've done unspeakable things and had no memory of it.

Shuddering from all the 'what ifs,' he put up his fishing pole, wondering why the fish weren't biting. He'd hoped to have something to appease his wolf before nightfall. Wasting time here meant he'd have less of a chance to get as far away from Tø as he could.

So, discarding his fishing pole, he continued his search for words as he walked on, listening to the forest, hoping his pursuers had moved on. Nearly four weeks of quiet likely meant *they* had, but he didn't put anything past *them. They* could be waiting behind any of the trees, plotting an ambush.

"Ophelia," he said again, warily gazing around at his surroundings. "The way I treated you was wrong. For that, I apologize. I know you just wanted to spend the day with me for whatever reason. While I don't understand why you would ever want to do that, I appreciate the sentiment. No one has shown me such kindness. At least not for a very long time. Meeting you and staying in Tø has been an answer to my prayers. I hope you can find it in your heart to forgive me."

He meant every word.

He just hoped she would realize it.

Ophelia had spent the morning stewing in resentment, which was unusual for her. She tried her best to be happy-go-lucky no matter the circumstances. This bubbling feeling of bitterness in the pit of her stomach made her nauseous. How unlike her. Her disgust with herself only made the feeling worse. She hated it.

She hated even more that a raincloud had formed above her head and had yet to dissipate. Puddles followed wherever she went, forcing her to keep a mop at her side in a sorry attempt to sop up the rain and her emotions.

The afternoon was spent pacing the entirety of her cottage, slipping and sliding on the wet floorboards that would no doubt grow mold in a few days' time. Now, as the sun began to set—her anger disappearing with it—she was mustering up the courage to confront Seamus when he arrived home.

Ophelia was definitely disappointed in him, but as she sat stewing in her anger, she realized she was disappointed in herself, too. He wasn't the only one acting unfairly, and he wasn't the only one in the cottage with secrets they refused to tell. Still, no matter how she tried to spin it, none of it changed the fact that he'd hurt her feelings. He owed her an apology as much as she did him.

The more she thought about it, the more she realized it

would break her heart if he didn't come home tonight. Their cottage would feel so empty without him.

It was then she noticed she'd been thinking of the cottage as 'theirs' and not 'hers' all day.

Nightfall drew closer, and there was still no sign of him. He said he'd spend the whole day at the lake, but she assumed he'd be back by now. Worry was eating at her; the thought of not knowing where he was worsening the nauseous feeling she'd had all day. Åssi might've gone with him. Perhaps he had gone home with him for dinner? It was a long shot, but it was a good start.

Trying her best to calm herself and not jump to any conclusions, she quickly made her way into town, roaming the streets until she found herself on Åsmund's doorstep. She knocked several times, peering in the window to see him lounging in the den with his children. He waved to her with a friendly smile as his wife, Orla, opened the door.

"Dear child, you look as though you've seen a ghost. Is everything all right?" she asked slowly, mild concern on her face.

"Yes, I was just looking for Seamus. I thought he said he'd be visiting today," Ophelia said absentmindedly, peering inside their home as if she thought he was hiding from her.

"He's not home from fishing?" Åsmund asked, eyes alight with worry.

Ophelia shook her head. "Did you go with him this morning?"

"No. He asked to borrow a rod and said he'd return it when he came to work at the beginning of the week," he explained, standing, giving Orla a knowing look.

"I'm sure he's all right, Ophelia, dear," Orla said, putting a comforting hand on her shoulder. Ophelia twitched away, unable to hide her frown. At least they couldn't see the disgust in her eyes.

Åsmund, like herself, didn't seem convinced by Orla's words. "You're going to look for him, aren't you?"

Ophelia only nodded, clutching her cloak tight to stop her hands from shaking.

"If you aren't back within the hour, I'm assembling a

search party.”

“Thank you, Åssi,” Ophelia trembled, turning back down the path.

The sky was purple when she finally made it to the lake. There sat Seamus’s fishing rod, but he was nowhere to be seen. She called his name a few times, but all she got in return was her echo.

However, there was a trail of footprints leading away from the muddy lakeshore.

“No going back now,” she whispered as she took to the path.

Why was he out in the woods this late? He should’ve been packing up and heading home for the night. In fact, he should’ve done that hours ago.

“Mr. Norland?” she whispered, weaving through the trees. “Seamus?”

Silence.

Nary the hoot of an owl or the scurrying of a squirrel.

Just silence.

Ophelia could read the forest as if it were a book. Something was wrong—*really* wrong.

“Seamus!” she screamed at the top of her lungs.

Not once had Ophelia been afraid of these woods. But as the sky darkened and the boot prints disappeared into the shadows, she felt as if every branch was out to get her. The Wilds had claimed many victims because of these trees. They had seen their fair share of bloodshed in their long lives, and Ophelia knew they would see more long after she was gone.

“Seamus!” she yelled again.

Pounding footsteps startled her. In the dark, she could make out a hunched-over figure lumbering toward her. They were panting heavily, branches breaking under their feet.

“What are you doing out here?” came Seamus’s voice. He sounded like he was in pain.

“Me? What are *you* doing out here? You should’ve been back hours ago!” she screeched, rushing to his aid. He was clutching his side, eyes shut tightly. “What happened to you?”

"I'm f—fine. Y—You can't be out here," he coughed, steadying himself against a nearby tree, swatting away her hands.

Ophelia opened her mouth to protest when a loud snap cut her off. Seamus doubled over, crying out in pain. His hands clenched into tight fists, pulling clumps of mud from the ground.

"G—Go," he choked out, another snap filling the air. Startled, he jolted up, holding his head in his hands.

Ophelia stumbled back. Maybe 'hands' wasn't the right word. Where fingernails had been, there were now long, thick, jagged claws. The claws were horrifying on their own, but the long gray fur jutting out over his skin was what made Ophelia's heart skip a beat.

Another snap filled the silence, and Ophelia realized the sound was coming from him.

It all made sense now. His temper. His appetite. The way his wounds had healed. The way the livestock was afraid of him.

He *wasn't* who he said he was.

He *wasn't* human.

But he *was* just like *her*.

He scrambled to his feet, his long claws digging into the tree next to him, causing clusters of bark to fall to the ground like drops of blood. "Run, kid," he said, his voice rough as if he'd been screaming for millennia.

"You're a werewolf," Ophelia whispered.

He whipped his head around to look at her, his wild eyes glowing pale green in the dark. His nose and cheekbones were pointier than she remembered.

"It's okay! I won't tell anyone, promise!" she said, her voice far too cheerful for the current situation.

He snarled at her, barring his sharp teeth. "I can't control it!" he growled.

Ophelia took a step back, colliding with a tree. She knew she should be running as fast as she could but was frozen. Wonderment and fear waged a war inside her chest. Frightened, freezing wind whipped at her hair, stinging her face.

Seamus opened his mouth—most likely to lecture her—

when his leg buckled beneath him. The sound of his bones shattering made Ophelia's stomach churn. He whimpered like an injured dog, shutting his eyes tight.

"Go!" he spat through gritted teeth, glowing eyes cast toward the ground.

The full moon was rising over the trees. Even if she were to run, his wolf would catch her.

"Seamus, listen to me," she said softly. "The more you fight the transformation, the worse it will be."

He looked up at her, a crazed look in his eyes. "Do—Do you have a d—death wish?" he snapped.

"Debatable," she whispered, pressing herself flat against her tree. "We need to get you out of here. Åssi will be putting together a search party by now. If they see you, they'll try and kill you."

"What? Why would he be—" he swallowed hard, struggling back up to his feet "—putting together a search party? What in Snake's name have you done?"

Steeling herself, Ophelia reached for his arm. "We were worried about you."

Before she even touched him, he shoved her away, causing her to hit the tree behind her so hard the wind was nearly knocked from her lungs. Drool was seeping from his lips, and his claws were flexed, ready to strike. Those brilliant green eyes were glowing so brightly that they reminded Ophelia of stars.

Catching her breath, she said, "Just try and take a deep breath."

Dodging another shove, she took him forcefully by the arm, helping him limp into the darkness. Seamus groaned, wrapping his arm around her shoulders. His muscles tensed, making her wonder how long they had until he transformed completely.

"You don't think—think I've tried that?" he snapped. His breath came out in quick bursts as she heaved him along.

"Can't you see I'm only trying to help?" she snapped back. "There's a fallen tree you can hide in overnight. They won't look for you there," she said as evenly as she could.

Seamus stopped, tipping to the side, almost sending them both to the ground. He snarled as another bloodcurdling snap filled their ears, his leg buckling again. It took all of

Ophelia's strength to keep him upright. She had to find a way to keep him calm. The howls of pain coming from him would surely alert Åssi and the others to their whereabouts.

An idea began forming in her mind—one she knew she would regret.

"I'm so sorry," she said quickly, pushing him away.

"For what?" he breathed, stumbling forward, grabbing a low-hanging branch to keep from falling flat on his face.

"This," she grimaced, placing a hand on his chest.

Light erupted from her hand in the form of lightning. Seamus's legs gave out as he and Ophelia crumpled to their knees. His eyelids fluttered as he stared at her, limbs hanging loosely at his side. It wasn't enough of a shock to truly harm him, but she hoped it numbed the pain and messed with his nervous system enough to slow the transformation. That's how Lochlan would describe it, anyway.

"Wha. . . didja jus do. . . ?" Seamus asked, his head flopping forward to rest in the crook of Ophelia's neck.

"I'll explain in the morning," she mumbled, dragging him back up to his feet and pulling him deeper into the forest. "You know, I've read books about werewolves," she said, adjusting his arm over her shoulders.

"Th—That's nice, kid," Seamus whispered, leaning most of his weight on her. Even in a state like this, his sass was as sharp as ever.

"I've always thought your kind was rather interesting," Ophelia continued.

He glared at her, rubbing his chest. There were scorch marks on his shirt, but he was too out of it to care. That or he was more concerned about what *he* would do to *her* than the other way around.

Soon enough, they came to the old tree she'd mentioned. Thankfully, it looked uninhabited.

Seamus stumbled inside, collapsing to the floor, panting heavily. Ophelia couldn't imagine the amount of pain he was experiencing. He was a prisoner in his own body, succumbing to a curse he shouldn't have had to carry. Watching as he lay there, writhing and shivering on the cold ground, made her heart twist from sorrow. Sympathetic ears were streaming down her cheeks. She wished she could do more to help.

With a heart-wrenching howl, he rolled away from her, fur breaking forth from under his tunic. His legs and arms creaked and cracked as they changed from human to wolf.

Ophelia turned away, clamping her hands over her ears. How long she stood like that, she didn't know.

After a while, all was quiet. Somehow, this was worse than the constant whimpering and howling. Daring a look back, her hands dropped from her ears, her breath caught in her lungs.

As the shadowy trees became indiscernible from one another and the moon shone down beams of silver, the man had disappeared, replaced by a giant, seething gray wolf.

The wolf struggled to its feet, its pale green eyes like lantern light. It growled deeply, staggering toward Ophelia, thick slobber hanging from its jowls. The Witch couldn't help but feel she was about to become the wolf's dinner.

Slowly, she edged to the side, making her movements as small as possible. She'd dealt with wolves before. They lived up to their reputation as monstrous beasts with short tempers. And those were just the ones that didn't have an angry human trapped inside them!

The wolf growled, fur standing on end, tail between its legs.

"You're safe here. I'm not going to hurt you. I promise," Ophelia whispered, tiptoeing out of the old tree.

The wolf did not seem to care or share the same sentiment. It lunged at her, its heavy paws colliding with her chest, sending her to the ground and causing her mask to shift to the side as her head collided with the frozen ground.

In the orb-like eyes boring holes into her soul, she could see her reflection.

The wolf sniffed her, steaming drool dripping onto her face. Despite herself, she groaned in disgust, twitching to the side. One of her arms was pinned by a massive paw with abnormally sharp claws. Its other paw was on her chest, stealing the breath from her lungs.

"Get off!" she screeched.

Wind whistled through the trees, sending down a cascade of snow from on high. Thunder rolled in the sky, the dark suddenly illuminated by bright blue lightning.

"Seamus!" Ophelia snapped.

Alarmed, the wolf stepped back, its ears twitching at the sound of its name—of his name. It shook with fear, growled deeply, and backed away into the empty log.

Unsure of what else to do, Ophelia flicked a lightning bolt toward the wolf, startling it. Deciding Ophelia was not worth its time, it ran full speed out of the log, disappearing into the shadows.

Rolling onto her stomach, she stared after him, struggling to catch her breath.

It was going to be a very long night.

CHAPTER TEN

LAMENTS OF THE LONELY

Seamus woke with a start, rain pelting him in freezing waves as he sat staring at the horror before him. What remained of his clothes hung loosely around his body, every inch of fabric stained with blood. The rain had washed most of it from his skin, but the earth was tinted a deep red, the bloody puddle around him a trophy. Scrambling to his feet, he stumbled away, sick to his stomach. There was a warm, metallic taste in his mouth. Whatever he'd eaten the night before was about to come back up.

Fragments of memories flashed in his mind. None of it made sense, but he was sure he hadn't been alone in the woods last night. Most of the blurry images that came to him were just colors. Red here, blue there. He thought maybe he saw the outline of a figure in a cave of sorts, but other than that, his wolf's mind had betrayed him yet again.

It was a feeling rather than a thought, but he knew he'd hurt someone. Even despite the blood, he knew he'd done something unforgivable.

Goosebumps erupted over his skin.

A sound in the distance caught his attention. He clamped a hand over his right ear, listening only with the left. Voices. He swore, taking off in the opposite direction, praying he'd end up at the cottage before—

He skidded to a stop, nearly colliding with a tree.

His head swam with images of Ophelia.

She'd been with him before he transformed.

His breath caught as he looked around wildly. He'd hurt

her. He must have! This blood must be hers. Consumed by revulsion, he started rubbing his hands on his pants until they were raw. It was all he could do not to tear his blood-stained flesh from his bones.

Goosebumps erupted over his skin. He had to find her, had to know if she was okay.

Without a moment of hesitation, he took off at full speed, jumping fallen logs and jagged rocks, weaving around trees, and ducking under branches that grappled toward him, waiting to trip him up.

Minutes turned to hours before Seamus finally reached the cottage's doorstep. No matter how hard he rattled the doorknob, it remained locked. He hoped against all hope she was just asleep, that the blood was from someone—anyone—else.

"Ophelia!" he shouted, banging on the door so hard he swore the old rotten wood cracked beneath his fist.

No answer.

"Kid, open the door!" he screamed.

Panic rising like bile in the back of his throat, he peered through the windows. No candles lit, no fire. She should be up by now! Where was she? Where were all the animals? He ran for the back, hoping to find her filling a trough or bucket with food, but again found nothing. The house and garden were empty. No Ophelia. No Eydis. No wolverine. Nothing.

Seamus's heart was pounding so loud in his chest that he was sure folks could hear it for miles. Anyone else and Seamus wouldn't have cared as much. But Ophelia was still a child. She had an entire life to live, yet he could have stolen it from her while intoxicated by the moon.

An idea struck him. He ran to the back door, knowing the lock was old and rusty. Maybe if he shook it hard enough, it would give way under his strength.

Thankfully, it practically crumbled beneath the gentlest touch.

Finally inside the house, Seamus screamed her name again, slamming open the door to her bedroom to find it empty. He'd never even glanced inside before. This was her sanctuary, and he'd never once tried to invade it. Seeing it now felt like a betrayal.

Sketches and pages ripped from old books were plastered on the walls, some torn and pasted together to create an entirely new image. Stuffed toy animals littered her bed, which had traces of hay and dirt left behind by the real animals that slept there each night. Paper stars hung from the ceiling, seemingly made from old medical texts. Books were piled on every flat surface, including the floor. Most had some sort of bookmark hanging out of them.

There was no question this place belonged to her.

It smelled like her, too, like mint and rainwater and pastries.

Seamus cursed himself, shutting the door softly.

Gruffly, he grabbed some spare clothes from his pack on the den floor, dragging his aching body to the washroom. As he scrubbed away the muck and blood, visions of furry paws drenched in blood assaulted the back of his eyelids. Screams of wounded animals echoed in his ears. His wolf must have had an eventful night. Trying to push down his unease, he changed into fresh clothes. Somehow, he'd acquired a purplish, starburst-like mark on his chest. His body protested as he lifted his arms to shimmy on a tunic. The rough wool of his tunic made the wound itch and burn.

He grizzled, heading back into the den just as the front door handle jiggled.

He panicked, darting to the floor and hiding next to the lounge.

Over his racing heart, he heard a familiar buzzing engulf the quiet cottage. He spun, looking over the armrest of the lounge.

A swath of blue fabric.

Ebony curls.

Purple lips and fingers.

A wooden mask made to pay homage to the Fox.

"Seamus!" *she* screeched, jumping out of fright.

"Ophelia!" he screamed back, relief and anger surging through him. "Where have you been?!"

"Looking for you!" she whisper-yelled. He could smell the panic on her. Hurriedly, she slammed the door shut, locked it, then pulled the drapes closed.

The cottage was plunged into darkness, the only light

coming from the smoldering ashes in the woodstove.

Seamus hadn't realized how hard he was breathing, how bad his legs ached from running, and most of all, how relieved he was to see her. He wanted to run over and give her the biggest bear hug she'd ever received to let her know how happy he was that she was okay, but to do so would most likely have the opposite effect. He'd noticed her aversion to touch and tried not to overstep his bounds, even on accident.

Ophelia still held the drapes on the kitchen window in her shaking hands. He could tell she was trying to calm her rapid breathing. The buzzing emanating from her grew to an almost deafening volume, a sharp crescendo against the raging wind outside.

Daring a look over her shoulder at him, her mouth dropped. "Blessed Amaranth," she breathed, hugging herself tight.

He inhaled sharply, stiffening. "I—"

"Are you hurt?" she asked, her voice filled with dread.

"N—No. I'm fine. But I—I—I think I hurt someone." He shivered, backing away from her before she could. . . Honestly, he didn't know what he expected her to do.

Her eyes widened. "That's not good," she said softly.

"You think?" he snapped.

What she said next shocked him more than anything else had that morning.

"Do *not* take that tone with me, Seamus Norland! I am the only one—*the only one*—" she hissed "—that won't look at you and immediately see a monster. I am a much better friend than an enemy!" She accented every sentence with a thrust of her finger in his direction.

All traces of the sweet and naïve girl he'd come to know had disappeared, replaced instead with that ancient feeling from when they'd first met.

The smell of hot apple cider flowed freely from her.

Hail battered the cottage.

"Well, what about you? Are you hurt?" he asked. He hadn't meant to be so short with her, but oh well.

"I'm perfectly fine, thank you. No thanks to your wolf, I might add!" She turned her nose up, hands on her hips. "The fright you gave me, Mr. Norland! I'd say you should pay for my therapy, but you'll never have enough funds to pay for the extensive help I'll need!"

Seamus felt as though he was slipping into hysterics. "*I* scared *you?*" he scoffed. "That's rich, kid."

For the first time, he was glad he couldn't see her eyes. He knew the look beneath her mask would have been enough to kill a man.

"As if you care for me, you fickle, fickle man!"

Seamus rolled his eyes, mirroring her pose. Hands on his hips, head held high, same scowl and everything.

"You're right, I don't! But that doesn't mean I want your blood on my hands!"

Ophelia's arms dropped. The spiced anger seeping off her immediately faded into that minty sadness he was used to. The buzzing turned from rhythmic to scattered, anxious notes.

"You said you couldn't control it. Whatever happened, it is on the wolf, not you." Her words were dull and emotionless. Her usual shaking had intensified to a full-on tremor.

What had happened? She'd been furious with him just seconds ago, but now even her sadness was seeping into nothingness. Emptiness.

He stared blankly at her, completely and utterly confused.

"Kid, listen—"

Tears seeped out from under her mask, running down her face, leaving behind glimmering trails that made him think of shooting stars. She wiped at them furiously, smearing the oddly sparkly tearstains. Swallowing hard, she made for the hall, but Seamus cleared his throat, causing her to pause.

"I'm sorry, kid; I didn't mean to cause you trouble," he said solemnly.

Ophelia's shoulder sagged. "I've been dealing with trouble for far longer than you've been around," she whispered.

"That may be true, but I didn't think my being here would—"

"And why *are* you here?" she blurted out, turning back to him.

Lightning tore through the sky.

"I don't see how—" He inhaled sharply, pinching the bridge of his nose, sighing, nodding to himself. After last night, it was fair enough for her to ask, but was he ready to divulge his tragic life story? He mulled this over briefly before finally saying, "I'm on the run, kid. That's the long and short of it."

"From whom? From what?" Ophelia demanded. "I will not take silence for an answer, Seamus Norland. If you intend on staying here, you will answer me. If you intend for me to keep your secret, you will answer me."

He rolled his eyes, making for the kitchen. "I'm telling you, kid, you don't want to know."

"Of course I don't! But look what not knowing has brought me! I *need* to know," she pleaded. "I need to know whether I can trust you. Whether—" She stamped her foot down in frustration, at a loss for words.

Seamus took a fresh loaf of bread from the cupboard and cut them each a slice. It was baffling how hungry he was, knowing he'd had many a midnight snack.

"I'm not ready to share that story just yet, kid," he said as he buttered a slice of bread and handed it to her.

When she didn't take his offering, he rolled his eyes and ate it himself.

He thought she would yell at him, that she'd scream or lecture him until he folded and bore his soul. Instead, she just shook her head in disappointment.

Seamus sat straddling one of the kitchen chairs, tearing little pieces of his bread off as he ate. "I'm truly sorry, Ophelia. I promise I won't stay a second longer than I have to."

Again, lightning crackled outside, though this time, it sounded like it was right outside the front door.

Ophelia took in a shaking breath, brushing herself off and straightening the cuffs of her jacket. "I will be sad to see you leave Mr. Norland. But what saddens me most is the knowledge that you run farther from yourself than you do from whoever or whatever is after you."

Ophelia lingered a moment longer before disappearing down the hall. Her bedroom door slammed shut the same second one last crash of thunder roared in the sky.

CHAPTER ELEVEN

TRAPS

Ophelia ripped her mask from her face, tossing it to her bed in a fit of anger. The wind outside was dancing around in her chest, every boom of thunder rattling her bones, each lightning bolt causing her heart to skip a beat. Try as she might, she couldn't coax the weather into clear skies. Even pacing her bedroom, hugging herself so tightly she would end up bruising her arms, wouldn't calm the ever-livid storm inside or out.

It wasn't that she was angry with Seamus or the actions of his wolf. He'd said he couldn't control it, and she believed him. Ophelia barely had a grasp on her own powers, so who was she to judge? And hers were meant to aid and protect her! She was meant to be in harmony with the elements. She couldn't imagine how Seamus felt harboring such a beast beneath his skin. Did he feel his wolf prowling deep in his mind in the same way she felt the hurricane swirling in her lungs?

No, she wasn't angry at him for that. How could she be?

What sent her over the edge was his constant aloofness, his nonchalant attitude toward his well-being, and how guarded he was. Couldn't he see she was just trying to help? She'd even take a lie at this point. At least that would give her something to go off when the time inevitably came for her to defend him.

Or, Amaranth forbid, *condemn* him.

By blood right, each snowflake marked her territory. Every tree, every hollow, and every person taking refuge in this wild and uncaring forest. Anything and everything the snow touched. This was her domain. Her home. Her creatures. She was honor-bound to protect these woods and beings. Especially those who were far from human.

Oh, Ophelia wanted to scream until her lungs gave out. Why was she always pulled in a thousand different directions? Why couldn't people and feelings be as they were in her books and psalms?

She cared deeply for Seamus, more so now that she knew how similar their stories could be.

She cared for everyone, even those that treated her like filth. She even cared for Lochlan! *Lochlan!* The same man who had used her for all she was worth!

Ophelia was growing tired of being quiet, letting the winds of life tumble her into place while she sat, unmoving, unable to protest.

This was *her* realm.

Her life.

H*er* cottage.

And those winds were meant to abide her, dammit.

Lightning sparked at her fingertips, the heat of it rushing through her veins, intoxicating her with power and deep, unbridled sadness. Her frostbitten fingertips screamed in agony with every sharp bolt. Taking a deep breath, she sat heavily on the edge of her bed, pulling her knees to her chest, ignoring how her lightning singed her dress. The thunder outside had stopped, but the thunder in her heart rattled on.

A knock on her bedroom door.

"Kid, can we please talk?" came Seamus's voice.

"Leave me alone," she demanded, though her voice was small and unsteady.

Despite her words, the door opened. Grumbling about his stubbornness, she hid her face by resting her cheeks against her knees. Searing pain surged through her arms as she forced the lightning to dissipate, the sparks burning her inside out with the effort. The last thing she needed was for him to see her magic. Thankfully, he seemed to have forgotten that little detail from the night prior.

Seamus sat beside her, his weight causing the bedframe to squeak. His feet tapped anxiously on the floor, the rhythm in tune with the rapid beat of her heart.

"I owe you an apology," he sighed, "You have done so

much for me, and I have repaid you with nothing but problems. The way I've been treating you is unfair. I hate how the people of Tø act toward you, yet I've been acting the same, if not worse."

Despite her heart telling her otherwise, Ophelia did not give him the satisfaction of responding.

"I don't understand the kindness you have for me, kid. I don't find myself deserving of it, but know I appreciate it. I do so hope you can find it in your heart to forgive me," Seamus finished. She hadn't realized his voice could sound so soft.

They sat quietly for a while.

Slowly, the electricity running through her stopped. She could still feel it; it was always there, just like the hurricane in her lungs. But its rampage had ceased. It wasn't fighting against her anymore. Peace wasn't the right word to describe this feeling—it would be a long time before she ever felt that— but she couldn't think of a better word.

Seamus cleared his throat, stumbling over his words for a few long seconds. "Why. . . aren't you. . . afraid. . . of me?" That question seemed to terrify him.

"Seamus," she began, sighing deeply, face still buried against her knees. "I do not blame you for the actions of your wolf. Even if you chose to take the bite, you never could have known how volatile a creature you would become."

He shifted uncomfortably beside her, scoffing. "Look at me, kid," he said softly. "Look at me and tell me I wouldn't have known."

She wanted to, she really did. She wanted to see an evil man, wanted to see Lochlan staring back at her.

But she didn't.

She couldn't.

Despite not having her mask to hide her own 'volatile creature,' she couldn't look at him and see a monster. There was nothing monstrous about Seamus Norland, at least not that she'd seen.

Blessed Amaranth, she wished she could turn to him and look him dead in the eyes without the protection of her mask. Would he feel the same? Or would he see a monster? Would he give her grace as she had given him? Would he understand? Would he accept what he saw as a part of her or shun her like everyone else?

Though these questions troubled her greatly, she only mumbled, "I don't have my mask."

A moment's silence before something gently tapped her arm. "Found it. I promise not to look while you tie it on." The bed frame squeaked again as he stood. There was a shuffling of footsteps, indicating he'd turned.

Ophelia covered her face with her hands, daring a peek through her fingers. Seamus stood towering over her, his back to her as he held out her mask. She leaned forward a bit to find his hand clamped over his eyes, too. It was almost comical.

Gratefully, she took the mask and tied the thick leather strings around her head in a neat little bow. The familiarity of its weight on her cheeks and nose was both comforting and disheartening. That mask was a child's safety blanket and a criminal's prison cell wrapped into one small package.

One last moment of uncertainty before she tapped Seamus's arm with a single finger.

Cheeks flushed, he turned back around. "I'm sorry, kid," he laughed awkwardly.

"I'm sorry too," she said, grimacing, "I'm sorry for pestering you so much. I don't know what came over me. I usually make myself scarcely seen and rarely heard."

He nodded, returning to his spot on the bed. "I've noticed."

"I have a lot to say, but no one ever listens," she replied. How would he respond to that? What response was she looking for? She didn't know why she said it. Maybe somewhere deep inside, she still wanted to test him.

"I think I understand the feeling," he sighed. "Maybe we can listen to each other?"

"I would like that very much, Mr—" Ophelia cleared her throat, smirking. "I would like that very much, *Seamus*."

The smile he gave her was the first real smile she'd seen from him. She desperately hoped what she said next wouldn't ruin it.

"Please know I'm not mad at you for keeping me at arm's length. Or for treating me 'unfairly,'" she said, making a show of air quotes. "You are only protecting yourself; I understand that. Though you say the only opinion that matters is one's own, I know how hard it can be to break away from the herd. Especially for a werewolf," she smiled playfully.

"Ahh, yes. The old 'pack mentality,'" he laughed, "You truly do not need to apologize, kid. I mean it."

He went to pat her shoulder, but she moved away before his fingers could graze her.

"Sorry," he said, awkwardly folding his hands in his lap.

"I—I don't really—uh—like being *touched*," Ophelia said, her voice small.

"Oh," Seamus said. "Well. . . How about this?" he asked, snapping in her direction. "That work instead?"

Ophelia laughed, snapping back.

For a fleeting moment, all felt right in the world.

Of course, as it was *Ophelia's* world, something had to ruin everything.

Seamus suddenly whipped his head around so fast she thought his neck would snap. All traces of the light-hearted smile and cheery disposition he'd had moments ago disappeared.

"What's wrong?" Ophelia asked, following his gaze toward the hallway.

Without a word, Seamus beckoned for her to follow him into the den. Tip-toeing, he crossed to the window, pulling back the curtains. Outside, the owls fluttered away as the reindeer reared, spooked by something just out of eyesight. Ophelia made for the door, Seamus stepping in front of her with a swift shake of his head.

A voice echoed through the air. Someone was yelling her name.

With a groan, Ophelia edged around Seamus, yanking open the front door to see flaming red hair blowing in the wind as Saoirse ran up the cottage path.

"Ophelia!" she screamed.

Seamus was at her side, peering over her shoulder. "Do we know her?"

"Yes, friend of mine. You've met her," Ophelia whispered, stepping out into the cold. "Saoirse! What's happened?" she called.

Skidding to a stop, she took Ophelia by the shoulders. Her eyes were wide with fear as she tried to catch her breath. "They set up traps. Torbod's got another fox caught in one. I can't get it out. There's so much blood."

"Wh—What?" Ophelia screeched, shaking Saoirse's hands away.

Saoirse swallowed hard, shaking her head violently. "*So much blood*," she breathed.

Without a second thought, Ophelia turned and collected her things. Whisking a basket off the ground, she haphazardly filled it with clean cloths and twine. Her hands were shaking so badly that she kept dropping things. Seamus followed close behind, picking up whatever clattered to the floor as he stared down Saoirse. He even handed Ophelia her cloak on the way out.

"I'll be back soon," she called, bolting out the door to follow Saoirse. Seamus gave her a dutiful nod as he closed the door.

Soon, she and Saoirse were running through the forest as fast as their legs could carry them.

Ophelia would forever be thankful Saoirse shared her love of animals. They'd taken it upon themselves long ago to dismantle traps and thwart any of the hunters' plans to kill unnecessarily. This made them rather unpopular in town, as one would imagine. Saoirse was a forager by nature, too. She spent most of her days in the forest, and whenever she stumbled upon an injured creature, she'd bring it to the cottage for Ophelia to look after. Coincidentally, this was how she'd met Narfi.

They'd been running for ages when Saoirse finally skidded to a stop at a hollowed log. Ophelia shuttered, hating how this mirrored last night. Saoirse knelt, cooing at a chittering gray fox. Ophelia knelt, too, eyebrows knitting together in worry beneath her mask. The fox's foot was stuck in some sort of metal trap with incredibly sharp teeth. It lay panting on the ground, thick, congealed blood pooling on its leg.

"These aren't Torbod's traps," Ophelia whispered, pointing at the emblem cast into the side.

Saoirse nodded, gingerly running her finger along the trap's branding. "He bought them from a caravan, apparently. Was bragging about it while the masses were looking for the wolf."

Ophelia grimaced. "Do you recognize the marking?"

"I believe so. I just can't recall where I've seen it. I'll let you know if I remember," Saoirse sighed, pinching the bridge of her nose as she stood.

Ophelia stroked the fox's head to try and calm it. "I think I can manage from here," she said, "Give Torbod a piece of our minds, okay?"

"Thought you'd never ask."

With that, Saoirse ran back toward town, startling the fox. Ophelia tried to soothe it as best she could, but the poor thing was beyond reach. Glancing over her shoulder to ensure no one was watching, she placed a gentle hand on the fox's chest. A tiny spark of electricity left her fingers and traveled over the fox. It calmed instantly, its rapidly beating heart and heavy panting finally slowing, just as Seamus's had the night before.

Ophelia touched the edge of the trap, grimacing. She'd never seen one like this before. It was far too advanced for someone in Tø to have. It must have cost a small fortune in metal to make. The only trappers with money to spare and time to invent new traps lived outside of The Wilds. These weren't the sort of things an ordinary caravan of traders would have lying around. Either these were stolen, or poachers were hunting Ophelia's woods.

Slowly, she wrapped her spindly fingers around both sides of the trap and pulled with all her might, a thick icicle wedging itself between the teeth until it loosened enough for her to remove the fox's leg safely. She scooped it into her arms, shielding it from the cold within her cloak.

The owls were in a frenzy when she returned. The stag who usually visited this time of day was nowhere to be seen. Neither were the bear cubs.

Seamus had disappeared, too—presumably into town— leaving her alone with her thoughts. Unfortunately, that wasn't something she was fond of on days like this.

CHAPTER TWELVE

TRUE COLORS

Ophelia had never fancied being a healer. Still, she tried her best to wrap up the poor fox's leg, hoping her efforts would be enough. She thought a lot about life and death, about what was on the 'other side.' Though she knew what was waiting for departing souls, she hated seeing beings at the end of their lives. That sort of thing was better left for Amaranth and Nightshade, the Spirits of Life and Death, respectively.

As Ophelia stood washing the blood from her hands, she thought back to seeing Seamus covered in blood, his face a perfect picture of terror. He looked wild without prompting, but the look on his face in the dark of the cottage nearly scared her out of her skin. It was true werewolves had always fascinated her, but she'd read story upon story of how dangerous they could be. She just hoped she'd be on the right side of things if Seamus ever snapped.

Hoped.

She did a lot of hoping. It was her curse.

A knock startled her from her thoughts. She shivered, drying her hands on her skirt as she returned to the den. As she passed through the kitchen, she snatched her discarded mask off the table, quickly tying it around her tussled hair.

If one more person came barging in today, she was going to start barricading the door. Luck did not seem to favor her today.

"Lochlan?" she asked, thoroughly disappointed as she opened the door.

Without asking, he pushed her aside and entered the

cottage, his robes dragging in twigs and mud. "I hear your stray has made himself useful around town."

"Yes," Ophelia said carefully, "he has. . ."

Lochlan's unblinking eyes swept over the cottage. The disgust in his gaze was so apparent it was as if he was shouting about it. Ophelia's stomach churned. Eventually, his eyes landed on the fox. He sighed heavily, straightening, turning to her with a *tsk tsk* and shake of his head.

With one of his stiff woolen sleeves, he gestured to the fox. "What have I said about allowing such creatures inside?" he groaned.

Ophelia cast her eyes toward the floor, wringing her hands. "Not to."

He nodded. "Then why is it sprawled out on your hearth?"

"It's injured."

Lochlan pursed his thin lips, crossing his hands neatly before him. A thick and heavy drought of silence fell upon them, leaving Lochlan to stand scrutinizing her with a scowl.

"Is there something you need, Lochlan? As you can see, I am in the middle of something," Ophelia whispered.

"You always have places to be and things to do, don't you, *Dømte En*?" he sighed, rolling his sunken eyes.

So badly did she want to say what was really on her mind, to tell him to stop calling her that horrid name, to say that he should stop poking around in business that wasn't his.

"With that, I agree," Ophelia finally mumbled.

There was a time when the Witch thought Lochlan loved her. After all, if it wasn't for him, she had no idea what would have become of her. Really, all he'd ever wanted from her was her secrets. *He* was the kind of man fairytales warned you about.

However, no matter her feelings, she also knew Lochlan held power she could never have, at least not with how her world, unfortunately, worked. One word from him to the wrong people would destroy her.

"Did you need anything?" Ophelia whispered, staring at the tops of her shoes.

"Do not mumble, child, it's *rude*."

Lochlan swept his robes over the lounge where Seamus had made his bed, knocking his pillow a little too close to the fireplace and startling the fox. Ophelia rushed forward to stop the cushion from catching a stray spark, but Lochlan turned to stop her. His fingers curled around her shoulder, his sharp nails digging into her skin. The look in his eyes was that of murderous rage, yet his face was stone-cold empty.

"*He* is like the fox. Neither belong here," he said through grit teeth.

Without thinking, she asked, "Why not?"

Lochlan's gaze darkened further. "With the Earl and Countess away, it is my job to take care of this town. I am many things, but an idiot I am not. There is no noble line connected to the Norland name. But I can tell you what it *is* connected to: *trouble.*"

"But he's a good man," Ophelia muttered, horrorstruck as the cushion burst into flames.

"Is he really? What exactly do you know about him?"

Ophelia fell silent. The answer was nothing. She knew absolutely nothing about Seamus Norland. Nothing other than the fact he was a werewolf on the run who liked to make wooden trinkets. Nothing except that for all his faults, there was still kindness inside him.

He was a mystery, and she had to admit, she'd questioned if he was the good kind. Maybe he was, maybe he wasn't. Maybe some people lied and kept secrets with good intentions. She certainly did.

Lochlan leaned down, his sour breath hot on her skin as he peered into the eyeholes of her mask. "He is the kind of person that will jeopardize your safety. I want him gone, Ophelia." His hand left her shoulder and trailed up her neck to her chin. Ophelia flinched, stifling a frightened squeal, turning her face as far away from him as her neck would allow. "I only do what is best for you, you know that—" he lifted her mask and stroked her cheek softly "—don't you?" His other hand took her wrist, his clammy fingers gripping her tight.

"Please remove your hands from me, Lochlan," Ophelia whispered, a dangerous tone underlining her voice. Her body trembled with fear, but her voice was steady. That's all that mattered. er body tremb

Lochlan's glare bore holes into her head, but ultimately,

he dropped his hands. He was about to say something when someone else knocked on the door. Ophelia quickly replaced her mask as Lochlan opened the door.

"Mr. Norland," he said, his voice full of disdain.

"Mr.—Actually, I don't think I ever had the pleasure of learning your last. . . name. . ." Seamus trailed off. Ophelia turned to see him staring at his blazing pillow. The fire reflecting in Seamus's eyes burned brighter than she thought imaginable.

"That'll be all," Lochlan yawned. "Thank you, Ophelia."

Ophelia blinked back tears, nodding.

Lochlan just bowed, giving Ophelia a knowing look as he slipped outside and slammed the door behind him.

"Are you okay?" Seamus breathed. He could barely speak, his voice like something metallic being drug along sharp rocks.

Ophelia only nodded as he rushed to the hearth to grab his pillow and stamp out the blazing flames. He swore heavily, rushing it to the washroom, where she heard it splash in the water basin. When he returned, he was fuming.

"Are you all right?" he repeated rather forcefully. His hands flexed, fingers twitching.

"I'm fine, Mr. Norland," she said softly, avoiding his eyes even though he couldn't tell.

Seamus looked her up and down, eyebrows furrowed deeply over his hazel eyes. He glanced at the squirming fox, nostrils flaring. Taking a deep breath, he straightened. He'd made up his mind about something. Slowly, his eyes trailed back to her. Ophelia recoiled as he approached her, his hand hovering inches away. Seamus was shaking with anger, hands grasping at the space between them. Blowing hot steam out of his nose, he finally dropped his hand to his side.

"Listen, kid. I've dealt with people like him my whole life. If he hurts you, you tell me. Understand? If he has *ever* hurt you, tell me," he hissed. "If he even touches you, you damn well better tell me. Got it?"

Ophelia nodded again, fiddling with a loose thread on her sleeve.

Seamus backed away, sighing heavily. "Your mask is crooked," he grumbled, gesturing loosely to her head. With that, he threw open the door and marched out without closing it.

Ophelia stared after him, straightening her mask. She so desperately wanted Lochlan to be wrong about him. For every selfish reason she could muster, she needed him to be wrong. Just when she thought she could finally trust the ever-mysterious Seamus Norland, something would send her spiraling all over again.

But not this time.

Sides were being drawn, and the choice was simple.

Truthfully, she knew Lochlan was right. Tø was the only place she was safe. Why risk this sanctuary, no matter its faults, for a traveler who was already causing her so much trouble?

Seamus being here was a liability. If he ever found out why she hid behind that mask, she had no idea what he'd do. She wanted to see the good in people, but people had yet to prove that she should. Every person she'd met—spare Saoirse—had proved to be a threat in one way or another. They took too much, left her high and dry, or exploited her for all she was. If the pattern continued, Seamus would be no different.

Still, she had hope.

For all his surliness, Seamus had been the only person in Tø to see Lochlan for what he was. Maybe he was going to be her downfall. Maybe he wasn't.

Steeling herself, Ophelia vowed that no matter what would come, she would stand by Seamus. Because, for whatever reason, she knew he would stand by her.

Seamus was about to do something he would likely regret for the rest of his life. He'd been where Ophelia was now. He'd spent a lifetime in fear of those exactly like Lochlan and those so much worse. He didn't want that for her. Though there was no reason to feel like this, Ophelia's safety was paramount to him. Maybe he held her in such high regard because she reminded him of someone he once held dear.

That thought alone was precisely why he raced to catch

up with that damned 'healer.' Fuming, he fell in step beside Lochlan, glaring at the crippled old man out of the corner of his eye.

Seamus cleared his throat, his voice shaking to suppress the snarl clawing at the inside of his throat. "Ah, I see we're heading in the same direction. What a coincidence."

The healer wouldn't look at him. "Yes. How. . . *pleasant.*"

Seamus looked sideways at the infuriating waste of space next to him. "You know, I don't think I properly thanked you for letting me stay 'round here," he said loftily.

Lochlan yawned lazily.

Seamus wrapped his twitching fingers around the back of Lochlan's neck. The old man's skin was dry, reminding him of a snake covered in a thick layer of dust. The sudden pressure on his neck made Lochlan pause.

Seamus smiled toothily, towering over him. "I've decided to return the favor with a little piece of advice."

"How kind," Lochlan murmured.

Seamus stepped in front of him, placing his other hand on the healer's chest. "Stay away from the kid, or the only person you'll be healing is yourself. Have I made myself clear?"

Lochlan was completely unfazed. "Quite," he said, leaning forward, blinking slowly. "You do not scare me, *boy.*"

Seamus's grip on his neck tightened, allowing his sharp fingernails to dig into Lochlan's scaly skin. "I should, *old man.* I really should."

"I should fear a lot of things, Mr. Norland. Pity," Lochlan laughed.

Seamus's lip curled in disgust. Before he could think it through, he shoved Lochlan to the side, crossing his arms over his chest. Lochlan only smiled, brushing himself off, lazily regaining his footing.

"I wonder, Mr. Norland, how you obtained all those scars?"

Seamus scoffed. "Keep talking. You'll have a matching set."

The healer gave him a smile that did not reach his eyes, accompanied by a curt nod. "Have a nice rest of your day, Mr. Norland. Not a nice life, I might clarify. Such a thing isn't a luxury you can find around here."

Charcoal clouds hovered overhead as Seamus marched back to the cottage. A gust of freezing air filled his lungs as he opened the door, which was left slightly ajar. The fire had gone out.

He did a double-take. The scorched logs almost seemed to glisten as if covered in frost.

Ophelia sat in front of the hearth, stroking the head of the fox. Seamus usually ignored the gloves she wore. The absence of them startled him. Her fingers looked as though they'd been frostbitten recently. Whether her shoulders shook from silent sobs or the cold, he couldn't tell. Maybe it was both. Seamus could feel the sadness radiating off her in frigid waves. He would never be able to articulate it exactly, but the beat of her heart sounded gray. For all the blue she wore, her emotions seemed to mirror the dark storm clouds rumbling outside.

CHAPTER THIRTEEN

THE FOX

Ophelia's efforts to heal the fox weren't going to be enough. As Saoirse had said, the poor thing had lost too much blood. Its leg was bent and broken in ways she did not think bones could bend or break. It would need to be amputated. Even if the fox survived, it would be miserable. A creature as wild as the fox would not do well without all four legs.

The weather had gone gloomy with the Witch's mood. She'd tried to stop it, she really had, but her emotions were just too powerful. She felt horrible when Seamus came home shivering from the wild winds outside.

With one look at her, he came to sit beside her as she stroked the little fox's head.

"You have an audience," he said, nodding to the window in the kitchen.

She peered over her shoulder to see an array of animal friends waiting patiently outside. She knew they, too, were saddened by the state of the fox.

"How is it?" Seamus asked.

"Not good," Ophelia whispered. "I don't think it has much time left."

Seamus hung his head low. "I'm very sorry to hear that. Is there anything I can do?"

"We can try to comfort it as best we can. You can pet it if you want; just be gentle."

Seamus gave her a funny look. Ophelia suddenly realized he might've meant if there was anything he could do for *her*. Clearing his throat, he lifted his hand over the fox but did not touch it. Ophelia smiled sympathetically at him. She reached for him, wanting to guide his hand and show him it was okay to pet it, but she jolted away at the last second. If Seamus had noticed, he didn't seem to care. His eyes were glued to the fox.

"It's okay," she whispered. He glanced sidelong at her. Only when she nodded reassuringly did he stroke the sleeping fox.

"I hope your day was better than mine," Ophelia said.

"Well, at the very least, my day was informative," Seamus said, dropping his voice to a whisper to match hers. "Sorry I disappeared for a bit."

Ophelia shrugged half-heartedly. "No hard feelings," she said without meeting his eyes. With her mask, it looked like she was staring him down.

Seamus gently rubbed the fox's ears. ". . . I meant what I said. I'm not afraid to put that man in his place on your behalf." His expression was like stone.

"I know." That she believed. "He wasn't always like that. There was a time when he didn't—" She sighed, choosing her words carefully. Sometimes, she wondered if Lochlan could hear her even when they were on opposite sides of town. "There was a time when he was in awe of me. When I was younger, I looked up to him. But he's changed over the years." She could hear the fear in her voice and knew Seamus could, too.

"I'm sorry."

She shrugged. "What's done is done."

Seamus went quiet, staring at the empty fireplace.

Ophelia had had lots of time to think while tending to the fox.

She inhaled deeply before speaking. "May I ask you something?" Seamus nodded for her to continue. "Can I trust you?"

"Why would you?" he replied with a dark laugh.

Ophelia shrugged. "The owls seem to think you're. . . special. . ."

Seamus furrowed his eyebrows in confusion. "The owls on the roof?"

"Are there other owls out there?"

"Generally? Yes," he scoffed.

Ophelia sighed heavily, resting her chin on her knees and shutting her eyes. "Is it okay if I sleep out here tonight? I don't want it to be lonely."

"Of course, kid."

Seamus stood and took his furs, blankets, and rock-hard pillows from the lounge. Careful not to touch her, he placed one of the furs around her shoulders and set a pillow beside her. Wrapping a thin, moth-eaten blanket around himself, he settled in next to her.

He was staring at the darkened fireplace.

She was staring at him.

For a while, the only sound was the rain pelting the side of the cottage.

"Seamus?"

Eventually, he glanced at her.

Something unspoken yet strangely sacred passed between them. They were two birds trapped in cages. His was rusty and neglected. All who passed figured he was left for the slaughter. No one stopped to free him. Hers was gilded and polished. All who passed thought she was lucky to be where she was. No one seemed to notice how many feathers were missing or how miserable she looked.

"I'll stay with you if that's all right," Seamus said ever so softly.

"I'd like that very much."

CHAPTER FOURTEEN

WOLF KILLERS

Morning came, and Ophelia's fears were confirmed. The fox hadn't made it through the night. Seamus tried to comfort her, but nothing he said would calm her. Lightning crackled in the sky, thunder rolled, and wind battered the trees until their limbs bowed in submission. Her bones felt like they'd cracked under the pressure of it all. Whoever did this was going to pay. The way so many people treated animals made her sick. Some had a complete disregard for life, no matter its form.

"Maybe burying it will help you feel better?" Seamus had offered over a late breakfast.

He'd cooked. Since his arrival, meals had always been Ophelia's duty. She could've whipped something up while he was asleep on the hearth, but she couldn't bring herself to do much of anything but cry. She'd retreated to her room, warmed by the comfort those four walls gave her. She hadn't intended to leave until Seamus knocked and came to check on her. Upon entering the kitchen, she'd found pancakes. Seamus had actually cooked. What a sight.

She'd nodded half-heartedly. "I think I'd like that."

Seamus had wrapped the fox in a clean cloth, and now he carried it into the woods, following Ophelia as she led him to one of the most sacred places in Tø. Behind him was a cavalcade of animals saddened to see their comrade be laid to rest. Still, they were glad Ophelia cared so much about their little lives. They wished they could repay her properly.

Deep in the woods was a clearing littered with teeny graves. Here, over the years, Ophelia had laid several animal friends to rest. Each death had broken her heart, but something about this fox, this fox she didn't have a chance to know, hit harder. Seamus had brought a shovel. He let her pick a plot and began digging a hole. They laid the fox to rest under dark skies and even darker moods. Ophelia used the rocks he'd dug up to create a heart over the grave. She sat there in the pouring rain for quite some time, praying to the listening ears above that the fox would have safe travels to the lush meadows in the cosmos. An owl had landed on her head, and a bear cub was curled in her lap. Several foxes were dotting the graveyard, their heads hung low. Eydis and the reindeer stood protectively behind her. Each of them was silent. That broke her heart. There wasn't a day that went by when they didn't chitter at her. If they could cry and wail, Ophelia knew they would.

Seamus stood at the edge of the clearing, lounging against a tree. Ophelia was thankful he understood why she was so upset. If he didn't, she appreciated he at least pretended to.

Sitting there with her entourage, she thought of Saoirse, wondering how best to break the news to her. She'd be livid and heartbroken, too. Ophelia doubted Torbod and the other trappers in town would ever have another peaceful day so long as—

The owl atop her head suddenly screeched, scaring the bear cub. The cub ran, Eydis chasing after it. The owl gave another cry of fright, then flew.

The foxes darted away into the forest, tails between their legs.

The reindeer reared, bolting after them.

Ophelia stood, looking to Seamus, whose eyes were set on something behind her. Fright and rage mixed in his eyes as he beckoned her back to him.

"Did you hear something?" she asked, scanning the trees but finding nothing even remotely alarming.

He shushed her, pushing her behind himself protectively. Ophelia frowned but knew in her heart Seamus wouldn't have done that unless he'd deemed it completely necessary. The way he was acting reminded her of how Eydis treated the cubs.

"Stay behind me," he whispered, staring wide-eyed into the woods.

The snap of a twig in the distance made Seamus's heart somersault in his chest. He swore under his breath, reaching up to touch his wounded ear.

"Seamus!" Ophelia screeched.

Cold hands were on his back as he fell forward, his face colliding with a rather nippy mud puddle. Panic surged through as he looked back at her, but her mask—and Seamus assumed her eyes, too—was directed at a jet-black arrow sticking out from the tree he'd just been leaning against.

Time seemed to pause. Seamus wondered what she was thinking. He knew she saw the symbol on the arrow's fletching, knew the cogs were turning in her head. Oh, how he wished to see her eyes. He knew there'd be something ancient swirling inside them.

Tripping over muddied skirts and her own feet, Ophelia ducked behind the tree as another arrow implanted itself in the ground near Seamus's head. He jumped to his feet, spinning so fast he made himself dizzy. Slipping and sliding on the wet ground, he hid behind the tree with her, wiping the muck from his face. Daring a peek around the tree, he locked eyes with an armor-clad warrior knocking another arrow onto their bowstring.

"Dammit," he spat, ducking back behind the tree to dodge another arrow.

"Ulvemordere. . ." Ophelia breathed. The beat of her heart was so loud Seamus could barely hear anything else over it. "W—Why are the Ulvemordere here?"

He gave her a knowing look and a vaguely apologetic grumble. She mumbled to herself, peering around the tree, stumbling back as an arrow flew past her face, ruffling her hair as it whizzed by. Seamus was about to scream at her to run when a clicking sound caught his attention.

Around the side of the tree before them came a crossbow, the shooter's face obscured by a black metal helm reminiscent of a wolf skull. Fur Seamus knew once belonged to a werewolf poked out from under their bracers and boots.

Without thinking, Seamus threw himself at their attackers, grabbing the crossbow and aiming it toward the sky as the Ulvemordere soldier pulled the trigger. Ophelia yelped behind him. There was a *thwack!* above, the crossbow bolt finding its resting place on a branch on high. Seamus growled at the solider, ripping their weapon from their veiny hands and tossing it aside. His attacker made for his eyes, sharp claws jutting out from their fingertips. Seamus head-butted them, instantly regretting it as his head filled with a high-pitched ringing. All he saw were imaginary stars as he stumbled backward.

His attacker took this momentary shock as a window. Claws bore into his skin, leaving behind five deep cuts that sent him to his knees as he clutched his side. This, thankfully, turned out to be a blessing as he was able to lunge at the attacker's legs and send them to the ground. They slashed and kicked at him, but Seamus just swatted the movements away, grappling for their helm. He ripped the helm from their head, using it as a bludgeon to knock them out. . . and then some. . .

Seamus struggled to his feet, panting hard, turning to see Ophelia holding her own against an opponent much taller and broader than herself, which baffled him. She had the soldier's bow in her hand, pulling with all her might. They had a grip on the string. What an idiot. The string snapped, startling them both. Seamus raced forward to help as the soldier shook away the shock and swung a punch, their fist colliding with the side of Ophelia's face. She stumbled back into Seamus, nearly sending him backward.

The impact was enough to dislodge her mask, sending it to the ground in a pile of broken pieces. Seamus could not see her face at his current angle, but he could see the Ulvemordere's eyes widening behind their own metal mask.

The soldier and Seamus glanced at the discarded crossbow. Unfortunately, the soldier was quicker. Quick as they could, they lunged for the crossbow and slid a bolt onto the rail. Seamus pushed Ophelia to the side, holding up the fallen Ulvemordere's metal helm as a shield as the remaining soldier took aim.

Suddenly, a thick pillar of ice shot up from the ground, their attacker's bolt implanting itself in it. Seamus peaked around the pillar of ice to see the Ulvemordere staring in disbelief. Seamus threw their companion's mask at them, causing them to stumble back and drop the crossbow. Seamus rushed forward, scooped it up, knocked in one of the bolts connected to the long strap attached to it, aimed and shot at the eyehole of their mask.

Perfect aim, as usual. Best not to think about *that* sound too much. . . He was always good with crossbows.

The soldier crumpled to the ground, blood gushing from their eye where the bolt had embedded itself inside their skull.

The mystical wall of ice shattered into a thousand snow-flakes that hung suspended in the air before falling softly to the ground.

Seamus turned back to Ophelia, who was holding her broken mask in her hands. He opened his mouth to speak, but his eyes fell upon her face. At first, he turned away and shield-ed his eyes out of respect—something about solstices and the Skogens Søstre came to mind—but what he'd seen had clicked. And it wasn't something he could ever unsee.

Slowly, he turned back around, unable to hide his shock.

The skin around her eyes and across the bridge of her nose was stark blue, with three lines like icicles curling over her cheeks. An intricate navy snowflake adorned her forehead.

Witch Marks.

Seamus could only stare. Of all the things his gruel-ing journey had shown him, what stood before him had never crossed his mind. All the Witches were meant to be dead. How had one—a young one, for that matter—escaped capture and execution?

Ophelia stood. Fear wafted off her in nauseating waves, the smell like rotting fruit. Her heart was practically rattling her bones it was beating so fast.

The soldier—a young man—he'd knocked out, began to stir. Instinctively, Seamus rushed in front of Ophelia, holding her behind him, protecting her secret. She yelped, swatting away his arms. Seamus hoped she realized whose side he was so obviously on.

The young soldier grappled to his feet, procuring a dagger from his arsenal of weaponry. He snarled, his puffy, bloodied face starting to heal. Trails of blood moved in reverse back into his nose. His eyes slowly opened, the subtle bruising fading. Seamus groaned as the soldier rushed forward.

In response, a gust of wind swept in out of nowhere. As

if by invisible hands, the soldier was thrown against a tree. He screamed on impact, curling inward. A final gust pinned him against the trunk as ice formed around his wrists, melding him with the tree.

Seamus looked over his shoulder at Ophelia, who was clutching his sleeve as she stared at the soldier, half her face hidden behind his burly arm.

"Impossible!" the Ulvemordere spat. "I'll kill you, s*kitten heks!*" he screamed, thrashing and kicking, trying to break free from his shackles of ice. "I'll kill you both!"

Filthy Witch, he'd called her. Seamus was seething with anger already, but that sent him over the edge. From the darkest corners of his mind came a guttural growl. He wanted nothing more than to squeeze the life out of this idiot with his bare hands. Ophelia attempted to hold him back, but her tiny hands couldn't hold him for long.

Seamus ripped free from her grip, removing a bolt from the crossbow's holster, crossing quickly to plunge the tiny yet sharp projectile into the soldier's throat. Ophelia squeaked, covering her eyes and turning away as the man before them gurgled his last bloody breath. Another sound Seamus didn't want to dwell on. . .

Seamus was panting heavily, eyes shut tight, ears pricked to hooves, and footsteps in the distance.

Looking over his shoulder, he saw Ophelia peering through her fingers at him, eyes—brilliant silver eyes—as wide as a full moon. Her purple lips were quivering in fright.

Seamus felt his shoulders sag.

This wasn't meant to happen.

He swore thickly, motioning her forward, but she stood stiff, just staring at the freshly dead man behind him.

"Kid, there's more coming our way," Seamus whisper-yelled, seething.

She swallowed hard, reaching for his sleeve, pulling him in the opposite direction of Tø. Breaking into a run, they shot off into the woods as fast as their legs could carry them, never looking back. Ophelia led the way expertly. They didn't stop running until they made it back to the cottage.

Ophelia stood shaking as Seamus locked the front door and pulled close the drapes on all the windows. He had a tight grip on his newly acquired crossbow, ready to fire if needed. Ophelia's own hands were shaking. They sparked with electricity as the gravity of what happened fell upon her. The broken pieces of her fox mask rattled in her satchel. The irony of that was not lost on her, but there were more important things to worry about right now.

A scream she'd been holding in since she first saw the Ulvemordere soldier appear escaped her burning lungs. Seamus winced, shushing her. He almost moved to clamp a hand over her mouth, but she beat him to it. They stared at each other for a good while, trying to catch their breath.

Ophelia was the first to speak. "You—You need to leave," she choked out, running her hands through her hair over and over, her frozen fingers leaving behind snowflakes.

Seamus made toward her, but she backed away, holding her hand out, allowing sparks to fly from her fingers.

"Stay back," she snapped.

Of all the possibilities—of all the outcomes—why this? Why *them*? This was all very far from what she'd been expecting. She stood staring at him as if he were a venomous snake about to strike. He was more than trouble; he was a walking corpse wanted by the worst group of people this world had ever seen.

Ulvemordere.

Wolf killers.

Seamus stood tall, his face darkening. "I'm not the enemy—"

"You brought them here!" she screamed, sparks turning to bolts of sharp, metallic-smelling lightning that swirled before her like a dance of death. "You're wanted by the Ulvemordere! That's why you've been running!"

"Yes, kid, and you're a Witch. Seems we've both been keeping rather nasty secrets. Happy now?" he snapped.

"No!" she hissed.

Seamus's nostrils flared. "You know, kid, you're lucky I just killed the only two who've seen your face. You're welcome, by the way."

"Oh, well thank you, *død mann*," she snapped, then

clamped her hand over her mouth again.

Dead man. She shouldn't have said that.

Seamus drew in a sharp breath, turning away from her.

"I'm so sorry. I didn't mean that," Ophelia cried.

Seamus rubbed the back of his neck, silent. His other hand was still gripping that damned crossbow, its strap swaying, the bolts gleaming like malignant little diamonds. He was scared and frustrated and bleeding. She had no right to snap at him or call him petty names like that. She was terrified, too, but he was right. They didn't know of her. They were only after him.

"Seamus?" Ophelia whispered, curling in on herself.

"I'm thinking," he said, his voice gruff with frustration.

The Ulvemordere were notorious. Forget Kings and Queens. If you hungered for absolute power, you joined *their* ranks. That blood-hungry cult of berserkers controlled the world. They were a ruthless, cutthroat, heartless cult. Even those who agreed with their heretical ways feared the sharp side of their weapons. Once joining, even thinking about deserting or resigning would get you killed. But why would you? Ulvemordere soldiers lived well beyond their means. What they wanted, they took, no questions asked. Their superiors were rich in ways the nobles couldn't even fathom. Of course, that meant those same nobles were in their pockets. Most complied without a second thought. Those who questioned authority wound up dead. They controlled the nobles; they controlled the peasants. They controlled the seas; they controlled the food supply. Even in The Wilds, a lawless country where their iron fist was often ignored, their presence was feared.

Their name was derived from their beginnings as poachers. Somehow, they'd gotten it in their heads that killing wolves and wearing their pelts would grant them otherworldly abilities—abilities that could rival Witches, the rulers at the time of their union. Wolves at the time ran rampant across Snøbolig and Høstlunden. There were whispers of wolves who could shift into humans. Rumor had it those beings used their powers for malevolent purposes. No one batted an eye at how many wolves the Ulvemordere killed. In fact, the history books say they'd been thanked and rewarded for their efforts. After a few short years, they'd amassed a following, troves of gold, and hundreds of pelts.

The problem? Ordinary wolf pelts don't grant humans any power or protection.

Werewolves, however? That's another story entirely.

The history books were unclear—Ophelia guessed this was because the Ulvemordere had written them—but one fateful full moon a thousand years ago, the first Ulvemordere hunting party had stumbled upon a pack of werewolves. Whether or not they knew those wolves were actually people was unknown. The details of the battle were lost to time, too, but it was clear the Ulvemordere were victorious. Once those wolves had been skinned and their furs processed, those who wore them suddenly had the same abilities werewolves did. Heightened senses, the ability to heal faster than any normal being—they'd even grow claws. They couldn't transform, but that didn't matter when you had the powers of two species on your side. The catch? Those powers disappeared as soon as they removed their pelts.

Upon this discovery, the werewolf population began to dwindle. It was genocide.

Of course, that wasn't enough. For the greedy, there is no such concept of 'enough.' This, coupled with evil, makes for a very dangerous philosophy to teach.

If stealing the pelts of werewolves gave the wearer power, what would stealing fairy wings do? What about unicorn horns? Goblin ears? Troll hearts? Dragon scales? The Ulvemordere's hunger for forbidden knowledge would never be satiated, but with every being they killed and studied, they gained a deeper understanding of how the world worked.

Their treachery was not discreet. The ruling Witches of the time were. . . not pleased, so to speak.

Soon, a war broke out.

There was a time when Witches ruled the earth, a time when Ophelia would not have been the sole Witch of The Wilds. If she'd been alive all those years ago, she would've made vastly different decisions than her predecessors. The people wouldn't have turned on her, that she knew.

The people thought the Witches only ruled because of their powers. They were ordained by the Spirits at the time, but of course, that little fact was scarcely uttered. Ophelia was bitter about that, but that wasn't the point. The point was that now that humans could steal the powers of any magical creature they wished, 'ordinary' folk figured it was time for a new regime.

All good things come to an end.

Humanity inevitably turns on the mystique.

The Ulvemordere could give humanity the same magic the mystique had hoarded since the beginning of time. They were welcomed with open arms, and as the war raged on, a new question began circulating.

What could be stolen from the Witches?

The answer was simple: their blood.

If a being drinks a Witch's blood, they'd gain their abilities for a short period of time.

The Ulvemordere killed and drained the blood of every Witch they could, using their powers against them. Even the strongest Witches of the time were no match for an army pieced together from bits and pieces of every magical creature imaginable.

The Ulvemordere won the war. The Witches? Their bloodlines slowly died, lost to history and folklore, always painted as villains. With the Ulvemordere ruling, humanity turned on the magical community.

Eventually, the species were regulated. Some were sanctioned to be killed at birth, namely Witches. Werewolves were hunted for sport, dragons were almost extinct, fairies who stepped out of line had their wings cut off—the list went on.

That's why Ophelia's kind was so rare, why she had to wear her mask.

If there is evil, there is good. If there is a dictatorship, there is a rebellion. If there is despair, there is hope. If there is life, then, of course, there has to be death.

All things in balance.

After years of control, the mystique was starting to push back. Another war was on the horizon. No one wished to speak of it, but you could tell just by looking around your own town. Especially if you lived in The Wilds. Resources were being diverted elsewhere without explanation. The Ulvemordere were stockpiling goods and weaponry, and so was the rebellion.

Another war was happening just now, one raging inside Ophelia's mind. Seamus had brought the worst of the worst with him. His being here could get her killed. But if he left, he would have no one to protect him. He couldn't run forever.

Ophelia paled, snapping herself out of her thoughts. "Is there a bounty on you?"

Seamus, who'd been quiet for quite some time, whipped his head around to stare at her in fright. "You're joking. You did *not* just ask me that." He had the crossbow held like a shield.

"Mr. Norland!" Ophelia yelled. "This is a very serious matter! Is there a bounty on you or not?"

"What do you think, kid?" he snapped.

Ophelia walked shakily to the hearth. If the fire were to ignite at that moment, it would have perfectly reflected her life.

"Maybe they don't know you're here," Ophelia said, trying her best to sound optimistic.

Seamus gave her a dull look. "There's two dead soldiers in the woods, kid. I think they know." He mumbled something to himself, pinching the bridge of his nose. "And your healer strongly implied he knew exactly who I was."

Ophelia's heart skipped a beat.

Lochlan had extended an olive branch to her, and she'd set it ablaze. He knew she'd want to protect Seamus, so he'd given her a chance to scare him off. Because if he knew the Ulvemordere wanted Seamus, then eventually, so would the Earl and Countess. That is if they didn't already. They'd gladly hand over Seamus if it meant protecting themselves and their town. Even if he was completely innocent. If they caught wind of Ophelia's misstep, they'd sell her to the Ulvemordere without a second thought.

"You need to leave. Now," she screeched, grabbing Seamus's pack from its place by the door, stuffing it full of hardtack and preserved meats. He'd bought a bedroll recently. Hastily, she tied that to the bottom of the pack.

She turned back to Seamus to find him staring at her shoes. With a quick glance down, she realized icy swirls had formed beneath her feet. He took a step back before finally looking up at her. His bushy eyebrows were knit together, his expression halfway between terror and concern.

Ophelia held the pack before her, knuckles white, the room chilling.

Sometimes, Seamus got this look on his face. His eyebrows would furrow, and he'd frown, and then he'd bring up something he must've been mulling over for some time. He had that look now, only his eyes darted all over her face. They lingered on the snowflake on her forehead longer than she'd like.

"Lochlan knows about that too, doesn't he?" he asked, gesturing loosely toward her face.

She nodded.

"You said he needed you when you were younger, right? Did you mean your powers? Would he sell me out even if it meant compromising your safety?"

Ophelia shoved the satchel into his arms, casting her eyes to the ground.

"Ophelia," Seamus said exasperatedly. "They are going to ride into Tø and ask all the wrong questions. Would he, or anyone else, point them in your direction?"

"I don't know," Ophelia said, though that was a lie. She wholeheartedly did know. Seamus did too, he was just being polite.

Very few knew what she was. Most had been paid to keep their mouths shut. That was all fine and dandy, but the Ulvemordere would offer more than Lochlan and the Earl ever could. Tø would be rolling in riches by the time they had her head on a pike.

"Get your things," Seamus demanded.

"What?" she blurted out.

"We'll tell Åssi we're taking a trip and won't be back until the weekend. We'll head in the opposite direction we tell him we're going and then circle back around toward the Cities." He spoke in short bursts, slinging his pack and crossbow over his shoulders, shooing her away wildly.

"I can't go with you," Ophelia said softly.

Seamus made a series of hysterical, enraged movements with his arms. "*Kid,*" he hissed, eyes ablaze.

"I will see you to the edge of town, but I cannot follow you further," Ophelia said, straightening. "I. . . I just can't. . ."

Seamus grumbled to himself but ultimately nodded, sweeping her out the door despite his better judgment.

Ophelia couldn't believe what was happening. She'd been harboring a fugitive with a bounty on his head for weeks.

That statement wasn't unheard of in The Wilds, but the fact that Seamus wasn't just a thief or a murderer changed things drastically.

A squeak escaped her as she stood on the steps, staring out at the garden. "Seamus. I've been housing a wanted wolf for weeks."

"The whole town has," Seamus said, waving her away. Suddenly, he stopped dead in his tracks, turning to her. "You're not—" He bounced on the balls of his feet with fright. "The *whole town* has been harboring a *fugitive.*"

Ophelia nodded, eyes wide. "Everyone is an accomplice. To them, at least."

Fast as they could, they raced down the path to Tø, slipping and sliding in the mud.

The owls cooed solemnly, knowing they'd done their best to try and warn their Witch. Unfortunately, their best hadn't been enough.

CHAPTER FIFTEEN

DAMNATION

Seamus was pounding on the door to the makeshift infirmary with all his might. There was a sound from inside before the door unlocked. Seamus kicked it inward before someone could open it, revealing a yawning Lochlan. Ophelia didn't have time to stop him before Seamus grabbed Lochlan by the hood of his robe. In one swift movement, he flung him against the wall.

"Mr. Norland!" Ophelia screeched. The heavy door slammed shut, making her jump.

Seamus's eyes were wild, glowing green. "What did you do?" he demanded, shaking Lochlan for effect.

"I'm sure I have no idea what you're referring to," Lochlan said.

Seamus took Lochlan by the throat, growling. Ophelia had never once seen Lochlan Gard afraid. Not until now. His sullen eyes bulged out of their sockets, his spindly fingers squeezing Seamus's wrist.

"Did you tell them I was here?"

"I—I didn't h—have to!" Lochlan choked out.

Ophelia drew in a sharp breath, eyes darting back and forth between them and the door, expecting it to be blown open again.

"You inquire enough a—about a name, the r—right people r—respond," Lochlan said in a garbled voice. "Or in y—your case, the *wrong* people."

Seamus released him, swallowing hard. He turned to look at Ophelia, eyes full of regret. His hand fingered one of the bolts on his crossbow's carrying strap, glancing back at Lochlan. Ophelia shook her head. Killing him wouldn't do anything. Though, if she were to be completely honest, she wouldn't exactly mourn the fickle physician.

Lochlan's lips curled into a smug smirk. He opened his mouth to speak when his gaze finally fell on Ophelia's face.

"Child, where is your mask?" he asked, horrorstruck.

Seamus spoke over Ophelia's sputtering squeaks. "*They* broke it. *They* saw her."

Lochlan paled. "Say it isn't so," he said to Ophelia.

"That's all you have to say?" Seamus barked.

Ophelia took a step back, grabbing Seamus by the sleeve. Clearly, he was not done with Lochlan by any means, but the longer he stayed here, the less of a chance he had to flee.

"Think for a moment of the implications, Lochlan," Ophelia hissed.

Lochlan glared at her. "What implications could—" A frightened gurgling sound escaped his throat. "Holy Spirits above. They'll come after me. Dammit, Ophelia! How could you be so careless?"

"They attacked us and broke her mask. She wasn't being careless!" Seamus spat.

"And what did she do to provoke them, hmm?"

Ophelia was surprised there wasn't steam blowing out of Seamus's ears by now. His face was so red, his jaw clenched so tight, she figured he was about ready to blow.

"What happened doesn't matter. What matters is that they'll be coming after the whole town, not just us," Ophelia said, tugging on Seamus's sleeve to get him to take a step back.

"So?" Lochlan laughed.

"We've got to warn everyone!" Ophelia shouted.

Seamus shook his head in disbelief, pinching the bridge of his nose. "Let me guess, you've been beaten around your whole life, looked over, abused, worked to the bone? But now that you have say over a whole town, you don't feel like such an illiterate, useless, annoying little man. Pray tell, what happens if there's no town for you to lord over?"

Lochlan was the first out the door.

With that, the three of them high-tailed it to the center of town. Well, Seamus and Ophelia high-tailed it. Lochlan sort of hobbled along like a dying horse. Everyone they passed stared after them, fear, confusion, disgust, or a mix of all three marring their features.

Seamus stopped abruptly before the old alarm bell atop the dried-up fountain, causing Ophelia to collide with him. Lochlan limply galloped to a stop. He was panting heavily, staring blankly at the ground. After taking a moment to catch his breath, Lochlan yanked the frayed rope, the old bell ringing a shrill tune. Villagers appeared around them, their faces full of morbid intrigue. Ophelia sourly remembered the last time that bell had rung.

"What's going on?" came Åsmund's voice.

Instinctively, Ophelia hid behind Seamus, trying to hide her face. Seamus glanced down at her, attempting to smile reassuringly.

Lochlan pushed his way to the group's center, silencing them all with a single shaking finger. "Ulvemordere soldiers are on their way here."

Confused murmurs washed over the crowd like a tsunami. Though the Ulvemordere were feared, the human folk knew they were safe unless they opposed their control. Even with Ophelia's presence—which some were catching on to—they'd be unharmed should she disappear, and they kept quiet.

"Did you tell them about the wolf?" Åsmund asked, skeptical. "Why would they concern themselves with us? Was it a werewolf?" He glanced at Ophelia, who was peeking around Seamus's arm, unbothered by what he saw.

Lochlan straightened to his full height, folding his hands inside his sleeves. When he wasn't slouching, he was quite tall. "Because, Åsmund, we've had a traitor amongst us."

Seamus went stiff. Ophelia's grip on his arm tightened.

"It *was* you, wasn't it?" Torbod sneered, fighting to get to the center of the crowd, pointing an accusing finger directly at Ophelia.

The crowd turned its collective head toward her. For a moment, all was quiet. Then, all at once, folks began to back away, tripping over each other. Mothers hid their children, shouting at their husbands to do something. Some just swore in shock. Some reached for cleverly concealed weapons they usually reserved for brigands.

"I didn't—"

"Shut your mouth or lose your tongue, *Dømte En!*" Torbod shouted.

"I told you she was controlling the wolf!" someone screamed from the crowd.

Torbod nodded. "You've always had it out for us. From the minute you got here, all we've had was trouble. The weather has been harsher, and the livestock thinner. You're always sabotaging our traps. Now, our cattle, too? What's next, our pigs? Our horses? Our children?"

"I didn't do anything to your cattle, Torbod," Ophelia said, her voice riddled with fear.

Torbod crossed to her, fuming. "Maybe not directly. But we all know you have a weird little connection to animals. I bet you sent that wolf to attack and kill them." He spat at her feet. "*Skitten heks.* You deserve whatever the Ulvemordere does to you. I hope they string you up by your neck and let us watch."

Seamus put a firm hand on Torbod's chest, fighting every urge to claw out his throat right then and there. His free hand twitched toward the crossbow at his side. This pompous man was the same shady villager who'd offered him a job at his farm. Angry wind whipped at the giant before him. A flicker of pain danced across Seamus's chest. He suddenly remembered it was storming the night of the full moon. Or at least, that's what the images flashing before his eyes made him believe.

"I would *never* do that!" Ophelia snapped. "If a wolf killed your cows, it did so on its own accord. How dare you accuse me of such things!"

Torbod sneered, leaning around Seamus's arm to get to her. "You fooled everyone else, but you didn't fool me. I don't put anything past you, you little—"

"I'd be very careful what you say next, Torbod," Seamus snapped, shoving him back so hard the man fell to the ground.

"Torbod, please, contain yourself," Lochlan said, sounding bored per usual. "I will deal with Ophelia, believe me, but she is not solely to blame."

Seamus's eyes flicked to him, the grip on his crossbow tightening. No compassion. No fear. Barely even apathy. He even yawned as he began to pace the circle of townsfolk. A crossbow bolt between Lochlan's eyes sounded really lovely right about now.

"Before you stands the real monster among us," Lochlan announced, gesturing toward Seamus with a flourish and a smile. "Ladies and gentlemen, Seamus Norland, werewolf."

Some members of the crowd began edging forward, hatred in their eyes. The fear and anger wafting off them burned the inside of his nose. The strongest scent, however, came from behind.

Lochlan laughed to himself, moving out of the way of an elderly man brandishing his cane like a spear. "Oh, but that isn't even the best part. Mr. Norland is an Ulvemordere defector."

Seamus raised his crossbow, setting a bolt onto the rail with one swift movement.

"Seamus, don't," Ophelia said from behind, her voice small.

Glancing over his shoulder, he found her entire countenance had changed. No longer was she the young woman with an ancient aura. Without her mask, without the mystery, she was just a scared child. Her eyes were cast toward the ground, and her trembling purple-blue hands hung loosely at her side. Seamus shook his head, disgusted with how these people treated her. He was even more disgusted with himself for letting them. He *was* a fickle, fickle man.

Turning back to the crowd, he had a few choice words swirling in his mind.

Lochlan had begun to circle again, eyes locked on Seamus. He was trying to get a rouse out of him, and Seamus knew it. Baiting him, using the people's fear against him and Ophelia.

"So that's that, then?" Seamus snapped. "You're just going to—" His ears picked up on a rumbling in the distance. He swore, backing away from the crowd, stumbling into Ophelia, metaphorical tail between his legs. "I hear hooves. Lots of them," he breathed.

Ophelia's heart skipped a beat.

All was silent.

Lochlan stood with a foot hovering in the air.

The rumbling was growing.

"Seamus," Ophelia said, her voice full of worry. "You need to go."

He gave a single shake of his head, adjusting his grip on his crossbow. Not once had he lowered it.

The ground was shaking beneath their feet. Battle cries carried on the wind.

Someone screamed at the back of the crowd.

The villagers jumped into action, running toward shelter and weapons—some even had the bright idea of running away.

It was chaos. Pure unbridled chaos.

"Seamus, you need to run!" Ophelia screamed, pushing him to the side.

"Not without you!" Seamus screamed back, sliding on the damp ground, nearly losing his footing. He reached for her wrist only to have her recoil.

"Please go," she pleaded, tears in her eyes. "*Please.*"

"Come with me!" he begged. Someone bumped into him as they ran by.

Ophelia put up a hand, shaking her head. "I can't. I shouldn't."

Letting go of his crossbow, he tried to grab hold of her before she ran off into the chaos, but he was too slow. One blink, and she'd disappeared into the frantic crowd.

He swore several times, turning on his heels.

Seamus hated feeling helpless.

Swallowing the bile rising in his throat, he ran to the edge of town, jumping fallen barrels and dodging scatter-brained patrons. The screams of terror echoing behind him made his stomach churn. Try as he might, he couldn't help but imagine one of those screams came from Ophelia.

A thin dirt path appeared before him.

He wanted to keep running. No, he *needed* to keep running.

Yet, he slowed.

Panting hard, doubled over, clutching his chest, he swore. Should the Ulvemordere capture him, he'd be skinned for his pelt, then burned. They'd make an example out of him, reiterating what happened to the dogs that disobeyed their masters. That thought terrified him.

He had to go.

He just had to.

That was his only option.

And yet, despite his better judgment, he spun back around and raced into the fray.

Fights were breaking out all around her as Ophelia wove through the chaos. Ulvemordere soldiers clashed against those able to fight back. Others fought each other. Some were stealing anything they could get their grubby hands on and making a run for it, but most were just trying to get out of the streets and barricade themselves inside their homes or businesses.

Ophelia knew she couldn't help them all. It'd been mere minutes, and bodies were already on the ground. It was all happening too fast.

Lochlan was nowhere to be seen. Of course, when push came to shove, he was gone. Was it any wonder he'd turn the town on her? This was all overdue, really. So why did it hurt so much?

Rough hands on her shoulders startled her out of her thoughts. She'd been hiding in an alley, trying to collect herself. She spun, ice expanding over her fist. Åsmund caught her wrist before she could bludgeon him to death.

"My wife and children are trapped," he said quickly, pulling her toward the butcher shop. The roof was ablaze, the door blocked by an overturned cart.

Tø was crumbling in every possible way.

"Please, *Vinterheks*," Åsmund cried, shaking her.

Winter Witch. Something bloomed in her chest upon hearing him say that. Not quite pride, but almost.

She nodded to him, shaking free of his grasp. Grasping

at the open air, she felt her muscles strain against her magic. The cart was heavier than she'd expected. She pushed her hand out with all her might and called upon the wind. A strong puff of air wrapped around the cart, slowly pushing it away from the door. A plume of dust swirled in the air where it'd been.

"Thank you," Åsmund whispered, racing off to find his family.

Ophelia looked down at her hands, watching her frost-bitten skin crackle and pop with sparks. Someone had come to her in their hour of need and trusted her to help. Taking a steadying breath, she turned toward the fray, knowing she couldn't run like Seamus. Ophelia would fight for these people until her dying breath, even if just one made it out of this alive. At least someone would be around to tell her story.

A pair of soldiers had a group pinned against a wall. Ophelia rushed forward, thrusting her hands forward, shooting ice spikes toward them. The icicles weren't sharp enough to pierce their armor, but the impact startled them enough that they forgot all about the people before them. The soldiers rounded on her. One had a mace, the other a broadsword. They charged at her, weapons swinging wildly.

For such feared warriors, they fought awfully sloppily. Every movement was random. Ophelia couldn't distinguish a pattern. Of course, this was coming from someone who'd only read about battles, not a seasoned warrior like Seamus.

The soldier with the broadsword came swinging first. Ophelia scrambled to dodge the slash of their sword, flicking a bolt of lightning in their direction. The soldier convulsed, screaming in anguish. Their beady red eyes shone like jewels in the darkness of their helm, their resentment and pain clear.

The one with the mace narrowly missed her, their weapon landing next to her foot. Ophelia kicked them hard in the face, sending them stumbling back.

One of the women in the group behind them ran forward with a shovel. With all her might, she swung. Needless to say, the soldier collapsed to the ground.

"Watch out!" the woman screamed, wielding her shovel like a sword.

Ophelia spun to see the other soldier had dropped their sword, opting for hand-to-hand combat instead.

There was no time to react before the soldier had her pinned to the ground, one hand clamped around her neck, the other procuring a dagger from their hip. Their iron gauntlet burned the bare skin on her neck, causing her to cry out in pain. Ophelia was clawing and kicking at the soldier to release her. Thin, sparkling layers of ice appeared on their body wherever her hands touched. Sparks of electricity danced over their armor. All the soldier did was laugh, squeezing his hand around her neck so tight she couldn't breathe. The iron they wore repelled her magic.

Just as Ophelia's vision began to blur, two sets of hands grabbed the soldier atop her, flinging them backward. Another set of hands yanked her up off the ground, which set her upright and dusted her off.

Ophelia watched in horrified awe as one of her saviors ripped off the Ulvemordere's helm, pulled back the strip of leather protecting their neck, and slit their throat.

Glancing to her left, she saw the face of the woman who'd hit the mace-wielder over the head. It was Ute. The resident fiber artist. While her work with a shovel had been much appreciated, Ophelia wondered why she hadn't opted to use her knitting needles.

Ute smiled brightly, patting Ophelia on the back. "You tried your best, Witch. No shame in a little help."

Ophelia smiled, rubbing her neck. She'd have bruises there, for sure. Subtle burns, too. "Thank you, Ute."

Ute nodded and bowed. The two men who had killed the Ulvemordere also bowed. Ophelia recognized them both. Neither had been kind to her in the past. Yet here they stood before her, bowing deeply, with looks of sorrow and remorse on their faces.

"What do we do, Witch?" one of the men asked.

Ophelia looked over her shoulder. Tiny, scared faces stared up at her in awe.

"Get anyone who can't defend themselves to the observatory. Children and elderly first. Barricade yourselves inside," she said, motioning them forward.

The men rushed off, hoisting the children into their arms.

Ute lingered for a moment. "Will you be all right?"

Ophelia nodded. "Get your family to safety."

Ute patted her shoulder, steeling herself before joining the others.

Ophelia couldn't believe what was happening around her. The villagers were rallying together, picking each other up off the ground, dusting each other off, and fighting side by side. Those who'd advanced on her and Seamus just moments ago were nodding in her direction with looks of determination on their faces. Tø would lose so many, but maybe it would gain something, too.

Sometimes, miracles are born out of tragedy.

Ophelia's sense of triumph didn't last long.

"*Heks!*" came Torbod's voice. She turned to see him pointing at her, a band of Ulvemordere soldiers at his back.

The Ulvemordere charged forward, their blackened iron armor absorbing the afternoon light. Ophelia threw her arms up into the air, a sphere of ice encasing her. Unaccustomed to maintaining something like this, she strained to fill the holes the soldiers were making in her shield. The hilts of swords and kneecaps were breaking into the sphere from all angles.

There were just too many of them.

Ophelia screamed with effort, sweeping her hands through the air.

Her protective dome shattered.

CHAPTER SIXTEEN

BATTLE CRY

Seamus ducked as a thick spear of ice whizzed past him.

Around him, matching projectiles implanted themselves into anyone unlucky enough to be in Ophelia's line of fire. Though a fair portion of the soldiers fell, the Witch was still surrounded. Balls of crackling lightning pulsated in her hands as her eyes darted back and forth between the Ulvemordere. She was cornered. She wouldn't be able to escape without electrocuting herself in the process. The metal of her attackers' swords would conduct too much electricity.

"Hey!" Seamus screamed at the top of his lungs. "Leave the girl alone!"

He bent, picking up a discarded dagger, his crossbow bouncing at his side. He braced himself to charge forward, wondering if he could take all of them.

He didn't even get a chance to try.

The air filled with sparks and arcs of lightning as the five remaining Ulvemordere soldiers went flying, the ground where they had stood now marred with scorch marks.

Ophelia stood in the center of a blazing ring, her clothes smoking, her eyes crackling with lightning, her sleeves ablaze. She breathed heavily, staring at the ground as if caught in a trance. Her limbs were shaking, her body trembling. The guilt on her face made Seamus sick. Close by, the Ulvemordere writhed in pain. At least one of them was dead, the others wriggling and seething, their armor crackling, the electricity cooking them alive as it found its way beneath the iron.

This was insanity.

Seamus slipped the dagger into one of his belt loops, rushing forward. Without thinking, he grabbed Ophelia by the collar, ignoring her groggy screeches of protest as he dragged her down a thin alley, only releasing her when he was sure they were out of eyesight for the time being.

He rounded on her in disbelief. "Are you crazy?" he whisper-yelled. "Do you have a death wish?"

"What are you even doing here?" Ophelia snapped back. She looked exhausted. Physically *and* mentally.

Seamus blew hot steam out his nose. "I came back for *you!*" he said. "You're not a hero, kid. You have no duty to these people."

"You know *nothing* of my duty or responsibilities!" Ophelia hissed back. She tried to slip past him, but Seamus crossed in front of her, taking her by the arm.

"I will drag you out of here unconscious. So help me, I will."

"Get your hand off of me," Ophelia said, her tone dangerous. The exhaustion was fading, replaced by that familiar ancient aura.

As Seamus made for her neck, Ophelia stomped down on his foot. Biting wind shoved him back against the wall to his left. His eyes widened as he stumbled to the side. He barely had time to react before she lunged at him, a sharp dagger of ice appearing at her fingers.

"I am perfectly capable of protecting myself," she seethed.

Seamus leaned away from the freezing dagger pressed against his neck, hands up in defense. "I never said you weren't! But I know the Ulvemordere. I know what *they* are capable of. You stand no chance against them. Not this many."

"I am not abandoning the people of Tø."

He sighed heavily, feigning defeat. Her dagger lowered, and he grabbed her by the shoulder, spinning her around until he had her neck locked between the crook of his arm and his chest. She struggled against him, clawing at his forearm with her sharp fingernails. Her fingertips had turned the same shade of blue as her Marks.

"Listen to me!" he roared. "What have they ever done for you? Why do they deserve your protection?"

At that she stopped struggling, her limbs falling limp. Seamus released her but kept a firm hand on her arm.

"They can't fight. They'll die," she said softly, staring at her feet.

Seamus had made one stupid decision today and wasn't keen on making another. He'd come back for her. *Just* her. He wasn't here to play the hero.

"Stars, child! Why are you hiding like this?" came a screeching voice. Seamus looked over Ophelia's head to see Lochlan. He was bloodied and sweaty, eyes wild with anger and fear. "Have I taught you nothing?"

Ophelia spun, a tight frown on her lips. "I was—"

Lochlan rolled his eyes, beckoning her forward. Ophelia visibly sagged, leaving Seamus wishing he'd just slammed her head into the wall, thrown her unconscious body over his shoulder, and made off into the woods. You know. Like any sane person would do.

"Hush now, I've taken care of everything," Lochlan sighed.

Before either of them could question what he'd meant, Lochlan took Ophelia's wrist and yanked her out of the alley. The movement had been far too aggressive for Seamus's liking, but he wasn't surprised. The second he'd laid eyes on Lochlan Gard, Seamus knew he'd possessed the ability to do terrible, terrible things.

Lochlan was pulling Ophelia through the quieter chaos, his billowing robes making him appear as a wraith leading an unsuspecting victim to her doom.

He probably was.

Had Ophelia no self-preservation instincts?

Seamus couldn't exactly blame her, seeing as he tore off after them without a second thought. Her safety was his only concern. He still didn't know why. He'd tried to put the pieces together while trying to find her, but nothing had come to him. It was more a feeling than a conscious thought. Maybe she'd enchanted him or something.

The three of them wove through the wreckage. Seamus bristled at the sight. Discarded toys, broken wagon wheels, doors, and windows kicked in. Livestock ran rampant, their cries mixing with those of women and children. It was sickening how quickly the Ulvemordere worked. They'd leave nothing behind by nightfall.

Lochlan led them to the observatory, only releasing his tight grip on Ophelia's wrist when they were safely inside. Already, the dead and dying littered the floor. Seamus lingered near the door, observing the damage he had once again caused. Everything he touched turned to dust. Two men motioned for him to move as they heaved a heavy bookshelf in front of the door. Ophelia was following Lochlan to his office. Despite himself, Seamus trailed behind, unable to tear his eyes away from the families he'd torn apart. The smell of heartache was bitter and salty, like an endless ocean full of dead fish.

". . . I don't want to hear it, child. You will do as told!" Lochlan's drawl drifted out from behind the old tapestry. Seamus caught the door to his office before it could close.

"But Lochlan—"

"Talk some sense into her, will you?" Lochlan sighed, gesturing wildly at Ophelia as he began stuffing a satchel with all manner of goods.

"Tried that," Seamus grumbled, wincing as the sound of an explosion filtered in from the village center. The distant smell of wolfsbane burned his nostrils.

"I should be out there! I should be helping! How many more bodies will it take before you realize that?" Ophelia asked, hot, angry tears flooding her face.

Lochlan gave her a bored look over his shoulder.

"You might not care about them, but I do! It is my duty to protect the creatures of these woods. I should—"

"I will not hear any more of this nonsense," Lochlan said curtly, shoving the satchel in her direction. "You cannot protect what has already been destroyed."

Seamus laughed darkly. "And whose fault is that?"

Lochlan glared at him. "Yours."

"Seamus," Ophelia warned, no doubt noticing his subtle attempt to reach toward the old fool.

"I didn't alert them to my whereabouts," Seamus snapped, ignoring Ophelia as he strode up to Lochlan.

Lochlan rose to his full, gangly height, looking down on him in disgust. "I would not put Ophelia in danger like that on purpose. I told you; I made inquiries about a name, and that information got to the wrong people."

Ophelia sighed heavily. "Excuse me, but—"

"You threw her under the cart as soon as you could!"

"My tactics may not have been thought through fully."

"'Tactics?' You call these '*tactics*?'" Seamus couldn't believe what he was hearing. "Just what exactly did you think you'd gain from all of this? Did you think they'd just—"

"Do you not hear that?" Ophelia screamed, pointing at the door.

Lochlan and Seamus fell silent.

The roar of hooves pounding up the path toward the observatory filled the space where their arguing had been.

Lochlan jumped into action, grabbing a crate filled to the brim with jars full of multi-colored liquids. With all his might, he pulled the crate out from under the workbench it had sat beneath. Dust filled the room as Lochlan struggled to move the heavy crate.

There was pounding at the observatory door. Seamus desperately hoped that old bookshelf would hold.

Lochlan grumbled to himself, lifting a hatch on the floor. "Quickly, now," he said, offering a hand to Ophelia. "In you go."

"Not without him," Ophelia said, holding her head high and pointing at Seamus. Somehow, that was worse than staring down an archer.

There was a crash, signifying one of the beautiful stained-glass windows in the sanctuary had shattered. The putrid stench of panic filled the air. Shadows shifted beyond the equally colorful window before them. Through the warped glass, Seamus could make out dark figures. Lochlan scowled. Seamus raised an eyebrow. Someone, somewhere, screamed.

"He will not die for me, Lochlan," Ophelia snapped.

A gust of wind thrust Seamus forward until he found himself tumbling down the chasm that was the hole beneath the workbench. Ophelia jumped in after him, helping him up off the ground with an apologetic smile.

The makeshift bunker fell into darkness. From above, they heard Lochlan struggle to replace the crate on the hatch.

Ophelia slumped to her knees, clamping her hands over her ears.

In the all-consuming darkness, Seamus lost track of time. He blinked a couple of times, calling forth his wolf's eyes. A low green glow cast soft shadows onto Ophelia's face. The hole they'd found themselves in was small. The top of his head grazed the wooden planks above. There'd be scarcely enough room if anyone else had been down here with them.

They couldn't have been down there for long when Seamus heard the stained-glass window above crack and shatter. Heavy footsteps pounded the floor above, knocking dirt loose. Seamus grimaced, listening to jars smashing onto the floor and papers being thrown across the room. The soldiers were talking over each other, their voices like garbled growls. They were doing their best to find him, that was for sure. Seamus pinned himself against the wall, praying his scent was obscured by whatever had been in those jars.

Something popped, and the smell of wolfsbane assaulted his lungs. Purple smoke seeped through the cracks in the floor. Seamus covered his mouth and nose, trying his best not to cough. A gust of air swirled around his head, the smoke dissipating. On the floor before him, Ophelia watched him with one giant silver eye that seemed to glow. Slowly, he dropped his hands and took a deep breath.

Nothing. No burning sensation in his lungs.

Neat trick.

The footsteps receded, and the tapestry hiding Lochlan's office sounded like a sword had ripped it in two.

Seamus slid down the wall until he sat opposite Ophelia, eyes glued to the Marks on the Witch's face.

What an idiot he was.

CHAPTER SEVENTEEN

REMNANTS

Ophelia had no idea how she'd drifted off. Then again, she used to conjure thunderstorms to put herself to sleep when she was a child. The sound of the Ulvemordere horses wasn't far off from that booming thunder. And now that she thought about it, glass shattering sounded a lot like lightning. That thought saddened her. What once brought her comfort would now terrify her for years to come; she was sure of it.

Her eyes flitted to Seamus, who was lying on his back, staring at the ceiling. She wondered just how long he had been on the run. Shivers ran through her as she thought back to what Lochlan had said. The ever-mysterious Seamus Norland was an Ulvemordere defector. That wasn't an easy feat. Almost unheard of, in fact. But Seamus had left. And the Ulvemordere—*the Wolf Killers*—would make him pay the ultimate price for it.

How lonely his existence must've been.

How scared he must be.

Ophelia couldn't help but question how all this had come about.

Something to ask later, perhaps.

Seamus snapped his fingers, startling her. His knees creaked as he stood. Apparently, even werewolves got arthritis. Ophelia stood, too, worrying the strap of the satchel Lochlan had given her. She had no idea what exactly he'd packed in it, but the sorry thing weighed a ton at least.

Seamus's voice was barely a whisper. "It's been a while since I've heard anything. Can you—" he waved his hands through the air awkwardly "—sense the box above us? Can you move it somehow?"

Ophelia begrudgingly let go of the strap and nodded. Raising a shaking hand, she called upon the cold air around her. Above them, a *whoosh* and a *scree* were heard.

"I'll go up first. Stay in the shadows just in case, all right?" Seamus said, already pushing open the hatch.

"What happens if someone is up there? I'd be stuck down here," Ophelia squeaked, voice cracking.

Seamus heaved himself out of the makeshift bunker, his voice strained as he said, "Let's hope it doesn't come to that."

The hatch shut, and she heard him replace the crate. His heavy footsteps shook the timbers above, sending a cascade of dust into her eyes. Before she had a chance to rub the dirt away fully, Seamus returned, his expression grim.

"How good are you with blood?" he asked, looking over his shoulder.

Ophelia grimaced. "Not."

"As expected," he sighed, offering her a hand out of the bunker.

Ophelia brushed herself off as Seamus peeked into the sanctuary, ears pricked to sounds Ophelia couldn't fathom. For the first and last time, she was glad to be in Lochlan's office. That hole had begun to feel like a grave. Her current surroundings weren't much better, but at least there was sunlight. The window depicting the Snake had been destroyed. Colorful glass littered the floor, which Ophelia was careful not to step on. There was a canister of some sort in the corner. Purple powder—ground up wolfsbane—clung to nearby surfaces. The substance was odorless to humans, but werewolves often noted it smelled bitter.

"Shut your eyes," Seamus said, waving her forward.

"That bad?" Ophelia squeaked.

Seamus turned to her, a kind but sad smile on his lips. "Best not to think too much about it." He offered her his hand, standing so as to block her from seeing what lay outside the door.

She hesitated before taking it, shutting her eyes so tight her nose scrunched up. His rough palms against hers made her squirm more than what might lay beyond the door. His skin reminded her of Lochlan's.

The smell beyond the tapestries was horrid. Ophelia had been around enough dead bodies to know the smell only set in after a day. Then, it dawned on her that the sun shouldn't have been shining.

They'd been down in that hole for a full day.

A guttural sob bubbled up her throat. It was all she could do to shove down the overwhelming anguish clawing at her heart.

"Almost to the door," Seamus whispered, giving her hand a soft squeeze. She wanted to shake away his grip so badly.

Soon enough, she heard the familiar creak. Crisp air washed away the putrid stink. Seamus dropped her hand and shut the door. She could feel his eyes boring holes in the back of her head.

"You can open your eyes, kid," he said softly.

Ophelia shook her head. If she opened her eyes, then all this would be real. The once lovely observatory would really be filled with the bodies of people she had once vowed to protect. The Ulvemordere would have really attacked. Her comfortable yet lonely life would really be over.

Maybe if she stayed there a moment longer, something miraculous would happen.

That's what happened in her books. Everything worked out in the end with books. That's why she liked them so much, why she read as though she hungered for words.

"Ophelia," Seamus said, less kind and more impatient than she'd have preferred.

Blinking against the bright sun, Ophelia looked around to see that this part of the world hadn't changed. The trees still stood tall. The graves along the path were untouched. Birds chirped as if nothing had happened. Sure, the ground was torn up from hooves and footfall, but Ophelia was sure she could explain that away if she tried hard enough.

Seamus nodded down the path, and together, they silently walked to town. The closer they came to the tightly packed buildings, the more evidence of destruction there was. Bloody mud puddles dotted the path. Broken brooms, shovels, and pitchforks were scattered in places they shouldn't have been. Some were covered in blood. Others jutted out of the ground as if thrown like a javelin. Overturned carts were accompanied by empty barrels and crates. Stalls had been ransacked. Every business had broken windows and doors ajar. Dead livestock lay around every corner. Bodies did, too. Not as many as Ophelia had expected, but enough. More than enough. The Ulvemordere had truly left nothing behind. Not a life. Not a measly trinket. If they'd had an efficient way to clear away all the blood, they would've done so.

Could a person die from heartbreak and guilt? If so, Ophelia felt she could keel over at any moment.

Seamus stopped dead in his tracks, face drained of color. "Stay here," he whispered.

"But what if—"

"Just stay here," he hissed.

A slow but steady heartbeat echoed in Seamus's ears. There was a survivor somewhere in the rubble. As quietly as he could, he lifted his crossbow. A bolt was still stuck in the flight groove. Looking past the sight, finger on the trigger, he walked silently through Tø. He hoped the Ulvemordere had truly left. He hadn't wanted to leave Ophelia standing alone in the wreckage, but he wanted to protect her from this destruction even more. Seamus refused to let Ophelia become a timid version of himself. He knew from experience that there was only so much heartache a person could take before it consumed them.

He cursed himself.

He hated dragging good people down with him. Why did it happen so often?

The heartbeat he was following grew louder. Seamus flicked out his werewolf claws as he rounded the corner of the general shop. Deep inside, his wolf was howling with murderous rage.

A corner of gray fabric appeared before him.

His finger twitched.

He almost pulled the trigger.

Seamus swore, begrudgingly coming to Lochlan's aide.

He'd gotten himself pinned under a cart. Though he thoroughly hated this man, he knew he had to help.

Mustering up his strength, Seamus pushed the wagon off the old healer. He grimaced at the sight beneath it. Lochlan was covered in blood. There was too much to tell where it had come from or if it was his. If it *were* his blood, Lochlan would soon become another body littering the mass grave that was Tø.

"You. . . You have to g—get her out of here. . ." Lochlan whispered, the effort causing him to wince.

"Save your breath, old man," Seamus said, leaning down to inspect the damage better.

Lochlan cackled the best he could. "As—As if I could use it at a later date."

Seamus rolled his eyes. He made to lift Lochlan off the ground, but the man stopped him.

"They have us, Norland," Lochlan breathed, his eyes wild. "And that means they have *her*."

Seamus sat back on his heels, hunched over on the ground before him like a greedy little goblin. "They took captives?" Odd.

Lochlan nodded. "They s—saw her. They *know*."

Seamus glanced down the alley he'd come down, expecting to see Ophelia peering around the corner. He'd damned that poor kid. She could have gone her whole life in peace—or at least peace adjacent—here in Tø. But he had to come along and screw it all up. Not to mention the lives that had been lost on his account.

It was always the same with him, wasn't it?

"Protect her," Lochlan whispered, the conviction of the preacher he once was taking over. He put a bloodied hand on Seamus's chest. "I place her in your charge."

"You're not getting out of this one, are you?" Seamus asked.

Lochlan smiled crookedly. "Not this time." His smile faltered for a moment. "Not today."

Seamus stood, not knowing what else to say. He gave a curt nod, leaving Lochlan to his thoughts. He figured putting him out of his misery would have been the humane thing to do, but Stars knew that man should be alone with his guilt for a while.

Or maybe Seamus was just cruel like that.

Maybe he wanted Lochlan to suffer, if only for a moment.

Ophelia wandered through what was left of the market, finding bits and bobs hidden beneath the wreckage. Most of the things inadvertently left behind were just junk, but she'd spotted something special to salvage. Although one of Ute's shawls had survived, it was caked in mud. Ophelia hoped she could restore it to its former state with a quick cleaning. It was bittersweet. This was only the second piece of Ute's Ophelia had.

The only silver lining was that she hadn't seen Saoirse's body nor Åsmund and his family. Maybe they got away. Maybe they were safe. She knew that chance was slim, but for now, she'd hold onto hope her friends would see her again.

"Don't do that!" came Seamus's exasperated voice. "I thought you'd run off!"

She spun to see him adorned with a bloody handprint and a face full of grim determination.

"What happened?" Ophelia asked, clutching the dirty shawl to her chest.

Seamus looked down at himself. "Touched something I shouldn't have," he said nonchalantly, then pointed to the satchel slung over her shoulder. He still had his few belongings strapped to his back. Hurriedly packing his things yesterday felt like years ago. "We're leaving. You have everything?"

Ophelia knew it was more of a courtesy question, but she did *not*, in fact, have everything.

"I need to stop by the cottage," she said, her voice trembling ever so slightly.

Seamus hesitated but nodded. After a moment of staring at each other at a loss for words, they fell in step beside each other, eyes locked on the top of their shoes.

When they finally made it back to the cottage, Seamus nearly plowed her over at the garden gate. The entire place was untouched. Even her animals were there waiting for her. There was a moment of tense silence before Ophelia threw open the garden gate. With a clap of her hands, thunder boomed in the sky, and lightning illuminated the garden.

"GO!" she screamed with all her might.

The owls took flight, the bear cubs ran crying, and the deer jumped the fence, disappearing into the forest with a click of their hooves. Eydis lingered for a moment, morose. Ophelia nodded, hoping Eydis understood it was okay to leave and that she'd be all right. The polar bear wasn't convinced, but they'd made a deal long ago. Should anything happen to Ophelia, Eydis was meant to take her place as protector. It was time to make good on that deal.

Eydis hobbled over to her, resting her chin in the crook of Ophelia's neck. The Witch wrapped her arms around her polar bear, burying her face in her soft fur one last time.

"Be good, Eydis," she whispered. Eydis made a humming sound, then walked off.

Ophelia's shoulders sagged once the last of the animals had fled. She'd truly lost everything in the span of a day. And what had she done to prevent that? Nothing.

"Way to alert everyone we're—"

"Shut up, Seamus," she whispered, throwing open the door to the cottage.

A quick look inside the satchel Lochlan had given her told her they were good on medical supplies for the time being. Hardtack, too. Ophelia took another bag from her room, filling it with clothes, extra supplies, and books. So many books.

The very last thing she grabbed—the thing she'd come here for in the first place—was a giant book with its own carrying strap. As her fingers traced the design on the cover, she cried. Relief that this tome was still intact flooded her. Hot tears streamed down her face. This book was all she had left.

"Got everything?" Seamus asked quietly. She'd forever be grateful he hadn't teased her about all the books.

She gave a curt nod, wiping angrily at her face. It embarrassed her that he'd seen her cry so many times. She'd had figured she was stronger than this.

In her hands, she held a mask. It wasn't a fox like her last one. It was a polar bear. She'd had it long before she'd met Eydis, but Ophelia had always thought the two looked oddly similar. As she tied on the mask, it felt like Eydis was still with her, forever watching over her.

Seamus looked forlornly around the cottage as she slipped out the door.

Then, out into the wild and scary world they went.

The owls hid high above in the treetops.

They'd been waiting for this moment since the Witch's birth.

2. The Wilds

Into the Cold

Seamus walked a few paces behind Ophelia, watching her intently. She walked through the forest as if the weight of the world was suddenly on her shoulders. In a sense, it was, though he could never let her know. Ophelia was not a fighter unless, of course, provoked. Telling her that the people of Tø had been captured on her behalf, that they'd most likely be tortured and turned into slaves, would *definitely* provoke her.

The 'kind and sweet Ophelia' would become 'hated and feared Ophelia' in a heartbeat. Imagining that made him shiver. Under no circumstance could he tell her. And under no circumstance could he let any more good people from Tø die because of him.

What a conundrum he'd found himself in.

He didn't know much about Witches, but he'd read the history books just like everyone else. He knew what she was capable of, knew why there weren't many of her kind left. In fact, before today, he'd thought the Witches had died out years ago.

As Ophelia fiddled with the buckle on her satchel, lost in thought, Seamus began to devise a plan.

Staying in Tø had never been the end goal. He should've stuck with that. It had only been a steppingstone. Before his last run-in with the Ulvemordere, he'd been on the way to some powerful allies.

He wouldn't necessarily call these people friends, but they shared a common enemy and goal. They hated the Ulvemordere almost as much as he did. Getting to them would be a trek, but he could safely deposit Ophelia at their doorstep, discreetly explain the situation, and go from there. She'd be safe; he'd be back on track. He could wash his hands of this without so much as a second thought.

"Where exactly in The Wilds are we?" Seamus asked.

". . . Between the border of Høstlunden and the Center Cities," Ophelia said, her voice small. "Why?"

Seamus adjusted the pelt pinned around his shoulders and the straps of his pack and crossbow, searching the abyss of his mind for the right words. "I know someplace we'll be safe. For a while, at least," he began. Ophelia slowed until they were walking side by side again. "I know a pair who lives near the border. They'll happily let us stay with them."

They'd let *her* stay with them. If he could convince Ophelia to show them her Marks, they'd revere her as a deity, practically worshipping the ground she walked on. Him, on the other hand? He'd be lucky if they didn't skewer him on the spot.

Ophelia eyed him. "That's several weeks' worth of travel."

He shrugged. "Walk faster?"

Ophelia cast her eyes to her shoes, her silence deafening. Seamus felt his shoulders sag seeing her so defeated. He hoped her wild spirit would return one way or another.

Then again, it had been years, and he was still at war with his own wild and untamable soul.

"We don't have enough coin to stay at inns in random towns throughout The Wilds for several weeks, Seamus," Ophelia said, a panicked undertone to her voice. "I doubt there are even enough inns for several weeks!"

That could prove to be true. Especially if they couldn't find a reliable map. But Seamus had been on the run for quite some time, and with time came wisdom. They'd be fine.

Or so he hoped.

"The forest is our inn," Seamus said dryly. "Free room and board."

"Well, what of the Ulvemordere? What if they catch up to us? What if they attack and try to kill us in the night?" That panicky tone of hers deepened as a crisp breeze ruffled Ophelia's hair. "I—I'm not a fighter."

"You seemed to hold your own just fine," Seamus assured her. "Didn't you say so yourself?"

Ophelia shot him a rather worried look. "I've never used my magic like that before! It feels—" she stopped dead in her tracks "—*wrong* to use it like that. I'm not meant for combat."

Seamus raised an eyebrow, gesturing for them to continue on.

For someone who claimed never to have fought before, she'd been awfully good at taking down all those soldiers.

Yet again, Seamus noted the ancient aura surrounding her. He was not a curious creature, but given what'd been ingrained in his head as a child, Seamus had questions. Theories, even. The histories had told him there'd only been one Winter Witch prior to her birth. Of course, there were other types of Witches, but none as rare as *Vinterheksen*. The Marks a Witch had noted their power over the people and the elements. The Witches of old had held titles and ruled kingdoms—*Witchdoms*—before the humans turned on them. The more prominent the Marks, the more power a Witch had. And more power meant more respect.

Or fear.

If memory served correctly, Ophelia would've ruled the entire Witchdom of Villeste Skog—the Wildest Woods—and beyond.

But that was then, and this was now. Witches had been burned at the stake, hung, or drowned simply for existing for hundreds of years. So many people proclaimed they'd been born at the wrong time, but Ophelia truly was.

"What?" the last Winter Witch asked, shifting uncomfortably. Seamus hadn't realized he'd been staring.

"Your mask," he said, trying to dispel the air of distrust between them. Strangely enough, he felt more wary of her than she was of him. "I prefer it to the fox one."

"Oh, thank you. . . Lochlan said he found it with me as a baby." There was no emotion to her words.

Seamus's eyes widened. "Really? Why didn't you wear it then?"

"Lochlan chose the fox. He found it ironic. The Fox rules over liars, aiding their illusions. Hiding behind his face is quite clever, I suppose," Ophelia explained, practically dragging her feet as she walked. "I wanted to wear the Polar Bear. I really did. I connect with her more. She represents hope. But Lochlan had the mask specially commissioned, and I didn't want to be rude. Not only that, but wearing the likeness of a certain animal is a life oath. Changing your mask is a cardinal sin for the Skogens Sostre. You're forsaking your supposed calling. Lochlan figured folks would catch on to the lie if I forsook the Fox."

Seamus scoffed. "And no one thought a child running around with a fox mask was weird?"

Ophelia shrugged. "Lochlan's weird. Everyone knew that."

"No kidding. . ." Seamus mumbled.

"Hmm?"

"Nothing," he sighed, clearing his throat. "Shall I call you the Polar Bear Goddess now?

A hint of a smile flicked across Ophelia's lips. "I don't think I've earned that title just yet."

Seamus just shrugged, smirking. "So. . . Are you any good with a sword?"

"Do I look like the sort who'd be good with a sword?" Ophelia asked.

He shrugged. He'd met all kinds of warriors throughout his life. Not judging a person's combative skills by their stature was something he'd had to learn as a child. Such lessons had instilled a peculiar sort of skepticism.

"What about archery?"

Ophelia crossed her arms over her chest and shook her head.

"Nothing? You live in The Wilds, kid," Seamus said, perplexed. "You've never had to defend yourself? Not even once?"

A piercing breeze cut between them. Ophelia curled in on herself, her hair swirling into the air like smoke. Seamus could hear her heart pounding away with a frenzied sort of fear. She stunk of mint.

"No," she said sharply. "Not once."

Lies.

Seamus decided it best to drop the subject. If she wanted to talk, she would. Otherwise, there was no harm in her silence.

The Witch hugged herself tight against the breeze, taking calculated steps away from him.

The wolf once again fell a few steps behind, wondering about her past.

A bright orange haze was cutting through the trees. Seamus hadn't realized how long they'd been walking until that very moment. They'd left early in the morning, but now he could see the first stars beginning to shine.

Dry firewood and shelter were among the things they'd need to survive a night in this cold.

The makeshift path they'd been following diverged ahead, forked by a large spruce tree. Yawning, Seamus stood at the fork, trying to decide which way to go. Eventually, he decided he was far too tired for such a momentous decision. Instead, he dropped his pack at the base of the tree and motioned for Ophelia to do the same. She hung her bag on a low-hanging branch, looking up through the branches with a puzzled look.

"I think this is as good a place as any," Seamus yawned, stretching, surveying their surroundings. He set his crossbow atop his pack, keeping only the dagger slipped into his belt loop. "Stay here while I try and find firewood."

"Shouldn't I go with you?" Ophelia asked, a twinge of fear in her voice. She followed his gaze into the dark, shivering slightly. In the low light, the trees started melting into one another, fanning out into an endless, hazy void.

"If we both go, no one will be here to watch our things."

"We haven't seen a single soul out here, Seamus. I doubt anyone will steal from us."

Seamus gave her a bored look. She sighed, muttering under her breath about how stubborn he was. On any other day, he would've argued.

"Don't go far."

He gave a thumbs up, withdrawing into the forest. The woods were still inexplicably quiet, setting Seamus on edge. He didn't want to stay out here a second longer than he had to. Quickening his pace, he picked up any fallen branch he found. In all honestly, 'branch' was a generous term for the mere twigs he'd found, but something was better than nothing. The forest was darkening quickly, moonlight replacing the bright glow of sunset. Normally, the dark was comforting. It was easier to hide in shadows, after all. But tonight, the pitch-black trees surrounding him made Seamus feel trapped. No matter how hard he tried, he couldn't shake the feeling he was being watched. Something else was out there with him. It wasn't human or animal—that he knew for sure. Still, it stalked him like a predator. He didn't fancy being prey, not tonight.

It was foolish to think such things, but Seamus swore the trees were moving. Maybe his tired eyes were playing tricks on him, but with each glance over his shoulder, he'd turn back to find a towering spruce tree blocking his path. Even an expert hunter could get turned around, especially in unfamiliar woods. Accepting that truth kept you humble. Seamus had seen too much to believe he was solely at fault for stumbling through the dark like this. His lovely traveling companion was proof that nothing was ever as it seemed.

Figuring he had enough firewood for the night, he made to follow his footprints back to Ophelia.

Something whizzed past in the dark, filling him with dread.

"Whose there?" he demanded, listening intently.

The woods were silent.

"Playing tricks like this will get you nowhere," he snapped, fingering the dagger at his back. "And believe me, friend, I am not an easy target."

Behind him, he heard the flutter of an owl's wings. He glanced back at it, watching with a scowl as the enormous thing soared overhead.

Eyes still on the owl, he stepped forward, colliding with a tree—a tree that had not been there moments ago.

CHAPTER NINETEEN

SPIRITS

Ophelia sat cross-legged on the ground, lost in thought as she drew pictures in the mud with a stick.

She'd always dreamt of running far away from Tø and Lochlan. All these years, that town had felt more like a cage than a home. Yet sitting here, riddled with grief, she'd give up her chance at freedom to return to that cage and find Tø unharmed.

A rustling followed by a giggle broke her from her thoughts.

A quick glance over her shoulder revealed a towering twig-thing woman dressed in clothes unsuitable for The Wilds by any stretch of the imagination. Her floor-length olive green overdress was embroidered with shimmering bronze ferns that elegantly danced over her curves. The sleeves and high collar were slit to reveal a translucent sage green blouse, the lacy edges resembling fern fronds. A capelet of leaves adorned her shoulders, pinned at the center with a bejeweled brooch. Her long silver hair was pinned back beneath a crown of ferns to reveal a kind face weathered by time. Her silver locks fell in loose ringlets down her back, the ends whipping back and forth in the anxious breeze surrounding Ophelia. Her hands were folded neatly beneath her stomach, her fingers adorned with green jewels and bronze leaves.

"Hello, Ophelia," the woman said, giving the slightest hint of a bow.

Ophelia stood and brushed herself off, bowing deeply. "Hello, Fern," she whispered. She removed her mask and held it behind her, her cheeks burning with embarrassment.

A sound like wind rustling through the trees, and Fern was standing before her, a sad yet resigned look on her wrinkled face.

"How are you fairing, my dear?" she asked, holding her head high, looking down upon Ophelia as if she were a Queen addressing her most trusted advisor.

Ophelia suddenly realized that standing before a Queen would never be as terrifying as standing before the almighty Fern, the Terrestrial Spirit of Magic. Ophelia had spoken with this Spirit a hundred times before, but each time took her breath away. She was an ancient entity, almost as old as life Herself. There was wisdom in those wrinkles. Little got past her.

Which was why this visit came as no surprise to the young Winter Witch.

"I've never felt so lost," Ophelia said, standing to look her in the eyes.

Fern brushed a loose strand of hair behind Ophelia's ear, causing her to shiver. "Amaranth asked me to check on you," she said, a softness entering her eyes. "Tø's section of the Garden has wilted."

Ophelia nodded. "There was an attack," she whispered, shifting uncomfortably as Fern finally dropped her hand from Ophelia's face.

"How many?" Fern asked, folding her hands behind her back. "Amaranth wouldn't say."

"I didn't count, my lady."

Fern's emerald eyes narrowed. She studied Ophelia before nodding to herself, turning to look out at the trees. "Who is with you?"

"A werewolf by the name of Seamus Norland," Ophelia said quietly.

A hint of surprise in Fern's eyes. "Ulvemordere, then?" she asked.

Ophelia only nodded.

"Did they see you?"

Ophelia cast her eyes to the ground. "I tried to be careful, I really did."

Fern's leafy capelet rustled. Ophelia couldn't tell if that

meant she was cold or irritated. "Trying is one thing. Doing is another."

"Apologies," Ophelia whispered.

Fern inhaled sharply, straightening. "Find someplace to lay low, Ophelia. We can't have you become a target now, can we?"

"No, my lady."

"Promise not to do anything rash?"

"Yes, my lady."

"Good," Fern said softly.

A laugh from the trees. Ophelia peered behind her to see a young boy dressed in armor made of bark. A crown of branches adorned his mop of mousy hair. His dark eyes glittered in delight from the shadows.

"Spruce," Fern sighed.

"Hello, Ophelia!" Spruce smiled, nodding solemnly.

Spruce was a tricky Spirit. He wasn't as powerful as Fern or Amaranth, but he and his brothers still had duties. Their job was to plant new trees and care for the world's forests. Spruce and his brothers were often seen as Spirits of Renewal, though each had their own calling. They may not be able to make people fall in love like Narcissus or heal like Salvia, but their duties were just as important.

His brothers took these duties very seriously.

Spruce, on the other hand, was a trickster. Ophelia often wondered if he'd been assigned the wrong plant. While his brothers cared for the forests, he was often causing trouble amid the trees. Especially for humans. Namely, those who logged more than they should.

"Fern," Ophelia sighed.

"He's harmless," Fern said, smoothing the wrinkles of her dress, glancing over her shoulder at the boy.

Ophelia raised an eyebrow, causing Fern to roll her eyes.

"What have you done to him?" Ophelia asked.

Spruce smiled brightly. "I wouldn't expect him back anytime soon."

A flicker of a smile lit up Fern's face. Ophelia had known her long enough to know she was fond of the young Spirit.

This, in itself, wasn't strange. Fern had a hand in creating each and every Spirit. However, Fern was usually a no-nonsense sort of creature. Though she'd created all magickind, she'd also created the rules by which they were bound. She had a very low tolerance for rulebreakers, often punishing even the most trivial things. But Spruce, for whatever reason, had never seen her wrath.

"Release him, Spruce," she said eventually, adjusting one of the rings on her hand.

Spruce frowned. "Do I have to?"

Fern looked sidelong at Ophelia. Something odd passed behind those dazzling emerald eyes. "Mr. Norland is Ophelia's traveling companion. They've decided they need each other for the time being."

Ophelia's eyebrows furrowed.

Spruce's shoulders sagged. With a flourish, he snapped his fingers. Whatever he'd done to Seamus had ceased. Most likely, he'd played tricks with the trees, boxing Seamus in and turning him around until he couldn't tell up from down and left from right. Ophelia had witnessed first-hand how those tricks affected humans. Spruce was not fond of woodsmen and hunters. Once long ago, they'd had their fun with Torbod, running him in circles until Spruce's older brother Pine scolded them.

"Return to the Garden, please, Spruce," Fern said, returning her full attention to Ophelia.

Spruce nodded, bowed, and then disappeared without a trace.

Fern leaned forward, peering into Ophelia's eyes. The intensity of her gaze made Ophelia shutter. "Things have shifted for you."

"In what way?"

"Time will tell," Fern said softly, straightening. "Time will tell."

With that, she was gone. One second, she was there, a sad smile on her face; the next, she'd blinked out of existence.

Ophelia just stood there, staring at the tops of her shoes, dread and exhaustion warring in her chest, creating an odd sort of numbness. There was only one thing she could think of that could've shifted in her life, something she'd been trying to avoid for a very long time.

"Ophelia!" came Seamus's voice, accompanied by his thudding footsteps.

She turned, smiling softly at him. Twigs stuck out of his hair; his eyes were crazed, faintly glowing green. Under one arm, he held a bundle of sticks, and in his other hand, he had his stolen dagger.

"I've been calling for you! Why didn't you answer?" he asked angrily.

"I didn't hear anything," Ophelia said innocently, for it was the truth whether he believed her or not.

He frowned, looking over his shoulder. "I don't like these woods," he mumbled.

"You were gone for a while. Did you get turned around?"

He whipped his head around to glare at her. "No."

His cheeks were cherry red.

Rocking back and forth on her feet, Ophelia surveyed their surroundings. Seamus huffed and puffed his way to the large tree where their belongings lay discarded. He was muttering angrily, digging through his pack with his free hand. She couldn't hear what he was saying and was too afraid to ask.

Had he realized the woods were toying with him? She knew werewolves generally didn't subscribe to the religion of the Terrestrial Pantheon, but she knew better than to make assumptions. He didn't seem like the superstitious type, but that didn't mean he wasn't.

She wrung her hands nervously, looking to where Spruce had stood.

She hoped Seamus was ignorant of the things hidden just out of sight. Their voyage would be much easier that way.

CHAPTER TWENTY

OWLS AND THEIR NESTS

With one final exasperated huff, Seamus wrenched a flint and steel from his pack, holding it up, appraising it like a jewel. He shrugged, turning and dropping the firewood he'd collected in a heap. Ophelia watched, ever curious, as he crouched down and arranged the twigs rather methodically. When finished, he sat back on his heels and struck the flint and steel. The sparks died immediately. By the fourth attempt, he was muttering atrocities under his breath. Ophelia shook her head, taking pity on him. She rubbed her hands together, tiny lightning bolts prickling her skin. Kneeling next to him, she hovered her hands above the firewood, smiling to herself. As her lightning danced across them, the twigs and skinny logs burst into flames.

"Show off," Seamus mumbled. A wry smirk tugged at his lips. "You're in charge of the fires, then."

Ophelia nodded her approval, sweeping her skirts beneath her, sitting cross-legged beside him. "Fine by me."

He turned and grabbed his pack, took out a tightly wrapped bundle of dried meat, and handed it to her. The smell of salty venison burned Ophelia's nose as she unwrapped her dinner. Seamus tore into his own as if he hadn't eaten in years. Ophelia frowned in disgust, tearing off tiny pieces of her salted meat to nibble on.

"So here's the plan," Seamus said, tossing their wrappings into the fire. "We head east toward Høstlunden and meet up with those friends of mine. We'll either go our separate ways or stay with them for a while. It all depends on how Helgi Kirkeby and his sister Tiril receive us." He grimaced at that, which made Ophelia uneasy.

"What are they like?" she asked, eyeing him cautiously.

"Tiril and Helgi?" he scoffed. "They're not the kind of people you can describe with words. They just 'are,' so to speak."

"Are they werewolves, too?

"Yup."

"You trust them?"

"With my life." He nodded as if to remind himself that was the truth. Ophelia couldn't help but wonder if he'd trust them with *her* life.

Seamus dusted the salt from his fingertips, stood, grabbed his makeshift bedroll from his pack, and shook it out. He placed it a safe distance from the fire, bundling up a pelt to use as a pillow. With a satisfied sigh, he sprawled out atop it, staring up at the sky. His eyes drooped, worry creeping across his face.

Ophelia stood, shaking the fallen spruce needles from her skirt. With a nod in Seamus's direction, she turned toward the tree. She slung her satchel over her shoulder, then grabbed the stub of a broken branch and pulled herself up, foot resting on a thick piece of bark.

"What are you doing?" Seamus asked, a hint of a laugh in his voice.

"I'm going to sleep up here," Ophelia said matter-of-factly, peering down at him. He watched her with one eye open, his head propped up under his arms.

"Won't you be cold?" he asked.

She shrugged, climbing further up, thin branches bending beneath her weight. "The fire's too hot. I prefer the cold."

"Of course you do," he sighed.

A moment of silence as she kept climbing.

She stole another glance over her shoulder to find him peering up at her, hands on his hips. He twitched each time she reached for a branch. Was he afraid she'd fall? Surely not. Why would he be? A piece of bark broke beneath her foot. He flinched, hands grasping at the air as the piece of bark hit him on the head. She smiled down at him, heaving herself onto a sturdy branch, sitting with her ankles crossed.

"How's the view?" he called up to her, picking the bark from his hair.

Ophelia gazed around at her surroundings. She wasn't high enough to see the treetops but was a good fifteen feet up. There was a nest resting amid the spruce needles above her. Beside her was a notch in the tree where a pine marten or a family of squirrels may sleep. Peering through the branches, she could see an owl peeking out at her from a nearby tree.

"Beautiful," she said.

Seamus looked around as though he wasn't convinced. "All right then. Don't fall. I'd rather not wake up to your broken neck."

Ophelia laughed, hanging her pack above her, taking out the small carrying case she kept her art supplies in. "No promises," she called down.

"Haha," he sighed, patting the tree trunk as he turned away. "Goodnight, kid."

"*Natt*, Seamus."

The branches obscured her vision, but she imagined he'd flopped back onto his bedroll by now. Ophelia swiveled on her branch, leaning against the trunk, removing her sketchbook from its carrying strap. She took a graphite stick wrapped in twine from her pouch and began sketching the owl. It hooted at her, ruffling its feathers. It seemed to pose, turning its head to the side, eyes trained on something she couldn't see.

It wasn't one of her owls. She knew their markings and the shape of their beaks well. This wee one was a long-eared owl, the feathers on its head resembling a cat's ears. Hers were Ural owls.

She missed them already. Maybe they'd follow her? She hoped they could find her. Eydis, too. Seeing them or any of her forest friends would ease the terror bubbling in her chest.

The owl gave a hoot, launching off its branch, fluttering over to her, landing in the nest above her head. It leaned down and nipped at the strap of her satchels, then began to groom itself. Ophelia smiled, calling it down to her as she closed her sketchbook and removed her mask. It fluffed its wings and fluttered down to her, landing in her lap.

"Hello there," she whispered, scratching under its chin. "How are you?"

It hooted at her, playfully biting her hand. It seemed to smile at her, eyes full of joy.

"I'm so glad to hear that!" Ophelia said, stroking the feathers between its eyes. "And me, you ask? Oh, I'm all right. I'll survive. I know I will."

The owl nuzzled her hand, cooing quietly.

"Why, thank you for the reassurance, my friend," Ophelia said, leaning forward, putting her sketchbook and pouch away.

She hadn't grabbed a pelt or the spare bedroll, but she had Ute's shawl. Thankfully, the mud had dried. She shook it out, wrapping it around her shoulders, tying it tight. It was like a hug from all the good people in Tø, the ones she missed. Like Saoirse.

The owl shut its eyes, giving one last coo as it snuggled into her arms.

"*God natt*, wee one. May you dream of better things," she sighed, petting its head as she drifted off to sleep.

Seamus's wolf ears allowed him to listen in on Ophelia's one-sided conversation with one of the critters that called that tree their home. Her voice was the softest whisper in his ears as he lay staring up at the star-filled sky.

". . . I'll survive. I know I will," she said. There was such sadness in her voice. It sounded as though she was on the verge of tears. "Why, thank you for the reassurance, my friend."

Seamus wondered if she could truly speak with animals. Did she hear a voice in her head as she sat, presumably petting the creature? Was it one of the animals she'd cared for all those years? Did it offer her words of encouragement?

"*God natt*, wee one. May you dream of better things," she said, her tearful voice full of sleepiness.

Seamus rolled away from the tree, watching how the shadows on the ground flickered in the campfire light. He hoped Ophelia dreamt of better things, too.

If he were to do one thing right in his life, it'd be getting that kid to the Kirkeby's. He knew they'd adore her, taking her in as one of their own like they had each other. They'd give her a room in their big old mansion, buy her as many books as they had the money for, and allow her to roam the halls without her mask, basking in the glory of the miracle she was.

Yes, if he were to do one good thing, one thing the Stars would smile upon, it'd be doing right by her.

155

CHAPTER TWENTY-ONE

ONWARD

Seamus woke to something drip, drip, dripping onto his face. While half asleep, his mind played tricks on him. Dreams held him for ransom, shifting reality, making him believe some ferocious beast was atop him, ready to strike. He groggily fought the air, pawing at nothing like a fox kit. The dripping wouldn't stop, the drool of the imaginary beast soaking every inch of him.

That's when he realized there was no beast atop him.

It was rain.

Seamus yawned, blinking his tired eyes, waking to a crick in his neck and a soft pitter-patter of rain. The tree he slept beneath was drenched, and the campfire was long burned out. With aching bones, he stood, squinting through the rain-drops that made it through the bows of the spruce.

"You up?" he called to the solitary Witchdom that was Ophelia's branch.

No response.

He leaned lazily against the tree trunk, straining his neck to see her. A hint of blue was still hidden among the branches. An owl was nestled in her arms, its eyes trained on him in a defensive sort of way. And was that a red squirrel curled up on her lap? It was hard to tell.

"The longer you sleep, the longer it'll take to get to the border," Seamus yawned.

He waited there, staring up at her unmoving form before turning to pack up his bedroll and cover their tracks. It was a miracle they hadn't been found last night. In hindsight, he shouldn't have built that fire. He'd been too tired to think straight and too cold to care. He shivered even now.

He hated the cold.

Before stumbling upon Tø and Ophelia, Seamus had been hiding out in a nice warm city, hunkering down amid alley cats and chimneys. Even with the snow, he'd been warm enough. The people there had had enough to spare, never batting an eye when things went missing. It'd been easy for him to stay hidden.

Seamus had lived a thousand lives in that city. He'd paraded around like an aristocrat, stealing cravats, vests, and shoes fit for a magistrate. He sold them afterward, never holding onto anything for long.

He'd been a beggar, toying with the heartstrings of anyone who listened to his sad, sad tale. Granted, each story had been different. He'd have to tell Ophelia one of them. She'd get a kick out of his storytelling skills. Or rather, lack thereof.

There was even a time when he pretended to be a priest of the Celestial Pantheon. That was what got him in trouble. Seamus had been crafty stealing that compendium, but not crafty enough, it seemed. One thing led to another, and he wound up pissing off the wrong people. Soon, the Ulvemordere came knocking. Thankfully, he was long gone before they found his hiding spot and all the loot he'd left behind. He always sold the most incriminating items, but here and there, he'd keep something small. Like a pair of nice wool socks or a shirt that wasn't full of moth holes. He'd had a bag, but it wasn't big enough to carry everything. People cared more about their bags than they did laundry. He'd learned that the hard way a few years back.

A twig snapped behind him, breaking him out of his thoughts. He turned, nearly jumping out of his skin when he saw Ophelia standing mere inches behind him. There was an owl on one shoulder, two cardinals on the other, and a whole family of squirrels in her arms. She looked more and more like a forest deity every day. It unnerved him.

"Don't do that!" Seamus hissed. A shiver like spiders scurrying up his spine spread across his back. How had she gotten down so quietly? He hadn't sensed her presence.

"Did you sleep well?" she asked, her silver eyes full of wonder.

He frowned but nodded. "As well as I could. You?"

"I did! I haven't slept in the trees since I was a child!" she exclaimed, giggling to herself.

Seamus couldn't understand her excitement, but at the very least, he was happy *someone* had woken up on the right foot.

"Do you have any idea where we are?" Seamus asked, gesturing around as he offered her some hardtack, forgetting she was carrying an entire colony of squirrels.

She peered through the trees then back down the path they'd come from. "I didn't leave Tø much, but I think I'd know where we were if we found the main road."

"And how do you suppose we do that?" Seamus asked.

Ophelia bent down, gently placing the squirrels on the ground. They seemed to bow before scampering back up the tree. The cardinals chirped, bidding her farewell, and the owl hooted a few times before following the squirrels.

"Can you talk to them?" Seamus whispered, staring her down in a way he hoped was intimidating enough for her to tell the truth.

All she did was smile as she adjusted the strap on her shoulder. "I say we take one of these paths and see where it leads us. Even if we end up adding another day to our trek, we'll get to where we're going eventually!" She took the hardtack he offered, munching away happily.

Sometimes, she had the grace of a young lady belonging to a noble bloodline. Other times, she was a finicky kid who knew no suffering.

She was such a baffling creature.

Seamus heaved his pack onto his back, checking to ensure their bedrolls were secured. He slung his crossbow over his shoulder, already annoyed at it. The way it bounced at his side was frustrating, to say the least. It was a valuable addition to their arsenal, but this setup wouldn't work in the long run.

Ophelia had an extra bag packed with furs and all sorts of random belongings she couldn't leave without, alongside her satchel and sketchbook. Her polar bear mask was hooked to the clasp of her satchel, bouncing with even the slightest movement. Seamus had thought it creepy when she wore it, but it was downright terrifying without a face behind it. The fox one had been worse. In a way, he was glad it'd broken.

"Which way?" he asked, pointing down the paths on either side of the spruce.

Ophelia rocked back and forth on her heels, chewing her lip. "My gut tells me to the right," she said eventually.

"Then to the right we go," he sighed, leading her along.

They walked in comfortable silence for a while, each lost in their own thoughts yet again. A few critters checked on them, or rather *her*. Suddenly, the forest was abuzz with sound. From the chittering of rabbits to the chirp of birds, the eerie quiet from before had dissipated. Seamus wanted to ask if Ophelia had anything to do with this. In fact, he wanted to ask her many ephemeral questions about her world and how it worked. It was strange being in her presence, knowing bears and foxes bowed down to her. Owls and squirrels—mortal enemies if he remembered correctly—were fast friends in her company.

Was that why he felt such a duty to protect her? Was his wolf enchanted by her, just like the rest of the forest? Seamus wasn't one for duty. All he'd ever seen was revenge and how to exact it. Yet this kid—this kid he barely knew—ignited some primal instinct in him. He'd wanted her to run far away from Tø and the Ulvemordere. He'd wanted to soothe her sadness over the fox. He'd wanted to make sure she was alright the second he'd awoken in the forest.

None of that sounded like him. Everyone told him he was a surly old dog, well on his way to being a grumpy old man.

But maybe she had a way with surly animals. Maybe she could speak to them and his wolf.

How else had she survived that night? He'd been so angry. He'd have figured she'd at least have a scratch or two. Yet there she'd been, unscathed, worrying over him instead.

He found himself staring again, tracing the icicle-like lines on her cheeks over and over again.

"Where do your friends live?" Ophelia suddenly asked.

Seamus cleared his throat, staring down the snowy path. "A place called *Dødbyen*," he said, redistributing the weight of his pack on his shoulders. He didn't have much, but it was heavy all the same.

"'The City of The Dead?' Sounds like a lovely place,"

Ophelia scoffed, watching him out of the corner of her eye.

"It is. Y'know, after you get past the thievery, thugs, and thingamabobs that'll kill ya dead," he laughed,

"Sounds like your sort of place," Ophelia concurred.

He shrugged, waving those words away. "You'd be surprised."

Ophelia edged slightly away, the movement so small Seamus wondered if it had happened at all. "Can I ask you a question?"

Seamus felt himself shrink. "Depends."

". . . why did you defect?"

He'd known that question was coming eventually, but it still caught him by surprise. *Curses upon curses*, he thought. He'd hoped she'd forgotten what Lochlan had said.

"Story for another time," he sighed, avoiding her eyes at all costs. Someone could drown in those churning silver seas. No wonder she wore a mask all the time. Despite her Witch Marks, those eyes were a danger in themselves. They reminded him of puppy eyes. One look and he was sure he'd do just about anything.

"Sorry for prying," she said. He could hear the embarrassment in her voice.

"I don't blame you," he said. "Just not something I enjoy reliving."

"I figured." He glanced down to see a sheepish smile and purple-red cheeks gazing up at him. "I have stories like that, too."

That saddened him.

The path they were following eventually began to widen and opened out onto a road that'd clearly been used a million times before. The dirt was densely packed, all snow cleared away. Puddles littered the road, oddly reminiscent of hoof prints.

"If we go back that way, we'll end up in Tø again. We're on the opposite side of town, near the river," Ophelia explained. "We can make it to Gulch by late afternoon. It's bigger than Tø, too. Easier to hide in. There's an inn we could stay at."

Seamus crouched to observe the muddy hoofprints. They'd been ruined by the rain so much so he couldn't tell if they were coming or going.

"We'd have better luck continuing until the next town. We'll stock up on whatever we can in Gulch, then spend another night in the woods," he said, shutting his eyes, using all his senses to take in their surroundings.

In his mind's eye, the forest came to life. He could see everything so clearly. Every bird high above, every rabbit burrowing down below, every deer watching them from the shadows. Even with his muffled hearing, he saw more than Ophelia's eyes ever could. He tried picking up the scent of the horses but found nothing. Depending on how long it'd been raining, he figured these tracks were old. Hopefully, the Ulvemordere had gone through Gulch already. If they played their hand right, they could stay on their tail without alerting them to their whereabouts.

"Does that work for you?" he asked, slipping in the mud as he walked on.

"Not like I really have a choice," Ophelia replied.

"That's what I like to hear."

Their footsteps squeaked and squelched beneath them, their shoes caked in mud. The rain was letting up, the sky a pale blue dotted with fluffy white clouds. Cold sunlight glinted off the remnants of rain, making everything glitter.

"Can we stop at the bookshop at least?" Ophelia asked after a while.

Seamus gave her a disapproving look. "Didn't you grab some books before we left?"

"One can never have too many books," she said, holding her head high. "Plus, you owe me."

"For what?" he scoffed.

Ophelia unclipped her sketchbook from its strap, a tiny plume of graphite dust floating through the air as she flipped through. Seamus caught glimpses of faces he recognized and animals he'd only heard of from folktales. Every page was filled with her drawings. From what little he could see, she was quite good. Eventually, she landed on the very last page, where two rows of tally marks had been scored into the corner.

"I've saved you more than you've saved me," she said matter-of-factly. "I do believe that earns me a trip to the bookshop."

"First off, what do you mean you've 'saved' me? Second, we could have wanted posters out by now. We're not stopping at a bookshop, kid," Seamus snapped.

Ophelia smiled brightly, pointing to each tally as she spoke. "When we first met, I saved you from your pursuers. After that, I protected you during the full moon. Lastly, I pushed you out of the way before an arrow could impale itself in your heart." She looked so pleased with herself. It sickened him. "You protected me from the Ulvemordere twice—thank you, by the way—but three is greater than two."

The audacity of this kid.

"Two of your rescues didn't happen when I was in immediate danger. I'd say that makes them insignificant," Seamus said, arms crossed tight over his chest. "And you're welcome, by the way," he added haughtily.

"They would've caught up to you sooner had I not taken you to town," Ophelia said, holding her head high. "And you could've hurt someone on the full moon by accident. Or yourself."

Seamus grimaced. She had a point. "All right, fine. You head to the bookshop; I'll get whatever supplies we can afford. We're lacking a few bits and bobs."

"A satisfactory compromise, I suppose." She held out her hand for him to shake. He shook it, rolling his eyes.

How had it come to this?

"Whatever, kid," he sighed. "If you're not at the designated meeting spot by a certain time, I'm leaving without you."

A jolt of electricity surged through his hand. "You wouldn't," Ophelia gasped, jerking back.

"I would," he said with a wink, flexing his hand to quell the sharp sting of electricity. Something told him she hadn't meant to do that.

"That is incredibly rude, Seamus," she grumbled, placing her mask upon her face.

He shrugged. "That was me being nice."

The dark eyes of a polar bear and the condemning frown of a Witch stared back in disgust.

CHAPTER TWENTY-TWO
AXES AND PARCHMENT

At first glance, Gulch wasn't that different from Tø. It had the same dilapidated buildings, crumbling homes, muddy farmland, and frostbitten people—but things like that mattered little in The Wilds. What Gulch in lacked creature comforts, it made up for in art. Throughout Snøbolig, art was valued more than life. Even in The Wilds, where criminals ruled the shadows, people still longed to create. Those who knit, painted, carved, sang, or wrote were just as important as the hunters who put food on their neighbors' tables. In a realm bearing witness to an ever-constant, ever-harsh winter, there wasn't much to do. Even the most feared criminal would be found curled up with a good book come nightfall. Children learned to read before they could speak. Socks, shawls, sweaters, hats, and mittens were considered fine goods.

Like many other towns, Gulch bragged of its artistic accomplishments to anyone who'd listen. At each entrance was a beautiful banner embroidered with the town name and animals in various colors, boasting the dyes the people here had access to. Gulch wasn't wealthy, but they lived comfortably, which was more than the people of Tø had been able to say.

"Where do you suppose we meet later?" Seamus asked, ignoring the fluttering banner overhead as they entered the sleepy little town.

"There's a statue at the town's center. You'll know it when you see it. I'll meet you there once the sun begins to set," Ophelia said, already making toward the bookshop. She'd only been here a handful of times, but Gulch wasn't a place she could easily forget.

"Sunset and no later," Seamus warned. "Be ready to leave before that, just in case. And don't—"

He did a double take, marching toward a wall mangled with wanted posters and local announcements. Eyes wide, he tore down one of the many wanted posters.

"Who's that?" Ophelia asked, leaning over his arm to see a man who looked vaguely familiar.

"It's me!"

Ophelia raised an eyebrow, though he couldn't see it. "Now, Seamus, I know you're wound up, but let's not lose our heads."

He scowled down at her. "Kid," he said, his voice barely a whisper as he looked over his shoulder to make sure no one was listening. "This is one of my old wanted posters. With the old bounty and my old face."

Ophelia took the poster and held it next to his face. It must've been *very* old, for the two faces had little in common. To an artist's eye, the proportions were right, but the man on the poster had a youthful glow Seamus must've lost years ago. The person on the post still had both ears, too, as well as no scars.

Seamus ripped the poster from her hands, crumpled it up, and then stomped on it for good measure.

"Go find your books so we can leave," he grumbled, kicking the crumpled paper and shooing her away.

Ophelia gave him a thumbs up, then skipped away, her bags bouncing along with her.

Gulch valued its fiber artists above all else. There were several competing fabric shops, all selling a different variety of wool, linens, and more. Ophelia stopped to peer inside one of these shops, the warmth of the patrons igniting a fire in her heart. Near the window, a mother and child were handing each other different colors of yarn, laughing and smiling as they fingered the tightly spun fibers. Ophelia wondered what they planned on making.

Beyond them was an older gentleman comparing two rolls of fabric as he talked with who Ophelia assumed was the store's owner.

Ophelia had always liked Gulch. Sometimes, she wondered how different her life would've been if someone here had found her as a baby instead of Lochlan.

With a heavy sigh, she forced herself to continue toward the bookshop, dragging her feet, taking in a town she was unsure if she'd ever see again. The way Seamus was talking, these may be her last few weeks in The Wilds. At least for the time being.

How odd a feeling this was. Her freedom was in the palm of her hands, yet the duty she'd been created for was slipping through her fingers. The more she thought about it, the worse she felt. How could she look toward the future with hope when so many had perished because of her? Because of Seamus? How could she wander through this town? Did her guilt show? Did the passersby see it? Did they wonder why she frowned? Could they see beyond her mask and instead see the twisted fear in her eyes?

The bookshop suddenly lost all its splendor.

There she stood in its doorway, fiddling with the buckle on her satchel, foot tapping to a discordant beat. She ached for the Spirits' guidance. Why couldn't they just tell her what to do? Why was everything a riddle? Ophelia hated riddles.

A heavy heart fluttered in her chest as she forced her feet to cross the threshold. The smell of musty old books and vanilla candles wafted into her nose, reminding her of Saoirse. Memories of her didn't quell the aching pain in her chest, but at least she could imagine Saoirse was hidden somewhere between the towering bookshelves. If she shut her eyes and listened, she could still hear her laugh.

There were books Saoirse loved that she hadn't had a chance to read. Maybe she'd pick up one of those.

Ophelia nodded to the shopkeeper, trailing her hand along the tattered spines surrounding her. Some of these books had been here for longer than she'd been alive; others were recent releases imported from neighboring cities. They even had a small section of used books from Høstlunden and beyond.

"Are you looking for anything in particular?" the young shopkeeper asked from the counter.

"Browsing for now, thank you," Ophelia said over her shoulder, disappearing behind a shelf packed with cookbooks.

"I'll be here if you need me!" she heard him say.

Seamus had followed Ophelia until she made it safely inside the bookshop. He lingered for a moment, wondering why she paused at the door. He'd heard the anxious flutter of her heart but couldn't fathom what had caused it. Part of him wanted to follow her inside to ensure her safety, but he trusted she could protect herself if need be. They'd made a deal, and he had to keep up his end of the bargain.

Though reluctant, he turned away and made for the general store. No one paid him any mind. Seemed no one recognized his face on the posters littered through the streets. If they had, he was sure he'd have been arrested on the spot. Seamus Norland wasn't exactly an inconspicuous man.

Maybe that was a good thing. In The Wilds, he looked just like every other thug sleeping on the streets.

The general store was quaint. He purchased some extra first aid supplies—though he hoped they wouldn't need them, you could never be too prepared—several packages of dried meats, some bread, jam, and cutlery, plus a metal container of hardtack. He figured they were set for a few days, at least until they made it to the next town. He'd asked around, and it seemed the river flowed on for miles. He didn't have a fishing pole, but it wouldn't be the first time he'd caught his dinner with his bare hands. It wouldn't be the last, either, if his luck continued like this.

He'd also purchased a small map of the surrounding towns. The writing was too small for his tired eyes to read, but he'd planned on delegating the map reading task to Ophelia anyway. She'd lived here all her life, after all.

Seamus was suddenly aware of eyes boring into him. He turned, seeing a young couple sidestepping around him, eyeing his crossbow. He looked down at it, realizing how menacing it was. It was all dark iron and fire-treated wood, the Ulvemordere logo—a candle dripping wax on a wolf skull—stamped onto the end of its stock. He grizzled, looking around at the shops surrounding him.

Someone had to have a different strap or sling for this thing.

After wandering through Gulch longer than he'd liked,

he stumbled upon smoke spilling out of a makeshift shed. The smell of burning metal mixed with the sweet scent of pastries baking somewhere nearby. It was oddly pleasant. It reminded Seamus of home, in a way. In one corner, a burly man stood over a rusty anvil dusted with metal shavings. Beside him was a workbench piled high with unfinished projects. Sparks danced through the air from the crackling forge nearby. On the walls, weaponry, cutlery, and farm tools hung in an unorganized fashion. Seamus frowned. He would've sorted everything properly. Why were there broadswords mixed with pitchforks?

The man at the anvil turned to him, an eyebrow raised. "What can I do for ya?" he asked skeptically.

Seamus was not one to dwell on appearances, but the presence of this blacksmith completely caught him off guard. He was muscular and taller than him by a long shot, his face covered in ash and soot. Atop his head, he wore goggles with blackened lenses, his hair sticking out at all angles beneath them. His beard was long and braided, the very ends glowing with embers. Over a dark gray tunic, he wore a heavy leather apron.

Seamus nodded at his crossbow, avoiding his piercing gaze. "Do you have any straps or know someone who does?"

The blacksmith eyed him cautiously but beckoned him to follow him to the workbench. Opening a drawer, he took out a small leather strap.

"This'll rest against your upper back, above your shoulder blades. That bow is small enough it won't hinder your movement. Plus," he began, clearing his throat, "it'll be easier to grab."

Intrigued, Seamus shrugged off his pack and set down his bow. The blacksmith handed him the strap, picked up his bow, and helped him attach it once he'd slipped on the holster. The stock of his crossbow slipped between two leather rings that easily snapped open and closed.

"Test it out," the blacksmith said, stroking his flaming beard, appraising him.

Seamus reached behind his back, unclipping his bow, swiveling it around, and pointing it at the ground. It was simple enough. He'd have thought the movement would've been harder to learn.

The blacksmith wore a greedy grin. "Seems like it suits

you! That'll be fifty coppers if you please."

Seamus fumbled with the clasps at his back, reattaching his bow. "Right. . . Will I get a discount if I get anything else?"

The blacksmith narrowed his eyes. He seemed to have been waiting for that question. "What's a guy like you need with all these weapons, anyway?"

"One can never be too careful in The Wilds," Seamus said, eyes on a pair of axes. "How much?"

He shrugged, following his gaze. "Another hundred each. Or. . . Maybe we can work out a trade?"

Seamus rocked back and forth on his heels. He'd already spent a fair amount on food and supplies. These were just wants, not necessities, but then again, he had another person to look out for now. His hands found the dagger tucked into his belt loop. He took it out, handing it off. There was a jewel in its hilt and a solid gold emblem on its cross guard, both of which could be scraped for more than it was worth.

"I'll trade this for the strap and some bolts," he offered.

The blacksmith turned away, holding the dagger to the light. "It's a nice piece, I will admit, but I'm sorry I can't accept it. I know what my work is worth and won't accept anything less. I don't mean to be harsh, but we've got to make a living."

Seamus sighed heavily, taking mental survey of his belongings. Besides his weapons, he didn't have anything else to barter. Still, he needed an arsenal he could trust. While ranged weaponry had always been a favorite, he was far better with close combat. Those axes would serve him better.

Unfortunately, he knew what he had to do.

"What will the crossbow get me?" he asked, feeling himself deflate.

The blacksmith turned back to him, eyes wide. "Both axes and their sheaths, easily. Would've cost you around two hundred otherwise. If you'd like, I can trade this dagger in for something a little sturdier, too."

Seamus begrudgingly handed over the crossbow, frowning. Still, they shook hands and exchanged goods. One day, he would wish he had that crossbow, but at least he had the axes.

"Pleasure doing business with you. As I tell all my customers, 'Chris is your guy if you need a smithy,'" the blacksmith smiled. "You're welcome to haggle with me anytime."

Seamus gave a solemn nod, bidding him farewell before leaving to find Ophelia's meeting place.

Once he reached the town center, he realized just how right Ophelia had been. That old statue was exceptionally hard to miss.

Carved into a dark stone was a giant rabbit, its fur pockmarked with stars. Seamus hadn't paid much attention to the world's religions until he was in his late thirties, and even then, he hadn't devoted himself to any Pantheon. Still, he knew The Rabbit and its significance. In the Celestial Compendium, The Rabbit had created all life. Just as Amaranth was said to have done amongst the Terrestrial teachings.

Seamus didn't care who created what or why. All he saw was a children's story.

With a yawn, he sat at the statue's base, organizing his pack, trying to stuff everything inside. It's a good thing it had pockets; otherwise, the jam wouldn't have fit. If he'd had the extra coin, he'd have bought a bigger pack.

Once everything was packed away, he leaned against the statue, observing the fleeting little lives around him. Everyone seemed to have places to be and things to do. How blissful it must feel to be unaware of the world and its workings. A neighboring town had been burned to the ground, yet these folk went on with their lives as if they hadn't seen or smelled the smoke on the wind. He envied their blind eyes and craved their ignorance.

Life got heavier and heavier by the minute. No wonder he didn't feel warmth gazing upon The Rabbit. How could She have created this world and let all the creatures ruin it and each other? Some Spirit She was.

Families came and went as the sun got lower in the sky. Seamus was sure Ophelia would've been back by now.

There was a pit in his stomach.

He knew he should've stayed with her.

Looking to the sky, he could just make out the stars hiding behind the remaining sunlight. He'd give her until the clouds turned pink.

That was the deal.

Seamus hadn't intended to go back on his word.

Ophelia must've spent hours lost in that bookshop. She'd found a few books to take on her journey, but her silent prayer to find Saoirse hidden in the corner wasn't answered. The place carried her ghost, however. She kept coming across her favorite books and kept mistaking the same redheaded patron for her.

Morning light had washed away her troubles, yet here she was, sinking beneath the waves of grief again. She had to get out of there and find Seamus before she drowned. Being around him set her mind at ease. At least they had each other, if only for a little while.

"Find anything exciting?" the young shopkeeper asked as she set her stack on the counter and dug into her satchel for her coin purse. He read through the books she'd chosen, adjusting his glasses, which were caked in a layer of dust. The fact he could somehow see out of them was a miracle.

"Always," Ophelia said.

"Is there anything else I can help you with today?"

Ophelia scanned the wall behind him. Leather bookmarks hung on the wall. She pointed to one—one embossed with a bear and its cub—then took a small bag of candied hazelnuts from a dish on the counter. Seamus was a snacker. The cottage pantry was proof of that.

"Do you happen to have any maps? The rain ruined mine," Ophelia said, hoping her lie was convincing enough. It didn't sound implausible, but she found that bookshops had very inquisitive employees.

"What kind are you looking for?" There was a strange light in the shopkeeper's eyes.

Ophelia raised an eyebrow beneath her mask. "What kind do you have?"

He smiled mischievously, beckoning her to follow him. Humming a jaunty little tune, he led her through the stacks until they came to a door with a heavy padlock. He took a key from his pocket and unlocked the door, sweeping her inside. The room was pitch black. Ophelia suddenly wondered what had possessed her to follow a strange man into the backroom of his shop. Seamus would not be pleased. Granted, she wasn't pleased with herself right now, either.

The sound of a match igniting filled her ears. A lantern was lit, carried by the shopkeeper as he led her deeper into the room. Scattered papers shifted beneath her feet, nearly tripping her. There were shelves on the walls, each housing objects consumed by shadows. None of them appeared to be the shape or size of a book. What was this place? The shopkeeper suddenly stopped, hanging his lantern on a chain dangling from the ceiling. He heaved a heavy box off the floor, setting it on a wobbly table. A thick plume of dust wafted up into the air as he opened it, revealing several rolls of parchment.

"I've just got these in from the inventors in Høstlunden," he said. "I'll warn you now, they're costly. But I'll give you a discount since you've just bought a copy of my wife's favorite book. If you ever head that way, you'll find a quaint little café and greenhouse. Tell the woman working there I sent you. She'll give ya a cup of tea for free."

With that, he took one of the rolled-up pieces of parchment and held it to the light. That mischievous smile of his glowed bright in the lantern light. As slowly as possible, presumably to add drama, he unrolled the parchment.

Ophelia frowned.

It was blank.

"This is a Wayfarer's Map," the mysterious shopkeeper said. He held it out before her, shadows shifting across its surface. At its center, a bug was scurrying about.

Ophelia leaned in closer, eyes widening. No, that wasn't a bug. Something was appearing on the map. She gasped, filled with wonderment. An intricate map of Gulch and the surrounding woods spread across the blank parchment. It even listed the shop names in a flowery script.

"How fortuitous," Ophelia whispered, taking the map from him.

The shopkeeper's mischievous grin transformed into the giddy smile of a young child. "All you have to do is think of where you want to go or the place you're at. It's been made with enchanted ink! Isn't that something?"

"These came from Høstlunden, you said?"

He nodded. "You'll never believe how I came across them. A strange old man dressed in the brightest colors you ever saw came knocking late one night. He had a caravan full of rare books. I suspect his goods were stolen, but—" he shrugged "—who am I to judge? I prefer to think he liberated them from horrible circumstances."

"How much?" Ophelia asked. A map like this was surely worth more than her weight in gold.

The shopkeeper appraised her. "Have you come in with Saoirse over the years?"

She nodded, rolling up the map.

He smiled. "It's on the house, then. Saoirse's father is close with my parents. We grew up together! I visit now and then, but I'll be making the trek across the border soon. I'll have to drop by and say goodbye soon."

Ophelia blinked back tears, hugging the map to her chest. "Thank you, sir," she whispered.

The shopkeeper took her map, sliding it inside a sturdy leather case as he spoke, "Friend of my friend, so to speak."

"Nevertheless, I truly appreciate this," Ophelia said, bowing deeply.

All he did was shrug and take the lantern from where it hung, leading her back toward the door. Ophelia paid for her books, bookmark, and candied hazelnut—she was sure he gave her a massive discount—then stuffed her books into her pack, scrambling off to find Seamus.

Even in death, Saoirse found a way to be there for her. Ophelia sent her a silent thank you, hoping she heard it. The knots in her chest loosened, and the ache in her heart dulled.

That is until she looked to the sky and realized how late it was.

Sunset had passed, replaced by dusk.

Ophelia's heart skipped a beat as she hiked up her skirts and ran full speed toward the town center, careful not to bump into anyone. Rounding a corner, the weather-worn stat-ue of The Rabbit appeared before her eyes. There was a small crowd in the square, but not one towering man with a face full of scars and half an ear.

Had he really left her? asked her heart.

Why would he stay? replied her mind.

A sense of hopelessness erupted in Ophelia's chest. The

bookshop had left her with enough coin for a meal but nothing else. So, this was it? She was left to wither away as a street urchin with only the books in her pack and her sketchbook. How could he do that to her? Even if she sold the pelts she'd brought, the money wouldn't last long.

"What are you looking so sullen for?" came a familiar voice.

Afraid her mind was playing tricks on her, she slowly turned to see Seamus leaning lazily against a wall, a frown on his lips, his arms crossed tight over his chest.

Relief flooded her, but she didn't intend to let him see. "I thought we made a deal?"

"The sun hasn't set yet," Seamus said nonchalantly.

Both ignored the fact that lanterns had been lit and stars were gradually appearing in the sky. Dusk was slipping away into night. He should've left ages ago.

"I found a map," Ophelia said proudly.

"Me too," Seamus said as he reached into his pocket and unfolded a tiny map with a rip in its center.

"Mine's better," she said, patting the case, which she'd attached to her sketchbook's strap. "I'll show you later. Are you ready to go?"

"Been ready," he said, eyeing her suspiciously. "What took you so long?"

Ophelia felt her cheeks turn red. "I lost track of time."

"I got turned around myself," he said, smirking to himself.

"Liar," she said, making a *tsking* noise.

"Bold accusations, kid. You could lose your tongue for that in some cities."

Ophelia just rolled her eyes, glad he couldn't see.

"C'mon," Seamus said, nodding his head toward the path winding around the statue of The Rabbit. "I want to get a fire started before it gets too dark."

Ophelia followed close behind, in awe of the fact he'd stayed. How strange. She thought for sure he'd left. Maybe he had? Maybe he'd come back just as he did before? How interesting.

Seamus fell back a few paces until he fell in step beside

her. The townsfolk around them were turning in for the night, bidding each other farewell as they closed their shops and made for home. Seamus watched them with a peculiar look on his face. Ophelia couldn't tell if he was disgusted with them all or yearning for a life like theirs.

Perhaps he felt a mix of both.

Perhaps she did, too.

CHAPTER TWENTY-THREE

PICTURES AMID THE STARS

Seamus led Ophelia to the riverbank, collecting firewood and tearing down posters of his younger self along the way. They'd found an overturned log and decided it was as good a place as any to rest for the night. Seamus had made a campfire, and Ophelia had ignited it. They'd unrolled their bedrolls, ate a quick dinner, and were now watching as the moon rose higher and higher in the sky.

"It's a beautiful night," Ophelia said as Seamus knelt to warm his hands by the fire.

Seamus looked up, eyes falling on The Rabbit's constellation. He grimaced but nodded his agreement.

"Do you want to see the map?" Ophelia asked.

She'd discarded her mask, much to Seamus's delight. He was ever-so glad to see her moon-bright eyes.

Sitting back on his heels, he gave her a look of mild curiosity. With a flourish, she procured a leather scroll case embossed with flowers. He could tell she was rather pleased with herself as she pulled out a rolled-up piece of parchment.

"Ever heard of a Wayfarer's Map?" she asked.

"I'm sure I haven't," Seamus laughed.

She turned it toward him, and he watched as their surroundings began to appear on an otherwise blank surface.

"It's enchanted!" she said excitedly.

"How'd you find that?"

She winked at him, daring him to pry further. "I have my ways."

"Did you steal it?"

Her eyes narrowed. "Of course not! I'd die before I stole anything, Seamus! How dare you think so little of me."

He rolled his eyes. "All right, all right, calm down." She held her head high, eyes full of expectance. Squinting, he wondered what that look meant before saying, "Good job. That'll come in handy."

Smiling brightly, cheeks turned rosy. He laughed to himself, shaking his head as she took out her sketchbook and began scribbling away.

Seamus grabbed a stick and stoked the fire. The cold was biting this evening. His face stung with even the slightest bit of wind. Whether there was Ulvemordere or not, they were renting rooms at an inn in the next town.

His heart about broke when he remembered how little coin he had left. Hopefully, he'd have better luck fishing tomorrow morning than he had on the full moon. He could sell some of his catch before they left Gulch, and if he were smart about it, they'd have enough for two rooms and some pocket change to spare. Ophelia could sell some of those pelts, too. They didn't need all of them.

"Seamus?" Ophelia suddenly asked, her voice small.

"Hmm?"

". . . did you really get turned around earlier?" she asked quietly, not looking up from her sketchbook.

Seamus paused, staring past the flames, studying her face. "I did. Why?"

Guilt flooded him. Ophelia's shoulders tensed as she sat staring at a blank page. "I thought you'd left."

"I promised I'd get you somewhere safe, didn't I?" Seamus asked, trying to make his tone as kind as he could. "I was only joking about leaving you behind."

"Oh," Ophelia said, sounding genuinely surprised.

Seamus threw his makeshift poker into the fire, coming to sit beside her. "I waited beneath The Rabbit for a while. When you didn't show up, I went looking for you. We must've just missed each other at the bookshop."

All of this was true. He'd promised to get her to Tiril and Helgi, and he wasn't planning on breaking that promise anytime soon. He'd worried when she hadn't shown, so he figured he'd go find her. What was the worst that could happen? He was already wanted by the Ulvemordere and running for his life. If she'd found herself in danger, adding 'escaping arrest in The Wilds' to his long list of crimes wasn't exactly something he was afraid of.

Ophelia began scratching away in her sketchbook again, lips set in a pout. Her minty sadness filled the air, cutting through the campfire smoke.

"I'm sorry, kid," he said as quietly as he could.

"It's okay," she mumbled. He was sure it wasn't, but he figured that was her way of politely dropping the subject.

Seamus sat back against their log, studying her. She was drawing the face of a young man with a beak-like nose, beady eyes, and a mischievous grin. She used her thumb to smudge the graphite she'd just laid down, shading his hair. Sitting back, she tilted her head and tapped her graphite stick on the page. There was a sudden air of uncertainty wafting off her. Her hand moved unsure across the page before she began sketching what appeared to be a map behind the young man's head.

"Who is that?" Seamus asked.

"I didn't ask his name," she said with a shrug, "but he gave me the map for free."

"How kind," Seamus said, unable to hide the surprise in his voice.

"He knew Saoirse," Ophelia added. She set her graphite stick in the crease of the spine, tilting the page for Seamus to see better.

That minty sadness of hers was stronger than it'd ever been before.

"Why are you drawing him?" Seamus asked, trying his best to distract her. He was starting to loathe the smell of mint.

Ophelia took the graphite stick and placed it behind her ear. Sighing, she flipped to the front of her book, landing on a page where Saoirse's likeness was depicted. She looked younger, though Seamus couldn't be sure. They hadn't spoken much. Beside her was a rough sketch of a deer drinking from the same river that flowed beside them.

"I keep my memories here," Ophelia whispered. "I've had this book for a few years now. I've tried to make the most of every page."

"May I see?" Seamus asked.

She looked at him sidelong, then down at his hands, which had crumbs and salt stuck to them. "Not right now," she said, a hint of disgust in her eyes.

"What's your favorite drawing you've done?" Seamus asked instead.

She searched the pages silently for a while, eyebrows furrowed in focus. Finally, she came to a page covered in drawings of foxes, bears, wolves, squirrels, badgers, pine martens, owls, and deer. Each was done in color, though Seamus couldn't tell what medium she'd used. He wasn't that into art.

"This is one of them." The minty air was beginning to dissipate. "A painter was passing through a few months ago. She lent me her watercolor paints for the afternoon. I quite enjoyed working with them. I went back and painted over some of my previous sketches, but this one is by far my favorite."

"Is that Eydis?" Seamus asked, tapping the bear in the center of the right page. Her use of blue and purple to shade an otherwise stark white polar bear astounded him. The drawing looked as though it could pop off the page and start giving him disapproving looks, just like the real Eydis had done.

She nodded, tracing the outline. "I draw her a lot."

Seamus suddenly remembered he'd been working on a carving of her bear companion. He turned and dug into his pack, finding it buried at the bottom, nestled alongside the half-finished fox he'd asked her to paint her favorite shade of periwinkle. He hid the bear in his palm, pointing out to the trees.

"Hey! What was that?" he said, startling her so badly her hair whipped him in the face as she turned to follow his gaze.

"I don't see—" She turned back to see a tiny carving of a bear held before her face. The minty sadness was replaced by sugary joy as she took the carving from his outstretched hand. "When did you make this?"

"I'd been working on it for a while. Do you like it?"

"Very much!" she said, petting it as though it were a living, breathing bear the size of her palm. "Thank you, Seamus. It's beautiful!"

He waved away her praise. "Yeah, yeah, you're welcome."

Ophelia held the bear over her heart, searching his eyes. Whatever she found within their hazel depths, she smiled at. "Thank you for not leaving me behind."

He rubbed his nose, giving a half-hearted shrug. "Don't mention it."

He was growing far too fond of this strange little Witch.

CHAPTER TWENTY-FOUR

KING FISHER

Seamus nudged Ophelia awake the following day, offering a piece of bread smothered with jam to the bleary-eyed Witch. He'd already eaten and had been up for a while, watching the sunrise as she slept silently beside him. The whole scene had been entirely too peaceful. Growing restless, he'd tended to their fire and began packing their things.

His eyes kept lingering on the riverbank. His wolf itched to bound into the icy depths and sink its teeth into a fresh kill. It craved blood, craved violence.

His wolf and him weren't exactly on speaking terms. He often referred to it as, well, an 'it' instead of calling the damned thing what it really was; a part of himself. His wolf had gotten him into a lot of trouble, and it seemed it didn't plan on stopping anytime soon. Most werewolves remembered their full moons. Most werewolves didn't shift at inopportune moments. Most werewolves *were* on speaking terms with their wolf. Furthermore, most werewolves didn't imagine their other form as an entirely separate being.

Ophelia stood, stretched, and yawned, rolling up her bedroll. "Thank you for breakfast," she said softly.

He grumbled and nodded, kicking off his boots. Now that she was up, someone would be there to watch if he slipped on algae-covered rocks and drowned. How fruitful.

"What are you doing?" she asked, following him to the riverbank with a concerned look.

"I'm going fishing," he said, smirking her over his shoulder. "We'll sell whatever I can catch."

He stripped down to just his trousers and rolled them up past his knees. Tossing his foul-smelling tunic and socks at her, he stepped into the river.

Ophelia dodged them, frowning. "You'll freeze."

"That's why I stoked the fire," he winked.

Ice-cold water stung his feet and calves. A brisk breeze burned his bare chest. He stretched, cracking his bones, rolling his neck. Ophelia sat on the riverbank, knees pulled to her chest. Her owl-like eyes watched him intently as he waded further into the water. He crouched, hands poised to catch a walleye or trout as it whizzed by. Gritty sand and sharp rocks scuffed the bottom of his feet as softly swaying plants tickled his toes.

His wolf was alert, ears pricked, eyes narrowed.

Something slimy brushed his ankle. He lunged forward, water splashing up around him, his hand grasping nothing but current. His eyes burned in his skull, the bright green reflection of his wolf's eyes glowing in the water.

Joy he hated calling his own surged through him. To his wolf, there was nothing better than catching something with his own two hands.

He was waist-deep in the water now, farther than he'd planned to go, but oh well.

Another fish rushed past. He dove beneath the freezing water, grasping its tail with clawed fingers. It wriggled beneath his hands as he brought it to the surface. Crimson trails of blood dripped down his hand, the smell of it intoxicating. He smiled, tossing the fish onto the bank.

Ophelia grimaced but applauded him.

He sat in the river for quite a while, but he hadn't caught much. Either he was still tired, or these fish were faster than he was used to.

A trout swam between his legs. A determined growl rumbled in his throat. Seamus held his breath and plunged into the water, claws slashing through the current. He sliced the trout's tail, causing it to falter. He swam forward, his teeth clenching around it. The metallic taste of blood hit his tongue. His wolf howled in delight in the depths of his mind.

He broke the river's surface, smiling with the fish still in his mouth at the horrified Witch.

"That's disgusting, Seamus," Ophelia frowned.

He tried to speak as the dying trout's tail flapped back and forth, smacking him in the face and spattering him with blood.

"What?" Ophelia asked, a hint of a laugh in her voice.

He removed the fish from his mouth, tossing it at her feet. "I said, 'It's fun!'"

"I highly doubt that," she said.

"C'mere, I'll show you," he offered, waving her over.

"I'm fine here, thanks," she laughed.

He shrugged, opening his mouth to say something when a walleye jumped out of the water. He dove again, overcome by instinct, happily leaving the surface behind.

This fish was fast. It fought the current, trying to escape him. Bubbles popped across Seamus's face as he swam with all his might after it. Before he could grasp it, a sharp pillar of ice jutted up in front of him, skewering the fish as it shot upward. He hung suspended in the water momentarily, gazing up at a shadowy form rippling above. He swam up slowly, only his head breaking the surface.

There was Ophelia, standing on a floating piece of ice, the frozen pillar and the dead walleye beside her.

"Is this how you do it?" Ophelia asked. She lightly tapped the walleye's tail, nearly slipping off her iceberg in fright when it moved.

"Kind of," Seamus said bitterly, but he smiled.

He was too deep in the water to stand now, his feet just barely grazing the riverbed.

"Look! Another!" Ophelia said, pointing behind him.

Seamus spun, eyes locked on another fish. He reached for it, an arrow-like piece of ice nearly slicing through his hand. The icicle embedded itself in the fish, and an identical icy projectile found its own target.

"Now you're just showing off," Seamus grumbled, feigning irritation.

Okay, maybe he *wasn't* pretending. She'd taken to this so quickly it almost frightened him. He'd spent years mastering the careful art of fishing with his bare hands, but Ophelia had killed three—well, now it was five—fish with ease compared to his handful on the shore. He frowned, his wolf pacing in his mind as he stared at her. His wolf was competitive, to say the least.

Still, he felt an odd sense of pride.

Ophelia hiked up her skirts, her iceberg expanding as the tip of her shoe touched the water and walked across. She collected her catch, water freezing beneath her as she stepped off the iceberg.

"We'll split the profit fifty-fifty if you can catch more than me before my toes freeze off," Seamus said, heaving himself onto her iceberg.

Ophelia held out her hand for him to shake. Seamus smiled toothily, staring her down. Time to even the playing field just a bit.

"Seamus Norland, don't—"

He gave a toothy grin, then pushed her, sending her backward into the freezing river. Laughing, he jumped in after her, floating above her as she crossed her arms over her chest and shook her head in disappointment. He rolled his eyes, waving her away, already spotting a loach. He spun in the water, grabbing it and sinking his sharp claws into its flesh. Smiling to himself, he swam back to the surface, slapping his catch onto the iceberg.

He repeated this process, surmounting a hefty pile of fish.

It wasn't until the seventh fish he realized he hadn't seen Ophelia in a while. His was the only pile, and there weren't any icicle-skewered fish floating in the river.

Panic gripped him. Without hesitation, he sunk below the depths, dropping to the riverbed, looking around wildly. What if she couldn't swim? What if she'd just drowned without him knowing? He twisted around, spotting ebony hair floating several feet away. He paddled against the current with all his might, smacking away stray pieces of horsetail, trying to clear the murky water until he reached her. His hand clamped her shoulder, and she turned to smile at him.

His lungs filled with water.

He felt himself gasp for breath as he looped his arms under her armpits and made for the surface. Ophelia wiggled free, tugging his arm and leading him back down. He kicked away, clamping his nose shut. Ophelia grabbed his wrists, shaking her head, trying to pull his hands away from his face.

She was crazy!

This kid was going to kill him!

As if she could hear his thoughts, she rolled her eyes, pointing to herself. Seamus saw her chest rise and fall softly as if they weren't several feet underwater. As if she was *breathing*.

That's when he realized it *wasn't* water filling his lungs. It was air. Slowly, he dropped his hands from his face. His lungs felt heavy and compressed, but he was breathing.

Ophelia nodded, a firm hold still on his wrists as she sunk toward the bank, her skirts billowing around them like thick clouds. Thick pillars of sunlight cut through the murky water as they descended, making tiny particles of sediment sparkle all around. Ophelia sat cross-legged in the silt, and Seamus guessed he was meant to do the same. He floated down to her, gazing around their brackish surroundings. His lungs filled and deflated against his will with mystical oxygen. Ophelia let go of one of his wrists, putting a finger to her lips. He gave an unsure nod, watching as she shut her eyes.

Were they just meant to sit here? Why?

This was all too weird.

She peeked at him, giving him a knowing look. That must mean he was supposed to close his eyes, too.

He couldn't shake the panic in his chest, but he trusted her to a certain extent. He wasn't drowning yet, so the odds were in his favor.

He shut his eyes.

A sense of peace washed over him. His body felt weightless, the current whipping around them, reminding him of the wind on a blustery day. Something touched his arm. Ophelia squeezed his wrist tight.

He opened an eye, the sight around them almost stealing the breath from his lungs.

Two otters, one smaller than the other, swam in circles around them. Beyond them, just visible in the dimness, was a whole school of loaches, their scales glinting like stars in the sky. The current had changed, flowing around them instead of into them. The Witch's hair whipped around in the water like smoke, making her appear as a benevolent river ghost.

Ophelia reached for the smaller otter, her hand gliding across its fur as it swam slowly by. It had curious eyes, much like the not-so-crazy young lady before him. Seamus lifted his hand, the bigger of the two otters coming to nuzzle his hand. The smaller one swam between them, ruffling Ophelia's skirts.

Seamus was grinning like an idiot, in awe of these critters and Ophelia's powers. There was no doubt in his mind that she had called to these otters. It seemed Ophelia had a connection to all creatures. Land, sea, sky—Seamus was sure she was seen as a friend to all. In the dark, his wolf eyes illuminated her face in a pale green glow. She was mystified by the otters, a hint of surprise on her face. He, in turn, was mystified by her.

They sat a while longer, enjoying the show the otters had put on for them as they chased each other and played with the loaches. Seamus had almost forgotten about the surface. It wasn't until Ophelia stood and tugged on his hand that he remembered the events leading up to this moment.

They swam to the surface, fresh, cold air burning their lungs.

"That was incredible," Seamus breathed.

Ophelia splashed him, paddling toward her iceberg. He followed. Seamus didn't know why it stood out to him, but that piece of ice was considerably smaller than it had been. Before, the iceberg bridge had touched the shore. Now, it floated in the center of the river, a few feet from the bank. How strange. He heaved himself up, offering Ophelia a helping hand.

"I see you've won our game," she said, gesturing to his catch. He'd completely forgotten.

He laughed, shaking like a wet dog, showering her. She smiled up at him with content eyes that seemed to sag slightly.

"Yes, well, I'll share anyway," he said, shrugging.

They picked up the fish and hauled them to the edge of the iceberg, wading the rest of the way back to the riverbank. Seamus took a clean shirt from his pack and tied up their catch, setting it aside. He was about to grab a dry pair of trousers when a powerful breeze swirled around him, drying him instantly.

He looked to Ophelia, watching as she wound the wind around herself. A second later, she was bone dry, her hair and skirts falling softly around her.

"How'd you learn to do all that?" he asked. He sat heavily on the ground before the fire, pulling on a pair of clean socks.

There was a far-off look in her eyes. "Years of practice," she said softly.

"Well, it seems to have paid off," Seamus laughed.

She was staring at him with a tilted head again, a question in her eyes. He followed her gaze to the tattoos on his arm and over his heart. Sometimes, he forgot he had them. It was rare for him to be in the company of a mirror.

"What do they mean?" she asked as he pulled on a wrinkled tunic littered with moth holes.

Seamus felt the color drain from his face. He pointed to the most prominent one, the two wolves over his heart. "This represents someone I've lost," he sighed, "the other is less of a tattoo and more of a brand." He grimaced, rubbing his left shoulder, a phantom pain spreading across his skin. "I'll tell you the story another time. We should head back to town, collect our bounty, then make a break for it."

That seemed a satisfactory answer.

He didn't want the truth of his past to ruin the traces of wonder left behind by the otters and Ophelia's magic.

But more than that, he didn't want his past to ruin *her*.

CHAPTER TWENTY-FIVE

OFF GUARD

Three uneventful days passed. They hadn't talked much, just focusing on the road ahead and their thoughts. Seamus kept to himself in the evenings, allowing Ophelia time to read or draw. Meanwhile, he'd practice with his new axes, trying to 'keep his body ready to fight,' or so he said. Ophelia had a feeling he was just restless.

Ophelia yawned as she unrolled their magical map. Seamus had reminded her of the name of their destination—Dødbyen—and tasked her with plotting a course. The Wayfarer's Map had worked its magic, showing her places she'd never heard of. There weren't a lot of towns in The Wilds, but there were more than she'd imagined. Other than the Center Cities, Dødbyen was definitely the most interesting. It was a dark slash on the map, a long chasm running between the borders of Snøbolig and Høstlunden. Seamus said it was an underground city. How exciting! Ophelia had never been to an underground city before! She couldn't wait to see this strange city in all its glory.

Seamus, on the other hand, was less enthusiastic.

Speaking of the wolf, Seamus was walking a few paces in front of her, snacking on the candied hazelnuts she'd purchased. Ophelia smiled, glancing up at him. She'd had a feeling he'd get a kick out of the otters. He hadn't been able to stop talking about them. She'd spotted them watching Seamus as he splashed around in the water. They'd been frightened but curious, too. As soon as Seamus had pushed her into the water, they'd found her. Ophelia hadn't been able to tell if they were siblings, friends, or a parent and child, but she liked to think they were the latter. On their walk back to Gulch, Seamus told her that he'd always liked otters. Ophelia was beaming while waiting for him outside the general store. When he returned, he placed a handful of coins in her palms, then stuffed a few bundles of dried fish in her pack. Apparently, he'd struck a deal with the shopkeeper. Seamus had gone down on his price, trading a few fresh fish for their preserved counterparts. He, too, was beaming. They'd made a fair bit off their shenanigans.

Shortly after, they'd set off again.

Now, three days later, Seamus had a skip in his step. While he seemed lighter than the days prior, Ophelia still noted the darkness in his eyes. She doubted he'd ever lose it.

Ophelia herself was falling behind.

Fatigue clung to her limbs, though she couldn't pin where it'd come from. She hadn't exhausted her powers in any way, or at least she *thought* she hadn't. That day with the otters, her iceberg had shrunk when they'd made it back to the surface. Yes, she'd been focusing all her power on Seamus's lungs, but she hadn't diverted any magic from the bridge nor asked the ice to melt. It should've stayed.

She yawned again, holding the map in one hand as she followed their path with her finger. A solitary inn was halfway between Gulch and the next town, Skumringsspir. Maybe Seamus would allow them a night's rest there. Ophelia had a feeling she'd need it.

"Can I ask you a question?" Seamus asked, turning and walking backward as he popped another nut into his mouth. The bag was half empty. Ophelia hadn't had a single one.

"Of course," she said, rolling up the map and stuffing it back inside its case.

"How do your powers work?" He had a quizzical look on his face. It made the scars on the left side—her left, his right—contort into snake-like shapes.

"What do you mean?"

He shrugged. "How can you—" he swept his hand through the air in a jagged motion "—make the icicles and whatnot?"

"Oh, uh, I'm not sure. I sort of just imagine it happening," she said, holding her hand out in front of her. "I can feel the elements, I guess. They talk to me."

"Animals don't, but the wind does?" he asked. He didn't seem convinced.

"I don't hear a voice; I'm not crazy." She frowned at him.

"No, not at all." He surveyed her, taking in her entire being—her mask, shawl, dark brown dress, and blue overcoat—and then pointed at her. "Do something, Witch."

"Why?"

"Humor me." There was a tricksy light in his eyes. It almost scared away the worrisome darkness.

Ophelia cupped her hands, feeling the air go cold around her fingertips. The breeze clung to her, wrapping her in a biting embrace as a tiny storm cloud formed above her hands. It rumbled, raining down needle-thin droplets.

Seamus stopped dead in his tracks, mouth hanging open, eyes wide. "And you can do that on a bigger scale?"

"If I wanted to," she said, reddening. Her storm cloud shot out tiny lightning bolts that sizzled across her palms.

His eyes drifted to his shoes as she walked past him. "Did you shock me?"

Ophelia coiled in on herself. "I am sure I don't know what you mean."

"On the full moon!" Seamus gasped, stomping up to her. "You zapped me!"

She grimaced, dropping her hands to her side. The storm cloud dissipated. "Oh, you meant *that. . .*"

"You weren't looking at the tattoos, but the giant, red, itchy, scorch mark on my chest. That *you* caused!" He shook his head disapprovingly.

Her cheeks were burning hot beneath her mask. She had been. She'd wondered why it hadn't healed and felt suddenly guilty. Ophelia cast her eyes to the ground, waiting for him to reprimand her or worse. "I—" She didn't know how to defend herself in moments like this. She'd hoped the details of that night would've stayed lost to his wolf's memory.

The second he stepped forward, she stumbled back, pressed against a tree. Seamus's eyes had gone dark as he dared another step forward.

"I felt electricity erupt inside me," he said, softer than

she'd expected. "It was excruciating. But familiar. The sound of it. The buzzing."

Ophelia shrunk, squeezing her eyes shut, afraid of what he would do.

"Do you feel that all the time?" he asked quietly. It was then she realized the darkness in his eyes was concern. "Are you in pain?"

Her eyes popped open in shock. "Not always," she said before she could stop herself.

Seamus frowned as he searched the eye holes of her mask. Slowly, he backed away. She could tell he was listening, his ears twitching slightly as he stared past the mesh and into the depths of her soul.

Ophelia turned away, eyes glued to the ground. "I'm sorry for hurting you. I didn't know what else to do. I panicked."

There was a laugh.

A hearty, genuine laugh.

"It's a neat trick, kid," Seamus sighed. Out of curiosity, she glanced back over her shoulder to see him smiling. He shook the bag of candied hazelnuts before her, not moving until she took one. "Next time, just, uh, aim for someone else, all right?"

Ophelia felt herself straighten as she ate her hazelnuts. "You're not mad?"

He only shrugged. "I guess I should've figured it out, huh?"

"Sorry," she said sheepishly. "We were both awfully freaked out that night. Does it hurt?"

He lightly tapped his chest, lost in thought. He winced a little, though he tried to hide it. "I'm fine."

"I'm so sorry, Seamus," she groaned.

He just laughed and shrugged again. "Like I said, kid, next time aim—"

Seamus's face had lost its color, shock, and anger, and something else Ophelia couldn't pin marred his features. Before she could ask what was wrong, he grabbed her by the collar, pulling her off the road and into the trees. He pushed her behind him, peering around a tree. Irritated he'd touched her without permission—again—she slapped his hand away.

"Wha—" Ophelia began.

He held up a finger, silencing her. Slowly, he touched his left ear, then placed his hand protectively in front of her. Ophelia listened as he'd instructed. In the distance, she could hear the thunderous sound of horses running down the path.

Seamus turned to her, his face set in indifference, his eyes betraying his fear. His voice was barely audible when he said, "Go quietly."

The ground shook the second they turned around. The Ulvemordere—or at least that's who they *thought* was coming around the bend—were too close. They wouldn't outrun them. They'd trapped themselves in the woods.

Seamus turned away, fingering his axes. Ophelia was suddenly overcome with relief that he had them. Seamus seemed to feel the same.

Still, it sounded like there were more Ulvemordere than they could take.

Drastic times called for drastic measures.

Ophelia backed up against a tree, stomping her foot on the ground. A thick column of ice formed beneath her feet, lifting her to a high branch. She stepped off, crouching. Any other day, she'd have climbed. Sometimes, she saw using her powers as cheating. Turning her attention back to Seamus, she reached out toward him, though he was at least ten feet or so away.

He spun, looking around wildly before finding her amid the branches above. "What are you do—"

Ophelia called upon the wind, imagining it lifting him and setting him down on the branch above her.

At first, nothing happened.

Seamus mocked her, waving his hands like a crappy street magician. "Get down!" he whisper-yelled.

Ophelia thrust her palms forward, begging the wind to listen. Seamus was a beast, but he wasn't *that* heavy! Surely she could do this.

His feet lifted off the ground. He hovered there for a moment, arms flapping, legs kicking. Ophelia felt a strain at the edge of her consciousness. Pain prickled up her arms.

"*Please*," she begged the wind.

Why wasn't it listening to her?

Seamus was suddenly flung upward into the tree. The gust of wind deposited him on a branch, though it didn't set him on steady feet. He leaned back, waving his arms wildly, trying to keep his balance.

Voices drifted in from the road. They could just barely see the iron armor of the Ulvemordere. Each wore the pelt of a wolf in one way or another. The majority had fur sticking out from under their armor, but some—maybe the commanders or lieutenants—wore an entire wolf on their backs. They'd traded in their iron wolf-like helms for the real thing. Lifeless canine faces sat atop their heads or shoulders. Each had a skull, glistening teeth, and matted fur. The only artificial adornment was the glass eyes, though one could easily mistake them for the real deal. Ophelia's stomach churned. How could a person wear a creature like that? How could they even *think* of doing such a thing?

Above her, Seamus's branch creaked. Ophelia looked up just in time to see him pitch forward, losing his footing. His hands flung forward, gripping a branch across from him. His heels dug into the bending branch beneath him, barely supporting his weight. There he was, standing at a diagonal, muscles strained to keep himself from falling, glaring down at her.

". . . I'm picking up a scent!" came a voice.

That glare turned to terror.

Ophelia shut her eyes, spreading her arms wide. She could feel the breeze, even when it barely blew. She whispered to it in her mind, begging it to pick up, hoping it would hide their scent.

A strong breeze surrounded them, nearly knocking Ophelia from her perch. Seamus's foot slipped. She had to duck, or else he'd have accidentally kicked her in the face. He dropped down next to her, shooting her a look she interpreted as 'Don't you dare ever do that again.' She mouthed her apologies, causing him to roll his eyes.

Between branches, they saw the Ulvemordere soldiers sniffing the air. Safely hidden in the trees, Ophelia took a moment to really look at them. They each wore different colored garments beneath their armor. Most of them wore bright yellow, but a few wore red. One wore black. Ophelia shivered. That soldier must hold the highest rank. She glanced at Seamus, wondering what the colors meant and what he'd once worn. Would it matter to her if he'd worn black? Would it matter to her if he'd been a general?

The wind stole the Ulvemordere's voices as they moved on, their horses clip-clopping away.

Ophelia waited several tense minutes before allowing the wind to settle.

"That was far too close for comfort," Seamus whispered.

Only able to nod, Ophelia gave him a knowing look.

This was what it'd be like from here on out. They'd be constantly looking over their shoulders, waiting for something to come barreling out of the woods. They'd gotten lucky the last few days, but luck seemed to be wearing thin.

Ophelia was about to voice her concerns when a cracking sound—much like the sound Seamus's bones had made on the full moon—echoed in her ears.

Their branch shifted.

"Uh, Ophelia. . ." Seamus began but was cut off.

They fell from their hiding spot, colliding with several other branches as they descended. Ophelia screamed, shutting her eyes tight.

Wind picked up around them, catching them before they hit the ground. They looked at each other, their mouths hanging open, when the wind cut out, slamming them onto the ground. They sat stunned for a moment, staring at each other.

The whole thing had been rather comical.

Seamus stood, dusting himself off, looking over his shoulder. "We need to establish a new set of ground rules," he said, eyes still full of horror.

"I didn't expect that to happen," Ophelia muttered, struggling to her feet.

Seamus turned away, speaking, but she couldn't hear him. Blood was pounding in her ears. She swayed to the side, almost losing her footing. Panting heavily, she reached for a low-hanging branch to steady herself. Her head felt heavy, her limbs weak.

At that moment, the only thing she wanted was to drift off to sleep.

"Kid," Seamus said sternly, cutting through the deafening pounding in her ears. She looked up to see his puzzled yet concerned face. "What's wrong?"

Letting go of the branch, she straightened, adjusting her mask, shaking her head. "Nothing, sorry," she said, folding her hands in front of her neatly.

Seamus looked her up and down, pursing his lips. He seemed unconvinced but was obviously too occupied with their close call. Sighing, he pointed to the map case at her side and then at the road.

"Find us a different route," he said gruffly.

Ophelia fumbled with the map, focusing on Dødbyen and how to get there as quickly as possible. The same map as before appeared across the parchment, but a new route had been marked in light blue ink. Seamus came around to look over her shoulder. They were still heading toward that inn—thank the Spirits—but after that, they'd jut off toward another town where a stable had been circled.

"Next time you want to go to a bookshop, I'm not complaining," Seamus breathed, taking the map from her.

CHAPTER TWENTY-SIX

GLAD TO MEET YOU
(I PROMISE I'M NOT LYING)

A few tense hours passed, but thankfully, they hadn't caught wind of the Ulvemordere again.

Strangely enough, it'd been Seamus who suggested resting at the inn. Ophelia had asked if that was safe, seeing as the Ulvemordere could very well be there, but it was unlikely. Too many horses, too many men, too small an inn. Still, he'd quickened his pace, stealing glances over his shoulder at her here and there.

Upon arriving at the inn, this theory proved true. There were only two horses in the paddocks, plus a pack mule. A few dirty canvas tents were set back against the woods, each with its own campfire. Smoke hung heavily in the air, making Ophelia squeamish. Friends and families sat laughing around those blazing fires, blissfully unaware of what fire could mean to the onlooker swathed in blue. Ophelia glanced toward Seamus, whose jaw was clenched tight. His lips were slowly twitching into a frown. Yet, all was normal, or so Seamus said. He couldn't pick up any hints of the 'usual Ulvemordere stench' as he called it.

By the time they stepped into the old inn, Ophelia nearly collapsed. Everything ached; every sense was numb. Warmth filled Ophelia's lungs as she breathed in the honey-thick and stale air of the inn. Pastries were baking somewhere nearby, mixing with the familiar smell of mulled wine. Seamus's stomach growled. Hers did, too, as if their stomachs were having a hunger-driven conversation.

"I'll be right back," Seamus mumbled, making for the

long counter where a woman was piling a plate high with boiled potatoes and sliced ham.

"Bring me something back," Ophelia yawned.

He gave a weak thumbs up before digging into his pack's side pocket for his coin pouch.

Left alone in the doorway, Ophelia took it upon herself to find a table. Legs aching, thoughts melting into one another from exhaustion, Ophelia decided on two plush yet tattered chairs near the door. Between the chairs was a table just big enough for plates and cups and an oil lamp. It was quaint and rickety, but it would do. The inn itself was just as run down as the furniture. Rusty oil lamps hanging from the ceiling, askew rugs, ragged curtains, and chips in the log walls gave the effect of a place that had done its one and only job for many, many years. There was even a fireplace with three sets of antlers hanging over it. Each had a wooden plaque, presumably describing the creature and who had killed it. Though dilapidated, the place felt homey. Hopefully, her room would be the same, serving as a pocket of safety for a few hours at least. How many children had been raised here? Untying her shawl and shrugging off her jacket, Ophelia draped them over the armrest of her chair, sinking into the pillowy seat. She could have fallen asleep just then had it not been for the notion of real food on its way to her. Hardtack and jerky had gotten old rather quickly.

Patrons walked up and down the staircase to her left, their footsteps causing the old steps to creak. Some held yawning children in their arms. Others walked arm in arm with lovestruck expressions. Ophelia wondered how long these patrons had stayed here. How many had stayed long enough to call this place home? What did their lives look like? Why were they here? Did anyone else wonder about these things?

Seamus returned with two steaming mugs of cider. He handed one off to Ophelia, settling into his chair.

"They'll have it out to us momentarily," he said, taking a sip of his cider. "Drink up," he smiled. The bristly mustache forming on his upper lip curved like a startled woolly caterpillar.

Ophelia blew on the hot, spicy liquid, letting the steam and smell envelop her. Hot apple cider usually had healing spices in it. If she was getting sick, she hoped this did the trick. She couldn't exactly afford illness, and the last thing

Ophelia wanted was to be a burden.

"I got us each a room," Seamus said, placing a key on the table beside her. "I, for one, am looking forward to an actual bed."

Ophelia nodded, yawning. Her eyelids weighed heavily upon her eyes. They stuck when she blinked, a telltale sign she should be in bed. She'd read that bears living outside of the country of Alle Årstider—in countries that experienced normal seasons—hibernated during the winter months. Too bad she wasn't a bear, else she might've followed suit.

Ophelia's mind wandered. How strange the other lands must be. Very few books were imported from the other lands, but she knew Alle Årstider, where she lived, was remarkable. Its four kingdoms, Snøbolig, Høstlunden, Dagslys Hul, and Vårretten, were all stuck in a single perpetual season. Høstlunden was Autumn all year every year, and Dagslys Hul and Vårretten were Summer and Spring, respectively. She and Snøbolig shared the same fate. Winter and bad weather clung to them like the plague. Ophelia didn't mind, however. The warmth of Summer made her skin crawl. It sounded atrocious.

Snøbolig may be harsh, but it was home.

Her powers may give her strife, but they were hers and hers alone. That had to count for something.

An older woman came and handed off their plates, giving a slight bow as she left. Seamus wasted no time digging in, his eyelids fluttering joyfully after each bite. He was speaking incoherently, most likely giving his compliments to the chef. Ophelia, never one to cause a scene, ate slowly. Seamus had finished and was pondering ordering seconds before she was even halfway done.

Ophelia eyed him suspiciously, wondering where he'd grown up. Seamus had the looks of a winter-worn man, but one could never tell. Snøbolig always took its toll early into one's travels. Maybe he hailed from Høstlunden? He seemed to know that place well, at least. Vårretten and Dagslys Hul were out. He was too pale to have come from the warmer climates. There was always the possibility he grew up on the mysterious island of Mørklagt Øy, where the Ulvemordere compound was. Ophelia desperately wanted to ask but figured that'd put a damper on Seamus's mood. A question for another time, perhaps.

"You going to eat that?" Seamus asked, eyeing her plate greedily.

All that remained was a half-eaten slab of pork, some cheese, and berries. Ophelia was nibbling away on a honey cake, not full but too tired to bring the fork to her mouth. Sighing, she slid her plate to him. His greedy eyes turned ravenous. He was like a hungry puppy begging for a treat.

"Much obliged," he said, stabbing the pork with his fork, lifting the whole thing up off his plate to chew on.

"Good dog," Ophelia said as quietly as she could, covering her mouth with her hand, hiding her smirk.

Seamus paused mid-bite. "I heard that," he scowled.

"I didn't say anything," she lied, feigning innocence.

He raised an eyebrow but dropped the subject, turning to survey the few patrons in the inn. She thought she saw a flicker of a smile on his face, but it was gone before he turned back to her.

"So, about those rules," he said after finishing off her plate. "I'll go first; no throwing me up into trees."

"Unless it's an emergency," Ophelia added.

"Let me rephrase that: under no circumstances will Ophelia Av'Skogen throw Seamus Norland up into a tree or anywhere else for that matter," he corrected, leaning forward. "All right, your turn."

"Really?" He just nodded. "Oh, uh. . ." She thought long and hard about these 'rules,' looking around, trying to find the right words. All the other patrons clung to each other. Couples held hands, parents used their thumbs to wipe crumbs from their children's faces, and friends shook hands or hugged. It was all very sweet, but it set Ophelia on edge. "Okay, second rule: unless I explicitly say otherwise, don't touch me. I know you were just trying to protect me, but I don't appreciate you grabbing my collar like that." She shifted uncomfortably in her seat, refusing to look at him.

Seamus's eyebrows knit together, but he didn't protest. "All right, got it. My turn: I lead, you follow. I can get a read on things pretty quickly. If I say it's time to go, it's time to go. Bookshops be damned."

"I'm okay with that," she said with a shrug. "Rule four: animals are still friends and not food. Don't think I've forgotten just because we've left the cottage."

"What about the fish?"

"I couldn't care less about fish, if I'm honest. They gross me out."

He tipped his head in mildly surprised agreement. "Well, what about the mask rule?"

"Oh, well, that sort of fizzled out, hasn't it?" Ophelia asked, wringing her hands. "I mean, you know what I am now," she added quietly.

"True, but I still have questions."

"I've no secrets," she said, though she wondered if that sounded convincing or not.

"And the tidying rule?" he asked.

Ophelia gave a sheepish grin. "I've been slacking on my side of that, huh? You've been packing our things each morning."

"I don't mind. Fizzle that one as well?"

After a moment's hesitation, she held her hand out to shake.

Just as he took her hand, a tall man with stringy blond hair came up and slapped Seamus on the shoulder. Though he looked rather fragile, the force of his friendly clap on the back was nearly enough to cause Seamus to topple forward into his plate.

"Seamus, old friend!" he said, his voice flowery. "How *have* you been? Still parading around as a vagabond, I presume?"

Seamus whipped his head around to find where the voice had come from. Ophelia noted the sudden change in his demeanor. He sat stiff, his fists clenched around his knife and fork. Guess the time for bonding—or whatever the rule-making thing had been—was over.

"Egill," Seamus said gruffly, eyebrows furrowed deep over his eyes. He frowned as the man pulled up a chair and sat between them.

The strange man was as thin and gangly as a praying mantis, his eyes piercingly yellow. His long, pointy, pierced ears stuck out from fraying holes in a woolen cap much too small for the size of his head. His long wool tunic was littered with moth holes, making it rather useless when you thought about it. Thankfully, he wore a heavy leather coat, mittens, and gigantic boots, all of which were lined with fur. It was obvious he wasn't used to the cold. Now, *that* was a man hailing from Vårretten or Dagslys Hul. He looked a freezing fool, but Ophelia suspected otherwise.

Egill nodded toward Ophelia but didn't look at her, the colorful beads in his hair clinking together almost rhythmically. "Who is this pretty little thing?"

Seamus's nostrils flared. "What do you want, Egill?" He'd turned his knife toward him, ready to strike at any moment.

Whoever this Egill was, she immediately didn't like him. Seamus was right. He did get a good read on situations. Should he ever give her a reason to doubt someone, Ophelia would.

The man smiled, revealing several golden teeth. His crystal-sharp eyes glinted with mischief. "Word amongst thieves is you've gotten yourself into some trouble." He leaned over to Ophelia, eyes still trained on Seamus. "Your companion here is worth top dollar, but I'm sure you know that already." His voice was almost aristocratic, though there was an underlying gruffness that made Ophelia think of rotten fruit. *Spoiled* rotten, more like.

Seamus leaned forward, voice low. "If you're here to collect my bounty, you have another thing coming, *butterfly*."

Egill rolled his faintly glowing eyes. That unearthly yellow sent shivers up Ophelia's spine. It was the color of yellow jasmine. A beautiful flower, yes, but a poisonous one, too. As such, it was an awfully fitting color for the Faye Folk. Ophelia hadn't had the pleasure of meeting a fairy in person, but she knew not to call them 'butterfly.'

"If I wanted you dead, you'd be dead, *mutt*." Egill's smile turned malicious.

Ophelia bristled, wondering what the history books would say about these two. If anyone else had called Seamus a mutt, she was sure they'd be dead before their head hit the floor.

Seamus leaned back, eyes full of hatred. "Pin-wing."

Yet another name you shouldn't call a fairy. It implied that the Faye Folk were nothing more than oddities, cut from the same cloth as the bugs often pinned inside picture frames. Just some lowly decoration or entertainment for others. Something pretty to look at and nothing more.

What was it with these two? Were they just going to trade insults all night?

"If I'm a pin-wing, you're crudely done taxidermy," Egill snapped. "Are we done?"

"What do you want, Egill?" Seamus repeated, his growing frustration evident.

He glanced at the five or so other people in the room. Ophelia wondered what he was thinking. Surely, he didn't intend to fight this unnerving fairy. He wasn't stupid. Reckless, yes, but not stupid.

"Can't I check up on my friends?" Egill asked, looking hurt.

Seamus kept his eyes on the other patrons, smiling tightly. "If I spot your friends, I'll be sure to point them out." He tapped the table with his knife in an anxious beat. Though she couldn't explain why, this made Ophelia discreetly move away from Egill.

The fairy's smile dropped. He finally turned to look at her, scowling. Shifty eyes took her in. It was obvious he didn't like what he saw.

"What's with the mask?" Egill asked, flicking the snout of it.

"Religious purposes," Ophelia snapped, edging further away from him.

"Seriously?"

Ophelia held her head high. "The eclipse has passed. With it, all that is beautiful has hidden itself away—even I."

Egill leaned close to Seamus, eyeing her carefully. "She's a vain one, isn't she?"

"Shut up, Egill."

Egill only cleared his throat, shaking his head in disgust. "Listen, we need to talk, Norland—" he pointed at Ophelia "—alone."

Seamus eyed her, his eyes lingering on her mask. He swore under his breath but nodded, following Egill outside. Ophelia had half a mind to follow them but knew better. Instead, she finished off her honey bun, took out her sketchbook, and pretended to draw. She could see them outside the window, glad her mask hid her eyes. They were too far away for her to hear even mumbles, but she could at least get a read on the situation. If things did get violent, she wanted to be able to step in if needed.

After all, there was no rule against protecting her self-proclaimed protector.

CHAPTER TWENTY-SEVEN

So Long, Old Friend

Seamus and Egill sat shoulder to shoulder before a campfire near the inn's front door. A cart with wobbling wheels passed. Seamus almost ran to catch up with it, hoping he could fling himself in the back. Wherever it was headed had to be better than sitting next to this insufferable fairy.

"I've been meaning to find you," Egill said, his voice dark.

"What's happened?"

Seamus had known Egill Daae for a very long time. They weren't friends by any means, but they could count on each other when push came to shove. It was a truce of convenience, though Seamus often wondered when that truce would end. Could today be the day?

"You tell me," Egill laughed. He took a swig of his hip flask, offering Seamus a drink, which he politely refused. "I woke up to your face plastered everywhere I looked. I thought we'd gotten past that." He took another long swig, coughing as whatever he drank burned his throat. From the smell, Seamus could tell it was some kind of brandy. His nose shriveled against his will. "Your posters are old, though. Don't have nearly as many scars, and you've still got both ears. And what's with the beard?"

"Yeah, well, it's been a while since they caught up to me," Seamus sighed. "And I *like* the beard," he said, mumbling something else under his breath.

"What was that?"

"I said 'thank you.'"

Egill looked over his shoulder, smirking to himself. "Heard you were stealing from the wrong folks. That never ends well. But the whispers say you've done something much, much worse."

"What exactly have you heard?" Seamus asked, staring into the fire, hoping it'd burn away the dread bubbling in his stomach.

"Oh, don't make me rehash what happened in Tø with you," Egill said with a roll of his eyes. "I don't have the nitty-gritty of it, but rest assured, someone's drawing up your brand new ugly mug as we speak."

"Egill," Seamus sighed.

"Well, I've heard you burned down a town."

"Lies."

Egill tipped his flask at him. "I figured. You were never one for real fires, only the imaginary sort." A pause. A laugh. "Well, there was that one incident with the baron and the inventor's wife—"

Seamus cleared his throat, cutting him off. "Who'd you hear it from? It's only been a few days." Seamus was suddenly suspicious. Egill generally gave him a sense of unease, but this was different. And why, oh why, was he in The Wilds? Of all places, of all inns, why here? Why now?

"I ran into a friend who heard from their cousin's wife, who spoke with their niece's fiancé, who told him that the Ulvemordere had sent a raiding party into The Wilds. I knew it *had* to be you, but I wasn't convinced until yesterday morning." Egill scratched his chin, swirling his flask. "I was passing through, heading back toward the Cities, when a small group of 'em ran in and started stirring up trouble. Gave your description, said you had a hostage. They mean business, Seamus. They've split into groups, heading in every direction."

Seamus sighed heavily, rubbing his eyes. "We saw a squadron this afternoon. They nearly found us."

"And who is this 'us?'" Egill asked. "What's the girl got to do with it? She's *obviously* not a hostage. They aren't plastering *her* face everywhere, either. Though come to think of it, they can't with the mask and all," he laughed, taking another draught. "Lucky her, am I right?"

Seamus ran a hand through his hair, shrugging. "I

picked up a stray."

Egill had a puzzled look on his pointy face. "That's not like you." Skepticism floated in those unnerving yellow eyes of his.

"She's just a kid," Seamus sighed. "I screwed up her life. I feel responsible."

Egill weighed that, draining his hip flask completely. "If only you felt the same about every sorry creature unfortunate enough to meet you."

Seamus's eyes traveled to Egill's back. Tiny stubs where wings should be moved beneath his coat.

"Yeah, well, meeting her was an accident," he groaned.

Egill offered his flask one last time. This time, Seamus almost took it. Alcohol had never been his friend, especially after taking the bite. A moon-drunk werewolf was one thing. A legitimately intoxicated one was another. Seamus rolled his eyes, pushing Egill's flask out of eyesight.

For a while, they sat in silence, just staring into the campfire. Seamus wondered what was going on in Egill's mind. That fairy's name came with a certain measure of terror. Most who knew him would call him an evil genius. Seamus usually shared the same sentiment.

"Your name's been circulating for a couple of months now. You're drawing too much attention to yourself," Egill said, not meeting his eyes.

"I know."

"You're usually so careful, mutt. What went wrong?"

Seamus gestured over his shoulder with his thumb. "Take a guess."

Egill stole another look back at the tavern. They could see Ophelia hunched over the table, scribbling away in her sketchbook. Seamus wasn't fond of leaving her alone in there, but at least she knew to keep her head down and keep to herself. From the sound of it, she'd had a lifetime of practice doing just that.

"Where are you heading?" Egill asked.

Seamus eyed him, finding nothing but a dull look of intrigue on the fairy's face. "Høstlunden," he chose to say, knowing Egill could always catch him in a lie.

"So, you've heard then?"

Seamus raised an eyebrow. "Heard what?"

Egill gave a toothy grin, leaning in close. "They're assembling beneath the Hunter's Moon again."

Seamus's eyebrows knit tight over his eyes. "Another shoddy plan in the works?"

Egill only nodded.

"What kind of plan, pin-wing?"

Egill smiled. "Come with me, and I'll tell you."

"Egill—"

He wiggled a finger in Seamus's face, making a *tsk*ing noise. "Knowledge isn't free, mutt."

"I'm not in the mood for your tricks. What are they planning? I was going to leave the kid with Tiril and Helgi. Are they part of it? If they're getting into trouble, then—"

"Like I said, your name has been circulating. The great Seamus Norland, Ulvemordere defector," he scoffed. "How many years have you been throwing punches toward the Ulve? How many years have you been running? You're making a dent, mutt. Every day, it gets bigger. You're a figurehead." The excitement in Egill's voice sickened him.

"There are thousands of Ulvemordere. How could I have made a dent?"

Egill gave him a knowing look. "There are rumors amongst sympathizers. Now, I'm not sure if this is true, but folks are saying you coerced a town—a whole town!—into fighting back. You stood up to them, and people are hearing about it. Again, word travels fast."

"How?"

"One of the townsfolk escaped," Egill whispered.

Seamus's heart began hammering in his chest. "Who? What are they saying?"

Seamus was filled with sudden regret. Who would've made it out of the Ulvemordere's grip? All he could think of was Lochlan. Had he survived? What lies was he spreading?

Or maybe it was Torbod?

No, if it was Torbod, Ophelia's true identity would've been made known immediately.

He could only hope it was someone like Saoirse or Åsmund. Someone who would keep Ophelia's secret or, at the very least, only share it with those they deemed worthy.

"We could rally an army, Seamus," Egill whispered. "We could turn that dent into a crack! Isn't that what we've always wanted?"

Seamus rubbed the back of his neck, looking out at the dark trees beyond. This was not the sort of news he was expecting.

"Kirkeby's are promising protection for any and all, but they're just a couple of bejeweled misfits. They're not of the people. But, if you're with them, people will come running to support us. A hundred Ulve defected after you! Think of how many more will join us with you at the helm of a revolution," Egill uttered hungrily.

"We've gone down this route before, Egill. It never ends well," Seamus spat.

"The kid must be special if you think they'll take her in. But they won't do it for free," Egill said, placing a hand on his shoulder.

Seamus felt his blood begin to bubble. This was a mistake. He should've ignored Egill and locked himself in his room until he got bored and left.

It'd only been eight days, and what had happened in Tø was already attached to his name. Before he'd arrived in that sorry little town, he'd stirred the pot, yes. But this was different. This was bad, this was very, very bad.

"We're stronger now. What happened to Ingrid won't happen again," Egill said, squeezing his shoulder tight. "You have to stop beating yourself up over things you couldn't control."

"I played a game of kings and pawns. I knew the risk. I don't fancy another round," Seamus snapped. "I was never any good at chess, anyway."

Egill sighed heavily, removing his hand and shaking his head in disdain. "That same group that killed your pack—your *family*—is still out there."

"Your point?"

"Don't you want revenge?"

"Egill—"

"Let's go after them," Egill said, throwing his arms wide. "First order of business, track down a squadron. Send a message. I've got a perfect target with your name on it." He gestured loosely to Seamus's axes.

Seamus sighed heavily, looking back at the tavern. Ophelia waved at him through the window. He gave a curt nod, turning back to Egill. "I can't do that," he said.

"Ditch the kid with the Kirkeby's, Norland," Egill sighed. "She'll figure it out just like we did. Coddling her will do more harm than good."

"I made a promise."

"Will you at least give it some thought? The Hunter's Moon is months away; you've got time."

"It's a suicide mission, Egill."

Egill only laughed. "Just like the old days." He leaned forward, his bitter breath hot against Seamus's ear. "It's Jette. I know where she is."

It was as if someone had lit a fire inside him. Seamus stood, fists clenched. "One of these days, I'm going to push you off a very high cliff. Remember, pin-wing, I stole your wings. Imagine what else I could do. How's that for 'the old days?'"

Egill stood, brushing himself off. "I'll meet you at our special spot, mutt." The fire reflecting in his yellow eyes set Seamus on edge. "I know you'll be there, one way or another. I can see it in your eyes."

With that, Seamus turned back toward the inn.

CHAPTER TWENTY-EIGHT

SHOULD'VE LISTENED

Seamus knocked on the table, startling Ophelia from her thoughts, causing her hand and pencil to jerk across the page of her sketchbook. Seamus's eyes were full of worry, though he was doing his best to hide it. Ophelia thought it best not to mention how he'd almost ruined her drawing.

"What did he want?" Ophelia asked, looking out the window to see Egill waiting by the side of the road. Ophelia thought it odd he had no bags with him.

Seamus sighed heavily. "To get under my skin, as per usual."

"He seems like an ass."

"He *is* an ass," Seamus corrected. He worked his jaw, staring at their empty plates. "You can go on up to your room, Phee; I'll take care of everything here. You seem tired."

So did he. Exhausted, in fact.

"Oh, I can—"

"I've got it," he said, giving her a very melancholic grin.

Ophelia hesitated but ultimately took her room key and drug her bags up the stairs. The steps creaked and sighed beneath her weight, the runner shifting, nearly tripping her. The landing opened up into a long, dark hall that seemed to stretch on for miles. Shadows sucked away the light of the oil lamps, creating a void of darkness. Squinting down at her key, she found her room was a few doors down on the right.

The key stuck in the lock, but the door ultimately gave way. The room was small, nothing luxurious. There was scarcely enough room for the bed, a chest, and a table, but it'd do for the night. Ophelia dropped her bags near the chest, then flopped down on the dusty bed, tossing away her mask. Whereas the common area smelled of delectable delicacies, the air here smelled of perfume and musk. Remnants of past inhabitants had seeped into wooden walls, begging to be remembered. Had there been ample light, Ophelia was sure she would've found bits and bobs left behind by patrons long gone. Warmth seeped in from under the door, the faintest smell of smoke and cider mixing with the musk and perfume.

As she lay on that musty old bed, Ophelia's eyes closed against her will. Her legs dangling off the bed, and her arms were pinned painfully beneath her, but she didn't mind. Muffled voices from below found her ears. It sounded like someone was humming a lullaby far away. Her legs twitched. She felt as though she were falling, but logically, she knew she was still on the bed, her face buried in the covers. The tension of the last few days faded, her tight muscles relaxing, her body melting into the soft and warm bed.

Long ago, there'd been a time when a party had been held at that old cottage she'd called home. Ophelia had never liked crowds. She remembered slipping away to her bedroom and falling asleep much like this.

She could almost feel them around her, those peculiar people of Tø. She nearly mistook a strand of hair falling on her face for someone's fingers brushing her cheek. Usually, she'd flinch away. For now, she was too tired.

Her thoughts went dark, the emptiness in her heart consuming her busy mind.

A knock on the door startled her. Ophelia sat up, blinking away her sleepiness and rubbing her face. Her body was abuzz and aching.

Half asleep, she staggered to the door, opening it a crack. Seamus stood staring at his feet, lost in thought. Remembering she didn't have her mask on, she only opened it enough for him to see one eye.

Seamus leaned against the doorframe, arms crossed, eyes drooping. "Just making sure you got up here safe," he said simply. He had her shawl and jacket draped over his arms. "Plus, you forgot these."

"Thank you," Ophelia yawned as he handed them off to

her.

"Sorry if I woke you," he said softly.

"You didn't."

He stared at her face, tracing her Marks with his ever-observant hazel eyes. Ophelia suspected something was on his mind but that he didn't know how to ask or phrase the question. Even if he did, she doubted Seamus would say anything. He kept his secrets close to his heart. They must play alongside the tattoo of the wolves chasing each other's tails.

"Lock the door, don't open it for anyone. I'll knock thrice, pause, then knock again come morning. If you need anything, come get me. I'm right across the hall, two doors down." He glanced that way, squaring his shoulders as someone walked by, blocking her from sight. Ophelia turned away, busying herself with a rusty nail sticking out of the floorboards. Seamus cleared his throat. "Anyway, kid, goodnight."

"Goodnight, Seamus," Ophelia said.

He pushed away from the door frame but lingered in the hall, looking sullen.

"Is there anything you'd like to talk about. . . ?" Ophelia offered.

Seamus's jaw clenched, and he shook his head. With a final nod, he grabbed the handle and shut the door.

Ophelia didn't know much about that fairy, Egill, but she knew he was bad news. Whatever he'd said to Seamus had obviously stuck with him. This did not bode well for either of them.

Ophelia didn't know how long she'd been asleep, but she was sure it hadn't been long. A sound had woken her. Something like keys jangling in someone's pocket. Or bells. Maybe it'd been bells. She sat up, yawned, and looked around her pitch-black room. The candle must have burned out. She snapped her fingers, a ball of lightning forming in her hand. Its cold silver-blue light illuminated the room, scaring away the shadows. In the dark, she couldn't see anyone or anything out of the ordinary. Perhaps the sound had come from downstairs? If that was the case, it wasn't her problem. Ophelia snuffed out her light, her back to the door.

There was that sound again. It *tink, tink, tink*ed somewhere close. This time, it sounded like something was tapping on the windowpane. Begrudgingly, Ophelia crawled out of bed and went to the window, finding nothing. Beyond the window, the world was cast in darkness.

Dark, that is, except for a single torch lighting up the road.

Ophelia scuffled back, tripping on her heels and falling back onto the bed.

At least ten, maybe more, Ulvemordere soldiers were standing in the road. A single too-bright torch illuminated their armor, helms, and taxidermized pelts, casting gruesome shadows on the ground.

Panicked, Ophelia pulled on her jacket and shawl, grabbed her bags, pulled on her mask, and then tip-toed into the hall. Quickly, she found Seamus's door, testing the handle. Locked. She tapped the door softly, remembering the pattern he'd told her earlier.

The stairs creaked. Ophelia turned just in time to see a soldier slinking up the steps. They seemed to form from shadows piling on one another, creating a menacing figure with fluffy ears atop their head that looked more like horns. There was a soft yet deadly laugh as they procured a dagger from a sheath at their hip. Ophelia pressed herself flat against the wall, arms raised, ready to fight. She'd often felt like prey, but now she really was.

Beyond the door, she heard shuffling. It creaked open, and something whizzed past her face. The Ulvemordere dropped to the ground, twitching and gurgling. A rather sharp fork had found their throat. Ophelia grimaced as Seamus peeked his head out, another fork at the ready. He used his foot to open the door, beckoning her in with a nod of his head.

"They've got us surrounded," Seamus whispered, shutting the door softly behind her. "I was coming to get you but heard footsteps in the hall."

"I heard a clicking or a jingling," Ophelia said, looking out the window. In the campfire light below stood a single-file line of soldiers.

"There's a bomb in the hall," Seamus mumbled.

"A *what?*" she hissed.

He shushed her. "After the footsteps, there was the

clicking of a timer. Most likely a smoke bomb. They know I'm here."

"How?"

"Any number of reasons, though my bet is on that guy at the general store. He looked at me like a lamb marked for the slaughter," Seamus mumbled, shaking his head.

A hissing sound came from the hall as thick purple smoke seeped in under the door.

"Wolfsbane," Seamus said, using his tunic to cover his nose.

Ophelia put her hand to the door, encasing it in ice, cutting off the airflow. Enough smoke had gotten in to coat the floor, but hopefully, it wouldn't affect Seamus too much. Wolfsbane was deadly to werewolves, though only in concentrated amounts. This was most likely meant to knock him out.

"Well," Seamus coughed. "Since that way's closed off, do you fancy a jump?"

Ophelia turned back to the window, grimacing. Just as she was about to protest, there was a crash from the hall. Glass had shattered somewhere. Ophelia seemed to have the same thought as Seamus; it'd come from her room.

"Window it is?" Ophelia asked.

Seamus frowned but nodded. "Still on speaking terms with that wind of yours?"

"Always."

He readjusted his pack, then nodded toward the window.

"Gentlemen first," Ophelia grimaced, taking a step back.

"Naturally," he said with a shrug. Grumbling to himself, he tossed his fork away, exchanging it for the axes at his hip. Steeling himself, he used them to point at their exit. "Help a guy out?"

Ophelia nodded, thrusting her hands toward the window as he ran forward. Seconds before he made impact, the window shattered, a sharp breeze sending the pieces flying and aiding Seamus in his jump. Ophelia rushed to follow, swirling her hands through the air, surrounding him in the breeze, slowing his fall.

The door behind her creaked, her ice shattering. Startled, she turned. A metal wolf skull was stuck between the boards. A scream escaped her. There was a thump, signifying Seamus tumbling to the ground and the roar of Ulvemordere soldiers advancing on him.

Spinning back around, Ophelia didn't hesitate to jump after him. A sharp breeze whirled around her, helping her land light on her feet. Before she had a chance to take in what was happening, she yelped, narrowly ducking as a soldier swung their broadsword. She rolled away, cutting her hand through the air, a knife-sharp crescent of ice colliding with her attacker. They stumbled back, hunched over, but were otherwise un-fazed. One of their friends came to their aid, ready to strike.

A well-aimed axe found their exposed neck. Ophelia covered her ears and looked away, turning to see Seamus was surrounded and down to one axe.

He grabbed hold of the closest Ulvemordere's helm, slamming them face-first into the ground.

Movement behind her made her stumble forward.

A glint of metal.

Searing pain.

The soldier with the broadsword had recovered. If Oph-elia hadn't moved in time, she'd have more than a thick gash on her arm.

The soldier swung their broadsword at the same time Ophelia stomped her foot, causing a column of ice to jut up beneath their feet. They went flying, arcing overhead, scream-ing in fright. There was a crunch as they landed somewhere behind her. Ophelia didn't stick around to see if they got up.

Eyes covered with a shaking hand, she felt around the body of the previously downed Ulvemordere, looking for Sea-mus's axe. Once she found the handle, she yanked it free and rushed to her wolf's aide. He was surrounded but held his own. Two soldiers were sprawled out on the ground, their helms ajar. Two men around Seamus's age had appeared from their tents and were fending off three other soldiers. Seamus stood panting in a circle of four more.

Ophelia pushed her hands forward, causing a great gust of wind to knock the soldiers off their feet. Seamus turned to look at her, spotted his axe, and held out his hand. She ran to him and handed off his weapon, grimacing as he wiped the blood off onto his thigh.

"You go right; I'll take the left," he said, growling as the soldiers got to their feet. "Headshots will do nicely."

"On it."

One of her targets was helping the other up. Ophelia took that moment to slash her hands through the air, sending twin lightning bolts toward the struggling soldiers. They shrieked, her lightning sparking across their armor, cooking them. The sizzling was horrifying. She tried not to think of it too much, else she would've spewed the contents of her dinner all over the battlefield.

Seamus was occupied with his own problems, so she turned to help the kind fellows near the tents. One had a log, the other only their fists. Ophelia doubted they were doing much against the soldiers. With an elegant flourish, she pointed to the sky. The soldiers slowed, their legs freezing, ice trailing up their bodies. As soon as the first one froze, the two men pushed it over. A blood-curdling crack echoed over the chaos.

Again, Ophelia tried not to think too much about the ramifications, instead turning back to Seamus.

One of the soldiers was down and dead. The other had him in a chokehold, his neck pinned under their leg. Seamus ripped off part of their armor and bit down hard. The Ulvemordere screamed, tightening their hold. Seamus had gone blue in the face. One hand was clawing at the Ulvemordere, trying to pry another piece of armor off; the other was reaching for one of his axes. It was too far away, and that soldier had too tight of a grip on him.

Ophelia thrust her hand forward, but nothing happened. She tried again, but there wasn't even a weak breeze.

Still nothing, even with a stomp of her foot.

Everything had gone eerily quiet. Not the battle, but the world. The elements.

Fatigue swept over her.

Seamus's eyes rolled back into his skull, his arms falling limp.

Frustrated and terrified, Ophelia screamed in anguish, thunder rumbling in the sky. Lightning cracked overhead as she rushed forward, skidding on the uneven ground. She placed her hand on the Ulvemordere's chest, imagining all the air being sucked from their lungs. They grabbed hold of her, their claw-like gauntlets ripping into her skin. Ophelia squeezed her eyes shut, holding her breath. The iron of their armor burned her hands, but she could feel her magic seeping into them through the cracks in their iron plates.

Their grip on her arm loosened.

Slowly, their arms dropped to their side.

Seamus sucked in as much air as he could, causing her to turn. He was gasping for air, pushing the soldier's legs away, looking downright murderous. He scrambled to his feet, struggling to breathe as he took his axe and—

Ophelia looked away, covering her ears and shutting her eyes. She sat like that for a minute, shaking, unwilling to look at her surroundings.

Something nudged her foot. She peeked, seeing Seamus swaying over her, bloodied axes hanging loosely in his hands.

"Time to go," he choked out, pointing his axe over his shoulder.

The Ulvemordere that had been stationed at the front had formed a semicircle around them. A line of kneeling soldiers with bows and crossbows took up the front. Behind them was a row with their arms raised, some sort of cylinders in their hands. Another row further back stood ready with their swords and daggers.

Standing before them was a short yet muscular figure cloaked in black armor and undergarments. One hand held a flickering torch, and the other gripped tight around a baton with a bejeweled tip.

Ophelia got to her feet, ignoring how Seamus kept swaying side to side. "Why aren't they attacking?"

Seamus was about to respond when the black-clad soldier pointed their baton at them.

Those posed to throw their cylinders threw them, the canisters colliding with the ground, sending up plumes of purple smoke. Arrows ripped through the air, narrowly missing their targets.

Seamus roared, and Ophelia took that as a sign to run as fast as her legs would carry her.

She cut through the trees, arrows whizzing past her. Though her muscles ached, and her legs felt as if they'd give out at any second, she kept going. If the Ulvemordere wanted them dead, that was one thing. If they wanted to capture and torture them, that was another.

Ophelia had only just escaped one captor. She wasn't keen on letting another take her.

Something caught her ankle, and she tripped, falling flat on her face.

She tried to stand, her ankle screaming in protest. It wasn't broken, at least she didn't think it was, but it very well might've been sprained. She struggled to a standing position nonetheless, hunched over, hands on her knees.

A twig snapped behind her.

A sharp icicle formed in her hand as she spun, placing her frozen weapon against—

"Seamus!" she said, surprised and relieved.

Her icicle illuminated him. He stood wide-eyed, hands up in defense, leaning away from the icy dagger at his throat. He was breathing hard, sweaty and pale, blood trickling down his face from his hairline. They stood like that for a moment, assessing each other's wounds, listening to the woods, waiting for the next wave of attacks.

Ophelia's icicle shattered in her hand, the pieces crumbling into snowflakes as they fell. Their only source of light vanished. She hadn't meant to dispel the icicle, but Seamus didn't need to know that. He swallowed hard, head dipped, hands slowly lowering to his hips. Ophelia took a step back, staring at her hands.

"You're bleeding," they said in unison.

"I'll heal," Seamus said, his voice strained. "You'll need bandages."

"I'm okay," Ophelia said distractedly.

Something was wrong with her magic. Twice now, it hadn't done as it was told.

There was that exhaustion again.

Seamus dropped to his knees, looking over his shoulder, that murderous rage still lingering in his eyes. Ophelia hugged herself tight, trying to force herself to calm down and breathe.

"What's wrong with your foot?" Seamus asked.

She looked down, not realizing she was favoring her right, her left knee bent slightly. "It's nothing, I'll be okay."

Seamus gave her a knowing look. "Can you run on it?"

"It's not broken."

"That's not what I asked," he said, lips set in a deep frown.

As gently as possible, she put pressure on her ankle. White hot pain erupted up her leg. She bit back a sob, putting on a brave face. She wouldn't be the weak link. She wouldn't be the one who got left behind.

Seamus grappled to his feet, dusting himself off. He reached for her arm but paused, his hand hovering in midair momentarily. She looked down, grimacing at the silver blood dripping down her sleeve.

"That looks deep," Seamus said, dropping his hand. "You're bleeding a lot."

"I'm okay, I promise," Ophelia said, standing tall.

"Kid," Seamus scoffed, shaking his head in disdain.

"I swear I am!"

"Tell that to the tears flowing down your face." He gave her a sympathetic look as he wiped blood out of his eyes. "C'mon, let's get you somewhere we can patch you up."

CHAPTER TWENTY-NINE

HEART TO COLD, COLD, HEART

Seamus led Ophelia through the trees in a zig-zagging pattern. Whether this was because he was trying to lose their tail or if he was unsure of where to go, she didn't know. She could, however, tell he was irritated with their slow pace. He walked a few feet ahead but kept backtracking to ensure she hadn't fallen too far behind. Meanwhile, Ophelia was hobbling along, nursing a foot that was swelling in her boot.

Seamus said he could see perfectly well in the all-consuming darkness, but she couldn't. She kept tripping and almost banged her head on a branch several times.

To add insult to injury—literally—it'd begun raining.

Seamus was taking this the worst. He seemed to think the world was out to get them. They were inconvenienced, yes, but Ophelia knew the rain had come to protect them. It washed away their scent, hiding them from their pursuers.

The Ulvemorderc and the werewolves they hunted were similar in that way. They both had some of a wolf's enhanced abilities. How they used those gifts, however, differed greatly.

Seamus had stopped up ahead. Ophelia limped over to him. Together, they stood overlooking a steep slope, peering through the dark and the rain toward something in the distance.

"There's a rock over there that'd provide enough shelter," Seamus said. His glowing green eyes swept over her. "Do you need help getting down?"

"I'm good," Ophelia said, her voice small.

Seamus carefully stepped onto the slippery surface of

the slope, gliding down the rest of the way. Ophelia sat, sliding after him. She could tell Seamus wanted to help her off the ground, but he stayed a respectful distance away. She labored to her feet, giving him a solemn nod.

The rock he'd mentioned was a thin slab of stone sticking out at a strange angle from the slope. With the last of their energy, they hurried beneath it, finding there was just enough room for them to sit shoulder to shoulder.

Seamus insisted she sit against the slope, content with having his back to the rain. Ophelia stiffened as she removed her mask, the cut on her arm stinging. They shrugged off their packs, creating a barrier on either side. Seamus finally tore his eyes away from her, rustling through his pack, digging into one of the pockets for the first aid supplies Lochlan had given them. They didn't have much, but it would do.

Ophelia untied her shawl, frowning at the unraveling stitches. Ute wouldn't be pleased. Biting back tears, she peeled off her jacket. Witch blood was an array of different colors, but it usually matched a Witch's eyes. Hers was silver. The longer she bled, however, it would eventually turn red. Red was bad. Very, very bad.

Trails of pinkish-red streams mixed with her silver blood. She'd lost a fair bit. Ophelia hadn't realized one could lose so much blood from such a weird wound.

Wincing, she rolled up her sleeve, taking the astringent-soaked cloth Seamus was offering her. She dabbed gently at the cut, biting her lip against the stinging. Seamus was right; it was deep. The more she dabbed at it, the more it bled. Unsure of what else to do, she grabbed a fresh cloth, wiping at the wound until it was mostly clean.

Seamus watched her through his eyebrows as he tended to the cut on his forehead. It was strange, his need to help her. It didn't make her feel helpless, and she was sure he didn't see her that way, either. It also didn't feel like his need to help came from a manipulative place. He didn't expect anything in return, nor would he hold it over her head. It was genuine. He just didn't want to see her hurt or struggling. Yet, he respected the boundaries she'd set, only breaking them in life-or-death situations or moments of panic.

That meant a lot to her.

It also meant a lot knowing he'd picked up on how she

flinched or winced without her explaining it. Yes, she'd set a rule, but he'd noticed not long after they met.

One day, she'd tell him why she hated when people touched her against her will. One day, he'd understand. But for now, she picked up a bandage roll and held it out to him.

"I'm low on hands," she said, shaking it in front of his eyes.

She trusted him. She hoped he knew that.

Seamus gave a half laugh and took the bandage roll, leaning forward. "Tell me if it's too tight."

She lifted her arm, holding up the edge of her sleeve so it wouldn't interfere. Seamus gently wrapped the bandage around the wound, taking great care not actually to touch her skin with his fingers. His fingers twitched slightly. Could he feel the cold resonating off her?

"How's your ankle?" he asked, his voice hushed.

"Throbbing," she said, watching in awe as he tied the bandage in a neat little bow.

"Swear to me it's not broken?"

She shrugged, reaching down to untie her laces. It took a great deal of effort to get that stubborn boot off her swollen foot, but she got it eventually. She peeled off her sock, wriggling her toes, slowly circling her foot.

"Hurts when I move it down," she said through gritted teeth. "And when I put pressure on it, obviously."

Seamus frowned. "What do you want to do?"

"Give it the night?" she shrugged.

"All right," he grumbled. He took a pelt from Ophelia's pack and rolled it into a tight ball, nudging her leg gently with it. Lifting her foot, she let it rest on the rolled-up pelt. "That'll do ya for now."

"Thank you, Seamus," she whispered.

He tipped his head toward her, pouring more astringent on a cloth. Frowning, he dabbed at his knuckles. The skin was torn up so badly you could almost see the bone. There was no trace of pain in his eyes, just annoyance.

"How long will it take you to heal?" she asked.

"Knuckles will take longer since I use my hands so much, but my head should be right as rain by sunrise. Bruises linger, though. I'm sure my neck will be sore for a while," he explained. "Thanks for the save, by the by. That'll be another tally under your name, huh?"

Ophelia nodded. "You're welcome. I'm sorry it took me so long. I'm not sure what happened." It was scary to admit that, but she felt guilty. He could've died, his windpipes crushed by that soldier, and it would've been her fault.

Seamus was quiet for a moment, his shoulders sagging as he put away their supplies. "Are you doing okay? Mentally? Supernaturally? I can take a guess about physically."

Ophelia pulled her other leg up to her chest, hugging it tight, resting her chin atop her knee. "Could be worse," she said.

"I noticed you struggling with your magic," he mumbled, avoiding her gaze. Rain battered his back, but he didn't grumble or flinch. Even the annoyance was gone now that he'd wrapped his hands. "That normal?"

He swung his legs around so he faced the same way she was, shimming back against the slope. He shifted a few inches away, trying to keep a space between them despite the small outcropping. His elbow hung out from under their rock. In seconds, it was soaked.

"I don't know what caused it," she said, leaning back against the slope, staring at her hands.

"We'll keep an eye on it. You mentioned it felt wrong using your abilities to fight, so we'll figure something else out," he said, his voice hopeful yet resigned.

Ophelia turned to look at him, studying the faint wrinkles around his eyes and beard beginning to grow along his jaw. Tonight seemed to have aged him. He sounded as though he could fall asleep at any moment.

"Are *you* okay, Seamus?" she asked.

He turned to study her as well. "I'm okay, kid. Worry about yourself, all right?"

"We're a team now, y'know," Ophelia scoffed. "The worry goes both ways."

Seamus looked away, crossing his arms tight across his chest. His hazel eyes were dark with something Ophelia couldn't pin. He was suddenly a thousand miles away, lost in a memory or thought she couldn't access.

There was a sudden awkwardness so palpable it made her skin crawl. She cleared her throat, observing their surroundings.

"I left the Ulvemordere thirteen years ago," Seamus began, "I was sent on a mission to kill a rabid werewolf, but I couldn't do it. She had a baby in a basket strapped to her back. She was frail, beaten down, barely hanging on to life.

I was born into it. I'd never seen the outside world from another's perspective, but in that moment, I did. How many parents had I killed? How many children? How many families had I fractured? It was dizzying. I'd been questioning things for a while, but not like that. I saw that woman, dressed in bloodied clothes—she told me later she'd given birth alone several days before—and felt *sympathy*."

Seamus shifted uncomfortably, not meeting her eyes. "I dropped my weapons, removed my helm, and tore their insignia from my shoulder. That was that. I was done. I'd been told I was on the right side of things my whole life, raised as a child king, working toward taking my place upon a gnarled and thorny throne. In that moment, it all seemed finite. I wasn't going to kill that woman, and I'd walk barefoot through glass before I even touched that baby." He shrugged it off as if it were nothing, but it wasn't 'nothing.' This was his life's story, and it meant the world to her, knowing he trusted her enough to share it. "So we ran. She was a young thing, scarcely older than you, maybe—wait a second, how old *are* you?"

"Eighteen," Ophelia said.

That shocked him just a little, but not enough to stop his story. "Anyway, I helped her track down her pack. That baby was sick, you see. So was she. Eventually, I was too. They'd come down with some sort of fever. The three of us were knocking on Death's doorstep by the time we found her family.

She and the baby healed up quick, but I wasn't going to make it. The alpha of that pack came to me and gave me an ultimatum. I could take the bite, see if it took, or I could call it quits, and they'd end my suffering. I chose the latter. He bit me anyway, that damned fool."

He smiled at that, looking out into the rain as if he saw the alpha's face in the sleet.

"As you can very well see, the bite didn't kill me. I was reborn as a very angry, very untrusting wolf who, if I'm being honest, just wanted to die." He turned to her, that smile of his widening. "But that old fool wouldn't let me. I was a crippled cattle dog to him, and he'd do everything in his power to breathe life back into me. It took a while, but eventually, I was no longer an Ulvemordere soldier. I was a wolf through and through."

"I sense a 'but' coming up," Ophelia said, straightening her knee, both entranced by his story yet ready to fall asleep. Listening to him talk soothed her, in a way.

"Pack life was good and all," he said, shrugging. "But I tasted bile every time I looked around. All I could think of was the other packs, the ones I'd slaughtered alongside my comrades. So me, that stupid old dog, and his bright-eyed daughter devised a plan."

He went quiet for a moment, leaning back against the sodden earth, staring up at the stone slab over their heads as if words were scrawled upon it.

"I'd only been gone four years. That didn't mean a thing to the Ulvemordere. They figured I'd been held captive, seeing as I'd made some pretty powerful enemies in my time. They took me in, drinking up my lies, seeing me as—" he rolled his eyes, grimacing "—as a deity. Their king had returned! Little did they know I'd come doused in the blood of a dead Ulvemordere, one I'd killed with my own hands the night before.

My wolf was out for blood, and blood is what it got. I'd infiltrated a base in Høstlunden, and I gave them all the same ultimatum my alpha gave me. They could take the bite, see if it stuck, or die. Most of them were too prideful, but a few took the bite. Two made it, and the rest died. The risk is higher when you've stolen a pelt, but a handful of them had decided it was worth it. The remaining? Well, let's just say I made a name for myself that day."

Ophelia pondered that and the silence that followed. It took a lot to change one's mind, and it was harder still to keep yourself on track once you've made a life-altering decision. Yet Seamus had, and here he was, still fighting the Ulvemordere to this day.

"Where is your pack now?" she asked. "I'd like to meet them. Is that where we're heading? You said Tiril and Helgi were werewolves."

Seamus turned to her, smiling sadly. "You know, I really

think they'd have liked you, Ophelia, especially my wife, Ingrid. You remind me of her in a lot of ways. She was that bright-eyed daughter of the alpha I mentioned. Boy, can you imagine the look on his face when I said I wanted to marry her? At first I thought he'd slit my throat, but he put his hands on my shoulder and said, 'I thought you'd never ask.'"

"Wh—What happened to them?" She regretted the question as soon as it left her lips, but it was something she felt she had to know. This was why he was telling her such a long story, wasn't it?

"I did, kid." He turned away, rubbing his eyes. "I skipped over some important information, but we'd made some friends who hated the Ulve just as much as we did. You might have heard, I'm not sure what kind of news you get, but we were about to wage war on the Ulvemordere. This was six years ago.

We never stayed in one place for long; we covered our tracks and kept our heads down, but it wasn't enough. The Ulvemordere caught up to us—they caught up to several packs and caravans—and did what I'd done. They slaughtered us. They came on a new moon when our powers were weak."

He scratched the back of his neck, then picked at his ragged fingernails. Ophelia wanted desperately to find some way to comfort him.

"They left me alive but killed everyone else. I was drugged, tattooed with the mark of a traitor, then locked away to rot."

"But you got out," Ophelia said, unsure what else to say.

"I did," he replied, his voice barely audible. His words were steeped in salty tears. If he'd been crying, she couldn't tell. The rain had always been good at hiding one's sadness. "Once the drugs wore off, I was so overcome with grief that I lost complete control. To this day, I still don't know the whole story. I've got bits and pieces, but I try not to dwell on them. It's not that I don't remember; it's that I don't want to. I've done my best to block it all out. I can't, however, forget waking up half-naked in the woods, drenched in blood, though. My wolf was never the same after that. We fight constantly. He hates me, and I've begun to loathe him for being so disobedient. If anyone understands your power struggle, it's me."

"So you're not just a traitor. You're a freedom fighter?" Ophelia asked. He nodded.

"All that is to say, kid," he began, clearing his throat, "destruction seems to follow me. I've got a handful of other stories that'll make your head spin, but I'm too tired for that. You can follow me if you like, but chances are it won't end well. Tø was just a taste."

Ophelia had suspected that ages ago. His story hadn't changed a thing for her. Even when Lochlan let slip he'd been a defector, she hadn't looked at him any differently. Call it divine intervention, but she trusted Seamus Norland. Today proved she was right for doing so.

"I don't want this burden to fall on your shoulders," he said finally, his eyes falling on her swollen ankle. "I will do my best to get you somewhere safe; I promise you that. Just don't expect any miracles."

What he forgot to acknowledge was that she, herself, was a miracle.

"Get some rest, kid. We've got a long day ahead of us," Seamus mumbled, shutting his eyes.

CHAPTER THIRTY

SELF-DEFENSE

phelia had fallen asleep long before him. Seamus had taken comfort in the soft sound of her breathing. Having someone with him, no matter the circumstances, was comforting. This was a very selfish thought, and he knew it. Regrettably, he'd felt the same crashing at her cottage.

All his life, Seamus had been surrounded by people. This draught of loneliness had only come about when his pack died. Six years he'd been alone. Before that, he'd always had someone to look out for him.

The Ulvemordere had lumped him into a squad the second he was born. Alongside nine other promising soldiers, he ate, slept, sparred, and grew. Those idiots might as well have been his siblings. Leaving them, betraying them, that had been his one regret. Despite his age, he'd always risen quickly through the ranks. Seamus had surpassed them, was promoted to sergeant, and then eventually to lieutenant colonel. It'd been his duty to lead them and their battalion to victory, and he'd made good on that hundreds of times. To grow up with these people, then to turn on them at the drop of a hat. . . No wonder his people hated him so. Joining the enemy was suicide. Even sympathizing with the enemy was punishable by torture. Sometimes death in extreme cases.

Yet Seamus hadn't feared his squad's wrath, for there wasn't a fleeting second he wasn't alone. He'd traded one family for another. Yes, he'd been bitter at the time, wishing his newfound alpha hadn't turned him. But as quick as the transformation had happened, his heart changed too. Their pack was small, but it was tight-knit. They, too, ate, slept, sparred, and grew together. They laughed and cried together. Fought an unmovable force together. Lifelong bonds were formed while fighting side by side, the kind of bonds not easily broken.

In the end, how had he repaid them? With death.

His hands may not have struck them, but he was still to blame. His past had caught up to him, and the nine soldiers he'd called family killed the werewolves he'd grown to love.

And then, of course, there was Egill. That fickle fairy may very well be his brother, given all they'd gone through together. The pin-wing was a fool for trusting him back then and an even bigger one for seeking him now. Seamus may not have ripped his wings from his back, but what had he done to stop the troll who took them? Nothing. Truth be told, Egill may still have his wings had Seamus kept his mouth shut.

So, yes, Ophelia's company was comforting, but he knew how this would end. One way or another, tragedy would strike. He had many betrayals to his name; why wouldn't there be another? Despite his best efforts, the people of Tø consumed every quiet moment and what Lochlan had said. Could he sit by and let Ophelia fall into the same pit of despair? But how could he rescue them? How could he drag her into a war her kind never should've fought to begin with?

These thoughts plagued him even in his dreams.

Nightmares were not new to him, but the subject matter of these were. Ophelia had snuck her way into his subconscious. He'd dreamt of their battle at the inn, but it had ended very differently. Both of them had died. Seamus had made his peace with death, but seeing Ophelia lifeless, even in his dreams? That was a reality he wasn't willing to accept nor bring to fruition.

The next morning, beneath the stone outcropping, he sat listening to the soft rustling of pages and a graphite stick sketching away above him. The sun had washed away the rain, so she must've thought this was the perfect time for drawing or reading. It was strange how tightly she clung to such hobbies, though Seamus couldn't exactly judge her. He'd picked up whittling as a child, and there hadn't been a time in his life when he wasn't carving something. Even the Ulvemordere had a thing for art, though they didn't exactly make the same kinds as the townsfolk. He shivered, thinking of all the gruesome mediums his kind had used.

Stowing these thoughts for a later day, he crawled out from under the outcropping, peering up at the Witch. Her eyes darted down to him, but he had the strangest sensation she hadn't really seen him. Their maps were unfurled before her, a light breeze twitching their corners. Seamus stretched before crossing his arms on the edge of the outcropping where she sat. The map he'd bought from the general store was covered in marks and the ramblings of a busy mind.

A thought struck him. She was meant to be their way-finder, but even wayfinders needed some semblance of combat training.

"God morgen, Seamus," she said, lost in thought.

"And to you," he yawned. "What exactly are you doing?"

"I've been trying to plot a path to Dødbyen," she began, "one where we'll be hidden from prying eyes."

"Found anything?"

She set down her graphite stick, handing him his map. Seamus smiled to himself. The margins were covered in tiny drawings of rabbits and bear cubs. Was he mistaken, or was there a wolf hiding under her thumb, too? Besides Ophelia's drawings, several paths were crossed or scribbled out. Only one route was left clear—obviously drawn in by her.

"I've taken a moment to eliminate potential hazards," she said haughtily, suddenly an astute scholar. "The crossed-out paths lead toward towns the Ulvemordere will likely be searching, seeing as they're the most straightforward routes."

"What of this?" Seamus asked, pointing toward the path she'd added. The route jut off from the main road, and while it wound through The Wilds, it was a relatively straight shoot toward Dødbyen.

Ophelia only shrugged. "I'm not sure of this path's purpose, but it weaves around all the major towns in The Wilds. Given the history here, I assume it's an old smuggler's route. It's just far enough outside the towns so as not to be suspicious or alert folks to thundering hooves in the night," she explained, dragging her finger around the path. "What do you think?"

"Good work. How'd you come across it?"

She gestured toward her magical map, looking quite proud of herself. "I just held it and hoped we'd find a safe road away from prying eyes.”

Seamus's eyebrows went up in mild surprise. He took the map, thinking of Egill and how he'd love to get his hands on something like this. Then, of course, his mind wandered back to their conversation at the inn. He sighed, trying to steady his hands so as not to tear or crumple it inadvertently. He hoped Egill wasn't getting into any trouble. Should he have gone with him? Was there time to find him? Did he just lose his chance at revenge, of finding clues about the missing people of Tø?

Something deep down inside him told Seamus that letting Egill run off alone was a horrible idea. He should've asked where exactly he was going. . .

As soon as the thought formed, the map began to shift. It'd displayed a map of Snøbolig, complete with Ophelia's smuggler's route, but now, the path had moved.

Seamus frowned. “Why'd it do that?”

Ophelia stared thoughtfully into his eyes. “What were you thinking of?”

All he did was stare at the map, feeling the color drain from his face. Of course, he couldn't say, not really. It wasn't like he didn't *want* to tell her about Tø, about Egill. Still, it was as though he physically couldn't. The mere thought of telling her the truth made his stomach churn.

“Our looming journey,” he mumbled.

“Are you sure?” Ophelia asked, feigning innocence. Bless her attempt at phishing for information. “That's an incredibly specific path.”

It was. And Seamus knew exactly where it led. He'd always been good with navigation, but more than that, he was good at stumbling upon things he shouldn't. The Witch sitting before him was proof of that. The route the map had constructed led them out of The Wilds and through the more tamed part of Snøbolig. It wound around some ruins, then went off toward Dødbyen. It'd take so much longer to get there if they took this route, but. . . But what if the map was trying to tell them—or rather *him*—something? What if this was the better option?

Then it hit him. Why not use the map to find the people of Tø? Ignoring Ophelia's look of concern, he thought of Åsmund, of Saoirse—even Torbod and the Ulve. This map could find them; he knew it.

A long minute passed, but the map didn't change.

Ophelia cleared her throat. "Do you think this route would be better?" she asked, a gleeful light in her eyes. "You've traveled more; maybe the map can tell? Maybe I didn't phrase my question right. Plus, if mine is a smuggler's route, who's to say it isn't still in use? Yours may be safer."

Seamus's mind was telling him not to follow his path, but his heart was screaming at him to throw caution to the wind. Ultimately, his main goal should be getting Ophelia to safety. After that, he could follow the blasted map Stars-know-where.

But. . .

What if she kept the map?

What if something happened to it?

What if, what if, what if—

Maybe he'd got it backward. Maybe the logical part of him, the part of his mind that was still wired to think in battle tactics, was trying to tell him that following this path here and now was the only option. Maybe it was his heart pleading with him to stay with Ophelia.

"That route doesn't appear on yours," Ophelia said distractedly. Seamus hadn't realized he'd been staring at her for so long. "The smuggler's route does, marked as just a normal path, but yours doesn't. From what I can tell, it's not an actual path, more of a suggestion by the Wayfarer's Map itself." She took his map and placed it beside hers. There was a noticeable empty space on his crumpled map where that route should be. "If this path only appears on an enchanted map, why would the Ulvemordere look there?" she asked. Her words were steeped in magic and mystery.

Seamus looked back and forth between the maps, weighing their options. "It's a good bet. . . But why?" He hadn't meant to say that last part aloud.

Ophelia shrugged. "It could've led somewhere that no longer exists? An old town, maybe? See those ruins there? Something must have happened to exclude it from your mass-produced one."

The ruins were definitely of note; she was on to something there. Parts of the world hidden by enchantment weren't unheard of. He'd once seen—no, he'd once *plundered*—a village disguised by veils of glimmering fog in Vårretten.

"Why does the path appear out of nowhere? That's what I'd like to know. It starts right here, with us," Ophelia said, gesturing to their surroundings.

"It is weird, isn't it?" Seamus added.

"Sounds like you want to find out why."

He laughed drily. "Not out of curiosity; don't twist my words."

"Wouldn't dream of it!" she said, shaking her head solemnly.

Seamus folded up his map while she rolled up her own. After stowing them both away, she hopped off the outcropping, wincing ever so slightly.

"How's the ankle?" Seamus asked, glad to change the subject.

"Much better, but sore," she sighed.

Seamus narrowed his eyes. "It's going to be a long walk either way. You up to that?"

"I'll be alright, promise!" She surely had a pep in her step this morning.

Seamus wasn't convinced, but he knew arguing would get him nowhere. Instead, they ate a quick breakfast, and he voiced a portion of the thoughts swirling around his mind.

"So, I've been thinking," he began, studying her as he spoke, "we need to do something about your lack of combat training."

She furrowed her bushy brows, a pout on her lips. "What do you mean?"

He took one of his axes from its place at his hip and held it out for her. Though he nudged her arm with it, she didn't move to take it.

"In case I drop one of these, or if I die and you can't access your powers—don't give me that look—I want you to be prepared," he said. She frowned deeply, looking at the tops of her shoes.

Seamus cleared the ground of debris that may trip them up. Such luxury would scarcely be available in a real battle, but he was trying to teach, not scar her for life. At least not today.

They stood side by side, a safe distance apart, each wielding an axe.

"I've always liked axes," Seamus said, watching her out of the corner of his eye. "The same movement you use to chop wood can be used to take off a head or a leg."

Ophelia's lips curled in disgust.

"The blade will do damage no matter how you swing it, but you want to build momentum. Don't try to be cool. You don't fight for kudos; you fight to kill and defend." As he spoke, she shifted uneasily at his side. "Follow my movements."

Together, they swung their axes over their shoulders, then slashed them through the air. Seamus instructed Ophelia to do this a few more times, allowing her time to get used to the axe's weight and how it moved in her hand. They switched sides, then started alternating the movement, making a deadly 'x' in the air.

"Strike up or down, same effect," Seamus said through gritted teeth as he swung his axe down hard.

These movements were repetitive and self-explanatory but necessary. Those who practiced flashy cuts and feints on dummies fought sloppily in actual battle. They'd spent so much time focusing on the new and shiny moves that they forgot all the basics. It was arrogant the way they fought. Embarrassing, the way they fell. While he knew Ophelia didn't have an arrogant bone in her body, he wouldn't allow her to suffer the same fate.

"Now, swinging an axe is good and all, but notice how the momentum causes you to expose your shoulder or chest? That leaves you vulnerable. How are you going to remedy that?" Seamus asked, taking a breather, resting the handle of his axe on his shoulder.

". . . wear armor?" Ophelia asked.

Seamus raised his eyebrow, not sure how he should respond to that. "That's a thought, but what if you don't have access to armor? How do you protect yourself with a weapon only?"

"You parry?"

Pride swelled in Seamus's chest. "Exactly!"

Ophelia reddened. "Read it in a book."

"All right, now watch carefully," he said.

He sliced his axe through the air, same as before, but this time, he quickly switched hands, grabbing it in the middle and immediately slashing back up. Had an enemy been before him, they wouldn't have had time to react. Ophelia tried a few times to copy him, fumbling with the axe, nearly dropping it on her toe the first few times. He grimaced, offering little help. An adjustment of grip here, correcting her footing there. Mostly, he wanted her to figure it out on her own.

Flashes of memories in Seamus's mind made his skin crawl. All he could think of was all the recruits he'd trained. The roar of a hundred voices screaming in unison and the rhythmic pounding of armored boots echoed in his ears. He could almost smell the sweat and blood mixing with the scent of freshly oiled weaponry.

For a second, the trees around him faded into the tall walls of the Ulvemordere compound. The outcropping they'd slept under transformed into a forge. Sparks ignited in his eyes, threatening to burn everything to the ground.

Shaking away these memories, Seamus took a step back.

Ophelia paused just before she made the move without a mistake. "What's wrong?"

He looked back and forth between her eyes. They were too silver maelstroms swirling with worry. "Just observing," he lied.

With a dissatisfied expression, she went back to practicing.

Swing the axe.

Grab the middle with your offhand.

Slash it back at your enemy.

Over and over and over again, he made her run this drill. They should be off by now, but Seamus didn't want a repeat of last night. That had been a narrow escape, and he knew it. One second more, and his windpipes would've been crushed. He would've died, and if Ophelia hadn't regained control of her powers, she would've too. Or worse, the Ulvemordere would've drug her back to their compound and—

He shivered, not wanting to think of what they may do to her.

Anxiety was building inside him like a geyser ready to

burst. "All right, that's enough axe practice for today," he said, his voice gruff.

Ophelia didn't hesitate to hand back over his weapon. He had a feeling she hadn't liked this little lesson. When he'd been her age, he hadn't either. He'd almost been one of those arrogant recruits who got themselves killed over stupidity.

"Are you sure you're okay, Seamus? You seem—"

"Completely fine." He gave her his best nonchalant smile, even adding a wink.

"Want me to start packing up, then?" she asked. Her eyes looked longingly at the outcropping their belongings lay beneath.

Seamus shook his head. "We're going to work on hand-to-hand combat for a minute first."

The way life seemed to drain out of her at that almost made him laugh.

Stowing his axes, he stood before her, fists up. He lightly punched the air a few times, noting how she stepped back with every movement.

"Hit me," he said, rocking back and forth, wiggling his eyebrows, daring her.

She clasped her hands daintily behind her, shaking her head. "I don't want to hurt you," she said softly.

"Kid, you *can't* hurt me."

"But you said bruises linger," she said, hands on her hips.

He shrugged. "I'll muddle through."

"Seamus," she groaned, looking to the sky.

"Listen, would you rather lack the necessary skills to defend yourself and end up dead?" he asked. She scowled deeply. "That's what I thought, now hit—"

Now, Seamus was not a stupid man. However, even geniuses can be tricked, fooled, or taken by surprise. There was no shame in underestimating a situation.

This was what he had to remind himself of when the following ensued.

As soon as the words left his mouth, Ophelia's fist collided with the side of his face, and something scrapped and clicked in his jaw. Seamus stumbled back, losing his footing and falling flat on his back in surprise. Suddenly, he was staring up at the sky, wondering what on earth had just happened. Stabbing pain erupted across his jaw as he tried to open and close his mouth.

"Blessed Amaranth!" Ophelia gasped. "I'm so sorry!" She clamped her hands over her mouth in shock.

Seamus could feel his jaw was hanging loosely to the side. He touched it lightly, wincing. That was going to leave a mark. Shutting his eyes against the pain, he popped his dislocated jaw back into place, ignoring Ophelia's gasp of disgust and fright.

"I'm so sorry! I didn't mean to! It was an accident!" she screeched.

All he did was lift his head to smile lopsidedly at her. "See, that's what I'm talking about."

"What?"

He struggled to his feet, moving his jaw around as he did so to make sure it was moving properly. "If that was you holding back, I'd hate to be on the receiving end of a real punch," he chuckled.

"Are you okay?" There were tears in her voice.

"Kid, I've had worse than a dislocated jaw," he said, gesturing to his ear, which unfortunately couldn't heal like the rest of him. Cuts, bruises, broken ankles? No problem. Missing limbs, eyes, or chopped ears? Apparently, that's where a werewolf's magical healing abilities stopped.

"I know—"

Seamus leaned close, smiling brightly. "I'm proud of you more than I'm in pain."

Ophelia stood clutching her fist to her chest, tears welling in her eyes. Her face was red, her Witch Marks purple. Seamus's smile slowly faded. Had he pushed her too far? He was trying to go easy on her, but had he slipped back into his drill sergeant role without realizing it? Or was she more sensitive than he'd originally surmised?

"I'm okay," he said softly. "I'm not mad at you, either."

"Can we pack up and go now?" she asked softly, not meeting his eyes.

". . . sure, kid."

3. The Great Big World

CHAPTER THIRTY-ONE

HOLD ALL QUESTIONS UNTIL THE END, PLEASE

After a few short moments of indecision, they'd chosen Seamus's route. If the Ulvemordere were still looking for them in The Wilds, it'd be safer to leave. Crossing over the river, they followed the mystical path in winding spirals. Three restless nights, three dreary mornings. Neither of them had slept well, but Seamus was taking the brunt of it all. Ophelia knew he was trying his best to hide his weariness, but that seemed to prove difficult. He seemed dazed, walking aimlessly a few paces behind, stumbling down the path. Ophelia eyed him cautiously but never brought it up.

Now, Seamus's stomach growled. So did Ophelia's. They'd skipped a few meals as of late, not wanting to risk another run-in. Until they crossed the border and ventured into Greater Snøbolig, Ophelia doubted they'd have a good meal anytime soon.

This only contributed to Seamus's fatigue. But why? What was wrong with him? Had the wolfsbane really affected him that badly? Or was he hiding an injury? Was it something else entirely? Ophelia frowned to herself, glancing over her shoulder at him. Seamus had taken the map, trying to calculate how much of a gamble each approaching town was. Whether they wanted to or not, they'd need to take another detour. Either from hunger or irritation, eventually, he decided any town was a safe town for the afternoon. Ophelia didn't care where they ended up so long as he had time to rest.

The town they arrived at was so similar to Gulch that Ophelia almost thought they'd made an enormous circle and ended up back where they started. However, upon further inspection, this town was much more run down. The banners were faded and frayed. In some places, the cobblestone was cracked or outright missing giant chunks. Nearby, a horse nearly tripped, its hoof stuck in one of the holes. Its rider swore, sliding off their saddle to help. Windows were caked with dirt and blanketed in snow.

The visage of Gulch disappeared, and Ophelia was suddenly standing in Tø's town square, stomach bubbling with nausea. She could try to convince herself she was just hungry, but that'd be a lie.

"Lunch first, then we stock up," Seamus said, looking longingly at a tavern in the distance. There was a sleepiness in his eyes Ophelia didn't like. Not one bit.

Still, all she said was, "Agreed."

Together, they stumbled through the sleepy town, keeping a watchful eye for wanted posters. So far, so good, but Ophelia didn't want to get her hopes up just yet. After that mess at the inn, they'd find posters soon enough.

Inside, the tiny tavern was nearly packed to bursting. It seemed this was the place to be this afternoon. Women sat perched on the knees of men who stared longingly at them. The look in their eyes reminded Ophelia of how Seamus gazed at a nice, juicy steak. Children crowded together in little armchairs. People of all ages sat on the floor. The tavern turned its collective head toward the center of the room. A few tables farthest away from the center of the room lay empty. Ophelia imagined these had the worst view. Unfortunately, Seamus would want to sit there.

"Hang back, I'll order," Seamus said with a yawn. He patted the sagging coin purse at his hip. Money was definitely going to be a problem sooner or later.

Quietly worrying as always, Ophelia wove through the tables—some seemed to have been pushed toward the back wall to make more room—settling on a small round one near a support beam. Stretching, she dropped her bags to the floor. Try as she might, she couldn't see the center of the room. What had everyone so excited? If she'd had Seamus's ears, maybe she could've picked out an individual voice from the crowd. Everyone was talking over each other, their voices blending together.

After the last week, this busy tavern was a welcome

sight. From the chattering people to the flickering candelabras, it all gave Ophelia a sense of peace.

Seamus found her a short while later, precariously balancing several plates and two mugs, all the while trying not to bump into anyone or anything. The sight was quite comical. Ophelia smiled to herself, receiving a glare from Seamus in return.

"What'd you find?" she asked.

"A little bit of everything," he said with a shrug as she took her steaming plate and mug. "Apparently, there will be live music. Some big-time band from Høstlunden is visiting."

Ophelia's eyes widened in surprise beneath her mask. "How interesting! Why did they pick this of all towns to perform at? It's so. . . *unique*. For lack of a better word."

Seamus shrugged. "I bet someone will talk your ear off if you ask."

Ophelia gave a slight nod, taking a sip of her cider. The boiling liquid burnt her tongue, warming her from the inside out. Suddenly, one by one, the tall candelabras dotting the tavern were snuffed out by a young woman dressed in gold. The drone of voices bouncing off the tavern walls lowered. Soft, melancholy music began to play. Ophelia swayed along to the melody, picking up her fork, wasting no time digging into lunch.

"Was only four pieces a plate, too," Seamus said through a mouthful of food, using his fork to point at her.

A sorrowful voice drifted through the tavern, calming the crowd with its wistful notes. Every patron fell silent. Seamus bobbed his head to the tune, sipping his cider.

Ophelia paused mid-bite, realizing she knew these lyrics.

Except they weren't lyrics. At least, that's not what they were *meant* to be.

It was a poem.

Nightshade for death and Begonias beware,

Anemones mean enemies, or so I've been told,

Geraniums give way to the thoughts in your head,

And Hemlock will kill ya long before you are dead,

The air chilled. Seamus sputtered as he drank his cider, his lips frozen to the cup. Through the open tavern door, a whistling wind swept over the patrons until it found them.

"Hush," Ophelia whispered.

A bouquet on your doorstep, tied with a bow,
He smiles to himself as he walks all alone,
'What a shame,' they'll say, 'Taken too soon,
By the love of another and the light of the moon,'

Ophelia stood, discarding her meal and leaving Seamus, fighting his mug for freedom of his lips. She could feel her heart beating rapidly in her chest, pounding against her ribcage in fear and rage. Ignoring scowls and scoffs, she pushed her way through the crowd. The breeze snaked through the room, threatening to extinguish the candles.

That sorrowful voice continued singing a song that had never belonged to it.

And ohhh, ohhh, no,
They should have warned you sooner,
And ohhh, ohhh, no,
Before they stood over your grave,

Oh, I know he gave you flowers,
But they don't mean what you think,
Yes, I know he gave you flowers,
But he did the same for me,

On a stage far too small for the grandiose being, he stood a young man—not much older than Ophelia—dressed in a sheer yellow tunic embroidered with golden daffodils. He had cream ruffs on both wrists and around his neck, which matched the sash on his waist. On his feet were pointed shoes like that of a fool. His enormous yellow breeches were tucked into dark brown tights, causing them to balloon out, adding to his court-jester appearance. His hair was a strange, gray-ish-blonde, and his skin was rich, ruddy brown.

Despite all this, the thing that stood out the most was the floral design on his face—yellow daffodils done in the style of rosemaling. The petals each had a dusting of glittery music notes.

The musician played a golden hurdy-gurdy as he tapped his foot, singing as loud as he could, his expression now solemn as he turned his face skyward. Behind him was a woman on the hammered dulcimer and an elderly man plucking away at a harp.

Ophelia's nostrils flared with anger.

He knew what he meant when he gave them away,
No Asters or Roses had he bought that day,
You took them with grace, inhaled real deep,
And now you lie in eternal sleep

And ohhh, ohhh, no,
They should have warned you sooner,
And ohhh, ohhh, no,
Before they stood over your grave,

And ohhh, ohhh, no,
They should have warned you sooner,
And ohhh, ohhh, no,
Before they stood over your grave,

And I know he gave you flowers,
But they don't mean what you think,
Yes, I know he gave you flowers,
But he did the same for me,
And now they stand over my grave. . .

The song ended with mournful notes plucked slowly on the harp. The singer bowed his head with a sorrowful smile as he took in the crowd's applause. He lifted his head, turning the wheel of his hurdy-gurdy, preparing for another song. But as fate would have it, his eyes landed on Ophelia.

The fear of Death herself lit up the singer's face. He stood frozen on the stage, staring her down. For a moment, she thought he might've run.

He cleared his throat, tucking a strand of ash-blond hair behind his ear. "I'm so sorry to cut this short, folks, but it seems there's a matter I need to attend to." He bowed, handed his instrument to the woman playing hammered dulcimer, stepped off the stage, then took Ophelia by the elbow and led her outside.

"How dare you," Ophelia spat.

"Hush!" he screeched.

Ophelia wriggled free from his grasp, hot, angry tears trailing down her cheeks. "That is not yours to use!" she said, shoving her finger into his chest.

All the bubbling emotions she'd been trying to keep at bay were about ready to explode.

The young man stood tall, twisting a stray strand of hair around his finger. "*She's* not going to use it," he shrugged.

Ophelia felt her mouth drop open. "You did not just say that to me."

"I only meant that—"

"Jonquil!" Ophelia snapped.

Jonquil, Terrestrial Spirit of Creativity, clamped his hand over her mouth. "Shh! Someone could hear you!" he said, golden eyes wide with fright.

Ophelia glared at him. While yes, he couldn't see *her* eyes behind the polar bear façade, it still made her feel better.

"If I remove my hand, will you behave?" he asked softly.

Her eyelids flickered in frustration, but she nodded. Ever so slowly, he let go of her, giving her his showman smile.

"Listen," he said, sighing heavily, "I'll be honest; I didn't think either of you would ever hear me play."

"And that makes using one of Saoirse's poems for your shows okay? Shows you're not even meant to play, I might add!" Panic was spreading in Ophelia's chest. Hearing Saoirse's poem, especially sung by Jonquil, felt as though her supposed death had been cemented.

Jonquil rocked side to side, mulling that over. "I think she'd like to hear her poems put to music. It's how I honor her memory."

"Then honor her memory in private!"

Ophelia's heart was pounding so hard she imagined it would explode if this kept up. Lightning was barreling through her nervous system, causing her muscles to tighten. She hadn't seen Saoirse's body, but she knew if she were still alive, they would've found each other by now. Saoirse always had a way of finding her.

Jonquil twisted to the side, gesturing to himself with a flourish. "Does anything about me tell you I do things without the need for attention? It's a beautiful song, Ophelia. I deserve to play it."

She rolled her eyes, shaking her head in disbelief. "You may have inspired her poems, but that doesn't mean you have the right to play them." She wiped at the tears seeping out from under her mask, wishing he could look into her eyes and see just how angry she was.

Jonquil took her by the shoulders, shaking her violently. "Do you know how *torturous* my curse is, Ophelia?" he asked, eyes crazed. "How *terrible* it is to fill others with such passion and zest, yet all the while being unable to create something I don't *loathe* with my *entire* being?" He leaned in close, peering into one of the eye holes of her mask. "Do you know how hard it is to stay relevant amongst mortal creatures? Soon, the people will realize I'm a fraud! A thief! Oh, Blessed Amaranth, how dirty am I! I'll be burned at the stake for stealing such sacred things! Please, please, *please*, dear Ophelia! Let me have this!"

"Jonquil, you're a Spirit. If they try to burn you at the stake, all you'll feel is dull warmth as your knickers turn to ash," Ophelia scoffed, shrugging him off.

"And then what? My secret will be revealed! They'll cage me up and force me to inspire them! Oh! The *horrors*!" He rested his head on her shoulder, sobbing uncontrollably. "They'll invent a genre of music so horrid folks will say their ears bleed upon listening! They'll—Garden, spare me—they'll invent *abstract art*!"

Ophelia rolled her eyes, trying and failing to push him away. "You do realize you could inspire them to paint with their own blood, thus causing them to bleed themselves dry while you escape, right?"

Jonquil stood, looking her dead in the eyes, all trace of terror and tears gone. "While that is a *slightly* worrying thought, you do have a point," he said thoughtfully.

"I usually do," she sighed, calling upon the breeze to dry his tears from her shoulder. It curled around her, whistling in her ears. Sometimes, it acted like a clingy kitten. The whistling often made her think of a cat's purrs. Now, all she could think of was an angry mountain lion about to pounce.

Jonquil smiled brightly, leaning down to her eye level. He was so very tall. If it weren't for his flowery appearance and penchant to cry at the drop of a hat, he'd be terrifying. They were quite similar in that way.

He straightened and fluffed his ruff, bowing deeply to her. "Why thank you, dear Ophelia. You've given me hope yet again! How splendid!"

"What are you even doing here?" Ophelia asked, exasperated.

Jonquil gave her a rather pointed look, frowning. "Uh. . . performing? Ever heard of such a thing?"

"Why *here*?"

"Oh. . . You meant it literally. . ."

Ophelia shook her head, thoroughly fed up. "When did you start tailing me?"

Jonquil went scarlet. "Not long after Fern and Spruce left. But—But—But—Before you get mad, I was hired, so I'm not *just* here for you. There's some sort of big party tomorrow, and I'm meant to play a few shows."

Ophelia frowned, tapping her foot impatiently on the ground. "You're unbearable!"

He turned away, bent backward, and smiled up at her. "I know! Isn't it fun?"

She wanted to say no, but instead, she asked, "How's the Garden?"

"In a tizzy as of late. Amaranth has confined herself to her greenhouse, Nightshade is swamped with work, and Salvia and Fern are butting heads again," he sighed, straightening and turning on his heels. "How's the mortal realm?"

"Frustrating."

"Still a woman of few words, I see?"

If only he knew. "So. . . You heard? About Tø, I mean," she asked, making nervous circles on the cobblestone with the tip of her boot. "Is. . . Is Saoirse really. . . ?"

He nodded, a mournful look on his face. "I'm so sorry to hear they've been captured."

"'Captured?'" Ophelia's heart stopped. "What do you mean 'captured?'"

Jonquil gave her a funny look. "Amaranth says the. . . I'm not entirely sure I'm meant to be telling you this."

"The Ulvemordere took prisoners?" Ophelia finished for him.

"If anyone asks, I didn't say a damn word, you hear me?"

"Your mom's going to kill you," Ophelia breathed. "Revealing the secrets of the universe *and* playing for mortals. Disgraceful, Jonquil, really."

He shivered, pulling his ruff up to hide his face. "Deary me. . . I'll be flambéed."

They stared at each other for quite a while, mulling this over. Why hadn't Fern told her? Of course, if there were a chance to save the people of Tø, she'd take it. That was her duty, wasn't it? The Spirits always talked of her destiny, of what she was meant to be. Maybe saving Tø wasn't part of that destiny. If that were the case, she'd rather change her path. Lochlan and Torbod might not deserve her kindness, but people like Saoirse, Åsmund, and his family did. She was their Vinterheks. Ophelia was honor-bound to protect them. She'd failed once. Never again.

"Ophelia, are you feeling all right?" Jonquil asked, his perfect little eyebrows furrowed deep over his golden eyes. The daffodil on his face shifted as though affected by the wind.

"Yes, I'm fine. Why do you ask?" Ophelia felt her heart skip a beat. This was all so dizzying. The world was blurring. A strong gust of wind could've knocked her over just then. Instead, it collected at her back, steadying her. The lightning coursing through her arms and legs kept pulsing, each bolt of anxiety accompanied by a shock of pain.

Jonquil considered her, slowly letting go of his ruff. "No

reason," he mumbled. His expression softened, and he smiled down at her, clearing his throat. "Well, I've got a show to get back to! And, just so you know—" he dropped his voice to a whisper "—I'm playing *a lot* of shows lately. I'll see you around, Snowdrop."

"Break a leg," Ophelia said with as much enthusiasm as she could manage.

Because she *wasn't* feeling all right. Her arms hung loose at her side, her legs trembled, barely holding her upright. Each heartbeat sent electric pain through her body. She looked down at her hands, glancing over her shoulder before removing her old woolen gloves, finding her fingers to be purplish-blue. Once Jonquil disappeared inside the inn, Ophelia rolled up her sleeves to see faint marks traveling up her arms resembling lightning bolts. The marks stung when she touched them, no matter how gently.

They were an accident, these marks. She hadn't meant to burn herself from the inside out, but she couldn't help it. She'd not been this anxious—or angry—in a while. Anxiety usually manifested as frost, but anger was always lightning. Sparks danced across her fingertips, leaving behind teeny tiny ice crystals. Her skin burned. Her heart fluttered.

"Ophelia," came Seamus's voice.

She yelped, gruffly pulling down her sleeve, hiding her burnt and frostbitten hands from him. The worry in the sound of her name was suffocating. She turned to him, praying the visible part of her face was the picture-perfect depiction of innocence and detached joy.

"Who was that? Do you know him?" he asked, his voice dark with worry.

"J—Zimri?" Ophelia asked, clearing her throat. Jonquil's mortal name tasted sour on her tongue. "Y—Yes. He's an old friend of mine."

Seamus didn't seem convinced, but he didn't press the subject. With a wary look around, he waved her back inside the inn. "Him? Really? Why are you—Whatever. . . Well, come finish your plate. There's an inn a short walk away. Got enough coin for the night, what do you think?"

"You sure that's a good idea?" Ophelia asked distractedly. She'd barely heard what he'd said.

His shoulders sagged. Dark circles marred his under

eyes. "I need a nap, kid."

"All right," she said softly, giving a slight bow before averting her gaze.

'Nap' correlated to 'map' in her mind. If Saoirse and Åsmund were alive, maybe the Wayfarer's Map could find them. She thought back to the strange look on Seamus's face when he'd held it. Had he tried to find them? Did he know the Ulvemordere had taken prisoners? Ophelia couldn't imagine how he'd learned such things, but he had encountered that Egill fellow. Maybe he'd said something? If he knew, why hadn't he told her? Was he trying to protect her? Half her town had died; the other half was supposedly imprisoned. Surely, he understood that meant a declaration of war on the Ulvemordere's part. Of course, he knew! He had to! But did he realize how badly she wanted to avenge those folk and save the ones left behind? He'd lost his pack. He had to be feeling the same way.

Why would he take away the same revenge from her that he seemed to lust for?

Why would Fern?

"Ophelia," Seamus said again, snapping to get her attention. She hadn't realized she'd just been standing there staring at him.

"Sorry, I'm coming," she mumbled.

All hopes of freedom and living the life she deserved fizzled out.

Again, Ophelia was trapped. This time, by purpose.

She didn't have to be, of course. She could turn a blind eye like the rest of the world. But was that what she wanted? She didn't know. All of this was far too much.

Beneath her skin, lightning continued to burn her muscles and boil her blood. She winced as she walked past Seamus, ignoring his concern.

Two paths lay before her. Both led toward things she'd always wanted, but which did she crave more? Which was the right decision? Couldn't someone pick for her? Blessed Amaranth, why didn't the Spirits just pick her up and place her where she was meant to be? Life would be so much easier that way.

CHAPTER THIRTY-TWO

TWO HORSES, A POLAR BEAR, AND A PEACOCK

The inn Seamus had found was just as packed as the tavern. What had this town in such high spirits, he didn't know, nor did he care. All he wanted was a warm bed and a few hours of peace.

"Are you feeling all right, Seamus?" Ophelia asked as they walked up to their rooms.

"No moon tonight," he sighed.

Ophelia's shoulders sagged. "Ahh, yes, I've read about that. Will you be okay?"

Seamus only shrugged, pointing to his room. "Ask me in the morning."

Seamus's wolf reacted to the moon the same way the tides did. He could feel its power ebb and flow depending on the phase, most notably during full and new moons. Full moons would have been exhilarating had they not filled him with such heartache over the years. But new moons? New moons had always been terrible. He was sluggish, lethargic, and other fancy synonyms that meant 'I feel like shit.' The effect always came out of nowhere, too. Even while aware of the coming celestial cycle, one minute, he'd be running wild with Ingrid; the next, he'd find himself curled up in a ball, his head split in two by a pounding headache.

Today was no different. He'd never admit it to Ophelia, but he practically fell asleep standing up. Yawning, Seamus unlocked the door to his room. From the doorway, Ophelia watched as he dropped his bag and examined the room. Not much to write home about, but it'd do. Crossing to the bed, Seamus picked up one of the pillows, aghast. He'd never felt something so. . . *lumpy. . .*

"Is it all right if I explore the town?" Ophelia asked.

"Why?" Seamus asked without looking at her. Instead, he shook that blasted pillow as hard as he could. This did little to resolve the mysterious lumps.

"Oh. . . I. . . just want to take a look around."

This time, Seamus did look at her. A raised bushy eyebrow accentuated his scowl. "Why?" he repeated.

Ophelia rocked back and forth on her heels, shrugging. "No reason."

Seamus gave her a bored look but nodded and waved her away. "Don't get into any trouble."

A dramatic gasp. "Me? Trouble? Why, Seamus, I'm a perfectly normal, law-abiding citizen!"

"So was I, kid. So was I," he sighed. Frowning, he beat his pillow against the wall. Finally satisfied with the state of it, he tossed it back on the bed and flopped down stomach-first.

Chewing her bottom lip, Ophelia lingered. "Are you sure you'll be okay, Seamus?"

A grumble of uncertainty.

"If you need anything, you'll come find me, right?"

A thumbs up.

"Okay. . . Well, enjoy your nap, Seamus. I promise to stay out of trouble."

Seamus buried his face in his pillow as the door closed behind her, sighing heavily. Mark his words: an hour from now, something horrific would happen.

Jonquil.

All Ophelia wanted was to find Jonquil. He and his troupe disappeared shortly after their enlightening little talk. Knowing him—and his mother—he had more to say and not a lot of time to do so.

Though she couldn't help but worry about Seamus, she

skipped down the hall, glad to know he at least confided in her. The innkeeper waved to her, smiling. She returned the gesture, a pep in her step. Even if she didn't find Jonquil, she'd still make the most of her time here. Aimlessly walking around Tø had been a favorite pastime. The town itself never changed, but the people did. It was amazing how varying moods affect environments.

The crisp air curled around Ophelia as she walked the streets, looking in through dusty windows at lives unaffected by the horrors that'd brought her here. The normality here was as comforting as it was unnerving, just like Gulch. Still, it was nice to be alone with her thoughts and—

"Well, your Mr. Norland seems delightful," came Jonquil as he fell in pace beside her.

"You're terrible at reading people, you know," Ophelia laughed.

"I was being facetious."

"Really? Hard to tell sometimes."

He just smiled, putting an arm around her shoulders, leading her down an alley, mischief in his eyes once again.

"Where are we going?" Ophelia asked, trying to wriggle away.

He squeezed her tighter, his smile growing sinister. "I have more things to tell you that I shouldn't."

"Uh oh. Do you know where Sao—"

"No, but I know something that will cheer you up."

Jonquil wiggled his eyebrows, silently leading her around the corner. In the shadows of a noisy shop, he pointed across the street to a stable.

"Two horses," he began, "one a quiet dappled gray, the other a domineering piebald. Both are fjord horses and show signs of abuse."

Ophelia's blood chilled instantly. "What happened to them?" she cried, suddenly feeling frenzied.

Jonquil only shrugged. "Gretchen—dulcimer player, possibly tone deaf, but we work around it—went to check on her appaloosa and said she'd heard them whimpering and the crack of a whip. She peeked and saw them cowering away from their riders."

"Oh no!" Ophelia cried, making for the stables. Jonquil pulled her back by the strap of her satchel, wagging a finger in her face. "What, why?"

"You're going to rush over there and do what exactly?"

Ophelia held her head high, avoiding his piercing gaze. "I'll think of something on the way." A sharp gust of wind ruffled their hair. It wasn't pleased.

"Oh, of course you will! But, the way I see it, you need someone to be a distraction," Jonquil said, ignoring the breeze.

"You are quite the distracting creature."

"Why thank you, Ophelia, I do so try to be!"

"Okay. . ." she mumbled, arms crossed in thought as she and Jonquil made their way to the stable. "Are there stable hands present?"

"One."

"Can you handle them?"

"I can certainly try!"

Ophelia nodded, smiling to herself. "All right, then I'll free the horses."

"What of the riders? What if they're there?" Jonquil asked, his grin rivaling hers. "Gretchen was rather scared of them."

"Oh, I'm sure you'll come up with something," Ophelia whispered as they approached the stable hand.

The tall, gangly young man looked up from his book, eyebrows furrowed. "May I help you? Come to collect your mounts?"

Jonquil was beaming now. This was just the kind of thing he loved. Toying with humans—especially shitty ones— was a favored hobby amongst the Spirits. They weren't necessarily meant to intervene in mortal matters, but sometimes, even Spirits had to break the rules. Jonquil took that unspoken rule as the gospel. No wonder he got in so much trouble.

Jonquil leaned into a small window that opened into a small room where the stable hand sat on a bundle of hay. There was a flash of gold in the young man's eyes. A goofy, drunken grin spread across his lips.

"Do you want to be a stable hand for the rest of your life?" Jonquil asked.

He shrugged. "It pays." The gold in his eyes pulsed.

Jonquil looked over his shoulder at Ophelia, giving her a look that screamed look-what-I-can-do.

"So, you enjoy this line of work? There isn't anything else you'd rather be doing?" he asked the stable hand.

The man thought for a moment, bookmarked his page, and then nodded. "Well, I've always toyed with the idea of being a sculptor. No one around these parts to mentor me, unfortunately. I'd have to go into the Center Cities." The gold pulsed again, this time brighter.

"What's stopping you?" Jonquil asked. "Money?"

"Mostly."

Jonquil nodded sullenly, pretending to think for a moment. Suddenly, his eyes lit up, and he turned back to the young man. "Hey! Isn't there some sort of program in the Cities? A fund for aspiring artists?"

"Is there?" the stable hand asked excitedly.

"Yes! In fact, I think you should drop whatever it is you're doing and go find out! Right now!" Jonquil said, digging into the pockets of his enormous, comical trousers. Eventually, he procured a single golden peacock feather. "Take this with you."

The stable hand, thoroughly awestruck, stood and took it. "But what is it?"

Jonquil took him by the collar, gazing deep into his eyes. "The key to everything, horse boy. The key to everything. Now, go forth and make Peacock proud."

"I will, sir, thank you. Thank you very much!" the young man said. Feather and book in hand, he took off, screaming, "Goodbye, father, I'm off to pursue my passions!"

A middle-aged man poked his head out of the stall he'd been mucking, looking confused. It took him a moment to realize what his son had said, but when he did, the sheer look of horror on his face made him drop his rake and race after him.

Jonquil laughed maniacally, sweeping Ophelia into the stable. "Too easy. Oh, how I love the mortal realm. Such impressionable minds, such stupidity," Jonquil smiled, turning to look down at the bemused Witch beside him. "Not you, of course, Ophelia. You're smarter than even we give you credit for. And I, for one, think you're a bloody genius."

"Really?"

Jonquil just winked, then spun on his tiptoes and bowed.

"Was he one of yours, then?" Ophelia asked, curtseying as she walked by him.

Spirits could see their motifs surrounding their followers and those under their protection. Jonquil had once described it as being able to view someone's sole purpose. How wonderful it must be to see such things.

"Oh, yes. He was practically swimming in daffodils and peacock feathers," he laughed.

"You know, you've just caused a family a great deal of strife," Ophelia said, crossing to the nearest stall, finding the appaloosa he'd mentioned earlier. It whinnied at her, nodding its head toward the far end of the building.

"Please, he's probably been slacking off for years, hoping his dad fires him," Jonquil sneered. "I only encouraged him to do what he'd wanted to for eons."

Ophelia rolled her eyes, nodding to herself. She scratched behind the appaloosa's ears and then made for the stalls it'd motioned to. In the darkest corner of the stable stood a towering black and white fjord horse, its nose and neck littered with fresh pink marks. Its eyes were covered, its jaw clenched tight over a harness. Ophelia frowned, reaching out to it. Its nose twitched, sniffing her hand, stamping at the ground. Behind it, crammed into the same stall, was the dappled gray. It whinnied in concern, cowering behind the piebald. Though they were both fjord horses, the gray one was considerably smaller and potentially malnourished from the looks of things. It was hard to tell in the low light.

"So, to recap," Ophelia began, taking the lock to the stall door in her hands. A thin layer of ice began forming around it. "You've played a show as yourself, used your mystical impressions on a young mortal, and are now helping me steal two horses?"

"Unfortunately."

Narcissus might really kill him this time.

"You're an enigma, Jonquil, I'll give you that," Ophelia mumbled.

The lock shattered, spooking the dappled gray horse.

Ophelia began to hum, reaching out to stroke the piebald. It leaned into her hand, sniffing the top of her head.

"Would you like those nasty blinders removed?" Ophelia asked.

Jonquil took a step back, eyes on the stable's entrance.

The horse nodded, leaning down so she could unbuckle them along with the bridle. Once the blinders were removed, it blinked a few times, taking her in. It showed its teeth, seemingly smiling.

"Don't worry, we'll get you out of here," she said softly, stroking its mane. After a quick scratch behind the ears, she made for the dappled gray.

It backed away quickly, shaking its head wildly, neighing and whinnying, and attempting to rear. The piebald stamped its hoof a few times, then smacked the other horse with its tail. Instantly, it calmed and hung its head low.

Jonquil sucked in a sharp breath. "Uh, Ophelia. . ."

"Shh," she hissed, then took gentle hold of the dappled gray's bridle. "Don't worry, we won't hurt you. Promise." The horse didn't seem convinced, but it let her unbuckle its blinders and bridle the same as the piebald.

"Phee. . ." Jonquil whispered in a singsong tone. "We have a problem. . ."

Ophelia peeked out of the stall, following Jonquil's gaze to where the father of the stable hand and two sour-looking older men stood arguing. The piebald had its eyes trained on those men, its expression murderous.

"Move," Ophelia said, almost a second too late.

Just as Jonquil stepped out of the way, the piebald rushed forward and made for what Ophelia knew to be the horses' former riders. The riders yelped in fright, scattering, and swearing, cursing the stable owner. The dappled gray poked its head out the same way Ophelia had, eyes wide. Meanwhile, the piebald chased the bigger of the two riders, nipping at his bum.

"It's a spritely thing, that's for sure," Jonquil said, tapping his chin.

"Shall we help?" Ophelia asked the dappled gray. There was no mistaking the way it shook its head. "Ahh, I see. Then shall we collect your friend before they get into too much trouble?" The horse nodded, nudging her.

Ophelia climbed into its saddle, patting its neck, carefully avoiding the cuts and raw patches its rider had caused. The horse nibbled Jonquil's hair, trying to get him to join the strange girl in the polar bear mask atop its back.

Jonquil shook his head, ducking behind it. "I'll help in my own way, love," he said with a wink.

Ophelia patted the horse's neck again, and off they went, flying through the stable, past the dulcimer player's horse, the befuddled father of the longing sculptor, and the gleefully destructive piebald.

"This way!" Ophelia shouted, waving the behemoth over.

There was light in its eyes alarmingly similar to the look Seamus sometimes got. It neighed, reared, then took off after its friend and the laughing girl who'd free them.

Their former riders were screaming, horrified, and full of rage, calling for their horses and threatening Ophelia in a multitude of ways. Just as they made for the other horses in the stable, a shimmering golden peacock barreled toward them at full speed. High-pitched screeches of murderous joy mixed with the screams of grown men running for their lives. The piebald on Ophelia's left seemed to laugh. The dappled gray rolled its eyes.

Just as Ophelia snapped the reins and urged the horses on, she spotted something stitched onto the kneepad of the piebald's saddle.

Suddenly, reality and the gravity of what just happened rushed over her.

Ophelia paled, steering the horses toward the inn.

It seemed she and Jonquil were in the same boat.

Seamus was going to kill her.

CHAPTER THIRTY-THREE

COME RAIN OR FRYKT

There was a pounding in Seamus's head. So loud, so abrasive, it felt like it was coming from all around him. It woke him from a dreamless sleep, his thoughts thicker than the gravy he'd heaped onto his mashed potatoes a few hours prior. Eyes shut against the throbbing, he pulled the blankets over his head.

That's when he heard it.

The tiniest whisper.

"Seamus? Are you awake?" Ophelia. "I need to talk to you. Urgently." Through the door, he could smell rotting pomegranate.

All remaining sleepiness was gone in a flash. The throbbing in his head lingered, but the sound was gone. Well, gone in the sense that it wasn't confined to his mind. The pounding had come from a series of frantic knocks just outside his door. Grumbling to himself, he peeled back the covers and staggered over to the door.

"Did I wake you?" Ophelia asked. He'd only opened the door a crack, peering through at her with eyes he knew were rimmed with dark circles.

"No."

Was that hay in her hair? "Oh, okay. . . Well, remember when you told me not to get into any trouble?" she asked sheepishly, curling in on herself.

Seamus's whole body went stiff, his grip on the door frame tightening. "I do recall something about that," he said as flatly as possible. Someone would've owed him a barrel's worth of gold had he placed a bet on this outcome.

The polar bear mask averted its gaze as Ophelia twisted a strand of hair around a gloved finger. "This is a good news, bad news situation, I promise," she said, her voice barely audible.

"Bad news first."

She bit her lower lip and shook her head. "You sure?"

Seamus leaned his forehead against the door, groaning. "What happened?"

The only word he caught was, ". . . stole. . ."

"I didn't quite get that."

"Mmm. . . Ishtoleshomehorshes. . ." she mumbled out of the corner of her mouth, her words melting together. Irritatingly, she was still playing with her hair, refusing to look at him.

"Kid—"

"I stole some horses!" she blurted out, holding her head in her hands. Her shoulders shook with a silent sob.

Seamus threw the door open, astonished. His jaw dropped so fast it almost dislocated again. "You *what*?" he screeched. He didn't know what kind of trouble he'd been expecting, but this was not it.

"Don't make me repeat it!" she cried, "I'm sorry, but they were being abused, and I couldn't just—"

"How many horses did you steal? Oh, Stars, do I really want to know? Why in Rabbit's name would you do that? Are you insane?" Seamus snapped, turning on his heels and quickly shrugging on his jacket.

"Just two. . ."

"Oh! 'Just two!' Oh, well, that makes *everything* okay! Good job, kid!" he said mockingly, giving her a wink and a thumbs up. "You *are* insane, aren't you?" he snapped, throwing his arms wide.

"I'm sorry! Do you want the good news at least?"

He rolled his eyes and brushed past her, pointing down the hall. "I suppose," he groaned.

"We don't have to make the rest of the journey on foot!" she said, feigning excitement, hot on his heels as they made their way quietly out of the inn.

Seamus glared at her, a thousand choice words on his mind. She folded in on herself, gazing at her feet. That confirmed it. This kid had absolutely no self-preservation instincts. Oh, this Witch was going to be the death of him, that's for sure.

Still, she had a point. Horseback was better than walking on foot for Stars-know how much longer.

"Take me to them," he sighed, "and for the love of all that is good and holy, they better be packhorses."

Ophelia edged in front of him, peering down the hall to ensure no one was looking. Skipping past him, she beckoned Seamus to follow. As soon as they stepped through the back door, Seamus's ears filled with avian screeches and the terrified screams of men. Somewhere in the chaos, there was a laugh.

Seamus glared at the back of Ophelia's head as she led him down an alley.

"What exactly did you do?"

"Nothing you wouldn't."

Seamus rolled his eyes, rubbing his temples. Eventually, they ended up in an alley near the tavern. Hidden behind a few crates and barrels, the face of a horse was staring at him.

Once again, Ophelia shrunk in on herself. "You remember how I said this was a good-new-bad-news situation?"

Seamus glared at her. "Yes. . . ?"

"Okay, well, would you be terribly upset if I said there was more bad news than good news?"

"Don't say it," Seamus groaned, turning away, hands on his hips. "Ophelia, I swear on my life if you say what I think you're going to say, I'm going to pop a vein."

"Seamus—"

"Don't say it."

"But, Seamus—"

Seamus waved away her words, pacing before her. "You couldn't have, oh, I don't know, stolen some loose change? No, horses! Horses, Ophelia!"

"I really think you should turn around. . ." Ophelia sighed.

Taking a deep breath, Seamus steeled himself, slowly

turning to face her. For once in his life, Seamus was at a loss for words. All he could do was throw his hands in the air and point at the bright red symbol adorning each horse.

"I'm sorry! The stable was dark, and I was more concerned about freeing them!" Ophelia cried. "Oh, Seamus, I'm so sorry!"

Seamus didn't even know how to express how angry he was. He just kept pointing at the horses, then at Ophelia, then back at the horses. There, stitched onto the kneepads, was a candle dripping wax onto a wolf skull—the telltale mark of the Ulvemordere.

Eventually, he found his voice again, "You stole horses from two Ulvemordere soldiers?" he snapped.

"They were being *abused*!" Ophelia bit back.

Seamus looked around, searching for someone to share in his disappointment, finding nothing but empty shadows. "Was screaming our names from the rooftops not flashy enough for you?" he yelled. "Dammit, Ophelia!"

"I said I'm sorry!"

"Oh, well, that fixes everything!"

"Seamus!" she groaned, visibly sagging. "I wouldn't have taken them if I had known."

"I don't believe that for one second, you little shit!"

Ophelia went quiet, refusing to look at him. The piebald horse on her left stamped its hoof, blowing hot steam out its nose. The little gray one held its head against her, giving Seamus a rather nasty look.

"Oh, there you go. Gang up on me, why don't you?" Seamus sighed, crossing his arms.

". . . Can we keep them?" Ophelia asked, stroking their noses.

Seamus had two options here. Either keep the horses so Ophelia wouldn't hate him forevermore or attempt to return stolen goods to people who would try very hard to kill him by any means necessary.

"I suppose," he grumbled. "But they're your responsibility."

Ophelia jumped up and down with glee, clapping her hands. "Oh, thank you, Seamus! You won't regret this, I promise!"

He already did. Very much so.

"Is that it?"

"What do you mean?"

Seamus gave her a bored look. "No more surprises, right? Nothing else you need to tell me? Because right now, I think I'll keel over from any more shocks."

"No, that's all," Ophelia smiled.

"Thank the Stars," Seamus groaned. "All right, I'm heading back to the inn. If you decide to get into more trouble, please don't tell me until morning."

"Goodnight, Seamus."

"Yeah, whatever. . ."

CHAPTER THIRTY-FOUR

TROUBLE

Come morning, the inn was empty, spare for the innkeeper lounging near the fireplace. The only sound was the crackling embers and the creaking boards beneath Seamus and Ophelia's feet. At some point during the night, she'd slipped back inside and crawled into bed. Seamus only knew this because their rooms were side by side. Excited, girlie giggling had woken him up. At least one of them was happy. Well. . . maybe Seamus was happy, too. The thought of getting off his feet for a while wasn't unpleasant.

"Mornin' folks," said the innkeeper.

Seamus nodded to him, warming his hands over the fire. Most mornings, he woke shivering. He used to hate the cold, but he was slowly growing fond of it. After all, he who fears the cold has never felt the warmth of the hearth. Furthermore, those who hate the cold hadn't the pleasure of meeting a Winter Witch.

Speaking of his lovely, stubborn, hard-headed Witch, she stood beside him, smirking at the flames.

The innkeeper shuffled something at his desk. "Say, have either of you seen any stolen horses?"

Groggily, Seamus replied, "What's a horse?"

"I'll take that as a no," the innkeeper laughed.

"Where'd everyone disappear to?" Ophelia asked, attempting to change the subject.

"Most folk have gone to the square. They've an execution to attend," the innkeeper yawned. "Decided I'd rather stay and tend to these flames than witness another fire go out."

Beside him, Ophelia stiffened.

Seamus bristled. "Mighty fine choice you've made," he said. He pointed toward the double doors that led to the kitchen. Now, it was his turn to change the subject. "Anyone back there? We're famished."

The innkeeper shook his balding head, uncrossing his ankles, kicking his bony legs up onto his desk. "There'll be food at the execution. You'll be passing through that way anyhow. Breakfast and a show."

"How long—"

"We should get going," Ophelia said, her voice tight.

The air around her had gone electric. Seamus felt the side of his face prickle. Both he and the innkeeper glanced at her. Her lips were set in a defiant pout, face turned toward the door. Quickly, they said their goodbyes to the innkeeper, thanking him for his hospitality and tipping him on their way out. Outside, throngs of townsfolk were flocking toward the square. There was excitement in the air, smelling of sugary pastries smothered in honey butter. Overnight, the town had been decorated with blood-red banners that flapped ominously in the breeze. This was no ordinary execution. Twice in twenty-four hours had he seen the Ulvemordere insignia.

"We'll go the long way around," he said over his shoulder. "No need to—"

But Ophelia was gone. One second, she'd been hot on his heels, nearly nicking him with the tip of her boot. The next, she'd vanished.

Seamus whipped his head around, searching for a pinprick of blue fabric amongst the growing crowd. The mob pushed him forward, leading him toward a makeshift wooden stage where the execution would be held. There was no noose, no chopping block, no basket for a severed head. Besides the armored guards, the only thing on the stage were iron chains. Manacles were attached to those chains. The rusty iron absorbed the sunlight, sending shivers down Seamus's spine.

Two of the guards held black banners stitched with a different scarlet symbol. These bore a broken hourglass and a sword.

Panic rising in his throat, Seamus ducked behind a stall selling morbid little trinkets to commemorate this momentous occasion. So far, they hadn't seen his wanted posters since leaving Dødbyen, but those guards on the stage could know his face. Best to stay out of sight. Seamus pretended to be interested in the wares, picking up a tiny wooden figure made to resemble an Ulvemordere General. If he'd been alone, he would've ripped the tiny soldier's head off and stomped it into splinters. In fact, he would've done the same to each toy soldier. Setting fire to it may have been more effective, but it wouldn't have been as satisfying. Nor enjoyable.

Momentarily, he turned his attention back to the crowd. A few stalls away, he spotted Ophelia. Discarding the toy soldier, he wove through the excitable patrons, trying to keep his face neutral. Sure, there were people around him who'd be sickened by the upcoming display, but not men with faces covered in scars and battle axes strapped to their sides. Showing emotion would be suspicious.

"Don't run off like that!" he whisper-yelled when he reached her, his back to the crowd.

She ignored him. Though he couldn't see her eyes, he knew they were fixed on the stage. Seamus frowned, yanking her sleeve, trying to discreetly steer her toward an alley.

"I want to stay," Ophelia muttered, her voice steeped in hatred.

"Why?"

She worked her jaw, shaking away his grip. "I want to see them for who they are."

"I'm sorry, did you forget that we're *wanted criminals*?"

"I need to see this, Seamus," she said softly, turning back toward the stage.

Seamus's heart somersaulted in his chest. Ophelia had already seen them for who they were. They both had. What had gotten into her?

Before Seamus could weasel the truth out of her, a fanfare began. Tabors and shawms mixed to create a harsh, brain-rattling beat. Swallowing hard, he turned toward the stage, arms crossed tight over his chest. Beneath the fanfare, Seamus could hear chainmail clinking against plate armor and the heavy footsteps of iron-clad feet. He heard screams, too, but the musicians tried their best to drown out the cries for help.

Two burly Ulvemordere soldiers, their heads crowned

with the hollowed faces of wolves, held tight to the upper arms of a flailing elderly woman. She was screaming as loud as she could, trying to wriggle free of her captor's grip. They held her low to the ground, dragging her across the wooden stage, her knees scraped raw by the rough boards. To give her credit, the guards struggled to clasp the manacles onto her wrists. She was a gaunt woman with bones that glimmered through her wrinkly skin. She looked more dead than alive. Soon, she would be.

Seamus shifted uncomfortably, horrified yet unable to look away. He wished this was the first Ulvemordere execution he'd seen. Wished he could say he'd never been part of one.

The Ulvemordere forced the woman to her knees, their hands clamped tight on her shoulders. Not once had she stopped screaming. Her words were unintelligible, but Seamus knew what they meant.

She wanted freedom. Wanted to live.

The fanfare faded as a tall and slender man walked onto the stage from between the banner-bearing guards, his arms crossed behind his back. His soldiers stood at attention, bowing slightly as he walked by. The man wore a patchwork cloak of pelts, forgoing his armor for mud-stained trousers and a tattered jacket littered with medals and awards of excellence. His eyes were crimson and shone with glee as he came to stand before the squealing woman.

Uncrossing his arms, he revealed a scroll.

The crowd fell silent.

Seamus's breath caught in his throat. Involuntarily, he slid into the shadows, hiding behind Ophelia as if she were a shield. His wolf cowered, whining like a scared pup. Seamus recognized the man immediately. Seeing Jette had been one thing, but the man on the stage instilled such fear in Seamus that he forgot his training.

Arild Melhus.

The man who'd been his closest confidant.

The man he'd trained to be his successor should anything happen to him.

The man who'd killed Ingrid.

Seamus had seen potential in him all those years ago. Arild had been nothing but a scrawny teen when he'd taken him under his wing. Now, he wore the ceremonial garb of a General.

Referring to him as 'the General' took the edge off the all-consuming terror Seamus was fighting. So, for now, that's what he'd call him.

The General unrolled a portion of the scroll, speaking so all could hear him, a smile tugging at his lips. "Before you stands Madame Mawde Carre, trow, accused on several accounts of misused magic," he began, "Crimes of the accused are as follows: thievery as aided by magic, distribution of misfortune, and identity fraud as aided by magic."

"Lies!" Madame Mawde Carre screamed.

The General's crimson eyes widened in delight. "Upon jury review, Carre is to be stripped of her magic and executed."

The crowd began to murmur. What in the ever-darkening night sky did that mean? How could one be stripped of their magic? Seamus glanced down at Ophelia. Her fists were clenched tight at her side, a deep frown on her lips. To anyone else, she'd look aghast at the crimes. To Seamus, who knew her well enough to recognize the martyr in her, she looked ready to fight. No doubt she was devising a plan to rescue the unfortunate trow.

Trows—an ugly subspecies of goblins—were malevolent and finicky shapeshifters known for their trickery, as most goblins were. Seamus didn't doubt the old crone had committed those crimes, but he *did* doubt she deserved to die. There were worse creatures out there. He should know. He was one of them. But unfortunately, the Ulvemordere didn't see things that way. Misused magic was misused magic. No matter the crime. No matter the cause. No matter the wielder. It was all punishable, usually by death. And, depending on the species, being born with magic before you're old enough to use it was punishable just the same. Take Witches, for example.

The General spoke again, the crowd's murmurs vanishing. "According to eyewitness reports, upon interaction with Carre, they'd notice an array of odd occurrences." His eye twitched as though those words tasted sour on his tongue. "Some reported stolen goods; others immediately noticed misfortune. The most notable account is that of a Miss Diorval Hogg, whose grandfather died moments after Carre visited the Hogg household."

"She killed him!" a young, warty girl near the stage yelled. "Murderer! Murderer! Kill the trow!"

The crowd took Diorval's words to heart, chanting those words over and over, their voices so shrill and loud that Seamus had to cover his ears. Ophelia shook her head disgustedly. Her hands flexed. Seamus could tell she was trying very hard to keep her emotions in check.

"Liars!" Mawde screamed. "I ain't killed anyone!"

The guards carrying the banners stomped their feet until the crowd settled.

"Several other patrons came forward with stories—" the General unrolled more of the scroll "—including but not limited to; financial hardship, heartbreak, and generalized bad luck. All can pinpoint the start to meeting Carre or her arrival to the town of Geiravör."

Mawde wailed in agony, her body sagging beneath the grip the soldiers had on her shoulders.

"As to accounts of identity fraud, several children are reported to have seen Madame Mawde Carre's true face multiple times. If Carre is, in fact, a trow, she will be punished accordingly. If she proves herself human, she will be held for further investigation," the General finished.

Another Ulvemordere dressed in dark robes walked onto the stage. She stopped behind Mawde Carre, offering the long metal box she held to the General. He strode casually over to her, his medals clinking like tiny bells. With a simple flick, the latch on the box opened. Seamus couldn't see what was inside, but those closest to the stage gasped in awe. The General reached inside and procured a metal baton, its shaft made of twisted metal—presumably iron. At one end, an intricate iron setting held a dark red stone.

Seamus had the strangest feeling he'd seen it before.

Had it been Arild that night at the inn?

"In accordance with local law, Madame Mawde Carre is allowed a closing statement," the General announced.

"I hate you all!" Mawde cried. "I was good to you. I ain't never caused trouble. Take your issues up with your Spirits, for they will judge you on your dying day!"

Angered outcries tore through the crowd.

The General leaned forward and whispered something

in the trow's ear. Her eyes went wide, her efforts to break free doubling.

The General, eyes agleam, placed the jewel-tipped end of his baton against her neck. The gem began to glow as veins of throbbing red light traveled across the trow's neck and face. She arched back, consumed by so much pain she couldn't even scream. Tears leaked out of her glowing red eyes as her face sparkled and began to sprout fur. Her nose shrunk, sinking into her face like a heavy book on a thick blanket. It reminded Seamus of a very wrinkled bat, in a way. Her long, bony arms shortened, puffed up, then pulled apart until she had four arms instead of two. Her wrinkly human hands softened and grew gnarly nails.

As her human features continued to fade, Seamus realized a sickening truth. Trow were towering menaces, their skin always a muddy shade of the rainbow, and their long, pointed ears dipped toward the ground. Their faces almost resembled pigs, and they smelled like one, too.

They were horrid little creatures.

Madame Mawde Carre was *not* a horrid little creature.

Which meant, of course, she wasn't a trow.

Ophelia lunged forward. Seamus quickly grabbed her arms, holding her back. He looked away from the horrible sight as the hobgoblin's skin turned ashy, those glowing red veins appearing on every inch of visible skin.

Ophelia couldn't look away. Her mouth hung open, tears slipping out from under her mask.

Seamus's stomach twisted. That could be her up on the stage. They could be draining *her* of magic.

"Monsters," Ophelia whispered furiously. Thunder rumbled above.

There was a soft thump from the stage. Seamus stole a glimpse over her shoulder.

Mawde Carre lay limp and lifeless on the stage, staring unblinkingly in Seamus's direction, drool pooling under her.

She was dead.

Whatever that baton was, it had killed her.

The General waved the glowing tip around, muttering something to the woman who carried the box. She nodded, took the baton, walked away, and replaced it in its case. Seamus had no doubt that baton now held Mawde's magic. How the Ulvemordere had managed to create a weapon like that and what they planned to do with it were questions he couldn't answer.

Some beings you couldn't steal from. Their blood wasn't magical. Their pelts didn't grant the wearer special abilities. Grinding up their wings wouldn't heal all that ailed you. Still, the Ulvemordere had been searching for ways to take their power. Seems they finally succeeded.

Seamus finally understood why Ophelia had stolen those horses last night. Seeing this made him realize that the impending fight was bigger than personal vendettas. This was about freedom for all.

Mawde's body was drug away by the same guards who led her to her death. A procession of Ulvemordere followed them, the fanfare resuming. The whole display was celebratory. The patrons laughed and cheered and clapped.

The banner-bearers and the General were all who remained on the stage.

"On behalf of all Ulvemordere, we thank you for allowing us to test our newest invention on such a heinous being. The Ulvemordere is forever in your debt," the General said with a deep bow. His face was void of emotion when he stood. But Seamus had seen the wicked smile he tried to hide from the town as he bowed. "Please visit our caravan to collect your share of the reward money."

Ophelia turned away at that, trying to disappear amongst the townsfolk as they dispersed. Seamus followed close behind. Close enough to throw her over his shoulder and run if she decided to cause trouble. He could smell her hatred, thick and spiced like curry. It stung his nose and made his stomach churn. The more horrible things they encountered, the less Seamus saw of the girl he first met that day in the forest. He hoped she would never let any of it break her spirit.

With the rest of the town preoccupied, they went to find the horses. This seemed to brighten Ophelia's spirits a little, but not by much.

Neither of them spoke until they left the town's border.

"She wasn't a trow," Ophelia said, her voice small, leading the dapple gray by the reins. "She was a hobgoblin. She was practically harmless."

Seamus felt his shoulders sag. "I know, kid."

"The townsfolk didn't," she replied.

"I know."

"She was innocent! They blamed her for their troubles when really life was just running its course." She shook her head angrily. "None of it was her fault."

Seamus only nodded. "There's nothing we can do."

"We could've saved her," Ophelia spat, throwing her arms wide.

This startled the piebald, who nudged Seamus as if to say, 'Please calm her down.'

"We *should've* saved her." Ophelia's voice shook with fury barely held back. Seamus knew she wasn't angry with him or even herself. She was just angry. That could be dangerous.

"There were too many, and I'm still recuperating from last night. We would've been shot down or skewered or drained like she was," Seamus said with a shrug. Arild's face had haunted his nightmares for years, but if he ever harmed Ophelia, Seamus was sure he'd never sleep again.

"We've taken on more. . ." Ophelia mumbled.

Seamus fell in step beside her. "And barely made it out alive! Kid, I know your heart is in the right place, but you can't save everyone."

"I could if I tried," she sobbed, turning to look at him.

Oh, Stars, not the tears! The tears were her most lethal form of magic. It was hard to listen to logic when he saw those tears.

"We can't save everyone," he repeated, looking away. "It's not fair, it sucks, but that's just how these things work."

She scoffed, wiping furiously at her tears. "Well, I think it's about damn time someone rewrote the rules."

CHAPTER THIRTY-FIVE

DAYDREAM BELIEVER

What had happened in Geiravör would stay with Ophelia for the rest of her life. The horrors of Tø were one thing, but seeing a being so lustful for power had erased any semblance of sympathy she had for the Ulvemordere. In fact, it was crazy to think she'd had any, to begin with. Still, when Seamus told her his life story, she saw them in a new light. How many felt just the same as he had? They couldn't all be so terrible, could they? Apparently, they were.

More than anything, she wished she would've saved that hobgoblin. Why did she get to live, but Mawde Carre had to die? It wasn't fair.

At least she'd saved the horses. For now, she'd take that as a win, even if Seamus felt this would all come back to haunt them later. She'd done her part, even though it was small. The horses were happy, so she'd tried to be, too.

It'd been a relatively quiet afternoon. The more time they spent on this mysterious road, the more apparent it became that no one had traveled it in a good long while.

Ophelia quite liked riding alongside Seamus. They raced once or twice, their snowy surroundings passing by in a blur. He didn't need to know this, of course, but she'd never ridden a horse. Bears and deer, yes, but never a horse. She could see why so many chose them over other mounts, though her mind kept wandering back to Eydis. If circumstances were different, Eydis would be here, too.

This horse would do, nonetheless. He seemed to like her,

which was a relief. Most animals did, but there were always the scarce few that didn't. She'd been worried his former riders had done too much damage, that he wouldn't warm up to her, but the opposite proved true. The dappled gray was an elegant fellow, suiting Ophelia quite nicely. He was ever so careful, eyes constantly scanning the ground, avoiding even the smallest twig or rock that may trip him. Ophelia suspected the horse already had a name, but since she didn't know it, she'd begun calling him Rain—for his coat reminded her of water droplets on a window, and he calmed her just as rainstorms did.

Seamus's horse was everything Rain wasn't. She was humongous, a terror on four legs with a sense of humor that would rival any court jester. She took great joy in trying to buck him off if he began to drift off to sleep. One time, she'd succeeded. Rain had whinnied, almost as if he was laughing.

Seamus had named his horse Frykt, for that's what she gave him. Fear.

Despite his prankster horse, Seamus also seemed to be in a better mood. He was quiet still, however. There was something on his mind; Ophelia knew it. There was quite a bit on hers, too, so she couldn't exactly justify picking apart his silence. Still, it set her on edge. She kept waiting for a lecture or for him to bring up the hobgoblin, both of which she dreaded.

Rain picked up on her anxiety. Now, he'd fallen a few paces behind Frykt, content to follow. Ophelia had taken a book from her pack and was trying ever so hard to focus on the story, but she couldn't. Her mind was a bubbling cauldron boiling over with worry. Besides Mawde Carre, all she could think of was their training session. She knew she should be grateful Seamus felt the need to equip her with a means to protect herself, but she wasn't.

What he'd said then had stuck with her.

If I die and you can't access your powers, I want you to be prepared.

Not a day had passed that she didn't hear them echo in her ears. Did he really think he was going to die before they made it to Dødbyen? Or was he just being pessimistic? Either way, Ophelia didn't care. As long as they were in each other's company, she wouldn't let anything happen to him. Seeing him so lifeless without the moon as his anchor only doubled this feeling.

While she acknowledged they were in this mess because of him, she understood the burden of her presence. Seamus may have gained an extra set of eyes, but he'd also gained another mouth to feed. Another thing to protect. Another thing to worry about. Relying on him wasn't fair, though he'd forced their hand. If all she could offer him in return was her magic, then he'd have it. Though she wanted to voice this, she found it hard to speak her mind. She didn't want to fight with him, knowing he would disagree.

Ophelia liked Seamus. He was strange and insufferable at times, but he was a breath of fresh air all the same. She felt a duty—a responsibility, more like—to take care of him. After all, it sounded as though they'd been in similar situations throughout life.

And then, of course, there'd been the look on his face as he tried to teach her how to wield his axes. He'd gone ashy, a far-off look in his hazel eyes. Ophelia had read enough books to know what that meant. A memory had surfaced, one he'd rather forget. Had he thought back to the Ulvemordere? Obviously, they'd been the ones to teach him the art of combat. Or maybe he'd remembered sparing with his pack? Ophelia wanted to ask but didn't want to overstep her bounds. If he wanted to talk about it, she had a feeling he would have by now.

For now, all she could do was read her book and try not to pin her own biases and worries on him. She didn't know everything. Not about him, not about the world, not about herself.

Sometimes, that bothered her.

Just as it did now.

Hours later, she'd taken out the map, ensuring they were still heading in the right direction. With Rain and Frykt, Seamus suspected they'd cut a few days off their journey. As long as they kept going without any other hiccups, they should be able to make it to Dødbyen well before the next full moon.

After confirming their path one last time, she'd tried to think of Saoirse, willing the route to change. No matter how she phrased the question or what she thought of, the map refused to change.

Seamus's silence had continued. Typically, Ophelia welcomed the quietude, but this wasn't the comfortable sort of silence. It was the kind of quiet you found yourself drowning in. Ophelia wanted nothing more than to rescue him, to pull him out of that turbulent sea. Part of her now understood why he had wanted to tend to her wounds so badly. She couldn't help feeling responsible for his mood, even though she'd done nothing wrong—at least, she didn't think she had.

She'd apologized for the horses, but after some thought, he'd found no fault in her actions.

If she'd done something else to upset him, she couldn't pin it.

Sometimes, she couldn't tell when she'd done something wrong or why the 'something' was wrong to begin with.

Sometimes, she felt wrong for just existing.

But not now. Not with him.

The draught of silence continued for five days. They kept to the woods and themselves. Conversation was strictly business. All Seamus ever asked was whether they were going in the right direction and if her ankle was fairing any better.

To be frank, it ached still, but she was muddling through. Hopefully, she wouldn't injure it further. A sprained ankle was one thing; a broken one was another.

Ophelia was tired, too. Sleeping on the ground, in trees, or atop Rain's back started to wear on her. She could tell Seamus felt the same, but he'd never say it out loud.

Ever stoic, ever stony-faced.

That wasn't him. Not the real him, at least.

It seemed they'd both hidden behind a mask all their lives.

It was late afternoon now. Ophelia was back sitting in a tree, munching on lunch, staring up at the sky through sparse branches. The trees were starting to thin. From the looks of things, they were almost out of The Wilds. Ophelia had never been allowed this far away from Tø, never seen what lay beyond the boundaries of Vileste Skog. She'd heard the entirety of Snøbolig was beautiful. Tall trees covered in crystalline snow were only the tip of the iceberg.

Ophelia was trying to be optimistic, but that only filled

her with guilt. If the Ulvemordere hadn't come along, she'd never have gotten the chance to travel like this. At least not with Lochlan around. This was a grand adventure, yes, but she couldn't allow herself to be too excited. People had died for her freedom. How was any of that fair? And in the grand scheme of things, was she really free? Would she ever be?

Ophelia wondered if Seamus ever felt the same. To her knowledge, he was the sole survivor of his pack. Did he ever have these conflicting feelings? Was he as wonderstruck as he was remorseful?

There was so much she wanted to ask him, but she didn't want to be the reason for his nightmares.

Ah, the nightmares.

Ophelia had woken many a time to the sound of his whimpering. His hands clutched his pelts and bedroll, a cold sweat pooling on his makeshift pillow. He kicked and thrashed and screamed in his sleep, but come morning, he acted as though none of it had happened. As if the claw marks in the ground had always been there. As if he were okay. Whether these nightmares were new or not, she didn't know.

Just another question she wouldn't dare ask.

Sometimes, she hated her overly inquisitive mind.

Just as she did now.

The trees had disappeared about an hour ago. All that lay before them was untouched snow and the open sky. Ophelia blinked, and the world had turned into a blank canvas. So much and yet so little to see. Not once had she seen so much of the sky. How fascinating. . .

An odd mix of anxiety and excitement swirled in her chest. What lay ahead? What sort of people lived beyond The Wilds? What parts of her world would they get to see? She desperately hoped that one day, she'd get to see the ocean. There was something wild and untamable about the ocean and its many creatures. That was the one thing she'd always dreamed of as a child: the sea.

Pirates, too, of course. Ophelia had always loved pirates. She'd read many books about them, both histories and fantasies. Most days, she dreamed of all sorts of maritime beings. Sometimes, all she wanted was to curl up with a book and imagine herself as a captain or first mate.

But not now. Now, she was ready for an adventure of her own.

CHAPTER THIRTY-SIX

HERE WE GO AGAIN

Sometimes, Seamus forgot his age. He wasn't a rebellious young man anymore. He was in his forties, his body starting to wear down. All those training exercises, all those battles won, all those days on horseback—everything was catching up to him.

While thankful to be off his feet, he swore Frykt had come equipped with the most uncomfortable saddle ever created. His rear had gone numb ages ago, his back just about ready to follow suit. Not to mention, his knees were screaming in agony. How long had it been since he'd commandeered a horse? Apparently, it'd been long enough to forget how to ride without breaking every bone in his body.

Ophelia, on the other hand, couldn't be happier. Beneath the polar bear façade, he imagined her eyes were glittering with delight. Her horse trotted gracefully, its long, lean limbs falling into a perfect rhythm. It held its head high, refusing to look at Seamus or the beast of fjord horse he rode.

In contrast, Rain's rider was staring holes into Seamus's skull.

He knew his silence had unnerved Ophelia, but his mind was too occupied for conversation. Seamus knew where they were and, more importantly, why this route only appeared on a map steeped in magic.

"We need to make a detour," Seamus finally sighed. There he went again, singing lies. "Remember that fairy we came across at the inn?"

"He's not exactly someone I could forget."

"Well, he mentioned something I'd like to look into. He needs my help with a—"

"Side quest?" she interjected.

"I'm not familiar with the term."

"It's when the main characters of a book get roped into doing something completely unrelated to their main goal," she explained. Rain nodded as if to confirm she wasn't just making that up.

"Ahh, I see." Seamus thought for a minute, tapping his chin. "Like going to the bookstore? Or stealing horses?"

Ophelia's lips flattened into a thin line. "Sure."

"Anyway. . . if all goes accordingly, this may end up—" He paused, almost slipping up and mentioning the people of Tø were alive and in the Ulvemordere's grasp. Clearing his throat, he said, "It's just something I need to look into." Seamus let that sit between them for a minute, a mischievous eyebrow raised to hide the deception. "So yes, I suppose we're going on a side quest."

This seemed to intrigue her, but he could tell she wasn't entirely convinced. Absentmindedly, she fiddled with the buckle on her satchel, making an incessant clicking noise, much to his chagrin.

"Do you trust him?" she asked quietly.

"Egill?" he scoffed. "Not by a long shot."

She frowned. "But, this side quest, it's important enough to at least pretend to?"

"Very much so."

". . . Does. . . does it have to do with your pack?" she asked.

Frykt's ears twitched as Seamus shifted uncomfortably in the saddle. "In a way."

"How long will it take to reach Egill?" Ophelia asked, catching his eye before he had a chance to look away.

"He's got a hideout up ahead, but I'm not sure where our quest will take place," Seamus explained.

Ophelia scratched her horse's neck, then swung her legs around until she sat sideways, cross-legged in her saddle. She rested her elbows on her knees, her face cupped in her hands. She looked like a bored toddler seated atop a horse much too big for her.

"Is this why you've been so quiet? Because you didn't want to tell me where we were going?" she asked.

Seamus felt his cheeks go red. ". . . are you mad?"

She only shrugged. "Did he tell you anything about our quest? What are we meant to do?"

Seamus puffed up his cheeks, blowing hot air out of his pursed lips. "I'll be honest with you, kid, I'm not entirely sure. But, yes, you're right. He brought up the people who killed my pack, so I know he's onto something big."

When Egill had a plan, you trusted it, even if you didn't necessarily trust him. That fairy may have flaws, but he was reliable when worse came to worse. This was the only reason Seamus was risking meeting up with him. They should be heading straight to Dødbyen, but with that attack at the inn that night, he'd been too on edge to think of anything else. All around him, walls were closing in. Seamus had never been one for cages. Neither had Egill. In that way, they'd found common ground.

Seamus may have outdated wanted posters, but a fairy without wings was shunned by everyone everywhere. Most assumed he'd forfeited his wings because of some horrible crime. The Faye Folk had their customs, wings were sacred, and though fairies were born with them, the privilege to use them freely had to be earned. Just as such, that privilege could be taken.

Egill had a liar's face. There'd been a time when he tried to prove his story was the truth. His wings hadn't been forfeited; they'd been stolen. Though it wasn't his fault, very few beings believed him. With his reputation, not even his own kind sympathized.

Fairies were duty-bound creatures. They grew up with a set path given to them by their families at birth. The men took after their fathers, and the women followed their mothers. To stray from this path was punishable by excommunication or worse.

Even before his kind turned on him, Egill had strayed.

His father was a musician. Egill was tone-deaf. Couldn't play an instrument to save his life. Fairies valued talent and skill more than anything, so given this rarity, he took to his mother's path. She'd been a dancer. No matter how hard he practiced, Egill kept tripping over his feet.

Again, he was given leeway to try and find at least one thing he was good at.

Eventually, he did find something. He was a thief through and through. Seamus couldn't quite remember the events leading up to his exile, but he knew he stole an obscene amount of gold from numerous Faye Folk. So, labeled a talentless criminal, he was banished, never to return to Dagslys Hul again. He'd almost lost his wings then, but one thing led to another, and he'd escaped. Shortly after, he'd met Seamus and Ingrid. The three of them were a menace to the Ulvemordere. They were clever, toying with the Ulve and evading capture as if it were a game.

The only problem was they were bound to lose eventually. One fateful day, their luck ran out. Seamus and Ingrid came out unscathed, but the Ulvemordere had sheared Egill's wings clean off his back.

Egill changed after that. His heart was full of bitter resentment for his people and the Ulvemordere. Seamus often wondered if the fairy hated him, too. He wouldn't blame if he did. Seamus chose Ingrid's safety over Egill's. It was his fault they'd taken his wings, a fate worse than death to most fairies. A fate he'd bypassed once, only to succumb to in the end.

That was why this was such a risk. As the years dragged on, Egill's hatred only grew. It was only a matter of time before he snapped. Seamus just hoped Ophelia wasn't around to see that. It'd be a very bloody day, and Seamus didn't know if he was strong enough to take that blasted fairy down.

He would, however, take Egill's unpredictability to that of a stranger any day.

"Why don't you trust him?" Ophelia asked. She seemed to have read his mind again.

"That's a loaded question."

Ophelia weighed this, staring straight ahead. "This side quest? It involves the Ulvemordere?"

"Unfortunately."

"Will we be fighting?"

"Most likely," Seamus sighed, "Though I doubt a broken fairy, a stubborn werewolf, and a benevolent Witch will strike fear into the Ulvemordere."

She tapped her fingers thoughtfully on her mask, scowling. "I suppose not."

When had she removed her gloves? Seamus didn't remember her fingers being such a dark purple.

"Hey, how're you doing?" he asked, surprising even himself.

"I'm all right. Why do you ask?"

He gave her a bored look. "Oh, I don't know, Phee. Don't know what came over me," he said lazily.

She frowned. "How are *you* doing?"

"My butt is about ready to fall off, but I'm otherwise perfectly fine. *Oppe og ikke gråter*," he laughed. *Up and not crying.*

Ophelia sighed contently. "*Jeg også.*" *Me too.*

For some reason, that sentiment was sadder coming from her.

CHAPTER THIRTY-SEVEN

WAGGING TONGUES

Soon, Seamus was tying Rain and Frykt to a tree at the base of a hill. A short, broken staircase wound around it, weaving between clumps of rocks that looked suspiciously like broken pillars.

"What happened to ditching the kid?" Egill called from the top of the stairs, arms crossed tight over his chest. Ophelia frowned at that but kept quiet. The word 'kid' made her feel exceptionally small coming from him.

Seamus gave a dramatic shrug as he climbed the steep incline toward him. "Stars help me; she likes my company."

Ophelia gave each horse one last pat on the head before following Seamus. "Hello, Egill! I don't believe we've been properly introduced. My name is Ophelia. It's a pleasure to meet you," she said in her sweetest voice. She curtsied, bowing her head, trying her very best to be polite. Though she didn't know Egill, she didn't like him one bit.

Egill squinted at her, seemingly appalled. "Holy Hemlock. . ." he mumbled.

"You get used to it," Seamus said with a knowing nod. He offered Egill his hand, pulling him into a loose embrace. "How're things?"

"Little better, little worse," he admitted. "Make it to the Kirkeby's?"

"We're working toward it," Seamus yawned, giving him a knowing look.

"Ahh, I see." Egill rubbed his chin, nodding to himself. "Detour?"

"Detour."

"Spectacular."

Ophelia glanced at Seamus, confused. He gave Egill a tight smile, one that'd be perceived as kind were it not for his clenched fists and stiff shoulders. Egill didn't seem to notice. All he did was laugh to himself, clamping a hand onto Seamus's shoulder.

"It's so good to see you again, old friend. You've no idea how much I've missed you." His eyes flicked down to Ophelia, a hint of disdain in his gaze. "Come, both of you. I'll let you in on a little secret."

With that, he turned and made his way through the ruins. Ophelia hesitated momentarily, then grabbed Seamus's arm, holding him back. She nodded toward Egill, hoping her frown gave off a questioning air.

Seamus leaned in close, looking deep into the eye holes of her mask. His entire countenance had changed. "Keep your guard up."

"Always."

He gave her a curt nod before shaking free of her grip. Sprinting, he caught up to his 'friend,' wrapping his arm around Egill's shoulders. They laughed about something.

Ophelia's stomach churned.

She had an awful feeling about this.

Egill wound them through the ruins until they arrived at a curved group of crumbling pillars. Inscriptions, worn away by time, were just visible beneath all the ice. The ruins weren't grand in any way. It wasn't a palace, wasn't a dilapidated old house. Deep in her heart, she knew this place was important somehow. In the center of the pillars was a fire. Trash, dirty clothes, half-eaten rations, and a moldy bedroll littered the ground. Ophelia scrunched up her nose in disgust.

For reasons she couldn't explain, this felt wrong.

This was not a place of warmth.

This was not a place of leisure.

If anything, it was a place of worship.

To what or whom, she didn't know. It wasn't a greenhouse or an observatory. It looked to her more like a village of pavilions.

Ophelia had the strangest feeling she'd been here before.

Egill sat cross-legged on the old bedroll. His surroundings greatly contrasted his outward appearance. He was so flowery. So handsome in the way only Faye Folk were, with his long, pointy ears which curved upward and piercing yellow eyes. Still, he seemed to frequent this spot. Everything here was his and his alone. You could tell so much about a person based on how they lived.

Yes, these ruins were beautiful, but they'd been sullied.

Yes, Egill was almost ethereal in his looks, but from what Ophelia had surmised, he seemed to have a blackened heart.

"I'll spare you the dramatics," he said in his haughtily irritating voice. "A band of rebels attempted to raid an Ulvemordere outpost. Needless to say, they failed. Idiots," he grumbled, then smiled and continued in a more jovial tone. "There was a public execution. Rumor has it the Ulvemordere are testing new equipment. And this isn't the first we've heard of it."

"What kind of equipment?" Seamus asked. He sat on a piece of stone that could've been a gazebo's roof, hands tented under his chin.

Egill shrugged. "They've created some sort of device. Something that extracts magic at its source."

"So we've seen," Seamus sighed.

"What all do you know about it?" Ophelia asked before he had a chance to. She was standing a few feet behind, eyes scanning the pillars, trying to decipher the carvings.

Egill turned to her as if seeing her for the first time. There was such animosity in his eyes. What was his problem?

"Truth be told, not much," the fairy sighed. "All I've heard is it only harms magickind. Humans are completely unaffected."

"And this outpost, was it a testing facility?" Seamus asked.

"I've not a clue."

Seamus ran a worried hand through his hair, eyes glued to the ground. His knee bounced up and down rapidly, his shoulders tense. Ophelia could just about imagine what was going on in his head.

"When was this?" she asked.

Egill's eyes twitched with irritation. "Three weeks back. What's it to you?"

Ophelia scowled. Every time he opened his mouth, the less she liked him.

"No reason," Seamus said. There was a twinge of anger in his voice. Ophelia figured it was all he could do not to ring the fairy's neck.

Egill frowned, his eyes darting back and forth between them. "Anyway. . . I'd bet they're using these devices to weed out magickind. Some of us can pass as humans, you know. That's dangerous in their eyes." Why, oh why, did he look directly at Ophelia when he said that?

"Every day, they find a new species to hate," Seamus mumbled, shaking his head in disgust.

Egill laughed darkly. "If only they'd go back to just hunting werewolves, aye?"

Seamus went stiff as a board, his eyes narrowing on the fairy. Egill wore an impish grin, revealing teeth too pointy for Ophelia's liking. Seamus stood, flexing his shaking hands. Their whole 'friendship' seemed to revolve around trading insults, but that comment had dug a little too deep.

"Yes, things would be easier that way, wouldn't they?" Seamus spat. "Looks like you're running low on firewood. I'll be back soon."

"Oh, come on, mutt, I'm only having a bit of fun. The world has gone to shit. If we can't laugh, we'll die. That's just the way of things." Egill rustled around in his heavy coat, procuring a flask. He tipped it toward Seamus, then drank it dry.

"Jokes are meant to be funny," Ophelia said, catching Seamus's eye as he sulked off.

Egill waited until they couldn't hear Seamus's footsteps before speaking. "So, kid, what's your deal?" He pointed to her mask, scrutinizing its every angle. Normally, this would unnerve Ophelia, but this man had no power over her, and she wouldn't let him think he did. "I thought the Skogens Søstre kept to themselves. How'd you end up with the dog?"

"I don't appreciate you calling him that," Ophelia said as sweetly as she could. "It's not very nice."

Egill tossed aside his flask, struggling to his feet. With heavy footsteps, he clamored over to her, eyes full of malice.

"*I'm* not very nice. In general." He stood with his hands on his hips, making himself as tall and big as possible. Nothing more than bully, really.

Ophelia straightened her skirts, not looking at him. "Really? Could've fooled me."

"Who do you think you are to speak to me like this? Have you no respect for your elders?" he asked, taking another step forward.

"I've found true respect is earned, not demanded." That was the truth of it.

Egill bore his pointy teeth, seething. He made to close the space between them, ready to do who knows what. But Ophelia put up a dainty hand, tilting her head at him.

"Is that wise?" she asked.

"Excuse me?" he spat.

"Hurt me; he kills you. Is that a wise decision?"

Egill's nostrils flared, but he took a few slow steps back, sizing her up. "You really think he cares that much? You know damn well he doesn't really want you around. You're either collateral or worth more than I initially thought. Either way, you're just a means to an end. You're stupid if you can't see that."

Lightning surged through Ophelia's body. She crossed her arms quickly, hoping he hadn't seen a stray spark. "How long have you known him?"

"Ten years."

"Funny. You think you'd have come to know him better by now." With that, Ophelia decided it best to explore the ruins before she got herself into any more trouble.

"Ah, so you think you're the exception? You think you're the expert on all things Seamus Norland, aye?" Egill scoffed. "Did he tell you who he was? Who *they* raised him to be?"

Ophelia paused, her heart dropping. "He may have mentioned something about that. . ."

"Well, lass, let me refresh your memory. The mutt was bred to be King. He'd killed hundreds of werewolves in his time but never took a pelt. Do you know why?"

Ophelia begrudgingly looked over her shoulder at him, frowning. Egill only smiled, knowing he'd baited her. Of all the books by all those pompous authors, not one had come close to using words as cunningly as fairies.

"There'd been a pelt chosen for him eons ago. The pelt of the First Wolf," he whispered, fingering the rabbit fur poking out of his gloves.

"What?" That one word was dripping with anger. Not because Seamus had kept this from her but because Ophelia hated letting Egill get the better of her.

Egill sat back, grinning maliciously. "Read about it, love. You may learn something," he said, gesturing to her sketch-book.

Ophelia rolled her eyes beneath her mask, then turned and walked away.

CHAPTER THIRTY-EIGHT

SOME AND NOW NONE OF YOU

Seamus returned, a bundle of firewood tucked under his arm, to find Ophelia wandering around the ruins. She smelled of rotten pomegranates again, and he was fed up with not knowing what that meant.

"Why do you smell like pomegranates?" he asked as they walked back to the center of Egill's camp at a snail's pace.

Long ago, Egill had found these ruins and claimed them as his own. They were as good a place as any for a fairy no one wanted around. He'd built his own little kingdom here.

"What do you mean?" Ophelia asked. She was walking up a piece of stone pillar that had fallen at an angle, arms out wide.

"You smell like pomegranates," he replied simply.

Ophelia just shrugged, wobbling a little, trying to keep her balance.

"You're minty when you're sad. Honey-sweet when happy. A little like curry when angry. But I can't figure out the pomegranate," he explained. He shifted his bundle of wood to the other arm so it'd be easier to catch her if she fell.

"You. . . You can smell my emotions?" she asked softly.

He nodded as she made it to the top of the pillar. She knelt, looking down at him with her head tilted in confusion. Or maybe she wasn't confused. Maybe she was just calculating. He stood beneath her, squinting against the mid-afternoon sun. A halo of light shrouded her. The snowy branches surrounding her made it look like she had wings.

"So, pomegranates. What's going on in that head of

yours?"

"I'm anxious," she said rather simply. "Incredibly anxious."

"Interesting."

"Can you smell other people's emotions? Is everyone different?" she asked. Her halo of light shifted as she tilted her head to the other side.

"Yes, and yes, but I'm going to be honest with you, kid; no one else has such strong and distinguishable emotions." Even one-on-one with Egill or Ingrid, the change in scent had been far too subtle.

"I've never been very good at keeping my emotions under wraps," she laughed. She jumped off her pillar, a slight breeze slowing her fall.

"I beg to differ."

She scoffed. "You'd be surprised."

Seamus furrowed his eyebrows, watching her hand instinctively rub her forearm as though she were trying to lull a deep ache. She'd done the same thing after talking to that Zimri fellow. While he doubted that the flowery musician had hurt her, that interaction still bothered him.

"Is there anything you want to talk about?" he asked.

He wanted to grab hold of her shoulder, spin her around, and make her talk to him, but he kept his word and his distance. Still, he needed her to know she could tell him anything. No matter how big or small, he'd listen without judgment. If the problem could be fixed, he'd fix it. If not? Well, he'd surely make a damn good effort anyway.

Ophelia glanced at Egill, who was only a few feet away, curling in on herself. "I don't think he likes me much."

"Egill doesn't like anyone," Seamus snorted. "What did he say?"

"It's not important."

It so obviously was.

"Listen, kid, if he—"

"Oh, believe me, I made it clear if he harmed me in any way, you'd kill him," Ophelia laughed darkly.

Seamus's eyes narrowed, and his lips pulled into a deep scowl. "A person can hurt you in many ways, Phee. Not just with swords or fists. What did he say?"

"He's just an ass and I don't like him," she sighed. "Can we drop it now?"

"If that's all, then sure."

"It is."

"All right."

Ophelia made toward the stairs, ignoring the displeased look Egill gave her as she walked by. Seamus had noticed his hatred toward her but had hoped she'd been oblivious. He could handle Egill's attitude but knew she couldn't. With stomping footsteps, he walked up and dropped his bundle of firewood on the fairy's lap.

"I'm going to tell you this once, and only once; that kid is not to be messed with. Her safety is more important to me than you could—"

"If you truly believed that, you wouldn't be here," Egill yawned. "Are we done?"

Seamus knelt, looking him dead in the eye. "What in the ever-darkening night sky did you say to upset her?"

Egill smiled his toothy little smile. "The truth. That one day, you'll up and leave because Seamus Norland has never cared for anyone other than himself. Not even his mate."

Seamus grabbed him by the hood of his gaudy coat, shaking him. "I'll kill you dead, pin-wing."

"You've lost your sense of humor, mutt." The idiot had the audacity to laugh. Seamus wanted to break his neck.

But he didn't. Because the Witch would disapprove. So instead, he shoved him back, standing. "I mean it, Egill. Lay off it."

He put his hands up in defense, feigning innocence. "All right, all right, I've gone too far. I'm deeply sorry."

Seamus growled, pointing to the fire. "Carelessly stoke the flames; you'll end up burned."

"Yes, my lord."

Ophelia spent the rest of the night with the horses. Seamus had tried listening to what she was saying but only picked up a few words. She was sad; that much he knew. Anxious, too, apparently. Had it just been the two of them, he would've done something to cheer her up. Say, diving into a stream to catch fish with his teeth or something. That'd done the trick last time.

Seamus was experiencing deja vu in the worst sort of way. This 'side quest' was shaping up to be a horrible decision, but he knew this was the right path. No matter where it led, he had to follow it.

Egill had filled him in on all the dirty details. They were to ride into this Ulvemordere outpost, take out the guards, plunder, and pillage, leave their mark, and then bolt. Sounded easy enough. There were hundreds of these outposts throughout the kingdoms. Each served a different purpose, but only a few dozen Ulvemordere staffed them. While yes, a band of rebels hadn't been able to hold their own against this outpost, those band of rebels weren't Seamus and Egill. Egill was a psychopath on his best days, and Seamus had presumably trained half the staff. He'd know their weaknesses and, more importantly, how to take them out.

Dinner had been tense, to put it lightly. Ophelia and Egill didn't even glance at each other, sitting on either side of Seamus, acting as though the other didn't exist.

Ophelia had eaten quickly and was now settling in for the night. She'd set up her makeshift bed as far away from Egill as she could without leaving the safety of the campfire light. This meant she had to sleep with her mask. Seamus could only imagine how uncomfortable that'd be.

He unrolled his bedroll beside her, settling in with his back to Egill's campfire. As of late, he'd found it easier to fall asleep beside her than when they were apart. Knowing she was near seemed to ease his every worry. Stars, how pathetic was that?

Ophelia propped herself up on her elbows, staring at him in silence.

"Are you sure there isn't anything you'd like to say before I drift off into dreamland?" he asked, fluffing the pelt he used as a pillow.

"He is a terrible person, Seamus," Ophelia said softly. "I'd prefer we not go with him."

Seamus stole a look over his shoulder. Egill sat staring into the fire, sipping away on a bottle of mead. He agreed, but in his heart of hearts, he knew they had to see this outpost for themselves. He kept thinking back to Arild, that baton, and how horribly wrong their skirmish at the inn could've gone.

Where had that weapon come from? There'd never been such a device when he was a soldier. If these weapons were being mass-produced, then Ophelia was in more danger than he'd originally feared. And if Egill were right that they were attempting to use these devices to round up magical creatures, then the whole world would be bathed in blood. The Ulve had done horrible things with their hands alone. But now? Aided by a heretical device like this? They'd only seen a fracture of what was to come.

"Sometimes we have to do things we don't like," Seamus said simply.

Ophelia frowned, turning her back to him. "I highly disagree."

Seamus lay on his back, staring up at the sky. "You don't have to tag along. We can drop you somewhere on the way. You and the horses. You'll all be safer that way."

Ophelia said nothing, but he could hear her heart pounding in her chest.

"I'd come back for you," he said, putting his pinky in the air. "Promise."

He'd never meant something more. If anything were to happen to her, he'd fight tooth and nail to get her back. The runes had been cast. This was his fate.

Until they made it to Dødbyen, at least.

Ophelia turned to look at his hand, frowning. "You risk a thousand years of bad luck breaking a promise to a Witch. I hope you know that."

"Thanks for reminding me."

CHAPTER THIRTY-NINE

PLAY STUPID GAMES

The next morning, the three of them were off. Egill didn't have a horse, so he rode with Seamus. This made the pesky fairy and the surly old wolf absolutely miserable. Ophelia found it to be the funniest thing she'd ever seen. Her cheeks ached from how long she'd been smiling.

That smile was gone now. It'd taken five long, tense days, but they'd made it to the outpost. They'd tied Rain and Frykt far enough from the outpost to avoid being spotted, instead sneaking through the woods on foot. It was early in the morning, so early it was still dark.

They hid in the trees, shrouded in shadow. In a clearing sat twelve black a-frame tents. Ophelia shivered, glad for the darkness. Though she couldn't pick out the lines from the shadows, she knew the Ulvemordere's logo was stitched on each tent. Ophelia had to keep reminding herself of their power. The tents themselves were unassuming, but the people sleeping inside them were a scourge upon the land. For the most part, the outpost felt empty. How lifeless and easy to pillage it seemed. Flickering fires dotted the camp. The faint sound of metal hitting metal seemed to accentuate the silence. A blacksmith was hard at work, forging weapons meant to destroy. Ophelia had always seen swords, daggers, and the like as a means to protect life, not kill. Too bad the Ulvemordere didn't share the same sentiment.

"Last chance to leave, Phee," Seamus whispered. He was lying beside her, peeking over a rotting log. "You've got enough money for room and board at that town we passed. It's your call."

Ophelia knew he wanted her to leave, but she wouldn't. If what Jonquil had said was true, someone in this camp may know where her people were being held. And if her suspicions were correct, Seamus was thinking the same.

"I'm staying," Ophelia said, giving him a reassuring nod.

"Oh goody," Egill sighed.

"Knock it off," Seamus spat. "Stow it, both of you. You're going to get us killed."

"I didn't say anything!" Ophelia hissed.

"You were thinking it," Egill mumbled.

Seamus groaned, pinching the bridge of his nose. "*Anyway*," he said through gritted teeth. Ophelia could tell he was already regretting this. "I count ten guards around the perimeter. Besides the smiths, everyone else is probably asleep or just waking up."

Egill pointed in the dark to the tent at the back of the camp. "Jette is there," he said.

". . . who is Jette?" Ophelia asked slowly.

Seamus hung his head low, taking a steadying breath.

"Jette was one of the soldiers in Seamus's command. Coincidentally, she also led the attack on his pack," Egill said haughtily. "If you 'knew' him, you'd know this already."

Ophelia ignored him, eyes on Seamus. "We're not only here for information, are we?"

"I told you, kid, we want to send a message."

"This isn't sending a message, Seamus, this is murder," Ophelia whisper-yelled.

"Why do you think I wanted you to stay behind? This is what war gets you, Ophelia." He slammed his fist on the ground, glaring at her. "If you don't like it, leave. It's better you learn this now than when—"

He didn't need to finish that sentence.

While she knew the path before them would be caked in blood, this still wasn't right. She knew Seamus, knew his temper. Jette and the rest of his soldiers may have betrayed him, but they were brainwashed just as he had been. If they could get through to this woman, to any of them, no one had to die today. Maybe that's why Ophelia was here. Perhaps she could talk some sense into them.

Voicing this, of course, would get her strapped to Rain and sent back to some random town like a misbehaving toddler. Best to keep her true intentions quiet for now.

After all, wasn't that what Seamus and Egill were doing?

Seamus's mind was on fire. His wolf hungered for battle, for the taste of blood on his lips.

Jette was here.

They'd been friends once. Jette was one of two women in his squadron and was one of the best swordsmen this world had ever seen. Before he defected, most had assumed the two of them would marry. It made sense, logistically. Jette came from wealth and was in the people's favor. Seamus was meant to lead the Ulvemordere. They'd be royalty. He'd been lying if he said there wasn't a time when he'd yearned for that future.

Now, all he yearned for was Jette's head on a stake.

"Egill, you're the distraction," he said. He made to point at him, realizing he'd been digging his nails into the frozen dirt beneath him. "Flit in, cause trouble. We'll be along shortly."

Egill nodded. For a split second, the air seemed to boil. Egill sparkled, then was gone. Tiny specks of fairy dust hung in the air like multi-colored snowflakes. Egill may not be able to fly, but he had an arsenal of other talents he could use.

"Now listen," Seamus hissed, rolling onto his side and looking Ophelia dead in the eye. Or at least dead in the eyehole. Curse that mask. "If I tell you to run, you run, all right? And absolutely no magic. You're a Skogens Søstre, not a Witch. Got it?"

"How, praytell, am I meant to protect myself then?" Ophelia asked.

He frowned, glancing at his axes. "I'll lend you one of these," he sighed.

"Aren't you the same man who said a broken fairy, a stubborn werewolf, and a benevolent Witch won't strike fear into the Ulvemordere?" She had him there. "I'm using my magic, Seamus. Besides, it seems you intend to kill everyone in sight. No one will live to tell the tale."

"I don't intend to—" A very loud *POOF!* came from the camp. Seamus peeked over the log to see a small, glittery mushroom cloud of fairy dust. "That's our cue."

Seamus grappled to his feet, wrenching his axes free from their sheaths. He ran as fast as he could, keeping to the shadows, hiding behind a tent. Ophelia was close behind, hands sparking. He put a finger to his lips and then motioned for her to stay put as he crouched and snuck around the other side of the tent.

Confused Ulvemordere, their weapons drawn, signaled silently as they stalked through the rainbow haze. Since Egill had spent so long without wings, his other powers were stronger. He'd found fairy dust had a million uses outside of aiding a fairy in flight. One of those uses was creating explosives out of thin air.

Seamus ran up behind one of the soldiers, hidden by the dust. He wrenched their fur mantle off of them, tossing it aside. Spinning, they yelped in fright. They lunged at him, but without their fur, they were powerless. Well, maybe not *completely* powerless. They swung their massive fists, forcing Seamus to duck low. He took this opportunity to lunge at their midriff, sending himself and the flailing soldier to the ground. This was almost becoming his signature move.

With a slice of his axe, target number one was dead.

"You were saying?" came a disgusted voice from behind. "Talk later, attack now," Seamus spat.

Through the haze, he spotted Egill. Three Ulvemordere had him cornered. He was blinking in and out of sight, laughing as he stole their weapons and used them against them. He nodded at Seamus, then disappeared again.

Four dead. Who knew how many more to go.

Somewhere behind, Ophelia squeaked in fright. There was a crack of lightning and a groan of pain. Another loud *POOF!* and the haze thickened. Fairy dust burned the inside of Seamus's nose. No amount of waving his hand in front of his face cleared his sight. A blurry blue form was glowing a few feet away. Seamus wanted to run toward her, make sure she'd killed target five, but Egill was whistling for him.

That only meant one thing.

Jette.

Blinded by the pain in his heart, Seamus ran toward the sound. He spotted Egill cowering in a corner, his hands steeped in red.

In a sing-song voice, he said, "She's still in the tent."

"Keep an eye on Ophelia," Seamus said, then ran toward revenge at full speed.

Egill yelled after him, "That's not my j—Oh, whatever!"

Seamus burst through the tent, cutting off a frantic soldier trying to explain what was happening beyond the black canvas walls. The soldier turned, hands on his weapon. Behind him, hunched over a table littered with maps, was a woman with silver hair and long X-shaped scars over her milky eyes. Bits of stark white fur peeked out from under her iron arm.

"What? Why have you—" she began, then sniffed the air. Her thin lips pulled into a cruel smile as she clicked her tongue. "Seamus Norland, what a surprise."

Her husky voice shook the frantic soldier out of his shock. He howled, swiping clawed hands through the air. Seamus took a hit to the shoulder, almost unable to react in time. Slightly panicked, he drove his bleeding shoulder into the man's chest, knocking the wind out of him. He fell backward, clutching his chest.

Jette held up a hand before Seamus could kill target six.

"You are not at liberty to kill whomever you please, Norland," Jette whispered. "This is between you and me. Leave my men out of it."

The soldier took that as his cue to leave. Still gasping for air, he scrambled to his feet and bolted out of the tent.

Jette dragged her sharp white claws across her maps. Each had tiny bumps on them, so she could read them despite being blind. While the Ulvemordere had accommodated her in that aspect, no one had ever questioned her ability to fight. Her sense of smell and hearing was scarily accurate. Though blind, she had a type of 'sight' many in their ranks had envied.

"Why have you come here?" she asked, shutting her eyes and inhaling deeply. "I'll know if you're lying."

Seamus shifted his footing, carefully keeping an eye on her hands and expression. A twitch could be the difference between life and death.

"I don't fancy talking," he said, flinching as she opened

her milky eyes.

"You never do, do you? All you ever were—all you ever will be—is blood and violence. You may have forsaken us, but you cannot escape that destiny," Jette said, lips curling into a smile. "Does it kill you? Do you yearn for destruction? Is that abomination inside you still trying to claw its way out?"

In the bellows of his mind, that blasted wolf of his growled. Seamus imagined each rumble to be a rather unsavory insult.

"Does it fight for control over your ruined vessel?"

"Shut up," Seamus said. It'd come out quieter than he intended, lacking the threatening aura he wanted to convey.

Jette nodded to herself, running a hand through her hair. "It's almost comical, really. You betray us, then your pack, then yourself."

"I didn't betray my pack," Seamus spat, tightening his grip on his axes.

"It's your fault they're dead, though, no? Or have you shrugged off another torturous responsibility?" That smile of hers grew lethal. "Well, this has been boring. Your move or mine?" she asked, hand on the hilt of her shortsword.

Seamus drug his axes across each other, the shrill sound causing her to wince. "Ladies first."

She licked her lips hungrily, arcing her blade through the air, missing him by mere millimeters. This had been intentional, and he knew it. Her gleaming sword was pointed at his jugular. One misstep or sneeze, and he'd be dead.

"At the tip of my sword is our ruin or our redemption. Why won't you come home? Why won't you return to the old ways?" Jette growled. "You are not too far gone to repent."

"That place was never my home," Seamus said through gritted teeth. He hooked his axe around her sword, pushing it down with all his might.

Jetter took a step back, swiping her sword through the air angrily. "Prove it!" she screamed. "Storm our isle, burn the pelt. Prove the prophecies wrong."

Seamus slashed his axes in an 'x,' trying to catch her off guard. Jette sidestepped out of the way, scowling.

"You're a coward, Seamus," she spat. "You're scared of it, aren't you?"

"Stop talking and fight!" he yelled. "Shut up!"

"You do not get to lord over me anymore!"

Seamus gave a roar of frustration, ducking out of the way as she stabbed her sword forward. In one swift movement, he had his axe hooked on her forearm, pulling her close. She tried to counter that with a headbutt, but Seamus was too quick. He took her arm, then swung her over his shoulder and slammed her onto the ground. Before she could regain her composure, he kicked her sword out of reach.

He stood over her, seething, his blades aimed at her throat.

She spat at his feet, eyes flashing red. The fur sticking out from under her armor shook with anticipation. "I asked you what you wanted. Why are you here?"

"Tø. What do you know?"

"Still soft, I see," she laughed. Seamus watched her off-hand as it gradually found the dagger at her hip. "Looking for the hostages, mutt?"

"Start talking, Jette."

She gave him a sympathetic look. "How bold of you, Seamus, to think you can come here and get the better of me. It'll be no small joy killing you and your companion. Have you brought the Witch?"

"Tell me where the people of Tø are being held, or I'll kill you," Seamus spat.

"You'll kill me either way," she laughed. "I'll keep my secrets. Unlike you, I'm still loyal to the Abyss."

Seamus jerked to the side as she took her dagger in her clawed hand and sprung to her feet. She lunged forward, aiming for his heart, eyes a blazing scarlet. Seamus attempted to swat away the attack, but as he went to drive his axe into her throat, Jette caught his forearm with hers, hooked his arm with her dagger, pulled it down and away, then drove her clawed hand into his side.

Ophelia screamed somewhere outside. A biting wind blew into the tent.

"Dammit," he spat through gritted teeth.

A faint green glow lit up her face, his eyes burning. Every inch of skin itched. His wolf begged him to let it lose, but he wouldn't. In his current predicament, he'd be easier to kill that way.

Seamus kicked Jette back, roaring in pain as her jagged claws were ripped from his side. Before she could react, he reached out and hooked his axe onto her shoulder. Pulling her forward, he tore off her breastplate and then sliced her stomach with his other axe.

They stood like that for a second, eyes locked, their hatred slowly unraveling.

"I gave you a choice, Jette. It never had to end this way," Seamus choked out, clutching his side.

She dropped her dagger, plunging her claws into his arm. "No, it didn't," she said, spraying him with blood as she spoke. "But it did. Congrats."

Ripping the axe from Jette's shoulder, he grimaced. That was brutal, even for him. Her hand slowly slipped down his arm, and for once, he had to look away as she collapsed to the floor.

What was up with him? This sort of stuff used to invigorate him.

Revenge tasted bitter on his tongue.

Ophelia was right; this was plain murder. None of this made him feel better. He just felt like a monster. He swayed on the spot, looking down at the blood seeping out of the thin cuts at his side. Jette should've killed him. The way she'd angled her claws, she hadn't done any actual harm. Yes, he was bleeding, but all she'd done was take off a layer of skin. If she'd hit anything important, he'd be dead by now.

Had she spared him?

No, no, she was just off her game. The Ulvemordere didn't spare people—especially traitors.

His head spun as he looked down upon her lifeless body. It was all he could do to keep himself upright, stumbling back, afraid he'd—

Someone was behind him, attempting to steady him against their back. Seamus glanced over his shoulder to see Ophelia. Her hands were encased in bright blue ice, her labored breaths appearing as storm clouds before her face. The air in the tent was suddenly unnaturally cold—colder than snow, colder than ice.

As Ophelia swept her arms wide, knife-sharp sheets of

ice shot out, implanting themselves in the ground, tents, and—Seamus grimaced—a few Ulvemordere who hadn't had time to pull on their armor.

"Egill!" she screamed, the sound too guttural for the fragile creature struggling to support him. "It's time to go!"

No response.

Someone shot at them, but Ophelia swatted the arrow away with a lazy flick of her wrist. A stomp of her foot and a thick wall of ice shielded them from the Ulvemordere.

"Can you get yourself out of here?" she said through gritted teeth.

"Going to have to," Seamus groaned, finally finding his footing. He turned, grabbing her arm.

"Egill!" Ophelia screamed again. Still, he didn't say anything. Ophelia shook her head, taking a deep breath. Something seemed to click in her mind. "We're leaving him behind."

"Fine by me," Seamus said.

Ophelia spun, eyes immediately falling on the dead woman at their feet. She gagged, looking up into his face. "Blessed Amaranth. . ."

"I know."

"Does it hurt?"

"What?"

"Oh, Finnicky Foxglove, is it bad?" she asked, her voice hushed.

That's when he realized she hadn't been looking at Jette's body. Seamus glanced down at his side. For a split second, he'd forgotten about the wound. A second wave of pain washed over him. He winced but shook his head. "I'm fine."

A heavy fist pounded against Ophelia's ice shield, startling her so badly that she nearly jumped out of her skin. Without looking down, she stepped over Jette, making for the other side of the tent. Doing a double take, she paused at the map table. As Seamus cut them an exit through the back panel of black canvas, Ophelia began frantically stuffing the maps into her satchel.

"Kid—"

"Shush, Seamus," she spat.

"We need to go!" Seamus roared, fed up with her curiosity and the searing pain resonating through his body.

He grabbed her by the strap of her satchel, pulling her through the makeshift exit. Blinking away the harsh sunrise, they found the way to be blocked. Just their luck, two soldiers stood shoulder to shoulder, wicked smiles painting their faces. The fur mantles they wore sprang to life, expanding across their backs and arms. The fur spread, consuming their faces until a gaunt wolf head formed. In seconds, two fully transformed Ulvemordere stood before them. They growled, stomping their massive, canine-like feet. They stood some eight feet tall, their bodies a mutilated mix of human and wolf.

"Ahh sh—" Seamus began.

Ophelia shoved him to the side. The sound of a cracking whip rang through the air, loud enough to stun Seamus and cause him to cover his ringing ears. Through one eye, he watched one of the Ulvemordere collapse, their chest smoking. The other, eyes wide, turned and ran with their tail between their legs. The top of their head was on fire.

"Impressive," Seamus mumbled.

Ophelia shrugged, taking him by the wrist. Together, they ran as fast as they could through the woods, forced to take the long way back to the horses. Rain and Frykt were in a tizzy when they finally found them. They were rearing and grunting, pulling with all their might against the tree they were tied to. Ophelia soothed them as Seamus cut their reins free. Just as a group of Ulvemordere reached them, they swung themselves into their saddles.

"Yah!" Seamus screamed. Frykt bolted, Rain close behind with—

Seamus couldn't believe his eyes. Ophelia stood tall atop Rain, ice spreading across her legs and her horse's back, merging them together. She was slowly bringing her outstretched hands together, her arms shaking violently. The trees around them were bending, folding over, creating a web of frozen limbs and trunks impenetrable by the Ulvemordere.

Thunder rumbled, followed by lightning that painted the early morning blue. Six navy lines seeped out from under her mask. Were her Marks. . . elongating? Wind was collecting around her in swirling gusts that pushed and pulled her as though trying to snap her out of some deep trance. Ophelia twitched, shaking her head.

"You can do that?" Seamus screamed over the sound of cracking wood and whipping wind.

Thunder rolled overhead, dark clouds blocking out the sunrise. Lightning crackled, spooking the horses, nearly causing Frykt to buck him off. Ophelia said nothing, her shoulders sagging. The ice at her feet had melted, leaving her and Rain soaking wet. Shakily, she sat, spinning around to face him. What little he could see of her face was snow-white. Slowly, her Marks retreated under her mask.

Anger surged in Seamus's chest. At himself for dragging her into this mess, at Egill for, well, being Egill, and at Ophelia for not staying with Tiril and Helgi like he'd wanted.

Ophelia slumped forward, resting against the back of Rain's neck.

"Hey!" Seamus screeched.

He slowed Frykt just a little until they were galloping beside their companions. He reached for Ophelia's mask, yanking it off her. She stared at him, eyes wide, her Marks the only color on her face. Moments ago, he'd sworn they had grown and darkened. Now, they were scarcely more than gray.

"You okay?"

All she could do was nod.

Seamus swore, looking over his shoulder, knowing the Ulvemordere would catch up to them eventually. Ophelia may have slowed them, but they could go around. They had their own horses back at their camp. It was only a matter of time.

"Seamus," Ophelia groaned, struggling to sit back up. "I need to tell you something."

"What?" he snapped. Stars, what now? She better not have left anything important behind. He was *not* going back for her sketchbook.

She took a steadying breath, glaring at him. "You're an idiot."

He only scowled because it was true.

CHAPTER FORTY

FULL OF TERRORS

Rain and Frykt carried them as fast and far as they could, but Ophelia could tell they were growing weary. She was too. That trick she'd pulled had saved them, yes, but it'd worn her out. All living things had the slightest trace of water, or so Lochlan had said. The trees were frozen solid, and the ice had called for her to use it. She'd done it before, but never like this.

Somehow, she'd convinced Seamus to stop and allow the horses a moment to rest at the town they'd passed on the way to the outpost. Half-asleep, Ophelia sat on an overturned trough as Seamus paid a stable hand to watch over their horses for a few hours.

"We need rations," he said when he returned. Without looking at her, he snapped, prompting her to follow.

Ophelia yawned, nodding. "I'm starving."

"We'll eat on the road."

Upon further inspection, they were low on quite a bit—namely, funds. Seamus was growing antsy, running around the town, trying to get everything they needed before nightfall. In his mind, they only had minutes. Ophelia figured otherwise.

"Seamus," Ophelia said with a heavy sigh. "We should rest here. We're both exhausted and you're still healing. A night at the inn doesn't sound bad, does it?"

Seamus grumbled something under his breath before turning. "No," he snapped. Blatant fear shone in his eyes. "We've already spent too much time here. We restocked what we needed. I'm not sticking around any longer than we have to."

"I know you're upset, but Rain and Frykt can't keep running like this. And so far, no one has—"

"So?" he roared.

Ophelia stumbled back a few paces, colliding with a passing patron. That one word was so angry and loud that it pierced her heart.

Seamus blew hot steam out of his nose, grabbing her by the collar and pulling her out of the middle of the bustling street. "Watch where you're going, kid," he huffed with a shake of his head.

"Sorry," Ophelia said, her voice small. She hadn't meant to upset him like this. Coiling in on herself, she looked away, staring at the gravel beneath her feet.

"These aren't hunters, Ophelia," Seamus snarled. She looked up to see him staring out at the crowd, his eyes ablaze with hatred. "They aren't poachers or trappers. They are—" He turned back to her, his voice barely a whisper. "*Ulvemordere*," he spoke that word as if it were poison.

"I know—"

"The fact they haven't caught up to us yet is nothing short of a miracle. But it's only a matter of time before that changes," he snapped. "I killed Jette. She wore white; she was one step below a general. That's a problem. That's a *big* problem."

"Yes, and who tried to talk you out of that? This side quest could've—"

"It wasn't a 'side quest!'" he barked. Almost literally. "Jette, she—she played a part in killing my pack. I would really appreciate it if you would get that through your thick skull." He flicked her mask to emphasize his words.

Ophelia looked him up and down, her lips pursing. "What's gotten into you? Why—Why are you treating me like this?"

He rolled his eyes, running shaky hands through his hair. "Jette had information I needed, and I didn't get it."

Ophelia sighed heavily and nodded. "I know—"

"You don't know!" Seamus spat. "You—You—You could never know, never understand."

She doubted that highly. "I could if you'd just *talk* to me!" she pleaded. "What is this really about? Does it have to do with the pelt? Or T—"

"Who told you about that?" Seamus said, his voice dangerously low.

Ophelia curled in on herself, shrugging. "Egill."

Seamus shook his head, scoffing. "Forget about the stupid pelt and whatever else he said; it's not important."

"Obviously it is, else you wouldn't be acting like this. Seamus, talk to me, please. Whatever happened, we can get through it together; don't shut me out."

"It is not your job to 'fix' me, kid, all right? Somethings you just can't fix."

"Seamus—"

He crossed his arms tight over his chest, staring at his shoes. "I'm tired of this, tired of you, tired of everything. You— You can't change the world, Ophelia, Marks or not. You act like this is just a story! Like everything is going to end in sunshine and rainbows. Like we have a choice! I'm tired of how nonchalant you are."

"'Nonchalant?'" Ophelia laughed darkly. "When have I *ever* been 'nonchalant' over anything? And we *do* have a choice! You didn't have to kill her. You could've talked to her! *I* could've talked to her. That was my plan before Egill shoved me out of the way when I tried to run after you!" she spat.

Seamus yanked his coin pouch from his belt, shoving it against her chest. "One day, you'll learn not all problems can be solved by words and words alone."

"I do know that! I just—"

"Some people cannot and will not be saved. You have to make peace with that."

It sickened her that she knew he was talking about himself. "Seamus—"

"I will not hear another word about this."

"I just—"

"Listen," he said, sweeping his arms wide and gesturing to their surroundings. "If you want to rest, want to stop by the market, but some paints, fine by me. Run off to your idyllic little fantasy world where a kind word can fix everything. Be my guest. Don't come running to me when reality smacks you up alongside the head!"

"I don't live in—I just thought that—"

"I don't care what you thought! It doesn't matter!" he snarled. "Go—"

"Stop talking over me!" Ophelia spat, stomping her foot. "Let me finish! It matters to me!"

"You think I care what matters to *you*?" Seamus whispered. He took a step toward her, baring his teeth—which were unusually pointy—his words rumbling in the back of his throat. "We are not partners. You are *nothing* more than collateral. You do understand that, don't you?"

Ophelia felt her shoulders sag. "'Collateral?'" she snapped, stepping forward. His nose pressed against her mask.

"You are the means to an end. I only keep you around because of what you can do," he whispered. "If something happens to you, so be it. If you get dead, I don't care. I did my part," he hissed. "If you want to stay here, take a moment to water the horses and get some shut-eye; it's not my fault if you get killed in your sleep."

"I *chose* you, Seamus. And I can just as easily choose to leave *you* for dead."

He scoffed. "With your perpetual self-sacrificial act? Please. You'd throw yourself to the literal wolves for me!"

"And you wouldn't do the same for me?"

He took a step back, shaking his head in disbelief.

"You're going to stand there and tell me that you don't care whether we both make it to Dødbyen in one piece?" Ophelia asked, grabbing his arm before he could walk away. "You're going to stand here, look me in the eye, and tell me that you wouldn't let my death eat at you for the rest of your life?"

"Let go," he growled, but she only clutched him tighter.

"You wouldn't do everything in your power to protect me?"

"Why would I?" he snapped back.

Ophelia took a deep breath, tipping her mask up enough that anyone paying close enough attention would see her marks. Seamus gruffly pulled her mask back down.

"Are you crazy?" he whisper-yelled, wide with fear.

"Are *you*? If you say I'm collateral and don't mean anything to you, why are you so worried if someone sees? Why do you care if I end up—"

His eyes had gone electric green. "I DON'T KNOW!" he screamed, ripping her hand away from him, his claw-like nails digging into her forearm, ripping through her skin like a knife through butter.

Ophelia recoiled in pain, clutching her arm to her chest, eyes wide.

"I don't know," he repeated half-heartedly. "I just do."

Seamus stood huffing and puffing, staring at his hand covered in her silver blood. As what had just happened finally sunk in, his eyes widened, shock replacing anger. His head snapped up, his glowing eyes narrowing at her. Never once had his eyes seemed so animalistic. It frightened her. She'd never been afraid of him until now.

"I—" he began, reaching for her. "It was an accident. I swear on Rabbit's name—Phee—I—"

She stumbled back, eyes flicking down to the wound he'd given her. So deep. So much blood.

A tiny voice she thought she'd finally snuffed out spoke up. *He's just like Lochlan.*

Another whispered: *You're an idiot.*

But the loudest voice was the one she believed. *Something isn't right.*

"*What is wrong with you?*" she whispered-yelled, eyes filling with tears as she continued to back away from him.

Seamus had a hand out toward her, his fingers curling into a fist as he dropped his arm to his side. "I don't know. I didn't mean to—"

"That is *not* good enough!" she cried.

He shut his eyes tightly, squeezing his fists so hard his knuckles had gone white. He bore his teeth like he wanted to yell at her again, but ultimately, his face and posture softened. He reached forward and yanked his coin pouch back. Ophelia had forgotten she was holding it. "I'm going to find an inn," he said dryly, turning away.

With that, he left Ophelia in the middle of the busy street. Hot, angry tears slipped out from under her mask as she watched him disappear into the crowd.

The logical—maybe even the selfish side of her—told her

she should run and never look back. She could take the horses and go anywhere in the world. She'd find someplace safe, somewhere no one would find her. For once, she'd think only of herself and her own needs.

But Seamus was right. She was self-sacrificial.

Something was wrong with him, and of course, she was worried. All this nonsense about a 'First Wolf' and some ancient pelt had been the tipping point. There was something he wasn't telling her, and that scared her more than anything. Secrets did not bode well for them. Isn't that how they had ended up here? More than anything, Ophelia wished they could trust each other fully. Even if Seamus thought she wouldn't like what he had to say, she wished he'd just say it. She would much rather hear a harsh truth than have him treat her like this for the rest of their journey.

As much as she didn't want to, she'd have to find him at the inn. Sucking up her pride would be better than him disappearing into the night, never to see her again. His words and actions may hurt, but the thought of going on without him was like a knife to the heart.

CHAPTER FORTY-ONE

BAD MOON RISING

Seamus slammed open the door to the first inn he found, ignoring the gawking eyes that turned his way. Grumbling, he dragged his seething self toward the long wooden counter in the corner. Sat behind it was a plump woman. She squinted at him, a look on her face he wouldn't exactly describe as friendly. Seamus inhaled deeply, digging out enough coin to pay for a night.

"Staying for the night. Two rooms," he mumbled, haphazardly tossing her a handful of coins, grimacing. Barely anything left for breakfast now.

The innkeeper caught the coins, holding them up to the flicking candlelight next to her. A wry smile lit up her wrinkled face. "Just the night? Can I offer anything else?"

He gave her a bored look and a slight shake of his head. "We won't need service, we've got rations."

"Your loss. Our cook is world-class," the woman laughed as she counted his coins. "Will your companion be on their way soon? We close doors at sundown. No one in or out."

Seamus gave her a questioning look.

"Sun goes down, moon comes up. And you know what they say about the moon. Brings out all sorts of creatures," she said as she turned and tapped the wall behind her.

Seamus could just make out a circular picture on the wall. It was made of three wooden rings, each a different color, covered with numbers, months, and moon phases. It was a lunar calendar.

The symbol at the top, signifying today's moon, made his blood go cold.

Tonight was a full moon.

CHAPTER FORTY-TWO

STALLING

Ophelia fiddled with the clasp on her cloak with one hand while the other held tightly to her satchel. Humankind was afraid, and to be honest, Ophelia understood why. They'd been fed propaganda all their lives. Their magical counterparts had been blamed for everything from plagues to lousy weather. These villagers were no different. You could see it in the goods they sold. The way they tried so hard to market magic as if it were a toy or oddity at best. Prying eyes followed her, lingering on her mask. A few folks whispered to each other. Some backed away. Not everyone was friendly to the *Skogens Søstre*, either. Though she didn't blame them for fearing things they didn't understand, she did blame them for what their fear caused. The Ulvemordere were proof of humanity's ability to use fear as a weapon—both their own and that of others.

Ophelia wandered around for a while, surveying shops and stalls that piqued her interest. Her joy was bittersweet, mixed with the scathing sorrow she felt toward Seamus.

Just when she thought she'd pushed Tø to the back of her mind, it once again became an obsessive thought. She saw things Saoirse would like and trinkets Åsmund would buy for his wife. There were even things that Lochlan would pause to look at.

Shaking away these thoughts, she continued through the market, purchasing several small pouches of herbs. Nightshade and Salvia had taught her a few tinctures that could come in handy. Especially seeing as she needed to tend to the claw marks on her arm and Seamus's wound. He'd said it was healing, but for some reason, she didn't believe him. While she wasn't skilled enough to make any miracle ointment, the herbs she'd found would do for now. Too bad they hadn't befriended an open-minded healer.

With the last of her spending money, she bargained herself a cut of pork. Food was always the way to Seamus's heart. Maybe he'd apologize for his uncalled-for behavior if he knew he'd get something out of it.

She held her head high, scoffing at the thought. As if his pride would bend for such a thing! The gall of that man was beyond her. . . His emotions changed faster than the flap of a hummingbird's wings! Glancing down at her wrist, she frowned. Four thin, silver-colored slashes. They'd stopped bleeding, but they stung every time she moved her hand. Grumbling to herself, she yanked down her sleeve. He was lucky those cuts weren't deep.

The sky was shifting colors as the crowd began to thin. Up ahead, she spotted an inn—so far, it'd been the only one she'd seen—and made her way toward it.

Ophelia did a double take.

A pair of boots lined with fox fur caught her eye. She stopped and stared longingly at them. Glancing down at her own boots, she found the seam between the sole and the top had finally popped. Her toes were probably more frozen than normal. Normally, that wouldn't bother her, but how cold was too cold? Though she was a Witch, she was still mostly human.

"Miss!" a voice called from up ahead.

At the doorway to the inn stood a woman waving her hands wildly, beckoning her forward.

"Is everything all right?" Ophelia asked, tilting her head to the side out of confusion.

The woman stared at her, mock sympathy in her eyes. "It's almost moonrise, hon. Best get inside. We've a few beds left."

"Oh, thank you," Ophelia smiled, following the woman inside.

The air inside the inn felt sticky and smelled of old ale. She scanned the common room for Seamus's brooding figure, her stomach growling.

CLAP!

She turned to see the woman barricading the door with a heavy log.

Ophelia bristled. "Might I ask the purpose of that?" Dread bubbled up inside her. She hated being locked in.

"Necessary precautions," the woman sighed, taking a large keyring hanging from one of her many belts. "Can't be too careful on a night like this."

"What do you—" Ophelia began, but dread turned to unbridled terror as her mind began to make sense of it all. How long had it been since they left Tø? Almost a whole month. Which meant— "Full moon," she breathed, eyes widening beneath her mask.

"Don't worry, dearie. The hunters have the woods covered. And if any nasty little wolves have slipped in tonight—" she lowered her voice, chuckling "—well, let's just say they should steer clear of the food. I heard there's an outpost not far from here. Those nasty critters will be in for a rude awakening come morning."

Ophelia's heart squeezed with worry, a dizzying sense of panic seizing her rapidly beating heart. No wonder Seamus had been so insufferable and wishy-washy as of late. The pull of the moon was exasperating everything he had already felt. On top of that, he'd probably been too worked up and worried to even notice.

"I—I need to find my companion," Ophelia squeaked, trying to keep her voice steady.

The woman thought for a moment. "Surly fella? Missing half his ear? Would be handsome if it weren't for the attitude and unruly beard?"

Ophelia nodded, scanning the room again on her tiptoes, thinking he might be sulking in a dark corner. "Yes, that'll be him."

The woman sighed heavily, placing a comforting hand on her shoulder. "Poor man said he was going out to look for you. I advised against it, of course. But, oh well! He seemed crafty. I'm sure he'll be fine by morning." She leaned in close, a crooked smile marring her face. "That is, of course, if he ain't one of them," she laughed.

Ophelia stood gawking at her. Lightning crackled beneath her skin, making her heart skip a beat. "What—What do you mean?"

"Town rules. No one in or out after sunset," she said with a shrug. "I can show you to your room. He already paid."

Ophelia was frozen, just staring at the door.

This town had every precaution set up against werewolves. They even had hunters in the woods. There must be a pack nearby. If the hunters didn't find him, the other wolves would. And if she knew anything about werewolves, it was that they were territorial. They wouldn't just *let* Seamus walk onto their land.

Knowing she would regret it later, she swept her hand through the air. The log barricading the entrance lifted from its confines, and the door blew open. Without another thought, Ophelia took off into the night, clipping her mask onto her belt in order to see better in the growing darkness.

She ran at full speed, unsure where she was going and what to do. All she knew was that she had to find Seamus, even if it took all night.

Even if she got bit by a rogue werewolf or shot by a hunter.

Even if the Ulvemordere were waiting for them.

If Seamus didn't know it was a full moon, he was a danger to others.

If he did, she was sure he was a danger to himself.

Ophelia skidded to a stop, surrounded by dark, foreboding trees. The last time she had taken off after him like this, her entire world had fallen apart.

How had she ended up here?

All her life, she'd tried to be careful—sometimes, a little *too* careful. Despite that, she'd thrown everything away for a surly old wolf! No wonder Lochlan had wanted him gone. Since she'd met Seamus, she'd damned a village, ended up wanted by the Ulvemordere, stole enemy horses, and had to deal with Egill—the list went on and on and on! Those were just the things she could think of off the top of her head!

Yet here she was, standing in unfamiliar woods, looking for *him*, hoping nothing bad had happened. Despite how he'd treated her, despite knowing he'd bolt once they got to Dødbyen, here she was.

Blessed Amaranth, she was so stupid!

A yelp and a snarl in the distance made her jump. Someone nearby swore as a wolf—*her wolf*—howled in pain. Before she knew it, she was running toward the commotion.

The trees thinned ever so slightly, revealing two beings in dark armor circling her wounded wolf. Even without the half-healed gash on his side, she knew it was him. Deep in her soul, she felt connected to him beyond the world of the living.

One of the beings—the bigger of the two—looked up at her. Hints of the leather aketon beneath their pauldrons, breastplate, and plackart shone crimson, starkly contrasting the gray woods surrounding them. A wolf's head sat on their shoulder as if biting into their pauldron. The teeth glinted as if covered in drool. A wolf tail hung from their belts. One of their arms was wrapped in fur. Their face was barely visible behind a black hood and face covering. But their eyes? Oh, their eyes glowed red beneath the shadows of their hood, instilling terror into the Witch they surely intended to kill.

Ophelia whistled. Her wolf whipped its head around to look at her. It was bigger than she remembered, its electric-green eyes like stars in the dark. It barked at her, backing toward her, eyes trained on its attackers. In the distance, howls of concern and anguish ricocheted off the trees.

"And now we've collected the full set," came a familiar voice.

Egill.

Ophelia felt her blood boil as lightning traveled up her arms and sparked in her heart.

Egill put up a hand, stopping the Ulvemordere solider in their tracks. "You have a choice, little Witch. Know whatever you decide will have everlasting consequences." His impish grin sparkled in the moonlight.

Seamus stood protectively before her, growling, pawing at the ground. Ophelia would forever be thankful she was on this side of that wolf's ferocity.

"What are you doing?" Ophelia asked, the terror in her voice palpable.

Egill mocked her, shivering dramatically. He laughed, wiping a nonexistent tear. "Oh, sweet Ophelia. You're *so* daft. What does it look like I'm doing?"

"Siding with the enemy," Ophelia snapped.

"Am I? Oops." Egill rolled his glowing yellow eyes, sighing heavily, still holding up his hand to hold back his companion. "Listen, kid, I go where the money flows freely. Your little pet has a bounty on his head that could set up my children's great-grandchildren for life."

"He's your friend!"

"That word doesn't mean to *me* what it means to *you*," Egill laughed. "Now, either move or. . . well, let's just say you won't like what happens next."

Ophelia shrugged off her bags, allowing her lightning to breach the surface. Sparks danced across her skin, lighting up the dark.

Egill's smile disappeared. "Pity."

The very second he dropped his hand, the Ulvemordere ran forward. They took a curved sword from their belt, aiming for Seamus. Seamus barked, lunging forward.

Unfortunately, Ophelia didn't see what happened next. Egill blinked away, leaving behind only fairy dust. The air above her grew hot and shimmered slightly. Ophelia stumbled to the side as the fairy materialized and dropped from the sky. Two opalescent daggers impaled the ground where she'd been standing. With a flick of her wrist, Ophelia sent a sharp breeze in his direction. His straw-like hair danced in the wind, his beady eyes squinting and watering as he stared her down.

"That ain't fair, Witch," he snapped.

Seamus yelped behind her, but there was no time to help him.

Egill stood from his crouched position. He stalked toward her, twirling his daggers around his unnaturally long and bulbous fingers. Ophelia stomped her foot, causing a sharp shard of ice to jut up from the ground where Egill had just been.

Ophelia turned in a slow circle, eyes searching the shadows for even the tiniest glimmer. Something moved to her right. She clenched her fists tight, encasing her hands in jagged ice spheres. She swung blindly, nothing but air colliding with her fist.

A disembodied laugh rang in her ears.

"My, my, what a *mighty* Witch you are," Egill whispered, his breath hot against her ear.

Spinning, Ophelia's fist crashed into an armored hand. The Ulvemordere turned his wrist, her bones shifting across each other in a way they definitely shouldn't have. The ice sheathing her fist cracked and fell to the ground. The cold metal of their iron gauntlets crushed her fingers, burning her skin as though fresh out of the forge. They smiled wickedly as Ophelia flung a knife-sharp piece of ice at their chest. It melted on impact. They were covered in too much iron. Her magic was useless.

Crippling pain erupted in the back of her skull.

The Ulvemordere soldier released her, sending her crumbling to her knees. Ophelia whimpered half-heartedly, instinctively reaching up to touch the back of her head. Egill appeared beside the soldier, a thick branch resting on his shoulder.

Her attackers blurred in and out of sight before she collapsed forward, the world going dark.

CHAPTER FORTY-THREE

UNDER A VERY BAD SIGN

Seamus woke with a start, blinking at the light with bleary eyes. Birdsong filled his ears. It echoed strangely in his skull, making his thoughts swirl. Drunkenness flooded his aching body. Though his vision was beginning to clear, his thoughts were still cloudy. He waited for the memory fragments to appear in his mind, but they never came. The cold bit at him. He was naked except for his pants. Thank the Stars for pants. Of course, they weren't doing much. They were more like ragged bloomers now.

He tried to move, his limbs screaming in agony.

A sickening feeling spread over his chest. Panic. Unbridled panic.

Something was very wrong.

He looked around wildly, realizing his hands were tied behind him, around the trunk of a tree. His ankles were bound, too, purplish ropes digging deep into his skin. They burned as he tried to wiggle his way free.

Wolfsbane.

He swore.

A laugh beside him. "And so, the dog wakes."

Seamus turned to his right, where a familiar face was smiling wickedly. "Egill," he spat, his voice only a rasp.

"In the flesh," he said as he bowed. "*Thanks* for saving my skin back there, by the way. So *glad* you doubled back for me," he said, his words containing all the sarcasm the world had to offer.

Edging past Seamus, he began to hum, his melody

mixing with the birdsong. He walked around slowly to—Seamus sucked in a breath—where Ophelia was bound to her own tree. She sat slumped over, her breathing soft as though she were sleeping. There was a silvery bloodstain on the tree where her head had rested. Egill knelt, lifting Ophelia's chin toward Seamus. Her face twitched in pain; her purple lips pulled into a deep pout.

While yes, this was all very concerning, what struck Seamus was the fact her mask was gone.

"Now, isn't that something?" Egill smiled. "A wolf *and* a Witch. Isn't. . . Isn't there a fable about that?"

Seamus struggled against his binds, his wolf begging him to let it loose.

"Relax, Seamus. I won't hurt a hair on that pretty little head of hers," he paused, making a show of weighing his options. "Actually, I will." With a blood-hungry grin, he slammed Ophelia's head into the tree.

"Stop it!" Seamus yelled, his shoulder slamming into the ground as he fought to loosen the ropes keeping him from tearing that pin-wing apart. One wrong move, and he'd dislocate his shoulder.

Egill crossed back to him, grabbed him by the hair, and pulled him upright. He knelt, shoving his knee into Seamus's side. Unfortunately, that was the same side where Jette had stabbed him. Seamus was huffing with anger and pain, a deep growl rumbling in his throat. With one hand clamped around his throat and the other fingering a blade sticking out of his boot, Egill leaned in close.

"You will stay quiet, or I will make you rip her heart out," he snarled, "with your *teeth*."

"I hate you," Seamus spat. Literally.

Egill opened his mouth to say something else, but before he could, Seamus head-butted him with all his might. Egill fell back against the cold, hard ground, laughing. He stood, brushing himself off, crossing to Ophelia. In one swift movement, he had his opalescent knife against her throat. A trail of silver blood seeped out from under the blade.

"Egill I swear on Rabbit's name if you—"

"Egill," a new voice said. Seamus turned to see a muscular woman he didn't recognize. Her hair was hidden beneath her hood, half her face obscured by a covering. "The *heks* is to be kept alive."

Ophelia's eyes fluttered open at that. "Looks like you'll have to kill me another time, butterfly," she croaked.

Seamus almost laughed.

"Just because I can't kill you, *skitten heks*, doesn't mean I can't make you bleed," Egill said through gritted teeth, pushing the tip of his knife farther into Ophelia's throat. She gasped in pain, her silver eyes widening, flashing blue.

From where Seamus sat, he could see her hands clench into tight fists. Where he was bound in wolfsbane-soaked rope, she had heavy iron shackles. He knew what was going through her mind. Knew she was straining to fight past the iron.

"Ophelia," Egill whispered, his sing-song voice like poison. "Go back to sleep, *dømte en*," he said softly.

Ophelia smirked. "That doesn't work on me, pin-wing. Witch magic eclipses fairy magic."

Egill shoved her head back again, standing with a scowl.

A growl like distant thunder resonated off the Ulvemordere woman. Beneath her armor, she wore scarlet undergarments, marking her as a lieutenant. Scowling, she nodded to Egill. Reluctantly, he followed her, their voices hushed.

The panic seizing Seamus's chest tightened its grip when he turned back to see Ophelia staring blankly forward, looking dazed.

"Ophelia!" he hissed.

She sighed heavily, turning to him. It seemed it was all she could do to keep her head up and eyes open.

"What happened?" he whispered, looking over his shoulder at their captors.

"Mmm. . . don't know," Ophelia said groggily. "It's blurry."

Seamus watched in horror as her head dipped down against her will. Relief flooded him when she looked up again, eyes wild.

"I—I—I'm awake," she coughed, shifting uncomfortably.

Seamus shook his head in disbelief, just staring at her. Her heart fluttered in fear, her constant buzzing the loudest it had ever been.

"Lean forward," Seamus demanded.

"Hmm?"

"Forward. Lean forward," he repeated through gritted teeth.

She complied, revealing the back of her to be caked in pinkish-silver blood and blackened dirt. Seamus swore. "They got you good, huh?"

She nodded, wincing. "I'm really tired." Her eyes shut as she leaned back against the tree, her body sagging. "I think I'm concussed again. Or still? I don't know."

"Pup, I need you to stay awake," Seamus said quickly.

"I know," she breathed. Rather mockingly, he might add.

Seamus wanted to scold her for that unnecessary tone. Instead, he whistled at her to get her to look at him. "I'm going to get us out of here, okay?"

Her tired eyes blinked slowly at him. "And why would you do that?"

Seamus furrowed his eyebrows.

Flashes of a fight—of words he so desperately wished he could take back—appeared before his eyes. *Ahh, there it is*, he thought. *My inevitable screw-up.*

"Whatever I said, I didn't mean any of it, kid; I'm so, so, *so* sorry," he said quickly.

"Yeah, right," she scoffed, settling against the tree. All she did was stare ahead into the forest, her eyes glazed over. "You'd do anything to get rid of me."

"Pup," Seamus said sternly, though not unkindly. "The moon—"

"Makes you do strange things," Ophelia finished, her words tumbling over each other. "You can keep saying it, but it doesn't mean I'm going to believe it." Her eyes shut as she took in a shuttering breath, her head lulling to the side.

Oh, he'd really done it now. However, fixing the emotional damage could wait until later. If he didn't look away, he'd worry himself to death. So long as he could hear her heartbeat, he knew she was okay. Truth be told, there was little solace in that, but it'd do for now. He'd meant what he'd said. Seamus was going to get her out of here one way or another.

Ophelia was in excruciating pain. The iron shackles at her wrists burned like a blazing fire. Already, blisters had formed. As she readjusted her weight, the edge of the shackles cut into them, sending a new wave of stinging pain up her arms. Her head was pounding from where Egill had hit her over the head, making it hard to think straight. Something sticky—blood, apparently—glued her hair to the base of her neck.

Before she'd heard Seamus's voice, she'd been fading in and out of consciousness. It wasn't until she'd heard him snap at Egill that she could snap out of her daze.

Of all the things to go wrong, of course, it had to be this.

Through the haze, she'd heard something about a pack being rounded up. 'Everything was going to plan.' That's what the soldier had said. Someone had been dismissed, Egill had made a snarky remark, and Ophelia had slipped back to sleep.

This wasn't going to end well. Saying they had to get out of there was an understatement.

Biting back tears, Ophelia tried to focus on her breathing as she imagined a thick layer of ice spreading out over the shackles.

Nothing.

"Don't," Seamus warned. She peeked at him. She'd never seen him this scared before. Decidedly, that look wasn't something she was fond of.

Ignoring him, she shut her eyes again.

Iron blocked magic, burning it away as easily as a flame to a spiderweb. All manner of magical beings were affected by it, but Witches especially found it a nuisance. While this was a universal fact, Ophelia had once read skilled Witches could counteract the iron and, in some cases, become immune. It was all about strength and will of mind. Ophelia didn't see herself as strong but believed in her resolve.

She could do this.

She had to.

After all, she was Vinterheksen, Protector of the Wilds, and Witch Queen of Snøbolig. The woods were her domain and where her magic was most potent. The magic that lived in tree roots and floated on the wind would bend to her will. All she had to do was ask.

A fuzzy feeling spread across her face as she bit her lip, feeling a prick of cold dance across her fingers. She focused on that feeling, imagining the cold sweeping over her arms, enveloping the shackles, and the iron freezing to its core. With a deep, shaking breath, she yanked her arms apart with all her might.

There was a soft shattering sound, and suddenly, she was free.

Seamus swore, laughing. A gleeful, delighted laugh that made Ophelia shoot him a disapproving look. "Hurry up and untie me," he said, a bright grin cutting his face in two.

Was that pride? Toward her?

A sharp, biting wind ruffled her hair as soon as the shackles fell from her wrists. She could almost hear whispers as though the wind was genuinely trying to communicate with her. It wanted to help, that much she knew. But it was trying to say something else, something it'd never shared with her before.

Ophelia stumbled to her feet as the shackles on her ankles shattered, too.

"Watch out!" Seamus screamed.

To her right, the air grew hot. Panicked, she stumbled back, narrowly dodging Egill's opal blade. With a snap of her fingers, two knife-sharp icicles appeared in her hands. Ophelia lunged at him, slashing her mystical weapons through the air, praying she'd land a blow. Egill rolled his eyes, effortlessly ducking and dodging every infuriated slice.

"You're a naughty, naughty child," Egill spat, showering her with shimmering sparks as he disappeared.

Ophelia shut her eyes, feeling for even the slightest change in atmosphere. Her back prickled with heat, so she spun, pushing her hands forward. Egill was thrown backward just as he began to rematerialize. He collided with a tree, sliding down the trunk, holding his head in his hands.

"I'm *not* a child," Ophelia mumbled.

"Egill," came the voice of the soldier.

"Hush," Egill winced as he stood, pointing one of his

daggers at Ophelia. "You know what, getting my ass beat for killing you is a small price to pay. I'll gladly rid the world of you, you annoying little Witch."

"Come try it, pin-wing."

"Knock it off!" Seamus snapped.

Egill lunged forward, blinking out of existence for mere seconds before appearing before her. He jabbed at her, met with nothing but a shock. Ophelia smiled, watching his body tense beneath the power of her lightning. Again, he vanished, unable to land a blow.

This little dance went on far too long. Egill was toying with her, trying his hand at cheap but deadly shots. Each time, he'd get a little closer, a little angrier. It was raining now, the world filled with anxiety over the Witch's safety. Ophelia used this to her advantage, turning rain into hail and battering him with it. She'd thrown all she could at him—lightning, snow and ice, wind—but it only fueled his aggression.

Still, she could see him tiring, just as she was. This was the great and powerful Egill Daae? Ophelia had but an inkling of combat training, and yet she felt they were equals. This was not the big bad fairy Seamus had described.

Over and over again, they poked and prodded at each other until, finally, one of Egill's daggers nicked her shoulder. An eruption of white-hot heat shot through Ophelia's body, stealing the air from her lungs. For a split second, her vision blurred.

As quickly as the feeling came, it was gone.

Egill took a step back, smiling. "Oh, I'm sorry. Did that hurt?" he asked, dragging his finger along the blade.

Silver blood dripped down his finger, glowing softly in the golden light of morning. Egill licked his finger, reveling in the taste of her blood. Immediately, his eyes turned silver, and sparks broke out across his fingertips. With far too much ease, he twisted his wrist, conjuring a small ball of lightning. Smiling wickedly, he arched back and tossed it at her.

Ophelia braced for impact, absorbing the electric sting, dazed for only a moment.

This magic was hers, no matter who wielded it. If he thought he could best her like this, boy, oh, boy, was he wrong.

Egill stomped his foot, causing the mud beneath their

feet to ripple. With another stomp, the mud sprang to life, arcing up like a wave. Quick as she could, she threw up her hands and sent the wave back at him.

Egill swore, wiping mud out of his eyes. "You're a wretched little thing, you know that?"

"Likewise," Ophelia sighed, tossing one of her icy daggers at him. It shattered in the air, showering him with hundreds of small but deadly shards.

Egill ducked, using his hand to shield his face.

A quick glance over her shoulder and Ophelia saw Seamus's eyes glowing a dangerous, electric green. His features were morphing, lengthening, and sharping as the seconds ticked on.

Turning back to Egill, she stomped her foot, and another wave of mud sprayed him. It clumped and spread around his legs, freezing him in place.

"You think that'll stop me?" he laughed, his skin beginning to sparkle.

Ophelia ignored him, rushing forward to free Seamus.

Just before she reached him, a sharp, stinging pain tore through her shoulder. Staggering to the side, she looked down to see a crossbow bolt had implanted itself beneath her collarbone. A sob escaped her as she fingered it. She heard Seamus scream her name but was too occupied by agony to register what was happening around her.

Warmth consumed her as hands grasped at her throat. She turned, sending a blast of freezing air into Egill's stomach. He slid in the mud but was otherwise unfazed. Ripping the crossbow bolt from her shoulder, she swept her hand through the air. An arc of lightning shot forward to greet him, but all it did was cut a tree in two as Egill flitted away.

Ophelia's knees knocked against each other as she swayed. Pressure was building in her head, once again causing her vision to blur.

All of a sudden, the world went quiet.

Egill appeared behind her in an instant, wrapping his arms around her throat, squeezing with all his might. Ophelia struggled against him, trying to send waves of electricity into his body, but she could feel her strength seeping away. All Egill did was laugh and clamp a hand over her mouth, pinching her nose closed in the process.

"Night night, Witch," he whispered.

Ophelia kicked and thrashed, clawing at his arms, his skin freezing beneath her fingers. A sinking feeling erupted in her chest as her lungs screamed and begged for air. The world swayed, her vision fading.

Unfortunately, that gave her an idea she knew Seamus would never in a million years approve of.

That look of vicious rage on his face told her he did care for her. At least enough to go full murder-wolf on her behalf.

If he thought that crossbow bolt had landed somewhere lethal. . . If he thought Egill had the upper hand. . . Who knew what he was capable of?

What she was attempting was risky. She'd only done it a few times before, and even then, it'd been on accident. Not to mention, Lochlan had always been there to revive her.

Shutting her eyes, she gripped Egill's arm as tight as she could, forcing a powerful jolt of lightning to travel through him and collide with her heart. Her chest tightened, her heartbeat slowing. Not enough to do any long-term harm, but enough to scare Seamus. Though they'd never really discussed it, she knew he was always listening, always able to hear her heartbeat. However, with his wounded ear, if she slowed it enough, he wouldn't hear the whispery beat.

Seamus roared from behind her, shaking the ground as Egill tossed her to the dirt, her consciousness slipping away.

She knew her wolf well.

CHAPTER FORTY-FOUR

YOU WERE MY PROTECTOR, YOU WERE MY BEST FRIEND

Seamus was panting heavily, hot, angry tears flooding his face. The second Egill dropped her limp body to the forest floor, he had broken free of his binds, filled with a strength he hadn't realized he possessed. Rage like molten lava coursed through him.

He couldn't hear Ophelia's heartbeat.

Egill turned to smile at him, gesturing to Ophelia's body. "I wonder what'll happen now that you don't have a one-woman army to protect you," he said, all too proud of himself. "Care to find out?"

Seamus gave a roar of anguish, racing forward. Egill sidestepped at the last minute, slamming his elbow into Seamus's back. Seamus lost his footing, receiving a face full of mud for his effort. Thinking quickly, he turned to the side, reaching for Egill's foot, causing him to fall the second he tried to move. Seamus was atop him in an instant, pinning him. If he tried to flit away, Seamus would be taken with him.

The world was blurring. As if his body was controlled by someone else, Seamus threw one punch after another, Egill's blood spattering him and the ground around them. Egill fought to take hold of Seamus's throat, squeezing with all his might.

Suddenly, there were hands on Seamus's shoulders, pulling him backward. Thick claws dug into his skin as the lieutenant swung him around and slammed him into the ground. Seamus struggled to his knees, the breath stolen from his lungs. The woman laughed, kicking him back down. She lifted her foot to stomp his throat, but Seamus rolled away, finally making it to his feet.

With a snarl, he lunged at her.

They wrestled and rolled on the muddy forest floor for a moment—throwing punches, trying to gauge each other's eyes out with their claws—until Seamus finally got a good grip on the woman's jaw. With all his might, he turned her head, her spine snapping beneath his powerful hands. The sound was horrendous. Her body hung in his arms for a minute. He chose to ignore the gravity of what he'd done, forcing down the sudden guilt and self-loathing.

All he saw was the world dripping silver with Ophelia's blood.

Tossing the dead soldier to the side, he staggered to his feet, looking to where Egill had been. All that was left of him was a faint shimmering.

Seamus screamed in anguish at the top of his lungs until they gave out, and he fell to his knees. Around him, there was a noticeable lack of wind. The hail was gone, too, leaving nothing but silence.

This wasn't how any of this was meant to go.

Glancing over his shoulder, he found Ophelia's limp body lying in a puddle of mud. Suddenly overcome with exhaustion, he crawled toward her. As his hand grazed her shoulder, a bright spark of white lightning shocked him. Startled, he rolled her over.

No heartbeat. She wasn't breathing.

He swore, blowing as much oxygen into her lungs as he could manage. A rush of electricity traveled up his fingers. Every spark felt like it drained him of what little energy he had left—as if it was sucking the life force from him.

If that's what had to happen, so be it. Stars knew she deserved life more than him.

A single, weak heartbeat echoed around him.

His own heart jumped as he took her pallid face in his hands.

Arcs of electricity erupted up his arms as Ophelia's eyes shot open. Up she sat, reacting so quickly that their foreheads collided. Seamus took hold of her as she doubled over, clutching her chest, her heart fighting to regain its rhythm. She leaned heavily into his arms, her rapidly beating heart the only sound for miles.

"Hey, hey, hey. Calm down," Seamus said breathlessly, hugging her tight.

She coughed a few times before swatting him away, frantically struggling to her feet. Seamus was on his in an instant, offering her his hands, but she waved them away. Pacing, she rubbed her chest, eyes shut tight.

"I'm fine," she choked, swaying for a moment. Her Witch Marks had changed. They weren't as bright a blue as he remembered.

"Y—You're fine?" Seamus yelled, taking a shocked step back. "Your heart *stopped*!" he screamed, causing her to cover her ears.

"I—I know," she replied quietly, her voice full of pain. "I did it on purpose."

"*What?*" he asked, his voice grave with worry and anger. His wolf was pacing in the bellows of his mind. It didn't like that statement. Seamus sputtered, hands posed as if he wanted to choke her. "You *stopped* your own *heart*?"

Breathlessly, she said, "I'm fine."

That may be true, but Seamus was about to kill her for doing something so stupid! How does one even stop one's own heart? Was she crazy?

"I can't breathe," Ophelia choked out, swallowing hard.

Seamus put his hands on his hips, shaking his head. He searched the silence for her constant buzzing but did not find it. Nor did he find a steady heartbeat. "Just try and calm—Hey!"

At the exact moment he stepped toward her, her legs buckled. Seamus swore, rushing forward. He caught her by her shoulders as she pitched forward, their hearts dropping in unison.

"Kid, you okay?" Seamus asked, his voice dark with worry.

Gripping his arms tight, she nodded. Together, they slumped to their knees, and Ophelia allowed him to coax her head to rest on his shoulder. Her gloves were smoking, and in a few places, there were glowing orange holes. Seamus hugged her tight, listening to her heart skipping beats and breaths coming in short bursts.

"Calm down, kid. I'm here. I've got ya," Seamus said softly.

"I'm sorry. . ." she whispered.

"It's okay; you were just trying to protect me."

Oh, he wanted so badly to be angry with her—to scream and yell and shake some sense into her. But all that could come later. Right now, he just needed to know she wasn't about to die in his arms. Seamus didn't know why, but he didn't want to move until she was better. He wanted to hold her and know she was safe in his arms, that her blood wasn't on his hands.

The grip she had on his arms loosened.

Seamus looked down, stiffening as her glassy eyes fluttered shut. Terror gripped him as he took Ophelia by the collar.

"Woah, woah, woah, hey!" he said quickly, shaking her as her head rolled loosely to the side.

Seamus swore again, cupping her face in one of his hands. Her skin was unnaturally hot to the touch. Like iron in the center of a blazing fire.

"Ophelia, look at me," he begged, shaking her again, brushing the hair from her face. "Pup, I need you to stay awake. Look at me, pup. Come on." He hated the pleading tone in his voice. "Ophelia, *please*. Kid, wake up!"

Those magnificent silver eyes flickered open, though he wasn't entirely sure she could see him. Her Witch Marks were more gray than blue. What did this mean? Ulvemordere soldiers were meant to kill Witches, yes, but he'd never come in contact with one until meeting her. He wasn't equipped for this, not in the slightest.

One thing was for sure, however. Ophelia had pushed herself too far.

"I'm tired," she whispered, struggling to keep her eyes open.

"I know, pup, but you've got to stay awake, okay? How do I help? How do we fix this?" he asked, tilting her chin to force her eyes to meet his.

For a moment, all she did was stare at him. "I have a fever."

"Yeah, I noticed," Seamus said gruffly. "Going to offer any more helpful insights?"

Before Ophelia could respond, Seamus whipped his head around, listening intently. In the distance, he heard hurried footsteps. Where there was one Ulvemordere, there were many. Seeing as Egill hadn't returned, he'd probably alerted the rest of their pursuers to their location.

"Can you stand?" he asked, taking Ophelia by the elbows.

"Dunno," she whispered.

"Good enough."

Heaving her off the ground, he looped his arm around her torso, leading her to a nearby tree. Once he was sure she wouldn't keel over, he stripped the Ulvemordere of her belongings, pocketing whatever he saw fit. Quickly, he collected their bags, which had been discarded near their captor's fire.

Turning back to Ophelia, he knew there was no way she was going to hobble out of there as quickly as he needed her to.

"You're not gonna like this, but I'm gonna carry you out of here, all right?" he said, leaning down to her eye level. "That okay?"

She nodded, wrapping her arm around his neck as he lifted her off the ground.

What a day.

CHAPTER FORTY-FIVE

TALK TO ME

After a while, Seamus deposited Ophelia by a tree, disappearing into the woods to dress in clean clothes. He'd tried to assure her that Egill hadn't followed, that she'd be safe alone for a few minutes, but he couldn't even seem to convince *himself* of that.

Ophelia's mind was swimming, her body alight with agony and electricity. She felt as though she were waking up after being asleep for centuries. The plan was to go back into town and get the horses, but Ophelia thought she'd be better off walking. Atop Rain, she knew she'd succumb to her exhaustion.

"How ya feeling?" Seamus asked as he came to kneel beside her.

Ophelia shrugged, taking the hand he offered her. "Foggy."

Seamus grimaced, heaving her up off the ground. "Can I yell at you yet?"

"Whatever for?" she asked, trying to find her footing. Seamus tried to steady her, but she shook her head and waved his hands away.

"Oh, I don't know Phee. Maybe because you *stopped your heart*?" he shrugged, hands on his hips.

Ophelia grimaced. "Well, technically, I only *slowed* it," she said, curling in on herself, waiting for him to start screaming at her.

Seamus stared at her a moment, then rolled his eyes. "I guess that's better; just don't ever do it again, ya hear? You scared the shit outta me."

Ophelia's shoulders sagged, averting her eyes from his disappointed gaze. "I was sort of, kind of, maybe counting on that."

Seamus straightened, eyes narrowing. "What?"

Ophelia felt her cheeks turn red. "Well, I was hoping you would freak out, and you know. . . Go all self-sacrificial," she said, holding her head high.

If he wanted to yell at her now, he had to give her at least some credit. So far, she'd not met anyone else except Seamus, who could pull off such a sassy in a state like this.

Seamus's eyes twitched in frustration. "Are you okay?" he asked rather loudly, throwing up his hands in defeat.

She smiled weakly. "I'll be fine."

"I don't believe you, you little shit."

Ophelia laughed, shrugging. "You can listen all you want." To emphasize that, she tapped her fingers on her chest to the beat of her heart. "It's steady now."

Seamus shut his eyes, his ears pulling back like a dog alerted to a strange sound. After a while, he nodded. "Next time, just tell me when you have a grand idea. Got it?"

"Got it."

He straightened, nodding curtly, gesturing to the muddy road they'd found themselves on. "Are your feet steady, too?"

"I suppose."

Once they made it back to town, they quietly retrieved their horses. No one paid them any mind, not even the stable hand. Rain and Frykt seemed confused but didn't say a word.

About an hour later, the horses walked behind them as they wove through the trees. Ophelia was right to assume that walking would fend off her exhaustion, though now her legs ached. Seamus had fallen in pace beside her, joining in solidarity.

"Are you sure you're okay?" he grumbled, looking at her sideways. "You've been taking a lot of hits lately."

"Yeah, I'm okay. I mean, I'm a little dizzy, but—" she shrugged "—it'll pass. Not the first time I've done this."

"You have no idea how severely that worries me," Seamus groaned, shaking his head disapprovingly.

Ophelia gave him a sympathetic smile. "One thing I can thank Lochlan for: he did everything he could to understand my powers. For better or for worse."

"Promise you won't keel over?" Seamus asked, bristling at Lochlan's name.

She nodded. "Promise." She stopped, putting a hand on her forehead. "Well, I am a little warm right now, but I'm sure that—"

Seamus rolled his eyes, giving her a sideways glance. "Be serious."

"I am," Ophelia said defensively.

"Kid."

"I'm fine, Seamus, really. I swear."

Another roll of his eyes.

Frykt stomped up to her, nudged her, and then blew hot air in her face. Rain whinnied in agreement.

"Oh, knock it off. It's bad enough coming from him," Ophelia sighed.

Rain's eyes went wide. Frykt nipped at her ear.

Ophelia swatted them both away. "I am *not* being insufferable."

The horses gave each other rather bored looks.

"Well, now say what's really on your mind," Ophelia mumbled, crossing her arms over her chest.

Seamus and the horses went quiet, nothing but the sound of hooves and footsteps filling the air. For a moment, Ophelia thought she'd weaseled her way out of a long lecture, but of course, something just had to go awry.

The wind whistled in her ears. Its worry and disappointment surged through her, tightening her lungs.

"I know," she whispered half-heartedly, hugging herself tighter. "I was reckless. I'm sorry."

Hurried footsteps. "Hey," came Seamus's agitated voice.

She peered over her shoulder, sickened by the concern on his face. They mirrored each other, both clutching themselves tight in a poor attempt at warding off what had happened.

He tipped his head down, forcing her to look into his eyes. "Thanks for saving my skin again."

She didn't like the way he looked at her. It was too close to how people stared at the dead and dying. It was the sort of fear saved for the direst moments. Ophelia couldn't exactly blame him for looking at her like that. She *had* been dead and dying. At least to him.

A lump was forming in her throat. All she could manage was, "Gladly."

"That being said," he began.

"Seamus—"

"Hey," he said sternly, "it's time for me to be the adult, okay?" He held her gaze, crossing in front of her, blocking her path. Hands on his hips, he continued, "Today could've ended in disaster. You—You—That was freaking terrifying. You scared the shit out of me, Phee."

The wind circled him, playfully ruffling his hair. It agreed. Frykt snorted as if to say, 'Well, that much is obvious.'

"I'm sorry," she sighed again, breaking his gaze. It was all she could do not to crumble before him. He'd scared her, too. For a second there, she'd thought they were both goners. Especially him.

Seamus shifted. She heard him scratch his neck and grumble to himself. "Listen, kid, I know you've been relying on the unseen your whole life, but you're not alone anymore."

She almost broke her neck from how fast she looked up at him. He was running a nervous hand through his hair repeatedly, his lips set in a deep pout.

"The only thing out here you should be talking to is me. Ignore the other voices; just focus on mine," he said, his voice small. The wind around him picked up, nearly toppling him, but it wasn't angry. "Okay, okay, knock it off. I'm sorry," he spat over his shoulder, swatting at it. He inhaled deeply, eyes shut when he turned back to her. "All I'm trying to say is that you worry me."

"I'm okay now," she said, her voice a strangled whisper.

Seamus took a deep breath, eyes wild with fury. "I don't believe that. You know I don't. But fine, let's say you are. What about tomorrow? What about a week from now?" All trace of carefully constructed kindness was gone. "I don't understand how your magic works, which means I can't help you if something happens. And I *really* can't help you if you don't let me in on the plan."

"It won't happen again," she said, suddenly defensive.

"Trust me, I want to believe that—I do. But you're too sensitive to this stuff. The environment reacts to you whether you want it to or not. Look at what you did to the trees! I don't even understand how you did that. It's like you can't shut it off, and that's—" He buried his face in his hands, shoulders shuddering.

The wind softened, wrapping around him like a blanket, trying its best to soothe him. Rain and Frykt had positioned themselves behind him. Frykt nudged him, beckoning for him to continue.

Seamus finally looked up at her, his tired eyes red and blotchy. "It's scary for me."

"I didn't mean to sc—"

"I don't give a damn about that," he said almost angrily, waving her words away. "I'm more afraid of something happening to *you.*"

All she could do was stare.

"So yeah, thanks for saving my skin," he said, turning away. He patted Frykt's neck, taking her reins and leading her away. "Just don't do it again, all right?"

Lochlan had always pushed her far past her limits, scolding her when she begged for rest. Even Saoirse, whom Ophelia would trust with her life, had convinced her to use her abilities for things they weren't meant for. Never for anything malicious, but she knew Ophelia had a hard time saying no. Lochlan had seen her as an experiment. When they were younger, Saoirse had seen her as a plaything. Neither had felt nice at the time. Nor did they now.

But then there was Seamus. He was arguably the only person who *should* be using her powers for personal gain. Yet he refused to. He didn't even want her protection.

"I don't mean to worry you," Ophelia said, noting how his shoulders sagged as he ambled away.

"We're a team, remember?" he said, giving her a wry smile over his shoulder. "That's what happens."

Ophelia hesitated before hoisting herself into Rain's saddle and trotting up next to him. Seamus's eyebrows were knit tight over his hazel eyes, his smile wavering.

"Is there something else?" she asked softly, tilting her head toward him. She knew he could hear the sadness clawing at her throat.

His face went blank. An emotionless statue of Seamus Norland had taken his place. There was a chasm between them, impossible to cross. Slowly, he looked away, warming his hands by blowing on them. Harsh sunlight marred his face, casting a dark shadow behind him. Ophelia felt that shadow held the real Seamus. The one walking beside her was not whole. She couldn't help but wonder if he'd ever been.

A thought crossed her mind, and before she could stop herself, she asked, "What will you do when we get to Tiril and Helgi's?"

Seamus's shoulders tensed. He wouldn't look at her. "I've been fighting for a long time," he said with a shrug. "Maybe it's time to try something else."

No part of her believed his words. Not even the quiet, hopeful part.

There was such anger in him, the kind of anger you can't put to bed. Whether he wanted to admit it or not, she knew he wished—no, *hungered*—for revenge.

"So you'll stay with them for a while?" she asked, already knowing the answer.

He worked his jaw, nodding. "Yeah, for a bit."

As if. Ophelia knew she'd be lucky if he didn't leave the night they arrived or sooner. Her chest tightened at that.

"Will you go after Egill?" she asked.

He rolled his eyes, shaking his head. "I don't want anything more to do with that pin-wing," he scoffed.

"So, you'll be heading somewhere to settle down then?"

He glanced at her, a distrustful glint in his eyes. "What's with all the questions?"

"Worry goes both ways."

"Yeah, well. . ." His words trailed off as he let go of Frykt's reins.

Ophelia had a feeling Seamus didn't know what he

wanted in life. On the one hand, his wolf begged to avenge his pack. On the other, he was a tired soldier ready to retire.

The plan was obviously still to ditch her and run. She'd known that for a while. But the more she learned about him, the more convinced she was that he wasn't meant to go through life alone. He was a wandering soul, more dead than the ghosts on the shore. More lost than a pirate at sea without a map.

He was a runner, too. Though it seemed he'd only recently picked up that trait. She was, too, in a sense. Neither of them had really gone after what they wanted. In fact, they'd been running from their deepest desires. But what were those desires? What did they want? If Seamus was unsure, Ophelia was confused at best.

Seamus wanted to avenge his pack. Ophelia wanted to avenge her town. Yet here they were, trotting away from the people who'd hurt them. Seamus wanted to find peace. Ophelia wanted freedom. Yet he was stuck in emotional turmoil, and she kept finding ways to trap herself.

What kind of life was this?

The fact of the matter was, this *wasn't* a life—at least not one she wanted to live. Surely, Seamus agreed. Neither of them had lived the kind of life anyone would aspire to have. They were fools to think anything would change upon entering Dødbyen.

"You've something else to say?" Seamus asked. He still wouldn't look at her.

"I've quite a lot, actually," she replied.

"Yeah? Save it for another time," he mumbled. "Not in the mood for more of your ramblings right now."

Ophelia glared at him, digging into her satchel for one of her books.

Seamus hadn't been lying when he said he worried for her; she knew that was the truth. Still, something was bothering her. Something had changed in him just now, and she didn't like it.

Again, she glanced at his shadow, wishing she could talk to the real Seamus Norland for more than a few seconds.

CHAPTER FORTY-SIX

BARING OUR TEETH

A few hours passed, and Seamus begrudgingly climbed back into Frykt's saddle. Growing tired, Ophelia handed off the map, resting against Rain's neck, allowing herself time to take in the scenery. Seamus was avoiding Ophelia's gaze at all costs, eyes glued to the Wayfarer's Map. In the quiet, she lay on her back, arms dangling off either side of Rain, soaking in what little wonder remained in her world. The cold afternoon sun made icicles dripping off spruce trees glisten like jewels. Fresh snow sparkled, adding to the crystalized appearance of the world. A gentle breeze rocked barren branches. The horses walked with a gentle gait, their hoof steps reminiscent of music. It was all sort of hypnotizing—soothing, even. The fear of the unknown still lingered in Ophelia's chest, but the moment was beautiful, and she wanted to revel in it despite her unease.

Succumbing to the serenity, she allowed her eyes to shut.

Birdsong echoed in her ears, mixing with Rain's breathing and his clip-clopping hooves. Lightning sent her body abuzz.

Clip-clop. She felt her grip on her satchel strap loosen.

Clip-clop. The birdsong was distorted, suddenly sounding muffled, almost sinister.

Clip-clop. There was a scream.

Ophelia's eyes shot open. She lay staring at a stormy sky, water lapping her face. Slowly, she sat up. Coarse sand dug at her palms. Seaweed clung to her skirts. Blinking to clear her blurry eyes, she found herself on the shore of a churning sea.

A black-clad army of fully transformed Ulvemordere stood at the ready, their weapons drawn.

Ophelia struggled to her feet, turning to run.

Her feet sunk deep into the sand, the particles knife-sharp against her skin. All she wore was bloodied rags. She screamed for help, trying to wrench her feet free from her sandy prison to no avail.

Fed up staring at the Wayfarer's Map, Seamus stowed it and reached in his pack for a pocketknife and the thick stick he'd pocketed a few days back. He broke a piece off and began to whittle away, letting the wood tell him what it wanted to be. While he couldn't hear the voice of the forest like Ophelia could, he'd found a few ways to understand it.

This stick had long been dead. If you thought about it, Seamus was carpentry's version of a Necromancer, breathing new life into an otherwise unusable piece of leaf litter. He had to chuckle to himself at that. Imagining himself with any amount of magic beyond his wolf's capabilities was a ridiculous thought. The world would weep, for the destruction he'd inadvertently cause would be great.

Subconsciously, he glanced at Ophelia. It was easy to imagine the destruction *she* could cause. If Ophelia ever snapped, all would rue the day they crossed her.

Yet, here she was. Snoring softly atop her horse.

Apparently, violent things come in tiny, unsuspecting packages.

For a while, Seamus kept whittling, trying to capture Frykt's likeness. He thought maybe he should carve Rain, too, then have Ophelia paint them. The set of them would be a nice trinket to have.

Again, he glanced over to see her head had lulled to the side in a rather uncomfortable manner. Her lips were set in a tight frown, her breathing coming in short bursts, her hands twitching.

The ache in his chest took him by surprise. The terror and rage he'd felt seeing her lying lifeless like that would take a while to shake off. That is, of course, if it ever went away at all. Where had this sudden attachment come from? Try as he might, he couldn't pinpoint when it'd started. It was almost like that attachment had been there since the beginning.

The whole ordeal was so odd.

From somewhere above, a shrill avian squawk cut through the quiet. She sat up, twisting her head around wildly.

"Hey," Seamus said softly, eyebrows furrowed. "You're okay."

"I fell asleep," she said groggily, struggling for a moment to twist back around in her saddle. "Forgot where I was for a second."

Like he always did, Seamus wished he could see her eyes. "Nightmare?" he asked.

She stiffened, ignoring his question, fiddling with Rain's mane. "How much farther to Dødbyen?"

"Not long now," Seamus shrugged.

She nodded to herself, shifting away from him slightly. Her head twitched slightly toward him like she was looking at him out of the corner of her eye. Seamus could hear her heart thumping wildly as she fiddled with the strap of her satchel, chewing her bottom lip. He frowned. So it *had* been a nightmare. Poor kid. Hopefully, she'd open up about it later.

That's when it hit him.

There wasn't going to be a 'later.'

This was the very last time they'd be traveling together. Come tomorrow, he'd be long gone. He'd slip away in the night, never to be seen again.

His stomach twisted into knots. He, too, shimmied away. The empty air between them was cavernous.

"You can talk to me about it, you know that, right?" Seamus asked. If she didn't spill it now, she may never have a chance to.

"I know," Ophelia mumbled.

He tapped his fingers on Frykt's reins impatiently. "So. . . What did ya dream about?"

"I don't particularly feel like talking about it right now. Thank you for the offer, though," Ophelia replied softly.

Seamus felt his body sag.

Again, Ophelia shifted away. She may well have been on the other side of the world at this point—physically and metaphorically. Seamus couldn't help but wonder what was going through her mind. Was she scared? Yes, she'd been lonely all her life, but she'd never been *alone*. Not really. Stuck at the Kirkeby's empty mansion, she would be. Was that why she'd had a nightmare, or had something else triggered it? They'd certainly gone through enough nightmare-inducing tragedies as of late.

More importantly, Seamus wondered if she'd come to the same conclusion he had. That no matter how badly they wanted to stay in each other's company, it was always going to end with nasty full moons and Ulvemordere.

Oh, how he wished things were different.

4. Dødbyen

CHAPTER FORTY-SEVEN

FRIEND TO ALL

At Seamus's request, they hid the horses a short walk from Dødbyen. They said a quick goodbye to them, instructing them to run should anyone attempt to steal them. Frykt nodded. Rain sighed.

With that, they took off to Dødbyen's entrance.

Ophelia's mind was abuzz with anticipation. Not quite excitement, not quite anxiety, something in between. Never in a million years would she have thought she'd see such a place. Not much was written about Dødbyen. As with all dark places, it was better to let your eyes adjust to the gloom than light a fire. She suspected she knew more than most—readers often did—but even then, the truths surrounding the City of The Dead were hazy at best.

Seamus was the only person to ever give her a first-hand account of the place.

He didn't seem thrilled to be returning.

The closer they got to the city, he'd gotten increasingly antsy. Now, just a few minutes away from the entrance, he was jumping out of his skin with fright.

Ophelia had noticed a few things about him in their time together. To the untrained eye, he kept up his façade of calm. But Ophelia saw the way his eyes couldn't stay fixed ahead for too long. The way he kept a loose grip on one of his axes, playing it off as if he were resting his hand on his hip. The way he stood way too close to her. Always the protector.

"Is Dødbyen really that bad?" Ophelia whispered. She didn't know why she felt the need to whisper. Maybe it was because she thought they'd be jumped by thieves at any second.

Seamus glanced at her as if seeing her for the first time. He seemed surprised she was walking so close to him. He grimaced, taking a few longer strides until he was once again at a respectful distance.

"How do you mean?" he asked.

"You're nervous. Very little truly makes you nervous," Ophelia replied.

He scoffed. "That's not true."

"Normally, things just make you sort of angry."

He opened his mouth to protest, but seeing as Ophelia was right, he only shrugged. "Okay, yes, I'm nervous. What's it to you?"

"See, now you're annoyed, which is arguably akin to dull anger," Ophelia said with a smug smile.

"You didn't answer my question."

"Oh. Well, if you're nervous, then—"

"Shush," he snapped.

He stopped suddenly, face white as the moon. Slowly, he stepped to the side, veering off the path, weaving between trees whose trunks were rubbed raw of bark in some places. How odd. Ahead, Ophelia could just make out two beings standing near the edge of a dark void. As always, Ophelia followed Seamus into the woods.

"Sorry, you were saying?" he mumbled.

"It's just if *you've* found a reason to be frightened, then I've found a reason to drop dead out of despair," Ophelia shrugged.

He gave her a confused look. "What?"

"Why are we hiding amid the trees?" she asked, hands clasped behind her back, rocking side to side, surveying her surroundings. "Oh! Are we taking a secret entrance? I've heard there are all sorts of covert tunnels around Dødbyen. Or are we meeting up with a band of rambunctious rogues? Do we have to smuggle ourselves in? Will they help?"

In response, Seamus said, "Why do you talk like that?"

Ophelia furrowed her eyebrows. "Pardon?"

"You talk like a snooty librarian."

"As if you've ever talked to a librarian, let alone a snooty one."

"You know, I never hear you talk to your animals or the wind the way you talk to me," Seamus said thoughtfully.

"Yes, well, animals are kinder than people, aren't they? And the wind greets me with the same kindness I offer up."

Seamus rolled his eyes, silently leading her toward a boulder at the edge of the tree line. The trees were dense and dark enough to engulf them in shadow, but Seamus ducked behind the massive rock nonetheless. He squatted, peering around the boulder, mumbling to himself. Ophelia took a quick peek around the other side. Five guards stood watch over a pulley system of sorts.

"We need a lie," he said over his shoulder. "A good lie."

Beneath her mask, Ophelia looked at him as if he were crazy. "What exactly do you mean by that?"

"Or, y'know, we could just knock 'em out, take the lift down—" he dusted his hands of invisible muck "—easy as that."

Ophelia raised a confused eyebrow, wishing he could see her rather judgmental look. "Why can't we just go up and ask for a ride? We've enough to pay the fee," she pointed out, frowning.

Seamus's face darkened. "I'm not exactly. . . *welcome* here. . ."

Ophelia sighed heavily. "Why does that come as no surprise?"

Seamus only shrugged. "You catch on quick."

"Are you going to tell me why?"

His cheeks were glowing such a bright red that he may have been mistaken for a rose. "Let's just say I'm the reason Dødbyen upped their security."

"What did you do?" Ophelia asked, eyes wide. "Did you steal something valuable? Murder a corrupt nobleman? Oh! I know—"

"Your brain just doesn't shut off, does it?"

"Not at all."

"To answer your question, *I* didn't kill the man—that was Egill. I *did,* however, steal the valuable thing. And it exploded, destroying several businesses," he said in a hushed tone, almost as if he were embarrassed. "I'm also generally disliked by everyone who meets me, if you haven't noticed. Very few want me around. I'm sure even you will be glad when you're rid of me."

Ophelia rolled her eyes beneath her mask, once again glad he couldn't see how irritated she was. She peered around the boulder again, eyes on the wooden structures that housed the lift's pulley system. Rusty gears and chains peeked through the trusses, sticking out like sore thumbs. Set a few inches behind the main mechanisms were gigantic wheels with heavy chains set into notches at their centers. The chains were unraveling, feeding through the gears as the lifts descended. Two dragons—obviously adolescent, given their size—were chained between the spokes of the wheels. As they walked in circles, the spokes dug into their scaly chests.

Without the dragons, the lifts wouldn't work.

Ophelia frowned.

No animal should be used to power human inventions. Especially dragons.

"Absolutely not," Seamus hissed, following her gaze.

"I didn't say anything," Ophelia whispered, still frowning.

"You didn't have to."

Ophelia glanced at him, shriveling under his stern glare. "They're practically babies, Seamus."

"Gigantic babies that'll burn you to a crisp if you get too close," he corrected.

"They deserve to be free!"

Seamus's lips were set in a deep scowl, his dark eyes filled with rage. "We're not risking our lives to save those— those—those *things*, Ophelia. It's cruel. I get it. Weep about it later."

"See, I wept about the hobgoblin, and my tears told me I had to do better."

"You did *not* just say that to me."

Ophelia stood tall, shaking out her skirts. "You distract the guards; I'll free the dragons."

With that, she took off running, ignoring Seamus's bark

of protest.

There was a whoop of fright from a guard as she skidded to a stop in front of the first dragon. She ignored the sounds of panic around her, stroking the dragon's neck. Its scales were white and iridescent, glinting a rainbow of colors. The skin beneath the scales was raw where the chains had dug in. It growled, flashes of purple light seeping out of its iron muzzle. The tops of its curling horns were scuffed from ducking beneath the gears of the pulley system.

"Hush now," Ophelia whispered, carefully squeezing her hands around the chains so as not to touch the raw skin. "I'm here to rescue you."

She shut her eyes, imagining the chains freezing to their core. Spiky ice crystals were forming beneath her hands. The chains were starting to crack.

Seamus screamed her name a few feet away. She glanced over her shoulder to see him surrounded by guards.

The chains binding the dragon shattered. It shook and stomped its feet, rattling the ground beneath her. The heavy chain on the wheel slipped, one of the spokes colliding with the back of the dragon's neck, causing it to rear. Ophelia stumbled back, hands out, gesturing for it to settle down. It whipped its head around to stare at her, magenta eyes full of malice. Ophelia stood as tall as she could, holding her ground as the dragon approached her. She grasped its muzzle, the iron burning her fingers as she stared deep into those swimming pink orbs.

There was a voice in her head.

Let go.

"I'm trying to help you," Ophelia whispered, shutting her eyes and resting her forehead against the dragon's snout.

Why?

"Because I've been where you are," she said.

The iron muzzle cracked and fell apart, freeing the dragon and its magic. Ophelia stood stiff as a board, softly stroking the place between its eyes. The smell of soot and dying embers tickled Ophelia's nose as the dragon purred.

Thank you.

"My pleasure," Ophelia smiled, bowing to the magnificent creature.

The dragon spread its tattered wings, the webbing reminiscent of an aurora borealis. Sunlight beamed through the webbing, drenching Ophelia in a cascade of color. A sense of peace coursed through her.

Blessings.

"Thank you," Ophelia said, stepping out of the way as the dragon took to the skies.

Under any other circumstance, Ophelia would stop and stare as it twisted through the sky. Instead, she turned on her heels and raced to the other dragon.

"You're in so much trouble!" Seamus screamed as she ran by. He had a tear-stricken guard pinned beneath his boot as he swung blindly at another with his axe.

"I know!" Ophelia screamed back.

The second dragon was smaller. Its scratched black horns and the spikes down its back resembled antlers. Its face was long and slender, reminding her of a deer. Black fur tipped its tail and wove between the spikes. Ophelia had never seen a dragon like this, not even in her books. The rest of its body was familiarly serpentine, spare for the hooves on its back legs. Its scales were a dull gray tipped in silver. Its eyes were milky white. It didn't struggle or flinch as Ophelia touched it. Instead, it leaned into her. She freed it just the same as she had its companion, guiding it out from between the spokes of the wheel. It looked over its shoulder at her, surveying her. It shook its wings, electricity buzzing in the air. The webbing was pitch black yet sparkled like the night sky.

Ophelia bowed to the dragon.

It bowed back.

This time, she did stop and watch as the dragon took flight. Its wings left trails of stardust as it glided high above. The Witch stole a moment of wonderment to imagine what it must feel like riding a dragon. Nothing else would compare, she guessed.

"You're welcome," Ophelia said, waving to it.

"Kid, watch out!" Seamus screamed, startling her.

She turned just in time to see a guard sneaking up behind her.

CHAPTER FORTY-EIGHT

BEST LAID PLANS

Ophelia pushed the wheel with all her might, forgetting there was a spoke behind her until it crashed into the back of her skull. She stumbled forward, gingerly touching her head. Just as the guard caught the spoke and flung it back to her, she looked up. Unable to duck out of the way, the second spoke hit her so hard she staggered back, colliding with the first again. A sickening *THUD!* rang through the air.

"Ow," she mumbled before collapsing to the ground.

Seamus rolled his eyes as he headbutted his attacker. Their nose popped as it cracked against the back of his skull. Their arms loosened as they slipped backward, freeing him. How they'd snuck up and got him in a chokehold, Seamus didn't know. This unfortunate fight was nothing but a blur of dragon scales and war cries.

Ophelia's attacker was rushing at him. Seamus dove to the side, rolling away head-first, jumping back up when he landed, grabbing his axe off the ground, spinning it around in his sweaty hands. He flipped his hair back, shaking the blood-sodden locks from his face. Either that looked cool or cocky because his attacker discarded their broadsword, beckoning him forward.

"Your choice," Seamus laughed, lunging forward.

He swung the axe, his attacker catching it with strength no man should have. His eyes flashed green, the telltale sign of a werewolf. Seamus groaned, kicking him between the legs. His attacker squeaked, collapsing to his knees. With the handle of his axe, he knocked the sour wolf unconscious.

He stood shaking for a minute, his wolf screaming in agony. Werewolves weren't meant to harm one another, but pack mentality only went so far in the human mind. He spat out blood, cracked his neck, then turned toward the Witch.

With shaking limbs, she stood, brushing herself off, bonking her head yet again on the spokes of the old wheel.

Seamus gave a disdainful sigh.

"Did you get—Oh. Good job," she said, looking around, rubbing the back of her head, a pained pout on her lips.

"How's your noggin?"

She shrugged, walking up to him, that pout turning to a frown. Seamus shook his head, turning to the unconscious guards before him. Surely, they had something of value on them. Ophelia rocked side to side, feet shuffling to keep herself upright. He squinted at her, searching the werewolf's pockets.

"Happy now?" he asked, glancing up at the sky where two dragons were dancing amid the clouds.

She just stared at him.

"You okay?" he asked warily. Oh, Stars, not again.

With a shaking hand, she pointed back and forth between her eyes.

Seamus mimicked her. "I don't know what that means, kid."

"Fuzzy," she choked out.

"'Fuzzy?'" Seamus repeated, standing slowly, pocketing some coins.

She nodded, reaching up to remove her mask. Her nose and cheeks were red, and purple splotches dotted her Witch Marks. Seamus grimaced, wiping his hands on his pants as he walked toward her. He snapped, drawing her attention to his hands, which he held at her eye level.

"How many fingers am I holding up?"

Ophelia's glassy eyes seemed unfocused. She squinted, blinked, then rubbed them, shaking her head to clear it. Much to Seamus's chagrin, her eyelids drooped.

"Are you moving them just to mess with me?" she asked.

"Nope," he sighed. He put up one finger, slowly moving it back and forth in front of her face. "Follow."

She followed his finger, eyes jerking unsteadily in their sockets.

"You're concussed," Seamus said, dropping his hand.

"I'm fine, Seamus, really," she frowned.

"Okay, okay, if you insist. But just do this one last thing for me, okay?" He moved to the side, gesturing forward loosely. "Take a few steps for me, if you please, dear *Vinterheks*."

She glared at him, holding her head high as she walked briskly past him.

The first two steps were fine, but by the third, she was staggering. On the fourth, she swayed. On the fifth, she hit the ground hard.

"No, not concussed at all," Seamus whispered, looking to the dragons, wondering why he was being punished like this.

With a heavy sigh, he came to kneel beside her. She stared unblinking at him, cheeks now red from embarrassment rather than blunt force trauma.

"How's the view?" he asked.

"Lovely. Care to join me?"

"Not particularly." He went to hoist her up off the ground but paused, scowling. "I'm going to lift ya up. Is that all right?"

"Yeah," she sighed.

He took her by the shoulders, hauling her off the ground, setting her upright on unsteady legs.

"I'm going to wrap my arm around you. Are you okay with that?" She nodded. He looped his arm around her, noting the dirt and twigs stuck to her. His hand hovered before her face. "May I?"

"I trust you," she said groggily.

Concussed or not, he was sure she'd never understand how much that meant to him. He smiled, brushing her off, looking over his shoulder to make sure no other threats had lurked out of the shadows.

"My head hurts," she breathed, reaching up to rub her temples.

"Oh really? Never would've guessed."

"No one likes a smart ass, Seamus—Wait, where's my

mask?" She whipped her head around, scanning the ground.

"You took it off," Seamus sighed.

"Did I?"

"Stars, kid, you're worrying me."

"Sorry."

Seamus just shook his head, leading her to where her mask lay. He bent, picked up the mask, then placed it over her face.

"Thank you," she said, a drunken smile on her lips.

Seamus gave her a bored look. "Faint on me, and I leave you where you drop."

"Noted."

With that, Seamus pointed toward the steps leading away from the lifts. "Fancy a walk?"

Ophelia sighed.

"Should've left the dragons," Seamus smiled.

That drunken smile held steady as she tilted her head back to watch them flit across the sky. "They're happy now. So am I."

Seamus rolled his eyes, dragging her to the steps. They hobbled down them as fast as they could, hoping more guards weren't waiting for them somewhere below.

Seamus had no idea how long they'd been on those steps, but his legs ached, and Ophelia was walking fine on her own by the time they made it to the first level of the underground city. A few feet away, where the lifts normally descend through a hole in the platform, was a whispering crowd.

"Oops," Ophelia whispered.

Seamus shushed her, stifling a laugh, gesturing for her to follow him down a dark alleyway. Dull crystal-powered lanterns lit their way, casting the world in a rainbow glow. Seamus allowed his posture to straighten and his steps to slow the farther down they went. All the guards knew his face, but they should be fine as long as they kept to the shadows. At least until the guards up top woke up.

Then again, they'd recently run into a figment of his past despite his best efforts.

Damn, Egill.

The steps stopped on another platform littered with stalls and vendors selling all sorts of strange and mystical things. In reality, those 'love tonics' and 'magical-looking glasses' were all fakes. The real potions and cursed objects were farther down.

"Seamus," Ophelia whispered, an odd lilt to her voice.

He turned to where she was pointing. He felt himself deflate, though he wasn't surprised by the sight. There was his old wanted poster, staring back at him with that snarky smile and those glittering eyes. Ah, to be young and carefree. He imagined there were thousands of those old posters strewn throughout Dødbyen. Yay.

Up ahead was another lift, which, thankfully, wasn't powered by a dragon Ophelia would beg him to set free. This one was powered by two scrawny humans wearing tattered clothes. Humans or animals? Which was morally better to exploit? That was the question.

Not keen on philosophical debates, Seamus dug in his pocket for the loose change he'd stolen earlier. He flicked a few coins into the young lads' hands, then stepped onto the lift with Ophelia.

It shook and swung a little as it descended. Ophelia shifted closer to him, almost grabbing his arm for stability. Seamus side-eyed her as she stared out at the buildings across the chasm. This chasm stretched on for miles. If you didn't fancy walking all the way around, you could take the rope bridges across. Or, if you were lucky enough to have wings, you could easily flit around the levels. Seamus elbowed the presumably wide-eyed Witch, pointing to two fairies with jewel-bright wings hovering in midair, laughing loudly. They wore the flashy costumes of performers beneath fur coats, their skin dusted with glitter.

There was that drunken smile again.

"You'll see all sorts of colorful characters down here," Seamus said. "Be on your toes."

Colorful light flickered on the mossy walls of the chasm. The sounds of thousands of creatures going about their days found Seamus's ears, setting him on edge. He hated crowds—hated them even more when there wasn't an easy escape route. Already, he regretted this decision.

With a glance at Ophelia, he realized he was hating it all

for more than one reason.

"Are you sure you're okay?" he asked warily.

She shrugged. "I'm getting there. As long as I don't get another fever, I'm all right."

"What constitutes a fever for you? You're constantly freezing."

"You just answered your own question, Seamus."

The lift tilted forward as he leaned over the railing to gaze below. Ophelia squeaked with fright. He heard her shoes slide across the wooden floor and the chains beside her rattle.

"You're fine, kid," Seamus laughed.

Behind him, she was clinging to the railing for dear life. The dark eyes of her polar bear mask seemed to widen, though he imagined her eyes were shut tight.

"I am decidedly *not* fine," she snapped.

He laughed to himself, leaning heavily on the railing, causing the lift to tip further forward.

"Stop it!" Ophelia screeched.

Seamus ignored her, looking down upon the bustling underground city. Few places on the surface were more treacherous than this. Though the formal name was Dødbyen, the locals lovingly called this city Abyss. Apparently, City of The Dead just wasn't cutting it. Nowhere else had earned the same moniker as the fateful void beyond the stars where all evil eventually ended up. Nowhere except Dødbyen.

"Please step back from the edge, Seamus," Ophelia squeaked.

"Don't tell me you're afraid of heights," he laughed, reclaiming his place at the center of the lift. It jerked and swung before settling. Ophelia hurried to his side.

"I'm not," she said, hands folded neatly in front of her. Seamus imagined her knuckles were white under her old, ratty gloves from how hard she was squeezing her palms.

Seamus gave her a knowing look, smirking despite her pout. "Ahh, Vinterheksen, exalted and mighty. Bested by her fear of heights and a rickety old lift."

An arc of electricity shot up his arm. He winced, stumbling to the side. His chest tightened, his eyes watering.

"Ahh, varulv, stoic and sure. Bested by a concussed Witch."

"All right, all right, point taken," Seamus laughed nervously, rubbing his aching arm. "So. You admit you've got a concussion?"

She was quiet, looking at the tops of her shoes.

The lift came to a stop. A young woman bowed to them, opened the gate, and swept them into the streets.

"Stay close," Seamus whispered, weaving his way through the crowd.

Seamus kept his ears on the sound of Ophelia's buzzing and his eyes on the massive waterfall in the distance off to their left. Together, they dodged carts full of poisoned pastries and bottled dragon fire. Ophelia's eyes were on the market stalls, scanning them for Stars-know what.

"Stay focused," Seamus said over his shoulder.

Ophelia nodded, quickening her pace until she fell in step beside him. Occasionally, she'd slow and wander a few feet away, distracted by something shiny.

Seamus could tell she was growing weary.

"Is there something specific you're looking for?" he asked, grabbing her by the strap of her satchel before a cart filled to bursting with foul-smelling potions could run her over.

"Not really," she said groggily. "Just looking."

"You're goin' down, aren't you?"

"Very much so," she sighed, her shoulders sagging.

Seamus took one last glance at the waterfall before turning his attention to the buildings jutting out from the chasm walls. He spotted a glowing sign that read 'tavern,' yanked Ophelia's strap so she'd follow, then hightailed it up a short set of stairs.

"We'll rest here for a moment; let you get your footing," he explained, opening the door to the very busy, very loud tavern. Both of them winced.

"Thank you, Seamus," Ophelia yawned.

"Don't mention it," he muttered.

Seamus watched her out of the corner of his eye as he paid for overpriced pastries and drinks. Ophelia stood rocking back and forth on her heels, preoccupied with the paintings on the tavern's wall. He frowned, pushing her toward a table in the corner.

He found it odd that they were always eating in the corner of hole-in-the-wall inns and taverns. Guess they really were criminals now. Only the shadiest of folks constantly hid in corners.

They ate quietly, both trying to melt into the shadows and disappear among the crowd. A fight had broken out at the bar. Drunken laughter and boisterous conversations drowned out the sound. Scantily clad women were vying for the attention of idiotic men. Children were pick-pocketing the elderly. Ah, Dødbyen. Home of criminals. What a joy! They fit right in.

"And. . . um. . . just. . . um. . . what was I saying?" Ophelia suddenly asked.

Seamus turned to look at her. "What?" he asked loudly.

She was looking out the grimy window to her right, tracing patterns in the muck with her finger. "I'm sorry for running off like that. I was being stupid. I. . ." She rubbed her neck furiously, staring at her empty mug of cocoa. "I don't know where I was going with that."

Seamus traced the curves of her mask, noting each immaculately carved strand of fur. "I prefer concussions to stab wounds. I'll tell you that right now," he scoffed. "But I'd prefer neither if I had to choose."

She busied herself with taking in the patrons of the tavern. The movement was small, but he was sure her eyes flicked down to the salt and nutshell-covered floor. Was this the sort of place she'd jot down in her sketchbook? If she did, he'd want to see what faces in the crowd she chose to add. Who stood out to her? *What* stood out to her? He knew for sure she'd draw the dragons, but what else?

And why was that horrid minty smell seeping off of her again?

"Ophelia," he said sternly.

Still, she wouldn't look at him.

"Kid, I'm not mad at you," he sighed. "I just—I just worry."

Her shoulders stiffened. The mint went bitter.

"I wish you wouldn't run off into danger like that. I get that you hate seeing animals hurt; I do. But you *have* to learn when and where to pick your battles." He sat back in his chair, watching her carefully. It was too loud in the crowded tavern for him to easily pick out her heartbeat, but he was sure it was thundering away inside her chest.

"I don't know why I didn't think of the other spoke," she said quietly. Her hands searched for something to fidget with, finding nothing.

Seamus only shrugged. "You said it yourself: you're not a fighter. Instinct kicks in, and sometimes instinct can get you killed." He snapped his fingers so she'd finally look at him. "I've had more concussions than I can count. More than I can remember, actually." His thoughts faded away as he tried to recount the last time he'd been laid up in bed, his head pounding so bad he couldn't open his eyes. "Look, all I'm trying to say is that you didn't do anything wrong. Your strength is your softness, your compassion. Mine is my fists. I'll let you guess which one I value more."

"You're too kind to me, Seamus," she said softly, a smile tugging at her lips.

"Guess you're starting to rub off on me."

That smile of hers twitched as she wrung her hands nervously. "I need to tell you some—" Her words died on her lips. "It's not important," she sighed.

Seamus's eyebrows furrowed. That minty sadness had disappeared, replaced by the lip-puckering stench of overripe pomegranates. Part of him doubted that smell only meant anxiety.

"What's on your mind?" he asked. "Talk to me."

"I'm just tired," she sighed, absentmindedly tugging at the loose pieces of yarn hanging off her shawl, head propped up on her free hand. Seamus had almost forgotten about their skirmish at the inn and the wounds she'd sustained. He hadn't noticed the frayed hole in her shawl until now.

He did, however, keep noticing she used that excuse quite often. 'I'm tired' didn't seem to mean the same thing to *her* that it did to *him*. His thoughts drifted to Lochlan and the experiments she'd mentioned. Saying she was tired must've meant something between them. Whether the experiments stopped or she muddled through after she said that, he didn't want to know. His guess, unfortunately, was the latter.

Again, he thought back to what Egill had said. If Lochlan happened to be the one running his mouth—if he'd survived—Seamus would make sure his was the last face that man ever saw.

They ate in silence after that. The pomegranate smell hadn't disappeared. Just as he had on the ride here, Seamus wondered what she was thinking, what she was feeling. They had very little time left together. He'd hoped to have figured her out by now. Yet there she sat, still a complete and utter mystery. He wanted to know her, know how her mind worked, know what those brilliant silver eyes saw when no one else was looking. She fascinated him in a thousand different ways. She was a miracle and an enigma, something most prayed for daily. But here she was, inches away, the innocence of childhood and the agonizing responsibility of her destiny warring inside her heart. He wanted to take it all from her. Every minty sadness, everything that made her stink of rotten pomegranates. Instead, he'd fill every chasm in her mind with whatever brought her sugary happiness.

That's what he *wanted* to do. Desperately.

But he couldn't.

For he was Seamus Norland, The Damned. He wouldn't allow her to sink to his level. Wouldn't allow her to rot under his touch like everything else.

That's why they'd come here, wasn't it? He was meant to deposit her on the Kirkeby's doorstep and run. That was the plan. That's what they had agreed on. *That's what he had to do.*

His throat tightened at the thought of leaving her behind.

Seamus had told her he wanted peace, but that couldn't be farther from the truth. He wanted revenge. There were hundreds whom he wanted to fill with the same pain he felt every second of every day. He was ready and willing to do unspeakable things, but that was a side of himself Ophelia could never ever see. Too much of his darkness had already crept into her light.

It was time to leave, time to part. No matter how badly he wanted to stay, he'd drawn a bad hand, and they were bound to lose.

"You ready?" he asked gruffly, trying to clear the lump from his throat.

She nodded, stacking her empty plate atop his. He deposited their plates, cups, and cutlery at the counter, and then off they went into the crowd.

Every step made Seamus feel as though he were on his way to the gallows. There was a tightness in his throat, but it wasn't from a noose.

At this point, he would've preferred a noose to the sadness in his heart.

CHAPTER FORTY-NINE

NEVER MEANT TO DO YOU HARM

Ophelia had an ache in her chest and an overthinking mind, but she was trying her very best to hide it. Seamus wove through the crowd, heading toward the waterfall with extraordinary speed. Try as she might, she could hardly keep up. Each time she did catch up, he'd quicken his pace. Was something wrong? He hadn't alerted her to any danger.

How strange.

The closer they got to the massive waterfall, the louder the rushing water was. It filled Ophelia with a sense of excitement and wonder, but most of all, she could feel the effects of her concussion washing away. Sometimes, she pondered whether the elements would heal her if she asked. A theory to test another time, perhaps.

Seamus cut around the edge of the waterfall and into the shadows. Behind the fall was a thin and slippery path. Icy mist drenched them as they took to it, careful not to slip into the churning water beside them. Ophelia couldn't see the bottom of the swirling pool. That was never a good sign. Those murky depths probably went on for ages. All manner of creatures could be hidden in those depths.

Eventually, the path led them to a passage carved into the chasm wall. On either side of the corridor, glowing crystals lit up the walls, just like the ones hanging in lanterns throughout the city. Each was a different color, reminding Ophelia of the aurora dragon's wings. She hoped it and its friend would be okay, hoped they'd flown far away.

Seamus drug his hand along the walls, his reflection distorted in the fragments of crystal surrounding them. Where his fingers touched, the crystals glowed brighter.

"Isn't that something?" he asked.

Ophelia nodded, tapping one of the crystals. Its pink surface rippled with light. "I've never been to the Center Cities. This is my first time seeing crystal-powered light."

"I figured as much," Seamus smiled, beckoning her forward. He picked up a loose shard off the cave floor, twisting it in the low light. Their faces were warped on its surface, making them look quite silly. He handed it to her, pointing to her pack. "Pocket it."

"That's stealing, Seamus," Ophelia laughed.

"So?"

Ophelia shoved the stone into her bag, grinning mischievously. "I doubt—Wow," she breathed.

They turned a corner, and the pathway abruptly opened into a vast cavity with a mansion smack dab in the middle. The ground had shifted from slippery rock to squishy moss. Where trees should be above ground, there were towering glowing mushrooms. The ceiling dripped with a steady flow of underground rain. Bioluminescent algae clung to the walls, mixing with the cold glow of the mushrooms. A gate made of pure gold protected the mansion; beyond it, towers of rocks littered the front garden.

The house itself stood two stories tall and looked more like an incredibly small castle rather than a mansion. It even had a few turrets! The exterior was painted cream, though the warmth seeping out of the windows made it seem like it was fashioned out of pure gold. The windows themselves were magnificent, too. They were tall and pointed at the top, made of amber-colored glass. A massive porch wrapped around the front and left side. There, smaller glowing mushrooms grew up from between the wooden slats.

"What is this place?" Ophelia asked, awestruck.

"It's a. . ." He rubbed his temples, thinking hard. "Damn, it's right on the tip of my—Ah! Subsurface biosphere!" he exclaimed, rather proud of himself. He swept his arms wide, looking up at the ceiling with wonderment.

"Those are big words, Seamus. Are you sure you know

what they mean?"

"Not at all."

Ophelia laughed, watching a chittering colony of bats do loops above. Salamanders crawled on the walls. Strange glowing bugs wove between her feet.

What a peculiar place.

She loved it immediately.

Ophelia wondered who'd found it and why they built such a horrid city on the other side of the waterfall. Maybe they hadn't. Perhaps this was meant to be a utopia, but as with all good things, it fell into ruin.

"Something on your mind?" Seamus asked.

"When you said you had friends, I wasn't expecting these type of friends."

"Why? What do you mean?"

"Well, these people are obviously well-to-do," she laughed, gesturing to the mansion in all its gilded glory.

Seamus scoffed, feigning hurt. "What makes you think I can't have well-to-do friends?"

Ophelia gave him a pointed look. "Seamus Norland, you take great joy in catching fish with your teeth."

He reddened. "Point taken," he laughed. "Let's not mention that inside, shall we? Don't mention our escapade up top either."

Ophelia nodded, waiting for him to open the gate. Several moments of silence passed before she turned to look at him. He just stood there, rocking back and forth on his heels, hands tightly grasping the straps of his pack. Ophelia raised an eyebrow, tilting her head to the side, donning her trademark pout.

"What now?" he asked exasperatedly, glancing sideways at her.

"Why are we just standing here?"

"I'm. . ." He paused, gesturing loosely to the gate. ". . . allowing you time to. . . take in the. . . intricacies of the metalwork. So you may sketch it later."

"How thoughtful," Ophelia laughed. "And here I thought you were stalling."

"See, I *am* learning," he said proudly.

"Learning how to be an insufferable liar," Ophelia said under her breath.

"I heard that," Seamus grumbled, giving her a disapproving look.

"I know," Ophelia smiled as she pushed open the gate. Seamus's face lit up in horror as she waltzed through it. She ignored his unintelligible squeaks, wondering why this place made him squirm so much.

"Just—Listen!" Seamus screeched, grabbing her wrist.

Ophelia spun, confused.

His eyes were full of remorse. They stared at each other for a moment. The drip-drip-dripping of the ceiling stopped, and artificial raindrops seemingly suspended in midair.

"I—" He searched what little he could see of her face. Ever so slowly, he let go of her wrist, hanging his head low. "Never mind."

"Is everything all right?" she asked as he brushed past her.

"Yeah," he sighed.

Ophelia lingered at the gate as he marched up to the mansion's front door. He pulled a rope, and the sound of a bell bounced off the cavern walls. She hated it when he was vague and brooding. Usually, that meant there was a lot on his mind that he felt he couldn't say. He whistled for her, nodding toward the door. Ophelia steeled herself, skipping up to him. They waited patiently for the door to open, looking at everything but each other.

Eventually, the door opened to reveal an elderly woman in a cream-colored maid's outfit. She took one look at Seamus, frowned, and then whisked them inside. The maid bowed before departing, leaving Seamus and Ophelia in the foyer to gawk at the splendiferous architecture before them. Well, Ophelia gawked. Seamus looked bored.

The stark white walls seemed to pulse with light and warmth. The grand staircase before them was dramatic in all the right ways, just like the ones often described in Ophelia's books. Plush carpet the color of mulled wine squished beneath their feet. A chandelier with glowing crystals fashioned to look like flaming candles hung from the ceiling. It was all so beautiful.

Then there was Seamus. Every surface was polished and gleaming, and here he was, a mud puddle on an otherwise spotless rug.

Who owned this place?

Who were they?

How exactly had he met them?

"Seamus!" came a high-pitched man's voice from a golden archway to their right. Soon followed a pudgy body dressed in a velveteen suit two sizes too small. He had a kind, purplish-red face and was missing an eye. His perfectly coiffed black hair was streaked with gray. "Stars, boy! Where have you been!"

"Hei, Helgi," Seamus said, bowing ever so slightly. "God kveld."

"'Good evening?'" the man scoffed. He shuffled across the carpet, shaking his head in disappointment. "Is that all you've to say for yourself? How long has it been, boy? We thought you were—Oh." The man's gaze fell on Ophelia. He considered her, his one eye flicking back to Seamus in a questioning sort of way. "Who do we have here?" he asked, his voice wistful.

Seamus didn't move to introduce her. Ophelia followed his eyes to the sprawling staircase. A tall woman whose hair was pinned up in intricate braids descended the stairs, her blush pink tea gown trailing behind her. She was significantly younger than the man, or at least she appeared to be. Her eyes were a striking blue, her hair a rich black.

She smiled kindly at Seamus, taking her place beside the pudgy man. "Hallo, *varulv*," she said, her voice deeper and huskier than Ophelia had expected it to be.

Seamus frowned though he bowed deeply. "Hallo, Tiril."

"Whom have you brought?" the woman asked, eyes glued to Ophelia's mask.

Seamus turned to her, giving her an apologetic smile. "Forgive me for this," he whispered, clearing his throat.

With one hand tucked behind his back, he used the other to grab hold of one of her mask's ears. Ophelia flinched away as he snatched the mask from her face. Her hair fell softly on her shoulders as she reached up to cover her Witch Marks with her hands. Seamus grabbed her hand before she could, giving her a solemn shake of his head.

"Helgi og Tiril Kirkeby," he said, standing as tall as he could. Tiril's eyes glittered with anticipation. Helgi's jaw just about shattered on the floor. Seamus stepped to the side, dropping Ophelia's hand. "*Vinterheksen*, Ophelia Av'Skogen."

"*Så det begynner*," Tiril whispered. She picked up the hem of her tea gown and knelt, bowing her head. Helgi placed a hand over his heart, his knees cracking as he, too, knelt.

So it begins, Tiril had said.

Ophelia looked to Seamus, who seemed to be a thousand miles away. He refused to look at her. His entire demeanor had changed. Whoever stood beside her was not the Seamus Norland she'd come to know. Out of habit, her eyes flicked to his shadow.

"*Mange velsignelser*," Helgi said, looking up at her with his one pale blue eye. *Many blessings.*

"*Takk*," Ophelia said, curtseying. She leaned over to Seamus, nearly toppling over since he'd moved so far away. "What is happening?" she mumbled.

Still, Seamus wouldn't look at her. "They won't stand unless you say they may."

Ophelia felt her cheeks redden. She coiled in on herself, smiling sheepishly. "You—You may stand," she said.

Tiril helped Helgi to his feet, both starstruck as they admired her. They had a mansion built to mirror a palace, yet they regarded *her* as royalty. Ophelia had never felt so out of place. She was content to hide her Marks beneath that silly old mask. She liked the anonymity, the way she could blend into a crowd. Seamus knew this, yet he'd put her on display for these strange people.

How dare he.

She glanced at him. He'd gone pale, his eyes devoid of emotion.

"*Vinterheks*," Tiril said, her voice full of wonder. "It is an honor to meet you."

"Oh, thank you. It's an honor to meet you as well," Ophelia said with a smile, forcing herself to tear her eyes away from the finicky wolf at her side.

Tiril and Helgi practically melted.

"A feast," Seamus said, clearing his throat. "A feast to celebrate this momentous occasion."

Helgi snapped his fingers, pointing at him with such exhilaration that Ophelia was sure he'd burst. "A splendid idea!"

Tiril nodded, taking him by the elbow. "Leave your bags, we'll send someone to take them up to your rooms. Please. Make yourselves at home." Together they disappeared through another golden arch to the left. Ophelia noted the arch was covered in carvings of ferns.

As soon as the Kirkebys's footsteps faded, Ophelia rounded on Seamus, ripping her mask from his hands, smacking him on the head with it. Seamus winced, cowering as she wound up to hit him again.

"I make bad decisions when I'm hungry, okay?" he said sheepishly.

"Oh, you'd do anything for food!" she snapped. "You just ate!"

"I said I was sorry!" he groaned.

"That was not your secret to reveal!" Ophelia spat, clipping her mask to her sketchbook with a scowl.

Seamus put up his hands in defense, edging away. "They're religious zealots! Kid, they'll protect you with their lives. You're a living deity to them."

"I never asked to be!" Ophelia hissed, dropping her bags to the floor and kicking off her boots before she made for the archway to the right.

"When have I ever steered you wrong?" Seamus asked, following close behind.

Ophelia ignored him, for she was again awestruck by the room they had entered. Inset bookshelves lined every wall, all culminating around a fireplace where a sleeping drake lay amid dying embers. Glowing crystals in intricate metal cages lay nestled between books, casting the room in a soft rainbow glow. Ornate furniture and a table filled with sweets sat in the center of the room. Suits of armor from across the world and cabinets filled with strange artifacts littered the spaces between shelves. Higher up, tapestries hung from the peaked roof. Some depicted battles, while others showed animals playing in a field. A bear skin rug lay before the hearth. A dog slept there, paws up in the air, tongue hanging out of its open mouth. A cat slept on the back of a brocade lounge.

Ophelia crossed to one of the bookshelves, fingering the spines of several tomes. Some were merely fictitious stories, others were histories, but many were religious texts. It seemed Tiril and Helgi were theologians.

Something brushed against her ankles. Ophelia looked down to see that the gigantic cat had jumped from its perch to greet her. It wrapped its feather-duster tail around her leg, purring softly. It had long, spotted, tawny fur and enormous green eyes that seemed to squint into a smile. A *skogskatt*, or *forest cat*. Ophelia had heard they were as hard to procure as they were expensive. Much like some of the books surrounding her.

"Seem like your kind of people, don't they?" Seamus asked. She could hear the smile in his voice.

"I'm not speaking to you right now," Ophelia snapped, not daring a look over her shoulder.

"Okay, okay, that was an asinine thing to do, I admit. I apologize," he mumbled. The cushions on the lounge sighed beneath his weight as he sat down, and the coffee table shifted as he kicked his muddy boots onto its glass surface. "You had to know this was the plan."

Ophelia just rolled her eyes and knelt to pet the cat. Its purrs were loud as thunder, its fur soft as a cloud. A wet muzzle nudged her arm as the dog sauntered up beside her. It was a reindeer herder, a medium-sized dog with pointy ears and a black and tan coat. It panted happily, licking Ophelia's hand. She smiled, scratching it behind its ears.

Seamus had turned in his seat, mystified. "Those two hate each other. They hate people even more."

Ophelia gave him a smug look.

There was a pitter-patter of scaly footsteps as the drake came over and crawled up Ophelia's back. It yawned, a tiny spark popping from its mouth as it settled around her neck. Its forked tongue lazily licked her cheek before it shut its eyes, content to sleep across her shoulders. It was small for a drake, no more than three feet long. Its spiky scales were brown, spare for the soot-like spots of black around its eyes. Its belly was warm on Ophelia's neck, and just like the dragons she'd freed, it smelled of campfire smoke.

"Your beasts like her," Seamus announced as Tiril and

Helgi entered the den.

Ophelia's cheeks reddened as she stood, careful not to drop the drake. It gently wrapped its tail around her throat, nuzzling the space between her jaw and ear. The dog and the forest cat followed her to one of the chairs, waiting patiently as she settled into her seat. The cat hopped into her lap, curling itself into a ball. The dog lay across her feet, yawning before it rested its head upon its front paws.

"Ivar the cat, Sköll the dog, and Maj-gun the drake," Tiril explained. "My goodness, I haven't seen those three get along in years. Ivar and Sköll tend to butt heads. Boys will be boys, I suppose. Maj-gun rarely puts up with their antics. She can be a drama queen."

"Ophelia has a way with surly creatures," Seamus said. There was misery in his voice.

"I'll say!" Helgi laughed. "I suppose it was you who freed our dragons, then?"

Ophelia stroked the cat, narrowing her eyes at him. "Is that a problem?" Seamus shifted uncomfortably at her tone.

Helgi paled, shaking his head furiously. "No, *Vinterheks*! Not at all!" He laughed nervously, pulling the collar of his shirt away from his neck. "No, it was but a simple question."

Ophelia leaned back in her chair, eyes fixed on the supposed zealots. If they saw her as some high and mighty being, she might as well play the part. That's what Seamus seemed to want, after all. Seamus was scared for her, but perhaps he deserved to be scared *of* her, too.

"See to it, no animal—dragon or otherwise—takes their place," Ophelia said, still slowly petting Ivar's head. Maj-gun chittered her approval.

Suddenly, she realized she was talking and acting like Arild Melhus, the General. The one who'd siphoned the hobgoblin. Her haughtiness disintegrated after that. Seamus must've noticed her deflate. He gave her a questioning look, which she promptly ignored.

"A wonderful decree!" Helgi said, applauding her.

"Those old lifts need to be serviced anyway," Tiril said. Her eyes darted back and forth between Helgi and Seamus, a bead of sweat forming on her forehead.

Seamus smoothed his bushy beard, smiling mischievously behind his hand.

Helgi cleared his throat, leaning forward. "Dinner shall be served later this evening. Our cooks need time to account for guests."

Seamus shrugged. "We're not in any hurry."

"Speaking of, what brings you here, Seamus?" Tiril asked.

Seamus uncrossed and recrossed his legs on the coffee table. Flecks of mud dusted a sugar-coated cookie. "You heard of the Tø incident?" he asked.

Ophelia studied him. Seamus Norland was long gone. In his place, sat a thief parading around as a wealthy businessman. He acted as if he owned the place—owned *them*. Ophelia figured he could fool just about anyone into believing he actually did.

What was it Egill had said? That Seamus had been raised to rule? Was this the Seamus Norland he'd been while with the Ulvemordere?

Helgi nodded. "There've been whispers."

"Ophelia was hidden amongst the townsfolk," he said, gesturing lazily to where she sat. "If not for her, I could very well be dead. Anyone can fake a Witch Mark, but I've not met a single person who can match the power she holds."

Tiril and Helgi—who'd been trying ever so hard not to stare into Ophelia's soul—turned to Seamus.

"Did the Ulvemordere see her?" Tiril asked.

Seamus gave a curt nod. Before he could say anything else, Helgi implored them to recount their whole journey scene by scene. Inevitably, the subject turned to the hobgoblin, which infuriated Tiril so much that she about burst from anger.

Once they were finished, Helgi whispered, "Oh, this is awful news." Shaking his head, he sat back in his chair, scratching his chin. "What an adventure the two of you've had. They've surely put out a warning to look out for you."

"Yes, but not amongst the people," Seamus said matter-of-factly. "I've seen a few of my old wanted posters but nothing about Ophelia."

Tiril nodded, taking a sticky pastry from the coffee table. "It'd be widespread panic otherwise." Her eyes flicked up to one of the tapestries above.

Ophelia could just see the glint of a sword woven with metallic thread. Such a sight made her heart drop. She shifted uncomfortably in her seat, turning her attention back to the books around her.

Tiril and Helgi's eyes drifted back to her. She was more than a deity to them; that was for certain. Seamus knew this. They were true believers, religious zealots indeed. What was the play here? Nothing was making sense. She stole a glance at him, finding nothing but ice-cold emptiness on his face.

"Seamus, why have you brought her here?" Tiril asked, suddenly alarmed.

Seamus just shrugged. "I figured she'd be safest here."

"Oh, Jumping Jackals, Seamus!" Helgi spat. "You know very well Dødbyen lacks proper defense mechanisms. Were you followed?"

"I'm not an idiot, Helgi."

Both Tiril and Helgi gave him a look that clearly stated they felt the opposite was true.

"Forgive me, Vinterheks, but your presence here will be. . . troublesome, to say the least," Helgi said, turning green as he spoke.

"Nonsense," Seamus laughed. "Isn't this what you've always wanted? You've got your martyr—your miracle."

"Their *what*?" Ophelia asked.

Seamus waved her words away, shooting her a glare. "The two of you have spent your whole life searching for someone like her. And here I am, delivering her on your doorstep."

Helgi and Tiril shared a look. Tiril finished off her pastry, thoughtfully licking the honey off her thumb. Ophelia sensed an air of irritation resonating off her.

"Seamus, we spent our whole lives searching for someone like *you*," Helgi said, frowning as he stroked his beard. "This—this *child* is not our miracle."

"See, I disagree. Imagine, if you will—" he began, folding his arms behind his head, leaning back against the cushions with a yawn "—a new contender vying for the thorn-covered throne that is Snøbolig."

Ophelia shivered, subtly shaking her head. Seamus

watched her out of the corner of his eye. He was on thin ice, and she hoped he knew that.

"It is the birthright of Vinterheken to rule Snøbolig. From coast to coast—Port Fantastik to the Høstlunden border—it is all her domain," he continued. "That is not only truth but law. The Ulve know this. So do the people."

Helgi looked Ophelia up and down. "What are you saying?"

Seamus smirked to himself, pointing his thumb at Ophelia. "I'm saying I've just given you the Witch Queen of Snøbolig. For a price, of course. My question is, what are you going to do with her?"

"Excuse me, but you're not 'giving' me to anyone," Ophelia snapped. "I am not something to lend, sell, or barter away. Nor do I fancy being passed around like a chess piece!"

"No one will use you as a chess miss, Lady Ophelia," Tiril said, gesturing for her to settle down.

"So, you would sit by and watch as more towns like Tø are wiped off the map?" Seamus asked. "What happened to duty? To purpose? You said you wanted to change things, that you didn't want to sit by and watch more people get hurt. What happened to that?"

"And what happened to the man I knew an hour ago?" Ophelia asked. "This is not how I wanted to do things!"

Seamus's nostrils flared, his right eye twitching. Turning back to Helgi, he said, "You're meant to be building a rebellion. What would happen if you announced amongst these people that a Winter Witch has been found? That you, Helgi, found her?"

Helgi's eyes glittered with greed. "Well. . . Well, I'd be something of a legend. . ."

"Brother, mine," Tiril snapped. "What the Lady does with her title is not for us to profit off. That would make us no better than the Ulvemordere!"

Helgi rounded on her, pointing to Ophelia with one of his sausage fingers. "Tiril, her existence changes everything!"

Tiril opened her mouth to counter, but Ophelia stood abruptly, cutting her off. Ivar mewed in protest. Seamus whipped his head around to look at her, warning signals blaring in his eyes. He was trying to communicate something quietly, but Ophelia didn't stick around to try to deduce what he had to say.

"I do want to make a difference, but I will do that of my own free will. Neither you, Seamus Norland, nor them will get to choose when and how that happens," Ophelia spat.

With a *humpf!* She made for the foyer, Tiril on her heels. Their bags were gone, presumably somewhere on the second level. Tiril sighed heavily, directing Ophelia to the stairs.

"Come now," Tiril said softly. "Let the fools jabber on."

CHAPTER FIFTY

THE KINDEST BETRAYAL

Helgi stared at Seamus, his face full of fatherly disdain. "You are quite the anomaly, aren't you, Seamus?"

Seamus removed his feet from the coffee table, leaning forward, hands clasped beneath his chin. "So I've been told," he sighed.

"You know, you're right. She is a miracle." Helgi reached forward and took a cookie from a silver platter. "But she's a curse, too. Logistically, I know why you've brought her to me—excuse me—*us*. But you're damning us, Seamus."

Seamus bristled at that but didn't speak his mind. "Having her here is risky, I understand that, but she doesn't have anywhere else to go. If you let her, she'll be a figurehead. I see this having a fortuitous outcome."

Helgi broke his cookie in half, tossing part of it to Sköll. The old dog caught it midair, happily munching away on the sugary delight. Maj-gun returned to her place amongst the embers. Ivar hissed at Seamus before following Ophelia and Tiril upstairs. Typical. He hated cats.

"*You* are *always* a risk, Seamus, old boy," Helgi laughed. The long scar running down the right side of his face curved as he smiled. "But, I must admit, even the most dire circumstances end up paying off one way or another. What do you want in return for the girl?"

Seamus had thought long and hard on this. In actuality, there was nothing he would exchange for Ophelia. Still, he knew what he was doing and what he needed to say.

"Oona's manor," he said, allowing a wicked smile to play across his lips.

Helgi, unable to hide his surprise, sat back in shock. "You want my wife's vacation home?"

Seamus nodded. "Been a while since I had somewhere to lay my weary head. It'll be a nice change of pace."

"You're trading the last Winter Witch for a house?" Helgi asked slowly, in awe of how shallow Seamus could be. "A *house*, Norland. My dead wife's house."

"Seems pretty fair to me."

"You're acting like you haven't changed since we last spoke, but I know you have. There's worry in your heart, Norland. I could pick up that putrid stink from miles away." Helgi's eye flashed green, immense concern swirling behind his iris. "This isn't like you. What's going on? Is there something else you want?"

There were rarely secrets amid werewolves. The Kirkebys were the closest thing Seamus had had to a pack in ages. They knew him inside and out. Being known that deeply made Seamus's skin crawl.

"I just don't want to see the kid get hurt," he said with a shrug.

"And yet, you propose we take her into battle," Helgi laughed. "You can't have it both ways."

"I know."

See, that was the problem. Ophelia, one way or another, would end up leading a militia. Whether it would be her choice or not, it didn't matter. That was the outcome. That was her destiny. Seamus, however, didn't want to be around to see what happened after that. Ophelia was going to get herself killed, and Seamus would not have her blood on his hands. Pawning her off on the Kirkebys was just him trying to get it through her thick skull that someone would use her for personal gain wherever she went. What she did with that knowledge, he didn't care. He'd done his part; it was time to leave.

"We cannot promise her safety," Helgi said. "We could post our most trusted guards outside her bedroom door and never let her leave without an escort, but that wouldn't do anything. You know that, right?"

Seamus just rolled his eyes, sitting back, gazing into the fire. Absentmindedly, he wrung his hands, anxiously tapping his foot.

Helgi mumbled a very hurtful curse alongside his name. "You're not being truthful."

"Why does it matter?"

"Because all we've ever tried to do is protect and care for you," Helgi scoffed. "The least you can do is tell me what's really bothering you. You needn't hide from me, nor Tiril."

"I ran into Egill. He says you've got a plan regarding me, and I—"

Helgi sat forward rather suddenly, eyes wide. "When? When did you speak with him?"

"Not long ago," Seamus said, tilting his head to the side in confusion.

"He's here? In Dødbyen?" Helgi asked, jumping to his feet.

Seamus shook his head, suddenly unsure of himself. "What's wrong?"

Helgi eyed him suspiciously. "I'm just surprised, is all. What did he say?"

Seamus recounted his earlier conversation with the fickle fairy, unable to hide his discomfort. He couldn't sit still, couldn't focus on one thing for too long. Everything set him on edge. The crystal lights were too bright, the crackling fire too loud. As he spoke, Seamus noticed the old wolf before him was just as restless. If just one person sympathized with him about Egill, it'd be him. Helgi was usually a picture-perfect image of indifference. Seamus was sure he'd stay stone-faced throughout even the most brutal forms of torture. The Ulvemordere had stolen his eye many years ago. It was rumored Helgi hadn't even flinched. Spare his jovial appearance and sweet tooth, Helgi Kirkeby was a terrifying creature. But now, he shrunk in on himself, shaking in his pointy shoes like a baby lamb.

"Egill's right on one account. We have been planning a. . . *soiree*. . . on the Hunter's Moon to—oh how do I put this?—'celebrate' the. . . 'accomplishments'. . . of our. . . 'friends.' Yes, yes, that doesn't sound one bit nefarious, does it? Officially, it's a ball. *Un*officially—" he laughed rather boisterously, trying to hide his worry "—well, I'm sure you can put two and two together. We'd love to have you there, Seamus. We've big things planned. I'm sure you could help. . . 'host'. . . 'things'. . ." His use of air quotes made Seamus want to stick a fork in his remaining eye. "While there is always room for you at our table, Seamus, I must warn you this *soiree* is months away."

"I'm not looking to join a party planning committee, Helgi," Seamus said with a roll of his eyes.

"Oh, but I meant—"

"I know what you meant."

"Are you—"

"I'm sure."

Helgi reddened.

With a sigh, Seamus continued on. "I'm getting old, and I'm getting tired. I don't want to be part of this fight anymore, and I don't want to live in fear, either. Oona's manor is hidden deep in the forests of Høstlunden, far enough away that no one will ever find me. For once, I just want peace." He nodded to himself, trying to convince himself of this. It was easy to lie to Ophelia and the Kirkeby's, but he'd been finding it harder and harder to lie to himself. "I don't want to be a figurehead like Ophelia. Not anymore. All that got me was heartache, and I pray things will be different for her."

"Seamus Norland, you were born with lightning in your veins," Helgi sighed, shaking his head. "What makes you think you can find—or better yet, *deserve*—peace?" That was not exactly the response Seamus had been looking for.

He shrugged, taking a page from Ophelia's book. "I'm just very tired, Helgi."

Clicking his tongue for Sköll to follow, Helgi turned to leave. "The manor is yours if that's what your heart truly desires. Tiril and I will do our best to protect the child, but I fear our old bones will do little against the Ulvemordere. You know damn well what will happen when the world becomes privy to this secret. You also know, Seamus, what happens to those we deem living deities."

With that, he left Seamus to his thoughts. Alone in the stuffy den, he glanced up at the tapestries gently swaying overhead. The low light of the crystals made it hard to see, but he knew one of those sorry excuses for a rug had his image woven into it. He did know what happened to false deities and hoped Ophelia would never have to experience what he had many, many moons ago. Truthfully, a part of him wondered what happened to actual deities and whether she was one.

Sighing heavily, Seamus took a saucer, piled it high with sweets, and then left for his room.

Whatever happened next, it wasn't his fault nor his decision to make.

CHAPTER FIFTY-ONE

LADY IN WAITING

Up the stairs, Tiril and Ivar led Ophelia down a hall plastered with cream wallpaper. Every inch of the wallpaper was embossed with an array of flowers, the raised designs dusted with shimmer. Tables sat beneath portraits, each with a different bouquet. Ophelia recognized the impressionist depictions. Though the painter had made a valiant effort, the faces meant to encapsulate the Spirits were very far from how they actually looked. Ivar mewed happily as Tiril opened a set of golden double doors. Beyond was a hall with navy blue walls and silver door frames. Paintings of animals made of stardust hung on the walls. The carpet disappeared, and marble floors resembling the night sky took its place.

"Reija!" Tiril called down the hall. "I need you again, dear! Please come see me!" She closed the doors, smiling over her shoulder at Ophelia.

Turning, Tiril led her back down the hall, stopping at a door not far from the landing. With a flourish, she threw open the door to reveal a room aglow with warmth. A four-poster bed was pushed against the lefthand wall, the drapes drawn back to reveal a mattress overflowing with pillows and blankets. At its base, someone had neatly stacked her bags. Behind it, a tall window looked out over the back garden. To the right was a vanity, armoire, and partition, and the cream surfaces were painted with a thousand tiny wildflowers. A velvet, blush pink robe had been laid across the back of the vanity chair, seemingly awaiting her. Sweet-smelling steam wafted through the air from behind the partition. It all reminded Ophelia of a princess's quarters.

"You may help yourself to anything in the dresser that fits," Tiril said, crossing to the armoire and opening it to reveal all manner of dresses, blouses, and skirts. "Reija will be with you shortly. I've asked her to draw you a bath. Please wash up before dinner." She bowed, making for the door.

"Tiril," Ophelia said, surprising even herself. "Thank you for your hospitality."

"Oh! You're very welcome, Vinterheks."

Ophelia rocked back and forth on her feet uncomfortably. "You may call me Ophelia if you like. There's no need for titles."

Especially titles she sometimes felt she didn't deserve.

Tiril was practically glowing with delight. "If you so wish," she said. With another bow, she turned to the door. Hand hovering above the door handle, she said, "We know you are not an object, Ophelia dear. Seamus had no right to say such heinous things. He can be rather stupid."

"I've noticed," Ophelia muttered.

Tiril smiled. "Please come find me if you need anything."

With one final nod, she whisked out the door, the hem of her tea gown swirling after her.

Ophelia looked around the room one last time before begrudgingly peeling off her shawl and jacket. Grabbing the velvet robe, she made for the bathtub hidden behind the partition. The water was slightly pink in hue and filled with tiny foggy bubbles. Yes, this room definitely belonged to a princess. It felt odd knowing all this was meant for her. If being the almighty Winter Witch consisted solely of life's luxuries, she wouldn't mind becoming a public deity. Too bad her title also came with war room meetings and battles never won.

Free of her muddy and smelly garments, Ophelia stepped into the warm water, the bubbles popping across her ever-frozen skin. After washing away days of blood and muck, she sunk beneath the surface, shutting her eyes, imagining herself floating thousands of nautical miles beneath the ocean. That was something she'd always wanted to do, to see the deepest, darkest trenches of the sea, to test how far she could go. She was always calmer underwater. All she could focus on was holding her breath and the movement around her. Peeking through the pinkish water, she stared at the ceiling, reveling in this stolen moment of peace.

Her mind was quieter than it had been in days.

Her eyes closed softly as she imagined all the air in her lungs swirling in her chest.

If she wanted to, she could stay there for as long as she pleased. When you could control the elements, finding loopholes to problems such as breathing underwater was easy.

Sometimes, she'd hide beneath the river to escape Tø.

Her face crested the surface as she realized that's what she was doing now. How easy it was for her to hide. How naturally it came to her.

The sweet smell of the bubble bath turned bitter.

How long was she going to hide?

Suddenly sick to her stomach, Ophelia begrudgingly left the safe confines of the bathtub and wrapped her robe tightly around her body. Sighing, she took a comb from the vanity and began to brush the tangles from her hair as she stalked toward the tall window beside her bed. The back garden was littered with rock structures and topiaries, which wove around a path leading to a greenhouse. Ophelia couldn't make out individual plants beneath the foggy glass, but she was sure it was a fernery. A fernery was a place of worship for those devoted to Fern's teachings and ponderings. Maybe she should venture that way. Fern was always a source of wisdom in times of trouble, much like this. The older she got, the more Ophelia seemed to rely on the fastidious Spirit.

A small voice accompanied a knock on her door. Opening the door just a crack, she found a young lady roughly a few years older than her. The girl smiled kindly at her and gave a bow. Her brilliant purple eyes were full of kindness, and her sand-colored hair seemed to glow.

"Miss Kirkeby asked that I assist you in getting ready for supper," she said.

Ophelia let her in, allowing the young servant to lead her to the vanity. The servant, whom Ophelia presumed to be Reija, held out her hand for Ophelia's brush and tapped the chair. She sat, handing off the brush. The young servant swept her blonde ponytail behind her shoulders, setting to work. Ophelia tried ever so hard not to flinch as she brushed and began to braid her hair.

"Am I pulling too hard?" Reija asked.

"Oh, not at all. Apologies," Ophelia said, averting her eyes from the mirror. She'd been staring at poor Reija with a displeased expression. How very un-princess like. How rude.

"Have you looked through the wardrobe?"

"Not yet," Ophelia said distractedly.

Reija reached forward and opened a drawer on the vanity. Inside was a jewelry box. "Accessorize first, I always say."

Ophelia lifted the heavy lid, gawking at the glittering contents. There were dangling earrings, multi-layered necklaces, dainty bracelets, and sparkling rings, all in an array of metals and jewels. One necklace in particular caught her eye. It was a silver chain dotted with tiny sky-blue gems. She picked it up, holding it to the light. The gems were blue topaz if her suspicions were correct.

"Oh, that's stunning!" Reija said as she tied off one last braid in Ophelia's hair.

There were dozens of tiny braids woven with silver ribbon dripping down from beneath a larger braid atop her head. Reija had left out a few strands around her face, framing her Witch Marks rather elegantly. She finished off Ophelia's hair with a chain of diamonds attached to two combs on either side of her head. It'd been a while since Ophelia was allowed to admire her beauty. For once, she wasn't ashamed to adore what she saw in the mirror. Her Marks were shunned, but she'd always loved them. She'd always been thankful for her powers, no matter the trouble they'd caused.

Reija smiled, squeezing her shoulders. "Pretty as a princess."

Ophelia reddened, the icicle-like marks on her cheeks turning purple. "*Tusen takk.*"

Reija winked, sweeping her over to the armoire. She took dress after dress from the wardrobe, showing off the front and back of each until Ophelia settled on a hickory-colored gown with a high-necked sheer underlayer. Its sleeves were puffed, standing on their own, making Ophelia look rather regal if she said so herself. The bodice had a sweetheart neckline and tied with an enormous bow at the back. Saoirse would say it accentuated all the right places. The multi-layered skirt just barely touched the floor, hemmed with a ruffle of the same sheer fabric the underlayer was made of. It was the sort of dress that made you look like a decadent dessert, and—according to the books she'd read—that was always the right choice for these sorts of things. Ophelia wondered how long this dress had sat in that armoire. Surely, the other ladies visiting would've brought their own or, at the very least, picked something in shades of pastel pinks and greens. Ophelia was quite fond of pastels herself but found they clashed with her Marks.

"May I help you with anything else?" Reija asked, fixing the bow at her back one last time.

"Might you lead me back to Tiril? I'd like to tour the grounds if that's all right."

Reija nodded, leading her back down the stairs and to the dining room where Tiril and her maid were setting the table. It seemed they'd brought out all the pickle castors they owned. Each was made of a different color glass and held a different pickled vegetable. Ophelia had never seen so many in one place! There were tall vases, each filled to overflowing with pink and red flowers. Four settings had been placed atop a lacy tablecloth: four copper plates, four sets of cutlery, four cups, and four bowls. Ophelia couldn't help but smile, but she still tasted bile. It was all so noble. So picturesque.

"It looks lovely, Miss," Ophelia said, eyes drifting toward the portrait of Tiril, Helgi, and an older woman on the far wall.

"Why, thank you! I—Oh! And look at you!" Tiril came to spin her around. Ophelia's cheeks were burning with embarrassment. "That dress suits you so well!" Tiril exclaimed as she straightened the bow at her back. Uncomfortable shivers ran up Ophelia's back, but she didn't want to ruin the mood by asking Tiril to please step away.

"The Lady would like to tour the grounds, ma'am," Reija said, admiring her handiwork, untucking a stray hair from behind Ophelia's ear.

"Did I spot a fernery?" Ophelia asked, choosing to go incredibly stiff instead of flinching away as they fussed about.

Tiril nodded, looking rather proud of herself. "Come, let me show you!"

She offered Ophelia her arm, and not wanting to be rude, Ophelia took it. Arm in arm, they ventured out to the back garden, taking their time as they passed under towers of stone and mossy topiaries.

Once they made it to the fernery—with some struggle— Tiril opened the large glass double doors. Hot air engulfed them as they entered, finding every inch of bare skin and burrowing deep. Fog clung to the floor, moving in swirls around their feet as they waded through the densely growing foliage. Marble statues hid between the bright green fronds, their sullen faces staring blankly at their surroundings. Spherical pale-yellow crystals hung from thin chains, mimicking sunlight. Ophelia wondered if they even had the same properties. Truth be told, she didn't know much about crystalline energy.

"I had this built alongside the house. There are over one hundred species of fern here." Tiril said, sweeping her arm through the air. "Fern has always been my favorite Spirit. Can you tell?"

Ophelia nodded, a thin smile on her lips. "I've always been partial to her as well." And Jonquil, Moonflower, Holly— the list went on and on.

"Ah! You have wonderful taste, Vinterheks!" Tiril laughed. "Oh, sorry, I mean *Ophelia.*"

Ahead, the ferns parted to reveal a bronze statue in the likeness of Fern herself. Her hands were cupped in front of her, a thin stream of water pouring forth from her fingers into a notch in the floor. The water made a swirling pattern on the floor, a thin stream surrounding two plush pads for kneeling.

"Do you like it?" Tiril asked nervously. It seemed Ophelia's answer would either send her heart soaring or break it in two.

"It's beautiful!"

Tiril put a hand over her heart, bowing. "*Takk.*"

"May I stay here a while? It's been a very long couple of weeks. I find myself at peace around nature," Ophelia said, kneeling upon one of the pads, hands resting on her knees, head bowed.

"Of course! Stay as long as you like!" Tiril gave another bow before departing.

Ophelia peeked over her shoulder before shutting her eyes and placing her hands together in prayer. She let her mind wander, thinking of all the things she'd experienced as of late. It had been quite an adventure thus far. She wished she could tell Saoirse about it all. She'd say the whole thing would make for a wonderful book.

A breeze rustled the ferns, their leaves filling the quiet

with a sound as soft as the flap of butterfly wings. The mist churned and parted as the crystals above clinked softly against each other.

Ophelia lifted her head to gaze at the statue of Fern. Her eyes were glowing a pale green, illuminating the soft wrinkles on her face. The crown of ferns she wore was made of emeralds, the faceted fronds glinting in the low light. Though the statue didn't compare to the real Fern, it was exquisitely done. The folds of her dress were so well executed that one would think the statue was clothed in the softest silk.

"I've seen worse," Ophelia said, turning to the figure kneeling beside her.

Fern—the real, living, breathing Fern—smiled at her, her crow's feet pinching, giving her a motherly sort of look. "I believe Jonquil is to blame. The only statues I've seen that even remotely look like us are the ones of him."

"He can be very self-centered," Ophelia laughed.

"Comes from his mother." Fern folded her hands on her lap, staring at her statue with scrutinizing eyes. "I do like the crown," she said thoughtfully.

"It's a nice touch," Ophelia added.

Fern reached down to wiggle her fingers in the stream circling their cushions. "You wanted to speak with me?"

"I've found myself in a strange predicament," Ophelia sighed, shifting to a cross-legged position. "I seek your advice."

"Why me and not, say, Lotus? She is the Spirit of Enlightenment, after all," Fern said matter-of-factly.

"Or Celosia," Ophelia said. Celosia, the Spirit of Knowledge. A close friend of hers, yes, but she preferred Fern's company. And Lotus was. . . an interesting being, to say the least.

"What is troubling you, seedling?" Fern asked as she spun a whirlpool in the stream with her spindly finger.

Ophelia slouched, tucking her hair behind her ear. "I've become a pawn in a very annoying game of chess. It seems I am to be put on display, paraded around as a deity, and used to conquer."

Fern listened quietly.

"There are talks of revealing my identity to the world. Of 'reclaiming my throne' to dismantle the Ulvemordere," Ophelia explained with a roll of her eyes.

She jumped into a very long-winded recount of everything that had happened as of late. Fern just played in the water, childlike despite her age. When Ophelia finally finished, Fern turned to study her as always.

"What do you believe of destiny, seedling?" she asked, catching her by surprise.

That was a very tricky question. "Undecided."

"Oh, please," Fern scoffed, "humor me."

"I believe," Ophelia began, rolling her eyes, "that destiny is decided at birth yet forged as you go. It's just there. None can escape it, but you may be able to change it."

"How hauntingly melodramatic," Fern yawned. "Have you been hanging around Jonquil again, then?"

Ophelia skirted the subject but guessed Fern already knew about their little escapade—she always did. "I'm feeling rather morose this evening; forgive me," she said instead.

"Apology accepted." Fern had a wistful smirk on her lips. "So, you believe in destiny, then?"

"I suppose so."

"Where does it come from?"

Ophelia thought long and hard about that, eyes glued to Fern's statue. "I think there is an 'idea' when Amaranth plants a seed, but it is up to the person She creates to figure it out. You can follow Her 'idea,' cultivate it, and watch it grow, or you can prune the leaves until you're left with something else entirely. If I'm to be honest, I don't think Amaranth fully knows a person's path. Not until their plants begin to grow, at least."

"What 'idea' do you believe Amaranth had when She created you?" Fern asked, turning to her.

An electric shiver ran through Ophelia's rather tense body. There was only one answer, though Ophelia desperately searched for another. "I'm the first Winter Witch in a thousand years. I'm destined for greatness."

"According to you, you don't have to be," Fern teased.

"But what if what I want and what should be are not the same?"

"That is something you must determine for yourself, my dear Snowdrop," Fern sighed. She sounded sad.

Ophelia hugged her knees to her chest. "Can't you just

tell me what I'm supposed to choose?"

Fern flicked a few drops of water on her. "I am not all-knowing."

"I really should've asked for Lotus and Celosia, huh?"

Fern laughed heartily. "You'll know better for next time." She admired Ophelia lovingly, reaching out to cup her face in her dripping hands. "I may not be of much help, but others might. Speak of your concerns; I'm sure your words will find listening ears." All was quiet for a moment, then Fern's expression turned serious. "Those you trust can become. . . *guiding lights*. . . should you let them."

Ophelia furrowed her eyebrows, knowing she was meant to glean something spectacular from that. Fern stood and made a show of bowing to her statue, a sly smirk on her face. She faded from sight, leaving nothing but two curly fern fronds in the shape of a heart in her wake.

"I do so enjoy our talks, Fern," Ophelia said as she stood and brushed herself off. "Thank you."

CHAPTER FIFTY-TWO

GLIMMERS AND TRIGGERS

Seamus made his way down to the dining room as slowly as he could. In the right company, he was quite fond of playing the part of contemptuous aristocrat. However, such a role was tiring, and all he wanted was a juicy steak and something warm to drink.

Grumbling to himself, he finally jumped off the last step and swung into the dining room, taken aback by what he saw.

It was *her*, he knew it was—Seamus was pretty sure he could find Ophelia deaf and blind—but the young lady laughing alongside Tiril was not *his* Ophelia. This was a lady in waiting, a young Queen, or something of the sort. *This* was the fabled Vinterheks.

She was stunning in that rich brown gown, her hair bouncing up and down as she laughed with enough warmth to rival the sun. How ironic, given how cold she was. The sight stole his breath away, filling him with such pride. It was like gazing upon his own flesh and blood, filled with adoration at the sight of his beautiful dau—

He cleared his throat, shaking away that thought.

He shouldn't have gotten so attached.

Ophelia turned to him, all rosy cheeks and smiles. "Hello, Seamus!" she said with a wave. There was a certain content sleepiness in her eyes. She fit in well here. Better than she had in Tø.

Seamus nodded at her, hands clasped behind his back like a nobleman. "You clean up nice, my lady."

Her smile widened as she looked him up and down. Seamus glanced at the navy vest he'd thrown on over a dusty tunic with puffy sleeves. He'd only changed since he knew Tiril would throw a hissy fit otherwise. She had a distaste for clothes that smelled of horse shit. Seamus didn't blame her. He'd even taken time to wrangle his matted hair and rumpled beard. Hopefully, they all appreciated his efforts.

"You're quite handsome when you aren't dressed as a brigand," Ophelia laughed.

He glared at her playfully. After a moment's hesitation, he offered up his hand. At first, he didn't know if she'd take it. Did she remember her earlier comment? That she trusted him? As he'd hoped, she took his hand, and he led her toward a seat at the center of the table. Her touch lingered, a hint of worry on her face. Seamus chose to ignore this, acting as if he hadn't noticed. He took his place opposite her, Helgi and Tiril at either head. The few servants the Kirkebys had begun placing platters of food before them, making Seamus's mouth water.

"Looks delicious as always, Tiril," Seamus said, leaning across the table to slap a hefty spoonful of boiled potatoes onto his plate.

Tiril waved away his compliment, blushing.

All in all, it was a lovely evening. Seamus had expected to be greeted with a broadsword to the stomach, yet here he was, enjoying a hot meal with the three people he trusted more than he trusted himself. Even though he knew they did not share the same sentiment, the company was nice enough.

"I showed Ophelia the fernery," Tiril said as she buttered a roll.

"And how did you like it?" Helgi asked, clearing his throat. Tiril's words had caught him by surprise. His eyes kept drifting to Seamus, a barely hidden scowl twitching across his lips.

Meanwhile, Ophelia was beaming. "It was beautiful! I quite liked the statues. Who did them?"

"A handful of sculptures and metal workers across the lands. Was there one in particular you liked? Most say the statue of Fern." All trace of worry slipped away. Helgi was over the moon. If they only had one thing in common, it'd be their appreciation for the arts.

"There was a horned man I quite liked. He had striking eyes," Ophelia said thoughtfully.

"Kid's something of an artist herself," Seamus said, pointing at her with his fork as he sat hunched over his plate. There was no room for acting haughty when it came to food. He'd eat like a pig and snort like one, too. Manners be damned.

Ophelia's smile flickered, alarms blaring in her eyes. Seamus gave her a questioning look as she hid behind an ugly vase full of pungent flowers.

"What is your medium?" Tiril asked.

Ophelia dabbed at the corner of her mouth with a napkin, eyes darting to the portrait of Helgi, his late wife, and Tiril.

"Graphite, mostly," she said, reaching for her water cup.

"Watercolors, too," Seamus added, confused as to why she was acting so modest.

"So, I was right in assuming that was a sketchbook you carried?" Tiril asked, clapping excitedly.

Ophelia nodded, falling dead silent.

"May we see some of your pieces?" Helgi asked through a mouthful of collard greens.

Ophelia's eyes flicked to Seamus, silently begging him to step in. He cleared his throat and sniffed, turning to Helgi. "How did the last boar hunt go?" he asked, skirting the subject.

"I didn't join," Helgi sighed. "I'm getting old and tired." That last remark was as sharp as his steak knife.

"Nonsense," Seamus said with a roll of his eyes.

Tiril clicked her tongue disapprovingly. "He's sprained something somewhere twice this year. Blessed Amaranth, he'll end up alongside his wife soon enough!"

Ophelia was quiet after that, but she did mouth a discreet 'thank you' when Helgi and Tiril were distracted by their plates. Seamus smiled apologetically, tipping his half-empty teacup in her direction. Stars, she was so weird sometimes.

"Did Seamus tell you how we met?" Helgi asked suddenly.

Now, it was *his* turn to get all quiet and cagey.

"I don't think that's a story to tell over dinner, old friend," Seamus said softly.

Helgi shrugged half-heartedly. "Raging battles help me digest."

Seamus glared at him, causing Helgi to tremble in his seat. "Maybe next time."

"When Seamus was still a part of the—"

"Ophelia," Seamus interjected, staring daggers into his plate. "Did you tell Tiril that Tø had an observatory?"

Tiril's heart fluttered with wonder. "What was it like? Each one seems to be different."

"It was rather pretty, but I do believe most of the money at the time of building was spent on the telescope. Still, it was fashioned out of marble and was filled with the teachings of the Celestial Pantheon," Ophelia explained. "Tø wasn't a religious town in my time. The observatory had been turned into an infirmary."

"I can think of worse uses," Helgi laughed. "Reminds me of that one time we found a greenhouse being used as a—Oh, I shouldn't say with children around."

Ophelia grimaced, turning back to Tiril. "You both seem to know a fair bit about both Pantheons. Are you theologians?"

Seamus inhaled deeply, glad to have dodged an arrow for now.

"That's what we like to believe," Tiril smiled. "But no, not really. Helgi and I grew up in Vårretten. Our parents both worshipped the Terrestrials. It wasn't until Helgi met his wife, Oona, that we began researching the Celestials and Their teachings."

"It's quite interesting the more you read. We've found that there are similarities between both religions. Some deities seem to have overlapped," Helgi added. "They may as well be the same stories from different points of view. If only we could ask."

A strange expression passed over Ophelia's face. Something of a mix between guilt and anticipation. Seamus could see the gears turning in her mind as she weighed something.

"Like Jonquil and The Peacock?" Ophelia asked, her voice small as if those words would get her into cosmic trouble.

"Exactly!" Helgi and Tiril exclaimed. She jumped at the volume of their voices.

Helgi leaned over the table, his sleeve dipping into a gravy boat. "Have you noticed how The Rabbit's parables seem to be a precursor to the laments of Amaranth? Or how the creation of man is so similar in both stories?"

Ophelia tapped her fingers on the table nervously. "Vaguely."

That was a strange response. Ophelia had no need for anxiety or shyness around Tiril and Helgi. They were her kindred spirits. So why was she acting as though she'd been caught red-handed? Seamus often wondered what knowledge that Witch had. Half the time, she seemed to know more about the workings of the world than she cared to admit.

"We've actually been looking into that connection lately. As you can imagine, Helgi and I believe all those old stories are historical truths," Tiril said as she chased a pea around her plate. "If that's the case, then the Celestial and Terrestrial teachings are not only a guidebook but a warning. Those 'stories' may be the key to ending the war between the Ulve and magic users once and for all."

"Speaking of the Ulvemordere, we've received news from the Center Cities not long ago. Seamus, I think you'll want to hear this," Helgi said, eyes aglow with expectation. "It lends truth to what Egill told you."

Seamus felt that arrow he'd dodged zoom back around and collide with his spinal cord. He just about sprayed tea out his nose.

"Has something else happened?" Ophelia asked.

Tiril and Helgi shared a look. Helgi gave a prompting nod, reassuring her as he always did. "Magic is heavily regulated in the Center Cities, as you well know. For a while, the powers that be were lenient. However, there are rumors of pushback and missing civilians," Tiril explained. She wouldn't avert her eyes from her plate.

"The Ulvemordere presence is growing day by day. They've taken over and pushed out those who—forgive me for saying such, Ophelia—have been elected into power and thus rightfully rule. We've got allies there. They're stuck, fearing for their lives. Insurrection in the slightest is reason for trial," Helgi added. "Not even humans are exempt."

Seamus nodded. "So I've noticed. I was hiding in plain sight around the Cities for a while. No good came of it."

Snøbolig had never been neutral spare for The Wilds. The country was overrun with Ulvemordere. It always had been. They'd even taken over the surrounding ocean, their main compound hidden on an island beyond a swirling mael-strom. Werewolves were said to have originated in Snøbolig. Given the Ulvemordere's relationship with his kind, Seamus wasn't surprised they'd taken over the supposed birthplace of his people. What did surprise him, however, was how tolerant the other magical folk were. The trolls specifically.

With some effort, Ophelia cleared her throat. "They've taken mo—Sorry, they've begun to take hostages? Is this normal? I thought they killed and left nothing behind."

"Here and there, human folk are rounded up, questioned, then sent to the mines for a 'lesson in obedience.' But as of late, a handful of magickind have gone missing. There are rumors of experiments, though I'm not sure which is worse. I've seen those mines. I wouldn't send my worst enemy there," Helgi grumbled. He took a swig of his sweet-smelling mead, shaking his head in disgust. "Anyway, whether those claims are true, I don't know. They're rounding up magickind for something sinister, that's for sure."

"They're monsters," Tiril said in a hushed tone.

Neither of the Kirkebys had changed, which meant every death still weighed heavily on Tiril's conscience. Helgi may excel in combat, but Tiril excelled in strategy. She was the logical, methodical one. Any failure was a direct result of her poor planning. Or at least that's how she saw it.

"They really are," Ophelia murmured, pushing her plate away, all appetite lost.

Seamus watched the life drain from her eyes. No doubt she was thinking of Tø. Seamus shot a warning look at Helgi, his mind wandering to his last words with Lochlan.

"If I help you, may I ask for just one simple thing in return?" Ophelia asked, startling them all.

Tiril and Helgi nodded, hanging on her every word.

Ophelia rolled back her shoulders and held her head high, avoiding Seamus's gaze. When she spoke, he could tell she was trying her best to sound like she deserved her title and the authority that came with it.

"I've reason to believe the Ulvemordere have taken hostages to lure me out. This weighs heavily on me. I will not see another being die because of my powers and Marks."

Tea shot out of Seamus's nose, spraying the entire

spread of food before him. He coughed and choked, reaching blindly for a napkin as he stared wide-eyed at her.

Tiril and Helgi gave her a questioning look. "The people of Tø?" they asked.

"I may not have been adored by the town, but I had friends there, and I'd do anything to get them back. If you can help me with that—" Ophelia sighed heavily, looking to the ceiling "—then I'll—I'll be your chess piece."

"Ophelia—"

"That's why you brought me here, isn't it? If you're 'giving me' to these people, I might as well play the part," she snapped. The air around him chilled.

Seamus rolled his eyes, slumping in his seat. He never should have said that. "All right, great. See? You've got your martyr," he said hotly.

"We'll do all we can, Ophelia, I promise," Tiril said, giving her a sympathetic smile. "I'll see what I can find about your friends if you give me their names."

Helgi nodded, saluting her with his mug of ale. "If they're in the mines, I'm sure we can work something out with Cathal. Good job, you showed up then, aye Norland?"

"I am not talking to Cathal," Seamus blurted out, surprising even himself. "Cathal can kiss my—"

"Language," Tiril said, narrowing her eyes at him.

Seamus rolled his eyes, mocking her. "I'm forty-eight years old, Tiril. If I want to swear, I'm gonna swear."

Several servants began clearing away dinner and bringing out dessert. No one touched even a speck of sugar.

"Cathal has a soft spot for you, you know that," Helgi said, giving him a disapproving look. "If anyone can get through to him, it'll be you. Plus, he'll be more than happy to meet a Witch."

"No, no, no. See, you must've heard wrong. Cathal doesn't have a soft spot for me; he likes that *I am* a soft, squishy, fleshy abomination that he can kill with a carefully aimed glare," Seamus frowned.

"Who is—" Ophelia began.

"Not important," Seamus sighed.

"Cathal is. . . an old friend, so to speak. He knew Seamus long before we did," Tiril explained, winking at her.

"If Ophelia's people are in his mines, we're going to have to speak with him," Helgi said, ignoring the fact that everyone else was ready to move on from this stupid, stupid subject.

"And by we, you mean you," Seamus laughed.

It was undeniable that the wheels were turning in Ophelia's mind as she slowly put two and two together on who this mysterious Cathal might be.

"Unfortunately, I have too many irons in the fire," Helgi said, his tone borderline a yell. "Our resources are stretched thin. We need all the help we can get. I implore you to think of the bigger picture here."

Again, Seamus rolled his eyes. "Hunter's Moon, my ass. Egill was right, then? You do have a plan for me."

Helgi bristled at this. "Egill is an idiot."

"While I agree, at least he had the forethought to warn me of *your* stupidity, Helgi."

Tiril gave a gasp of disgust.

"Norland, I will not have you speak to me that way under my own roof. You are a guest here; you will act like one," Helgi said as he banged his pudgy fists on the table. Ophelia yelped in fright.

Seamus fingered his butter knife, thinking of how he could inflict pain upon Helgi Kirkeby, The Ruthless. "What exactly are you proposing, Helgi? Don't tell me you want me to knock on the Ulve's front door and ask them to kindly step down. It doesn't work like that."

"Seamus, you know what you mean to them," Tiril said flatly. "You—"

"You still believe that stupid prophecy?" Seamus laughed.

Ophelia looked up from staring at her plate, eyebrows furrowed, confused.

"Humor me a moment, will you?" Tiril snapped. "Why do they fear you if it's not true? And why shouldn't we believe it?"

"What prophecy?" Ophelia asked. "Egill said something similar, remember?"

Everyone promptly ignored her.

"Even if the prophecy is false, if we've enough firepower

at our backs, who are they to stop us?" Helgi asked.

"You literally just said you're stretched thin! Where do you suppose we get that sort of power?" Seamus asked. He pointed his butter knife at Ophelia. "She can't defeat an entire army. Please tell me you know that."

Tiril gave a motherly sort of sigh. "If you talk to Cathal—"

"Absolutely not! I'm not speaking with Cathal," Seamus snapped, tipping the entirety of his teacup into his mouth, allowing its contents to burn his throat. "He's a foolish old codger whom I'd very much never like to see ever again," he coughed, waving his butter knife around as if it would ward off their words. "Egill was more than enough."

"Maybe it's time to mend old—"

Seamus pushed his chair away from the table, shaking his head violently. "I'd rather not."

Ophelia, who'd been quiet up until now, raised her head to look at Seamus. "I don't want to turn a blind eye."

Seamus's heart about burst with anger. Before he said something truly stupid, he bowed, bidding them all farewell, making for his room.

Over the last thousand years, millions of rebel groups had tried to threaten the Ulvemordere's reign of terror. Each and every one of them had failed. Each and every one had died a gruesome death. If the Ulvemordere were rounding up people and experimenting on them, of course, that terrified him. Images of Lochlan experimenting on a young Ophelia haunted him. But what could they do? The Ulve were always devising new and exciting ways to kill magical folk. Even if they could rally an army, it'd all be for naught.

This wasn't the dawn of a new day; this was perpetuating old cycles.

And who in their right mind would take up arms with them? It would be no different than damning themselves to the darkest corners of The Abyss!

Ophelia only wanted to dive headfirst into danger because empathy clouded her judgment. He knew this was what she wanted—what they all wanted—but he'd hoped meeting these weirdos would change her mind. Was Seamus the only one who could see their stupidity? Was he the only one who could see how Helgi flip-flopped between plans solely because of greed? When he looked at Ophelia, Seamus knew he saw gold. And all Tiril saw was her storybooks come to life. Ophelia wasn't stupid, nor naïve, not really. Couldn't she see that this was going to end badly?

Curses! He *knew* coming here was a bad idea. He shouldn't have fought the notion so hard. He'd placed an opportunity in Ophelia's lap like a dog bringing a dead bird to its master. Would she take it? Would she allow herself to be deified? Was that truly what she wanted?

They both talked a big talk about honor and duty, but when push came to shove, what would Ophelia choose?

And would Seamus be able to live with himself knowing he'd set her on this path?

What in the ever-darkening night sky had he had expected bringing her here? None of this had been thought through.

CHAPTER FIFTY-THREE

If You Die, I Want to Die with You

With a sigh and shake of his head, Seamus swung open the door to his room and flopped down on the bed. He was exhausted and aching, his head pounding as he stared at the ceiling. This place made him feel like a scared child lost in the wilderness. It brought up memories and histories about himself he'd much rather forget, though no one seemed to let him. No wonder the townsfolk referred to *Dødbyen* as Abyss. Visiting the Kirkeby's had surely left him craving the sweet embrace of death.

He wasn't sure how long he laid there, but the sounds of dinner and the servants' busywork had died long ago. He was sure everyone had gone to bed.

No better time to escape than now.

No time like the present, no fear like the past.

Seamus began to pack his bags, looking toward the future with distrust and dismay. Once he got out of here, he could go down any number of paths. The problem? He knew they'd all lead to the same destination.

At least a few of those paths didn't involve taking up arms with the Jewel King.

During dinner, a servant washed and dried his smelly old clothes. Grimacing, he stuffed them back in his pack alongside a few tunics and pants from the dresser. Surely, the Kirkebys wouldn't miss anything. They had more than enough to spare. However, he did lose the velvet vest and traded it for his tattered jacket. The fur lining comforted him like a safety blanket a child refused to give up. In a way, it reminded him of his wolf.

Just as he went to sift through the contents of the bedside tables, tiny, dainty footsteps echoed out in the hall. A knock on the door followed. He swore under his breath, tossing his pack over the bed before greeting Ophelia. She slipped inside, lingering near the door as Seamus plopped down on the bed.

"To what do I owe the pleasure?" he asked with a wary smile.

Ophelia wrung her hands, rocking back and forth on her heels. "I wanted to say goodbye," she said softly. There was kindness in her eyes but not in her voice.

Seamus's face fell. "How. . . ?" He let that word hang in the dense air between them.

Of course, she'd known.

This had been the plan all along. There really hadn't been any trickery.

"Where will you be going?" she asked, smoothing the wrinkles of the pale blue dressing gown she'd changed into. She matched their star-covered surroundings. Tiril always placed him in the Celestial wing of the mansion. How sardonically poetic.

"You know I can't tell you that," Seamus sighed, working his jaw. His eyes stung like someone had splashed him with scalding water. What was wrong with him? Why was he acting like this?

Ophelia came to sit next to him on the bed, picking at loose threads on the bed linens as she spoke. "What if you find yourself in trouble? *Someone* should know where you're going." Those moon-bright eyes of hers were dense with storm clouds.

"I can handle myself, kid," he said sternly, though not unkindly. "I do, however, appreciate your concern."

He stood, patting her on the shoulder as he rounded the bed. He picked up his pack, checking it one last time.

"You should take the candlesticks," Ophelia said, scanning the room.

"What?"

"Steal them, I mean. Amaranth knows they've got plenty," she explained. "Sell them, barter them, melt them down—whatever works. There's a jewelry box in my quarters you could raid as well."

"By the Stars, I think I've rubbed off on you," Seamus breathed, genuinely aghast at the notion.

All she did was smirk over her shoulder.

That's when he heard the thundering heart, the terrified crescendo of lightning coursing through her veins.

Guilt flooded him.

Worry flooded him.

Leaning lazily on the bedpost, he gave her his best aristocratic smile. "You like it here?"

Ophelia's smile brightened. "Oh yes, very much. The library is extensive. I look forward to theorizing about the cosmos with the Kirkebys."

She was lying. Straight to his face, she was lying.

Seamus figured that permitted him to do the same.

"I had a feeling," he said with as much gusto as he could manage. "I w—" he cleared his throat "—wouldn't be leaving you here if I didn't think you'd like it. If—If I didn't think you'd be safe."

"I know. You've been very good to me, Seamus." Her smile faltered as she turned away. They both knew that was a lie.

Seamus discarded the tealights from a candlestick and shoved it in his bag. Was he making the right decision? He knew Tiril and Helgi would treat her well. They'd treat her as their own, like a daughter.

A pang of. . . *something*. . . hit his chest.

Cringe?

No.

No, he was happy for her.

Fear?

No.

No, he trusted them.

He stopped folding a blanket, looking back at Ophelia, who was distracted by the crown molding on the ceiling.

Jealousy?

Yes.

That was it.

Bitter, bitter, jealousy.

In another life, another time, he would've stayed. They could've been a fam—

Seamus shook the thought away before it could cement in his mind. If Ophelia stayed with him, he'd ruin her. Look what he'd done already! She had nothing because of him. Leaving her here was mercy. It *was* the right decision. He had to believe that.

"Can I ask you something?" Ophelia mumbled, eyes still on the ceiling. Seamus couldn't help but follow her gaze to the constellations depicted above. What did she see? What was she thinking? Furthermore, why did he keep asking himself that?

"Of course," he replied, his voice gruff from the lump in his throat.

"Do you ever get tired of running?"

Yet another arrow wedged itself in his spine. How many more could he take before keeling over?

"Kid—"

"I'm serious," Ophelia said, swiveling around to stare into the depths of his soul. Her silvery eyes seemed to pulse. He swore there was something swimming in her irises. "In some ways, I've enjoyed it, though believe me, I feel guilty admitting that. But I've seen the world, if but a fraction of it! I've seen *my* world. And we've met so many interesting beings. It's been quite an adventure! Yet, I want a place to rely on. A place to return to when I grow weary. Don't you want that?"

"That kind of life isn't meant for me," Seamus said with a shrug.

That was precisely why he couldn't stay here.

Why he couldn't stay with *her*.

"You liked Tø enough to stay."

He grimaced at that. "Yeah, well," he scoffed, "that was a mistake. Look where it got us."

Her façade of excitement shattered. Tiny sparks danced across her fingers, burning the bed linens as she stared at him. No part of Seamus wanted to hurt her any more than he already had. Yet he'd been acting like an ass all evening in hopes she'd never forgive him for leaving. Making her hate him enough that she'd burn this room to a crisp was easier than saying goodbye, even if he made her resent this house and see it as yet another prison. Even if his words forced her to leave in the night just as he was. That'd be a better outcome than her walking in his shadow. Egill was right. It was time to throw her to the wolves so she'd learn how to protect herself. That's how he'd survived this long. Just like Helgi. Just like Egill. Just like every other sorry creature he'd ever known.

"If I could go back and change things, I wouldn't have met you," he said as levelly as he could. "If I had just continued on, then—" Ophelia's heart skipped a beat. "—then none of this would have happened. Meeting you was a huge mistake. I'd take it all back if I could."

A single tear slid down her cheek as she whispered in a broken voice, "I know you don't mean that."

He worked his jaw, feigning nonchalance as best he could. "Believe what you want, kid."

"So that's it then?" Ophelia asked. Her thundering heart hammered against her ribcage, angry and discordant. "You'll run until there's no more dirt to tread? How shameful."

The smell of rotten pomegranates wafted into his nose.

Seamus morphed his face into a deep-set scowl. If it were anyone else, he'd have up and left as soon as those words left her mouth.

"Is running all you know how to do?" she snapped. He could see the regret in her eyes even as she spoke, but he didn't exactly blame her for saying such things. She had a point, as she always did.

His eyes softened, but the frown stayed. "What exactly do you expect me to do?"

"Fight back! That's why I'm here, right? So I can change things? So these people can use me as a figurehead?"

Those words hung heavy between them. Seamus felt as though he'd keel over from shock. The bedpost behind him was suddenly the only thing keeping him upright.

"No, I just thought—" Seamus pinched the bridge of his nose, finally admitting what he'd been lying to himself about this whole damn time. "I don't know, Ophelia, all right? I don't know why we're here. Where else could I go? Where else could *you* go? We've nothing to our names, we have no—"

"What we *have* is *each other*," Ophelia snapped. "That might not mean anything to you, but it does to me. I meant it when I said I trusted you, and I *know* you trust me."

"Ophelia—"

"And I also know you were only trying to get a rise out of me earlier! Yet, you believed what you said, that I could challenge the Ulve if I wanted to."

"Phee—"

She threw her arms wide, looking around with wild eyes. "You just admitted you've nowhere else to go, so why are you running?"

Helgi's words floated in his mind. Despite how he craved it, no part of him thought he deserved peace. Still, he knew what he was made for. He'd been born a warrior, blood on his hands before he opened his eyes. It was useless trying to change that fate. If only Ophelia knew what exactly he'd been running from. There were secrets he'd yet to share—secrets more dangerous than Witch Marks.

Seamus was a man of duties and promises kept. But the farther everyone tried to drag him into the void, the more he wanted to throw responsibility to the wind. He was made to be a martyr, a leader, but he was growing tired of that burden. What was left to fight for, anyway? Nothing. How easy it'd be to damn the world. Farmland and freedom somewhere in Vårretten sounded awfully nice right about now.

"How do you expect me to go up against the Ulvemordere alone?" Seamus asked. It was a question he'd asked himself many times before, never finding an answer. Maybe his Witch had some sort of mystical insight. "How do you expect me to save everyone alone?"

"You wouldn't *have* to be alone," Ophelia offered. "You'd have me and the Kirkebys!"

He made a show of rolling his eyes, shaking his head in disgust. "Two washed-up librarians, a stubborn werewolf, and a benevolent Witch won't exactly strike fear into an ever-growing army of lunatics."

"Where there are few, there'll be many," Ophelia whispered, eyes pleading with him to agree.

"Stick to the arts, kid," he laughed, "you're good at them. Add poetry to your roster." Ophelia glared at him. "As much as I hate to say it, Lochlan was right. You should not be fighting against them. You are not a soldier; you're not a—"

"Then what am I?" Ophelia asked, exasperated, standing and throwing her hands up in the air.

"You can be a thousand different things, kid. Pick a profession that won't kill you, will ya?"

Ophelia stood tall, the hem of her dressing gown whipping back and forth against her ankles. "A thousand years."

"What?"

"The last recorded Winter Witch was born a thousand years ago. His name is the first on the long list of Witches who have died for their powers. I am the first of my kind in centuries, and I'm just supposed to peddle books and paint?"

"You love books! You can't shut up about books!"

She rolled her eyes. "If I have powers, then why shouldn't I use them? It's personal now, so why not?"

Seamus crossed his arms over his chest, tilting his head to the side. "If the Ulvemordere hadn't shown up, would you have ever thought this? Would you be preparing to march up to their stronghold and blow it down with a cleverly aimed gust of wind? Or would you have gone on and turned a blind eye?"

Ophelia's shoulders sagged as she stared at him. There it was again. That ancient aura. The eyes that held wisdom far beyond her years. "Seamus," she began. She sounded exhausted. "That is *all* I've ever thought about. Do you know how much better the world would be with them gone? Do you have any idea how many people need me? Need *us*?"

Of course, he did! Few didn't! Maybe people would rally behind them, but rejoining this silent war was the same as signing his death certificate. Hundreds would follow, and thousands would die. Yes, they'd have an army, but at what cost? Turning a blind eye wasn't easy, but it was safe. That's what Seamus wanted for himself and that damn Witch! Safety! Couldn't she see that?

But they all had a point, didn't they? Could they ever find peace without revenge? Could Tiril and Helgi really grant Ophelia safety?

No, no, he was being stupid again, letting her get under his skin. He shook his head, a poor attempt at clearing his thoughts.

"You and I are not the right people to take them down, kid," Seamus sighed. With that, he threw his bags over his shoulder and made for the door.

"If not us, then who, hmm?" Ophelia asked. He could tell she was genuinely curious who he had in mind. "I'll say it again. You seem to think I'm important, else you wouldn't have said all those things to Tiril and Helgi."

"I set the bait; they took it," Seamus laughed. "Arrogance doesn't look good on you."

That rotten pomegranate smell intensified as she stomped her foot on the ground. A strangled cry of anger bubbled up her throat.

"Listen, kid, I've a long journey ahead of me, and all you're doing is getting in my way. If you'll excuse me, it's high time I left," Seamus spat, attempting to step past her.

Something clicked in her mind at that. "I'll follow you," she said, grabbing his wrist to stop him. Her fingers were ice cold, leaving frost on his sleeve.

"I'll keep running."

"So be it."

Seamus leaned down to her eye level, willing his wolf to show itself. His eyes glowed electric green, reflecting in hers like fireflies dancing across a stormy sky.

"You shouldn't carry this," he whispered, his voice barely audible, so dark with worry and anger it almost sounded like a growl. "You don't want this. *I* don't want this."

"But I choose it anyway," she said, mimicking his tone. "Even if you leave. I've made my choice."

She was breathing heavily, her hand clenched so tightly around his wrists that her knuckles were white. He imagined the world above was riddled with thunder and pelting rain. How self-righteous. She fancied herself to be a Spirit, didn't she? Figured if she tried hard enough, she'd be all-powerful. All-knowing even.

He knew firsthand this wouldn't end well.

All he saw when he looked at her was himself, and he hated it.

"I would gladly die to protect my people—to protect *you*, Seamus Norland," Ophelia said quietly. She said it softly, so simply, as if she hadn't just wrecked his whole world. "Blessed Amaranth, especially you! If anything happened to you because of me, I wouldn't be able to live myself. How am I meant to protect you—any of you—if you're not at my side?"

"*I'm* meant to protect *you*. Not the other way around," Seamus said, trying his best to keep his voice level.

"And how can you do that if you leave?"

"Tiril and Helgi have promised to—"

"I don't care about what they promised!" Ophelia cried. A bolt of electricity left her fingers, shooting up his arm, causing them both to wince. "You said you'd get me somewhere safe, but I don't feel safe here."

"Kid—"

"No. You will *not* talk over me; you will *listen*," she spat, squeezing his arm tighter. "As long you're in Snøbolig, you're my responsibility. The people of Tø were my responsibility, too, and I will not fail you as I failed them."

"No one blames you for what happened, ya hear?" Seamus snapped. "For the last time, that wasn't your fault!"

Her silver eyes had gone charcoal. "We've had this conversation before, haven't we? About whose opinion of you matters most. You say you don't blame me, but I blame myself. Isn't that all that matters?"

"Ophelia Av'Skogen," Seamus said shakily. "No one—be it me or anyone else—is worth dying over. That is both an order and a fact."

"And I am?"

"Kid, you're a miracle. Of course, you're worth dying for!"

Her eyes darted back and forth between his own. "People keep saying that. I wonder what it means."

"It means the world needs you," Seamus said rather aggressively.

Damn her, she'd backed him into a corner. She was baiting him into this, and he knew it, but the truth of those words still took him by surprise.

"The world needs you, too. I know it," she said softly. "So whether you choose to fight or keep running, I'm coming with you."

He let his bags drop to the floor, overcome with grief.

At that moment, he realized he *did* have something to fight for. He had a very persistent, very annoying little Witch with stars in her eyes and hope in her heart.

Yes, he saw himself in her. But he also saw Ingrid. She was a perfect mix of them both.

"I will not allow you to ruin yourself for people who will never give a damn about you," he snapped. They were so close that their noses were almost touching.

"I know you won't. And if you feel so deeply that the only way to protect me is to run far from here, I won't protest. But I beg you, Seamus, run toward something worth believing in," she hissed. "Run *with* me. You're not a lone wolf anymore."

Hot steam blew out his nose. Neither of them moved. Neither of them breathed.

Seamus suddenly realized it wasn't revenge or peace he truly wanted. What he'd been missing all these years was companionship. He missed his pack, missed Ingrid. He'd just labeled the hurt and the desire for his old life as something they weren't. Maybe that's why those things warred in his mind constantly. Perhaps all he wanted was someone to fight alongside him.

"Will you follow?" he asked, that persistent lump in his throat slowly dissipating.

"Until there's no more dirt left to tread," she whispered.

He searched her eyes for even the slightest hint of hesitation but found none. "Then we make a plan, and it better be a damn good one," he said, turning away. He couldn't believe what he was saying.

Without another word, she turned and left.

Seamus felt his heart break in two, stealing the breath from his lungs as he sat heavily on the edge of his bed. He loved that kid so damn much. The only problem? Everything he loved—everything he even touched—went up in flames.

Helgi had said lightning was coursing through his veins, and he knew that was true. Seamus had tried so hard to keep the sparks away from Ophelia, but they were kindred souls in that way.

They'd already hurt each other denying how badly they

needed one another.

It was all downhill from here.

But as the Stars would have it, it seemed they wouldn't have it any other way.

CHAPTER FIFTY-FOUR

CONSTANT AS THE STARS

Seamus lay wide awake, staring at the ceiling, knowing in his heart that this wasn't the path Ophelia was meant to be traveling. Still, it was the path she'd chosen, and she'd picked it herself. No one was making this decision for her, and Seamus would try his best to respect that.

He'd made his own momentous commitment today, too. That kid would be his life purpose, if only for a little while. Now that he'd promised to stay, a great weight had lifted off his shoulders. Yes, it'd been replaced by another weight in the form of keeping the damn kid alive, but that was only half the battle. In fact, that might prove easier than the impending test now offered to him.

Who would he be for her? What was his role other than a protector? Who was Seamus Norland deep down inside? To all those questions, he didn't have answers. One thing was for sure, however. The answer lay within Ophelia. She brought out the best in him, even when he didn't want her to. That was scary, knowing some outside force could affect him so much. But who was he to complain? He'd dealt with the moon all these years.

The moon.

Laying there, staring up at the painted constellations, his lips twitched into a sad smile.

Moon-bright eyes that only saw the best in him.

Was this what it felt like to find a home in someone? To be terrified of losing them, yet ready and willing to charge into battles so long as you stayed by their side? Was this kinship toward her how ordinary families felt toward one another?

More questions he couldn't answer, but he was quite fond of the notion that one day he'd find the answers.

The door to his room opened, revealing Helgi. "Would you care to join me at the tavern?" he asked.

"Why? So, I can watch you drink yourself sick and eat stale peanuts?" Seamus laughed, sitting up.

"Yes, or maybe we can catch up since I haven't seen you in several years," Helgi scowled.

Seamus stood and stretched, reaching for his jacket. "And yet, we picked up right where we left off."

Helgi grumbled his agreement, playfully rolling his eyes. Together, they made their way downstairs. There, they found Tiril, who was carrying a tray of tea into the den. She paused, eyes on Seamus, her expression blank.

"Is something the matter, Tiril?" Helgi asked, attempting to take the tray from her. "You're up awfully late."

Tiril swiveled and held the tray as far from him as she could without spilling. "Are you heading out?" she asked, her words directed to Seamus.

"Unfortunately, I'm the drinking buddy for the night," Seamus replied.

She nodded, a far-off look in her eye. Eventually, she sighed, inclining her head toward the den. "May I speak with you a moment?"

Helgi deflated. "Meet me when you can, I suppose."

With that, he left without saying goodbye.

Seamus reluctantly followed Tiril into the den. The sweets and treats from before had been cleared away, leaving room for the tea tray. Tiril busied herself with concocting the perfect cream and sugar mix, then handed a steaming cup to Seamus.

"Am I in some sort of trouble?" Seamus asked, settling in beside her on the lounge.

She smiled sadly, shaking her head. "No, no. I'd just like you to myself for a moment, that's all."

"Ahh. . . I see. . ."

They sipped their tea for a while, Tiril staring deep into Seamus's eyes while he fumbled with his tiny cup and saucer. Those things were *not* meant for someone with hands as big as his. He looked as though he was toying with a child's playset.

"You're hurt," Tiril said suddenly. "I still smell blood on you."

So that's what was bothering her, then? "It's just a nick. I'm all right. It's getting better. Hardly notice."

"You should've healed by now."

Seamus cast his gaze on his shoes. Was this how Ophelia felt when he lectured her? It was as though a thousand eyes were suddenly trained on him, and each could stare directly into his soul. Needless to say, it wasn't a pleasant feeling.

"I'll manage," he said simply.

Tiril didn't seem convinced. "If you say so, Seamus, dear."

The kind gesture of tea and company had gone sour. Now, all Seamus could think about was the ache at his side and all the bruises plastering his body. Already, he was regretting a night in the tavern. Tiril seemed to think the same. She'd gone from staring at him to staring into her cup as though it held some cosmic secret.

"If it makes you feel better, I'll stop at an infirmary and get it properly bandaged so my guts won't spill out or anything," Seamus laughed. Tiril wouldn't look up from her teacup, but she did frown. "That. . . that was a joke."

Ever so slowly, she turned away, reaching into her pocket. For a moment, she hesitated, then quickly placed a leather-bound book between them. Seamus didn't know why, but he swore he'd seen it before.

"What's this?" he asked, setting down his teacup.

"A gift," Tiril said, voice scarcely a whisper. "Read the page I've bookmarked, if you please."

Seamus rolled his eyes but ultimately did what he was told.

"What on earth does 'Guidance, forged by Northern Stars' mean?" he asked when he finished reading. "'Soul, forged by Abyss?' Tiril, I've read this before, but it's still just words on a page for me," Seamus laughed, shutting the book and tossing it aside.

"What exactly did the Ulvemordere tell you about the pelt of the First Wolf?" Tiril asked.

"This again? Tiril—"

"Seamus, you may not believe in things unseen, but I do. Humor me a moment, won't you?"

Seamus rolled his eyes, leaning back to stare at the tapestries above. "That it killed whoever tried to wear it, that it had a mind of its own, seemingly possessed. I know it sprang to life when I was born. Why do you ask?"

"Had it reacted to anyone else?"

"Not that I know of."

Tiril pursed her lips, giving him a knowing look. "A mystical werewolf pelt comes to life the second you're born, yet no, you can't believe there may be a prophecy about you? No part of you believes it?"

"I'm sorry, Tiril, but I don't. It's just words in a book anyone could have written."

"Not all books are fiction, Seamus."

With that, he agreed. But it didn't mean there was truth in every tale.

Before he had a chance to argue this point, Tiril continued. "For just a moment, let us believe that you are meant to take up the pelt of the First Wolf, that you're meant for something more. What would that mean to you?"

"I can't take up a pelt. I'm not human anymore, you know that. Should I try and wear the pelt of another, it'll kill me," Seamus scoffed. "This is common knowledge, I fear."

Tiril flicked his nose, scowling. "I said, humor me."

"You're relentless."

"Thank you."

Seamus was at a loss for words, watching the tapestries gently sway on high. Tiril had always fancied needlework, and she was good at it, too. Once upon a time, she'd promised to make something for his and Ingrid's child, should they have one. She talked of reading the child stories, of spoiling them senseless. No matter how hard she tried, Tiril had always clung to things that would never happen. She was a dreamer, and while it was nice to have dreams and desires, one had to stay grounded in reality.

The wolf that pelt belonged to was intertwined with a religion he didn't know if he believed in. Should this prophecy or story or whatever it was be true, Seamus would have to reevaluate his entire life. Everything he thought he knew and trusted would be a complete and utter lie.

He wasn't a dreamer. Such things scared him. That's why he wanted to run so far so badly.

But Ophelia was a dreamer, same as Tiril. Still, he knew them as two of the strongest people he'd ever known. Yet here he was, thinking himself weak most days. Was there such a thing as being too realistic? Was his pessimistic nature starting to eat at him?

"All right, let's say I take up the pelt. Then what happens? What does it do? What does that make me?" he asked, not exactly ready to toy with the idea but not wanting to sit in such overwhelming silence any longer.

"Witches are meant to carry within them the souls of their predecessors. That's how someone entirely unrelated to the previous Witch is granted their powers," Tiril explained. "What if *you* carry within you the soul of the First Wolf?"

"That would imply the existence of reincarnation, something I can guarantee you I don't believe," Seamus laughed.

"What happened to pretending?"

Seamus sighed, turning to look at her, seeing nothing but hope in her eyes. He didn't want to have to say it out loud, but Seamus was not the person you came to if you needed an extra spurt of hope.

"Tiril, the Ulvemordere believed the First Wolf was a Spirit," he sighed. "I don't know much about religion, but I know the Wolf was tied to North Star. Are you implying I may be some version of that entity?"

Tiril's hopeful eyes grew wider. "If you are?"

"I'm not! Believe me, I'm not," Seamus laughed.

How was he meant to believe this? He, Seamus Norland, The Damned, a reincarnated Spirit? Meant to do what? Save the world? This was insane—mental, even. More than anything, he wanted to deny it. He desperately wanted to stand before her and scold her for such foolish concepts. There was hope, there was yearning for a better future, and then there was parading around as jesters. But this book in his hands was familiar to him. The look in Tiril's eyes unnerved him. It almost felt as though choosing not to believe this as truth would break her in two.

"If I was, how would you know?" he asked, barely able to string together a coherent sentence.

"Oh, darling boy," Tiril sighed, "I have known you were destined for greatness since I first met you. It was only a matter of time before I figured out why."

Seamus stood, looking down at the tiny book in his enormous hands. He walked to the fire, knowing he could easily toss it into the flames and be done with all this. He also knew, that if he really truly wanted to, he would've left Ophelia's side ages ago. But, in truth, both those thoughts disgusted him. As fearsome as he wanted to be, there was a softness in him that knew Tiril wasn't crazy for wondering. That Ophelia wasn't reckless for thinking she could alter the way things had been for a thousand years.

This was why he made a point to refrain from reading up on the Celestial religion. If there were Spirits up there, sentient Stars with his best interest at heart, why weren't they here? Why weren't they making the world a better place? Why couldn't they stand before him and tell him this themselves? He didn't know much about North Star but knew the Spirit had been revered in old times. She'd been a navigator, both spiritually and physically. Werewolves revered her, a close second to the moon. Many creatures looked to her in their darkest moments, trusting she'd lead them toward their end goal. She was more than a 'guiding light.' She was *The* Guiding Light—the only North Star. People had put their faith in this being, trusting the thoughts in their heads or the random 'signs' they'd seen to be sent from above. They made decisions based on feelings, not facts, and look where it had gotten them.

If this North Star, or First Wolf—whatever you wanted to call it—truly existed, then she'd made a right mess of everything.

And if he, by some miracle, was meant to take her place, how could he possibly be any better?

Shaking his head, he flipped aimlessly through the book, landing on a page that made him go cold with insurmountable fear and the feeling that he'd just answered a question he never wanted the answer to.

What ye, Star Seed, must do,

Look not to thine brothers, thy sisters, nor friends,
Not thine fathers, thy mothers, nor elders,
No, oh seedling, cast thine eyes to the Stars,

Listen good, listen well, Star Seed,
Thy eyes scarcely trick thine mind,
Thine mind scarcely trick thy heart,
Trust, oh seedling, cast thine eyes to the Stars.

"What are you thinking?" Tiril asked, coming to stand beside him.

Seamus quickly shut the book, forcing it back into her hands. "That this is a load of bullshit," he lied.

"Seamus," Tiril sighed, shaking her head in disdain. "I know it's a long—"

"It's more than a long shot, Tiril," he laughed, stepping back. "You're placing hope in something that has never once been proven to exist. Excuse me if I don't believe you."

Her brilliant blue eyes sparkled as she said, "That's the fun of it."

Seamus frowned, hugging himself tight. "What does Ophelia say? Did you tell her?"

"I haven't, but I'd say Ophelia knows more than she lets on," Tiril sighed. "I've a theory about her, too, you know."

"What do you mean?"

Tiril was quiet for a long moment, staring into the fire, watching Maj-gun laze amongst the flames. "I just think it's odd, that when the world needs them most, both a North Star and a Winter Witch have appeared. That in itself is strange, but yet you've found each other. Against all odds, you've found each other."

"How is that odd?"

Tiril turned to him, a fiercely hopeful smile on her lips. "Because this isn't the first time the two of you have been a family."

All Seamus could do was furrow his eyebrows and fight to keep his mouth shut.

"Well then. . . I shall leave you to your thoughts," Tiril sighed, giving him a wink. "Think well and good on what I've told you."

"You too, you crazy old bat," Seamus mumbled.

Tiril slapped his arm as hard as she could. "Seamus Norland! How dare you call me cra—"

"All right, all right, I'm sorry," Seamus sighed.

Tiril's face softened just a touch, a tiny smile tugging at her lips. "I'm sure I can find it in my heart to forgive you."

CHAPTER FIFTY-FIVE

FRIENDS IN UNLIKELY PLACES

Ophelia had left Seamus's room to pack her things and try to get some sleep but instead found herself tossing and turning into the wee hours. Begrudgingly, she sat up, knowing she couldn't lie there any longer. Ivar, Sköll, and Maj-gun were all asleep, sprawled out across her bed and the pillows in the way animals often slept when they were well and truly content with their human companions. Careful not to wake them, Ophelia crawled out of bed, poking her head out into the hall. The crystal light in the halls shone bright, but that didn't do much in the way of telling her what time it was. Leaving the door open so as not to lock her furred and scaled friends inside, she slipped down the hall to see if Seamus had stayed true to his word.

The door to his room was open.

Her heart sank at first, but upon closer inspection, all his belongings were still haphazardly thrown across the room. Though it looked like a tornado had blown through, nothing was missing. She smiled to herself, knowing he wouldn't leave without supplies. Seamus was reckless but not stupid.

With that thought in mind, she hurried downstairs to see who she could find.

The den was empty, as well as the kitchen and dining room. Ophelia wasn't one to go poking around people's homes in the dead of night, so she resolved to return to her room until morning. Whenever morning was, that is. How was she to tell? She didn't think she could live underground like this, never knowing what time of day it was. Never being able to look out at the stars. The cave was beautiful in its own right, but it was sad in a way, too. She'd never felt more cut off from the world than she did here.

With that thought in mind, she turned back toward the stairs.

"May I help you with anything, Miss?" Reija asked.

Ophelia yelped, nearly jumping out of her skin. She'd not heard Reija's footsteps in the hall, yet there she was, waiting for her just outside the dining room archway.

"Oh, no, I was just looking for Seamus," Ophelia said, giving a bow.

Reija's eyes widened with mild surprise at that. For a moment, she was flustered. "Ahh. . . I see. . . Well, my lady, Mr. Norland has gone out for the night with Master Kirkeby. Shall I fetch you when he returns?"

"Oh, uh, that's okay, Reija, really. I don't want to trouble you," Ophelia said, edging past her.

Reija gave a solemn nod, almost looking. . . hurt? "Are you in need of anything else?"

This was a very tricky situation. Standing before Ophelia was a woman who wanted nothing more than do something, anything, for her. Yet, standing before Reija, was a young lady whose stomach churned at the thought of someone waiting on her hand and foot.

"Reija," she began, trying to sound like a noblewoman, "While I recognize you are duty-bound to the Kirkeby household, you don't have to go out of your way to—"

"Tiril thought you might say so, but I assure you I have no qualms with caring for you, Lady Ophelia," she said, straightening. "In fact, I take great joy in it. It's not every day you're at the beck and call of a Witch."

"Oh. . . but. . . I don't want you to be at my beck and call. . ." Ophelia said softly, avoiding her eyes.

Reija studied her for a moment, lips pursed. Ophelia hoped she hadn't offended her in any way. She'd hate to be a terrible guest.

"Are you going back to bed, my lady? Mr. Norland says you've had a long few days and need your rest."

Ophelia doubted she'd be able to get back to sleep after this whole ordeal. "Would I be allowed to read in the den 'til morning?"

A smile tugged at Reija's lips. "Of course, Miss."

She gestured to the den, leading Ophelia inside. Ophelia stood out of her way as she tidied the pillows left askew and cleared away empty plates.

Once she'd left, Ophelia took a chocolate-covered cookie and began pacing the den, looking for a book that suited her fancy. Saoirse would quite like it here. She'd also quite like Reija.

There she was again, thinking of Saoirse.

Was she alive? Was she with the rest of Tø, hidden away at one of the Ulvemordere's outposts or compounds? Or was she well and truly lost?

A thought struck her. Maybe the maps she'd taken from Jette's tent had information on such things? She'd had an inkling of this when she'd seen them, consumed by the thought of finding her town and putting things right, but up until now, she'd forgotten all about them. Suddenly invigorated by the prospect of knowledge, she spun.

And there was Reija, waiting patiently in the archway. "Yes, Miss?"

Ophelia was trying to find the right words to politely send her on her way when another idea popped into her mind. "Reija, do Tiril and Helgi have any maps with the locations of Ulvemordere bases?"

"A few, yes. Would you like me to show them to you?"

"If it isn't much trouble, yes, please."

Reija bowed slightly, crossing to one of the suits of armor decorating the den. Standing on her tiptoes, she reached up and twisted the head of the spear the suit held a few times. Beside her, one of the bookshelves swung gently forward. Ever elegant, she pulled the makeshift door open with a flourish, revealing a small room where all sorts of weaponry hung on the walls. In the center was a long rectangular table with wooden pieces depicting ships and caravans, horses and armies, as well as beings like trolls, wolves, and fairies.

Careful not to disturb anything, Ophelia leaned over the table to inspect the craftsmanship of the wooden pieces. Though she couldn't be sure, she had a feeling Seamus had carved each of them.

"Tiril moves the pieces around the map to show where

our allies are, should she know. You'll find a wolf wearing a crown here in Dødbyen. That is your Mr. Seamus Norland," Reija explained.

"Why does she do it?"

"Tiril is a nurturer at heart, really. She believes herself honor-bound to care for her rebels as if they were her children." Reija stood quiet for a moment, content to watch Ophelia flit around the room, taking it all in. "Is there anything else, Miss? I'm happy to bring over your plate of biscuits."

"Rei—"

"I would much rather be put to use instead of muddling about if it makes you feel better."

"You won't stop asking until I give you something to do, will you?"

"That is correct, my lady."

"All right. . . I suppose you may bring me something to eat while I fetch some things from my room."

Reija was beaming. She practically danced out of the den and into the kitchen, her smile bright enough to rival the sun. At least Ophelia could take solace in knowing she'd made her happy.

Quickly, she hurried back up to her room and grabbed all the maps from her bag. Somehow, she'd amassed quite a few of them. She hadn't realized just how many she'd stolen from Jette's camp.

Upon returning to the secret room in the den, Ophelia found a steaming bowl of stew and Reija, who was sifting through a drawer on the long table.

"Tiril has blank maps around here somewhere. I thought you may get use out of one," she said absentmindedly. "Please tell me if the stew is up to your standards."

"I've been living off Seamus's shoddy campfire meals for weeks on end. Anything is better than that."

Reija laughed to herself, continuing her search.

Ophelia placed her maps on the table, careful not to disturb Tiril's pieces. Then, she took her bowl and began studying the differences between her magical map of Alle Årstider, Tiril's, and the ones she'd stolen. Just as she'd seen with the route to Egill's hideout, there were places on the Wayfarers Map that didn't appear on the others. How many secret towns were there? How many mystical places were hidden just out of sight?

"Hey, can I ask you something?" Ophelia asked, mind overwhelmed with secrets no one would answer.

"Of course, Miss."

"Do you know anything about the prophecy that was mentioned over dinner?

Reija looked up, smiling. "Unfortunately, Miss, I wasn't one for superstition until I met you."

Ophelia didn't know how she was meant to take that, but she figured it best to drop the subject—for now, at least.

"Ahh! Here we are!" Reija said, sounding quite pleased with herself. Leaning across the table, she handed her a pocket-sized map. The rough outline of Alle Årstider and prominent town names were there, but it lacked the standard illustrations and detail. "Tiril had these commissioned to fill out and send at a moment's notice. We've codes used to mark places on the map that may need the rebel's help."

"Smart, really," Ophelia said.

Reija nodded, coming to stand at her side. There was a questioning air about her. She wanted to ask what Ophelia was up to, but she may have thought it wasn't her place.

"Do you know which pieces mark the outposts?" Ophelia asked.

Reija pointed to sets of black tents, looking quite pleased to be included. Ophelia marked them on her blank map, cross-referencing them with the maps she'd taken from Jette. Ophelia noted there were quite a few places on Jette's maps that were not marked on Tiril's. Reija noticed this too and went to fetch a few more tents, placing them on the map wherever they needed to be. Tiril would be ecstatic, or so she said.

"Does Tiril keep records of these outposts?" Ophelia asked.

Reija thought for a moment, then nodded. "She does, but they're kept in her quarters. I can fetch them for you in the morning. Or, of course, you may ask her yourself, should you feel so inclined." She whispered the last part. She was sure Reija would find great joy in getting the records for Ophelia herself.

"May I ask you something?" Ophelia asked, standing.

"Anything, Lady Ophelia."

"Why am I important to you?" The question just sort of came out. In fact, it wasn't the one she'd intended to ask at all.

Reija seemed taken aback as if she didn't already know. "Lady Ophelia, you're a walking legend. You're proof that the old ways have not died and that there is hope for magickind. I do believe saying you're 'important' is not a strong enough word."

"You sympathize with magickind, then?" That much was obvious, but it was a kinder way of phrasing, 'But you're human, aren't you?'

"I do. If I may speak freely. . . ?"

"Yes, of course." It saddened her that Reija had to ask.

"Thank you, Miss. You see, my hatred for the Ulvemordere knows no bounds. They stole someone important to me, and I intend to make them pay for that. If I cannot strike them down myself, then the least I can do is aide you, my lady. Or Lady Tiril and Master Kirkeby, of course."

"May I ask who they took from you?"

Reija sighed heavily, avoiding her eyes. "My sister. Our mother was half-mer. My sister was born with a penchant for the sea and a dusting of the most brilliant purple scales you'd ever seen. She was quite the fisher, too. We lived in the boglands of Vårretten, where food is heavily regulated. The Ulve did not like that she could catch fish better than them, yet refused to sell her talents. When they found out she was half-magic, she was executed. In a way, they took my mother, too. Heartbreak does funny things to people."

"I'm so sorry, Reija," Ophelia said. She almost pulled her into a hug. Almost.

"It is not your fault, Miss."

"Believe me when I say I will help you avenge your sister's death." That was the truth of it.

"I look forward to the day you sit upon Snøbolig's throne. I hope I may offer my services then, my lady." With that, she bowed and excused herself.

Ophelia looked back to her maps, suddenly realizing just how much her existence could mean to people. Though she was aware of her miracle status, she'd wanted to fight back for selfish reasons, but now, knowing there were people who'd feel exactly the same as Reija instilled in her a new hunger for redemption. Snøbolig and the rest of Alle Årstider would one day be restored to the mystical, whimsical, magical place it was meant to be.

That would be Ophelia's life purpose. *This* was her destiny. Fern would be proud. She couldn't wait to tell her.

"Miss?" came Reija's voice. Ophelia turned to see tears flowing down her face. "Please call on me should you need anything. Anything at all, no matter how small. It's why I'm here."

"Thank you, Reija. I will."

Already, people were rallying behind her, fed up with how the world worked. How many more would join her should she reveal her presence to the world?

CHAPTER FIFTY-SIX

A TASTE OF COURAGE

Ophelia went to bed shortly after looking over the maps, intending to read until someone came to get her for breakfast. Instead, she finally fell asleep, her head resting on Sköll's back. She could've slept longer had it not been for the gentle knock at her door.

"Yes?" she called, stretching and rubbing the sleep from her eyes.

"May I come in, Miss?"

"Yes, of course, Reija!"

The door opened to reveal the ever-lovely Reija, who seemed to be in much better spirits than when they'd last spoken.

"Tiril has asked you and Mr. Norland to join her and Helgi in the map room after breakfast to discuss your findings," she said, grinning ear to ear.

"Wonderful! Thank you, Reija."

"Happily, Miss," she said with a bow. "May I help you get dressed?"

"I suppose," Ophelia laughed. "But, uh. . . Please don't tend to my hair. I can do it on my own." More like she hated the feeling of people touching her hair.

"Of course, my lady."

Reija threw open the door to the wardrobe as Ophelia went about brushing her hair. It may have been her imagination, but Ophelia swore there'd been fewer dresses in that armoire last night. Plus, all the pink and green ones had disappeared. Now, there were only blue, gray, and brown gowns. Ophelia smiled to herself. Tiril really did know how to take care of her guests. She must've switched them while she'd been downstairs.

"How about this one, my lady?" Reija asked, taking out a smoke-gray dress. She held it up to herself and spun as if to show just how glorious it was.

"It's beautiful!" Ophelia said. In the mirror above her vanity, she saw her eyes gleam with delight.

"I took notes of what you did and didn't like last night. Hopefully, we've filled your wardrobe with dresses more suited to your taste," Reija said, looking quite proud of herself.

"You have no idea how much I appreciate that," Ophelia said, almost tearing up.

The dress Reija had picked had a sweetheart neckline just as the brown one she'd worn before, though this had a separate bolero with long, glittering, sheer sleeves that brushed the floor. The skirt was made of the same material and spilled out around her feet like a waterfall.

"I do good work, don't I?" Reija asked.

"Phenomenal."

"I'll meet you downstairs, my lady," Reija said, bowing as she left.

Ivar, who had been watching protectively from her bed, hopped down to study her. He seemed to approve, seeing as he dragged his tail across her legs, purring. Once she'd tidied her things, he walked her to the door, seemingly proud of Reija's choice of dress.

"You're rather chipper this morning, aren't you?" That was Seamus, who was absentmindedly doing up the buttons on his sleeves as he joined Ophelia in the hall. He was wearing a dark navy overcoat embroidered with swirls oddly reminiscent of the shapes her magic made.

Ophelia was so relieved to know he'd stayed. "I am."

He glanced up at her, nodding to himself. "Tiril filled your closet, too, I see."

Ophelia swished her dress back and forth, then spun. "It's quite pretty, isn't it?"

Where had all these clothes come from? It was almost as if someone had conjured them.

"You'll find she'll spoil you. It's in her nature, I fear."

"So it seems," Ophelia laughed. "Did anyone tell you of the meeting we've planned?" she asked, taking the arm he offered her. Her smile was infectious, causing Seamus's face to split in two.

"Yes, I've been fetched," Seamus said thoughtfully. "I suppose you've finally looked over the maps you snagged from Jette?"

Ophelia just nodded, her smile turning mischievous.

Breakfast was a quick affair. Helgi was hung over, and Tiril had a far-off look in her eyes, but overall, Ophelia couldn't be happier. Seamus had explained the situation, sharing an odd look with Helgi, who laughed boisterously at the fact that Seamus would be taking Ophelia with him after all. Now, the four of them, plus Reija at Ophelia's request, sat around the map table.

"Tiril, are any of the places previously marked on your map used to hold prisoners?" Ophelia asked, handing over the map she'd marked up the night prior.

In turn, Tiril handed her a weathered leather-bound book with papers sticking out of the pages. "Not that I remember, though some of these are just as old as I am. Their purpose may have changed."

"They'd have better luck constructing a new place entirely. I doubt any of the old locations are being used for anything other than troops. The Ulvemordere are smarter than they seem, and their outposts aren't necessarily a secret," Helgi yawned. Reija poured him a cup of tea, nodding along as he spoke.

"Very true," Seamus said. He stood on Ophelia's right, arms crossed, face full of stone-cold determination. "May I see that, Tiril?"

Tiril handed him the map and a dripping quill, instead turning her attention to the maps Ophelia stole. After skimming through Tiril's records, Seamus marked off the outposts and camps least likely to house prisoners. With that, they were left with seven options. Seamus took Jette's map, the one with the tiny bumps all over it, shutting his eyes and dragging his fingers across it to read it. Vague descriptions of each of the remaining camps narrowed it down to four. One camp near

The Center Cities in Snøbolig looked promising, but the three in Høstlunden did just as well. One, in particular, was on the coast, giving the Ulvemordere ample opportunity to move prisoners around Alle Årstider discreetly.

"We'll send word to the rebels in Høstlunden and go from there. Those willing to do reconnaissance will be sent out in due time, not to worry," said Helgi between sips of tea.

"Should we really wait until then?" Tiril asked. "Stars only know what has happened to these people. Why make them wait any longer?"

"We shouldn't be hasty, Tiril, dear. We've just lost a group due to poor planning—you know I don't blame you, let me finish—I will not see another group or four lost," Helgi said. The passion with which he spoke shook the room.

Tiril sagged in her seat, avoiding his gaze. "The thought of their continual suffering sickens me."

Reija had been staring at Ophelia for quite some time, her fingers tapping a discordant beat on the steaming teapot she held.

"Yes, Reija?" Ophelia asked.

Tiril, Helgi, and Seamus turned to her, almost startled by her presence.

"Lady Ophelia, am I to speak freely?" she asked, her voice small.

"Always."

Reija set her teapot down, crossing to stand on Ophelia's left, addressing her employers and Seamus. "Noomi overheard you talking about Cathal and his mines. I, too, am of the opinion speaking with him will be fruitful."

Helgi nodded, looking relieved he hadn't been the only one wanting to press that subject. "Seamus, you must speak with him."

Seamus rubbed the back of his neck. "Why does it have to be me? You know the history. I'm sure there's another way."

Tiril shook her head. "If there is one, I can't see it. I doubt the missing magickind will be in the mines, but Ophelia's people could very well be. I would advise you also to pick his brain about these new weapons. Who else would be supplying the materials? Who else would know where the prisoners are being held? They transfer beings to his mines all the time;

he'll have at least *some* information. Cathal tries to be neutral, but he knows more about the Ulvemordere than he cares to admit."

"And this Cathal is. . . ?" Ophelia asked carefully. The name was familiar, but she couldn't quite place where she had heard it before.

"Cathal Sandvik, commonly known as the Jewel King. As Tiril said over dinner, he is a dear friend of ours. He supplies us with the crystals that light our city," Helgi said with a scowl. "He also supplies the Ulvemordere with their iron. You tend to have immunity if you can supply the enemy with something worthwhile, especially if you own all the stock in a certain good."

Ophelia knew of the Jewel King. Cathal—it was strange knowing his name—was as ruthless as they come. He was a centuries-old terror made of magic and stone. The Jewel King title was synonymous with destruction. But even trolls powerful enough to kill an army of a thousand men needed to make a living. For generations, the Jewel Kings had owned the mines in Snøbolig and Høstlunden. If there were mines in Dagslys Hul and Vårretten, she was sure he'd own them too. Thankfully for everyone in the warmer climates, there weren't many mountains.

"All right, well, Seamus and I will speak to Cathal on your behalf and see what he knows," Ophelia said, earning herself a scowl from Seamus. Reija, however, gave her a reassuring nod.

"Sounds like we'll be planning a raid soon enough. Maybe even two, depending on where everyone is being held. Just like the old times, isn't it Seamus?"

"Yeah," Seamus mumbled. "Just like."

"I shall inform Cathal of your arrival," Helgi said, standing.

Tiril cleared her throat, trying to catch Ophelia's eye. "Is there something else?"

"Well. . ." Ophelia hesitated, trying to find the right words. "What if we *do* find that the people of Tø are being held in the mines?"

"This is reconnaissance only, Ophelia," Helgi warned. "We don't need you two stirring up trouble. We will regroup and form a rescue party once you return. You're going in vastly outnumbered. There's no sense in playing the hero now."

"Well, dammit, Helgi, now you've jinxed us!" Seamus sighed.

"What?" he laughed.

Seamus smirked into his cup. "Last time I told her not to get into any trouble, she stole our horses."

"You have a penchant for rescuing animals, don't you, my dear?" Tiril asked.

Ophelia shrugged. "Helping those in need is one of life's greatest gifts."

CHAPTER FIFTY-SEVEN

FAREWELL

A week later, after Helgi had sent word to Cathal and the rebels, it was time to make the trek to the Juvel Hjem mountains. Several groups across Høstlunden would attempt to raid and pillage Ulvemordere camps. If all went well, they'd share their findings during a 'soiree' under something called the Hunter's Moon in the coming months. The plan was set, and Ophelia was hopeful her people and those affected by the Ulvemordere's recent actions would return safely soon enough.

Spending time with the Kirkebys had been a welcome respite. When they weren't drinking in the luxuries so freely given to them, Reija showed Ophelia around Dødbyen while Seamus trailed behind. She'd grown rather fond of Reija and was sad to leave her behind, but she knew this was far from the last they'd see of each other. She'd quite miss Tiril, too. Ophelia could definitely see herself living happily within these walls, but both she and Seamus were growing restless.

This goodbye was bittersweet. It marked the dawn of what everyone hoped was a new age. Helgi had mumbled, 'the dawn of The Winter Witch' under his breath. If she were honest, Ophelia liked the sound of that.

Not wanting to linger, Seamus had proposed they leave early in the morning. This didn't sit well with Tiril, who'd begged and pleaded they stay for one last breakfast. Seamus only agreed after she started crying.

Between mouthfuls of food, Tiril, Seamus, and Ophelia had engaged in riveting conversations, laughing boisterously. Helgi had been quiet, barely touching his food. After two weeks spent watching him eat an army's worth of delicacies, Ophelia found this exceptionally baffling.

"Brother mine, what ails you?" Tiril laughed.

Helgi pushed his plate away, attempting a smile. "Nothing, nothing. I just wish we all had more time together."

"Are you getting sentimental in your old age?" Seamus asked.

Helgi glared at him. "Perish the thought."

"When our intrepid adventurers return, I'm sure we'll have many more meals like this," Tiril said, tipping her cup to Ophelia.

"Yes," Helgi whispered. "I look forward to your return."

It was evident that Tiril and Helgi were not pleased they were leaving so soon. Helgi had already begun planning which old times he'd show to Ophelia. Tiril was preparing a letter, asking a friend of hers to fit her for a few dresses. There'd even been talk of putting in a tiny door for Ivar, Sköll, and Maj-gun so they could come and go from her room as they pleased. Reija had even mended her coat and shawl and fashioned her a new pair of gloves.

Still, they spared no expense preparing Ophelia for the long journey ahead. They'd insisted she trade her smelly old satchel and pack for ones better suited for a traveling deity. Attached to the bottom of her navy blue pack was a plush bedroll supposedly stuffed with pegasus feathers. They'd also allowed her to pick whatever she liked from the wardrobe. There weren't many items suitable for trekking through the wilderness, but she took what she could. The dresses she'd worn during her stay were left behind, but Tiril promised they'd always be waiting for her.

That room overlooking the fernery was hers, too, she'd said. The Kirkeby's doors would always be open for her. Seamus, too, of course, though they didn't say this aloud.

"I suppose it's our fault you're leaving so soon," Helgi sighed as he and Tiril led them to the tunnel leading back to Dødbyen.

Seamus grunted his agreement.

"Thank you so much for all you've done for us," Ophelia said with a bow. "I'm forever in your debt."

"Darling girl," Tiril whispered, "the pleasure is ours and ours alone. Repay us by making it back here in one piece, all right?"

Seamus mumbled something that sounded suspiciously like, 'It's your blood on her hands otherwise.' Ophelia elbowed him in the ribs. He winced, refusing to look at her.

"And keep us updated! It isn't that hard to send a letter, Norland," Helgi spat.

"Ink is expensive," Seamus snapped back.

"I'll make sure to send a letter at each town we pass through," Ophelia laughed.

With one final goodbye, she and Seamus were off, meandering through Dødbyen, unsure of what lay ahead. Ophelia was invigorated. This was what she was meant for, no?

She hoped Fern was proud of her. Amaranth, too.

Jonquil wouldn't be. That much she knew for certain. He was of the same opinion as Seamus, always saying she should keep her head down and stay out of trouble. Then again, it wasn't like him to stick his neck out for anyone or anything. He kept to his hurdy-gurdy or lyre and preferred things that way. There'd been a war once, one not dissimilar to the one on the brink of waging today. His mother, Narcissus, Spirit of Love, held his refusal to fight over his head like an anvil.

Jonquil, in many ways, was a disgrace to all Spirits.

Especially his mother.

Ophelia couldn't help but love him for that reason.

She also couldn't stop smiling. Hope fluttered in her heart. These past few weeks had been a journey in their own right, but what would come next would be epic. Meeting Tiril and Helgi had been the chance of a lifetime, and she refused to waste it. No matter how long it took, she'd rescue the good people of Tø.

"So," Seamus began, his husky voice cutting through her thoughts. "The Jewel King spends most of his time in Juvel Hjem. Those mountains are about a three-day trek away on horseback. That is, of course, if we don't run into trouble along the way."

"We'll just have to be careful," Ophelia said.

Seamus gave her a very pointed look. "I'm not sure that's something either of us can do. If you haven't noticed, we get ourselves into the strangest situations. Need I remind you of the tree you flung me into? The one we fell out of?"

"Oh, speak for yourself, Seamus. I can be careful."

"I doubt that highly," he scoffed.

Ophelia rolled her eyes. "Need I remind *you* the Ulvemordere were none the wiser to my existence until a certain werewolf came barging into my town?"

He glared at the top of his shoes, crossing his arms tight over his chest.

Ophelia had a dreadful feeling she shouldn't have said that. Her cheeks burned with anger beneath her mask, cursing herself as she edged a few inches away from him. He was lost in thought, his pace quickening as they wove through the bustling city of Dødbyen.

Head a little clearer than it had been when they arrived, Ophelia was able to take in the dark beauty of this place. Every time she walked these streets, she saw something new. She especially liked the way the colorful crystal lights cast everything and everyone in a rainbow of color. As they passed under signs with glowing crystal letters, Seamus's hair seemed to change from pink to yellow to red. Instinctively, Ophelia's hand searched in her bag for the shard of crystal she'd pocketed. Maybe one day, she'd have it made into a necklace or ring.

Under the crystal lights, in the small alcoves between carts and businesses, performers showed off their many talents. Some swallowed swords or contorted their bodies into otherworldly shapes. Some juggled fire. Some danced. Every alley was a mini circus. Each set of performers—mostly Faye Folk—had a small crowd surrounding them. Even Seamus seemed intrigued by a few of the acts. Ophelia did, too, of course. Going to a circus was one of the many things she'd always wanted to do. However, some of the acts frightened her. Especially the fire jugglers. She could feel the heat resonating off of them, her skin prickling at the thought of getting too close. Discreetly, Ophelia snuck around to the other side of Seamus, placing him between herself and the fire-wielders. He glanced down at her but said nothing. Together, they wove through a group of clapping patrons, watching a woman spin around on a hoop hanging from the platform above her. Now *that* was entertaining.

"Have you ever met a troll?" Seamus asked, his body finally relaxing.

"No. What are they like?"

Seamus weighed this for a moment. "Not fun."

"Ahh, I see," Ophelia said thoughtfully. "You get along well with them, then?"

"Well, would you look at that? We've got a comedian on our hands, folks. Gather round, gather round. You'll laugh so hard your sides will split," Seamus said dryly.

"Is she really?" a bemused passerby asked, his eyes on Ophelia's mask. Behind him, several heads turned to listen.

Seamus did a double take, shaking his head. "No."

Ophelia stifled a laugh. "Come now, Seamus. You've got to be careful what you say in Dødbyen."

"Kid, you're on thin ice. I'd stop while you're ahead."

Ophelia rolled her eyes. "I figured by now you wouldn't be so—how do I put this kindly. . . Ah! Yes, *unbearable.*"

Seamus slowed to a stop. "Just so we're clear, I don't like any of this. I'm only tagging along so you don't get burned at the stake, you hear?"

"I know."

"I don't think you do," Seamus spat. "You're the only thing I—" he began, his words steeped in anger. He swore. "It doesn't matter."

It didn't matter to him, but it mattered to her. She smiled to herself, knowing she'd weaseled her way into some part of his heart. Maybe he'd never admit it, but she knew. Same as she knew the wind would always be there to catch her if she fell from too high a height.

5. Juvel Hjem

CHAPTER FIFTY-EIGHT

ONLY TICKET OUT

Seamus had never been so sad to leave Dødbyen. Usually, it was all he could do to stay more than ten minutes. Today, however, he only wanted to hide in the stuffy Kirkeby mansion.

With a heavy heart, he led Ophelia up the stairs to the first platform. She still had her eyes on all the performers and wares. It seemed to take great effort for her not to stop and ogle over every little thing. One of these days, her curiosity was going to get her hurt. Today was not going to be that day.

Two guards stood watch over the lift they intended to take. Unfortunately, Seamus recognized them from the dragon-rescuing incident. One was the werewolf he'd taken a cheap shot at. His wolf paced in the depths of his mind, but it wasn't as antsy as he'd expected. How strange.

"While the Kirkebys have forgiven all your transgressions, let it be known we haven't. Once a thief, always a thief. Once an arson, always an arson," one of the guards said as they opened the gate for them.

"You know, technically, none of that was my fault," Seamus said thoughtfully. "I was just a pawn, really."

"Yeah," the other guard laughed. "And 'technically,' I'm an Earl." He made a great show of air quotes to get his point across.

"Oh, come now, love. You're not fooling anyone with that face," Seamus called down as the lift rose. He saluted them and waved, "See ya in jail, fellas."

"I'll want my money back next time we meet, Norland," the first guard said.

"Fat chance," Seamus mumbled.

"What was that, *dødmann?*"

For some reason, this comment enraged Ophelia. She leaned over the edge of the lift, pointing rather menacingly at him. "If you care so deeply about your gold, you should've kept a better hold of it!"

Seamus pulled her back from the railing, both to keep her head from hitting the platform above as the lift rose higher and higher and out of fear she'd say or do something she'd regret. Tiril and Helgi had presumably granted her local immunity, but that didn't mean everyone would take that into consideration.

"You done?" he asked.

"Quite," she smiled.

As the lift passed through the hole in the first platform, she situated herself in the corner. Absentmindedly, she fiddled with the buckle on her satchel, making an incessant clicking noise, much to Seamus's chagrin.

"How'd you know they took prisoners?" he asked slowly. They hadn't discussed it until now. For some reason, he could tell she hadn't wanted to talk about it under the Kirkeby's roof.

Ophelia scoffed. "Why does everyone keep bringing up some grand purpose you're meant to fulfill?"

"You first."

"Not everyone fit in the observatory, and there was a distinct lack of bodies in the town square." The way she spoke was odd. The lilt to her voice made him distrustful of her words, but he didn't know how else she would've reached this conclusion. As far as he knew, no one could have told her. "Your turn."

He inhaled deeply, moving to stand beside her, gripping the chains on either side of him for support. His legs felt weak. He wanted to lie to her and say he'd come to the same conclusion but couldn't.

"I found Lochlan," he began, his voice tight. He was in bad shape. There was nothing we could've done for him. He told me the Ulve took prisoners, that they wanted to lure you just as you'd suspected. He didn't want you running into danger and asked me not to tell you."

"You should've anyway," Ophelia said. He'd expected anger, but her voice was empty and emotionless. She didn't even smell like pomegranates or mint.

"I know," he said.

"Anyway, that's not what I meant, Seamus," she sighed.

"Well, that's all you're getting." The last thing he wanted was to indulge in one of the Kirkebys' 'theories.'

Seamus had the funniest feeling she rolled her eyes beneath her mask. As the lift ascended, she fell quiet, making circles on the floor with the tip of her boot.

"I want to save them, Seamus. It's important to me," she said softly.

"That might not be possible, kid. I'm not putting their safety before yours, you hear?"

The lift shook as it settled at the top of the chasm. A glaring guard opened the gate, offering them no pleasantries as he beckoned them forward. Their horses were waiting for them, equipped with new gear. Both of them looked agitated, especially Frykt. As soon as Rain saw Ophelia, he calmed and trotted over to her, neighing wildly. The guard tending to them helped mount their belongings, then waved them away. Seamus didn't pay him. Tiril and Helgi had suggested he should, but he just didn't feel like it.

"I wouldn't put them before you, either," Ophelia said when they'd galloped out of earshot. "But I would put them before myself. I hope you understand that. I'd put all of you before me."

That's what worried him. "Well then, I'll just have to keep an extra eye on you, huh?"

She smiled brightly at him. Weirdly, her horse seemed to do the same. "I suppose so."

CHAPTER FIFTY-NINE

Now That I'm Grown

After being cooped up in that mansion for a week, Ophelia had hoped to stretch her legs for a while. Instead, she found herself stuck in a haze, eventually resigning to the saddle. Rain was happy to oblige; in fact, she thought the horse had grown irritable without her atop his back. Seamus was atop Frykt, whittling away again. Ophelia sat cross-legged, plotting their course. Though the existential weight had lifted, Ophelia's worries were far from gone.

According to her magical map, they weren't far from Juvel Hjem.

Seamus yawned, holding his carving to the light. Ophelia frowned. His wrists were still raw from their encounter with Egill. Wolfsbane did more damage when ingested or inhaled, but from what she'd seen, the physical wounds took a while to heal.

Ophelia glanced down at her own wrists, shocked by the sight. Dark purple veins shot out across her frostbitten skin. When did that happen? Seamus would've pointed it out by now. The last time she'd checked, the marks hadn't been that dark. She flexed her fingers, finding her skin tight and stiff, her bones aching. As quietly as she could, she reached into her satchel and dug around for the gloves Reija had made. Had she really taught herself to ignore the pain so much that she hadn't noticed? That was a scary thought. After all those experiments Lochlan had done, the last month had finally pushed her over the edge. She'd gone utterly numb to the wear and tear of her powers. Her hands had been cold, but that was normal, wasn't it? Her wrists ached, but she'd been drawing an awful lot lately.

Frowning, she rolled up their magical map, glancing at Seamus to find him staring at her.

"That's bad, isn't it?" he asked.

"What's bad?"

He gave her a knowing look.

Her cheeks reddened. "I'm okay," she said, her voice small.

"You keep saying that, but I don't think you believe it." He made a few more cuts on his carving of Frykt, then swung his legs around so he sat side-saddle. Feet dangling off the side, he crossed his arms over his chest, taking on the role of a disappointed parent. "They've gotten bigger, I've noticed."

Ophelia twirled a strand of Rain's hair around her gloved finger. "It's been worse."

"That doesn't mean it isn't bad now," he said softly. "You've been sleeping late, I noticed. You're not still injured or whatever, are you?"

Ophelia just stared at him, searching his eyes for. . . she didn't know what. The Witch had been so used to being over-looked that the sudden attention was unbearable. She hated being in the spotlight. Why else had she wished to become invisible all these years?

"Do you want to hear a story?" she asked, unable to avert her eyes from his all-consuming gaze.

He nodded, leaning forward, the expectation of a child listening to a bedtime story on his face.

"I did," she blurted out, "I—I mean, I did have to defend myself. A long time ago. You asked me once if I'd ever had to, and I lied."

Seamus's eyes swept over her. She could tell he knew this story was not one he was ever meant to hear.

Ophelia sat stiff, eyes shut tight as she searched for the right words. "Lochlan wasn't a healer. He was an alchemist," she began, "and a horrible one at that."

The words poured out of her before she could stop her-self.

"For a while, he was kind. He was never loving, per se, but he took care of me in his own weird way," she began, already choked up. "For a few short years, I had a taste of nor-malcy. It was nice, you know. I made a few friends. Like—" she cleared her throat "—like Saoirse."

"It didn't stay like that, though," Seamus said.

"The older I got, my powers grew. I went from barely being able to conjure a single snowflake to creating a tornado inside the observatory. And the thing is, I was a very temper-amental child. You've seen firsthand how dangerous that can be." She gave him a knowing look. He nodded, face gray. "Loch-lan did his best to try and teach me how to wield these powers, but it was out of my control. Or, more importantly, out of *his* control."

Ophelia shifted uncomfortably in her saddle, looking out at the trees. "Throughout my childhood, he'd poked and prod-ded at me, but never too much. He'd never hurt me. Until, of course, he did."

Seamus's face was dark with hatred.

"He was very sick, Seamus. He'd never tell me what was wrong, but over the years, he'd grown frail. Others his age were perfectly healthy. I never understood why. Anyway, no matter what he did, he couldn't heal himself. I remember one day, he took a research trip to the Center Cities. When he returned, his entire demeanor had changed. He started receiving strange parcels in the mail. Unicorn horns. Ground-up fairy wings. Mermaid scales. The whole lot. Whenever I asked, he'd told me to mind myself and stay out of his way."

Seamus rubbed the back of his neck, lost in thought. "Sounds like he had an Ulvemordere friend."

Ophelia nodded. "I thought so, too. While they stayed out of The Wilds, I knew they hung around the Center Cities. I was a very imaginative child, Seamus," she said, holding her head high. "It's a blessing and a curse."

"I've noticed."

"Nevertheless, Lochlan began doing a myriad of strange experiments. When Lochlan can't solve a problem, it drives him mad. He'll do anything to 'fix' someone, no matter the conse-quences. That's why he was Tø's healer. He'd cured the uncur-able for years; he just couldn't cure himself." Ophelia shivered, fiddling with the buckle on her satchel strap. "If you can be-lieve it, I was worried about him. *Very* worried. And you know what happens when I have strong emotions."

"Your powers go haywire," Seamus said with a nod.

"Precisely," Ophelia sighed. "The experiments he'd done to himself had made his condition worsen. My worry for him had caused a terrible storm. I've been told it was the worst weather The Wilds had ever seen. A bunch of the livestock in Tø ended up dying. As you can imagine, this did not bode well for a town that relies on animal byproducts to survive. When Lochlan found out what I'd done, he was livid. I'd practically damned the whole village into poverty. Knowing I'd caused that broke me, but no matter what I did, I couldn't quell the storm nor my worry for Lochlan.

As I mentioned before, he ruled in place of our Earl and Countess. The villagers who didn't know what I was were scared for their families. The ones who did were scared of me. Lochlan locked me in the observatory and began a different set of experiments.

I knew he was angry with me, but I didn't realize what was happening until it was too late. I knew what my blood could do, so when he asked if he could use some of it, of course, I said yes. I figured if he could heal himself, I wouldn't have anything to worry about. The storm would stop, the villagers could buy new livestock without them dying, and Lochlan wouldn't be angry with me for being so careless."

"Phee. . ." Seamus whispered.

"He went from trying to teach and help me wield my powers to doing horrible experiments, searching for a way to strip me of my magic. There was no worry for my well-being; there was only bloodlust. He figured I was the key. That my life force could heal him. And me, being a naïve and impressionable young Witch, let him do whatever he pleased in an attempt to help him." The fear and anger in her voice made her sick. She was rightfully furious with Lochlan, but those feelings never helped. In some ways, they made her feel worse. All she felt was guilt. How horrible was that?

"There are jars of my blood mixed with all manner of additives hidden in the observatory. Many a day, he'd drained me near dry just to see how my body would react. Would I heal myself? Would I lash out and attack him? Would a storm blow the roof off his observatory? Would I simply die?" Seamus's eyes narrowed, his hands flexing as if he were about to fight the horrid old man. "Once he answered these questions, he found new ones. Why *didn't* my body heal? Why did I lose control of my magic when pushed too far? Was the weather reacting to me, or was I affecting it on purpose? How big of a storm could I conjure? How far could he push me without killing me? How much of my blood would allow *him* to conjure a storm? It was no longer about healing himself; he just wanted to cut me up and see how I ticked."

"I knew I hated him," Seamus grumbled.

Ophelia inhaled sharply, forcing her fidgeting hands to rest neatly in her lap. "The experiments kept me weak, so the storm outside stopped, but a new storm formed inside me. My magic had always had a mind of its own, but the more he did, the more I lost control. I didn't want to fight back, convinced I was doing the right thing, but my magic had had enough. I hurt him once, burned straight through his robes. Nearly killed him. Looking back, I wish I would've. But I didn't see it that way at the time. My magic had disobeyed me and had hurt a 'friend.' So, as the experiments continued and my magic tried to fight back, I forced every bolt of lightning back on myself. I was burning myself from the inside out."

She unbuttoned her jacket, pulling her shirt over her shoulder to reveal stark white raised marks in the shape of lightning bolts. Seamus sucked in a breath, wincing. He forced himself to look away, rubbing his eyes and shaking his head in disbelief.

"The thing is, Lochlan never wanted me to *die*. Why would he? If I died, his little science project would be for naught. Yet, the more he hurt me, the more I hurt myself. I was so scorched and frostbitten I should've died."

She could see the gears turning in Seamus's head. It was a good thing Lochlan was dead, or else he'd run back to Tø and forget about Cathal, Egill, and the Ulvemordere. She knew it'd be his life's purpose to track down that horrible old man and kill him with his bare hands.

"So, what happened?" he asked, his voice strained from barely held-back rage. "What changed, I mean? How did you escape?"

"I didn't," Ophelia laughed, earning herself a scowl. "He just. . . ran out of questions he could safely answer."

There was more to it than what she'd told him, but those secrets weren't hers to share alone. Her story was intertwined with the myths of the Spirits.

She'd met Amaranth and the others years before but rarely called on them. That day, when Lochlan finally gave up, he'd sent her out to collect some herbs from the forest. Ophelia had been so weak she'd collapsed, lungs and heart fighting to keep her alive. As her consciousness slipped away, she'd called for the Spirits, and they'd come.

Upon waking, she found herself in the fabled Garden the Parables of the Terrestrial Pantheon talked about. Amaranth, Salvia, and Fern were all nursing her back to health. They kept her in the Garden for days, healing her wounds as best they could, breathing life back into her. And though they tried their best, for reasons even Celosia and Lotus couldn't figure out, they couldn't fully heal her.

Jonquil had hovered nearby, playing his lute in hopes that'd help in some way. It had. He rarely played around the other Spirits. He must've been very worried.

Until now, only the Spirits had known her whole story.

"Then I got older, and some friends helped me realize he was a monster," she said with a shrug. "I wasn't able to escape him, not really, but I never let him hurt me ever again. Lochlan rarely allowed me to leave his sight, but at least I had my cottage. I couldn't leave Tø, but I had an ounce of freedom. It's sad, but I was content."

I never really healed from what he did, as you can see." She rolled up her sleeves, showing him the old scars and the fresh dark reddish-purple marks. "So, all that is to say, I accidentally trained my magic to attack me if I'm in danger," Ophelia sighed. It was almost laughable. "And I've been in a lot of danger lately."

She let her story hang in the air as Seamus sat staring at her with pity and guilt. Another heavy weight felt like it'd been lifted from her shoulders. While there was so much more she wanted to tell him, getting all that off her chest seemed to wash away the scars and the pain. Of all the people she could've told this story to, she was glad it was him riding alongside her.

"I. . . Kid, I'm. . ." Seamus's words fell flat. He had to force himself to look away, jaw clenched tight. "Kid, you know I would *never* let anything like that ever happen to you again, right?" he asked warily. Frykt whinnied as if agreeing.

"I know."

"I'd die before I let another evil hand touch you."

"I know, Seamus."

"You're—"

"Seamus," Ophelia smiled, reaching over and taking his hand in hers. I'm never safer than when I'm with you," she said, gently squeezing his hand.

"Damn straight."

Always Thinking of You

It was night now. Ophelia had fallen asleep while reading atop Rain's back. They weren't far from the Jewel King's domain, so Seamus figured it best to rough it out until they arrived at Juvel Hjem. Frykt and Rain had slowed from fatigue, and he himself was growing weary. His side ached as it healed. Rest would do wonders, but he couldn't sleep. Whenever he closed his eyes, all he saw was a young Ophelia happily letting Lochlan do unspeakable things to her. Knowing what he knew now, Seamus wished he could go back in time. If the opportunity ever presented itself, he would. No matter where in time he ended up, he'd drop whatever he was doing and run full speed to Tø. For there was a Witch that had needed him long before they met.

He was suddenly very glad he hadn't left her in Dødbyen.

Ophelia's life story had made him realize how similar they were. They'd both been fooled into thinking they were on the right side of things, only later realizing just how wrong they'd been. In a lot of ways, their lives seemed to mirror each other. It was a heartbreaking thought, yes, but it made him feel less alone. Knowing someone was there to walk—or, as of now, *ride*—beside him gave him great comfort.

He also took great pride in what it meant for her to tell him all that. It'd taken great courage and even greater trust in him. Seamus wouldn't let that trust in him go unreciprocated. Even if his life ended tomorrow, he'd spend the rest of his days protecting his pup.

Pup.

When had he started calling her that? It wasn't a term thrown around loosely for a werewolf. To call a child your pup was to admit you saw them as your own. Blood be damned, that child was yours now, and you better be willing to live up to the role of a parent. It'd been an accident calling her that, but deep down, he meant it.

She was his pup, whether she felt the same or not.

At some point, his body had given out, and he'd fallen asleep. Ophelia was up before him, back to reading. One of these days, he'd have to pick up one of those books and see what all the fuss was about. He'd never been much of a reader. The Ulvemordere had put little emphasis on such things.

"Good book?" he asked with a yawn.

"One of my favorites," she said distractedly, turning a page before bookmarking it. "Sleep well?"

"No."

"Me either," she sighed, shutting the book and thus rejoining the world. Dark circles marred her under eyes. "I don't care if Egill finds us or whatever. We're spending the night at the best inn money can buy after we leave Juvel Hjem."

"Well, with the money we have left, I can get you—" Seamus reached into his pack, taking out his coin pouch. Grimacing, he counted what little he had left. "A hay bale and a potato sack."

"My, my, what luxury," Ophelia groaned.

"Chin up, kid, we'll figure something out."

Unfortunately, Tiril hadn't convinced Helgi to lend them some spending money. There'd been something about how 'he rarely paid back what he owed,' which Seamus found offensive yet true.

Ophelia smiled to herself, putting on her mask as the trees began to thin, revealing the mountains. "We always do, don't we?"

Seamus yawned again, sliding off Frykt to stretch his legs. Ophelia followed suit, falling in step beside him.

"Will you tell me about the prophecy now?" Ophelia asked after a while.

Seamus shot her a disgruntled look. "It's nothing you

need to worry yourself over.”

“But *you* were the one that said the Ulvemordere were raising you to be king. You never expanded on that.”

“To be fair, you never asked.”

“Yes, well, it’s almost like other things have occupied my mind,” Ophelia frowned.

Seamus sighed heavily, mulling this over. How was he meant to explain something he tried incredibly hard not to think about? This ‘prophecy’ was meant to dictate his life, and he barely knew anything about it. All he remembered from his time with the Ulvemordere was some sort of artifact reacting to him as a child.

“If I knew, Ophelia, I’d tell you,” he said finally.

“Promise?”

“Promise.”

“If you say so,” Ophelia mumbled. “So. . . Egill? Was he trying to lead us into a trap, then?”

“Jette didn’t seem to know I was coming,” Seamus said thoughtfully, glad she’d changed the subject. “But whose to know? Egill has an incredible mind. Too bad he uses it for nefarious purposes.”

Ophelia was quiet, looking out at the trees. Seamus followed her gaze, trying to see the same things she saw, wondering what conclusions her mind was forming. Though she’d admitted to being naïve when younger, she was far from it now. He wondered if Lochlan let her read as a child or if that habit had come after she’d ‘escaped’ him. He’d heard once that reading made you a kinder, smarter, more thoughtful being. All those traits were evident in Ophelia. Seamus wanted to be like that, too, if he was honest. Though he doubted he could ever adopt such traits. He was too—he sighed heavily—*surly*, for lack of a better word.

“Do you feel any better now that Jette is dead?” Ophelia asked. The question was morbid in nature, but Seamus knew her well enough to know exactly what she meant by it.

“No,” he said. It surprised him how easy it was to admit that. “Not at all.”

“Then why did you kill her?”

“Rather her than me.”

"Did you try to get through to her?"

Seamus wanted to say, 'What's with all the questions?' Instead, he simply said, "No. But I did ask about Tø."

"Did she say anything?"

"She knew something but refused to say," he sighed. "Jette was always stubborn. That's why I kept her around. You wanted to be stubborn, too. No matter the circumstance."

"Were you close?"

"There were rumors we'd get married."

"Is that what you would've wanted?"

"Once. But not because I loved her."

"Did you marry Ingrid for love?"

That question took him by surprise. What was worse was that he couldn't answer the way he should've. Again, there was something he *wanted* to say, but he couldn't make his lips form the word.

Without looking at him, Ophelia continued. "It's okay if you didn't."

"But isn't that what marriage is? The purest and truest expression of love?"

"Not to everyone. Sometimes it's just business. Sometimes, it's a necessity to live. Sometimes it's forced upon you. Sometimes you marry someone for all the right reasons, but it doesn't last," Ophelia said with a shrug.

Seamus mulled that over, glancing at his hands. There should have been a wedding ring on one of his fingers, but there wasn't. He'd thrown it away a long time ago. "Does marriage equate to love to you?"

"Yes. I wouldn't marry someone I don't love," Ophelia replied matter-of-factly. "But romantic love isn't the only kind of love out there. And it's far from the kind of love I yearn for. There's the love of siblings, of friends, of parents and children, of pets and their owners. I think love should be celebrated in all its forms."

Seamus was confused as to how they went from talking about his dead ex-comrade to discussing the intricacies of life, but he didn't entirely dislike the conversation. This was why he liked Ophelia's company so much. He still thought her odd. Who wouldn't? But he'd grown to love her strangeness. Somehow, this weird little Witch touched a place inside him that had never seen the light of day. It made him realize that he, too, was odd and that they often shared similar ideals.

"I hope you experience all kinds of love, pup," he said softly.

She turned to smile at him. "I hope you do, too, Seamus."

Seamus turned his attention back to the road, smirking to himself. Up ahead, towering above, so tall the peak disappeared into the clouds, were the Juvel Hjem mountains. Littered across its many ridges were caves and villages carved into the rock. At its base was the entrance. Four craggy trolls stood guard in the distance, overseeing ores and jewels being carted away.

"Please tell me we're not fighting our way inside," Ophelia groaned.

"Not this time," Seamus laughed. "But, uh, point of advice; let me do the talking."

Ophelia bristled, displeased with the idea. "If you insist."

They led Rain and Frykt to a makeshift stable, steeling themselves for what lay ahead. Ophelia didn't know the Jewel King's temperament, but Seamus knew all too well that there was no predicting what would come next.

The trolls guarding the entrance to his domain crossed their spears—which were the size of tree trunks and just as tall. Since they were so huge and their weapons massive, they didn't exactly block their way. Still, Seamus took pause.

"Purpose of entry?" one of the trolls asked.

"Visitation," Seamus said as loud as he dared. There was a delicate balance between speaking to be heard and being rude. Trolls almost rivaled giants in stature. The phrase 'How's the weather up there?' was a genuine question.

"Who?" another asked.

"Cathal Sandvik," Seamus replied.

Trolls didn't have the same anatomy as humans. Where eyes should be, there were jewels. Trolls had no eyelids or pupils. Their eyes didn't move. Despite this, Seamus swore the guards gave each other a look of distrust out of the corner of their faceted eyes.

"Names," the first troll demanded. The two trolls that

weren't attempting to block their way stamped their spears on the ground.

"Seamus Norland," Seamus said, puffing out his chest. He turned to Ophelia, nudging her with his elbow. She stood frozen. He couldn't exactly blame her.

The second troll leaned down to her, turning its head to see her better. One of its eyes was cracked. It took in the shaking human being before it, its rocky mouth grinding as it frowned.

"Name," it said, taping the top of her head with a pudgy finger covered in moss. Its finger was nearly the size of her face.

"O—Ophelia Av'Skogen," she managed, giving an awkward curtsey.

Seamus cringed but said nothing.

Why he cringed, he didn't know. Something about 'Av'Skogen' irked him.

The trolls lifted their spears, turning as one to allow them entry. The four of them shepherded him and Ophelia through the cave, eerily quiet. Chances are they knew his name but not hers—unless, of course, Tiril and Helgi had detailed such things in their letter. Either way, he could sense their distrust.

Ophelia clung to his side, slumped as she walked. She smelled of pomegranates again, her anxiety enough to make him gag. He tried to give her a reassuring look, but his own fears were getting the better of him. Cathal was one of the few forces that scared him. Trolls were exceptionally hard to kill, especially those as old and powerful as the great Jewel King.

"Where are they taking us?" Ophelia whispered.

"I'm going to be completely honest with you, kid, I don't know. I'm assuming the throne room, but I'm not hopeful."

"Now's the time to tell me why you—" she glanced up at the trolls "—have a strained relationship with Cathal."

Seamus pinched his nose, trying to ease his sudden headache. "I'd intended to tell you sooner. Not enough time now."

"Wonderful."

"Truly."

Ophelia turned her attention to their surroundings, and Seamus did the same. Juvel Hjem hadn't changed one bit since he'd been here last. The same crystal lights that lit up Dødbyen hung from the high ceilings. Well, high for an average-sized being. They were honestly quite low for a troll, some twelve feet tall. Barrels and crates of supplies were pushed up against the walls, covered in dust. Broken tools lay discarded. Support beams sagged under the weight of the mountain. Seamus couldn't understand how the place hadn't collapsed after all this time.

Creatures of all kinds bustled around them, their clothes tattered and covered in dirt. A human, their skin caked in mud, struggled to push a cart full of coal up the slight incline of the cave floor, heading toward the light. Behind them was a ghostlike procession of other beings carting their own loads. Smaller trolls shouted orders, shoving any stragglers. There was no remorse in their eyes, but then again, how could one deduce a troll's feelings from such unmoving spheres?

Every couple of troll-sized paces, there was a tunnel. Some led to the mines; some led to refineries, and others led below to the workers' quarters or above to the troll quarters.

The conditions here were harsh. Working in the mines wasn't something a being chose freely, at least not a sane being. It was taxing on mind, body, and soul. Seamus knew these halls had seen many a death. Most of which were unnecessary. Most beings got little out of the job, but someone had to do it. Jobs like these mattered the most but were usually underappreciated at best. Seamus couldn't help but wonder if the miners' families understood the sacrifice they were making.

"I don't like it here," Ophelia said. Seamus glanced down at her to find she was hugging herself tight.

"Hopefully, we won't be here long," Seamus said with a reassuring smile.

For her sake and his, he hoped he was right.

CHAPTER SIXTY-ONE

JUVEL HJEM

It was an understatement to say Ophelia was shaking in her boots. Something about this place set her on edge. The farther the trolls led them into the mountain, the quieter the voice of the wind was. The air was stagnant here, smelling of nothing but metal, dying embers, and sweat. There was a tug at her consciousness somewhere beyond, but other than that, she felt the outside elements and herself weren't welcome here. As the ground began to slope and the light of the surface was snuffed out, Ophelia began to feel sick. The mountain seemed to be compressing her, squeezing the air from her lungs.

"I really don't like it here," she groaned, hugging herself as tight as she could.

"Just try and stay calm, Phee," Seamus said softly. In the low orange light, he found her hand.

The tug on her consciousness grew stronger as the trolls steered them around a corner. This hall was completely devoid of life, but in the distance, she heard the clink of metal against stone. At the end of the hall, stalactites hung like a million pointy teeth, leading to the stomach of a furious beast. The trolls, either unaware of or unbothered by the rocky beast, ushered them through the mouth. Ophelia clung to Seamus's arm, unsure why she was so frightened.

Beyond the mouth, the beast's stomach acid appeared in the form of murky water. The only light came from tiny glowing worms hanging from the ceiling. Occasionally, one would drop from their perch into the water with a soft *plunk!* The water seemed agitated, though Ophelia couldn't explain why. This had been the tug she'd felt on her mind. Stalagmites jutted out of the water, each carved with all manner of pictures. Some were worn, their pictures nothing more than bumps, showing their age. Others seemed fresh, as if the sculptor had just stepped away. In a sense, it reminded Ophelia of Egill's hideout. Slippery steppingstones, which seemed to have been made for strides belonging to trolls and trolls only, led to a center platform. Both Ophelia and Seamus either had to jump or stretch their legs as far as they'd go to get safely across. On the center platform, a troll lazed on a rather unimpressive throne. One arm propped up his egg-shaped head, his legs dangling over one of the armrests. He wore only a crown of jewels that matched his massive ruby eyes and a leather loincloth weighed down by multicolored gems. Pockets and shards of rubies littered his rocky skin, reminding Ophelia of a geode. Ophelia and Seamus were brought before him, the trolls behind them stepping aside, spears ready. The Jewel King sighed heavily upon seeing Seamus, resting his head upon his massive fist. Behind him were more carvings. These were inlaid into the cave wall, made of every jewel you could imagine.

"You're late," the Jewel King said. Though it seemed to take much effort for him to speak, his voice echoed through the subterranean throne room like an explosion. "Helgi sent word days ago."

Seamus bowed deeply, hand over his heart. "Forgive us, my lord, we got sidetracked."

Ophelia, too, bowed. In the grand scheme of things, they were equals by birthright. If the troll knew who stood before him, she guessed he would've bowed as well. Sometimes, the mask was a curse.

"Speak quickly, *boy*; Cathal grows tired of you already," the Jewel King yawned.

He rubbed two of his fingers together, the sound like gears grating against each other. Two human servants dressed in gray appeared from a hidden tunnel to the left. Together, they struggled to carry an enormous ruby tray across the steppingstones. Upon the tray were all manner of delectable delights fit for a troll. Golden bowls of candied beetles. A decanter of what appeared to be tree sap, given the bark floating in it. Clumps of moss dusted with sugar. Fish bones. Scrap metal. Ophelia was trying very hard to keep her face neutral.

"As I'm sure Helgi mentioned in his letter, we've come to you. . ." Seamus's words trailed off as Cathal reached forward and grabbed a handful of candied beetles. He cleared his throat, shivering slightly. "Apologies, my lord. As I was saying, I'm sure Helgi already explained, but we're here on business. We seek both your wisdom and your aid, my liege."

"Yes. . . Yes, Cathal remembers names. Seamus means to barter for souls?" the troll laughed. "What could he possibly have to offer?"

Seamus looked to Ophelia, frowning. Nothing. They had absolutely nothing to barter. "Well, before we discuss the terms of our trade, might we have proof the souls we seek reside in Juvel Hjem?"

If Cathal could slowly blink in disdain, Ophelia was sure he would've. "No."

Seamus went red, nostrils flaring. "Very well," he grumbled.

"Cathal believes there was more to Helgi's letter?"

Nodding, Seamus continued on. "It has come to light that the Ulvemordere have been rounding up creatures of all kinds, attempting to drain them of their magic."

"And? Cathal does not see why Seamus and Helgi have come to him." The troll grabbed a fish bone, suckling on it.

"My lord, we humbly request your aid and information," Seamus said with another bow. Ophelia again copied him. Seeing him like this, so complacent and submissive, was unnerving. "If this continues, it won't be long before the Ulvemordere comes after even the likes of you."

"And why would they? Cathal and the Ulvemordere have an agreement," he roared, sitting up, swinging his arms, nearly knocking over the servants in the process. The decanter of sap was knocked off the ruby platter. It rolled off the platform and into the water without a splash. "Seamus comes to Cathal, in his hour of need, asking for help after what his people did to us?" Cathal asked, his voice echoing through the chamber. Ophelia swore the stalagmites shook. "And Seamus can't even be punctual?"

Seamus's eye twitched. "Apologies, my lord."

"Cathal does not accept."

"Even so, I beg you to listen. I am—" he grimaced "—I am willing to put the past behind me if you are. There is too much at stake here. It started with the killing of werewolves, then the burning of Witches. Next were the fairies and their wings. Unicorns. Merfolk. You may uphold your end of the bargain, but you know the Ulve won't."

Seamus's carefully crafted persona was slipping. Ophelia could see the passion in his eyes, the hatred for the thing he once strived to be. If she were Cathal, she would've bent to Seamus's will. But Cathal didn't seem to share the same sentiment. He was some two-hundred-and-fifty years old. There was wisdom with age, yes, but when one stayed in their ways for so long, their judgment was often clouded. She'd seen that in herself, in Seamus, and even Lochlan. Especially Lochlan. Ophelia knew she wasn't meant to say anything, but if Seamus's temper got the better of him, this would end very badly.

"If I may be so bold, my lord," she said, taking a step forward.

Cathal leaned down, scowling. "Who?"

She curtsied, smiling up at him. "I am Ophelia Av'Skogen, a dear friend of Seamus's."

Cathal considered her, taking another handful of beetles as he leaned back. "Speak."

"If you were to look back at the history books, this wouldn't be the first time the Ulvemordere attempted to take control of the mines. If you remember, three kings your senior, nearly lost his life. Your line of lineage would've ended that day were it not for a—"

"Witch," Cathal said with a nod. "Sigfreður, The Peaceful. Cathal knows of him. What does Ophelia mean to imply by bringing him up?"

"Trolls are strong, yes, but they've always been stronger when aided by others. Look at your mines, my liege. Without the labor of other creatures, you'd not be as powerful as you are today," Ophelia said. She pointed at the servants, who shook their heads in warning. "No one is strong enough alone."

Cathal scoffed. "That is why the Ulvemordere sends Cathal their prisoners. No Ulvemordere, no workers. No workers, no mines. No mines, no Cathal."

"But—"

"Ophelia speaks of community, yet the man beside her thrives on solitude." The troll guards beside them laughed. "Have you not heard what he did to Cathal? To Cathal's people? Community is a luxury, child. One that is earned, not demanded." The anger in his voice was evident. The servants shook beneath the weight of the ruby platter, eyes wide.

Ophelia glanced at Seamus, who was staring at her with both admiration and fear. Slowly, she looked back at Cathal. "I can assure you Seamus Norland is not the man you once knew. I do not know what he did to you, but he is no longer with the Ulvemordere," Ophelia said, hoping her smile and that statement were enough to calm the troll's fury. "He renounced them years ago, as I'm sure you know. He has spent years trying to reconcile his wrongdoings. I have witnessed this first-hand."

Cathal stood from his throne, his mossy eyebrows knit in irritation. "And what has Seamus done to prove himself worthy? Cathal sees a man unchanged. For a human whose life ends in a blink, Cathal would think he'd have done better by now."

Seamus took a step forward, stumbling over his words.

"No, no, no, you shush. Cathal wants the girl to speak."

Although Ophelia wanted to curl up in a ball and hide, she stood tall as she could. She'd be lying if she said she didn't shift under his ruby gaze, but she held her ground as best she could.

"Seamus has proved the only person he doesn't care for is himself," Ophelia said, "He would risk life and limb to protect those unable to protect themself."

"This means nothing to Cathal!" the Jewel King roared. He slammed his fist on his throne, shaking his head in dismay. "Seamus switches sides as though his decisions won't have consequences. Cathal will not fight alongside someone so indecisive."

Seamus again tried to speak, but Cathal held up a hand, eyes still on Ophelia.

"The version of Seamus you met before is not the man he is now. He no longer poses a threat to you or your people. We are both allies, ready to fight for a day when troll, human, fairy, werewolf—everyone—can get along in peace," Ophelia said. She could feel frustration coursing through her body. How did the noblemen and women argue their points like this daily?

Cathal took a handful of candied beetles and threw

them at her. Ophelia flinched but refused to move.

"You speak like Sigfreður," Cathal whispered, his voice rumbling like boulders tumbling down a cliffside. "Why?"

"He has always been an inspiration to me."

Sigfreður, The Peaceful, had been the first and last Winter Witch. His people had loved him until the Ulvemordere spread their ideologies like the plague. He'd been a friend to all, caring for every wounded creature, animal or humanoid. Though the Ulve had done their best to burn his teachings, some of his books were circulating even now. Reading his teachings was all fine and dandy, of course, but Ophelia much preferred talking to him face to face. Except Sigfreður was no longer Sigfreður. Not really. Those who knew him best called him Holly, the Spirit of Peace.

"Ophelia is not who she says she is," Cathal said slowly. "Do not lie to Cathal, child. Who are you?"

Ophelia simply said, "A concerned citizen tired of the iron claws the Ulvemordere rule with."

"And what does Ophelia know of the Ulvemordere?"

Ophelia straightened, smoothing the wrinkles from her coat. "I know they are creating weapons that can drain beings of their magic. Forgive me for saying such, but I can take an educated guess as to where those crystals are coming from."

Seamus looked as though he wanted to strangle her.

Cathal shifted uncomfortably in his seat but nodded. "Cathal knows not what Ophelia refers to but is aware the Ulvemordere use his ores in their weaponry."

"My lord, I believe you know far more than you let on," Ophelia said softly.

Trolls had been the ones to discover the crystals that lit up towns like Dødbyen. By that logic, Ophelia could take a guess who'd discovered the jewels capable of siphoning magic.

The room fell quiet for a moment. All there was was a drip-drip-dripping coming from the ceiling. Cathal watched Ophelia carefully, his ruby eyes refracting her image tenfold. What did he see when he gazed upon her? Did he see a future dignitary? Could he see through her mask, straight into her soul?

Eventually, he sighed, turning away. "If Cathal breaks his pact with the Ulvemordere, he will lose more money than you have even dreamed of. Why should Cathal even consider your proposal? Ophelia is asking Cathal to betray those he views as allies."

"I cannot make you do anything. It is not in my nature," Ophelia said. "I only ask you to give this thought. The Ulvemordere may need a skill you have, but the mines should belong to the trolls. Right now, they don't."

"With love, kid, shut up," Seamus hissed, appalled.

"And why not?" Cathal asked. His voice was softer than she'd expected it to be.

"You're not their business partner," Ophelia sighed. She knew she was pushing her limits, but they had to get through to him somehow. "If the Ulvemordere tried to take the mines once, who is to say they won't try again? With these new weapons, they may finally be able to claim them. What is more important to them? An alliance with you or the raw materials in these mines?" She glanced at Seamus, who was shaking his head violently. "To them, you're just an employee," she said as levelly as possible. "Your 'deal' is barely compensation."

Cathal laughed. The water on either side of the rock rippled. Pebble-sized shards fell from above. Cathal sat back down on his throne, plucking a glowworm off his shoulder.

"Ophelia is smarter than she looks but not smart enough," he roared. "Seize him," he smiled, gesturing to Seamus before popping the worm into his mouth.

The guards behind them took a step forward.

"Wait!" Ophelia screeched. "Why?"

Seamus edged toward the water, hands on his axes. "Kid—"

Before the trolls could act, Cathal held up a hand. "Given the circumstances, Cathal believes the Ulvemordere is the lesser of two evils. Siding with Seamus is just bad business," he yawned. "And he knows too much." He slammed his fist on his throne three times. "Furthermore, Cathal never liked the stories of Sigfreður, The Peaceful. He was a fool. Ophelia is just as well."

The trolls lunged forward, swinging their spears in Seamus's direction. Compared to them, he was slender and agile, easily dodging out of the way. Ophelia reached toward the stagnant water, calling it forth. Two serpentine water spouts rose behind him, slithering in the air, ready to strike. Ophelia swiped her hands through the air, the snake-like streams colliding with the trolls. Slowly, they turned to look at her, unmoved by her theatrics. She smiled sheepishly, waving and tapping her foot on the ground softly.

The trolls—and Seamus—tilted their heads.

None of them realized the water pooling beneath their feet was frozen solid.

With another swipe of her hand, Ophelia called upon the wind. For a moment, nothing happened. Cathal laughed. Ophelia slashed her hand through the air with all her might. A gust circled Seamus, shoving him forward, his feet slipping and sliding on the ice. The trolls grabbed at him, grasping at nothing as they slipped and fell. Ophelia put up her hand, the wind depositing Seamus at her side.

"Thanks," he said, grabbing her by the collar.

They bounded across the stepping stones, running as fast as they could down the hall, more troll guards hot on their heels. They seemed to pour out of invisible tunnels, blocking their path no matter where they turned. That nauseous feeling in Ophelia's stomach worsened as they ran further into the mountain. Seamus cut to the left, slipping down a path seemingly meant for humans.

A high-pitched screech cut through the air.

Seamus was screaming at the top of his lungs, his hands clamped over his ears as he sunk to his knees.

Ophelia's entire body seized, her bones rattling. Her muscles felt like they were pulsing, the blood coursing through her veins vibrating, sending waves of pain through her. No matter how hard she tried, her body wouldn't move.

What had Lochlan said? Water was affected by sound, by something the new science called 'frequencies.' Was that affecting her now? Humans were made of water, but Ophelia's body was different. Pure rainwater ran through her veins, mixing with her blood, a sea of magic easily drained. She was paralyzed, watching in horror as a young troll barely taller than herself plucked Seamus off the ground and flung him over their shoulder. The sound stopped as the troll disappeared around a corner.

Ophelia collapsed to her knees, exhaustion taking the place of paralysis. Struggling to her feet, she made to follow.

Craggy hands took hold of her shoulders, flinging her against the cavern's wall. She groaned, gasping for air, searing pain radiating up her spine.

"Cathal wouldn't do that if Cathal were you," the Jewel King spat, pinning her to the wall with a single, giant finger on her chest.

"Let him go!" Ophelia choked out.

Cathal stood unfazed, pressing his finger harder into her chest, stealing the breath from her lungs. At the back of her mind, she screamed for otherworldly help, but no one came to her rescue. The wind couldn't reach her. She could almost feel it cowering in fear.

"Cathal has no qualm with you, child," he whispered, his tone dangerous. "Leave, and Cathal's guards will not follow."

He dropped his hands, giving her a knowing look. Ophelia gasped for air, glaring at him. Her powers were ineffective against him. It took years for rivers to wear down rock. What had given her the idea she could move the unmovable mountain that was Cathal Sandvik?

"Witches were once sacred to your kind," Ophelia squeaked out. "We could've been friends."

"What the Ulvemordere does with those crystals is none of Cathal's business. Ophelia is mixed up in things she doesn't understand," he said, stepping aside, gesturing for her to leave the way she'd come. "Do not come back to Cathal. Do not come looking for the names on that list."

Fine. Ophelia would leave.

Because if she stayed, she wouldn't be able to save Seamus.

Without hesitation, she turned and ran as fast as she could. Though her legs and lungs burned with the effort, she didn't stop running until she was on the surface and safely hidden amongst the trees.

She'd read countless stories about trolls. She knew their laws and how miscreants were treated. Seamus would have a trial before they made his bones into jewelry.

Until then, he'd rot in a cell—a cell that Ophelia would break him out of.

CHAPTER SIXTY-TWO

THE FOOL

Seamus was dazed, that infuriating sound still ringing in his ears. His head was spinning, too. The troll carrying him deposited him in a cell, ridding him of his weapons and pack. Snarling, they slammed and locked the door as Seamus grappled to his feet. The troll's sapphire eyes glinted with malice, their craggy face cutting into a smile as they tossed his belongings into a broken mine cart.

They'd really done it now, hadn't they?

Cathal wouldn't hurt Ophelia unless necessary, but Seamus knew she wouldn't leave without a fight. If she proved to be a nuisance, Cathal would dispose of her. He knew he should be worrying about himself, but seeing her freeze when that Stars-awful ringing erupted in their ears made his skin crawl. Seamus was sure she'd been in pain. Had the noise affected her too? And where had it come from? Presumably, it was from some new device loaned to the trolls by the Ulve. What had happened for them to start creating all these new weapons?

"Are you new?" came a voice to his right.

A young man with feathered wings was in the cell beside him. He smiled as wide as he could, revealing a few gold teeth.

"What?" Seamus asked, rubbing his ears, hoping that would stop the ever-present ringing.

"I asked if you were new," the winged young man said.

"Yeah, let's go with that," Seamus sighed, shaking himself clean of dirt as he made for the large iron bars before him.

"No amount of shaking, scratching, or pulling will make those things budge," the young man warned, ruffling his dark brown wings.

Seamus ignored him, taking the dagger hidden in his boot from its sheath. It'd been a while since he'd grabbed for it. He'd almost forgotten it was there. Squeezing his arm through the bars, he placed the dagger tip in the keyhole. He fumbled with the mechanism for a moment before hearing a snap.

The blade of his dagger clattered to the ground.

"Well, that's new," the young man laughed, his feathers ruffling. "Good try, old chap."

Booming footsteps from the tunnel to the right brought forth Cathal. He took one look at the broken blade on the floor and laughed.

"Seamus is as clever as always," he said.

"Where's the kid?" Seamus spat, tossing the hilt of his dagger in Cathal's direction.

Cathal smiled, rocking back and forth on his gargantuan feet. "She ran, wolf. Seems to Cathal betrayal is a trait Seamus admires or—dare Cathal say—*looks* for in a companion."

"Cut the bullshit," Seamus snapped, trying to hide his relief. He wasn't sure he believed Ophelia would simply run off without doing something stupid, but he knew Cathal wasn't lying. "You know she's right. They'll swoop in and—"

"What Seamus doesn't understand is that his actions have had consequences Cathal's people cannot remedy," the troll growled.

Seamus rolled his eyes, crossing his arms tight. "Does the word 'apology' mean nothing to you?"

"Does 'genocide' mean something to Seamus?"

"Gen—What in the ever-darkening night sky are you talking about?" Seamus laughed.

Cathal leaned in close, frowning deeply. "If Seamus does not already know, Cathal cannot explain it to him. Seamus's stupidity knows no bounds."

Seamus shook his head in disbelief. "So, what? Are you going to hand me over to the Ulvemordere? Put me on trial? Let me rot here a while?"

"Trial? Once Cathal informs his council of Seamus's repeated transgressions, you'll be executed," Cathal laughed. "You have conned your last con, Norland." His thunderous laugh followed him as he turned and walked away.

Shock stole the breath from Seamus's lungs as he dropped to his knees. Damn the Ulvemordere. Damn them all to the farthest reaches of the darkened cosmos. With a shaking hand, he pulled the collar of his shirt away from his neck. Any hope of escape had been squashed beneath Cathal's footsteps. He was no match for this many trolls. By nightfall, he'd surely be dead.

Stars, he prayed Ophelia came to her senses and left him here to die. *Please, oh Stars, please, leave me here to die.*

The tightness in his chest released as he leaned forward, resting his head against the cold metal bars. A wolf who'd known cages all its life knew the bars protected them from their captors. It was bound to find comfort in confined spaces. Similarly, a dead man walking was bound to yearn for the grave eventually.

"Stars, what did you do to deserve that?" the winged young man asked.

"You first," Seamus grumbled, rubbing his face in a poor attempt to dispel his unease.

"Me? Oh, Cathal found out I was a mole," the man laughed. "My Captain sent me to retrieve a special ore that is only found and refined in the depths of these mountains. . . Or so I'm told. . ."

"I see that worked out for you," Seamus said, already bored with his story.

"Yes, well, all is fair in love and piracy," he yawned. "Or, in my case, love and geology."

Seamus buried his head in his knees, trying to quell the ache in his chest. He held so much hatred for his younger self and all the stupid decisions he'd made.

Any being with magic threatened the Ulvemordere's grand design, but the trolls? Trolls had been around since the beginning of time. Being around for so long, most followed them without a second thought. How else would they have amassed so many workers for their mines? Especially with these conditions. They were seen as ethereal beings, said to have been around when Spirits walked among mortals. If there was any being to put your faith in, it was the trolls. Which, come to think of it, was why the Kirkebys held them in such high regard.

The Ulvemordere had seen this admiration and knew they had to exploit it. Sometimes, you have to side with the enemy to advance in life. Eventually, they had struck a deal with Jewel Kings of the past and were still reaping the benefits. The problem with the Ulvemordere was once they got their claws into someone, they wouldn't let go until they were bled dry. They were weeds in the garden with exceptionally stubborn roots.

It'd been tradition for the Jewel Kings to be cordial to the Ulvemordere. The trolls would do their part and would have their immunity. If not, trollkind would cease to exist. The trolls may be fearsome, but the Ulvemordere had proved themselves to be just the same.

The second Cathal and his trolls tried to reclaim their fiscal freedom, the Ulve retaliated.

Seamus knew he deserved the fury of Cathal's trolls. The Ulvemordere had forced—no, *guided*—him to harvest their heartstones. Gleefully, he'd carved out their cores, reveling in the adrenaline rush a kill brought him. He'd been *proud* to do that dirty work. What the Ulvemordere did with those stones, he didn't know. He'd once heard heartstones, when crushed, could be used as a drug. He'd always assumed that'd been their purpose.

Seamus had almost killed Cathal all those years ago. Maybe he should've. What had made him hesitate? He couldn't remember. Something, something deep down inside, had rattled his bones before he could strike a hammer on Cathal's chest. That terrible old troll had seen it. He'd taken a chance on the young fool before him.

The deal he'd struck on the Ulvemordere's behalf was to save his skin—a soldier for every troll and the promise that things would change once Seamus sat atop the throne. Foolishly, Cathal had believed him. His comrades had been rounded up and executed, each and every one of them gladly giving their lives. For the glory of the Abyss, kill or be killed. That was the motto; that was how they'd lived.

The trolls stayed safe, and Seamus lived on. The problem was, he'd broken their deal by leaving the Ulvemordere. Apparently, Cathal had never forgiven him. Seamus would likely never know what had happened in his absence. Whatever it was, he knew it'd been bad.

It'd been years since they'd seen each other. Helgi had

purchased the glowing crystals in Dødbyen as a sign of good-will. He was well aware of Seamus's history with the Jewel King. The Kirkebys had made sure Cathal knew of Seamus's attempts to right his wrongdoings, but that obviously wasn't enough. It seemed Cathal's hatred for him overshadowed his judgment.

Whatever made Tiril and Helgi believe Cathal would listen to him was beyond him.

"Thinking about what your last meal will be?" the winged pirate asked.

Seamus almost laughed. "Yeah, something like that," he grumbled.

"I—"

"Listen, bird brain, I'm not here to make friends, all right?" Seamus snapped.

That shut the gawking monstrosity up.

CHAPTER SIXTY-THREE

PROMISES WELL KEPT

Ophelia had waited in the forest until nightfall, watching from the treetops as the lights on the mountain blinked out one by one. Now, only two torchlights remained at the cave's entrance. She could just barely make out figures stationed there, ensuring those who lived and worked inside the mountain were protected through the night. At this distance, she couldn't tell whether they were humanoid or troll—couldn't distinguish a shadow from what cast it.

She had no desire to try and go through the main entrance, so why was she waiting here in the dark? Ophelia's heart raced as she worried the hem of her skirt. Seamus was the planner, not her. Already, she doubted herself, and she'd not formed even an inkling of an idea on how to free him from Cathal.

A dreary little drizzle fell upon her. Each drop tugged at her consciousness, her heartbeat in tune with the pitter-patter on her shoulders.

Ophelia climbed down from her treetop perch, straightening her shawl and picking pine needles from her hair. What would Seamus do? Surely, he wouldn't have run. He would've fought until death to save her, knowing damn well he didn't stand a chance against those trolls. She chewed her lip until it bled, staring through the trees.

Her worry transformed into terror as she realized she'd have to be smarter than him. She could sit and imagine Seamus running headstrong into harm's way, but such efforts would never work for her.

Beneath her feet, the snow turned solid, darkening,

spreading like ink on a damp sheet of parchment. Black ice.

In her heart, she knew her only option was to sneak in through one of the window-like holes on the mountainside.

Mustering what little courage she had left, Ophelia tiptoed through the forest, a watchful eye on the dim light emanating from the mountain's entrance. Once she was sure she'd be out of sight, she ran for the steep incline that led to the first window.

Ophelia's feet did not have the same determination as her mind. She skidded to a stop, foot hovering above the ground.

This was supposed to be the moment when a sign appeared from the Stars or Spirits, making the path ahead clear.

The pounding in her ears and the wind whipping at her in warning was more than enough to make her want to turn back. Every logical part of her was screaming to run away, to come back with someone stronger, someone more equipped to rescue him. But could she leave? Even though she had the best intentions, could she turn her back on him? Ophelia was born to protect all who inhabited her domain. Seamus was the last she'd sworn to protect. Could she live with herself knowing she'd risked his life instead of believing she could rescue him alone?

Raindrops hung in the air as her foot sunk into the snow.

No, she couldn't.

Seamus was her friend, and she'd choose him over herself a million times over. Hadn't she told him that?

The rain dissipated, and the wind ceased, leaving behind a sense of disappointment in the air.

"I'm sorry," Ophelia sighed. They wanted her to choose herself—to leave and never come back. But that just wasn't in her nature.

With a shaking breath, she ran up the slope to the nearest window, her legs screaming in protest. Peering inside, she found several troll children fast asleep. Or at least she hoped they were asleep. Their unmoving eyes stared blankly at the ceiling. Definitely not a safe place to slip inside.

She climbed on, peeking into every window. Each room she saw belonged to a happy troll family. She was trying to rescue Seamus quietly, not cause panic amongst innocent troll-kind. She'd have to climb higher still. One of these windows had to open into a hall or something. She'd search all night if she had to.

She could imagine the look on Seamus's face when she came to his aide. Something between relief and disdain. No doubt Ophelia would be reprimanded for staging a rescue like this. Still, she hoped he could find it in himself to be thankful. It wasn't every day she risked her life for a stray. Contrary to popular belief, she only took in those she deemed worthy.

By the Stars, she wished he could understand what she saw in him.

On Amaranth's name, she wished he'd see himself as a protector, not a destroyer.

That day in Tø, he'd come back for her, chosen to keep her safe. Didn't that prove there was good in him? She fully believed what she'd said to Cathal, that he was not the same man he once was. How could he not see that his choices hadn't been his own? When he'd committed all those heinous acts, he'd been but a child, barely older than she was now.

The Stars needed to send him a sign, something he couldn't explain away.

The moon crested the top of the mountain when Ophelia found the dark hall she was looking for. Nimble as her old wolverine friend, she ducked inside.

Sometimes, she wished for Seamus's eyesight. Navigating this void-like expanse would be so much easier if she could see in the dark. Removing one of her gloves, she snapped her fingers, her hand aglow with lightning. She also wished for Seamus's hearing. She'd love to know what was lurking just out of sight.

As quietly as she could, Ophelia tip-toed down the hall. According to her books, trolls kept their dungeons buried deep. She'd follow this hallway down into the bellows of the mountain until she found what she was looking for. Of course, she was counting on Cathal or his guards not finding her first.

On the other hand, Seamus would get himself captured solely to find her.

Should she do that? Cause a scene? Reveal her whereabouts? Declare war? Or would that screw everything up tenfold?

Shaking away the self-doubt, Ophelia quickened her pace, following the slight downward slope of the hall. The walls were closer here. This path wasn't meant for trolls. She must've found a space dedicated to smaller beings.

After hours of winding down the hall, Ophelia found herself back where she and Seamus had unfortunately parted. She knew where she was now, a blessing she wouldn't take for granted. Wracking her brain for the turns they'd taken, she found the tunnels that led back toward the throne room. If her books accurately depict troll culture and architecture, there'd be a door leading down to the dungeons—an easy way to transport those on trial straight to the Jewel King himself. Making herself as small as possible, she pressed against the wall, peering around the corner to find the throne empty.

That couldn't be good.

Ophelia's heart somersaulted as she stepped out into the open. Such a place made her feel unworthy. If she'd been born in a different time, she'd have a throne room that rivaled Cathal's. While Jewel King and Winter Witch of days long gone had been equal, Ophelia slowly realized her power would rival his, too. In ways that mattered more than changing the course of the wind or, in his case, locating rare ores.

Part of her was grateful she didn't carry the burden of a Witchdom.

A smaller part ached for that control. That part terrified her. The more she stood in the center of that throne room, the louder that part of her grew. Yes, Sigfreður had ruled peacefully, but that didn't mean he was a pacifist. She'd be expected to do the same.

Ophelia shivered, snuffing out her lightning light and scanning the intricately carved walls for a hidden door.

Her eyes kept trailing back to the throne. There was something off about it. It was too plain to match the room. Maybe this was Cathal feigning modesty; after all, this room had been carved centuries before he was created. But Ophelia couldn't help but think how his skin reminded her of a geode. Such an ordinary seat didn't match his grandiose appearance.

Ophelia took to the steppingstones as fast as she could, careful not to slip, the water swirling beneath her as she leaped across. Heavy footsteps echoed down the hall, startling her so badly that she nearly slipped.

"I know, I know," she whispered, trying to calm herself. "I'll be careful."

Quick as she could, she ducked behind the throne.

Here she was again. Back to wishing she could turn invisible.

Heart pounding, she sunk into the shadows, hugging her knees to her chest and shutting her eyes tightly. The footsteps grew louder. The throne shook ever so slightly as the Jewel King took his place.

"I may be able to look past letting the girl go free, but Seamus was meant to be *mine*," said a voice Ophelia unfortunately recognized. It was the voice of the General, the one who'd killed the hobgoblin.

Cathal laughed darkly. "Arild forgets whose throne he stands before."

"And you, Sandvik, forget where your loyalties lay," the General spat. "Release him to me immediately or suffer the consequences."

The throne creaked. Ophelia imagined Cathal leaning forward and gazing deep into the General's eyes. "Little human," he began, his voice rumbling with laughter, "Cathal knows what you want from the wolf. It is in Cathal's best interest to see you fail. Death is too kind a release for Seamus Norland."

Ophelia clamped a hand over her mouth to keep from squealing in fright.

Metal clinked against metal, and Ophelia pictured the General straightening his heavy, patchwork cloak. "I suppose I cannot expect a being without a brain to make logical decisions," he mumbled. "Very well. If this is the hill you die on, I wish you on your merry way."

Ophelia couldn't fathom having the gall to speak to Cathal in that way.

There was a huff and a puff before receding footsteps. Ophelia heard Cathal tap his fingers on the armrest of his throne, a low, displeased laugh escaping him. She dared a peek around the throne, catching the hem of the General's patchwork cloak. The throne shifted again, and Ophelia ducked back behind it, shaking in fright. She could hear Cathal pacing, his footsteps shaking the ground. The water around her rippled, just as afraid as she was. She wondered what it had seen. The Jewel King wasn't known for his gentility. Cathal's pacing stopped. Hushed unease hung in the air. He whispered something under his breath, but Ophelia couldn't quite make it out. Again, the throne shook as Cathal sighed heavily, the sound like thunder.

Ophelia sat there frozen for Spirits-knew how long. She'd thought for sure Cathal would've reached behind his throne and grabbed her by the scruff of her neck, deciding he fancied a midnight snack. Each breath could have been her last.

Yet here she was.

And Cathal was—

Ophelia felt her body relax as she dared another peek around the corner.

Cathal was asleep, snoring like a baby in a cradle.

Without a moment's hesitation, Ophelia jumped to her feet. Terror had made her hyper-aware of her surroundings. She'd spotted a sliver of light peeking between two carvings on the wall across from her. Quietly as she could, she ran across the steppingstones, hoping this was the hidden door. Face pressed between an amethyst dragon and a sapphire pegasus, she peered through the crack. Beyond the hidden door was a brightly lit, circular room with snow-topped carvings of trolls. Ophelia nearly dropped dead from fright. The carvings were far too realistic for her liking.

Behind her, Cathal groaned in his sleep.

With frantic hands, Ophelia searched for a way to open the hidden door. Under the dragon's wing was a notch, just big enough for a troll's hand. Though she pulled with all her might, the door wouldn't budge. A quick look over her shoulder to ensure no prying eyes had found her, she shoved her hand between the carvings. A column of ice wedged itself between the wall and door, opening it up enough for her to slip through.

Taking a deep breath to steady herself, she tip-toed through the chamber. She wondered how such a place had formed. Above, the mountain broke apart, revealing the night sky's glory. Soft snowflakes fell in spirals, clinging to her hair and jacket, their curiosity palpable.

The towering carvings before her seemed to represent the Jewel Kings of old. Ophelia recognized one of the cracked faces from her books. She'd stumbled upon a memorial. Ophelia often pondered how death connected all beings. How very human of the trolls to construct such a site.

She stood in the center of the chamber, staring up at the sky, the stars blinking their sleepy eyes. She wondered if the stars, too, held funerals, if they'd be the only ones to honor her like this one day.

Something caught her foot as she spun in a circle. The tip of her boot sunk down a small hole. Dropping to her knees, she brushed away the snow to find a rusty old grate.

Below, huddled in the center of a cell, moonlight glittering upon his skin, sat Seamus.

Ophelia smiled.

How fortuitous.

CHAPTER SIXTY-FOUR

LISTENING EARS

"This could have gone better. But I do believe it is a learning experience. All things happen—"

"Do *not* finish that sentence," Seamus said through gritted teeth.

There was a long moment of silence before Seamus realized who spoke. He looked up, eyes wide.

"What in the ever-darkening night sky are you doing?" he screeched, jumping to his feet as Ophelia waved down at him through a grate in the ceiling. Had that always been there?

"Rescuing you!" she called down excitedly.

"R—res—Ophelia!" he gasped. "Leave this instant!" he screamed, stamping his foot on the ground.

"They'll kill you!"

"Ophelia Av'Skogen, you will do as I say!"

"Ungrateful," Ophelia huffed. With that, she disappeared.

"Ophelia!" Seamus bellowed.

"Well, she seems like a wildfire," the winged young pirate laughed.

Seamus glared at him. Just as his mind formed the perfect snarky response, the grate above him shifted, sending down a dusting of snow. He looked up, watching in horror as the grate turned a silvery blue, the surrounding ceiling now covered in icy swirls. The grate creaked and cracked before collapsing inward, taking Ophelia with it. Seamus panicked, reaching forward, unable to break her fall in time.

A biting wind followed her inside. It wrapped around her legs and torso, slowing her fall, depositing her rather elegantly before Seamus. Ophelia smoothed her skirts as they floated down around her, a smug smile on her face.

"Ready to go?" she asked, looking around his cell.

"What do you think you're doing? You're going to get us *both* killed now!" Seamus spat, throwing his arms wide.

He could feel his wolf clawing at his insides. Oh, it was furious with her. He could hear its gravelly voice screaming from the darkest corners of his mind. How dare she put herself in harm's way to protect it, protect *him*. It held her in such high regard. Ophelia was kind to all creatures, but the kindness she'd extended to his wolf was a rarity. It liked her, and dare he say it, it saw her as a member of its pack. It wanted nothing more than to protect her.

"I wasn't going to let them hurt you, Seamus," Ophelia scoffed, hands on her hips. She gave him that judgmental little head tilt which infuriated him so.

A growl was rumbling in the back of his throat. "And how do you suppose we get out of here?"

Ophelia thought for a moment, her shoulders stiffening. "I'm working on it."

"Well, genius, can't go back the way you came. In case you hadn't noticed, I'm not exactly twig-thin like you," he spat, gesturing to the tiny hole in the ceiling.

Rocking back and forth on her heels, Ophelia took in the cell. "We'll just have to leave through the front door."

"Ophelia—"

"Great idea!" said the winged pirate.

Ophelia turned, smiling and waving. "Hello! Nice to meet you."

He bowed. "Ma'am."

Seamus groaned, his eye twitching as he shook his head.

Ophelia crossed to the cell door, a spring in her step. She wrapped her fingers around the bars before Seamus could stop her. Surprisingly, her hands didn't burn.

"In the old days, trolls didn't refine iron. It went against their belief system. Meaning—" she said over her shoulder as the bars turned ice blue "—they aren't equipped to hold people like me."

The metal bars moaned and shattered just as the grate had. Ophelia skipped through the hole she made, freeing the pirate in the same way. He gazed at her in awe, cheeks red. Seamus figured they weren't far off in age and knew what that meant for a young man. He rolled his eyes, shooting him a dirty look.

"Guards don't rotate for hours; we'll have to make a run for it," the pirate said, averting his stare from Ophelia to the ground.

"Great," Seamus sighed, retrieving his things from the mine cart.

The winged pirate shrugged, a sly smile on his face. "Trust me. I can get us out of here."

Ophelia opened her mouth to say something, a hint of a smile on her face. Seamus turned his glare on her, pointing an accusing finger at the winged pirate.

"We're not trusting this guy," he snapped.

"Has he given you any reason not to?" she asked, gracefully donning her gloves.

"He's a criminal, Ophelia."

"So are we."

"He's a pirate!"

Though he couldn't see her eyes, he imagined they were glittering in delight. "I like pirates."

"I do believe pirates like you, too," the young man whispered.

Seamus pinched the bridge of his nose. "You do realize—"

"While I'm living for this adorable father-daughter banter, we are currently in a very dangerous situation, and we should probably leave before—" The pirate broke off, shivering. Heavy footsteps resonated down the long hall. ". . . that happens."

Seamus put himself between them and the hall, ready to fight tooth and nail in order to allow Ophelia time to escape. Just as the corner of a shadow appeared on the wall, the winged pirate grabbed Seamus by the elbow.

"No need for that," he said with a toothy grin, pulling Seamus toward a dark corner.

Where crystal light couldn't reach sat a rickety old door. With a labored pull, the winged pirate opened it, waving Seamus and Ophelia inside. When they were safely inside the dark abyss beyond, the pirate closed the heavy door softly, leading them down a winding hall in silence. His wings dragged across the walls despite him folding them as tight to his body as he could.

Ophelia was between them, causing Seamus's wolf to squirm again. She shouldn't be in front of him. Any danger would reach her first. If she were behind him, such dangers would still be there, but something about taking the brunt of the hypothetical attack before them eased his mind.

The winged pirate stopped at another door. Through a crack in the wood, he peered into the room beyond. His golden wings shook softly, a single feather dropping to the floor. Seamus frowned as Ophelia flicked the feather into her hand with a twist of her wrist and tucked it into her satchel. He highly doubted she'd done that to cover their tracks.

"Kitchen's beyond," the pirate said over his shoulder. "Don't see anyone. Prepare yourselves nonetheless."

Seamus finally wedged himself between the pirate and Ophelia, giving her a knowing look. She'd risked everything to come back for him. He wasn't keen on letting her use this new-found bravery again anytime soon.

The pirate quietly opened the door, light on his feet as he entered the quaint kitchen. Flames torched the bottom of a cauldron, the smell of stew wafting into Seamus's nose. Half-chopped vegetables littered the countertops. Whoever was preparing the food this evening wouldn't be far away. No cook worth their weight in salt would step away from a culinary masterpiece for long.

Seamus shut his eyes, focusing on the sounds around him. The crackling of the fire melted away as he stepped into the kitchen. Muffled voices around the corner, floating in from—he breathed deeply, the scent of raw meat tickling his senses—the cellar.

"Ophelia?" said a tearful voice.

Seamus's eyes shot open. A girl with untamable red hair

stood up from under one of the workbenches.

"Saoirse!" Ophelia screeched, rushing over to her.

Saoirse took a step back, eyes wide. "No, no, no! You can't be here! You need to leave—You need to leave now!"

Seamus sniffed the air again, mildly alarmed. He smelled another wolf.

"Come with us!" Ophelia cried, reaching for her hand.

Again, Saoirse avoided her touch. "No, you have to go! They've just brought in another round of prisoners and all these fancy weapons. Some of the soldiers are still here! If they see you, you're dead."

Ophelia just stared at her, smelling so strongly of mint that Seamus could hardly breathe. "I've been looking for you," she said brokenly.

Saoirse swallowed hard, turning her back on them. "Go, Ophelia. It's not worth it."

Unfortunately, Seamus had to agree.

"Who else is here? We—"

"I never saw you," Saoirse snapped.

Grabbing Ophelia by the sleeve, Seamus dragged her to a door he hoped would lead them toward the outside world. The pirate followed, taking a large metal spoon off the wall as he went. Seamus couldn't tell if the massive thing was decorative or meant for troll-sized hands. He did, however, know why the feathered criminal took such a thing. It seemed he wasn't going back to that cell without a fight.

If, of course, he made it to the cell at all.

Seamus scowled and peeked his head out the door, finding nothing but another long hallway. Left or right. That was the decision he had to make. In the distance, he could hear the beginning of panic. Word was spreading fast that two prisoners had escaped. Like any logical being, he chose the path that didn't lead toward angry troll voices.

Hyperaware of the sound his footsteps made, he ran down the hall, the others in tow.

"Make for a window," Ophelia said from behind, her voice strained. Seamus could hear the fright and sadness in her beating heart. It sickened him.

"Smart thinking, my lady," the winged pirate said.

"Thank you," she replied half-heartedly.

With a roll of his eyes, Seamus gestured for the two of them to take the lead. Hands resting upon his axes, he followed their quiet footsteps through the dark. All the torches had been extinguished. Even the crystal light was gone.

Around the corner came a beam of moonlight. The three of them raced to it, the pirate making it first. He squeezed his shimmering wings together, struggling to crawl through the hole. Once he was through, he darted up into the star-lit sky, eyes trained on the ground below.

Seamus gently pushed Ophelia forward, helping her over the ledge. She stood in the snowfall, offering Seamus her hand as he swung his leg over the makeshift windowsill.

The sound of metal being drug across stone rang in his ears.

A musky yet metallic stench filled his nose, making his eyes water.

Ophelia's jaw dropped in shock.

CHAPTER SIXTY-FIVE

TROLLS SCARE THE SHIT OUT OF ME

Seamus was halfway out the window when he froze, his eyes wide. Over his shoulder, Ophelia could see two enormous trolls. Without a second thought, Ophelia beckoned the wind to push him, sending him tumbling out the window. Just as he picked himself up off the ground, a jagged troll shoulder slammed into the wall, shattering the rock like glass.

Ophelia stumbled backward, losing her footing, taking Seamus along with her as she plummeted head over heels down the mountainside. Sharp rocks and ice dug at their skin as they rolled down and down the hill until they finally landed on solid ground in a pile of sore limbs. It was a miracle Ophelia's mask had stayed on.

"Ow," Seamus groaned, wiping Ophelia's hair from his face.

"Sorry."

In response, he grabbed hold of her, rolling to the side, squishing her beneath his weight as an axe head the size of Ophelia's torso implanted itself where they'd been seconds before. Seamus scrambled to his feet, pulling Ophelia off the ground as the troll wielding it tried to wrench it from the earth.

"RUN!" Seamus screamed, shoving her behind him, nearly knocking her back down.

The second troll pursuing them slid down the slope, landing next to its comrade, a deep scowl on its face.

Ophelia took hold of Seamus's sleeve as the winged pirate landed before them, swinging his giant spoon. It collided with the first troll's head, barely cracking his rocky skin.

"Admittedly, I thought that would do more damage," the pirate said, backing away, shaking hands still gripping the now-bent spoon. His wings shivered, betraying the horror he was trying to hide.

The troll freed his axe from the ground as his comrade edged around him. He held two gargantuan cleavers caked in a layer of what Ophelia would pretend was mud and not dried blood. Mud was less terrifying. Yes, it had to be mud.

Above, brandishing a jewel-tipped baton, was the General. Scowling, he pointed the baton at her, then dragged it across his neck. With that, he turned and disappeared inside the mountain.

"Go, Phee!" Seamus screamed, his hands outstretched as if that stance protected her somehow.

Ophelia's skin was prickling with white-hot anticipation. Something was pulling on the edge of her consciousness again, whispering in her ear that it could help. Sharpshooting pain ran up her arms, her magic begging her to let it free.

"Cathal will make brisket out of you," the axe-wielding troll snarled. "Been ages since Gärdar had himself a harpy."

"I'm griffinkind, boulder-head," the pirate snapped, swinging his club-like spoon forward. It collided with the second troll's cleavers, sending sparks into the air.

Gärdar's axe swung down on him as Ophelia thrust her hands forward out of pure instinct. A roar escaped her throat as that white-hot prickling beneath her skin manifested into arcs of electricity at her fingertips. Her gloves burned. The troll's axe hung in mid-air. His comrade stopped fighting against the winged pirate, shocked. Wind whipped at Ophelia's hair as the troll pushed with all his might against his axe.

The wind was screaming alongside Ophelia. It knew the pirate as a friend. It'd carried him across sea and sky for years. It wasn't ready to let him die. Not now, not ever.

Nor was Ophelia.

Feeling as though she was pushing a boulder up that mountain alone, she shoved her hands forward, sending the troll flying backward. Ophelia cried out in pain, her bones shaking as though they fancied shattering. The second troll locked its eyes on her. Seamus charged forward, taking the winged pirate's spoon and grasping the dull side of one of the cleavers.

"Seamus, no!" Ophelia shrieked, clutching her aching arms to her chest.

That troll was going to kill him.

The ground beneath Ophelia's feet shook. Time seemed to slow as Seamus used the enormous spoon to knock the cleaver from the troll's hand, taking a finger or two with it. He thought himself clever, but he wasn't clever enough. The troll swung its other cleaver as Ophelia felt all the air escape her lungs. She was screaming at the top of her lungs, her arms shaking with unbearable pain as the ground beneath her shifted. A crack like a lightning bolt shot out from under her feet. The ground below the troll erupted shards of ice and rock bursting forth from its skin. It was screaming, too, with fissures fracturing across its skin. It was crumbling apart, holding its head in its hands as it split. Gärdar ran forward to help, but the crack in the ground sprang forward to greet him, the same fractures appearing on him, too.

Ophelia didn't stop screaming until the trolls collapsed, their bodies shattering into a million tiny pebbles as they hit the ground.

Ophelia gasped for air, her vision blurring.

The wind fell silent, recoiling from her, frightened.

Seamus was speaking to her, a horrified look on his face, but his words were lost on her.

She swayed, her heart fluttering.

Silence.

N u m b n e s s . . .

Darkness. . .

Hands on her shoulders,

shaking her as hard as they could.

Ophelia blinked, and she was staring up at a very pale, very sweaty Seamus. Taking her by the collar, he pulled her into a sitting position. How had she ended up lying on the ground?

"Can you hear me?" he asked, his voice gruff with worry.

She tried to speak, but her words came out garbled. All she could do was nod.

"There'll be more any minute. We need to go," the winged pirate said. He, too, sounded terrified.

Seamus heaved her off the ground, setting her on her feet, hands gripping her arms as hard as they could. "Talk to me. You collapsed, kid, talk to me. What happened?" There was a crazed look in his eyes. It reminded her of his wolf.

"Tired," was all Ophelia could manage.

Before she could find her footing, Seamus swept her off the ground, throwing her over his shoulder, nodding at the winged pirate.

"We're the ones they want. You'll be better off flying far away from here," he said to him.

The pirate considered him. "Will the Witch be all right? She doesn't look it."

"My problem, not yours."

The pirate hesitated before nodding. "I'll buy the two of

you some time. Thank you, my lady. I am forever indebted to you." He bowed, then—accompanied by a swirl of snow—took off, twisting rather elegantly in the sky, his hawk-like wings sparkling.

Seamus wasted no time hightailing it out of there, running toward the safety of the forest. Trees whizzed by in a dizzying sort of way.

Ophelia was slipping in and out of consciousness. The wind was still quiet. Why had it gone? Where she usually felt a buzzing beneath her skin, there was nothing. She beckoned to the clouds above, but again, there was nothing. Nothing except a sharpshooting pain in her chest. She groaned, allowing her body to go limp and her eyes to shut.

Her mind tried to wander, but all she found were foggy thoughts she couldn't quite grasp.

When she opened her eyes again, Seamus had her softly pinned against a tree by the shoulder. He was breathing heavily, his jaw clenched so tight she figured it would break under the pressure.

". . . Seamus . . .?" Ophelia asked, resting her head against the tree.

He whipped his head back to her, eyes wider than a full moon. "Are you okay?" he asked, gently removing her mask.

"Everything hurts," she whispered.

Seamus swore, eyes darting down to her gloved hands. She hadn't realized she was clutching his arm that tightly, let alone grasping it at all. Ever so gently, he pushed up her sleeve, revealing purple-black bruises. She winced as he touched her skin, biting back tears.

"Why would you do that?" he whisper-yelled. "What did you do?"

"I don't know," she said breathlessly.

Her vision blurred again, her knees buckling. Seamus caught her, stumbling backward as he tried to support her dead weight.

"Something's wrong," she gasped, her chest tightening. "Seamus, something's wrong with me."

"Hey, relax, kid, calm down," he whispered, hugging her tight. "You're going to be just fine." Struggling, he pushed her back up against the tree, staring into her wild eyes as she took labored breaths. "Look at me," he said, taking her chin in his hand, forcing her to meet his eyes. "Calm down."

"What did I do?" she asked, shutting her eyes as tightly as she could, reaching up to grab Seamus's arms again. Her fingers dug into his skin, but he didn't seem to mind.

"You just killed two trolls."

"Blessed Amaranth," Ophelia sighed, shaking all over.

Seamus was quiet for a moment. "I looked away for a second, and you'd collapsed."

"Sorry," she said, opening an eye.

He frowned. "That word is beginning to sound quite meaningless coming from your mouth."

Despite herself, she smiled weakly. "Sorry."

He kept one hand on her shoulder but dropped the other, studying her as she rolled up her sleeves and removed her scorched gloves. How many pairs had she burned through lately? Her fingertips were black and covered in soot. The bruises stopped just below her elbow. The marks resembled storm clouds, the thin lines of unbruised skin like lightning bolts.

"That's not good," she said, shoving her gloves inside her pocket.

Seamus gave her a disapproving look. "I'd hope not."

A breeze rushed past and ruffled her hair, taking the numbness with it. Its voice was back, whispering in her ear, worried. That was never a good sign, either.

"I think I need a healer," Ophelia said, not meeting Seamus's eyes.

"And where do you suppose we find one, hmm? Those aren't normal," Seamus said, gesturing loosely to her arms. "Neither is that." He pointed at her mask, which he'd tossed to the ground.

"Seamus, I'm really tired," Ophelia sighed. A sudden wave of exhaustion took over, her legs shaking from the effort it took to keep herself upright. "I can barely stand."

Seamus stiffened, a deep-set scowl on his face. "Don't you dare die on me, ya hear?"

"No promises," she laughed.

"That wasn't a joke."

Slowly, he let go of her shoulder, eyebrows knit tight over his eyes. Without looking away, he picked up her mask and handed it to her. As she clipped it to her belt with shaking hands, he took their magical map from the case at her hip. With one last disapproving look over his shoulder, he gestured for her to follow as he trudged on.

"We're a few hours from the nearest town. Cathal and his men will be looking for us there. We'd be better off backtracking," he explained, his voice gruff. He tried to clear the lump from his throat but couldn't.

"Or we stay in the woods and go to the town beyond. More wasted time otherwise."

He glared at her, working his jaw. "This whole ordeal has been wasted time, Ophelia."

"We saw Saoirse," Ophelia shrugged. "If she's here, doesn't that mean the others are, too?"

"Yeah, alongside Arild Melhus!" Seamus groaned. "Dammit! Dammit, dammit, dammit!"

"So long as we get back to Dødbyen, we'll be fine. At least you're not stuck in a cell," Ophelia shrugged.

Seamus glared at her over his shoulder. "Excuse me if I'm not over the moon."

6. A Real Family

CHAPTER SIXTY-SIX

Do You Ever Think of Me?

Ophelia was in tears. She'd begged and begged to go back for Saoirse and the horses, but that was a risk they couldn't afford. Especially in her state. Seamus was sure she understood this, but still, she'd gone on and on about how they'd abandoned them for no reason, practically throwing a temper tantrum. He pitied her. Having to see Saoirse like that was cosmic cruelty. Not only that, but Seamus had come to understand her love for animals and tried to soothe her as best he could. Rain and Frykt were resourceful creatures. He was sure they'd eventually find their way back to them. Whether she believed him or not, she relented. The tears hadn't stopped, but at least she'd ceased pestering him.

Seamus kept to the map, ears pricked to any sign of danger. Ophelia walked quietly beside him, wiping the occasional tear. As they walked, her condition seemed to get worse. She was almost delirious, groggy, and unresponsive to his questions. It went without saying how much that worried him.

"Not much farther now, pup," Seamus said, rolling up their map and stuffing it in his bag. "Mask on."

"I thought the nearest town was a few hours away," she said sleepily. She fumbled with her mask, tying it so carelessly that it sat crooked.

"Kid, we've been walking most of the day," Seamus said, unable to hide the worry in his voice. "It was almost sunrise by the time we left Juvel Hjem."

"Oh," she mumbled.

Seamus reached out and fixed her mask, frowning. His fingers grazed her skin, causing him to jump back in surprise.

Her cheeks were hot to the touch.

"Phee, you've got a fever."

"Hmm?"

He placed the back of his hand against her cheek, scowling. "You're lukewarm, which would be fine for me. But you told me to worry if you had a fever, and this constitutes as a fever."

She flinched away, hugging herself tight. "I'll be okay."

"Ophelia," Seamus said sternly.

"I've had worse."

"Kid, you're covered in bruises and burns, you've got a fever, and you can barely walk straight. What's worse?"

"You don't want to know," she whispered. "You really don't."

The town they stumbled upon was called Onding. It was small, dilapidated, and crowded, but it'd do. Besides, the more people packing the streets, the easier it was to disappear. Seamus shoved his way through the patrons, leading Ophelia by the strap of her satchel. Colorful banners hung off every building. Music wafted through the streets. It seemed they'd stumbled upon a festival of sorts.

A singular one-story tavern was nestled in the center of Onding, its doors wide open as if waiting for them. A sign boasted room and board, so Seamus figured it was as good a place as any for them to rest. Inside, the brightly lit pub was packed to bursting.

"Room and board for two, please," Seamus said, knocking impatiently on the service counter.

"All we've got is a room with one bed and with no amenities," the innkeeper said. Seamus could barely hear him over the noise.

He glanced at Ophelia, whose gaze was glued to her shoes. "That's fine, thank you," Seamus sighed. He paid, took their key, and then pulled Ophelia to their room.

Thankfully, the thick walls and door muffled the deafening sound of the party outside. It was a quaint room with a murky window and unlit candles, the only furniture being the bed, a wobbly nightstand, a table beneath the window, and two chairs. Ophelia yawned, her eyes locking on to the bed. Seamus nodded his approval. She gave a half smile, dropping her satchel and mask to the floor as she flopped down upon the stiff old mattress. She fluffed the pillow, burying her face in it, sighing heavily.

"We should leave by first light," he said, turning away. He set down his pack, unrolling his bed roll near the door. "It's almost a new moon. It's not safe to be—" He paused, looking over his shoulder to find her eyes were shut; meanwhile, one leg and arm were hanging off the bed. "Kid?"

He stood, coming to kneel next to her, watching her back rise and fall, listening to her heart and the faint buzzing that followed her like the plague.

"Don't tell me you've fallen asleep already," he sighed.

No response.

Carefully, he reached out to brush the hair from her face. He placed the back of his hand on her forehead, surprised to find her skin had grown warmer.

He knew she wouldn't listen, but come morning, he'd have a stern talking to her about not using her powers for a while. Ophelia was a fragile thing. Though strong enough to destroy two trolls and control the elements, it seemed that kind of power wasn't sustained long. Every being had its limits, and he knew if a Witch reached theirs, it'd kill them. He'd sooner have himself die than let that happen. Seamus was no healer, but he guessed she'd either crossed that threshold or was just shy of it. The bruises and scorch marks across her arms were proof of that.

"Ophelia," he whispered, a panicked undertone to his voice.

There was a certain peacefulness in how she lay there— the peacefulness of a corpse.

Seamus stood, shaking his head. Gently, he lifted her leg back onto the bed, ensuring it wouldn't fall off again. Scanning the room for an extra blanket, he found a stack beneath the bed. He shook one free of dust before gently placing it atop her, lifting her arm, and tucking the blanket under her hand. Just as he let go of her tiny hand and turned away, her fingers clamped tightly around his.

He stood there in disbelief, in awe of how small her hand was compared to his. How cracked and worn and bruised he was compared to her softness.

Ever so gently, she tugged his hand, her face twitching with something he could only describe as pain.

Eyes shut with worry, he sat on the edge of the bed with a heavy sigh, squeezing her hand tight. A shiver of fear ran through him as he watched her sleep. If she didn't wake by morning, what could he do? What was wrong with her, and how could he fix it? All he wanted was to fix it.

Ophelia's grip on him loosened.

With more reluctance than he'd care to admit, he let go of her. He stood, the hand that had held hers clenched in a tight fist. He lingered there momentarily, then crossed to the window and cracked it open enough to let the cold in. Returning to his pack, he dragged it next to the bed, settling in on the floor beside her.

Seamus knew his worry wouldn't allow him much sleep.

Seamus woke shivering, finding Ophelia had not moved an inch since the day before. Dread filled his chest as he sat up. At least she was breathing. Last he checked, corpses didn't breathe. Careful not to wake her, he felt her forehead. Her fever had gone down some, but she was still warm. He guessed she'd be out of commission for quite some time.

She'd caused an earthquake. That wasn't something he figured fit into the whole 'Winter Witch' magic category. Then again, neither did controlling lightning. Sometimes, he wondered if they'd all got it wrong. Maybe she wasn't a Winter Witch at all. Maybe she was something different, something more.

Either way, the amount of power she'd used yesterday had damaged her physically and spiritually. She was right; she needed a healer—the *right* kind of healer—someone who wouldn't bat an eye at the mask or the bruises. Someone who worked with their kind.

He knew of one, but that practitioner lived on the other side of the world. If Ophelia were wounded the way he thought she was, she wouldn't make it that far.

"You'll worry yourself sick, Norland," he grumbled, standing, his frozen bones cracking as he stretched.

Hopefully, he *was* wrong, and all she needed was a few

extra minutes of rest. They'd take it easy from here on out. That'd do the trick for sure.

Seamus decided it best to busy himself with something other than the terror in his heart. He rolled up his bedroll then left for the washroom, taking his time, reveling in the warm water against his skin. Once he'd changed into clean clothes, he ordered them breakfast.

Returning to their room, he found Ophelia still hadn't moved.

His heart sank.

Setting their breakfast on the nightstand, he patted her shoulder. "Up ya get, kid."

Nothing.

"Phee, wake up," he said, hating the pleading tone in his voice.

His wolf trembled in fear, something he wasn't used to.

Why wasn't she waking up?

"Ophelia," he said sternly, shaking her as hard as he could.

Startled, her eyes shot open. She looked up at him, confused, squinting against the early morning light seeping in through the window.

Seamus breathed a sigh of relief, gesturing to the heaping plate of food on the bedside table. "Eat. You need your strength."

She sat up, rubbing the sleep from her eyes. "Was I out long?"

"Just the night," Seamus said, forcing the plate into her hands.

"What time is it?"

"Later than I'd prefer, but you needed your rest."

"Sorry," she yawned, plucking a sausage off her plate. He really wished she'd stop saying that blasted word.

He hovered over her, arms crossed tight over his chest, a deep scowl on his lips. "We need to talk," he said.

She looked up at him mid-bite, eyebrows furrowed.

"You're pushing yourself too far. I'm not sure what that was back there with those trolls, but I never want to see you do it again." He put his hands on his hips, glaring at her to emphasize his point. "Next time you have the grand idea to do something stupid, consult me first, yeah? I thought I told you that already."

"I forgot," she shrugged. "And you were preoccupied."

He glared at her. "Try and remember next time."

"Sorry," Ophelia said. "I just acted on in—"

He sighed heavily, running shaking hands through his hair. "I'm not mad," he began, "You just worry me."

"S—"

"Don't say you're sorry. Whether you mean it or not, it doesn't have the effect you think it does."

"S—" She bit her lower lip, picking at her plate. "I'll. . . I'll consult you next time."

He gave a curt nod, gesturing to the door with a thumb over his shoulder. "Eat quickly, then get cleaned up. We're dangerously low on money, so I'm going to see if I can do an odd job or something before we leave."

"Stay safe, Seamus," she said through a mouthful of biscuit.

CHAPTER SIXTY-SEVEN

FESTIVAL

Ophelia sat bewildered on the edge of the bed. Yesterday was a blur. If she focused hard enough, she could remember all the little details, but her brain would rather sweep the whole thing under the carpet and move on. Her limbs ached, the dark, lumpy bruises on her arms grating like sandpaper as she moved.

Once she finished eating, she grabbed a clean set of clothes and wandered the inn until she found the innkeeper. He directed her to the washroom, which was preoccupied. She waited patiently until she could bathe properly, the hot water stinging her wounds. Thankfully, the soot on her fingers washed away. The damage wasn't as bad as she'd feared, but her fingertips were still burnt. They almost had a blue tint to them, too. How odd.

After dressing and attempting to dry her hair with a spare towel, she returned to her room. This inn or tavern or whatever it was wasn't as lavish as her room in Dødbyen, but it was a nice reprieve. She could happily stay here for a while. Amaranth knew she probably should.

Seamus did too, else he wouldn't have busied himself with odd jobs. She hoped he found a kind soul who needed extra help wherever they'd ended up.

Yawning, she took the liberty of packing what little had been taken out the night before. When had she gone to sleep? Last she remembered was the click of a door unlocking. After that, everything was pillows and blankets spare for the overwhelming feeling that she was finally safe. She also remembered someone tucking her in. She'd probably imagined it, but she swore someone had placed a blanket on her just as she drifted off. Probably a dream. She thought she reached for their hand. Had she really been so feverish she'd imagined things?

Not knowing when Seamus would return, Ophelia took out a book and read until her eyes grew heavy.

Somewhere beyond the veil of sleep, Seamus whispered, ". . . Ophelia. . . you with me?"

Her skin tingled as consciousness and feeling returned to her. Her heavy eyes opened, and there he was, kneeling at her bedside, very obviously worried.

"Back so soon?" she asked groggily.

He placed a hand on her forehead, a sad smile on his lips. "Spent most of the day helping the town set up for their little celebration. Earned a fair bit of change."

Ophelia yawned. "I was reading. Must've fallen asleep again." She glanced around the bed for her book, finding it on the nightstand, her leather bookmark peeking out where she'd left off.

It was then she realized she hadn't imagined someone tucking her in. It'd been Seamus. He must've marked her page, too.

"How're you feeling?" he asked. He sat on the edge of the bed, twitching hands resting neatly in his lap.

The grogginess of sleep clung to her. She yawned again, taking his hands in hers, trying to blink away the exhaustion. "Better than I was, that's for sure."

He was staring at their hands, his jaw clenched tight. "Would you like to visit the festival?"

For some reason, this took her by surprise. "Why?"

"You need rest, yes, but you shouldn't sleep all day," he said with a shrug.

"All right."

Seamus informed her the tiny town of Onding was celebrating Children's Day. Once a year, Onding celebrated its children, for they were the future. He'd said it was a day for parents to shower their children with treats and gifts. For some reason, the celebrations had been bumped up. The town was bustling with excitement. It seemed to be their favorite day of the year. Ophelia thought the concept was nice, though it made her a little sad. Holidays always made her feel like that. While she loved watching others enjoy these special days, she'd never had the same experiences.

Paper lanterns adorned with children's drawings of happy families floated above, suspended by colorful streamers. Ophelia sighed, averting her eyes.

"Do you want to paint one?" Seamus asked, his eyes glued to a long table a few feet away where paints and unlit lanterns were set out for anyone who wanted to participate.

"Oh, that's—"

"It's free," he said, smiling down at her.

Ophelia tapped her foot nervously, shrugging. Seamus was insistent, leading her to the table. He sat across from her, put together a wooden palette full of every paint color available, and then handed it to her with a lantern.

Beside her, a boy no older than five was trying his best to paint his father's likeness. A few seats down, so was a set of twins. On and on the children went, all painting their families. Ophelia stared at her lantern, feeling out of place.

Seamus handed her a paintbrush, a tired smile lighting up his face. "What are you going to paint?"

Ophelia twirled the paintbrush in her hands, her leg bouncing beneath the table. She had an inkling of an idea but didn't know whether she was allowed to paint it.

Just as she opened her mouth to ask, Seamus said, "You could paint your animals?"

That was a lovely idea. She'd paint Eydis, Rain, Frykt, and a certain wolf that was always watching over her. She took a graphite stick from the case above her sketchbook and sketched herself, Seamus's wolf, and all her animal friends. Seamus sat quietly, watching her carefully. When she was done sketching, she began to paint, trying her best not to pick apart her work too much. This was meant to be fun, so she'd try her best to see it that way.

When she was finished, she turned her lantern around to show Seamus.

He picked it up, holding it to the light. "Beautiful," he said. He ran his thumb over the wolf, smirking. "That guy looks familiar."

Ophelia felt her cheeks go red.

"Would you like to hang it with the others?" he asked, offering her his hand.

"Yes, please," she said, taking his hand.

Together, they walked to a separate table where volunteers lit the lanterns and hung them. Ophelia was asked to pick the color of the streamer she wanted—blue, of course—and then the volunteers hung her lantern in an empty spot above a picnic table.

"Is this something you'll add to your book of memories?" Seamus asked as they sat below their lantern, smiling up at it.

Ophelia studied him, wondering what was going on in his head. "Yes, I think I will."

She took out her sketchbook, flipping to an empty page. She drew the lantern, then him, adding a pair of fluffy ears. When she'd finished, she spun her book around and slid it over to him.

"The ears are a nice touch," he laughed.

"You can flip through it if you'd like." She knew it was something he'd longed to do for a while now.

"You sure?"

She nodded.

He sat back, pouring over every page, reading her life through the pictures she'd drawn. He didn't say anything, but Ophelia could understand him just by looking into his misty eyes, which reflected the drawings in their muddy depths.

"You're very good," he said softly, "you could make a career out of this."

"I could, but I won't. Art brings me comfort. I don't want it to be a chore if that makes sense."

Seamus nodded. He flipped through a few more pages, then spun the book around, tapping a drawing with a questioning look. "Is this that musician friend of yours?"

"Zimri? Yes, that's him," Ophelia said. There were lots of drawings of Jonquil and the Spirits. That page was full of him playing his lute and dancing amongst daffodils. She'd done it on one of her many visits to the Garden.

"How did you meet such a character?"

"He passed through Tø with his troupe one day," Ophelia shrugged. It wasn't a total lie.

They sat there until he'd seen every page, complimenting her drawings and asking questions about the memories and people depicted there. She'd lied and said that some of the Spirits were characters from books she'd liked. He couldn't fathom how she could imagine words on paper as actual living people. When he finished, he returned her sketchbook, thanking her for the opportunity and privilege to see it.

Absentmindedly, Ophelia flipped back to a drawing of Saoirse she'd done at the beginning of the year.

"She'll be fine," Seamus whispered, "The worst thing they'll make her do is candy some beetles."

Ophelia smiled to herself, nodding. If that were Saoirse's fate, she'd like to think she wouldn't mind. She'd always had a way of finding beauty in the strangest things. That was probably why she'd liked Ophelia so much.

"We'll go back for her, though, right?" Ophelia asked.

"Right," Seamus replied, giving a solemn nod.

They sat in comfortable silence, soaking in the people and things around them. Families dressed in traditional folk costumes called bunad danced to the fiddlers in the town center. Mothers braided their children's hair. Fathers played games with their sons. Grandparents told stories. Aunts and uncles passed around pastries.

That bittersweet feeling was creeping up Ophelia's spine again.

Seamus cleared his throat, tapping the back of her hand. She turned to him, opening her hand on instinct. He placed a handful of coins in her palm, smiling drunkenly.

"Oh, I already have a little extra coin," Ophelia said, pushing her hand back to him.

All he did was shake his head. "It's Children's Day. All the adults are buying nonsense for the kids. Consider this my contribution. Go get yourself something frivolous I'd disapprove of."

"Are you sure?"

He set his face in a comically stern expression. "It's an order, soldier," he said, lowering his voice as deep as it would go.

Ophelia was bouncing in her seat with excitement.

"Thank you!"

"Yeah, yeah, whatever," he laughed. "Be back by moon-rise."

"Okay!"

She wasted no time bolting for the carts and stalls. There were stalls with folk costumes, carts piled high with sweet treats, rows upon rows of toys and stuffed critters—everything and anything you could imagine. Ophelia watched parents pick up their tiny children so they could better see all the wares available to them. Older children, their faces red with embarrassment, awkwardly showed their guardians the things that caught their eye. It was all so overwhelmingly wholesome.

One stall in particular caught Ophelia's eye. Money jingling in her palm, she bee-lined for it. Stuffed animals with the softest fur hung from a makeshift storefront and littered a table decorated to resemble a forest.

"Hello, wee one. How may I help you?" said the woman running the stall.

Ophelia was immediately drawn to a giant polar bear at the back of the display. She reached for it, rubbing its ear between her wounded fingers. The lady at the stall glanced at the strange marks on her skin but said nothing. She picked up the polar bear and held it, admiring it.

"I've been holding on to this fellow for a while, hoping he'd find a good home," she said.

"Did you make him?" Ophelia asked. She took one of the stuffed toy's paws in her hand, squeezing it softly.

"I did!" the woman said excitedly. "What do you think?"

"I love him," Ophelia said. She heard her tone of voice change. She somehow sounded her age. Though most would think she was far too old for toys, when did a child truly grow up? "May I have him, Miss? I promise to take good care of him."

"Why yes, you may," the woman laughed. She passed the bear onto her, holding out her hand. "Ten copper, please, wee one."

Ophelia paid, then skipped away, hugging the polar bear tight, trying to think of a proper name. The bear was huge, almost too big to hold with one arm. She spun it around, looking into its button eyes, feeling as though she'd won some cosmic game.

So that's what she named him.

Seier, meaning victory.

Seamus had followed Ophelia's gaze, noticing the slight frown she had whenever she stopped to watch a young mother braid her daughter's hair. Seamus had eyed Ophelia carefully. That frown spoke volumes. As soon as she was out of eyesight, Seamus made for the woman with immaculate braiding skills.

"Excuse me," he said, feeling his face redden.

Why was he doing this?

The woman looked up with a questioning smile.

"Would you be willing to teach me how to do that? To braid hair?" Seamus asked sheepishly.

The woman snickered to herself. "Why would you want to learn how to braid?"

Seamus blinked a few times. "I. . ." His face was practically on fire by this point. "My. . . d—*daughter*. . . she has a lot of hair," he said, swallowing his pride as he gestured to his head wildly. "Like a full-on manticore's mane. I figured putting it in braids would make it easier to manage."

To his relief, there were no further questions. The woman nodded, gesturing for him to sit. She spent an hour teaching him all kinds of braids, finishing their lessons by showing him how to incorporate beads and ribbons. Seamus asked where he could purchase the beads she'd used, knowing such simple things would mean the world to Ophelia.

They parted ways, and Seamus set off to find his daugh—no, his *Witch*—a small pouch of beads rattling away in his pocket. He'd also bought a brush, which would be a nice upgrade from the old comb she usually used.

Ophelia ended up finding him first, shoving a half-eaten pastry in his face.

"Where'd you disappear to?" she asked, wiping jam from her lip.

Seamus gratefully took the pastry, giving her a slight

nod in thanks. "Had some things I needed to attend to." He glanced down at the giant polar bear plush in her arms, nearly mistaking it for the real thing. "I see you took your orders to heart."

"He's cute, isn't he? I named him Seier." She was glowing with joy.

Seamus wished she'd smile like that all the time. He patted the stuffed bear's head as he finished off her pastry.

"Are we heading back now?"

He nodded, and they wove quietly through the partygoers together until they found themselves back in the busy tavern. How rare it was to find someone you could share the quiet with. Everyone always had to fill the silence. Few appreciated it for what it was. After a quick dinner, they returned to their room, where Seamus began to pace. Ophelia watched him, bemused.

"Is something the matter, wolfie?" she asked playfully.

He reached for the pouch of beads in his pocket.

Why was he so nervous?

"So, I—I saw you—I noticed that—" The way his words tumbled out of his mouth made him sound like a stately stuttering scholar.

Ophelia tilted her head to the side, removing her mask. "Seamus?"

He grumbled to himself, reaching into his jacket, taking the hairbrush from the hidden pocket inside.

"I've noticed," he began, taking a sharp breath. "That when you scc happy families, you get antsy."

Ophelia straightened, watching Seamus run his hands over the brush's fibers. With a heavy sigh, he came to sit opposite her on the bed, searching her eyes.

"I know your heart craves the simplest of things. Like quiet dinners and good books. Painting and drawing. Watching the birds dart around the sky. Someone braiding your hair," he smiled. "So, if the opportunity arises, I'll try to give you those things."

"You asked that lady to teach you to braid hair, didn't you?" Ophelia asked, a bright smile on her lips. The storm in her eyes dissipated, revealing two bright moons.

His face reddened. "I did."

Ophelia turned, sweeping her hair behind her back as Seamus sat on the bed beside her. She hugged her polar bear tightly, never flinching as Seamus began his work. They were both aware of how absurd this situation was. A fearsome warrior reduced to a hairstylist. Tiril and Helgi would never let him live this down.

"Can I ask you something?" Ophelia whispered. Seamus had just started weaving three strands of hair into one, slipping on a few beads as he went.

"Always."

"Do you believe in fate and destiny?"

"I don't know. Do you?"

"I think so," Ophelia yawned. "Otherwise, I don't think we would've met."

The notion that some higher being had brought them together, that their lives had gone so horribly wrong so that they'd end up here, was almost. . . comforting? There was no one else in the world he'd rather be sitting here with other than her.

Seamus remembered when they first met and how odd it was that he happened upon her, of all people. At Tø of all places. He'd call that fate. Though he had fought the feeling for most of his life, he'd felt a presence guiding him. Whether it was her Spirits or his, he knew something was out there.

He'd felt that force grow after Ingrid's death, though that was when he fought it the hardest.

"Sometimes I think she led me to you," he said aloud, unable to stop himself.

"Ingrid?"

"Mmhmm."

"Why do you think that is?"

Seamus began to braid another section of hair, smiling to himself. "She used to feed the rabbits, too."

Ophelia turned to look at him, her moon-bright eyes full of wonder. "Really?"

"Rabbit was her favorite. She used to joke and say it was cliché, but she devoted herself to life and the preservation of it," he explained. "I think that's why I now hold such a grudge against Rabbit. Why couldn't she have saved Ingrid, her most loyal subject?"

Ophelia turned back around, quiet. It was the same sort of awkward quietude she'd had when Tiril and Helgi had talked about the links between Terrestrials and Celestials.

"I saw the rabbits, and I knew Ingrid was watching over me," Seamus said with a shrug. "And then I saw a young lady feeding them, and I knew I was safe. At least that's what I'd hoped."

"Polar bears represent hope," Ophelia said softly. "That's why I like them."

"Huh, I've never heard that before."

Seamus had made twelve braids, each adorned with wooden beads carved with runes. He took six of these braids on either side of her head and clumped them together with the remainder. Bringing them together, he braided them into one long plait, tying it off with a blue bow.

"Finished," he smiled, admiring his handiwork.

Ophelia gently touched the bow, nodding her approval. "Thank you, Seamus."

"Anything for you, pup."

CHAPTER SIXTY-EIGHT

TIDAL

"I'm almost sad to be leaving Onding," Ophelia said as they packed their bags the next day. "I quite like it here."

"Yeah, it's all right, isn't it?" Seamus asked as he folded up his bedroll.

Ophelia just nodded, sitting on the edge of the bed to tie her shoes. They'd stayed in their room for most of the morning, sleeping and reading, respectively.

"Children's Day was fun," she said absentmindedly.

"Yes, I'd have to agree with you on that, too."

Ophelia smiled up at him, watching as he dug through the nightstand to see what he could stuff in his bags. "I wonder what other kinds of festivals or celebrations exist throughout Alle Årstider. Tø didn't celebrate many holidays. We really didn't have the money to do so."

"There's a place in Vårretten that celebrates this incredibly smelly plant each year," Seamus said, grimacing. "Don't go to the boglands, Ophelia; it's not worth it."

"Does it bloom once a year or something?"

Seamus only nodded, staring into the distance as though remembering something terribly traumatic.

Ophelia cleared her throat, kicking her feet. "Do werewolves have any special holidays?"

Seamus looked up, reddening. He came to sit beside her as he pulled on his socks. "Full moons are normally one big party, but every couple of years, a no-moon day coincides with a meteor shower. You'll think it strange, but it's when we feel

completely in harmony with our wolves. There's something to
be said about werewolves and starlight, I'll tell you that."

"Well, the Wolf in the Celestial teachings is tied to the
North Star," Ophelia said matter-of-factly. "Strange, isn't it?
You'd think they'd be tied to the moon, but the Bat is."

Unfortunately, Seamus *had* heard that before.

"Anyway, when this strange little event comes about,
all the elders enter the forest and pass around this disgusting
drink. Everyone gets drunk out of their mind and tries to 'com-
mune with the Stars,'" Seamus laughed. "It's a sight to behold,
that's for sure."

"Did you ever get to experience that?" Ophelia asked,
eyes wide.

Seamus really hoped his face conveyed how hurt he felt.
"I said that the *elders* got to. Are you calling me old?"

Ophelia's cheeks began to turn pink as she said, "Well. .
. you're older than I am, at least. . ."

Seamus rolled his eyes, leaning down to pull on his
boots. Ophelia stifled a laugh, kicking her feet again. As Seamus tied his laces, she nudged him with her elbow.

"Seamus?" she laughed.

Exasperated, Seamus turned to her, caught between a
smile and a frown. "Okay, yes, I did join in once."

"What happened? Did you get to talk to the Stars?" she
asked, eyes glittering with expectance.

"Well, most of the pack spent the night running naked
through the woods—" Ophelia shriveled up her nose "—but I
spent it curled up in a ball hallucinating. Apparently, I had a
bad reaction to whatever was in their magical mystery mead."

Seamus shivered, remembering the burning fever and
how his mind swam, turning everything around him into a
dark, churning void. The morning after had been just as terrible. As far as hangovers went, that was the worst he'd ever
experienced. No one would tell him what was in that strange
concoction, but in order to get a werewolf drunk, it had to have
been something strong.

To make matters worse, for weeks after, everyone walked
on eggshells around him. No one would tell him if this was
the truth, but after that, Seamus always felt they saw him as
less than. The bite may have taken to him, but there was more

to being a werewolf than transforming every full moon. There were cultural things he never grasped, traditions that didn't make sense to him. He'd never say it out loud, but it must've been the Ulvemordere in him. Old habits die hard.

"What did you hallucinate, if you don't mind me asking? And how do you know that they weren't visions from beyond?" Ophelia asked, wiggling her fingers in his face.

"All I saw was a pulsing black void," Seamus shrugged. "I didn't hear a voice; I didn't see any premonitions that have since come to pass."

Ophelia leaned back on her hands, lost in thought. "How truly odd."

"Why?"

Ophelia, too, shrugged, hopping up off the bed. "In some stories, the Celestial realm is described as a 'starlit expanse of darkness.' Maybe the magical mystery mead did its job, you just weren't open to the message," she laughed.

That thing Ophelia always did? When she got embarrassed or anxious and made herself small? Seamus suddenly understood why she did it. He felt himself recoil and shrink, avoiding her gaze.

"Yeah, maybe. . ."

Packed and ready to head back to Dødbyen, they set out on the road. Children's Day festivities were still in full swing, so Seamus allowed Ophelia to linger in the streets of Onding. They stopped under their lantern, smiling up at it. Some of the smaller children asked them about it, happy to listen to Ophelia as she explained why she painted it in such a way. A few of the adults even complimented her on her talent. Seamus couldn't help but feel a sense of pride, living vicariously through her.

Walking through the square, Ophelia pointed out the stall where she'd purchased her polar bear plush, waving to the young woman selling her wares. Seamus nodded to her, bemused. It was nice to see his Witch act her age. She may be eighteen, but to him, she was still a child. Yes, she was wise beyond her years and a force to be reckoned with, but she carried this sort of innocence with her. Seamus hoped it stayed around for a good long while. If buying her stuffed animals, books, and art supplies kept her innocence, he was happy to oblige.

What she'd said earlier had stuck with him, too. She liked Onding, yes, but it was the community here he knew she craved. Looking toward the future, he saw them in a cottage not dissimilar to the one left behind in Tø. But unlike that cottage, the village nearby would be accepting of both Witches and werewolves.

"What are you smiling about?" Ophelia asked as they debated what to grab for lunch.

"Nothing much," he replied.

Ophelia tilted her head, befuddled. "Ominous."

He winked at her, then stepped toward a stall selling giant turkey legs. Once they'd paid, they continued to amble through the town until they ended up at the outskirts.

"Well, this is it," Seamus sighed, tossing the remnants of his lunch.

"Back to Dødbyen," Ophelia smiled, taking one last look around at Onding.

"Was this a satisfactory side quest, pup?"

"Very—Holy Hemlock!" she shrieked, about falling over from shock. "Our horses!"

There, a few feet away, were Rain and Frykt. Standing beside them was a figure in a dark woolen cloak, their hand clutching the horses' reins. The figure was gesturing wildly, their hand held beside their head as if trying to gauge someone's height. The elderly man they were talking to looked both frightened and bored.

"Rain!" Ophelia called, waving excitedly.

Upon hearing her voice, both horses whipped their head around. Rain bolted, pulling down the figure before they could release the reins. Frykt reared, whinnying madly. Ophelia ran to them, pulling Rain into a hug, overcome with joyful tears.

"Oh, I've missed you both so much!" she squealed, stroking Frykt's forehead.

Frykt gently nibbled on her hair, then pushed her forehead into Seamus's chest.

"Yes, yes, I missed you, too," he sighed, scratching her behind the ears. "See, I told you they were resourceful."

The figure, who'd been lying on the ground dazed, finally got to their feet, their face shrouded by an enormous hood. Seamus's hand went to axes, but before he could react, the figure lowered their hood.

Or rather, *his* hood.

"Pirate!" Ophelia exclaimed.

The winged pirate shook his head violently as if to clear it, dusting himself off. He looked up, then did a double take, his face split in two by the brightest smile Seamus had ever seen.

"I knew I'd run into you again!" he said, wincing as he threw his arms wide in triumph. "Glad to see you're doing better, my lady."

"Thank you," Ophelia said.

Seamus rolled his eyes. He could see a bit of pink spreading across her face. Oh, brother.

"I had a feeling these two belonged to you. They were bucking wildly, attempting to free themselves. Especially the spotted one," the pirate said, patting Frykt's hindquarters.

Frykt, in turn, slapped his face with her tail, looking disgruntled. Seamus hid his smile behind his hand, playing it off as though he were just smoothing his beard. Unfortunately, the pirate didn't seem fazed in the slightest.

"Ahh, yes, we got off to a rocky start. . ." the pirate said sheepishly. "I was only trying to rescue them, you see."

"Thank you so much!" Ophelia said, bowing.

The pirate reddened. "My pleasure."

"Kill me now," Seamus mumbled.

Frykt stamped her hoof in agreement.

Rain shot them both a dirty look.

"So. . . Where are the two of you headed now?" the pirate asked.

"Dødbyen," Ophelia said, earning herself a glare from Seamus.

The pirate laughed, nodding. "Oh, I've been to Dødbyen. Quite a kooky place if you ask me."

"It *is*, isn't it?" Ophelia smiled, turning to hug Frykt. If horses could blush, Seamus figured the giant beast would've. Instead, she wrapped her head around Ophelia's shoulders, avoiding Seamus's eyes. "Where are you going?"

"I'll be meeting back up with my crew in Høstlunden shortly," the pirate said, shrugging. He then grimaced, squeezing his left shoulder.

Ophelia tilted her head to the side, frowning. "Are you all right?"

"Me? Oh, yes, I'm fine. I took a tumble, but I'll heal," he sighed. "No heavy flying for me, though. Guess I'm making the trek on foot."

Ophelia looked to Seamus, her frown deepening. The eyes on her polar bear mask seemed to grow larger and. . . cuter? So did the eyes on the stuffed bear tied to her pack. Seamus shook his head, imagining a pleading look beneath her mask.

"No," he said.

"Seamus!"

"Absolutely not!"

Ophelia stuck out her tongue, then turned back to the pirate. "Dødbyen isn't that far from the Høstlunden border. You could hitch a ride with us if you'd like."

The pirate's face lit up with joy. "I'd really appreciate—"

"I just said 'no,'" Seamus hissed.

Ophelia rounded on him, arms crossed, attempting to look fierce. "We owe him that much."

Seamus only scoffed. "We owe him nothing."

"Oh, your dad's right, I—" the pirate began.

Ophelia shushed him. "Seamus, he risked his life to get us out of Juvel Hjem."

"So?"

"So, I think that means we owe him! Plus, he went out of his way to return Rain and Frykt to us."

The pirate cleared his throat. "It's all right, my lady, I don't—"

"And he's injured!" Ophelia interjected.

"That's not our fault," Seamus laughed. "We've already got too many mouths to feed. We don't need another."

"It'd just be 'til Dødbyen, Seamus," Ophelia said, visibly pouting.

"Kid, I doubt he wants to tag along with us."

"Well, let's ask him, shall we?"

Seamus rolled his eyes. "Let's."

"Mr. Pirate, sir, would you—Oh," Ophelia said, looking over her shoulder. The pirate was gone. Mildly alarmed, she spun in a circle, then looked beneath Rain and Frykt as if he was hiding under them. "Where did he go?"

"Our bickering probably scared him off," Seamus laughed.

Ophelia stood quietly with her hands on her hips for a moment, then made a great show of shrugging. "All right, well, I suppose that's settled then."

Seamus smiled to himself, climbing up into Frykt's saddle. "We're terrible, aren't we?"

"Maybe just a little."

CHAPTER SIXTY-NINE

TERMS OF ENDEARMENT

The dampening sound of the night had fallen, casting the world in blue. Seamus was lounging on Frykt's back, eyes closed softly, mulling over the last few weeks. Ophelia was atop Rain, drawing.

Everything was peaceful; everything was quiet.

All except Seamus's mind.

Without the distraction of Onding, his thoughts were running wild. No matter how hard he tried, he couldn't get the image of the hobgoblin from Geiravör out of his mind. That sight had plagued his nightmares, but now, after seeing Ophelia's unconscious body on the ground barely two days prior, her inevitable death plagued him. All he could think about was what else could've gone wrong. Mawde Carre, being drained, was burned into his retinas. But the face was wrong. All he saw was *her* face and *her* Marks. The scene played on repeat, but he saw less of the hobgoblin and more of Ophelia each time. Needless to say, he was on edge.

"Oh, yes, I quite agree," Ophelia said out of nowhere, startling him out of his thoughts. He sat up, turning to see her staring up at the sky. "Really? That's my favorite, too!"

If she were talking to Rain, he would've whinnied, neighed, or swished his tail. Same with Frykt. If not either of them, who was she talking to? Seamus looked around. There was no breeze billowing around them. No running water nearby. No creeping critters. Only falling snow and the pines.

And the moon.

A pang of guilt surged through him. Did she truly forgive him for that night? The full moon had taken a lot out of both of them, but at least Seamus was healing. The burns on his ankles and wrists were nearly gone. The cut at his side from Jette's blade was healed, too.

Ophelia, unfortunately, didn't have the luxury of mystical healing powers. Was she really all right?

She laughed to herself, shrugging. "I suppose so." It took him a minute to remember she *wasn't* a mind reader and *wasn't* talking to him.

"Are you talking to the moon?" Seamus asked, giving her a look he hoped conveyed just how crazy he thought her to be. She'd argue he'd chosen to spend all his time with her. If she was crazy, so was he.

She turned to look at him, smiling mischievously. "Now, why would I do that, Seamus?"

"So you *are* talking to the moon?"

All she did was laugh and look back up at the sky. "Why, yes, he *is* a cleverclogs, isn't he?"

"Can you actually hear the moon's voice? In the same way you talk to the wind or animals?"

Ophelia gave him the same 'you're-insane-and-you-know-it' look. "I don't hear a voice, Seamus. Well, most of the time, at least."

"So. . . All this time, you've just been talking to yourself?" Okay, maybe he was crazy, but she was a lunatic. Literally, it seemed. At least she was smiling again. He hated seeing her unhappy.

"Yes."

"Are you mental?"

"Decidedly so."

"Stars, kid," he sighed, grimacing. "We're getting your head checked out when all this is done."

"They'll want to check yours, too," she said matter-of-factly.

Seamus considered that, frowning. "Forget I said anything."

"Wisest decision you've ever made."

"So, the moon, aye?" he said, changing the subject. He looked to the sky, waving up at the glowing celestial body. "How is he tonight?"

“Well, for one, the moon is a *she*,” Ophelia said, pursing her lips. “And she’s all right. A little weepy, I’d say.”

“Ahh, I see.”

“You can talk to her if you’d like. She’s an old friend of yours, after all.”

Seamus rolled his eyes. “I wouldn’t call her my friend.”

“I do believe her opinion matters more than yours, Seamus.”

“Why?”

“She’s older than just about everything. And you’re. . . Seamus Norland. The surly old wolf.”

“And you’re Ophelia Norland, the annoying little Witch,” Seamus sighed contently. “Yet everyone everywhere seems to love you. Even the moon.”

Ophelia’s mouth hung open. Rain stopped dead in his tracks, equally aghast. Even Frykt seemed shocked. Seamus gave them all a questioning look, then realized what he said.

“You’re not really annoying. I didn’t mean that. Sorry. . . I’m not really surly, either. That’s why I said it.” He cleared his throat, scratching the back of his neck. “It was a joke, pup, I’m sorry.”

Ophelia just stood there with her mouth hanging open. “I’m—Yeah—Okay. Okay, cool. That’s. . . it’s okay.”

“I didn’t mean to hurt your feelings.”

“Y—You didn’t,” she whispered. Her voice was strained, like she wanted to cry. Oh, he was in big trouble. Now, *he* was the lunatic.

“I’m sorry, I take it back! I didn’t mean it,” Seamus said, putting his hands up in defense.

“No!” Ophelia screamed—almost angrily so. “Don’t take it back! Don’t take any of it back! Always call me that!”

He blinked at her. “Oh. . . Oh, okay. . . You’re an annoying little Witch, and I’ll call you that for as long as I live,” he said, his confusion apparent.

“Good,” Ophelia said, straightening. “Yeah, good.”

Seamus cleared his throat, pointing to the sky. “Um. . . You want to talk to the moon some more or. . . ?”

“Nope.”

"Yeah, me either."

They gave each other a wary look, then continued on side by side. The horses glanced sidelong at them and shook their heads. Seamus grumbled to himself angrily. Why was he always saying or doing the wrong thing? Sometimes, he thought he was being funny, but apparently, he was just being rude or plain mean.

He didn't want to be that person around her. Not only did he want to set a good example, but he was afraid he'd rub off on her—he was the adult, after all—he was terrified one more slip-up would mean she'd leave. If he didn't straighten up, sooner or later, she'd get wise. Then again, she had stayed longer than most. Stars, she *chose* him.

"Hey," he said, clearing his throat and scratching the side of his nose nervously. "I don't think you're annoying. I really don't."

"I know," she said softly.

"I'm sorry I'm so. . ." he sighed heavily, "*surly*," he finished, shaking his head in disgust. He hated that word.

The tiniest laugh. "I know you are, Seamus."

"I just—"

"Seamus *Norland*—" Why did she say his name like that? "—I'm not mad."

"You sure?"

She nodded. "Still, always call me *that*."

"Annoying?"

Her lips pulled into a thin pout. "Yeah. That." The sarcasm in those two words was not lost on him.

His brain was a giant question mark. What else had he called her other than annoying? Little Witch? Hadn't he called her that before? Why was she acting so weird?

CHAPTER SEVENTY

I'VE GOT MY MIND ON YOU

Ophelia's heart was soaring. Despite that nonsense with the trolls, the last two days had been the best ever—ever! There was no question about it. She could feel her cheeks grow warm beneath her mask, her lips twitching with a smile. Seamus gave her a funny look.

Oh, he was so silly sometimes. Pretending he didn't realize what he'd said.

Unless, of course, he didn't.

That was an even funnier thought.

He'd slipped up and accidentally said the one thing she'd been secretly hoping to hear all this time. Last names were special. You only gave them to partners and children. They were a symbol of love in the purest form. If he saw her as his child, Ophelia could die happy even at the hand of an Ulvemordere.

When this was all said and done, would he make it official? Tø was gone, so they had no residency. If they chose to live under Tiril and Helgi's roof or anywhere in Dødbyen, their word would be the law. He could formerly adopt her if he wanted to.

Oh, but she was getting far too ahead of herself.

Blessed Amaranth, that slip-up may have been a complete accident, and he may not even feel that way. Maybe he was just tired.

Still, she hoped he'd meant it.

She wanted very badly to be his daughter, to have his

name, for it'd be the only thing he could really give her. She'd cherish it forever and never let anyone or anything take it away.

"Rest here for the night?" Seamus asked, nudging her with his elbow.

Ahead, the trees faded into a clearing. Ophelia nodded. "As good a place as any."

As always, it was his job to set up camp. Glad to be rid of firewood-collecting duty, Ophelia stepped out into the clearing, gazing up through the snow. The tops of towering pine trees framed a navy-blue sky, snowflakes like shooting stars falling silently all around. Ophelia slowed to a stop, untying her mask and clipping it to her belt as she tilted her head to catch the fluffy flakes. Each snowflake was the gentlest kiss upon her face. Arms wide, she spun slowly, listening to the whispers of the wind and the quiet laugh of each flake. You know, the ones she 'really couldn't hear.'

"Seamus," she said as quietly as she could, eyes still closed. "Come here."

Shuffling footsteps, the crunch of freshly fallen snow. Something dropped onto the ground, presumably his bags. "Don't you tire of it? You see it every day," Seamus said, mirroring her tone.

"I'm not called The Winter Witch for nothing, Seamus," Ophelia whispered. "I love the snow more than words can express. It feels. . . like an old friend." She stopped twisting amongst the flurries, holding out a hand for him. He took it, and it felt like that meant something. Together, they stood beneath a holy embrace from the elements.

A little over a thousand years ago, when the first Winter Witch was born, the very first snow had fallen. Or so the stories said. In a way, all Witches carried the same life force as those who came before. If the stories were true—and Ophelia knew they were—then these falling flakes really were an old friend. Sigfreður may be living as a Spirit, but his human soul had died long ago. Ophelia always figured she carried a part of it with her.

Seamus cleared his throat, prompting her to open her eyes. He stepped back, bowed deeply, and offered her his hands. "Shall we?"

Ophelia glanced over her shoulder to see his belongings

lying discarded. She, too, shrugged off her bags and took his outstretched hands.

"You dance?" Ophelia asked.

He nodded. "You?"

"Never had the chance."

Seamus nudged her foot with his. "Stand on my feet."

Ophelia gave him a questioning look. "Won't I squish your toes?"

"Trust me," he said with a shrug.

Ophelia stood atop his feet, imagining herself as light as a feather. Seamus moved his right foot forward, left foot to the side, and right foot toward the left, repeating this motion until they were softly spinning at a steady pace throughout the clearing. Ophelia felt herself laugh, her cheeks burning from the enormous smile on her face. She'd had seen many young girls stand on their father's feet at festivals and in the communal hall at inns. She'd yearned for that experience, yearned for a family. Never once did she imagine she'd have one.

"Can you remember the steps?" Seamus asked. This whole time, she'd been looking at their feet. He, however, had been staring at her face.

She nodded, stepping off his toes. "Is this a waltz, then?"

"The same one all those princesses would dance in your books," he said with a content smile.

Somehow, her smile grew wider. They kept their steady rhythm, snowflakes dusting their hair, lashes, and clothes, casting them in white. They were ghosts, dancing under the moon, thinking of nothing but each other. Snowflakes swirled around their legs, encasing them in a spiral. It was dancing with them.

All worry washed away. The only thing weighing them down now was the snow.

Seamus shifted back, lifting one of her hands and twirling her around as fast as he could. He laughed. Ophelia hadn't heard that laugh in a while. She wanted nothing more than to be the reason he kept laughing, kept smiling, and kept living. He dipped her, then grabbed her by the waist and lifted her, spinning her one last time before setting her softly on the ground.

"And now you know how to dance," he said, sounding

insurmountably proud of himself.

"Why, thank you for the lesson," Ophelia said, giving him a dainty little curtsey.

He bowed rather dramatically, arms swept wide. "See? I'm good for something other than blood and violence."

That made her frown. "Seamus, you've always been more than blood and violence to me."

He stood up slowly, his smile gone, but Ophelia knew he wasn't angry or even sad despite the tears threatening to spill down his cheeks. He looked down at her through snow-covered locks, and in his eyes, she saw someone who'd been seen for the first time in their life.

"Thank you for coming into my life, Ophelia," he said softly. "I mean that. Truly."

Ophelia—blushing furiously—clasped her hands before her, shrugging away her giddy embarrassment. "You're welcome."

There was that smile again, that laugh. "Now, don't let that go to your head."

"Too late," she laughed.

He patted the top of her head as he walked by, heading off to make camp for the night. Ophelia made to follow him but paused.

She spun back around, arms again outstretched, face tilted to the sky. "Thank you for bringing him to me," she whispered to the many ears above who were listening and the many eyes watching over her.

For she was eternally grateful to the many Spirits surrounding her. Whether it be Amaranth, Fern, or even Jonquil, someone had finally answered her prayers. All this time, she had prayed, hoped, and wished for someone to love her as effortlessly as Seamus did.

She had found a family in that surly old wolf.

She'd found a father.

Seamus had cooked them a quick dinner, which they ate over quiet conversation. The evening was a stark contrast to what'd happened that morning. He couldn't help but hope the sense of peace he had stuck around over the next few days. Ophelia felt it, too, he could tell. This was the most she'd ever talked, rambling on about her book and how much fun she'd had at the festival. They'd finished dinner ages ago but were still up talking, watching the embers of their campfire dwindle to nothing.

"Where did you learn to dance?" Ophelia asked sleepily. She should be asleep by now.

Seamus sighed heavily. "You never knew what sort of skill you may need for a job. Let's just say I attended quite a few balls while working for the Ulvemordere."

Ophelia's face screwed up into a look cross between disgust and amusement.

"What?"

"I'm picturing you in a suit, your hair perfectly coiffed. It's worse than that charade you put on for the Kirkebys," she laughed.

"Oh, yeah, it definitely was," Seamus laughed, shaking his head in dismay. "Horrid sight, really."

She stared at him for a while, knees pulled up to her chest, her cheek resting atop them. The dark circles under her eyes were back.

Eventually, she yawned, standing. "Tusen takk, Seamus."

"Heading to bed?"

She nodded, unclipping her bedroll from her pack. "Hopefully I'll sleep better tonight."

"God natt, Ophelia."

"Natt, Seamus."

She unrolled her bedroll behind him and settled in for the night. He found it odd she chose to sleep on the ground, seeing as there were perfectly good trees all around. Maybe she was just too tired to climb.

Far from tired himself, Seamus decided to stay put by the fire. He dug in his pack for one of those sticks he'd pocketed on their journey, instead finding the half-finished fox he'd been working on weeks ago. He smiled to himself, content to whittle away into the wee hours.

Once he finished it, he placed it in Ophelia's pack for her to find later.

Still restless, he held one of the sticks to the light. Dancing with Ophelia had eased the knots in his chest, but he still kept thinking of the hobgoblin. The sorry being wouldn't have had a funeral. If she had any family, they'd never know she'd died. There was no one to honor her. No one except Seamus and Ophelia, at least. Seamus decided the stick he held wanted to honor the hobgoblin, too, so he got to work carving her likeness. He'd carve her with a smile, imagining her life before that town turned on her.

He figured Ophelia would appreciate this, though he didn't know if he should give the carving to her or not. There'd been reckless abandon seeping off her seeing that goblin die. It was probably best to keep this to himself for now.

He glanced over his shoulder, watching her sleep as he always did. Listening to her breathing, watching her back rise and fall, protecting her in even the smallest, quietest ways. She held the polar bear plush tight to her chest, burying her face in its fur. That feeling of peace doubled. He was glad to be here with her despite what was coming next and what had come before.

He thought back to their earlier conversation about the moon, laughing to himself. Stars, she was so weird, and he loved it.

Instead of calling her Ophelia Norland, the annoying little—

He froze, nearly cutting himself with his pocketknife, realization smacking him up alongside the head like a troll's craggy hand.

Ophelia Norland.

He'd called her Ophelia Norland.

Not Ophelia Av'Skogen.

Ophelia *Norland.*

He'd used his name in place of hers. By complete accident. That was why she'd freaked out, not him calling her annoying.

Always call me that, she'd said.

And he would.

Seamus slowly returned to the fire, realizing how much

he'd changed since being in her company. For the first time—truly—he was himself. He was Seamus Norland, the man who cared too much yet never enough. The man who'd inadvertently adopted a teenage Witch who talked to the wind, the moon, animals, and herself. And him. The man who was tearing down all his walls for one pup. The man who was finally allowing himself to love someone again, though this love, this fatherly love, felt more real than his love for Ingrid ever had.

He turned his face skyward, searching for the Rabbit among all the other constellations. Once he spotted it, the stars pulsed and seemed to sparkle.

For once, Seamus knew he was on the right path.

He also knew that the young Witch behind him loved him just as much as he loved her.

Ophelia Norland sure had a nice ring to it.

Maybe they would get it in writing one day.

CHAPTER SEVENTY-ONE

GOD MORGEN

Morning came, and that fuzzy feeling in Ophelia's chest remained. It was early, the world cast in a peach glow, the birds still asleep. She lay on her side, studying Seamus as he slept. It was a feeling more than anything, but she knew he often watched her the same way. It was a protective sort of thing. How mothers watch infants in their cradles. How children wake in the middle of the night and stare at their snoring parents. It gave her a sense of peace, listening to his too-loud snores.

She smiled to herself, quietly rolling up her bedroll and packing away her things. Done with her part of the cleanup, she set off into the woods for a walk. Rain and Frykt joined, trotting behind her, talking amongst themselves. Since they were far enough away from civilization, Ophelia could stow her mask for the time being. How freeing it was to weave between the trees, alone, unmasked.

The forest had been quiet the day before, but it was alive once again. There weren't as many animals now that they weren't in The Wilds, but there were still plenty of friends to make and critters to pet. She'd not been walking for more than a couple minutes when she glanced over her shoulder to see some fawns had begun to follow behind the horses. Their father lingered in the shadows, cardinals sleeping on his antlers. Flitting above her head were owls. It reminded her of the place she once called home and the friends she'd left behind. She thought of Eydis and how badly she missed her. That old polar bear had been with her through thick and thin. Where was she now? Ophelia prayed she was all right. She thought of the fox they'd buried, too, hoping her graveyard hadn't been desecrated. A sadness washed over her, but she wouldn't let it drown her. Not this time. She turned toward the fawns, kneeling to their level, allowing them to sniff and nuzzle her as they saw fit. Their father came to stand behind her, shaking his head so the cardinals would fly off and land on her shoulders. Rain and Frykt came to stand beside them, nodding to acknowledge his presence. The owls took their place. The deer gave a heavy sigh. He reminded her of Seamus.

"Is everyone well this morning?" Ophelia asked, sitting cross-legged on the forest floor.

The fawns stamped their feet excitedly. The cardinals ruffled their feathers.

"I'm so happy to hear that! Have you plans for the day?"

The fawns looked at each other, their eyes glittering with mischief. Their father blew steam out his nose, ruffling Ophelia's hair. The owls hooted their disapproval.

"Ahh, I see. Well, you should listen to your father, wee ones. He only wants what is best for you." The deer gave a nod, narrowing his eyes at his finicky fawns. "See? There are probably hunters around here. He doesn't want you to get hurt."

The fawns cried, and one of them—the smallest of the three—headbutted her shoulder. Their father gave a cry of shame. The cardinals sang songs of disgust. The owls blinked, emotionless. Frykt stamped her hoof, narrowing her eyes rather menacingly.

Ophelia turned to the deer, stroking his snout. "Oh, you've quite the handful here, don't you?"

He hung his head low.

"I wish you good luck," Ophelia laughed.

The owls swiveled their heads, hooting wildly, their laughs mixing with hers. Soon, every creature surrounding her laughed and cuddled up against her, more than happy she was here. She could've stayed there forever, content with their company. But Seamus was waiting for her, and she wasn't keen on leaving him behind for this motley crew. After a while, she bid them farewell, and the birds saw her back to the campsite.

Seamus still lay huddled beneath his blankets, twitching, eyes shut tight. Ophelia frowned, wringing her hands before coming to kneel next to him. Another nightmare, she suspected. When they slept beneath the stars, she often woke to him talking in his sleep or digging his claws into the earth, growling like he was now. He never spoke of it, which saddened her. Didn't he know he could confide in her? Surely, talking about the nightmares would help.

She didn't want to pry, but she'd come to enjoy caring for him in any way she could. It was the least she could do to repay him for everything he'd done for her.

"Seamus," she whispered, placing her hand on his shoulder and giving a gentle squeeze. "You're all right. I'm here."

Seamus jolted awake. There was a hand on his shoulder—a *cold* hand. He turned sharply, eyes adjusting to the bright morning sun. A faint green glow emanated off him, illuminating Ophelia's pale, worried face.

"Are you all right?" she whispered, her hand resting reassuringly on his shoulder. "You were growling in your sleep again."

All he could do was stare at her.

There she was, her worried eyes rimmed with dark navy circles, hair sticking out in every direction, and a cardinal sitting atop her head.

He swallowed hard, rubbing the sleep from his eyes. He sat up, noting how Ophelia didn't let go of his shoulder.

"Sorry if I startled you," she said as calmly and gently as possible.

". . . it's fine. . ." he said groggily, looking back and forth between her bright silver eyes.

She calmed everything.

She *was* everything.

Such fulfillment this child had brought him. He'd never wanted children before, yet this peculiar Witch with her drawings and somber smile had made him a nurturer. She was his child, his pup, his closest friend and confidant.

Without her, what was he?

Nothing.

He'd been nothing before, and he'd be nothing if—and

he prayed to the Stars this never happened—if there was ever an after.

All that was good, great, and wonderful was the best thing that had happened to him in a very long time, which was why his mind was splitting in two with nightmares. The more he loved someone, the worse the barrage of nightmares got. Sometimes, he couldn't even tell he was only dreaming.

Clearing his throat, he pushed off the ground, avoiding her eyes. He was sure he looked a sorry sight, but he'd stopped caring whether she saw him a mess weeks ago.

"Bad dream," he whispered. "I'm okay."

She sighed heavily. "I'm sorry. Do you want to talk about it?"

He shook his head violently. "No. No, I'd rather not. I'm just glad none of it was real." He tried to laugh, but it came out broken.

With a nod and a yawn, she, too, stood, surveying him. "Try not to dwell on it."

"I will," he said. Easier said than done.

She gave a nod of approval, then started on about her morning and the friends she'd made, how a deer had reminded her of him, and how glad she was they'd be on the road soon. She thanked him for the dance the night before, eyes alight with childlike joy. The tight knot in his chest loosened with every word. Though he'd vowed to protect her, that Witch had done well to protect her wolf in her own right. She was, after all, the only thing that could ward off the nightmares.

CHAPTER SEVENTY-TWO

KNOWN BY ALL

Onding wasn't that far from Dødbyen in the grand scheme of things. It was a relatively straight shoot from the outlying forests back to the City of the Dead, a simple trek filled with laughter between good company. Quickest two days of their lives, most likely. Despite the new moon and how tired Seamus had been, he'd had fun. Now that he thought about it, he couldn't remember the last time he'd felt like that.

Furthermore, Seamus was quite pleased they hadn't encountered any more trouble.

Ophelia was just pleased in general.

Even more so that they stood before the cavernous ravine, not a dragon to be seen. Leaving the horses with a stable hand, she wore a rather smug smile.

Two of the guards Seamus had beat up a little over a week ago began bringing up the lifts.

"Back so soon?" asked one of the guards. It was the werewolf with the attitude. Ophelia would say that seemed to be a shared trait amongst their species.

"Well, we knew you were just *dying* to see us, so we figured we shouldn't keep you waiting," Seamus said with a wink.

The guard rolled his eyes, looking to his comrades who were smiling mischievously. He scowled, making circles in the mud with the tip of his boot.

"No comeback this time?" Ophelia asked, brushing past him.

"I'm thinking. Give me a second. It will come to me," he

mumbled.

Seamus gave him an exaggerated, reassuring look. "Oh, sure. No doubt about it."

The guard opened the gate to the lift, more than happy to feed them to the criminal underbelly below. Seamus and Ophelia bowed mockingly, slipping onto the lift. Their laughs were barely stifled as it descended, leaving them with nothing but the scowling face of the guard above.

Once they reached the ground floor, they took their time heading toward the Kirkeby's mansion. Against his better judgment, Seamus let Ophelia shop around the market and watch some of the performances. Just as before, she quite liked the aerialists. There were a few trinkets her curious hands lingered on, too. Seamus took a mental note of these, storing that knowledge in hopes of using it one day soon.

There was one stall in particular she quite liked. Nestled between stalls selling 'healing' tonics and 'magical' clothing was an art shop. Watercolor palettes and jars of brightly colored paint glinted in the crystal light. While Ophelia was distracted, drifting off to the next stall wistfully, Seamus bought her a cheap set of paints, hiding it in his pack to gift to her later.

Smiling to himself, he counted his remaining coin, stumbling through the crowd to find her.

"Uh oh," Ophelia breathed.

Something tore.

Seamus looked up to see she held a piece of parchment in her shaking hands.

"No. No, you're joking. Why 'uh oh?' What do you mean 'uh oh?'" he groaned, pulling the string to close his coin pouch.

She turned the parchment around, and low and behold, it was like looking in a mirror. It seems the Ulvemordere finally got around to distributing updated wanted posters. Lucky him. Oh, and would you look at that? Under his bounty—fifty thousand gold pieces, by the by—was fine print reading 'Paid for in part by the Sandvik Mining Guild.'

WANTED
BY DECREE OF ACTING ULVEMORDERE
GENERAL, ARILD MELHUS

DEAD
A
O
R
ALIVE
SEAMUS NORLAND
50,000 GOLD
EQUAL TO 500,000 COPPER
-PAID FOR IN PART BY THE SANDVIK MINING GUILD-
CITIZENS ARE ALSO ADVISED TO BE ON THE LOOKOUT FOR MR. NORLAND'S COMPANION, A YOUNG
SKOGENS SØSTRE WEARING THE POLAR BEAR'S LIKENESS. SHE, TOO, IS ARMED AND DANGEROUS.
IF SPOTTED, PLEASE CONTACT THE NEAREST ULVEMORDERE OUTPOST.
THE YOUNG LADY IS TO BE KEPT ALIVE.

"Screw you, Cathal," Seamus barked, ripping the poster from Ophelia's outstretched hands.

"At least I don't have one," Ophelia sighed.

"'Citizens are advised to be on the lookout for Mr. Norland's companion, a young *Skogens Søstre* wearing the Polar Bear's likeness. She, too, is armed and dangerous. If spotted, please contact the nearest outpost. The young lady is to be kept alive,'" Seamus read out loud.

Ophelia yelped, grabbing back the poster. "I'm not armed and dangerous!" she screeched. She said it as if it were the only concerning part of the poster.

"I'd beg to differ," Seamus sighed.

Ophelia made a *hmph!* as she tore up the poster into incredibly small pieces, letting them fall to the ground like ashes. "This is absurd!"

"And very, very bad," Seamus added, though bemused. "Come on, we need to get to the Kirkebys before someone tries to turn us in."

The elderly maid who had greeted them once before welcomed them with a warm smile into the Kirkeby mansion. She was accompanied by Reija, along with a young male servant who seemed to despise the very breath he breathed. The maid gestured for them to drop their bags, then directed the servants to hang them. Ophelia made to protest that she was perfectly capable of lugging her things upstairs, but Seamus discreetly shushed her. She knew this was the way the world worked. Some people chose—or, in some horrible cases, were *forced*—to tend to others society deemed 'better' than them, but that didn't mean Ophelia had to like it.

"You may hang your mask here, Lady Ophelia. Tiril had it installed," Reija said with a slight curtsey, pointing to the wall opposite the coat rack.

Framed in gold was a polar bear head carved from glowing white crystal. Its mouth was open, ready to receive Ophelia's mask. Seamus coughed to cover his laugh as Ophelia awkwardly hung up her mask, her cheeks aglow with embarrassment. Why had Tiril gone to the trouble of commissioning such a thing?

Reija smiled contently, taking Ophelia's bags from where they lay. "Shall I run you a bath, Miss?"

"Oh, uh. . . N—no. Thank you, though," Ophelia mumbled, rocking back and forth on her heels. Though she had reservations about servitude, she ultimately didn't want to be a burden. If she wanted a bath, she could very well run her own.

Though she frowned, Reija nodded and went on her way, hoisting Ophelia's bags up the stairs. The young man tending to Seamus followed her, looking morose. The maid bowed, then went off to fetch Helgi and Tiril.

"Am I to bow, oh Winter Witch?" Seamus asked, shoulders shaking from a silent laugh.

Ophelia stood tall, hands folded neatly before her. "It wouldn't hurt."

Seamus snorted, rolling his eyes, making for the den. Ophelia didn't budge. Tilting her head ever so slightly, she arranged her face in what she hoped was a mildly annoyed look.

"You're not serious, are you?" Seamus asked, his laugh tinged with uncertainty.

"You know, there will be a day when I can justly have you jailed for your sarcasm," Ophelia said sweetly.

Seamus narrowed his eyes, obviously mulling that over. "I don't like you pompous, Witch."

Ophelia smiled, dropping the façade and skipping past him, her muddy skirt swishing back and forth like the tail of a happy dog. "Oh, but I do so love toying with you, Seamus."

"I suppose, in a way, I deserve it," Seamus sighed.

They settled into their seats, Seamus near the fire, warming his hands, Ophelia as far from the fire as she could get while still enjoying the comfort of a couch. Ivar, Sköll, and Maj-gun soon joined her, beyond happy she'd returned. Seamus wasted no time filling a plate with sweets of all flavors and colors. He even set aside a few chocolate-dipped biscuits for Ophelia, knowing she wasn't brave enough to graze on the confectioneries unless prompted to.

"You know, I never expected letters from Seamus, but you, Ophelia?" came Tiril, visibly distraught as she rounded the corner. "Oh, I figured we'd at least get *one* from you, my dear!"

Ophelia sunk in her seat, remembering her former promise. "Apologies, Tiril, the opportunity never arose. I'll do better next time."

Seamus scoffed.

Tiril took a cushion and hit him over the head with it. "What in the ever-darkening night sky did you say to Cathal, you blubbering oaf?!" she screeched.

"I didn't say a damn word!" Seamus snapped, standing, shielding his plate of sweets from Tiril's battering. You'd have thought that pillow was filled with glass, what with how he winced against her battering. "I was cordial!"

"Did you *see* the posters? Five hundred thousand coppers? Dammit, Seamus!"

"Would you stop with the pillow, woman?" Seamus said between mouthfuls of something covered in powdered sugar.

"He really did behave, Tiril. If anything, I'm to blame," Ophelia said sheepishly.

Tiril hit him with that velvet cushion as hard as she could. "Now you've got the Witch covering for you?"

Seamus gave Ophelia a bored look. "We'll get nowhere with this one. Makes her mind up and sticks to it, I'll tell you. The old bat's crazy." He crossed his eyes and stuck out his tongue, barely able to conceal his laugh.

Ophelia grimaced, covering her ears as Tiril began yelling vulgarities, each word accentuated by the soft *thud!* of that cushion against Seamus's arm. He just laughed, nearly choking on his plate of sweets. Maj-gun, who'd crawled onto her shoulders, seemed to roll her eyes. Ivar and Sköll seemed to be placing bets on how long this would last.

"Did I miss something important?" Helgi asked as he plopped down on the opposite side of the couch, closest to the fire.

"Just Seamus getting his ass kicked by a 'crazy old bat,'" Ophelia said, smirking. Tiril whipped her head around, eyes ablaze with fury. Ophelia sunk deeper into her seat, avoiding her gaze. "Sorry, Tiril."

"You're a bad influence!" Tiril spat, tossing the cushion aside and stomping off to stand before the fire.

"Why thank you," Seamus said.

"Oh, you—"

Helgi leaned forward, clearing his throat. "So, what have you brought us, Seamus? I expect good news, aye?"

Tiril scoffed.

Seamus sat his empty plate on the coffee table, dusting his hands off on his pants as he sat. "Well. . . We've got news, to say the least."

Seamus launched into a long-winded tale, recounting what had happened in their absence. Somewhere along the line, Tiril came to stand beside him, her irritation replaced with a motherly sort of concern. Ophelia listened intently, feeling as though she wasn't a part of the story even though she'd experienced everything firsthand. She felt oddly detached from the world, her eyelids heavy.

CHAPTER SEVENTY-THREE

Diry Paws and Furry Coat

Helgi and Tiril had listened intently, nodding along to Seamus's story, their faces darkening. Seamus recounted what Ophelia had mentioned about Arild and how he seemed to be a liaison for the Ulvemordere.

"To think what would've happened had that pirate not been there!" Tiril snapped, tossing the pillow aside, nearly landing it in the fire. "Stupid, stupid trolls! How can Cathal continue to side with those monsters?"

Seamus shrugged. "It's all just business to him."

"Well, it's wrong!" Tiril scoffed.

"Calm yourself," Helgi sighed, waving her over. "It'll do no good getting all worked up about it."

Tiril came to sit beside him, shaking her head. "Someone ought to."

After seeing what that baton could do, Seamus was of the same opinion. The Ulvemordere had reigned supreme on brute force alone, but now they were getting wiser. Something had shifted, and the tides of total world domination were in their favor.

When Seamus had been a part of their militia, there were whispers of prophecies to be fulfilled and secrets yet to be shared. For the most part, they'd just been enforcers. A thousand years spent in the shadows, doing as they please. It'd only been in the last three hundred years that they started crawling into the light. It'd been a long, slow takeover, but it'd worked. Hunting Witches and werewolves to near extinction, spreading fear, and upending lives. It was all coming to a head.

Seamus had never been one for prophecies, but the more it was brought up, the harder it was to ignore it. What if they were right? What if it were coming to fruition?

Helgi cleared his throat, shifting uncomfortably. "Did you see any sign of Egill after leaving Juvel Hjem? I'm not understanding his place in all this. While I realize he tempted your vengeance, what exactly did the Ulve wish to gain from sending him after you? Is there something you're not telling us?"

Seamus shrugged. "I've been pondering that as well. Jette didn't seem to expect me, at least, not really. I'm not sure how to describe it. She seemed surprised, yes, but not as though the possibility hadn't crossed her mind. I almost think Egill wanted me to do his dirty work. And no, Helgi, you oaf. I'm an open book."

Tiril weighed that. "Maybe. You don't think he was simply trying to trick you?"

"Egill doesn't do things solely for tricks," Seamus said with a shake of his head. "That isn't 'the Egill way,' so to speak."

"Or maybe Jette wasn't the real target?" Helgi offered. "Ophelia said he vanished, correct? Maybe he was after something else and used you two as a distraction."

"Could be. He was awfully insistent on me tagging along," Seamus sighed. "I find the whole thing strange. He is an odd one, I'll admit it, never really trusted the bloke, but. . ."

"This isn't like him, is it?" Tiril asked.

"No." Seamus turned his attention to the fire, reaching up to tug on his right earlobe.

A small but very loud part of him didn't believe Egill was really working with the Ulve. If he was conning anyone, he had to be conning *them*. Why, he had no idea. Egill had always been in it for the money, that was for sure. Sure, the pin-wing was a bitter fellow, but Seamus doubted he shared the Ulvemordere's ideals. Especially after they took his wings. There had to be more going on beneath the surface. Otherwise, Seamus feared things were about to go south real quick.

"What are you thinking?" Helgi had been staring at him, face blank but eyes full of fear.

Seamus just shrugged, kicking his feet up onto the coffee table. "He's playing a long con, I know it, but I haven't the foggiest why."

Helgi frowned, stroking his beard in thought. "I feel we're on the brink of war."

Seamus just rolled his eyes. "Haven't we been at war all this time? Something to the effect of a thousand years, or am I suddenly prophetic?"

"Well, yes, Seamus, but this is different. That war has been fought in the shadows. We'll wage this one in broad daylight," Tiril said proudly. "We'll have the people on our side, won't we?"

Seamus nodded. "That's the plan, aye pup?"

The three of them turned toward the wise young Witch, eager for her input, only to find her sound asleep. Soft snores filled the sudden silence. Seamus smiled to himself. Maj-gun was around her neck, Ivar in her lap, and Sköll had his head resting on her arm. It was quite an adorable sight, he had to admit.

"Is she all right, Seamus?" Tiril asked softly.

Seamus sighed heavily. "She's been taking the brunt of it all as of late. Scared the shit out of me during our little escapade in the mountains."

"What happened?"

"If I knew, I'd tell you."

Helgi frowned, crossing his arms tight. "Temperamental as a storm."

"Not really," Seamus smiled, standing. "She just has a lot to learn. Doesn't know when to call it quits—for better or worse."

Quietly, he came to kneel before her, patting Sköll's head. He blew in her face, trying to wake her without startling her. Ophelia blinked, looking around like she didn't know how they'd ended up here.

"A bed would be more comfortable," Seamus said softly.

Ophelia yawned, trying to rub the sleep from her eyes. "Agreed."

"Come on then, let's get you upstairs."

"Aren't we having a war room counsel?"

"Eh, you can sleep through it. These things are boring

anyway. You'd have more fun watching watercolors dry," Seamus mumbled, taking her by the hand and hoisting her off the couch.

Ivar and Sköll followed their two-legged friend and the despicable—by their standards—Seamus Norland up the stairs. The two of them waited patiently outside Ophelia's room, tails wagging happily. Ophelia yawned, fumbling with the door handle. Once inside her room, she staggered to the bed and flopped down upon it. Seamus came to tuck her in, scratching Sköll behind the ear as he settled in beside her. Maj-gun, by some miracle, had stayed nestled around her neck. Seamus had a funny feeling the drake liked her constant freezing nature.

Ophelia's sleepy eyes fluttered shut. "Thanks for taking care of me, papa," she said groggily. "Jeg elsker deg."

Seamus paused, hands holding the edge of the blanket, taken aback. It took him a moment to realize what she'd said. "I love you, too, pup," he whispered. "Get some good rest, okay?"

She mumbled something akin to an okay as he stood. Ivar settled in atop her chest, purring as loud as thunder.

"Take good care of her, all right?" he whispered, lingering in the doorway.

Ivar seemed to nod.

That was good enough for him, so Seamus took the stairs back down to Tiril and Helgi. A content smile played on his lips. Again, he saw a glimpse of the future. For a glimmering, fleeting second, they were in a cottage near a frozen lake, and all was right in the world. At that moment, he knew he could find it within himself to fight for that future. A future where a surly old wolf lives a quiet life with his daughter, the once and future Witch Queen of Snøbolig.

Now, *that* was worth believing in.

All right, maybe having a Queen for a daughter wouldn't necessarily make for a quiet life, but the vision in his head was better than what they'd dealt with so far.

Yes, from this moment on, he'd run toward that.

Tiril and Helgi were waiting for him at the bottom of the stairs, knowing looks on their faces.

"You're quite fond of her," Tiril said.

"I swear I remember you saying you hated children," Helgi added with a nod.

Seamus just shrugged. "She's my pup; what can I say?"

CHAPTER SEVENTY-FOUR

THEOLOGY, PROPHECIES, AND THE DESTRUCTION OF MAN

A gentle knock stirred Ophelia from her first peaceful dream in weeks. At first, she thought she imagined it, hoping she could fall back asleep. Yet, just as her eyes closed, another knock echoed throughout her room. Fighting the covers and Ivar to get off of her, she staggered to the door, yawning. There stood Tiril, still in her dressing gown, looking morose.

"May I bother you a moment?" she asked.

Ophelia nodded, gesturing for her to enter. "Is something the matter?"

Tiril only shook her head, edging for the stairs. "I'd like to show you something in the fernery."

Ophelia lingered in the doorway, watching as Ivar and Maj-gun titled their heads in confusion. Sköll was still asleep, none the wiser. Tiril gave her a reassuring nod, beckoning her forward. Sighing, Ophelia followed.

The fog in the fernery was heavier today, clinging to the floor, unwilling to move. Tiril followed the swirling stream, leading her beyond the statue of Fern to a part of the fernery hidden by lush greenery. Through the dense fronds was a golden archway resembling the ones in the house. Beneath it sat a pile of pillows. Tiril sat, patting one of the cushions so Ophelia would do the same.

"How are you, Ophelia, dear?" she asked once Ophelia had settled in beside her.

"I'm all right," Ophelia said, taking in her surroundings. "You?"

Tiril laughed to herself, shrugging. "I suppose I'm all right, too."

"Is this what you wanted to show me?"

"No," Tiril sighed. She gazed at Ophelia for quite some time, studying her. Ophelia felt herself shrink into the pillows, her cheeks reddening. "Try as we might, we haven't found the people you're looking for. I'm so sorry, my dear."

"Guess I shouldn't have gotten my hopes up," Ophelia sighed, clearing her throat to stop from crying. "At least I know S—"

"Ophelia," Tiril said, taking hold of her hands. "Do you know who he is? Who he was meant to be?"

"Seamus?" Ophelia asked, stiffening.

Tiril nodded, dropping her voice to a whisper. "Has he told you?"

"No, no, he hasn't."

Tiril dropped her hands, reaching into the mountain of pillows. After a minute of searching, she pulled out a book. It was bound in charcoal gray leather, scarcely bigger than her hand, thin as a graphite stick. On the front cover, embossed in silver, was a four-pointed star. Tiril opened it, flipping through the blackened pages. When she found the page she was looking for, she handed the book off.

The passage was in the old tongue and read:

Verily, verily, hast he traveled,
Guidance, forged by Northern Stars,
Verily, verily, look not to each other but to thine heavens,
Thine fall, brought unto thee by your own weapon,

Verily, verily, hast he been delivered,
Unto to ye, oh wicked brethren,
Verily, verily, the many are not one,
Thine time has come and gone,

Verily, verily, hast he left,
Soul, forged by thine Abyss,

Ophelia read the passage a few times, feeling as though she'd heard it somewhere before. She dragged her thumb across the page, racking her brain, coming up with nothing. In what book had she seen this?

"What is this?" she asked, closing the book and tracing the star on the cover with a shaking finger. Given the context clues, she knew what this was *meant* to be. But was it real?

"Helgi and I pride ourselves on procuring rare tomes. This is one of them," Tiril said, tapping it. "If you know where to look, you'll find secrets aren't as guarded as one would think."

"That didn't exactly answer my question," Ophelia said, attempting to return the book to her.

Tiril wouldn't take it, pushing it back to her. "Do you know of North Star?"

Ophelia nodded. "In the Celestial teachings, the Sun, Moon, and North Star were created as the anchors of the universe. They were responsible for life, death, and guidance, respectively. When our earth was created, they came to us in the form of animals. Rabbit, Bat, and—" Ophelia paused, looking up into Tiril's expectant face. "Wolf."

"The *First* Wolf," Tiril corrected.

Ophelia stood, shaking her head, clutching the tiny book to her chest. "W—What are you saying?"

"It is said the Ulvemordere killed the First Wolf and that when they did, the world was thrown out of balance," Tiril said casually, sinking further into the pillows. "With losing one of our anchors, what did we expect?"

"Egill said Seamus was meant to wear the pelt of the First Wolf," Ophelia said, suddenly feeling antsy. "That he'd not taken a pelt because one was set aside for him."

"Correct."

"So, Seamus was meant to be what? I'm confused," Ophelia said, turning to her. "Other than the King of Ulvemordere, I mean."

Tiril studied her for a moment, almost glaring at her.

"I've read many books in my time, Ophelia, same as you. I'm sure you know Witches are meant to carry with them the souls of their predecessors."

"I've heard as such," Ophelia said, beginning to pace.

Tiril cleared her throat a few times, muddling something over. Eventually, she sighed, turning to watch a glowing centipede crawl across the glass wall of the fernery.

Ophelia looked down at the book she held, opening to the first page. In a frilly font, it simply read 'The Guidance of North Star.' Against her better judgment, Ophelia let her eyes drift to where the statue of Fern lay hidden between emerald green fronds. What had she referred to Seamus as? A 'guiding light?'

"What does this have to do with him?" she thought aloud.

"The Ulvemordere have a pelt locked away on their compound, one they claim is the pelt of the First Wolf. According to Seamus, when he was born, it. . . reacted." Tiril slowly turned back to her, studying her face. Ophelia furrowed her eyebrows, halting her pacing. "The box it's locked in apparently began to shake, and guards reported growling from within."

"W—What are you saying? That Seamus is related to the First Wolf? To North Star? That the Ulvemordere found a way to *kill* a Spirit?" she asked, scoffing.

If it were true, the Spirits were in danger. Furthermore, if that were the case, she'd like to think Fern or Jonquil would've told her.

Tiril shook her head. "Do you believe Sigfreður's energy resides in you, thus transferring his magic?"

Knowing she was cornered, Ophelia only nodded.

"Then one may say it isn't impossible that the same thing happened to Seamus, that the First Wolf's energy resides in him," Tiril said, gesturing loosely to their surroundings. "Maybe *that* is why the pelt reacted to him."

"I'm not saying I don't believe you," Ophelia began. In actuality, she did believe it. More so than Tiril could ever imagine. "But how did you come to the conclusion that the Ulve's First Wolf is the Celestial Wolf? Or, North Star, I suppose."

"I didn't," Tiril laughed, "Helgi did. We found records from when Sigfreður ruled. Seemingly out of nowhere, he hired a cartographer, a werewolf named Ljot. We've only a few scrolls from the time, but Ljot was Sigfreður's closest confidant and advisor. Through her, your predecessor was able to rule in a way that earned him the moniker of Sigfreður, The Peaceful. It is said she knew things about their enemies, the world, and religion that a being at the time shouldn't have. That was why Sigfreður was such a threat to the Ulvemordere and other rulers."

"I've never heard of her," Ophelia said, unable to hide the accusatory tone of her words.

"We hadn't either. As far as I can tell, she was entirely erased from history. The Ulvemordere do not share the name of the First Wolf. They only state there was one. I'm not surprised on that account; it has always been their goal to dehumanize us. What better way than to take our names?"

Before Tiril had a chance to say anything else, Ophelia flipped to the back of the book, finding a signature and a paw print. The handwriting matched the title page and the passage she'd read. It was all made by the same being.

She wove the book before Tiril, giving her a questioning look. "This was Ljot's?"

Tiril nodded. "Appears to be."

"That doesn't mean Ljot was North Star," Ophelia said, raising a skeptical eyebrow.

"Maybe not, but I'll tell you this: in the days of old, Sigfreður's kingdom flourished. He truly was a friend to all, loving and kind, but he was young, too—a lot like you, Ophelia. Someone had to have been there to guide his decisions. He didn't have a council and didn't publicly list an advisor, so who was it? And if it *was* Ljot, why would he keep her hidden?"

"Because if she was a Spirit, she wasn't meant to interfere," Ophelia said.

Tiril nodded. "We could be entirely wrong—clinging to lies, even—but I would rather place my faith in the unknown than believe our world will never change. Høstlunden and Snøbolig have completely plateaued. We used to be pioneers of industry, and now? Nothing. The only beings allowed to make any sort of technological advancement are the Ulvemordere. They regulate everything from food to ideas to life. Life, Ophelia! In Sigfreður and Ljot's time, quite the opposite was true. There was peace, there was love, there was understanding.

There was creativity and a lust for knowledge. What changed? I'll tell you: the two people embodying these ideals were killed. Now, our countries are riddled with poverty, crime, and hatred. We were thrown out of balance, and I believe it is because Ljot, the first werewolf to be killed by Ulvemordere, was North Star."

Ophelia mulled this over, returning to sit beside her and sinking into the pillows. If a Winter Witch had returned after all this time, it wasn't impossible that North Star had as well. If, of course, Tiril and Helgi's theory was true. There was someone she could ask, but for the time being, there was still more she had to glean from Tiril.

"How much does Seamus know?" she asked, tapping Ljot's book.

"He knows the pelt called to him as a baby, knows he was meant to rule the Ulvem—"

"Tiril. . ." Alarm bells were ringing in Ophelia's mind. All of a sudden, everything was making sense. ". . . what happens when someone takes up a pelt?"

"How do you mean?"

"Well, if a werewolf had heightened abilities, say they were faster or stronger than their pack mates, would those traits transfer to the wearer?"

Tiril sat up, stiff as a board, nodding.

"What would've happened if Seamus had donned Ljot's pelt all those years ago when he was still human?"

"I'm assuming he would've had Ljot's abilities."

"Which means he would've been able to guide them toward victory, thus breaking Ljot's prophecy," Ophelia said, eyes wide with fright.

"Finicky Foxglove. . ." Tiril mumbled, taking the book from Ophelia's shaking hands. "They interpreted it wrong. If you're an Ulvemordere reading this, you'd assume the 'wretched beings' are magickind, no? They've twisted minds; you know they could've come to that conclusion."

Ophelia shivered, shaking her head. "So, either Seamus will be the Ulvemordere's downfall. . ."

"Or the reason they reign supreme," Tiril finished.

CHAPTER SEVENTY-FIVE

HOLLY

Ophelia had said her goodbyes to Tiril, then took off full speed, taking the lift out of Dødbyen. Now, she stood surrounded by trees, eyes shut, calling for an old friend.

"You're very loud," came Jonquil's voice. Ophelia opened her eyes to find him lying on his side, head propped up on his arm. "What is it?"

"I need passage to the Garden," Ophelia said. "Urgently."

Jonquil jumped jauntily to his feet, brushing himself off. "Is that all?"

"*Urgently*, Jonquil," Ophelia whisper-yelled.

He winked, then placed a gentle hand on her shoulder. Suddenly, the world began to melt away, the boughs above dripping onto the forest floor. Every color glowed bright as starlight, filling Ophelia's vision with flecks of rainbow reminiscent of crystal light. Beneath their feet, yellow daffodils sprung up from the ground as snow and mud turned to lush green grass. The trees continued to melt, pooling onto the ground, leaving behind flowers of all shapes and colors until a vibrant meadow stretched as far as the eye could see.

Where the cold Snøbolig forest had been, now lay Jonquil and his mother's patch of the fabled Garden. For miles, there were daffodils—yellow and white, representing each individual who'd devoted themselves to Narcissus or Jonquil. Beyond their flowers were others, the closest being peonies.

No matter how often Ophelia visited, this place always stole her breath away.

"Well, what's happened?" Jonquil asked, bending down

to a wilting flower. He ran his thumb across the petal, frowning. "Another?" he mumbled.

"I need to speak with someone," Ophelia said distractedly, turning away from the meadow.

Behind her was a forest, the likes of which Alle Årstider had never seen. Millions of multi-colored trees stood tall and unmoving, concealing within them the home and birthplace of every Spirit. From where she stood, Ophelia could make out torchlight resonating off the hidden city. The sight filled her with such warmth. This place had always been home to her.

"Who?" Jonquil asked, kneeling.

"Someone."

"Why?"

"Because."

Jonquil looked up at her, frowning. "Because *why*?"

"Because," Ophelia said with a stamp of her foot. "It's not important."

"If you say so, Galanthus. . ."

Ophelia sighed heavily, then picked up her skirts and wove between daffodils as carefully as possible. The last thing she needed was to step on one of the fragile flowers, inadvertently crushing the hopes and dreams of an unsuspecting artist. Or worse yet, accidentally destroy a fated love. Oh, Narcissus would surely have her head on a platter for that!

When she reached the forest's edge, she spotted Spruce dangling high above, waving down at her. Ophelia smiled up at him, wondering what on earth he was doing, then continued. A small path cut through the trees, leading toward a city few had even dreamed of. Treehouses connected by precarious bridges crowned a cluster of tall sequoias. A few Spirits went about their days, carrying armfuls of bulbs, seeds, or starts, heading off to plant them in their garden patches. Weaving between the trees was a river where lily pads and lotus flowers floated aimlessly. Distracted by the flowers, a white tortoise with a lovely pink shell strolled along the riverbank.

"Taking inventory, Lotus?" Ophelia called.

The tortoise slowly looked up, nodding. Lotus was one of only a few Spirits who chose to stay in her animal form despite human nature's ease. The other Spirits thought her quite odd because of it. Ophelia just thought her strange in general.

"Good morning, Ophelia!" came a familiar voice. The love she felt from nearly every Spirit in the Garden was always so baffling.

Ophelia looked up just in time to see a woman with long purple hair jump from a bridge. The edges of her dress curled and folded around her until a bright purple butterfly took her place.

"Good morning, Orchid; how are you today?" Ophelia asked, holding out her hand. The butterfly landed on her outstretched palm, fluttering its wings in excitement. "Glad to hear it."

The butterfly took off, encircling her momentarily before she flew toward the meadow. Of all the creatures that could encapsulate the Spirit of Beauty, Ophelia had always thought a butterfly was a perfect fit.

Taking her time—both out of anxiety and simple mortal joy—she made her way toward two trees that grew together to form an arch. She passed through, the remaining patches of flowers slowly trickling out until only bushes and ferns were strewn between the densely packed trees. Who she wanted to visit often spent his time here. He didn't care much for communing with the other Spirits. Why, he'd never told her.

Sure enough, she found a man in a sunlit patch of the magical forest, his long scarlet cloak trailing behind him. The edges of it were tattered, cut by the spiky leaves of the holly bushes he waded through. The bushes tilted toward him as he walked, grappling for his attention. Careful not to snag her skirts on the bushes, Ophelia hurried to keep up with him. There wasn't enough room to walk beside him, forcing her to follow as close as she could without stepping on his cloak. Ophelia smiled. The edges of it were embroidered with holly leaves and berries, the metallic threads catching the sunlight.

"I'll admit, I'm surprised you've come to me," the man said. Ophelia did not answer. She only followed. "Then again, you have a tendency to surprise us."

Holly—the once great Sigfreður, The Peaceful—slowed to a stop, smiling over his shoulder at her. He twisted to face her, scarlet eyes aglow with delight. He may have given up his Witchdom a thousand years ago, but he still had the regality of a King. Even the crown of holly leaves digging into his forehead was oddly noble.

Holly considered her, lingering on the dark circles beneath her eyes. "Is there something I can help you with, Galanthus?"

"I've come seeking your council, Holly," Ophelia said with a curtsey. "Have you a moment?"

Holly smiled down at his shoes, giving a small laugh. "Ever formal, Galanthus, dear. We've been over this, haven't we? We're equals, you and I."

That may be true, but Ophelia wasn't keen on disrespecting the Spirits. Even ones she shared blood with by technicality.

"May we speak?" she asked, clasping her hands behind her back.

He nodded, beckoning her forward. The holly bushes around them parted, crawling out of the ground and scurrying away on feet made of roots. Sweeping his cape behind him, Holly sat on the ground, removing his crown. Ophelia sat before him, unflinching as he placed it atop her head. The sharp leaves poked painfully into her skin, but she did her best to ignore it. Spirits forbid she show discomfort in his presence.

"What have you to say?" he asked, placing his hands neatly in his lap.

It was always strange looking at him. Despite his long silver hair and piercing red eyes, they looked alike. At least, Ophelia thought they did. Same nose, same chin, same sadness in the tilt of their smiles. Once upon a time, he'd even had her same ebony hair and silver eyes. Part of her was glad his appearance had changed in death. If he felt the same, he'd never mentioned it.

"What was it like when you were King of Snøbolig?" she asked softly, averting her eyes.

He sighed heavily. Holly was never one to speak without thinking. The silences surrounding him were filled with wisdom that could rival even Celosia.

"Might you be more specific, Galanthus?" he asked. "There's so much to tell."

Ophelia cleared her throat, adjusting the holly crown. "Ljot," she said simply.

Holly didn't seem surprised she'd said the name, but he did, however, frown. "Who has been filling your mind with such stories?”

“Was she the Wolf?”

Holly squeezed his eyes shut, turning his face away from her. “Ljot, like you and I, had many names.”

“What happened to her?”

“Nothing you don’t already suspect, I assure you.”

Ophelia nodded to herself, sitting in awkward silence for a moment. Eventually, she continued to speak her mind despite knowing the being beside her could smite her at will. Holly would never do such a thing, but the fact he was capable set her on edge.

“Did the Ulvemordere kill her?” she asked softly.

“One of them did, yes,” Holly said, turning back to her, wiping a tear from his cheek. “They found a way to strip her magic, turning her mortal. I’ve not a clue how.”

“I’m so sorry, Holly. You two were close?”

A sorrowful smile lit up his face. “She was like a mother to me, Galanthus.”

Ophelia shivered, a great sadness washing over her. Was this how hers and Seamus’s story would end, too? Would they lose each other? Oh, how she wished Tiril wouldn’t have said anything.

“There’s something else on your mind?” Holly asked.

Ophelia nodded, glad to change the subject. “When you were presented to the Witchdom, what happened? How were you received?”

“In my younger years, I was a novelty at best—something beings would willingly pay fare to see. As time went on, I believe the folk came to accept that I was to be their King. It helped that I was born into nobility, of course. That always makes things a touch easier,” he laughed. “Why do you ask?”

Ophelia’s eyes flicked up to his. That piercing scarlet was incredibly hard to look at. His eyes weren’t cruel like that of the Ulvemordere General’s, but they were still filled with vigor never to be trifled with.

“There’ve been people who’ve forced my hand,” she said carefully. “I don’t think I can stay hidden anymore.”

“You want to reveal your Marks to the world?”

“More than my Marks,” Ophelia sighed. “The Marks are

one thing, the title too, but it's the—"

"The hope you may bring?" Holly finished.

She nodded thoughtfully. "Everyone keeps telling me I can be a symbol, and I do want that, of course! I want to be as you were! But I'm afraid. I know. . . I know it's selfish."

Holly reached forward and took back his crown. He gazed sadly at it before returning it to his head, casting the same look upon her.

"I don't want you to be as I was," he said, "In many ways, I was foolish. I tried very hard to play the diplomatic pacifist, and look where it got me." He clicked his tongue, shaking his head. "Blessed Amaranth, don't get me wrong. I'm thankful for the role I play now and for the beings choosing to uphold the values of Holly, but. . . Had I done things differently, I'd have made a better world for you to be born into. And. . . Ljot wouldn't be dead. I'd still have my North Star."

"You mustn't blame yourself for that. You couldn't have known what was to come," Ophelia said, giving him a reassuring nudge with her knee.

"Ahh, yes, but that is the guilt of those who come before. We're meant to change things for the better, not leave the world in ruins for the coming generations." His eyes drooped, his sad smile twitching into a frown. "I, of course, must grapple with this most of all. It was my destruction that ushered in a thousand years of bloodshed."

The history books said the same thing, but Ophelia knew better than to attribute such things to him. He was born in an era of jealousy between the Witchdoms. He'd come from nobility, and yes, he'd had Ljot, but even the wisest advisors couldn't prepare someone for such unforeseen circumstances. They'd all lived in an idyllic time, unaware of the coming dangers. He'd been one of the youngest rulers at the time. The only Witch in Snøbolig. He'd done his best, and yes, he'd made mistakes, but blaming oneself only went so far. Snøbolig tried to live in peace, but that didn't mean there wasn't trouble. He may have been a Witch, but that didn't mean he'd had a coven. Seeds of jealousy had been planted long before he was born. Unfortunately, he'd just taken the brunt of it all.

Despite knowing all this, Ophelia asked, "How do I be better? How do I prevent myself from making the same mistakes?"

Holly leaned very close, winking at her. "You know why we call you Galanthus, don't you?"

"Galanthus nivalis is the scientific name for snowdrop. Or so the alchemists say," Ophelia said with a shrug.

"Do you know what snowdrops represent?"

Ophelia fiddled with a loose thread on her sleeve, nodding. Holly took her hands, giving her a playfully disappointed look.

"They represent hope," he said, "Hope is both cautionary and full of trust in things it cannot see. It is awe-inspiring, yet timid. Powerful, yes, but rare." He shook and squeezed her hands, ignoring how her head dipped down in embarrassment. "Hope is surprising if you ask me. And as I've said before, you always surprise me, my dear Ophelia."

"I don't feel very hopeful sometimes," Ophelia sighed.

Holly lifted her chin, smiling, gazing deep into a set of eyes that once belonged to him. "The Wolf kills the Deer. That's how my story ended—how it will always end. So it's a good job we made you a Polar Bear, then, hmm?"

With that, he kissed her forehead and stood, dusting off his cloak. He gave a deep bow, then drifted off to tend to his portion of the Garden and the many berries and leaves representing his followers.

Ophelia stood, brushing herself off. "Goodbye, Holly," she whispered, hiking up her skirts, spinning until she came face to face with— "Hemlock?" she asked, surprised.

Lounging lazily against a tree mere inches away was a deceptively young-looking man. From beneath the shadow of a weathered, moss-covered top hat covered, two glowing white eyes slit like a snake's scrutinized her. At the base of the top hat were bushels of hemlock blooms that cascaded over the brim like a veil. The man's lips curved into a frown as he pushed off the tree, his tattered overcoat clinging to the bark.

"Hello, Galanthusss," he whispered, his voice honey-smooth, almost intoxicating. Ophelia's heart was beating as fast as pouring rain. He flicked out his thin, forked tongue, tasting her scent as he circled her. "What bringsss you here?"

"A friendly visit," Ophelia said, stepping away from him.

Hemlock, Spirit of Fear, smiled toothily. "To Holly?"

Ophelia only nodded.

"Why might you be looking for him? Isssn't Jonquil whom you pessster?" he asked, shoving his hands into his pockets. One of his fingers poked through a hole.

"Holly and I are friends, too," Ophelia said, straightening in an attempt to hide her fear.

Hemlock could taste it, she knew. Was it similar to how Seamus could smell her emotions? What a strange notion. Now that she thought about it, such a thing seemed incredibly intrusive.

Hemlock sauntered up to her, slit eyes pulsing. "What did you asssk him? Did he anssswer your quessstionsss?" he whispered, leaning in close. His tongue brushed the tip of Ophelia's nose, sending shivers up her spine.

"Hemlock," came another voice. Ophelia glanced over her shoulder, finding Fern standing in a patch of sunlight a few feet away. "That is enough."

Slowly, Hemlock stood straighter, frowning. "Mind your mannersss, Fern. You're interrupting."

"Ophelia," Fern hissed, reaching a hand toward her.

Terrified as a child lost in unfamiliar woods, Ophelia rushed to Fern's side, hiding behind her. Hemlock always set her on edge. It was the human part of her, the part that feared heights, loud noises, and people she didn't know. The part that wasn't always welcome in the Garden. Most of the Spirits treated her well enough, but not everyone. Some felt both her presence and existence were blasphemous.

"You have better things to do than terrorize her," Fern snapped. "I'd suggest you get back to your duties."

Hemlock's long, forked tongue whipped back and forth in anger, but thankfully, he kept his thoughts to himself. Fern held out an arm, blocking him from getting any closer to Ophelia.

He hissed at them, then whispered, "Watch your back, ssseedling. There are ssscarier thingsss than I in your future. . ."

The sound of his laugh bounced off the trees, causing a whimper of fright to bubble up Ophelia's throat. She hated the way he made her feel, but it wasn't exactly her fault. Hemlock had always used and abused his abilities, reveling in torturing souls unfortunate enough to stumble upon tall cliffs, dark halls, and creepy crawlies.

"Why have you come here?" Fern asked, rounding on her. Her voice shook with anger barely held back.

Ophelia hugged herself tight, feeling her body deflate. "I came to speak with Holly," she mumbled, cowering under Fern's fierce gaze.

"You should not have," Fern whispered. For a moment, her eyes went glassy, then—like a bolt of lightning flashing across a pitch-black sky—she sprang to life. "Leave this instant," she said, voice full of fear. "Find Jonquil and have him take you back to the mortal realm."

"What's wrong?" Ophelia asked.

Fern looked down, green eyes pulsing with magic so potent it made Ophelia physically sick. "Until further notice, I do not want you in the Garden."

"But—"

"Leave, Ophelia," Fern whispered. "Please."

CHAPTER SEVENTY-SIX

TENDERNESS

"You're up early," Seamus yawned, nodding to Tiril as he stepped past her, making for the dining room. "Ophelia out with Reija?"

"Yes, she stepped out," Tiril mumbled. Sighing, she pointed to the den. "We need to talk."

Seamus grimaced. What had he done now? Off the top of his head, he could think of a handful of reasons she'd want to lecture him—the absence of letters while they'd been gone being one.

"Breakfast first?" he asked.

She pursed her lips, making a dramatic sweeping motion with her arm, gesturing for him to follow. Seamus groaned, taking exaggeratedly slow steps. Tiril sat him near the fire, gazing deep into his hazel eyes.

"You're doing a good job of watching over her," she said wistfully.

Seamus just shrugged, not keen on early-morning small talk. Twiddling his thumbs, he gazed around the den like a deer caught in a hunter's sights.

"Seamus. . ." Tiril mumbled, following his gaze, ignoring how his shoulders sagged. "May I ask you something?"

"If I say no, you'll have me flogged," he laughed, begrudgingly turning back to her. Tiril gave him a bored look, lips pulled into a thin pout. Seamus furrowed his eyebrows, stiffening. Something was wrong.

"Would you mind terribly if I thought of her as my granddaughter?" Tiril asked, her enormous pale blue eyes full of anticipation.

"You'll have to ask her," Seamus said, unable to hide the worry from his voice.

"I just wanted to ask. You've finally found something belonging solely to you. I wouldn't want to take that from you," she shrugged.

"Ophelia doesn't 'belong' to me, Tiril."

"You know what I mean, Seamus, dear."

Seamus scratched the back of his neck, searching her eyes for what was troubling her. "I suppose if you're asking my permission, the answer is yes. But again, you'll have to ask her."

"Thank you, I will," Tiril smiled. "You're about the closest thing I've ever had to a son, so I feel somewhat responsible for the two of you."

That wasn't news to him. Tiril had always been overly concerned about him, although he didn't exactly mind. The way she cared for him may very well be the reason he cared for Ophelia. However, up until now, it'd always been an unspoken sort of thing.

"Tiril, has something happened?" Seamus asked softly.

Though she smiled, there was sadness in her eyes. "No, not at all. I just worry."

"If anything happened, you know you can talk to me, right?"

"I know, Seamus."

They sat shoulder to shoulder for a while, each occupied by the décor, books, and tapestries surrounding them. Seamus suddenly loved this makeshift library and the notion that he had somewhere to return to should he grow weary.

Tiril shifted to look him directly in the eye. "I do so hope you take care of yourself in the way you take care of Ophelia."

Seamus nodded his agreement. "For her sake, I'll try." His cheeks reddened. "Tiril, what's really on your mind?" he asked softly, turning to sit cross-legged beside her. "Talk to me, please."

For a moment, she just stared at him, searching every soft wrinkle, every hair, every speck of dirt on his face, for. . . something. It wasn't scrutiny in her eyes. It was. . . sorrow?

No, not really. Fear? Maybe. Her eyelids drooped, and that pout deepened, but still, it was like trying to read a blank page.

"I wish you could see your potential the way I can," she said, stroking his face with the back of her hand.

"You told Ophelia of the prophecy nonsense, didn't you?" Seamus sighed.

"Someone had to."

Seamus laid his head on the back of the couch, shutting his eyes. Tiril was the only motherly figure he'd ever had. He hated disobeying and upsetting her. Still, she had her beliefs, and he had his own.

"I don't believe in coincidences, my dear. There is too much happenstance for me to turn a blind eye," she whispered.

"I'm not a hero, Tiril," Seamus replied, refusing to open his eyes.

Tiril pushed a strand of hair behind his ear, her touch leaving behind traces of sleepiness. "To Ophelia, you are," she said.

"I keep messing things up," he said groggily. "Heroes don't do that."

"Your mistakes do not define you, Seamus, believe me."

CHAPTER SEVENTY-SEVEN

KRINGLE

Ophelia stood frozen as the lift settled to a stop at Dødbyen's ground level. All she could do was wring her hands and worry. How that differed from her normal day-to-day state, she didn't know. Yet, this worry was different. Her interaction with Hemlock and Fern had left her with a dull ache.

She shouldn't have left the Garden. She should have demanded answers. Something was happening just out of earshot. Jonquil knew it, too, or he wouldn't have whisked her out of there so quickly. The second he saw her face, he'd fallen dead quiet. Such a thing was almost unheard of.

"Miss?" asked the man holding open the door to the lift.

Ophelia felt her cheeks redden. She gave an awkward bow, then hurried toward the mansion.

Was it her imagination, or were a million eyes suddenly trained on her? For a split second, she thought she'd forgotten to replace her mask. Over the years, she'd grown so used to the weight of it on her nose that she forgot it was there. Same with the black mesh on the eyeholes. The mesh altered her vision, making everything a little duller, a little hazier.

Sometimes, that's how she felt after talking with the Spirits. Hemlock *especially* made her feel this way.

A great feeling of empty loneliness washed over her as she walked down the rainbow-lit tunnel to the Kirkeby mansion. Distorted, multi-colored versions of her reflection stared back at her. Even her mask looked sad.

What was she? She wasn't human, not really. She wasn't a Spirit, though that was her destiny. She was a Witch;

she knew that. But what did that mean? Where did she belong? As far as she knew, she was the last of her kind. She was the sole survivor.

Peering around the bend, she made sure no one was coming. Confirming she was alone, she slowly untied her mask, gazing at her reflection. What had she expected to see? All she saw was the same old silver eyes and stark blue Witch Marks. Nothing had changed.

Had she changed at all? For a moment, she thought she had. She'd felt braver, stronger, wiser.

And yet, the second she saw Hemlock, all that disappeared.

Here she was, feeling lost and terrified again. Not even her mask had brought comfort. Usually, hiding behind it made her feel invisible. She'd always loved being invisible. She'd *craved* being invisible. Now, seeing the Polar Bear staring back at her, a great, bubbling dread began rumbling in her stomach.

"I don't know who I am," Ophelia whispered, her words echoing off the glowing crystals surrounding her. "Why don't I know who I am?"

Hemlock. These feelings had to be caused by him. The aftermath of his presence always left her weepy. Reminding herself of this made her sudden tears insignificant.

Unfortunately, that didn't change the fact that Hemlock only toyed with feelings that were already there.

Sometimes, Ophelia saw herself as an empty vessel. Everyone she'd ever met had poured their own desires and purposes into her. Still, there must be a hole somewhere near her feet, for it all leaked out sooner or later. Just like Hemlock had turned her whimsy into fear, everything she wanted out of life seemed to come from someone else.

That bubbling dread was turning to woe.

Shaking her head in frustration, she hurried to the mansion, ignoring the disappointment in the faces staring back at her.

The young serving boy met her at the door. He took her mask, hanging it on its hook, making Ophelia frown. Ignoring his questioning look, she went off to find Seamus, hoping he'd have some insight into why she was suddenly feeling so. . . hopeless.

"Are you all right, Lady Ophelia?" Reija asked, appearing from the dining room. Her eyebrows were knit deep over her purple eyes, her lips set in a contemptuous scowl.

"Oh—Oh, yes, I'm okay," Ophelia said, wiping a stray tear.

Reija's lips twitched. "Would you like me to take your coat and shawl?"

The thought of removing her outer layers made Ophelia feel incredibly vulnerable. This coat, with all its rips, tears, holes, and stains, had been with her through thick and thin, serving as armor, in a sense. Without it, she felt exposed. This shawl, with its tattered edges and loose threads, was a safety blanket. Without it, everything lurking just out of sight could snatch her up and drag her into the shadows.

"No, I'm all right," Ophelia sighed.

"Hmm. . . Yes, it's a bit cold in here, isn't it? I'll have Matei stoke the fire," Reija said thoughtfully.

Ophelia nodded to herself, gazing into the den where Seamus lay sprawled out on the couch with Sköll. Gentle snores drifted off of him, mixing with the light pop and crackle of the fireplace. He'd been sleeping in and dozing off quite a bit lately.

Reija cleared her throat, drawing Ophelia's attention. She hadn't realized Reija was still standing there. "Seamus tells me you're an excellent baker," she said, attempting a smile. "I was just about to head to the kitchen. Would you like to join me?"

Ophelia inhaled deeply, knowing Reija could sense her unease and was only trying to help mitigate a situation she could never understand. For that, she relented, bending to untie her boots.

"I'd like that very much, Reija, thank you."

Reija, pleased she'd gotten through to the finicky Witch, led her to the kitchen.

White wood paneling and copper cookware took up most of the walls, accompanied by the many jars of grains and flour lining long, tall shelves. Dried bundles of herbs hung from the ceiling, filling the room with a pleasant, earthy scent. A few bowls and cutlery sat on the enormous table in the center of the room.

"What would you like to bake, my lady?" Reija asked, standing beside the table, gazing around at the many ingredients Ophelia could pick from.

"I usually just make kringle," Ophelia said sheepishly.

"Shall we make that then?"

Ophelia nodded, reaching for jars labeled 'flour' and 'salt,' and then handed them off to Reija, who seemed rather smug. If basking in the familiarity of baking brightened her mood, then she guessed Reija would want her to bake forevermore.

"What sort of fruit or nuts would you like to use?" Reija asked, gesturing toward a door Ophelia hadn't noticed before.

"Oh, whatever is on hand," she shrugged.

Reija almost looked as though she pitied her. "Name any ingredient, and I assure you, we have it."

"Anything?"

Reija nodded, that smug smile growing tenfold.

"Pistachios."

Reija pointed to one of the shelves, bowed, and disappeared behind the door. A wave of cold swept through the kitchen. Ophelia suspected that door led to the cellar and wondered what sort of ingredients lay hidden below.

Ophelia sighed contently, pouring flour into a large mixing bowl. Reija returned shortly, carrying a small basket of eggs, a pitcher of water, and a bowl of pistachios.

"Did you have pistachios in The Wilds?" Reija asked as she cut thin slices of butter. "I wouldn't have thought so."

Ophelia shrugged, working the flour, butter, and water together. At the stove, began bringing some butter and a bit of water to a boil. "Produce shipments were few and far between. My. . . *guardian*. . . however, once brought back pistachios. They're known for their medicinal properties, and he was a healer, so y'know. . ." she explained absentmindedly. That was one of the few good memories she associated with Lochlan, though she hated giving the man any credit. "This is normal for you then?"

"Noomi, Tiril's handmaiden, used to own a bakery in her prime. Tiril ensures the pantries are well stocked so she may dabble whenever she pleases. That's one thing I love about Tiril. She makes sure we're happy, no matter the cost," Reija said, smiling to herself, pointing to her with a spoon. "If I were a wolf, I'd be glad to have her as my alpha."

Ophelia nodded but added, "Isn't she anyway? You're part of her family, no? That means you are part of her pack."

"Not necessarily," Reija corrected, "If I'm to be part of anyone's pack, I shall be part of yours and Seamus's."

That feeling of unease began to slide off Ophelia's bones. "I suppose you're right."

As Reija busied herself with making the pastry, Ophelia pressed the base dough flat into a baking sheet and set it aside. Turning to the shelves, she began chopping the pistachios.

"Are those pistachios?" Seamus yawned, stretching as he walked into the kitchen. He attempted to pluck one from the bowl, but Reija was too quick. She slid it away, frowning. "You've more than enough to share," Seamus mumbled.

"God morgen, Seamus," Ophelia said, taking a good look at him, trying to surmise why he'd been so drowsy as of late. Since the last full moon, she'd kept a quiet tally of the phases at the back of her book. The new moon had been a few days back, coinciding with their stay in Onding. If Ophelia had to guess, its effects still lingered.

"Phee," he said, nodding to her. "Where'd you disappear to?"

"I. . . just wanted to explore. I hope I didn't worry you," Ophelia said, avoiding his gaze.

"That shipped sailed months ago, pup," he sighed, eyes still on the bowl of pistachios. "How much longer on that kringle?"

"It isn't even in the oven yet," Ophelia laughed.

"Do you always eat your hosts out of house and home?" Reija asked, taking the dough and remaining cold ingredients and heading for the cellar.

"Only the ones I like," Seamus laughed.

Reija rolled her eyes, closing the door a little gruffly behind her.

"So. . ." Seamus said, hopping up on the table, crossing his arms tight. "Are you going to ask?"

Ophelia furrowed her eyebrows, tilting her head to the

side. "Ask what?"

"Tiril told me she filled you in on the whole 'I may be a reincarnated Spirit' thing," he shrugged.

"Oh, yes, *that*," Ophelia mumbled, heart doing somersaults. She turned away, busying herself with tidying up the table, never one to leave someone else's home a mess. "An interesting turn of events, no?"

"You believe it then?" he asked.

Ophelia rolled her eyes. As if he didn't already suspect that. "I do, but do you?"

"Does it matter?"

"Your opinion of yourself always matters," Ophelia laughed.

"Except in regards to the Moon?"

"Yes, or the Sun."

Seamus weighed this, staring at his feet. His toes peeked through the ratty old socks he'd purchased from Ute. That day seemed eons away. Ophelia suddenly glanced down at her shawl, realizing Ute would be disgusted with them. How dare they let her goods fall into such disrepair.

"Reija will mend them again," Seamus said, following her gaze.

"I don't want to trouble her any more than I already have," Ophelia sighed, hopping up onto the table next to him. "It makes me feel. . . icky."

"I suppose I can relate. Everyone believing me to be some savior from on high makes me feel rather 'icky' too," he laughed. "I mean, me, of all people! Can you imagine how horribly I could screw everything up?"

"I can't, actually," Ophelia said, looking sidelong at him. "I prefer to think you'd do a lot of good."

Seamus's face fell, his shoulders sagging. "I doubt that."

"Agree to disagree."

He smiled at that, nudging her with his elbow. "Sorry I didn't tell you about it. I don't find it important nor easy to talk about."

Ophelia shrugged. "I understand. There are things about me you don't know either, things I can't find the words for."

In her time at Seamus's side, she'd learned he'd come to her when he was ready. Yes, he'd kept things from her, but she knew his secrecy had come from a place of love. Anger over these things was easy. Finding grace within yourself was difficult. A part of her was hurt, but at the same time, she'd kept quite a bit from him, too. He may be a reincarnated Spirit, but she'd talked with Spirits all her life. How could she be cross with him if she couldn't be honest herself?

It suddenly hit her that she would have to tell him about the Garden, about Jonquil and Fern—all of them. She might be able to allot Seamus grace, but he was quick to anger. She knew he'd understand *why* she hadn't told him, but the anger would still be there. All he'd see were the dangers of not knowing. Especially since that meant he really *was* a reincarnated Spirit. If she told him, there'd be undeniable proof via Holly's words.

Maybe she'd keep quiet until they were on the road again. Better to break the news when she could easily run from a seething wolf ready to throw her over his shoulder and lock her in her room.

Though she was worried about how he'd react, being able to share the unknown with Seamus sent her heart aflutter. For so long, she'd navigated two vastly different worlds alone. Now, she had someone beside her, equally as confused. They were two mortal Spirits, overcome with duties they'd never asked for. The weight was heavy, but sharing the load made the burden at least a bit easier.

Reija came bounding back up the stairs, looking a little pale. "I'm so sick of spiders!" she spat. Dusting herself off, she rushed past them, muttering about how badly she wanted to leave Dødbyen.

Ophelia, on the other hand, was glad to stay as long as they could. This place was becoming home somehow, though she didn't necessarily see herself living here full-time. Plus, she knew Seamus would be happier near a lake or river. Ophelia, too, would rather be amongst trees than rock, but beggars were rarely choosers.

"What are you smiling about?" Seamus yawned.

"Oh, nothing," Ophelia laughed.

Sitting there, thinking of navigating their ever-weird lives together, made her oh-so-happy. One day, they'd have a house like this where they could rest their weary bones.

How strange.

In the company of those she trusted, Hemlock's grasp on her mind had vanished. The sickening, swirling fear she'd had was gone.

Ophelia was suddenly reminded of who she was.

She was Ophelia Norland, daughter to the one and only Seamus Norland. Spirits, reincarnation, prophecies—what have you—none of it mattered.

Sometimes, a family was a surly old wolf and a finicky Witch.

Sometimes, family was all that mattered.

Hurried footsteps echoed in through the hall, startling Seamus. Tiril blew into the kitchen, frenzied, holding a slightly crumpled piece of parchment. "Ophelia," she began, going pale. "You've got a letter."

CHAPTER SEVENTY-EIGHT

WE SCREWED THAT UP, DIDN'T WE?

Quickly, Tiril led them to the map room, calling for Reija and Helgi and passing the letter to Ophelia. There, the five of them huddled around the table, doing their best to ignore each other's worried looks.

The letter was addressed to 'Lady Ophelia Av'Skogen, Vinterheks' and bore the Ulvemordere crest. The fact that the letter wasn't addressed to 'Lady Ophelia *Norland*, Vinterheks' somehow hurt more than seeing the wolf skull and candle.

"Dearest Vinterheks," Ophelia read aloud, already tasting bile. "So sorry I missed you at Juvel Hjem. Mr. Sandvik informs me that you and your little army plan to make a move on me and mine. If you wished to start a war, all you had to do was ask. In compliance with the old ways, I invite you to my townhouse in Veil, Høstlunden. There, we may speak at length on your treason, treachery, and all-around stupidity. I believe this meeting to be in your best interest. I hope we may find a resolution to these matters. Meet me before the next full moon. Best wishes, Sir Arild Melhus, Acting Ulvemordere General. P.S. Tell Seamus hello for me."

"He would've wasted less ink had he simply asked you to view the elaborate trap he'd built," Reija scoffed, yanking the letter from Ophelia's trembling hands.

"Arild has always been one for theatrics," Seamus sighed, arms crossed tight over his chest. Ophelia may be unable to smell his emotions, but she could tell he was boiling with anger. "He knows where we are, and he knows what you want. He's just making sure we're aware of that."

“And I’m guessing if we don’t show up, Dødbyen’s next on the hit list?” Helgi asked.

Seamus nodded, pinching the bridge of his nose. “Wonderful.”

“But you know him, yes? That gives us at least a mild advantage,” Reija said, trying to sound hopeful.

“Arild was under my direct command when I was part of the Ulvemordere. He was transferred to my unit in hopes I could stamp out his unpredictable demeanor. He’s always been a wildcard,” Seamus replied, killing the light in her eyes. “If you think I’m stubborn, you better thank your lucky Stars you’ve never met *him*.”

Tiril sank shakily into one of the seats around the map table, looking like she was about to fall apart. Ophelia could only imagine what was going through her head.

“Veil isn’t far from Juvel Hjem’s Høstlunden entrance,” Helgi said, gazing at the maps. “He’ll have the trolls at his beck and call.”

“He has them here, too. Why wouldn’t he just attack us here and now?” Ophelia asked.

“What Dødbyen lacks in security measures, we make up for in criminals. There are too many beings here—magickind and human—that would put up a fight. It makes more sense to draw us out instead of attacking here,” Helgi sighed, holding his head in his hands. “Meeting us here would be their last resort.”

“So why not force their hand?” Reija asked, taking the words right out of Ophelia’s mouth. There was a fierce light in her eyes. If Reija had never once fought a battle, you’d never know.

“The people will be able to defend themselves, giving us time to escape, but Dødbyen would crumble. Literally,” Seamus said, grimacing. “I doubt that’s the outcome we want.”

“If you go to Veil, you’ll be sitting ducks,” Tiril whispered, staring at the tops of her shoes. “I don’t like this.”

“Me either,” Seamus grumbled, shaking his head.

Helgi suddenly looked up, snapping his fingers. “If he wants a fight, we’ll give him a fight. We’ve plenty of allies in Høstlunden. If we act fast enough, we can get the word out.”

“That’s a lot of letters to send in a very short amount

of time," Tiril said, rubbing her temples. "We've only got a few weeks to prepare."

Ophelia looked around at all the wooden pieces littering Tiril's maps, her heart heavy. "If we drag the rebellion into this, won't we give Arild exactly what he wants?"

Seamus nodded, inhaling deeply. "I've got a bad feeling this was the plan from the beginning."

"How do you mean?" Helgi and Tiril asked.

"It all boils down to Egill. He knows too much. He wanted us to have those maps, I'm sure of it. I'm one of only a few who can read Jette's brail," Seamus sighed, looking to Helgi. "Have you heard back from the groups checking those locations?"

Helgi looked away, sagging in his seat. "One problem at a time."

"If we don't warn the others now, we'll just cause more problems in the future. Pardon me, Mr. Norland, but the gathering beneath the Hunters Moon isn't exactly a secret, either," Reija scoffed.

"My point exactly," Seamus said with a roll of his eyes. "Egill had attended multiple times. As of now, we're the only ones who know of his betrayal."

"Not necessarily," Helgi said. Ophelia could see the gears turning in his mind. "Egill takes calculated risks, right? He's always got a backup plan. Someone else within our ranks must know and sympathize with him."

"He's got an informant?" Reija asked.

Seamus and Helgi nodded.

"Egill knows where the gathering will be held; it will be a bloodbath," Seamus whispered. "You know damn well they've been planning a raid for that day. The problem is, Arild has grown impatient. Why wait four months for the gathering, knowing he can get under Phee's skin? He and Egill are just proving a point."

"The Hunter's Moon is irrelevant," Tiril whispered. "If they have another informant within our ranks, then who knows what information they might have? Even if we cancel the gathering, warn the others, and wait for them to attack here, we're still putting countless lives in danger."

Ophelia sat back in her seat, twiddling her thumbs,

trying to think of how to remedy this. There'd be no way to find Egill's informant, so wasting energy trying to find them was useless. If anything, that'd draw more attention to themselves. And Tiril was right. No matter what they did, it wouldn't change the outcome. Arild's twisted olive branch was proof of that. He'd get the job done one way or another. How many people got hurt in the process was up to them.

"May I make a proposition?" Ophelia asked, sitting forward, clearing away the maps. Tiril and Helgi were on the edge of their seats. Seamus inhaled sharply but nodded. "No matter what we do, we're going into battle. At the very least, we can prepare ourselves. I say we send a message to your rebels and ask them to join us in Høstlunden. Not only will we be taking the fight straight to Arild and the Ulvemordere, but we'll be putting on quite the show."

"In what way?" Seamus asked.

"I've a grand idea," Ophelia smiled, standing.

"I'm not going to like this, am I?"

Ophelia reached into her pocket, taking out the small polar bear carving Seamus had made for her. She placed the polar bear beside Seamus's wolf on the map, then looked around at each of them.

"A pawn turns into a Queen, yes? If Arild wants to play chess, we'll play chess."

Ophelia expected a little pushback, a lecture at the very least. She did not, however, expect silence. Seamus turned away, tugging at his earlobe, muttering to himself. Helgi and Tiril leaned toward one another, whispering amongst themselves.

"You mean to announce yourself to the world, then?" Seamus asked.

"I do."

"Why? Well, okay, I know *why*, but. . . *why?*"

Ophelia looked to Reija, who gave a solemn nod. "A friend made me realize just how much I'm worth." Reija smiled to herself, holding her head high. "I do not fancy being paraded around like a relic, but if that is the price of freedom, I suppose I'll manage."

"Ophelia, you're damning yourself to a life of constantly looking over your shoulder," Seamus said, rounding on her. He wasn't angry, not in the slightest. All she saw in his eyes was fear.

"Announcing yourself as the last Winter Witch will draw more than the attention of the Ulvemordere. They aren't the only beings afraid of Witches," Tiril said, frowning.

"At the end of the day, it's her decision," Helgi said, giving her a reassuring wink.

"You're right, it is. Seamus, I told you to run toward something worth—"

"I know," he sighed, running a hand through his shaggy, greasy hair. "I know. If this is what you want. . ." he looked up at her, forcing himself to smile, ". . . then I'll stand by you."

"As will I," Reija said.

Helgi and Tiril glanced at each other, then nodded, standing. "Us, too," they said in unison.

They helped each other to their knees, bowing their heads. Reija followed suit. Ophelia turned to Seamus, who rolled his eyes, then lowered himself to one knee as well.

"Is that really necessary?" Ophelia laughed.

"Better get used to it, kid," Seamus laughed. "Or should I say, 'Your Highness?'"

The next few days were a blur of ink and parchment as Helgi, Tiril, and Ophelia penned letters to prominent rebels in their circle. Those closest had already sent their replies. So far, the reaction to the call for help had been unanimous. If the Ulvemordere threatened one rebel, they threatened them all. Long-hidden resentment and rage would wreak havoc on Arild and his army. The Ulvemordere wouldn't know what hit them.

Yet again, it was time to leave the partial safety of Dødbyen. Ophelia was growing tired of these goodbyes. She hoped this wouldn't be her last stay at the Kirkeby mansion. More than that, she hoped every soul within these walls made it home safe when all was said and done.

"One more time, just so I know you were truly listening," said Tiril as Seamus rolled his eyes. They stood before the waterfall, the spray drenching them.

"Tiril," Seamus grumbled.

"Appease me," she snapped.

Ophelia sighed heavily but smiled. "We're to rendezvous at an inn just south of Juvel Hjem's Høstlunden entrance. Should we find ourselves in any sort of trouble, we're to return to Dødbyen and send word with Noomi."

"Yeah, what she said," Seamus said, lazily pointing over his shoulder with his thumb.

"I just—"

"'Don't want anything to happen to you.' We know," Seamus finished. "Stars, woman, you'd think we were preparing for some epic battle or something."

Tiril shook her head, offering Ophelia a hug. Ophelia begrudgingly let Tiril wrap her up in a bear hug. Oddly enough, it wasn't all that terrible.

"Keep an eye on him, will you?" Tiril mumbled, stepping back as Seamus tugged on Ophelia's satchel strap.

"I'll try my best. You know how well he listens."

Tiril rolled her eyes. "Don't remind me."

"We'll see you soon, ya old hag," Seamus smiled, kissing the top of her forehead.

With that, they were off.

Words weren't needed. Both Ophelia and Seamus were terrified of what was to come, but at least they were together. At the end of the day, that was all that mattered.

They were just about to step onto the lift when Seamus turned to pounding footsteps.

"Lady Ophelia!" Reija called, running to catch up with them.

Seamus stepped protectively in front of Ophelia, frowning. "Is everything all right?"

She nodded. "I just. . ." Reija took a deep breath, bowing. "I would have you know I'll be traveling with Tiril and Helgi when they leave. I am. . . fulfilling my duties to them. My. . . contract, so to speak. . . is coming to an end. Meaning I'll be out of work. I was wondering if when this is all said and done, you might be looking for a servant?" She didn't stand to her full height until she was done speaking.

Seamus stepped to the side, giving Ophelia a knowing look.

"I think I will be, yes," Ophelia smiled.

Reija laughed, looking relieved. "I look forward to serving you, my Queen."

"Oh, don't jinx me!"

"Please, as if I could ever jinx a Witch."

Ophelia chuckled to herself, bowing to her future servant.

She hated that word. 'Servant.' Should Ophelia be accepted into this world as a Queen, the servant role would be nothing more than a job description. Should anyone treat her as less than, it'd be cause for punishment.

Reija would be her equal. It'd be one of her first decrees.

"I'll see you soon, my lady."

"Safe travels, Reija."

Reija gave one last bow, then went off to finish her duties.

Seamus stared after her, a look of satisfaction on his face. "You're going to make a great Queen one day, Ophelia."

"You think so?"

"Pup, if there's one thing in life I've been completely sure of, it's been you."

It was nice to be believed in for once.

7. HØSTLUNDEN

BIRCHWOOD & SNAKE OIL

The Høstlunden border was only a few hours away. Seamus had made the crossing a hundred times before, but Ophelia had only dreamed of such things. Høstlunden was eternal Autumn. A sea of orange, yellow, and red as far as the eye could see, steeped in pumpkins and nutmeg. Compared to Snøbolig, it was an entirely different world. What would crossing that border feel like?

Seamus had figured they'd run into a handful of beings, noting the passage between Snøbolig and Høstlunden was well-traveled. So far, they'd seen a noble convoy, a wagon piled high with crates, and a menagerie of mounts and their riders. It was all so exciting. Once, a bundled-up reptilian woman playing the flute waved from atop her camel. Jonquil would be delighted.

Now, as the border neared, a caravan pulled up beside them. Seamus directed Ophelia to move into the shadows with the horses, eyeing the driver cautiously. The wagon was painted with jewel-toned rosemaling—traditional floral folk art—and had a velvet covering on the roof. It was on the same path as them, presumably heading back to Høstlunden after a long visit.

The driver waved from atop her fjord horse, catching Seamus's eye. Her blonde hair was braided and pinned to the top of her head, reminding Ophelia of a princess. She wore a stark white undershirt beneath a plum-colored bodice and maroon apron. Both of which were embroidered to match the florals on her caravan.

Seamus put on his best smile as he slipped from the

saddle and walked up to her. From where she sat with the horses, Ophelia couldn't hear what they were saying. The woman laughed and blushed. Seamus fluffed his hair. The woman hopped off her horse and disappeared inside her wagon, beckoning Seamus to follow.

A long minute passed. Ophelia grew uneasy standing there alone. Frykt pawed at the ground, blowing hot steam out her nose. Rain whimpered.

Just as Ophelia was about to call for her surly wolf, he jumped out of the wagon with a mischievous smile. He reached into his coin pouch and handed a few gold coins to the woman, bowed, and then skipped on back to Ophelia.

"What was that about?" she asked.

Tucked under his arm was something wrapped in velvet. "Caravans always have things to sell," Seamus said as the woman hollered her thanks and rode off. "Now, this is more ceremonial than anything, but it'll do ya in a pinch."

He held out the tightly wrapped parcel, his mischievous smile growing somber. Slowly, Ophelia unwrapped the parcel.

A small silver dagger with a sparkling navy blue handle sat nestled in the fabric. It had a leather sheath of the same color, silver stars embossed onto it.

"This is for me?" Ophelia asked.

Seamus nodded. "Just in case axes aren't your thing."

"Thank you," Ophelia whispered, taking the dagger in her slightly shaking hands.

She didn't like weapons of any kind, but this dagger was beautiful. The blade was slightly curved and etched with stars, the pommel reminiscent of a full moon. As he'd said, it didn't seem made for self-defense. It seemed to be more of an art piece. Ophelia could appreciate that, at the very least. Maybe that's why he'd been drawn to it.

"It's small enough to hide in your boot, more like a knife than a dagger," Seamus explained. "Last resort sort of thing. Keep it close, but pray you won't need it." He winked at her, smiling brightly as she sheathed it and bent sideways to stuff it in her boot.

Seconds later, he was back in the saddle, begging her to race him to the border.

Frykt may be a powerhouse, but Rain was faster. He and Ophelia stood before Høstlunden's border, waiting for Seamus and Frykt to catch up. Try as she might, she couldn't snap the reins and push Rain forward.

"All right, you win," Seamus said with a laugh as he and Frykt pranced by. The two of them crossed the border with ease, unaffected by the sudden change in atmosphere.

Ophelia was frozen with wonder.

Behind her was familiarity. Snow and ice clung to her, just as cautious of her departure as she was. But in front of her? In front of her was curiosity, the gently swaying Autumn leaves beckoning her forth. She could feel warmth blowing in from the other realm, the breeze tickling her skin. How odd. Something so familiar suddenly felt alien.

Dry, brassy grass met thick, wet snow. It was as though some sort of invisible force kept the two from mingling.

Seamus turned Frykt so he could face her. They stood beneath a birch tree, the leaves floating down around them. Seamus looked as though he belonged to that other realm. The harshness of his features softened in the amber glow.

"What's wrong?" he asked, eyebrows furrowed. He must've sensed her unease.

". . . Oh. It's. . . It's just. . . I've never been to Høstlunden. . ." Ophelia mumbled.

Seamus smiled to himself, shaking his head in what Ophelia knew to be a silent laugh. Frykt blew steam out her nose, narrowing her eyes as Seamus dismounted. Though he stayed beyond the border, Seamus extended his hand toward her.

"It's not scary. I promise."

Ophelia couldn't bring herself to argue. Instead, she gave Rain a gentle pat and slipped from the saddle. After making a great fuss about straightening her skirts, she reached for Seamus's hand. Eyes shut tight, squeezing his hand as hard as she could, she found herself unable to move. Seamus chuckled to himself, pulling her across the threshold and spinning her.

"You can open your eyes now," Seamus whispered.

Slowly, Ophelia opened her eyes. Before her lay Snøbolig in all its glory. Her back was to Høstlunden, to the adventure ahead.

"I thought. . . I thought there would be a notable change," Ophelia said, bemused.

Rain snorted, then hopped over the border. Frykt came to greet him, nuzzling his forehead.

"How so?"

Ophelia shrugged. "I'm not sure. I am the *Winter* Witch, after all. Who knows how the Autumn realm might've reacted to me."

Seamus just smiled, clicking his tongue to get the horse's attention. Both Rain and Frykt came to collect their riders, visibly distraught. They must hate how often they left the saddle. Rain especially. Ophelia was sure he'd be content to carry her to the ends of the earth and back.

"Have you been to all the Provinces?" Ophelia asked, picking a fallen leaf out of Rain's silver mane.

"Not Dagslys Hul," Seamus said with a shrug.

"Really?"

"I'm not pressed about it. I heard the heat can boil your blood and melt your eyeballs," he laughed.

Ophelia wrinkled her nose, shivering. "I doubt I'll ever visit such a place."

Back atop their horses, they continued down the long winding road to the *Frog & Lantern Inn,* a tavern just west of Høstlunden's entrance to Juvel Hjem. There, the rebel council would convene, and Ophelia would present herself as the one and only Vinterheks. It'd been decided before they left that they'd take the fight to Cathal, attempting to rescue those imprisoned in the mines by the Ulvemordere—namely, Saoirse.

"Nervous yet?" Seamus asked as he scanned their surroundings.

"Like you have to ask," Ophelia whispered, taking out her sketchbook.

She flipped to the back, placing the bright orange leaf beside the pirate's feather. The tallies she'd drawn so long ago were there, marking who'd saved who. She'd almost forgotten about them.

That feeling of dread was sneaking up on her again. If she told Seamus about the Spirits, would that protect him? Or would she be doing more harm than good? The loyalty she had for the Spirits told her she shouldn't reveal such secrets without explicit approval, but. . . But what would happen if she didn't ask? Would it really be so bad?

Sighing deeply, she began, "Listen, Seamus, I—"

"Tiril, Helgi, Reija, and I will all be there to protect you. You've nothing to worry about," Seamus said quickly, slowing Frykt until they were trotting side by side.

Ophelia frowned at him. Had she not been wearing her mask, she would have glared. "You don't believe that, do you?"

"Oh, not at all. We've crafted ourselves a trap. If you make it out unscathed after talking with Arild, who knows what will happen at Juvel Hjem? We're luring them out, toying with them in hopes of giving them a show," he scoffed, "I'm— What's the opposite of optimistic? It's on the tip of my tongue."

"Pessimistic," Ophelia said with a wink, flipping to the last sketch she'd been working on. Maybe now wasn't the right time to tell him.

"Yeah, that," Seamus grumbled. "Pessimistic. Hopeless, even."

"I'll try to have enough hope for the both of us," Ophelia laughed.

"I appreciate that, pup."

A half-finished face stared up at her. She twirled her graphite stick a few times, sitting crossed-legged atop Rain. Try as she might, she couldn't remember if the pirate had feathers on his ears or not. A hazy image of him danced in her mind, incomplete but there.

"Is that the pirate?" Seamus asked, leaning over, squinting at her drawing.

Ophelia's face reddened. "I suppose."

Seamus gave her a bored look. "Why are you drawing *him* of all people?"

"What exactly do you have against pirates, Seamus?"

"They're no good thieves, for one. Dirty, lying, cheating sons of—"

"You'd think you'd get along swimmingly, then," Ophelia smirked.

Rain chortled, causing Frykt to roll her eyes.

Seamus scratched the back of his neck, reddening, about ready to defend himself when he let loose a shrill yelp of fright. With the speed of someone set ablaze, he began patting himself off, screaming inaudible words, grasping at his neck.

"What—What's wrong?" Ophelia asked, eyes darting over him, looking for some sign of a threat.

Seamus shook as hard as he could, eyes wide as a snake slithered across his back and began to coil itself around his arm. Unfortunately, as he leaned sideways, trying to pry the blasted thing off, his saddle began to shift. With no time to react, all Ophelia could do was laugh as he tilted to the side. There was a thud and a groan as he collided with the ground. Frykt about fell over from her odd, whinnying laughter. Rain's ears twitched with concern.

"Are you quite done?" Ophelia asked, standing on Rain's back to see.

There lay Seamus, holding an itty-bitty snake as far away from his face as he could. To add insult to injury, one foot was stuck in a stirrup. Try as he might, he couldn't wrestle his foot free. Grimacing, he tossed the snake as far as possible, then quickly released his foot and tried to straighten Frykt's saddle.

"Ahh, don't look now, the snake's back," Ophelia said, pointing behind him.

Seamus spun so fast he nearly tripped and fell. "Where? Where is it?" he barked.

"Ope, never mind. It's just a branch."

Glaring, he turned back to her. "That's not funny."

"I thought it was," Ophelia said, smiling as Frykt neighed her agreement.

"Stupid snake," Seamus spat, gruffly readjusting his saddle before climbing back onto Frykt's back. "Stupid, stupid snake."

Ophelia's eyes were glittering with delight. "That's it, then?"

"That's what?"

"Your thing."

"What thing?"

"The one thing you're afraid of."

Seamus's cheeks went as red as the leaves above them. "So, what if it is?"

"Oh," Ophelia laughed. "Oh, I'm *never* letting this go. Fickle wolf, bested by his fear of snakes."

Seamus mocked her in a high, squeaky voice. "You've still got that height thing, y'know."

"I was more afraid of the lift than the height."

"Liar."

"Scaredy cat."

Seamus whipped his head around so fast that Ophelia thought it might snap. "I am *not* a scaredy cat."

Ophelia only shrugged. "Your girly little screams say otherwise."

"Wiseacre."

"Your childish rebuttals only tell me I've hit a nerve," Ophelia sang.

Seamus rolled his eyes, but she caught a glimpse of a smirk before he turned away. "We're all scared of something."

Ophelia was fully prepared to tease him some more when she spotted something over his shoulder. It was gone in a flash, but she swore she saw the tip of a top hat peeking behind a tree.

Seamus followed her gaze, shifting uncomfortably. "It's not another snake, is it?"

Ophelia's stomach churned. Rain's ears went back. He could sense it, too.

Hemlock had followed her.

"No," she said, trying to keep her voice steady. "I thought I saw something, but I guess I was wrong."

Seamus gave a great sigh of relief, rubbing his eyes. "Thank the Stars." He dug his heels into Frykt's side, pushing her onward.

Rain came to a halt, looking over Ophelia's shoulder, eyes wide.

"Hush," she said, patting his neck.

Ophelia would not give *him* the satisfaction. She refused to look behind her, to play into the fear crawling up her spine. Hemlock had no hold over her.

"Come on, now!" Seamus called from ahead. "It's getting dark."

As Rain raced to catch up, Ophelia decided she'd keep her relationship with the Spirits quiet for now. Even if Hemlock had sent the snake after him, something told her that Seamus wasn't the real target. Whatever was happening beyond the shadows was meant for her to solve. Talking with Holly had upset the powers that be, and now she had to deal with the consequences. Dragging Seamus into it was useless. He had his own destiny to figure out.

CHAPTER EIGHTY

ARTISTIC EXPRESSION

Seamus chose a quiet, secluded patch of the old birch forest for them to rest. The Frog & Lantern was a few days away with little but an expanse of leaf litter to protect them. A few towns hid between woodland and brush, true, but after Dødbyen, Seamus was happy to sleep beneath the stars once again. Sunset had come and gone, leaving them with heavy, velvety darkness. Høstlunden nights were riddled with noise, unlike Snøbolig, where snow had blanketed everything in silence. Though Ophelia could sleep through it all, Seamus knew he'd have at least some trouble. If he quieted his mind and allowed himself to be still, he swore he could hear even the bugs crawling beneath his feet. Tiny, squelchy, slithering creatures. He shivered. He'd have to agree with Reija on this one. He hated spiders.

Ophelia wove silently between the densely packed trees, surveying their surroundings.

"Found a good spot yet?" Seamus asked as he cleared space for a fire.

With the goods Tiril had packed for them, they'd eat like nobles for the next week. Plus, there was the kringle Ophelia and Reija had baked.

Ophelia sighed, shaking her head. "None of these will support my weight. Guess it's the ground for me."

He laughed. "Pity."

"Do you need help with anything?" Ophelia asked, hovering behind him as he made a makeshift fire pit.

"I've got everything handled, more or less. Have you

tended to the horses?”

“Yes, they’re all right.”

“Wonderful. Well, then, you may stay here while I collect firewood,” Seamus said as he stood and wiped his hands on his jacket.

Ophelia stared at him a moment, making circles in the dirt with the tip of her boot. “May I join you?”

Seamus furrowed his eyebrows. “Really?”

She shrugged, dropping her bag and sketchbook before untying her mask and tossing it aside. “Why not?”

Finding no fault in that statement, Seamus beckoned her into the woods. Quietly, they collected what they could. Any dry twig, stick, or branch would do. Thankfully, such things were more prevalent in Høstlunden. Soon, their arms were nearly full.

Around them, the forest was alive with all kinds of sounds. Nocturnal creatures went about their nights, turning the woods into a symphony of footsteps, flutters, coos, and chitters. If Seamus were lucky, this arboreal melody would lull him to sleep. He wondered what Ophelia could hear. It’d been so long since he’d had human ears that he’d forgotten what all she could hear. Ophelia’s anxious energy was not lost on him, though he decided to chalk it up to plain old nerves. Not knowing what lay in the dark, what was causing whatever sounds she heard, it had to be troublesome. If it was anything other than that, he hoped she’d confide in him. If she didn’t, well, what was there to do, really? She’d offered grace toward his secrets; the least he could do was offer the same.

“Did you enjoy exploring Dødbyen?” he asked, attempting to ‘break the ice.’ No pun intended.

“Oh. . . uh. . .” In the dark, he saw her shoulders sag. “It was interesting, I suppose.”

“Did you make any frivolous purchases?”

She laughed, walking backward as she spoke. “No, unfortunately.”

“Hmm,” Seamus said, shaking his head. “Well, that just won’t do. Guess it was a good thing I picked something up for ya, aye pup?”

“You got me something?” Was it his imagination, or had Ophelia’s eyes literally sparked with excitement?

"Do you remember when you told me about the painter that let you use their watercolors?"

Ophelia stopped dead in her tracks. "You bought me watercolors?"

He nodded, piling a few more branches into her arms. "I might've."

Back at their crude little camp, Seamus set to work building a fire as Ophelia rolled out their bedrolls. It was all she could do not to pester him about the watercolors. Seamus took great joy in that. Teasing her—without inadvertently hurting her feelings—filled him with a warmth that rivaled the sun.

Once the fire was burning hot, Ophelia took out the pots and pans Tiril had lent them. After tossing together a quick stew, she began whistling, glancing back and forth between the fire and Seamus's pack.

"You're very impatient," Seamus yawned, using his hand to coax the aroma of the stew into his nose.

"I've lived an eternity of patience, Seamus. I do believe *im*patience is long overdue," she smiled.

"I suppose you're right," he replied.

As the stew bubbled and Ophelia busied herself with whatever book she was reading, Seamus allowed himself to sit back and enjoy the peace for as long as it lasted. Their quiet moments together had become ever so important to him. How he'd gone on so long without that Witch, he didn't know. Imagining his life before her felt like trying to remember a hazy dream. He knew it had existed, but it was too surreal to believe.

"What's your book about?" Seamus asked, turning to her.

"A young lady is tasked with solving mysteries in a strange, far-off swamp land," Ophelia said without looking up.

"Is it any good?"

"It's humorous, I'll give it that," she replied.

"I'll have to borrow it sometime."

This time, she did look up. "I'd much rather get you your own copy. Celosia knows you'd ruin mine."

"I would not!"

Ophelia shut her book, raising an accusatory eyebrow. "Your muddy paws leave prints wherever they go. There are thumbprints in my sketchbook leftover from the last time you flipped through it. Try as I might, nothing has removed the horrid little stains."

Seamus grimaced. "All right, all right, I'll get my own copy."

Satisfied with that, she turned back to her book. "If it makes you feel any better, I never lent Saoirse any books either."

"Why not?"

"Because of the state of the books *she'd* lent *me*."

Seamus laughed to himself, nodding. "Worse than thumbprints in the margins?"

"Far worse," Ophelia whispered, a far-off look in her eyes.

Left with nothing to do, Seamus studied her while she read. Her expression changed with the pages, leaving Seamus wondering whether she mimicked the characters. He'd ask but knew not to bother her once she'd read more than a few pages.

Yawning, his eyes drifted to a small movement behind her. As though she'd felt his gaze shift, Ophelia looked up at him. Ignoring her look of concern, he licked his lips and took a sharp stick from the pile of leftover firewood.

"Don't move," he whispered.

Without giving her time to protest, Seamus leaned forward and grabbed something long and wiggly from behind her. He yelped, tossing it aside before wiping his hand on his pants. Writhing on the ground between them was a snake. It hissed at them, making toward Ophelia's feet. Without hesitation, Seamus reached down and stabbed the stick into the snake's head. Ophelia covered her eyes, presumably glad it hadn't made a noise as it died.

"I hate snakes," Seamus spat. "I can't believe I'm saying this, but I miss The Wilds already. At least there weren't snakes in The Wilds."

Ophelia nodded, face hidden behind her book.

Gagging, Seamus picked up the lifeless snake and threw it aside. "I disposed of it. You can look now," he said softly.

"Sorry."

She peeked over her book, eyebrows raised in fright. "Disgusting."

Seamus agreed, nodding as he tossed the bloodied stick into the fire.

Ophelia frowned to herself, marking her place and setting aside her book. She sat frozen for a minute, scanning the trees, firelight flickering in her silver eyes. Her fingers twitched, a single spark traveling up her hand, lost beneath her sleeve.

"Did you see something again?" Seamus asked, following her gaze.

"No, not this time."

Turning her attention to the stew, she began ladling the steaming concoction into bowls, handing one off to him along with a roll. Once they finished eating—with no signs of snakes—Ophelia turned expectantly to her wolf.

"Well. . . ?" she asked, glancing at his pack.

"I'm sorry. Was there something you wanted?" Seamus asked in a sing-song tone.

Ophelia rolled her eyes but smiled. Seamus winked at her, then leaned over and made a great show of rustling through his pack. Finally, he procured a small metal tin and handed it to her.

Ophelia made to open it but paused.

"Why do you shower me with gifts?" she asked, staring deep into his soul with those moon-bright eyes.

That was a splendiferous question, one Seamus didn't have the answer to. "Because."

Ophelia gave him a knowing look, then gently opened the tin. Her eyes widened as she tilted it toward the firelight. "They shimmer!" she gasped. "Seamus, they sparkle!"

"You like them?"

"I love them!" she laughed.

To his surprise, she hugged him. Such a thing was so unheard of from her that it took Seamus a moment to realize what was happening.

"Oh, I can't wait to use these! Thank you so much, Seamus. I promise not to waste them," she said as she let go.

There was such life and happiness in her eyes.
Now that—*that* was why he 'showered her with gifts.'
Just like her impatience, such things were long overdue.

CHAPTER EIGHTY-ONE

LINDWYRMS

The following day, Ophelia was awakened by an ever-annoying *snap-snap-snapping*. Blinking away the harsh sunlight, she twisted to see Seamus nearly packed up and ready to depart.

"You were snoring," he said absentmindedly.

"Was not," Ophelia replied groggily.

Smirking, Seamus offered her a piece of kringle, then went about the rest of his duties. Once Ophelia had finished her breakfast and shook away her grogginess, she packed up her things and tended to the horses.

Rain wouldn't stand still, which was completely out of the normal. He was so calm, so stoic. Frykt was a ball of energy, raring to go even when you begged her to settle. Now, she'd gone quiet, grinding her teeth.

Rain whinnied, stamping his hoof a few times.

"Something's wrong," Ophelia said, turning to Seamus.

"Frykt wouldn't stop whinnying. Woke me up," he said, yawning. "Don't be surprised if I doze off."

In response, Frykt nuzzled the top of Ophelia's head, moving closer to her. Rain looked over his shoulder, eyes wide.

"Seamus, they're really spooked."

All the wolf did was nod, eyes trained on something above. Rain stomped his hoof again, glaring at him. It was obvious they wanted to leave. Unfortunately, Ophelia knew to trust her animal companion's instincts. Rarely had they been wrong. Before either of them could descend into equestrian hysteria, she climbed into Rain's saddle, scratching behind his ears. Even that didn't calm him.

"Do you hear anything?" Ophelia asked, scanning the trees.

"Nothing out of the ordinary."

A few hours later, when Seamus's rear had gone numb from being in the saddle too long, they stopped for lunch. To their right, a handful of paces into the trees was a ravine. According to Seamus, dragons had made the canyon their home. Vast networks of caves hid in the shadows, giving the beasts ample space to be, well, beasts. If he had let her, Ophelia would've gone exploring. Maybe the aurora dragon and its friend were somewhere below, reuniting with their kind.

"It's not uncommon in Høstlunden to mount dragons," Seamus said as he made exaggerated lunges around the small clearing they'd found. He'd said something about 'keeping limber,' but Ophelia hadn't been paying attention. Instead, she stood in the center of the clearing, sketching her surroundings.

Echoing through that ravine in the distance was a breeze. She could feel it calling to her, beckoning her forward. Again, she thought of what it might feel like to soar through the sky, not a care in the world. To feel the open air around you. . . It must be incredible. Reading her mind, a trickle of that breeze blew through the trees, causing fiery leaves to flutter down around her. They collected at her feet in the shape of a heart, mostly shades of red.

"That's very sweet of you," Ophelia laughed, holding out her hand.

The wind swirled around it, a small, wispy cloud beginning to form.

"Hey, we talked about that," Seamus scolded.

"It's just saying hi," Ophelia sighed.

She shut her sketchbook, clipping it in place before turning and leaning into the wind. It collected at her back, propping her up. Ophelia crossed her arms behind her head, crossing her ankles.

With a smug smile, she said, "You're just jealous you can't do this."

Seamus rolled his eyes but continued his 'keeping limber' efforts. Rain and Frykt—who were still acting unusually—were watching him intently. Neither of them could stay still, constantly jittering about. Ophelia had kept an eye out for Hemlock, but so far, she'd seen nothing.

As if struck by lightning, Frykt suddenly jumped to life, rearing. Rain spun, taking off full speed back toward the road they'd been following. After snorting madly at Seamus, Frykt followed.

Ophelia furrowed her eyebrows. "That was. . . odd," she whispered, trying to ignore a sudden wave of dread.

Seamus suddenly stopped mid-lunge, pointing up a tree. "Kid? Is there meant to be this many snakes in Høstlunden?"

Ophelia coaxed the wind to leave her, coming to stand beside him. There in the tree, hidden amongst the autumnal leaves, was a rust-colored snake curled around a branch. Another was slithering above it, and two more were higher up. Spinning, Ophelia found each tree had its own tiny den of snakes.

She stiffened. "Seamus."

He, too, was scanning the treetops, baffled. "What?"

"I think we've stumbled upon something we shouldn't have."

Wincing, he stood to his full height, shaking out his left leg. "Yeah? What else is new?"

"Do you hear anything out of the ordinary?" Ophelia asked quietly, grabbing his arm and pulling him close.

"Just a rapid stream nearby. Why?"

"In which direction?"

"Toward the ravine, I suppose."

Ophelia grimaced. "I don't think you're hearing a stream."

"Why are you acting so—" Seamus froze, the color draining from his face. He reached up and turned her face to the side. "What in Rabbit's name is *that*?"

Ophelia's heart skipped a beat. Slithering through the trees was an enormous dragon-headed snake. Its scales were striped—pumpkin and hickory in color—its underbelly and the spikes on its back a sandy beige. Its giant eyes were nothing but a black abyss, reflecting their image like a mirror. It circled them like prey, sizing them up.

"A Lindwyrm," Ophelia breathed. Seamus lifted his foot to step in front of her, but Ophelia stopped him. "No sudden movements."

"Aren't Lindwyrms extinct?"

Ophelia shook her head slowly, pulling him backward, looking over her shoulder to make sure this was the only giant serpent they had to deal with.

"Remember that snake you killed?"

"Yeah?"

"Lindwyrms have a hive mind. You killed a set of its eyes."

"I pissed off the giant dragon-snake?"

Ophelia nodded. "You pissed off the giant drag-on-snake."

"Dammit."

Around them, the birch trees began to shake and hiss. There'd been a time when Ophelia had felt a kinship toward snakes. She'd read once that they couldn't produce their own body heat. They were cold-blooded, just like her. Now? Now, she wished snakes and Lindwyrms were just a figment of her imagination. Stupid, stupid Hemlock! He had to be doing this. Either that or she and Seamus were the unluckiest beings in Alle Årstider.

"*This* is why I'm averse to killing animals!" Ophelia whisper-yelled.

"Kid, how was I supposed to know I'd summon a giant snake from my childhood nightmares?"

Ophelia groaned, carefully edging around him so they stood back to back. The Lindwyrm wove between the trees, tightening its circle. It could strike at any moment.

"You're just lucky this one is a baby!" Ophelia snapped.

"*That's a baby?*" Seamus shrieked.

"The babies don't have arms," she said matter-of-factly.

"*The adult ones* do?" Seamus looked as though he'd keel over from fright.

The Lindwyrm must have been at least eight feet long, its head the size of Seamus's torso, its body thick as a barrel of wine. Blessed Amaranth, it was a good thing the horses had bolted. As she and Seamus stood bickering, it continued to tighten its circle. The beast was far too close for Ophelia's liking. It was toying with them.

"What do we do? Do we run?" Seamus asked, his hand resting on his axe.

"Are you crazy? It'll swallow its tail and roll after us like a giant sentient wheel!" Ophelia snapped.

Seamus swore, looking over his shoulder at her. "So, what? We fight it?"

After weighing their options, she sighed, nodding. "Unfortunately."

Seamus slipped his axes from his belt, readying himself for an attack. He nodded toward the Lindwyrm, nudging Ophelia's arm with his elbow. Slowly, she raised her arms, imagining the snake's body freezing solid. The tip of its tail glistened with frost, which traveled up its body like thousands of tinier, less deadly snakes—sort of like the ones watching from their treetop fortresses.

The Lindwyrm's movements slowed until it stopped, frozen less than a yard away.

Seamus was backing away, a pleased look on his face. "Huh, I figured that'd—"

The ice encompassing the Lindwyrm's body shattered. It hissed and thrashed, slithering angrily toward them. Ophelia arched her arms over her head, a thick wall of ice materializing around them. The Lindwyrm—to their dismay—leaned back and blew a plume of flames at the glacial shield.

"*It breathes fire?!*" Seamus screamed.

"*Dragon*-snake, Seamus. *Dragon!* Now run!" Ophelia cried, grabbing him by the hand and yanking him away from the melting wall.

"I thought you said not to do that!"

"I changed my mind!"

As fast as they could, they raced through the trees. As they ran, Ophelia conjured a thick fog, praying it'd hide them long enough to find their cowardly—yet incredibly smart—horses. Seamus was behind her, muttering about how he would never have a peaceful dream again. Ophelia had to agree. Of course, that meant they'd actually escape the Lindwyrm. It couldn't follow them forever, right? There had to be somewhere it wouldn't follow. Maybe the sound of a nearby town would scare it off? Was there even a town nearby? Ophelia could only hope.

Oh, hope, what a finicky, fickle temptress she was.

Ophelia should know better.

She skidded to a halt as a second, much larger, much angrier Lindwyrm slithered out of the fog before her. Other than its size, the only difference was the pointy horns on its head. Oh, and the arms. Can't forget about the arms.

"I pissed off the dragon-snakes mom, too, didn't I?" Seamus asked tearfully, his voice shaking.

"Appears so."

"Well, pup, it was nice knowing you. Thanks for the laughs."

"You're welcome."

In a last-ditch effort, Ophelia swirled the fog around the Lindwyrm, forcing it down into its lungs. It choked and writhed, leaning back, ready to burn them to crisps. Much to its chagrin, the mist snuffed out its fire. Unfortunately, Ophelia didn't know how long that'd work. Using all the strength she could muster, she pumped it full of fog, a risky thought crossing her mind.

"I have a grand idea!" Ophelia yelled over whipping wind and something rumbling.

"Do it!" Seamus screamed back. She heard a screech, a scrape, and a squish as his axe collided with something scaley.

Ophelia spread her fingers wide, begging the fog to freeze and expand into ice. Thankfully, it obeyed. Spires of ice erupted from the Lindwyrm's mouth.

"Kid, kill it!" Seamus roared. It sounded like he was in pain.

Ophelia shut her eyes, imagining the snake's blood freezing and shattering.

Seamus screamed in agony from behind. She turned and saw the baby Lindwyrm had coiled its body around him and sunk its teeth into his arm. It squeezed him tightly, stealing the breath from his lungs. His eyes rolled back into his head as he gasped for air.

Over his shoulder, leaning against a tree, was Hemlock. He wore a wicked smile as he tipped his hat to her.

Instinct took over. Ophelia was screaming at the top of her lungs again, lightning burning through her fingertips. The baby Lindwyrm was freezing, its eyes glazing over. A primal, terrifyingly familiar feeling filled Ophelia's body. It was the same thing she'd felt when she'd killed the trolls.

Ophelia swept her arms wide, doing just as Seamus had instructed.

Wrapped beneath layers of this ancient sensation was guilt. This thing—this *monster* and its mother wanted nothing more than to kill them. So why did she feel such remorse?

Why did her heart shatter along with these beasts as their frozen bodies crumbled?

Unfortunately, she didn't have much time to wallow in her guilt and confusion.

Hemlock pushed off his tree, shaking his head as if to scold her. Before Ophelia had time to react, he disappeared into the shadows. With him went the dread, replaced by a sparking rage.

Seamus staggered to the side, standing in a pile of frozen Lindwyrm chunks. He looked up at her, glossy eyes wide. He took a step back, opening and closing his mouth several times as he reached up to touch an oozing and bloody bite.

"That was. . . not a fun side quest. . ." he said shakily. "And dammit, that hurt!"

HEMLOCK'S CHOSEN FEW

Ophelia raced to his side, hands hovering over his wounds. If only she'd turned back around to help. If only she'd killed them quicker. If only she'd rounded on Hemlock the second she'd sensed his presence.

"I'm sorry, Seamus, I'm so sorry," she said, tears stinging her eyes.

"I'm fine," he said gruffly, waving her away. "It's not that bad. It's just a giant snake-dragon-thing bite. I'm sure it's. . . fine."

"You're bleeding!" Ophelia shrieked. "Badly!"

He looked up with tired eyes, shaking his head. "It's not your fault, pup." He'd been saying that a lot lately, but she still didn't believe him.

He winced, flexing his arm. Ophelia looked away, gagging at the blood oozing out of him. Turning away was an equally terrible decision. Her stomach churned at the sight of the dead Lindwyrms. All she could do was cover her eyes and pray this was all an awful dream.

"I've had worse. I'll heal quick," Seamus said, an almost jovial tone to his voice. She heard him rustle around in his pack and unfurl their map. "And look at that! With all that running, we're closer to the inn now. Not by much, but y'know. . ."

"That's good," Ophelia said, feeling queasy.

Seamus laughed to himself. "Come on, let's try to find our horses."

They set off, finally leaving the frozen Lindwyrm chunks

behind. Their scales would've sold for a fair amount, but neither wanted to stick around, fearing another would slither out of the shadows. After walking aimlessly for far too long, they found themselves staring out at the ravine. Ophelia peered into the dark expanse below, catching a glint of something shiny in the shadowy depths. Somewhere in the distance, she heard a roar and the beat of leathery wings.

"I doubt the horses came this way," she said, scanning the cliff face for another Lindwyrm. At this point, she figured if there were one, there were many.

Seamus yawned, rubbing his eyes. "We'll find them. Either that, or they'll find us. I say we hug the ravine. At least we may get some sort of warning should another Lindwyrm rush us. Plus, I'd much rather take a tumble than be eaten should worse come to worse."

Ophelia frowned, stepping away from the cliff. "Not funny."

"Who said I was joking? You talking to the wind again?"

She shot him a glare, which he returned by wiggling his bloodied fingers in his face. That nearly caused her to lose her lunch. What a sight that would've been, her doubled over, green in the face, glaring at Seamus as he laughed. Despite herself, a smirk tugged at her lips.

The sun was just starting to set. How odd. In Snøbolig, it would've been dark already. She wondered how the Sun chose to shine on certain parts of the world, glad she'd never have to make a decision like that. Ophelia had, however, made the conscious decision to stay a safe distance from the ravine, afraid the surrounding ground wasn't stable. While yes, she fancied flying, today was not the day to test if she could.

Seamus was studying the map in silence as Ophelia watched the horizon. Grumbling, he rolled up the map and shoved it back in his pack. He had a far-off look in his eyes, lost in thought as he rubbed his sore arm.

"Are you sure you're okay?" Ophelia asked.

He squinted at her out of the corner of his eye, hesitating before nodding. Ophelia knew this meant he was unsure of himself, which worried her. As they'd continued on, his pace had slowed. He walked dangerously close to the cliff, eyes on the all-consuming darkness below.

"Seamus, please be careful," Ophelia said quietly. She fiddled with the strap and buckle on her satchel, noting how his steps seemed unsteady.

"I'm fine," he said softly.

"Come back this way," she pleaded, reaching a hand forward, not daring to go any closer. Too much weight on unstable ground or one wrong move could send them over the edge.

"Do you want to hear a story?" he asked, turning his gaze to the sunset.

Ophelia furrowed her eyebrows. She had a very bad feeling. The birch trees were going dark, hiding within them all manner of uncertainty. ". . . Sure," she whispered.

Seamus took a deep breath, teetering a little to the left. Thankfully, that was where solid ground was.

"The Ulvemordere compound had these big, long bridges between the guard towers. These things were some seventy feet up, and the railings were just a row of thin bricks. Perfect place to toss people to their death," he laughed to himself, staggering across a line of wobbly rocks lining the cliff. "It'd become a game amongst my battalion. We'd hop up on the rail, trying to balance on the bricks. If you lost, you lost it all. None of us did, though sometimes—" he nearly lost his footing "—sometimes I would test my luck. I wanted to slip off the side and s—"

This time, he did lose his footing. Eyes wide, he fell toward the open expanse, arms flailing. Ophelia threw her hands forward, a strong wind collecting around him. He hung in mid-air for a minute before the wind whisked him up and deposited him on the ground beside her.

He laughed, his eyes glassy, his pupils humongous. "But I guess if my life had ended there, I wouldn't be here with you, huh?" He staggered to the side, waving away Ophelia's hands as she reached forward to catch him. "I'm fine."

In her mind's eye, Ophelia saw the pages of an old, musty book flipping back and forth. There was something she was missing here. Something about Lindwyrms. What was it?

Her eyes traveled to Seamus's wound, and that's when it clicked.

Lindwyrms were *venomous*.

"No, you're not—Seamus!" she screamed as he pitched to the side, eyes drooping.

Ophelia tried to catch him but wasn't fast enough. He landed with a thud on the ground. His breaths came in short bursts as he lay there twitching, his eyes staring at the sky but seeing nothing.

"Seamus, can you hear me?" she cried, taking his face in her hands.

His eyes fluttered shut as he took a deep breath, his body going still.

"Seamus!" Her own breath caught as she laid her head on his chest, listening for his heartbeat. She could hear it faintly beating but wasn't sure how long that'd last.

Panicked, she tore the map from his pack, watching impatiently as the ink swirled to life. They weren't terribly far from a town. Maybe there was a healer. Maybe she'd make it in time.

"Ssstrange how the favorite child—Amaranth'sss preciousss pet—doesssn't know a damn thing about the world ssshe livesss in," came a voice from the shadows.

Ophelia stood, hands sparking. A few feet away, Hemlock was sitting in a tree. Wrapped around his arm was a stark black snake, its beady white eyes trained on Seamus.

"Curiousss, isssn't it?" Hemlock asked, nodding toward her wolf's stiff body. "A human would've been dead by now."

"Why are you doing this?" Ophelia snapped, stepping around Seamus protectively, poised for an attack.

Hemlock's long, forked tongue whipped back and forth. "Galanthusss, darling, if you do not know, I cannot help you."

Smirking, he slid from his perch, stroking his snake. He cooed and chittered at it, then coaxed it onto the brim of his top hat, watching Ophelia intently. Slowly, he stalked toward her.

The grass beneath Ophelia's feet began to smoke, crackling and popping with tiny sparks. "Back up," she spat.

"Or what? You can't harm me, darling. I'm a Ssspirit. Pet or not, you're *nothing*," Hemlock laughed.

"You're not meant to meddle."

All he did was roll his eyes. "And yet, that'sss all we do, isssn't it? We're told not to interfere, and yet we are resssponsssible for mortal dreamsss and wissshesss. We mold and ssshape them, yet we cannot meddle? It doesssn't ssseem fair."

"That's different!"

"How ssso?"

Ophelia inhaled sharply, afraid her next response would get her and Seamus killed. In truth, that rule had never made much sense to her either. Hemlock had a point. What was the difference between messing with humans and fulfilling one's duty as a Spirit? Of course, sending a Lindwyrm after Seamus didn't seem like Hemlock's duty, but he had caused fear. He could argue this point all day and still technically be right.

"Why him?" Ophelia asked, gesturing loosely to where Seamus lay.

Hemlock clasped his arms behind his back, nodding. "What wasss it Holly sssaid? 'The Wolf killsss the Deer.' But what doesss the Polar Bear do to the Wolf? Have you given that any thought?"

Ophelia glanced at Seamus, who'd gone pale, his face screwed up in pain.

"What if—Just hear me out on thisss. What if is the Polar Bear killsss the Wolf? What happensss then?" Hemlock asked. "If it were me, I'd dissstance myssself from the old man."

"Get out of my head," Ophelia snapped, turning back to him. "I do not consent to you toying with me. You hold no power over me."

"Except I do. That isss your fault. You're ssstill human, Galanthusss. That'sss the problem. You can die, and ssso can he."

"But we're Spirits, too, at least partially," Ophelia countered.

Hemlock's face split into a wide, evil grin. "Are you sssaying you're our equal?" he laughed.

"Knock it off, Hemlock," came another voice.

Ophelia yelped, startled by the being suddenly standing at her side.

Jonquil.

"You're not meant to be here, sssseedling," Hemlock hissed, eyes narrowing.

"Yeah, well, neither are you, mate," Jonquil mumbled.

He snapped his fingers, and a sparkling, golden lute

appeared in his arms. A shrill, disembodied tune echoed through the forest as he began to strum. Hemlock covered his ears, wincing. Daffodils sprang up around his feet, their petals scorching his pant legs. Ophelia may not be able to harm a Spirit, but *they* could hurt *each other*.

"Go away, you snake," Jonquil grumbled.

Hemlock stamped on the daffodils, glaring at him. "Really, Zimri? Petty, childish insults?"

Jonquil plucked a few gentle notes on his lute, causing the daffodils to disappear. "Oh, you've not seen the lows I can steep to. Ophelia, my dear, I suggest you make yourself scarce. This is going to get ugly."

"What about S—" Ophelia turned to see Seamus resting atop Frykt's back. Rain was sniffing him, eyes wide. "Oh, now you two show up."

Hemlock mumbled to himself, then took the snake from his top hat and thrust it forward. The blasted thing elongated and stretched, its face opening wide enough to swallow Ophelia whole. Jonquil played a power chord, sending a wave of energy to collide with it.

"Buh-bye, Snowdrop!" he snapped.

Ophelia grimaced, then ran to the horses, wasting no time climbing into Rain's saddle. With a snap of the reins, they were off.

CHAPTER EIGHTY-THREE

TRUST

Everything was a blur. Ophelia had never seen animals run as fast as Frykt and Rain. With lightning speed, they raced toward the town Ophelia had spotted. Several times, she thought Frykt might accidentally bump Seamus off. Rain kept clacking his teeth at her, frustrated with her carelessness. Ophelia felt trying to intervene would cause *him* to buck *her* off.

Tears streamed down her face, mixing with the sudden downpour. Thunder and lightning crashed overhead, filling the night air with an all-consuming sorrow.

She didn't know how long they'd been running, but when the bustling town finally appeared before her, the horses finally slowed long enough to take a deep breath. It wasn't long before Rain was galloping again; all the while, Ophelia was screaming that she needed a healer. The townsfolk burst into a panic, pointing her toward a crooked building in the center of their village.

Leaving the horses outside, she burst through the front door. A woman was in the center of the small, warmly lit entry. She took one look at her before jumping into action.

"What's happened?" she asked calmly, though her movements were rushed and anxious as she collected various supplies.

"M—My dad—I need help!" she screamed. "My dad's been bitten by a Lindwyrm," Ophelia cried. The woman paused to look at her. Ophelia knew what she was going to say before the words left her mouth. "It's dead."

A dark look passed over the woman's face. She gave a solemn nod, gesturing for Ophelia to step aside. Heart twisting in her chest, Ophelia did as she was told. She watched from the window as the woman rushed outside, calling for help. Two burly men carried Seamus inside and up a steep set of stairs. Ophelia followed, careful not to be in the way. The healer barked orders to her apprentices as Seamus was deposited in a bed far too small for his broad frame. One such order was to drag Ophelia downstairs and deposit her in a chair by the hearth. Afraid of being thrown out entirely, she didn't protest.

Rain and Frykt were peering through a dusty window, their worry palpable. Ophelia broke down in tears, leaning heavily against the windowsill. She overheard something about taking the horses to the stables, acutely aware of movement behind her. What she assumed was a stable hand appeared out of nowhere, attempting to lead them away. Frykt tried to protest, but upon seeing Ophelia shake her head, she calmed. Rain whinnied reassuringly, nodding as they were led toward the stables.

An hour later, Ophelia was sitting by the hearth, knees hugged tight to her chest. There'd been yelling and hurried footsteps overhead for quite some time, but now all was quiet. Ophelia prayed this meant Seamus was going to be okay.

Thunder still roared outside, accompanied by the occasional crash of lightning. The rain had turned to hail. Ophelia knew none of it would stop unless Seamus came waltzing down those stairs with a smug smile on his weathered face.

Why did this keep happening to them? Every single time they had a moment of peace, it was ruined most drastically. All Ophelia wanted was a day or two of uneventful rest. Was that too much to ask for? Didn't they deserve some peace and quiet?

Jonquil better have caused Hemlock a world of hurt.

"Miss?" came a calm voice from the stairs. The healer stood at the top of the steps, her face set in steely indifference.

Ophelia scrambled to her feet, her breath caught in her throat. The healer beckoned her up the stairs, disappearing around the corner. Ophelia took the steps two at a time, nearly colliding with the healer as she held open the door to the room where Seamus lay.

Ophelia lingered in the doorway, making sure he was breathing before entering. If he was dead, she didn't want to see it. That'd be far too much for her fragile soul to handle.

Her exhaustion nearly took over when she saw his barren chest rising and falling steadily.

"He'll be right as rain in a few days," the healer said, placing a comforting hand on Ophelia's back.

She led her to the bed beside Seamus's, shooing away her apprentices. Once she was sure they'd left, she pulled close the lilac curtains around the beds, cutting them off from the other patients. Ophelia sat heavily on the bed, taking in her wolf's battered body. He was pallid and sweaty, his left arm and shoulder wrapped tight with bandages. A bruise was forming across his right side. Honestly, he didn't look as bad as she'd expected. She'd been expecting the worst, so this was more than a pleasant surprise.

"Miss?" the woman asked. She'd asked a question, but Ophelia hadn't registered it.

"Hmm?" she responded groggily.

"I asked if you'd like me to wrap up your hands," she said softly.

Ophelia looked down to see her skin was raw and sticky, blisters littering her fingertips. She suddenly remembered she'd scorched herself with her lightning. Until now, she hadn't even noticed.

"Oh, yes, please," she whispered.

The woman nodded, disappearing momentarily before returning with a jar of foul-smelling liquid, some cloths, and bandages. She sat on the edge of the bed near Ophelia, gently taking her hands in hers and beginning to clean the self-inflicted wounds. The liquid she dabbed on her fingers stung horribly, but she imagined it'd be nothing compared to what Seamus would feel when he woke.

"You're both extremely lucky," the healer said quietly. "Those snakes have claimed many a life as of late. I've asked the stable boy to inform our Earl. You'll be receiving compensation for killing it, no doubt."

Ophelia only nodded.

"How *did* you kill them?"

"It all happened so quickly, I'm not entirely sure," Ophelia said, her voice small.

The woman gave her a strange look, causing Ophelia to shift under her gaze.

"He took his axes to them," Ophelia said simply. Her words were so dry, so lifeless.

The woman's lips twitched into a sad smile. "I know that's not the case, wee one," she said. "Your companion here should be dead. Even a baby Lindwyrm has enough venom to kill a grown man—it has, in truth. I could've only made him comfortable if he wasn't lost to us already. The fact he's still here—that he's healing—makes me believe he's. . . *special.*"

Ophelia stiffened, yanking her hand away. She was completely drained and unable to fight if that's what this would come to. How she'd managed to kill those snakes in the first place was beyond her. If this healer turned them over to the Ulvemordere, they'd both be good as dead.

"Hush now," the healer said, reaching for her hands. "You'd be surprised how many of his kind come through here. He's a werewolf, no?"

Ophelia glanced down at him. That bruise on his side would linger, but it did look at least slightly smaller than it had moments ago. She nodded, allowing the woman to resume tending to her wounds.

"I'll be sure to keep that to myself," the healer said. She took a thin strip of gauze and began wrapping her fingers one by one, using the excess to secure the bandages around her palm. Once she'd wrapped the rest of her hand, she moved on to the next. "Of course, I believe even a werewolf would have some trouble killing a Lindwyrm. Did he have help?"

Ophelia studied the healer. She was all freckles and braided red hair, her green eyes like two all-consuming voids. Like Seamus, she had a hint of wrinkles around her eyes and lips but still held onto a more youthful air. There was vast empathy in her words, but that cold indifference hadn't left her face, even when she smiled. She wore a stained dress and apron, though Ophelia preferred not to dwell on what it was stained with. She was the perfect image of a healer who'd seen too much too young. Yet she still held onto the kindness—to the bedside manner a doctor was meant to have.

In a word, she was nothing like Lochlan.

This put Ophelia at ease.

"He did," she said softly, surprised at how evident her exhaustion was in her voice. "Had help, I mean."

The healer nodded to herself. "I had a feeling."

She finished wrapping Ophelia's other hand, sitting back on the heels of her palms to look her over. Ophelia had the strange feeling she could see through her mask—she knew what hid beneath it, she was sure.

"You're safe here, wee one. Both of you," she whispered, leaning in close.

"Thank you," Ophelia said, forcing herself not to pick at the bandages and ruin all her hard work.

"Rest up, I'll bring you some food. Seems you've had a very long day," the healer said as she stood.

"I really have," Ophelia laughed darkly.

The healer studied her, pursing her lips. With an unsure movement, she reached forward, her fingers resting on the edge of her mask. "May I?"

Ophelia wanted to say no. That was the smart thing to do. She knew nothing of this woman; why should she trust her? This healer would be what, the ninth person to find out about her Marks lately? That was risky. The more who knew, the more danger she was in.

So yes, she should say no.

But she didn't.

Because, eventually, everyone would know. Why hide now? So, instead of shooing her away, she nodded and braced herself for whatever happened next.

With a tenderness Ophelia had scarcely experienced, the healer removed her mask and set it down on the table between her and Seamus's beds. She smiled sadly, brushing a stray strand of hair behind Ophelia's ear. She traced the curve of her jaw to Ophelia's chin, brushing her thumb across it in a very motherly way.

"Sleep, *Hellige En*," she said, her kindness finally reaching her face. "Dream of better things."

Hellige En.

Holy One.

A kinder name for Witches, something only said by those holding on to the old ways.

No one had ever called Ophelia that before.

CHAPTER EIGHTY-FOUR

WATERCOLOR FLOWERS

Ophelia had slept, yes, but she had not dreamt of better things. Instead, she'd been plagued by nightmares involving giant snakes chowing down on a golden peacock and a persnickety wolf. As one would imagine, she did not wake feeling well-rested.

The healer—Miss Syrena Skora—had given Ophelia free rein of the infirmary. Rather forcefully, she'd also given her a tour. There was a small room above that served many purposes. During the day, it was where Syrena and her team of medics treated patients. At night, she made the tiny, stagnant room her home. Below was a sort of resting place, allowing patients and their loved ones a moment of peace. There was a small kitchen at the back of the infirmary where the medics worked in rotation to feed those with extended stays. Syrena was rather keen on Ophelia lounging in the den, but she'd politely refused. She'd much rather stay with Seamus until he woke up.

This seemed to irk Syrena, though Ophelia hadn't a clue why. From what little they'd said to each other, she got the impression Miss Skora ran a tight ship. Any deviation from her well-thought-out routine was cause for irritation. She liked things a certain way, something Ophelia could respect. Hopefully, their presence didn't cause the healer too much strife. Ophelia would hate to be a burden.

Seamus, however, wouldn't bat an eye. Unfortunately, Ophelia knew that meant he'd most likely cause problems on purpose.

She watched him now, stomach twisted in knots. Not once had he stirred from his slumber. His brow was dripping with sweat, his breathing still harsh and ragged. Syrena had mumbled something about hoping his fever would break. Ophelia was inclined to agree.

Sometimes, when Ophelia was genuinely anxious, no matter what she did, she couldn't focus. Her go-to was reading, allowing herself to be whisked off into a strange, far-off world. Usually, when she read, she saw vibrant, colorful scenes and heard the characters' voices as if they were in the same room as her. Today, however, the words were just ink on a page. After reading the same paragraph repeatedly, she resolved to draw. That wasn't working either. She'd filled three pages with doodles of wolves and polar bears, peacocks and snakes, but none of her sketches looked right. Even when using the watercolors Seamus had bought, all she felt was emptiness. Trying to nap only brought on more nightmares. She'd even tried sitting in silence, allowing her mind to wander. That had been a very bad idea, so she'd gone back to drawing, trying to fill another page with Seamus's likeness.

To her right, the curtains parted and in swept Syrena.

"How is he?" she asked, depositing an armful of jars onto the bedside table between the two cots.

Ophelia just shrugged, steadying the glass of water she'd used to clean her watercolor brushes. Just as she was about to lift her hand, Syrena nearly knocked it over again, her elbow catching the side of it.

Blushing, she pushed her many jars to the other end of the table. "Still drawing, I see?"

"Trying to, at least."

"Well, you know what they say about idle hands. It's good to stay busy."

Syrena got to work undoing Seamus's bandages, grimacing. Despite her best intentions, Ophelia couldn't look away from his wound. His skin had gone the color of old parchment, the puncture wounds oozing with a yellowish liquid. It was all she could do not to gag.

Syrena looked up at her with a sympathetic frown. "You don't have to stay cooped up in here. I'll keep an eye on him, I promise."

Ophelia chewed her lip, eyes glued to the many jars of salves and ointments on the bedside table. Syrena was right; she didn't *have* to stay. Leaving his side, however, felt wrong.

If Seamus were to wake up and find her missing, he'd panic. That wouldn't do anyone any good. Seamus was many things, but 'calm, cool, and collected in times of trouble' was not on that list.

Sighing, she returned to her sketchbook, swirling her brush in her glass. The way the metallic particles spun through the water reminded her of a mystical whirlpool trapped in a potion bottle. Absentmindedly, she wiped the brush on her sleeve, then dipped it into a small pan of chartreuse paint. The color was perfect for Seamus's werewolf eyes.

"There's a look out at the edge of town," Syrena said, wiping her hands on her apron before taking a fresh roll of gauze out of its pocket. "Looks over the ravine. It's quite pretty."

Ophelia glanced at her, eyebrows furrowed.

Syrena's shoulders sagged. "Just something to think about, love."

Picking up on Ophelia's need for quietude, she got busy dressing Seamus's wound. This time, Ophelia had no desire to watch. Whatever she was applying to the bite smelled worse than a stable. Lochlan, too, had used foul-smelling tinctures, but this seemed excessive.

When Syrena was done, she sat on the edge of Ophelia's bed, picking at loose thread on her apron. "Well, did you give it any thought?"

"The lookout?" Ophelia asked.

"Mmhmm."

"No, not really."

Syrena tapped her fingers on her knees, looking around the small, makeshift room. "I think getting some fresh air would do you good."

"Why?"

"I have a penchant for these things."

"What if I refuse?"

Syrena stood, hands on her hips. "All right, you've forced my hand. Doctor's order, love. Out you go." She picked up Ophelia's mask from where it lay at the foot of the bed, holding it out to her. "You'll go crazy sitting there all day."

Ophelia squinted disapprovingly at her, pouting. What

she wanted to do was tell Syrena that she wasn't the boss of her, and if she wanted to stay, she damn well would. Instead, she cleaned her brushes and put her things away neatly. Frowning, she took her mask and tied it on.

"You'll thank me later," Syrena said, holding the curtain open for her.

Ophelia rolled her eyes beneath her mask, taking her sweet time descending the stairs. Ignoring the other patients in the den, she braved the world outside.

Most of the town consisted of tall, skinny buildings packed tightly together. Everything was painted in shades of brown, rust, and pumpkin, blending in with the surrounding forest. For a town in the middle of nowhere, the place was quite packed with beings of every kind. The patrons weren't as diverse as Dødbyen, but for a girl who'd spent most of her life around humans, diversity was diversity.

Even their clothes were strange to her. In The Wilds, people choose practicality over style. Though intricate embroidery and fiberwork were highly valued, most men and women dressed roughly the same. Thick jackets, woolen skirts, and all manner of knitted or crocheted goods filled every wardrobe in every home. Ophelia had seen a taste of what the wide world of fashion had in store while visiting the Kirkebys, but this? This was incredible! Those with more human frames wore such elegant clothes. Ophelia may have confused them with nobility had there not been so many wearing the same attire. Women in long, jewel-toned dresses with high collars, lace, and enormous, puffy sleeves. Men in pristine tailcoats and top hats carrying canes with small bouquets tied to the handles.

What struck Ophelia was the apparent religion in this town. She knew Høstlunden was far more religious than Snøbolig, but seeing mums, sunflowers, and dahlias wherever they would take root filled her with such warmth. Several beings wore boutonnieres; others had clumps of blooms pinned to their bodies or in their hair, each cluster meaning something different depending on the blooms. Mortals created bouquets to honor their Spirits or to simply inform others of their desires. Such a range of emotions surrounded Ophelia. She wished she had time to decipher each bouquet's meaning.

Eventually, Ophelia found the lookout Syrena had mentioned. A long, skinny gazebo was built on the ravine's edge. Maroon and fuchsia mums were planted all around it, making the gazebo appear to float on vibrant pink clouds. An elderly couple sat on a bench, laughing amongst themselves. Despite them, the lookout was empty. Ophelia waved to them sheepishly, wishing she was entirely alone. Ignoring their mild looks of concern, she sat on the gazebo's railing, feet dangling over the edge. Some twenty feet below, a dragon lay curled on an outcropping. Plumes of smoke drifted up from its snout, culminating in a tiny cloud-like spiral above its head. Its tail flicked softly up and down like a cat's, making Ophelia wonder if it was purring just as such.

With the thought of cats came images of Ivar. Oh, she missed that cranky old cat. He stuck to her like a mushroom to rotting tree bark. What were he, Sköll, and Maj-gun up to? Getting on each other's nerves, no doubt. All the while tripping Noomi and pestering Matei. Reija had told her all about it. The Kirkeby's pets had rather boisterous personalities.

Speaking of the Kirkebys, she should probably write Tiril a letter. She'd try to sugarcoat it as best she could, but she deserved to know what was happening.

The dragon below her stirred, shaking away its slumber. It yawned, stretching its wings as it stood. As if sensing her gaze, it looked up and stood on its back legs. Ophelia waved at it, smiling. The dragon beat its wings, soaring into the sky with record speed. It flew past her, the gust of air caused by its wings nearly enough to knock her backward. It spun through the sky, twisting and turning in impossible arcs, reminding her of the otters she and Seamus had met.

Poor Seamus. It felt wrong to be sitting here without him. He should be there, watching the dragon with her.

The discomfort that thought brought felt like bugs crawling under her skin. Not having him by her side was equivalent to being unable to breathe. Part of her was missing. While she was confident in his healing abilities and Syrena's medical knowledge, Hemlock had been right. They were both still human, still able to die. And when that inevitable day came, and Seamus died, a part of her would die, too.

Ophelia's stomach churned, the world throbbing and swaying around her.

"That's enough of that," she whispered, waving to the dragon as it flew back into the ravine. Instead of watching to see where it went, she spun and hopped off the railing. Again, she waved to the elderly couple, who gave her a slight nod.

On the way back to Syrena's infirmary, she stumbled across the stable. After bargaining with one of the stable hands, she took a bucket of oats to Rain and Frykt, content to tend to them for a while. Inside their stall were brushes, which Rain kept nudging. Ophelia took this as a request and began brushing his silver mane and tail. Strangely enough, that was quite comforting. Once all the knots were out, she began braiding his mane. Upon seeing this, Frykt stamped her hoof and neighed in what could only be described as jealousy. Ophelia laughed, happy to braid her mane as well.

Once both horses were satisfied, she bid them farewell, hugging them before she left.

When she finally returned to the infirmary, the lamplighters had just begun their work. Ophelia lingered on the doorstep, watching them dart about the cobbled street.

Just as she made to open the door, she heard something rustling in the alley beside the infirmary. Ophelia knew she should ignore it, but what if whatever lay in the shadows was a threat? Taking a steadying breath, she bent and took her dagger from her boot. Slowly, she crept into the alley, heart beating rapidly against her ribcage. Dagger held before her in what she hoped was a menacing way, she rounded the corner. There, poking out of a pile of trash, wagging happily, was a fluffy tail. Ophelia furrowed her eyebrows, letting her arms drop.

"Just a raccoon," she sighed, stifling a laugh. "Wow, I can't believe I—"

"'*Just* a raccoon?' After all this time, I'm 'just a raccoon?'" said the raccoon as it turned to her.

Despite knowing the speaker, Ophelia stumbled back, thoroughly startled.

"I'd like to think I'm more than *just* a raccoon," said the tiny, fluffy thing as it held up a fishbone.

A laugh bubbled up Ophelia's throat. "What in Amaranth's name are you doing here?" she asked, grinning ear to ear.

The raccoon began to shimmer, the dark stripes on its tail glowing as bright as a moonbeam. As the raccoon stood, it grew, its legs and arms elongating. The face of a raccoon stretched and shifted until the kind face of Ophelia's very best friend appeared. Before her stood a petite woman with long, jet-black hair striped with silver. Her eyes were the brightest shade of purple one had ever seen, her pupils white. Smiling, she adjusted a pair of spectacles—one lens a circle, the other shaped like a crescent moon. Ever elegant, she wore a high-collared lilac dress embroidered with silver moonflowers. Around her waist was a belt to which a magnifying glass, a notebook, and a magical quill were attached.

"Hello, Moonflower," Ophelia said, quickly stowing her dagger.

Moonflower, Spirit of Mystery, laughed to herself. "Gracious, Snowdrop! Were you going to stab a poor, innocent raccoon?" she asked, shaking her head in mock disapproval.

"Of course not!"

Ophelia had only had three true friends her whole life. Saoirse, Jonquil, and Moonflower. Each had come to her in a time of need, but Moonflower was truly extraordinary. Unfortunately, due to her duties, she spent most of her time traveling. Still, she visited and wrote to Ophelia as often as she could. There was an old Terrestrial saying that friendships were gardens. If you tended to them, love bloomed. Despite the distance, Moonflower did her best to cultivate an incredibly strong friendship with her Snowdrop.

"It's so good to see you!" Ophelia said, reaching for her hand.

Moonflower gave her hand a gentle squeeze, nodding. "I wanted to visit sooner, but I got swamped with work. Sometimes, it feels like I'm being pulled in every direction imaginable. I had wood trolls praying for discernment here in Høstlunden, fairies searching for lost relics in Daglys Hul, pirates hunting for treasure somewhere at sea, and some old fool in Snøbolig trying to find prisoners. So many mysteries, so little time. When I get the chance, I'll tell you all about them."

"I do believe I may have egged on the old fool," Ophelia laughed.

"Yes, I thought so, too."

Moonflower was often found alongside Celosia and Lotus, aiding those seeking secrets and knowledge. In towns with strict law enforcement, officers often wore uniforms embroidered with her motifs. Same with those who worshipped the Celestial Raccoon. Authors were also quite fond of her, praying to her whenever their stories needed an extra air of, well, mystery. As such, Moonflower herself was fond of books. One of the many reasons she and Ophelia got along so well. Cut from the same cloth, they were.

"You're not visiting for long, then?" Ophelia asked.

"Well. . ." Moonflower said, her voice small. "Yes and no. You see, I'm not really visiting. I'm here to. . . *collect*. . . you."

"Collect me? Why? What—Oh." Ophelia's heart about stopped beating. "I'm in trouble, aren't I?"

"I wish we were seeing each other under better circumstances. I'm so sorry, Snowdrop."

"This is because of Hemlock, isn't it?" Ophelia spat. "That blasted snake!"

Moonflower grimaced, readjusting her spectacles. "Actually, this is because of Holly. Or so I'm told. Honestly, it's a—ehem—a *mystery* to me. I only just returned to the Garden. Celosia's been catching me up to speed."

"Wonderful," Ophelia sighed. "Well, I suppose we should get this over with."

"Don't worry; you're not in as much trouble as you think you are."

"Really?"

Moonflower shrugged. "Amaranth, Fern, and Nightshade always let you off easy, don't they?"

Ophelia rocked back and forth, weighing this. That'd been the case thus far, but she knew eventually her luck would run out.

Moonflower lifted her hand, ready to whisk her off to the Garden, but paused. "Before we go, are you really traveling with a bumbling oaf?"

"He's more of an *endearing* oaf, but yes."

The Spirit raised her eyebrows in shock. "That's not what Celosia heard from Narcissus. Jonquil said he's a real piece of work."

"Moony," Ophelia laughed.

"I'm only working with the facts I've got. It's all hearsay until I find the truth," she said with a wink.

CHAPTER EIGHTY-FIVE

THE TERRESTRIAL PANTHEON

Moonflower gave Ophelia's hand another squeeze, and the alley melted away. Dusk faded to dawn as a sprout fought its way through a crack in the cobblestone pavement. The ground fractured and creaked as the sapling grew, its roots shooting out in all directions. In seconds, an impossibly tall weeping willow had materialized before them. Beneath their feet, a small cluster of moonflowers bloomed.

"You'll be fine," their creator whispered, dropping Ophelia's hand. "I promise."

With that, Moonflower bowed and gestured behind them. Ophelia gave her a reassuring nod, swallowing hard before turning toward the willow boughs. Peeking through the gently swaying branches, she saw the remnants of a crumbling stone structure.

"Enter," came a small, feminine voice.

The boughs split like curtains being drawn. Ophelia stood frozen, scanning her surroundings. She'd never been to this part of the Garden. The ruins here reminded her of Egill's camp. The aura they pulsed with was just as familiar as that dilapidated visage. The only difference was the arch of thrones. Fifteen of them, each occupied except two. The throne at the very center of the group was carved from jet-black stone and was covered in dead vines. To the right, beside an occupied throne, was the second empty seat. It, too, was carved from stone and covered in rotting plants. This one, however, had a four-pointed star etched into its headrest.

In the center of the ruins was a ring of multi-colored mushrooms. Holly, Jonquil, and Hemlock stood there, their backs to her.

This was the Terrestrial Pantheon.

Oh, Ophelia was in way over her head.

"Galanthus," said the voice from earlier.

To the left of the center throne stood a young girl in a frilly pink dress that puffed out like a pastry. She looked barely older than ten, but Ophelia knew better. This being was as old as time itself. Pale pink ringlets stretched the length of the girl's back, accentuated by fronds of amaranth dripping down from the top of her head. Her lips twitched into a frown as she sat on her opalescent throne, looking rather bored. Bushels of amaranth sprouted up from the ground, curling around her lovingly. On the headrest of her throne was a pink jewel shaped into the silhouette of a rabbit.

Amaranth, Spirit of Life.

Fern sat beside her, a far-off look in her eyes. Two of her favorite troublemakers had been brought before the Pantheon. Whatever could be going through her mind? Slowly, her eyes drifted to Ophelia, giving a slight nod. Ophelia's heart dropped to her feet. How she managed to stagger to the ring of mushrooms, she didn't know. It was all she could do not to keel over out of fright. Holly glanced at her, his face devoid of emotion as she squeezed between him and Jonquil.

The woman sitting on the throne between the two empty ones stood, opening her arms in welcome. The hem and sleeves of her long, silky dress were curved like bat wings, a nod to her Celestial moniker. A veil hid her face, turning her stark white hair a dark, foreboding gray. Atop her head, she wore a crown of nightshade, their bright purple petals a stark contrast to her monochromatic wardrobe.

"Shall we begin?" Nightshade, Spirit of Death, asked. Her voice was silky smooth, barely a whisper.

On Amaranth's side sat Fern, Salvia, Narcissus, Celosia, Birch, and Peony. On Nightshade's—spare for the empty seat— were Foxglove, Higanbana, Moonflower, Gladiolus, and Lotus. The Spirits nodded from their thrones, faces filled with a myriad of emotions.

Narcissus, Spirit of Devotion, looked murderous. "Why she must be here is beyond me," she said, pointing at Ophelia.

Ophelia glanced at Jonquil, who'd gone green. "I'd like to

know that, too," she whispered.

"Did we say talk amongst yourselves?" Nightshade asked. "If either of you cannot follow directions, we will not entertain this a second longer."

Ophelia felt herself shrink beneath the Spirits' scrutinizing gaze. "Apologies, Your Excellencies. I did not mean to be troublesome."

Amaranth impatiently tapped her fingers on her throne's armrest. Fury danced in her bright pink eyes. "Holly," she began, looking bored, "what have you to say for yourself?"

Fern sat unnaturally still, eyes glued to the ground. The ferns growing around her throne shook and curled inward as though anxious.

Holly stepped forward, hiding his hands in his sleeves. "As I have stated numerous times, the seedling came to me with questions, and I answered them. I do not see the fault in my actions."

"The fault lies in your failure to consult the rest of us." That was Narcissus.

Holly worked his jaw, refusing to look at her. "Your perspective has been considered, Narcissus. That does not mean I must agree."

"How dare—"

"That is *quite* enough," said Nightshade. "We will be civil." A flash of purple light shone through her veil, quieting Narcissus instantly.

"Galanthus, is this true?" Amaranth asked.

"Yes, I did come to him," Ophelia said, her voice small.

Fern shifted uncomfortably, clearing her throat. Without looking at her, she asked, "What questions did you have for him?"

Holly inhaled deeply, eyes fluttering in frustration. "You know very well what she asked of me, Fern."

"I—" Ophelia began.

"Hush," both Fern and Holly said, surprising one another.

"Your loyalty is admirable, but the seedling is not here as your witness," said Amaranth, sitting cross-legged on her throne, her face cupped in her tiny hands. "We will hear her words unfiltered, or I'll have you both removed."

Holly took a step back, nudging Ophelia with his elbow.

"I asked him about North Star," Ophelia said, stepping back. Jonquil shifted beside her, moving ever so slightly in front of her.

Amaranth wasn't surprised in the slightest. "And why, pray tell, did you feel the need to do so?"

Holly rolled his eyes. "Ama—"

"Holly, do not test her," Nightshade whispered, cutting him off. Once Holly had settled, she gestured for Ophelia to begin.

"I am under the impression North Star has been reincarnated," Ophelia said. She was acutely aware that both Fern and Holly wanted her to lie, but what good would that do? She stood before an entire Pantheon of Spirits. Several of which wished she'd never been born! "I wanted to know what happened to Ljot."

"And what did Holly tell you?" asked Narcissus.

"Truthfully, not much," Ophelia said, trying to ignore the way Jonquil glared at his mother.

Holly nodded, looking pleased.

"And yet, you know more than you ever should've," Amaranth mumbled. "Tell us, seedling, how did this all come about? Who has been filling your head with stories?"

Holly had asked the same question. Only then did Ophelia realize they might've been searching for a specific name.

"A mortal by the name of Tiril Kirkeby. She is a faithful patron of the Terrestrial Pantheon, I assure you. She's just curious, is all," Ophelia shrugged.

"Tiril is one of mine," Fern said, nodding. "She is faithful indeed."

Amaranth rubbed her eyes, shoulders sagging. "I don't care who she is or what she worships; I only care about the why and how."

Celosia, who'd worn a calculated expression until now, cleared her throat and adjusted her monocle. "I do believe the mortal is in possession of many religious texts. I've heard her pray to me many times, seeking knowledge. Lotus, too."

Lotus, who sat across from her, still in her tortoise form,

nodded slowly.

Amaranth cast a glare on them both. "Helpful, thank you."

Higanbana rolled his eyes. "Are we to entertain every mortal's flight of fancy?

"If the seedling is right in assuming one of our own has returned, we shouldn't dismiss her." That was a voice from Nightshade's side. Foxglove, Spirit of Trickery, lounged lazily on his throne, giving Ophelia a wink.

"Oh, well, I definitely believe her now," Narcissus said with a roll of her eyes.

Jonquil stepped forward, pointing at Ophelia. "Why on earth would she lie about this? What does she stand to gain? Ophelia has always been faithful to us. For goodness sake, she rarely even *prays* to us! We're more friends than deities to her, just as we are to each other!"

"Jonquil!" Narcissus snapped. "You are in enough trouble as it is. Do not speak unless you are called upon!"

Sensing Jonquil was about to do something he'd regret, Ophelia grabbed him by the shoulder, yanking him back. He glared at her, shaking her away, turning to Hemlock.

"Wipe that smug smirk off your face, mate; I'm warning you," he snapped.

Hemlock looked over his shoulder at Ophelia, smiling deviously. "They're all rather riled up, aren't they?"

There was that overwhelming dread again. All Ophelia wanted was to flee. There were Spirits beyond the willow that'd gladly take her back to the mortal realm. If she ran fast enough, maybe the others wouldn't catch up.

Amaranth stood, rocking back and forth on her heels. "Hemlock, you attempted to kill someone."

Hemlock cast his grin upon her. "Sssee, I would sssay I only tried to frighten him. That isss my duty, no?"

Fern rolled her eyes. "When you were created, we intended for mortals to pray to you *despite* their fear. You were meant to be a protector."

"And yet, that didn't ssstick," Hemlock scoffed. "If had, we wouldn't have the ever-lovely Gladiolusss, now would we?"

Gladiolus, Spirit of Courage, laughed darkly. "Hemlock,

you do realize you attacked a mortal, correct?"

Hemlock tipped his hat. "Did I? Sssee, I was under the impresssion he was one of usss. At leassst, that'sss what the ssseedling told me."

"I did not!" Ophelia snapped.

Hemlock gave a great, dramatic shrug. "Who elssse would I have heard it from?"

"You were lurking in the shadows when she spoke with Holly," Fern spat. "Mercy me, you act like *you're* the Spirit of Trickery!"

"Tricks, not lies, Fernie," Foxglove said, looking hurt.

"As if they aren't the same thing," said Lotus.

Foxglove gasped, standing. "They aren't!"

Multiple members of the Pantheon began yelling over one another in an attempt to prove themselves right. Amaranth blew a raspberry, looking to Nightshade, who was pinching the bridge of her nose beneath her veil.

Salvia stood, smoothing the wrinkles from her apron. She looked so very similar to Syrena it was almost frightening.

"Children," she said, her voice shaking the ruins. Somewhere, something crashed. The Spirits quieted, looking to her expectantly. "Petty squabbles solve nothing. If North Star has returned, our focus should be protecting the vessel."

Higanbana, Spirit of Ruin, shook his head. "I'll respectfully counter that. The last North Star brought destruction to the mortal realm. I say the vessel should be disposed of before they realize their power." How contradictory to his purpose that statement was. If anyone was content with the end of the world, it should've been him.

Holly put up a hand before Ophelia could speak her mind. "You know damn well none of that was Ljot's fault."

Higanbana rolled his eyes, pointing an accusatory finger at him. "You were blindsided by her, Hol. You did not know her as we did."

"You're right; I knew her better," Holly spat. "All she did was defend your actions, and yet you let that imbecile slay her. We are Spirits; we're not meant to die, and yet you lost one of your elders. Ljot has been gone for a thousand years, yet this Pantheon has not changed since its decision to banish her. You caused her fall, turned her bitter, refused to listen to her, and now you intend to do the same to Ophelia's companion."

"Ljot caused her own fall," Nightshade whispered. "It was her *decision* to become a fallen star. Her mortality was her *own decision.*"

Ophelia's mind was about to explode. From the look on Jonquil's face, so was his. What did Nightshade mean by calling Ljot a 'fallen star' and that she'd turned mortal? Ophelia hadn't thought that was possible. Truthfully, it shouldn't come as a surprise. If one could be transformed into a Spirit, who was to say a Spirit couldn't turn back?

Amaranth was watching Ophelia intently, eyes narrowed. "Speak your truth, Galanthus," she said. It was a demand. Nothing more, nothing less. To refuse would be blasphemous.

"I'm confused," Ophelia said simply, stepping behind Holly in fear of the repercussions that statement would cause.

"Of course you are," Amaranth laughed. "These are things you shouldn't be privy to."

"But—"

Hemlock raised a hand, a twinkle in his eye. "If I may, the return of North Ssstar sssurprisssesss you all, doesss it not?"

Amaranth's gaze flicked to her. In all the years Ophelia had known her, she had never seen Amaranth afraid. Now, such was evident. Fern, too, looked terrified.

"Which meansss," Hemlock began, stepping out of the mushroom circle, "none of you ssscoured the ssstarsss for Ljot'sss sssoul. Tell me, bunny, does the vesssssel have a flower?"

Amaranth's nostrils flared, her fists clenched tight. To anyone else, she would've looked like a disobedient child.

"Does it?" Higanbana asked.

Every Spirit held their breath, turning to her. The only one looking away was Holly, who shut his eyes and hung his head low. Amaranth took a calming breath, turning her back on them. Fern glanced at Ophelia, working her jaw.

Seamus didn't have a flower. Ophelia didn't know what that meant, but it was obviously very bad.

"Come now, bunny. Don't be coy," Hemlock laughed, "You can tell usss."

"Holly, what does it mean if Seamus doesn't have a flower?" Ophelia asked.

"It means, Galanthus, that Amaranth didn't create him," Hemlock said over his shoulder.

Ophelia's eyes went to the empty throne in the center of the ruins. Amaranth wasn't the creator of the universe. She and Nightshade were a result of its birth. No, there'd been something—some*one*—before them. The emptiness of the throne made Ophelia's skin crawl. As with everyone standing before her, this Spirit had many names, but their purpose was one and the same. The Jackal. Aconite. Most, however, called them The Abyss—the all-consuming darkness beyond the stars where every vile and evil creature went when they died. The very same entity the Ulvemordere worshipped and devoted their lives to. The beginning, the end, and everything in between.

"The Abyss created Seamus?" Ophelia asked, looking back and forth between Holly and Fern.

"Meeting adjourned," Amaranth mumbled, snapping her fingers.

The Spirits surrounding her vanished, leaving nothing behind but their respective flower or plants. Ophelia was left alone in the mushroom circle at a loss for words. Amaranth placed her hand on The Abyss's throne, sighing heavily.

"Do not let the pelt touch him," she said, never once looking back at the frightened Witch.

"So he is North Star, then?" Ophelia asked. "Should I tell him? About you, about them?"

Amaranth merely glanced at what would've been Ljot's throne. "You are lucky, my dear, to be caught between our worlds. You live outside the boundaries and rules we've set. You were right to wonder what you are. You were correct, too, in pondering your destiny. The truth is, I do not know the answer to either of those questions. You, seedling, have surprised even I. Your path is yours to make, Galanthus. If I am to give you one piece of advice, it is to follow your heart. It is the one thing I am sure of."

"Do. . . Do I have a flower?" Ophelia asked, hugging herself tight.

Amaranth finally turned to face her, smiling sympathetically. "You wouldn't be our Snowdrop if you didn't."

Ophelia spun a strand of hair around her finger, frowning. "Can I ask something else?" Amaranth nodded. "When I die, will I end up like Holly? A full Spirit? Or will that be the end of me? What about Seamus?"

"You already know the answer to that," Amaranth said, almost accusatorily.

SECLUSION

With a snap of her fingers, Amaranth sent her back to the mortal realm, leaving Ophelia more confused than she had been in a very long time. Until now, she thought she knew all there was to know about the Spirits, the Garden, and creation. Now, as she stood alone in the alley, she realized how wrong she'd been. How arrogant she'd been in assuming such things.

Ophelia tried the infirmary's door handle, frowning. Locked. A moth fluttered around her head, attracted to the lantern hanging nearby. Frustrated, she waved it away, knocking impatiently. Beyond the door, she heard hurried footsteps. A series of locks clicked and rattled before the door opened.

"Oh!" Syrena said, looking relieved. "Where did you disappear to? You scared me!"

"Sorry," Ophelia mumbled, slipping past her.

Syrena peeked out into the dark as if to make sure no one followed her, then closed and locked the door. "Is something the matter?"

Ophelia scoffed, crossing her arms tight. "I'm all right."

Whether Syrena was accustomed to moody teenagers or she simply didn't feel like it, she didn't press the subject. "Did you eat? There's plenty of leftovers in the kitchen."

At the mention of food, Ophelia's stomach growled so loud one could've mistaken it for thunder. Syrena smiled to herself, winking at her before heading off to the kitchen. Before Ophelia could decide whether to retreat upstairs or make herself comfortable before the blazing fire, she returned with a steaming bowl and mug. With far more excitement than Ophelia would've expected, she handed off the meal, gesturing to the couch before the fire. Gathering that a healthy guest was a rarity, Ophelia sat, trying her best to smile. Plus, she'd rather not be alone with her thoughts right now.

"Did you go to the lookout?" Syrena asked, sitting on the coffee table, eyes full of expectation.

Wide-eyed beneath her mask, Ophelia shifted ever-so-slightly away from her. "Yes."

"Well, what did you think?"

"It was peaceful," Ophelia said, sipping what turned out to be hot apple cider. "Thank you for telling me about it."

"You're very welcome! If you know where to look, you'll find this town has a goldmine of little joys like that," Syrena said, glancing at the staircase. "Your father's fever has gone down a bit. As promised, I kept an extra eye on him."

Ophelia leaned to the side, awkwardly setting down her mug of cider before digging into what appeared to be some kind of vegetable pie. "What does that mean? Will he be okay by morning?"

"Wolves are stubborn. When something tries to knock them down, they throw a harder punch," Syrena laughed, "In that way, I'm hopeful."

It wasn't necessarily a straight answer, but it would do for now. "Well, Seamus is nothing if not incredibly stubborn."

A flicker of confusion crossed Syrena's face. She twiddled her thumbs a moment before clearing her throat. "You're welcome to stay down here for as long as you like, but I've got to turn in for the night. I've got a busy day tomorrow."

"Is there anything I can help with?" Ophelia didn't know why she'd asked, but she did. Maybe it was a force of habit. All she could think of was Lochlan.

Syrena blinked a few times, mild shock swirling in her emerald eyes. "I couldn't ask that of you, love."

Ophelia only shrugged, taking a few more bites of whatever this delightful concoction was. "I have some experience with infirmaries. Even if you want me out of the way, at the very least, I can fold sheets and stock supplies."

Syrena stared at her a good long while, very obviously mulling this over in her mind. "If I think of anything, I'll be sure to let you know. For now, rest, *Hellige En.*"

Ophelia stayed in the den for a long while after Syrena went to bed. Overwhelmed by emotional turmoil, she could only sit and stare at the fireplace.

Half the Pantheon wanted Seamus dead. Hemlock had tried once to kill him, and she knew he'd try again. Higanbana would, too. There was no telling how many other Spirits would visit the mortal realm for the same purpose. It was only a matter of time before something went terribly wrong.

That thought almost sent her into hysterics. Hadn't the last few months gone terribly wrong, too? If worse was to come, she didn't know if that was something they could handle.

After leaving her dirty dishes in the kitchen, Ophelia retreated upstairs. Sitting on the edge of Seamus's bed, she untied her mask and set it aside.

"I'm scared for you," she whispered.

He'd tell her not to worry, that whatever happened to him shouldn't matter, but that simply wasn't the case. Seamus was worth more than he knew, both to their mortal enemies and the Spirits that sought his erasure.

In a word, Amaranth had tasked her with protecting him. If that ended in her death, she would just have to make peace with it. Even if it meant giving up her mortal soul and trading it for something she'd never asked for.

Ophelia hadn't been able to sleep for two days straight. Seamus still lay unmoving, though the color had slowly returned to his pallid skin. Syrena didn't seem surprised. Apparently, she was well acquainted with how the werewolf body healed.

Speaking of the healer, Ophelia quite liked her. She was kind but stern in a motherly way—a no-nonsense sort of woman. Still, she had crow's feet and wrinkles around her lips that told of a life spent smiling and laughing. Ophelia couldn't help but wonder what she was like outside of this stuffy infirmary.

While Miss Syrena Skora was a welcome change of pace, the infirmary was not. It reminded Ophelia all too well of Lochlan's observatory. Was this too-sterile yet grungy atmosphere attached to every infirmary? This was only the second Ophelia had been in. Truth be told, she hoped there wouldn't be any more added to that list. Ophelia didn't think she could handle another ordeal like this.

It was early morning now, the sun just peeking through the dusty old curtains in the den. The whole building was silent. There wasn't even a crackling fire to keep her company. Ophelia had been reading, woken by soft footsteps and light humming. Syrena and her medics were hard at work upstairs, but the stairwell stole the sound and whisked it away. In the quiet, Ophelia felt a grave eeriness descend upon the infirmary. It felt like a million eyes were watching her, waiting for her next move. Glancing out the window, she reminded herself a million eyes would not fit in such a small space. Still, that feeling lingered.

Long past breakfast, Syrena finally came downstairs. She looked somewhat deflated, dark circles marring her eyes.

"God morgen, Syrena," Ophelia whispered.

Syrena swiveled to greet her, all trace of weariness gone. "God morgen, my dear. How are you faring?" she asked, pointing to the bandages around Ophelia's hands.

Ophelia shrugged, flexing her fingers. Her skin felt tight and itchy, but she'd tried her best not to mess with the bandages too much. The last thing she needed right now was a lecture brought on by frayed bandages.

"Fine, thank you," she said.

Syrena gave a wink, then disappeared into the kitchen.

Again, the den descended into silence.

There wasn't much to do to pass the time. Once again, Ophelia tried rotating through her usual hobbies, but none filled the gaping hole in her chest. How had this happened? She'd been content with the dull familiarity in Tø. Yet now, all her favorite things had lost their charm. Even experimenting with her new paint set was beginning to bring boredom.

Syrena entered the den with a tea tray, which seemed to be the breakfast food of choice here in Høstlunden. Either that or Syrena and her medics didn't want to spend too much time pondering what to eat in the morning.

"I've thought of something you can help me with," she said, preparing a cup of tea and buttering a biscuit.

Ophelia practically felt her eyes glitter and gleam beneath her mask. A task! A side quest! Finally, something to distract her ever-worried mind!

"I'm happy to do whatever it is," Ophelia said, taking the cup and saucer she'd been offered. Taking a sip of the tea, she tried very hard not to wrinkle her nose. Far too bitter for her liking.

Syrena dug into one of the pockets on her apron, producing a folded sheet of parchment. "This is a list of supplies I've yet to restock. Would you be a dear and fetch these for me? I've written down which shops you can find them at."

"Oh! Of course!" Ophelia said, greedily taking the list.

Scrawled upon it in a swirling script were ingredients surprisingly familiar to her. Lochlan used most, if not all, of these. A simple task but a welcome one.

"Thank you, honey," Syrena said, offering her a biscuit. "Take your time. Feel free to explore the town some more. I'm in no rush." That was an exceptionally polite way of shooing Ophelia away. It almost made her laugh. "Lunch will be in a few hours, should you wish to join us."

Ophelia had checked off almost everything from Syrena's list. Everything was stored in her satchel, carefully packed to ensure none of the glass vials broke. Just a few odds and ends left, then she'd return for lunch. After that, she'd fall back into mundanity, slowly dying from boredom. Hopefully, she'd be given another task. As she'd said, even folding sheets would be better than sitting in silence.

Buntry—Syrena's bustling town—welcomed Ophelia as an oddity. The people here were curious, not at all frightened by a Skogens Søstre. Instead, they greeted her with questions and ponderings, though Ophelia wasn't quite in the mood to entertain them. She felt like a caged animal or perhaps a sentient statue.

It was all very overwhelming.

Would it be like this when she revealed her Witch Marks to the world? Would people come to her with questions they figured only she could answer? Had Holly experienced all this? She wasn't too fond of finding out, but such was the way of things.

"Well, what's wrong with him?" said a voice from behind.

Ophelia spun, surprised to find Egill lounging lazily against a lamp post. She scowled, hands on her hips. "What's it to you?"

Egill rolled his stark yellow eyes, readjusting his crossed arms. "He's my *friend.* I worry."

"Do you try to kill all your friends, then?"

"You didn't answer my question," he replied, slipping one of his opal daggers from its sheath. He glared at her momentarily, then began picking the dirt out from under his nails with said dagger.

"You're smart, Egill; I'm sure you can figure it out," Ophelia scoffed.

"Where's all this hostility coming from?" he sighed, examining his handiwork. After holding his hand up to the light, he returned to picking away his nails. "Can't we be civil?"

"You attacked us, tied us up, then tried to kill me. Excuse me if I find it hard to be polite," Ophelia laughed, turning.

Egill fell in pace beside her, not once glancing in her direction. "We all do wicked things, little Witch."

"What do you want, Egill?"

"You're meant to be meeting General Melhus before the full moon. In case you've forgotten, that's only a few days from now. Being tardy doesn't bode well for you," he said, pointing the tip of his dagger at her.

A surge of electric anger rushed through Ophelia's body. The tips of her fingers began to glow, the bandages smoking. "How can you align yourself with him? With *them?* Even without your wings, you're still magickind. How can you sit by and watch them massacre our people?" she asked, throwing her arms wide.

Egill fell quiet, gazing at her reflection in his dagger. After a while, he shifted the blade ever so slightly until all he saw was his own face. The longer he stared at himself, the deeper his scowl became.

"You're worse than them," Ophelia whispered, wondering why they were still walking together. "So much worse."

"I am well aware, little Witch," he said, sighing heavily. "I do not expect a *child* to understand. What you view as simply good and evil does not apply to everyone. There is nuance and happenstance and things you will never understand; try as you might."

"I am not a child," Ophelia mumbled, well aware of how

childish that made her sound.

"You are in my book," Egill scoffed. She got the feeling that was something to be proud of, though coming from him, it still made her feel small. "You've seen but a fraction of the world, met but a handful of beings. Until you have traveled this earth and learned all you can, you will never be more than an empty vessel. Even then, you can't claim to know everything. Yet, funnily enough, you will have gained understanding. If only a little, you'll begin to understand."

"I know more about the world's workings than you'd imagine," Ophelia snapped, stopping dead in her tracks. "You'd do well to remember that."

Egill spun on her, placing the tip of his dagger on her chin. "And *you* would do well to remember who my employers are."

Around them, passersby paused to watch. Hushed voices began to rise in panic, their words accentuated by pointing fingers and looks of fright. Egill scowled, glancing over his shoulder.

"I'd suggest you leave for Veil before it's too late," he whispered.

Before Ophelia could respond, he was gone in a puff of fairy dust.

CHAPTER EIGHTY-SEVEN

The Acting General

"Now. . . who is it you're going to see?" Syrena asked, the skepticism evident in her voice.

Ophelia felt her cheeks go red, and unfortunately, she wasn't hiding beneath her mask. "Tiril Kirkeby. She's sort of like my grandmother, in a way."

Syrena may not be a werewolf, but Ophelia was certain she could smell lies from a mile away. "Ahh. I see," she mumbled, frowning. "And when will you be back?"

Ophelia had spent most of the prior night pouring over the Wayfarer's Map, charting a course. Despite knowing how long this journey would take, her words came out rather shakily. "In a few days."

"And what shall I tell your father if he wakes and you're not here?" Syrena asked, arms crossed tight. She tapped her foot impatiently, that frown turning to a scowl. "I may have a very angry, very worried werewolf on my hands during the full moon."

"Tell him I'm with Tiril." Ophelia's face was about as warm as the face of a girl with ice in her blood could get. "I'll be back, I swear it."

Syrena raised her eyebrow but didn't ask any further questions. After packing her a lunch, she sent Ophelia on her merry way.

With Rain in tow, she went off to face the dastardly General Arild Melhus.

For two days, Ophelia and Rain were on the road.

Two days of quiet.

Two days of expectance.

And now, here she was.

Veil was not how Ophelia had imagined. Even under the guise of night, she'd seen it all so differently in her mind. She'd been picturing some well-to-do town not dissimilar to Buntry. Instead, Veil was little more than a washed-up mining town. The village lived alongside the ravine, a long, rickety bridge connecting it to the other side, leading to its twin city. Dark, foreboding buildings lined either side of a dirt street. Inside, shifting shadows floated back and forth. Were there people here? Civilians?

Rain blew hot steam out his nose as they trotted quietly past them. There were no torchlights or glowing crystals to be seen. The only light came from the moon, casting the world in a pale silver glow.

Hopefully, Seamus would be all right during the full moon. Maybe if he transformed, it'd heal him.

Frayed banners blew back and forth high above, their stitching barely visible. Veil was not just a town; it was an Ulvemordere hideout. Beneath the rumbling thunder, Ophelia heard growls. Stationed outside the buildings were men and women in iron armor, their hands flexing, fighting the urge to attack her. What she'd initially thought were boulders or craggy outcroppings were trolls. Their rock-like skin blended into the shadows, their bejeweled eyes sparkling in the moonlight. Overturned barrels and carts littered the streets with rotting fruit and vegetables. Here and there, trolls snacked on both the wares and what had been storing them. Everything smelled of death decay.

Rain looked over his shoulder, visibly distraught.

"Shh," Ophelia whispered.

Seamus would ask if she was nervous.

Sighing, she whispered, "Not as much as I thought I'd be."

In turn, he'd ask if she was sure she wanted to go in alone. He'd tell her that no matter what, he'd be there. Ophelia would laugh and say, 'If I need you, I'll call.' But there was no one to call for. Not anymore. It was just her and Rain. And, of course, the wind at her back and the thunder above.

Ahead, a flicker of orange lit up the dark. Ophelia urged Rain onward, realizing this was where she was meant to meet Arild.

Rain slowed to a stop, almost frowning as Ophelia slipped from his saddle. "If I need you, I'll call," she sighed, kissing his forehead.

Arild's townhouse was inviting and charming in the way only brick buildings were. It even had a pleasant wrap-around porch. Unfortunately, the man standing upon it sullied that.

Egill—stupid, stupid Egill—grabbed her arm as she stepped onto the porch, stopping her. Without so much as looking at her, he asked, "Did you come alone?"

Ophelia knew very well where she found the audacity to respond the way she did. She sounded like Seamus. "You may be scared, Egill, but I am not."

Egill narrowed his glowing, yellow eyes, scowling. "You have no idea who you're dealing with."

"I beg to differ," she snapped, shaking him away.

"You're going to regret this day as long as you live, little Witch, trust me," he sighed, letting go of her arm.

"Am I?"

"This isn't a joke."

"And yet, I laugh. What's wrong? I thought defiance was a trait you admired."

Head held high, she opened the door, immediately enveloped in warmth. It was a sticky sort of heat. Someone had let the fire burn too hot, especially for a night like this. Inside, Arild's townhouse was nearly empty. Two chairs sat beside the fireplace, facing each other, a bearskin rug between them. Hundreds of claw marks marked the wood floors, indicating hundreds of transformations.

To Ophelia's dismay, Egill had followed her inside and now stood near a grand staircase to the left.

Standing before the fire was a man in a patchwork fur cloak. He gestured loosely to the chair on the right, waiting for her to sit. Ophelia steeled herself, doing as she was told. She perched on the edge of the seat, ankles crossed, hands resting in her lap as she'd seen Tiril do.

"I don't believe we've been properly introduced," he said, turning to her, his hand held out for her to shake. "Arild Melhus, acting Ulvemordere General. A pleasure to make your acquittance, Miss Av'Skogen."

"Norland," Ophelia corrected, shaking his hand as it was the polite thing to do.

"Beg your pardon?" Arild asked.

"Norland," she repeated. "Ophelia *Norland*."

Egill audibly rolled his eyes, mumbling about how Seamus's stupidity truly rubbed off on her.

Arild's lips curved into a hungry smile. "Oh, believe me, *skitten heks*, that name comes with nothing but death. You should be careful attaching it to yourself. Words are power."

"Yes, and I intend to cast only kindness," Ophelia said, smiling as he sunk into the seat opposite her. "At least on those who deserve it."

Arild lounged lazily in his seat, head propped up by one clawed hand. The tips of his fingers were gray and furry, his nails sharp and jagged. They dug into his cheek, drawing blood, but he didn't seem to notice.

"Let's talk about that, shall we? This idyllic fantasy world you live in," he said, sounding too tired even to speak.

Ophelia kept her face neutral, nodding. "What would you like to know?"

Arild crossed his ankles as if to mock her. "How do you intend to eradicate the threat that is my people? What was it? 'Kill them with kindness,' as the saying goes?"

"Oh, no," Ophelia laughed. "No, *you* Arild, we'll kill the old-fashioned way."

"Ahh. . . I see. . ." He studied her for a moment, smirking. "Do you like. . . *games*, your Highness?" he asked, patiently awaiting her answer.

"Not particularly, no," Ophelia said through gritted teeth.

Arild laughed, gazing into the fire. "Trust me, I think this is one you'll want to play."

Behind her, floorboards creaked. Ophelia glanced over her shoulder, watching Egill ascend the stairs, a dark look on his face. Above, there were muffled, exasperated voices. Something fell, rattling the ceiling and shaking loose a plume of dust. Arild's smirk grew into a wide, toothy grin as two women in bright scarlet robes descended the stairs. Between them, they struggled to carry a massive, padlocked chest. Huffing and puffing, they set it before Ophelia and Arild's chairs.

Arild pushed himself into a more regal sitting position, back straight, head held high. "Would you like to guess what's in that box?" he asked, inclining his head toward the chest.

"Is this the game, then?" Ophelia laughed. "Doesn't sound very fun."

"Oh, but it is!" Arild said, tapping his claws on his armrest. "Humor me, Your Highness. Take a guess."

Ophelia didn't *have* to guess. She knew exactly what was in that box and what he was trying to do. He found this to be a joke. She held no power here, surrounded by enemies he thought could overpower her. They might be able to, in all honesty. She'd tire quickly against all of them. Yet, despite that, she still had her resolve.

Two terrifying men had had a hand in raising her. Though one of them still had much to teach her, the other had left her with lessons she'd never forget. Lochlan had fancied himself to be a King. He'd been many things, but stupid, he was not. For better or worse, he'd taught Ophelia how to handle herself with eloquence, even before those who didn't want to give her the time of day. Seamus had bestowed upon her a sharp tongue, but Lochlan was the one who'd taught her how words could be deadly. In turn, that had taught her how to guard herself from simple minds. This was not a joke, nor a game, or anything amusing in the slightest. Ophelia would choose peace over violence any day, but that didn't mean she was incapable of horrific things. That was just human nature. You cannot have one without the other, but it is how you balance those things that define you.

"What exactly do you want?" Ophelia asked, averting her eyes from the chest.

"Right now, I want you to guess," Arild said, scarlet eyes aglow with delight.

"I refuse to play these games. What do you expect to gain today? You know what that pelt is, and so do I. If you place it upon his shoulders, you're practically damning yourself."

Arild nodded, tapping his chin. The long scars on his face seemed eerily similar to Seamus's. "Yes, yes, you're referring to the prophecy, hmm? Am I—" he laughed "—am I meant to be scared? Do you know what will happen to a werewolf should they don the pelt of fallen kin?" Ophelia didn't give him the satisfaction of a response. "No? Well, let's show you, shall we?"

Arild stood to his full, towering height, snapping his fingers. Above, a door opened and then slammed shut. Muffled screams and cries for help echoed through the silent house. The whole ceiling shook with heavy footsteps and the sound of something—or rather some*one*—being dragged. Egill appeared at the top of the stairs, pulling along a woman with a bag over her head. Forcing her to stand, he shoved her, leading her down the stairs.

Egill brought the captive to stand behind the chest and the robed women, emotionless. With a dramatic flourish, Arild plucked the bag from her head.

Saoirse.

"Did I forget to mention her in my letters, or am I mistaken?" Arild asked.

Saoirse broke down into tears, barely able to breathe between shaking sobs. Scowling, Egill shook her until she found a way to calm down. Her eyes shone the same electric green as Seamus's when his wolf fought for control. Ophelia couldn't believe what was happening.

"I'm so sorry," Saoirse cried. "I'm so sorry!"

Ignoring Arild's look of triumph, Ophelia stood, trying to arrange her face into a sympathetic smile. "It's okay. It's going to be okay."

"A Witch *and* a liar. What a dichotomy," Arild sighed. "Make a move, *skitten heks*, I dare you."

"I'll kill you," Ophelia seethed.

There was a moment of silence before he shrugged, stepping to the side. "Ladies, if you please."

The robed women took keys from their sleeves and began unlocking the padlocks on the chest. As the locks opened and the chains dropped, the chest began to stir.

"Run and see what happens," Arild whispered, directing his words at Saoirse.

Ophelia felt herself go pale, afraid of even blinking. Egill hung his head low, nudging Saoirse's foot until she sunk to her knees. One of the women opened the chest while the other reached in and lifted a silver pelt into the light. It shook and thrashed, coming to life as though possessed. With all its might, it tugged toward the door, and Ophelia knew what it was after. Seamus. The pelt was calling to him.

"Beautiful, isn't it?" Arild asked, his voice wistful. "To think, such power resides within it, yet it can only be accessed by a single soul."

Saoirse's eyes went wide with realization. "I don't want it," she mumbled, shaking her head. "I—I don't want it. I don't want it."

Arild gazed longingly at her, like a hunter watching their mark. "As you can see, your lovely little friend here took the bite. Fortunately for us, it took; otherwise, we'd have no one to demonstrate on."

The woman carrying the pelt came to stand between him and Ophelia, clutching the pelt so tightly that her knuckles had turned white. On instinct, Ophelia shifted away, trying not to let it touch her. In response, it thrashed forward, forgetting about Seamus long enough to try to envelop her.

"It doesn't like you much, does it? Can't say I blame it," Arild laughed.

"Saoirse has nothing to do with this," Ophelia spat, hands crackling. "Let her go."

Arild clicked his tongue, shaking his head. "Ah, but she knew you were a Witch. You were aware there are punishments for that, right? You can't be *that* stupid."

"The girl had a choice, and this is what she chose," Egill said, one hand squeezing Saoirse's shoulder.

Arild nodded, gesturing loosely toward her. "I'm not merciless, Your Highness. The people of Tø were given a choice. Either stand by you and die a painless death, or rebuke your name, vowing to glorify the good and righteous Abyss. Saoirse, love, how many stood with you and that oaf? What was his name? The one that chose the noose? The butcher?"

Saoirse went very still, staring down Ophelia as though the Witch would strike her down if she spoke.

"Åsmund?" Ophelia whispered, feeling something shatter deep, deep inside her soul.

"Yes, yes, that was him. Admirable, fellow, I will say.

Never once wavered, even when his wife and children begged him to reconsider." Arild spoke with such mirth, such life. Ophelia was sick to her stomach, watching the room spin. The sparks at her fingers died. "I bet you're wondering how this one lasted so long, though, right?"

"I'm so sorry, Phee," Saoirse whispered. "I messed up. I'm so sorry."

"How long have the two of you been friends? Oh, what does it matter? Your friendship is about to end anyway," Arild laughed. "The fact is, I know all your little secrets, Galanthus."

Saoirse held her head in her hands, once again sobbing uncontrollably. It was only then that Ophelia realized she was bound with wolfsbane-soaked rope. Her wrists were rubbed raw and bubbled as the purplish liquid dripped down her arms.

"She may have chosen you over life, but she didn't choose you over her siblings," Arild sighed. "I'm not a monster, you know. I can show mercy. But test me, Witch, and I'll kill them next."

"Saoirse," Ophelia said, kneeling to her eye level. "Saoirse, look at me."

Saoirse's shaking hands fell to her lap. Pale green light illuminated her face, her eyes bloodshot and full of tears.

"It's okay. *We're* okay," Ophelia smiled. "They'll be okay, too, I swear it."

She tried to reach for Saoirse's hands, but Egill yanked her back, giving a warning look.

Ophelia stood, rounding on Arild. "What does this prove?" Ophelia asked, sweeping her arms wide. "You're a force to be reckoned with, I get it. What do you want from me, Arild? Hurting Saoirse—"

Arild lunged forward, taking her face in his hand. He squeezed her cheeks as hard as he could, his long claws drawing blood. "You can offer *me* nothing, little Witch. I know you don't fear me; I've made peace with that. But I also know that you don't care what happens to you. You do, however, care about what happens to *them*. If that's the only way to break you, Galanthus, then so be it."

Galanthus.

He'd called her that twice now. Yes, Saoirse knew Jonquil, but she'd never known he was a Spirit. Further still, she didn't know Ophelia's other names. Someone else must've told him that. Either the Abyss or its ears within the Garden. Probably Hemlock.

"What did it promise you?" Ophelia asked, staring deep into Arild's scarlet eyes, searching for any semblance of humanity.

"The likes of which you can never understand," Arild mumbled, shoving her backward as he turned to Egill and the robed women. "Get it over with."

Egill stepped back, scowling. Arild looked as though he'd won a different kind of game, some cosmic one only he knew the rules to. He nodded to the woman holding the pelt, that toothy smile spreading across his lips once more.

"It's okay, Phee," Saoirse whispered. "I'll be okay."

Ophelia couldn't help but back away, overcome by violent sobs. Try as she might, she couldn't bring herself to turn away as the pelt was lowered onto Saoirse's shoulders. The monstrosity enveloped her instantly, twisting around her like a cape caught in the wind. Saoirse screamed, reaching up to try and pry it off, but the pelt was too strong. Like some sort of sentient wrapping paper, the pelt continued to wrap around her, hungry like a snake.

As quickly as it had begun, it was over.

The pelt fell forward with a sickening thump, loosening its grip. The women in red pried the pelt from Saoirse's body, folding it neatly despite its struggle.

Saoirse—kind, loving, Saoirse—lay lifeless, staring blankly up at Ophelia. Her eyes were milky, and her body was covered in stark white constellation-like marks.

Arild took hold of Ophelia's shoulder, squeezing with all his might. "I would stop crying if I were you. It doesn't bode well for the soul."

Ophelia slapped his hand away, rounding on him. "You're a *monster*!" she cried. "A horrid, horrid monster!"

Arild closed the space between them, digging his sharp, iron claws into her neck. "Yes, that's the point," he snarled, blowing hot steam out of his nose, "therefore, we are equals."

"I am *nothing* like you!" Ophelia spat.

All he did was smile, tapping her nose a few times. "One

day, you will be. One day, you may even be worse. The more you have to lose, Vinterheks, the easier it is for fear to control you," Arild said, turning his back to her. He knelt before Saoirse, admiring his handiwork. "Your curse is your compassion. Mine is simply people like you."

He snapped his fingers, and Egill appeared at her side in a puff of fairy dust.

"I'll be in touch, *skitten heks*. I so look forward to playing chess with you," Arild whispered over his shoulder.

The world around Ophelia was suddenly too bright to look at. Panicked, she put up her hands to cover her eyes. The warmth disappeared, and Ophelia blinked, finding herself outside. Egill released his grip on her arm, his hands resting on the hilts of his daggers.

"You really shouldn't have come alone," he snapped.

Rain stomped up to them, blowing hot steam in his face. Her horse was a regal fellow, never one to speak without thinking. However, Ophelia imagined he had a few choice words for Egill.

"Tell your 'employer,'" Ophelia began, climbing into the saddle, "that I'll give him a war if he wants one. Checkmate that."

All the way back to Buntry, she cried. For Saoirse, for Åsmund, for Seamus—everyone. Even herself.

Arild Melhus needed to die, and Ophelia would be damned if it didn't happen by her hand.

CHAPTER EIGHTY-EIGHT

NIGHT TERRORS

Seamus was trying his best to shake away his unease as she and Ophelia walked toward. . . somewhere. Where were they going again? He couldn't remember. Somehow, they'd found themselves in a narrow valley on a thin, rocky path. Alongside the path was a stream. Seamus yawned, looking over his shoulder to ensure Ophelia was still close behind. A few feet back, she waded through the water, her skirts dragging behind her.

"Stay close," Seamus said, running his hand along the damp, rocky wall beside him.

Before Ophelia could respond, herding calls rang through the valley from above. They echoed in Seamus's body, rattling him to the core. The vibrations woke the sleeping wolf hiding beneath his skin. For a moment, he'd forgotten it was there. Now, he was suddenly hyperaware of the sounds surrounding them, of the metallic smell wafting through the air.

Panicked, he ran toward Ophelia, yanking her into the shadows.

"What's wrong?" she whispered.

Smoke washed away the smell of blood. All around him, invisible fires burned. From the cliffside overhead, he heard a wolf's cry. Pain rang through his mind.

"I—I need to get up there," he said, stumbling into a shaft of light, the cold sun burning his eyes. It was too bright; he couldn't see any figures on the horizon. "It's hurt."

"What's hurt?" Ophelia asked. She hadn't followed him into the light, choosing to linger in the shadows.

"The wolf!"

". . . what wolf?"

Seamus looked down at her, feeling crazed. "The howling wolf! Can't you hear it? Can't you hear the hunters?" he asked, throwing his arms wide.

The cries of the wolf ricocheted in his ears so loudly he could barely hear her response. It was as if that sorry beast was right beside him, wailing and howling with all its might, hoping someone would listen.

"Seamus, I don't hear anything."

He grumbled nonsensically under his breath, waving her away, scanning the cliffside for purchase. He could climb it, surely. He had to find that wolf. The hunters would kill it. He had to help it.

"Come on, I need your help," he said over his shoulder.

No response.

"Kid, I need you to—"

He peered around the rock where they'd been hiding to find a bloodied mess of the Winter Witch he'd come to love. Her mask lay broken beside her, revealing five stark silver slashes across her face. Her Witch Marks were ashy. Dark bruises covered every inch of visible skin.

The cries of the wolf above suddenly stopped.

Seamus stood frozen, staring at Ophelia's lifeless body. What had just happened? He looked away for two seconds, and what? She'd died? Surely not. This. . . this wasn't right. This couldn't be happening. This wasn't right! Something was incredibly wrong. He had to—

Wet, sticky warmth bloomed on the back of his neck.

Slowly, he turned on his heels, dread filling him.

Standing before him, its gray fur matted with clumps of snow, its eyes glowing green, was a gigantic wolf. Hot steam blew out of its nose, encompassing Seamus in a plume of metallic-smelling breath. Blood. This wolf had *blood* dripping from its mouth. It *drip-drip-dripped* down onto him, causing his stomach to churn.

Seamus called upon his own wolf, upon his claws, upon every primal instinct he had, but all he found was cowardice. His wolf was gone.

The giant canine before him shook the snow from its fur. That storm-cloud gray fur began to shift, darkening and shimmering. Flecks of white still littered it, but they weren't snowflakes. It was like staring up into the flickering sky on a cloudless night. Those green eyes blinked, melting into a milky white. The blood dripping from its mouth gleamed silver.

"What did you do?" Seamus snarled, looking over his shoulder, stomach churning at the silver gashes marring Ophelia's face.

"Me?" the wolf asked. He was sure he'd heard that voice before. "This is not my work, Star Seed."

Seamus felt himself pale. ". . . Ljot?"

The wolf lunged at him, enormous paws dripping in silver blood as it aimed for his chest. Seamus skidded back, slipping on loose rocks and colliding painfully with the ground. The wolf's front paws landed squarely on his chest, stealing his breath.

Oh, that damn wolf of his. It always caused him such trouble, yet it was never there when he needed it most. He screamed and cried and begged for it to crawl out of the dark cave inside him where it slept, but it never came. There was a real, tangible threat upon its master, yet it didn't care. It never had.

And he knew why.

It had always viewed him as a traitor, as someone unworthy of a pack. Unworthy of love. Of life. His wolf despised him, and for good reason.

The only reason they'd been on good terms lately was because of a certain Witch. It had a purpose, feeling a kinship with her. But without Ophelia, who was it meant to protect? That Witch was the only thing that'd calmed its mind. Not even his mate had done that. Ingrid had been an anchor, but the rope between them had easily frayed and snapped—even before she died.

But Ophelia? Ophelia was the invisible force that stilled choppy waters. She'd forced Seamus's ship to float idly on serene waves, forced him to take pause, to look around and see where he'd washed up. He'd found himself at her side. That's where he should always be.

The enormous wolf pushed its snout against his forehead. Its breath was sweet and sticky—like poison. Its fur pulsed, changing colors like an aurora.

"I damned my world," it whispered. "I will not let you follow in my pawprints."

Seamus grabbed hold of the wolf's legs, anger overtaking his numbed sadness. He pulled its legs apart with all his might, his fingernails extending into claws that ripped into the towering wolf's night-sky-like fur and flesh.

Seamus was plunged into darkness.

A horrid, tearing sound resonated through the air.

Something soft and warm lay in his hands where blood should've pooled.

He was suddenly very sweaty, panting heavily, lying unmoving on uneven ground, his heart hammering in his chest.

CHAPTER EIGHTY-NINE

SWEET RELIEF

Pinpricks of heat radiated across Seamus's left side. He groaned, blinking away the stinging light flooding his vision. The ceiling pulsed above him. There he was, lying in a bed, a torn pillow in his clawed hands.

Knowing what'd transpired had only been a nightmare should've eased his mind, yet that overwhelming feeling of dread held fast to his heart. Where was he? Last he remembered, the Lindwyrm had wrapped itself around his legs, and Ophelia was—

Ophelia!

Was she hurt? What had happened? He remembered sharp teeth and a scream as the world went all topsy-turvy. Seamus sat up with a start, looking around with wild eyes. To his dismay, she was sprawled out on a bed two feet away. On the nightstand between them was her mask, along with a few vials and some bandages. Around them, lilac curtains shut out the outside world. They must be in an infirmary.

His arm and shoulder screamed in agony as he tore the thin blankets off himself, struggling to stand. Gentle hands were on him in an instant, pushing him back down as he scrambled drunkenly to reach Ophelia's unmoving body.

"Your daughter is fine, Mr. Norland," a woman said quietly.

Seamus glanced up at the freckled face for a split second, utterly caught off guard by the words she'd used. "She's—She's—What's wrong with her? What happened? Is she all right?" he asked. His voice was strained, his words tumbling out of his mouth in an inebriated sort of way.

"She's perfectly fine, just exhausted. You, on the other hand, should be dead. Now lay back down and *do not* wake her. She hasn't slept for days—up worrying about you, I might add. I've only just gotten her to bed," the woman sighed heavily. "Dreadful timing, really," she whispered under her breath.

A crown of blue-violet salvia was resting upon her head. Seamus didn't know much about the Terrestrial religion, but he knew that meant she was a healer—and a skilled one at that.

Eyes fixed on Ophelia, he begrudgingly complied, haphazardly climbing back into bed, swearing. Every movement felt like someone had poured scalding water on his left arm. If he didn't know better, he'd have thought his wounds had come from the mystical wolf in his dream. He could still feel its paws on his chest. Was that Ljot, or had Tiril finally crawled under his skin and filled his mind with nonsense? Either way, that nightmare wasn't something he'd soon forget. The image of Ophelia dead at his feet was burned into his mind, settling beside the image of her killing those trolls. He shivered uncontrollably, running a hand through his hair, wincing at the movement.

The healer took no pity on him. All she did was click her tongue and shake her head.

"How. . . How long have I been out?" he asked gruffly, clearing his throat, trying to push away his worries as she tucked him back into bed. He'd not been sleeping; he'd been comatose.

Syrena frowned. "A little over a week. A normal man would've died within the hour," she said, giving him a pointed look. "Lindwyrms are not to be trifled with."

All Seamus could do was nod. His eyes drifted back to Ophelia, noting how her hand rested on the nightstand as if she were reaching for him in her sleep. His bandaged arm twitched toward her. He wanted nothing more than to look into her moon-bright eyes.

"Are you sure she's okay?" he asked.

The healer turned to gaze upon the sorry sight that was his Witch. Gentleness replaced all remnants of animus. Ah, she played favorites, did she? There was an unspoken truth hanging in the air. This woman had seen Ophelia's Witch

Marks. What did that mean to her?

"I do believe she needs more rest than even you," she whispered.

The vibrant blue skin beneath Ophelia's eyes had gone a dark purple, the rest of her skin so pale it was almost translucent. Seamus could just make out hints of light flitting back and forth across her face. The tiniest yet deadliest form of lightning to ever exist. Her hair was a matted mess, and her wrinkled clothes were caked in dried mud. It'd been a while since he stopped and really looked at her. Damn, she looked terrible.

The healer dusted her apron of some bitter-smelling leaves, nodding to herself as she turned away. "Try not to worry." Seamus couldn't tell if that was directed at him or not. "I'll return shortly. Fancy some dinner?"

Seamus gave a curt nod, his eyes sweeping over her. Her frock matched the salvia on her head. Her ruffled apron appeared to have been cream-colored once, though now it was stained with various colors. Best he could, he tried not to dwell on the red and brown splotches. Between the apron and frock was a lacy black skirt to which leaves, lint, and petals clung. Seamus's mind brought forth an image of Lochlan in his tattered old robe. Surely, that bristly old curmudgeon would frown upon this woman. That thought suddenly diminished a few of his worries.

The healer slipped between the lilac curtains and left through a door beyond.

"Pup," Seamus hissed when he heard the door close. "Ophelia, wake up."

Stomping footsteps creaked beyond the curtains before they were thrown open. "I told you not to wake her!" the healer snapped.

Seamus felt his face go red. Both with embarrassment and defiance. "And why should I listen to you?"

She stomped up to the bed, the curtains swaying back and forth as they closed behind her. Without an ounce of hesitation, she pinched his bandaged arm with all her might.

"Hey!" Seamus growled, flinching away, eyes wide.

"Oh, relax, *wolfie*. You'll heal," she spat. "Leave her be."

With that, she left for good.

Seamus lay staring up at the ceiling, trying to distract himself with thoughts that were not consumed by Ophelia.

Or Ljot.

Or the Ulvemordere.

Egill.

Dødbyen.

Tiril, Helgi, and Reija.

He scowled. This proved more difficult than it should have been.

Quietly and as carefully as possible, he reached for Ophelia's hand. As soon as his fingers grazed hers, his claws shrunk back into his nailbeds. His massive, bloodied, and bruised hand completely engulfed hers. Ophelia didn't move, but he swore she gave him a gentle squeeze. He could feel her pulse beating against his palm. That alone was enough to allow his body to relax. Yes, he could hear her heart. But sometimes that wasn't enough. Even werewolf ears could lie.

Seamus lost track of time, slipping in and out of consciousness as he held Ophelia's freezing hand.

No part of him wanted to let go, but as soon as he heard the click-clack of that blasted healer's heels, he dropped it. For whatever reason, that woman scared him.

The healer returned with a heaping plate of food and a steaming cup of tea. Seamus took it gratefully, not realizing until now just how hungry he'd been.

"My name is Syrena. I own this little hole in the wall," she explained, sweeping her hands through the air.

"Seamus Norland," he said with a curt nod.

"Pleasure," she smiled. "Oh! Before I forget, you needn't worry about paying me. Ophelia's taken it out of the prize money."

Seamus gave her a questioning look.

"You earned a bit of gold for your troubles with the Lindwyrm."

He nodded to himself, looking sidelong at Ophelia. "Good, good."

Syrena gently pushed the teacup up to his lips. "I promise it'll help you feel better."

He sniffed it warily, unsure what notes he thought might waft into his nose. How can one tell if tea is poisoned? Despite his wariness, he drank the cup dry in one sip. Warmth bloomed across his chest, encouraging his sleepiness.

"Thank you," he said, setting the cup aside as he reached for a sausage.

Syrena just nodded, eyes on his bandaged arm. "Last night was a full moon. Your body tried to transform, but it wasn't strong enough. How're you feeling?"

He shrugged, grimacing. "Like you said, I'll heal."

"Are you dizzy at all?"

"I was when I first woke up, but fine now," he said. "More tired than anything."

"You're both welcome to stay here as long as you need," Syrena said. Her words were jovial, but her lips pulled into a thin pout.

Seamus studied her for a moment. She couldn't have been much younger than him, yet there was wisdom in her eyes he was sure he'd never possess. He saw the same in Ophelia. He figured they'd become fast friends while he'd been asleep. There was worry in her eyes, too, hidden amid the green, swirling in the tiny gold flakes around her pupils.

"Is something wrong?" he asked, his eyes flitting back to Ophelia against his will.

"You're on wanted posters, Mr. Norland," Syrena said softly. "You've amassed a high bounty. Higher still each day you evade capture."

Seamus straightened. "And? What's it to you, carrot top?"

She rolled her eyes. "You're fortunate to have stumbled upon mine of all infirmaries," she said haughtily.

"Why's that?"

"Anyone else would've turned you in," she snapped. "Though if you call me 'carrot top' again, I may reconsider."

She stood, taking his plate—which wasn't licked clean, so he wasn't done with it—and stuck her tongue out at him.

Seamus grabbed her arm, glaring at her. "Well, if that's the case, *ginger snap*, put your listening ears on. If you do anything to put her in danger, I'll make you regret it."

Syrena shook free of his grip, leaning down to his eye level. "I'd never put *Hellige En* in danger. You may take everything else I say as a lie, but that is the truth through and through." With that, she flicked him hard on the nose. "Behave, wolfie."

She stood to her full height—which wasn't as impressive as she made it out to be—then straightened her rumpled apron. They both looked to Ophelia, watching her sleep soundlessly. The dark circles under her eyes had faded slightly, but not by much. She looked almost sickly, as if she belonged solely to the infirmary and its self-important healer.

"If you need anything, holler," Syrena sighed, then disappeared through the curtains.

PAST LIVES

Sleep had come easy for the first time in years. Whether that was the doing of the Lindwyrm or Syrena, Seamus didn't know nor care. He was just glad to sleep without a nightmare, knowing Ophelia was safe and sound a few inches away.

Morning came, and with it, he grew restless. His wolf had, too. While Seamus was glad to have had a dreamless sleep, his wolf kept thinking of his nightmare the day before. What in the ever-darkening night sky had that been? It'd felt so real. He could still smell that giant wolf's breath, the weight of its paws heavy on his chest as he got up and stretched. If he stayed any longer in bed, he may start hallucinating about the whole ordeal. He shivered, casting a sidelong glance at Ophelia, who was still asleep and snoring softly. His wolf whimpered, wishing she were awake.

Shaking his head in a poor attempt at clearing it, Seamus took a clean set of clothes from his pack and set off to find a washroom. He dressed quickly, scrubbing his face near raw before venturing out to find Syrena. She'd said to holler if he needed anything. Hopefully, that meant she'd feed him again if he asked nicely.

When she'd called this place a hole in the wall, she'd surely meant it. The small hospital ward—'small' as in six beds, all currently occupied—was on the second floor. The stairs wound up one more level to a padlocked door, presumed to be staff housing. The main floor, little more than a few feet across in either direction, was more of a den than the entry of an infirmary. There were two heavy armchairs near a brick fireplace on one side of the room and three long cabinets filled with all sorts of herbs and tinctures on the other. In the corner sat a small round table with four periwinkle stools and a matching tablecloth. Beside the table was a half-open door. Seamus could hear a quiet conversation and the clink of silverware filtering through from the room beyond. His stomach growled.

Syrena stood before the shelves, a small, tattered notebook in one hand and a quill in the other. Nearby, a jar of glittery orange ink sat dangerously close to the edge of the windowsill. Crates had been deposited by the door, their lids propped against the cabinets. She seemed to be doing inventory and restocking any empty jars.

"How are you feeling?" she asked without looking up at him.

"Stiff and hungry," Seamus yawned as Syrena scribbled away in her notebook.

"Haven't I already fed you?" she laughed. She shoved her notebook and quill under her arm, picked up an empty vial, and then peeled off the label.

"Sometime yesterday," Seamus said with a shrug. "What's breakfast like in these parts?"

Syrena glanced at him, eyebrows furrowed deep over her eyes. Slowly, she turned to look out the dust-covered window to her right. Her shoulders sagged as she sighed.

"Didn't realize what time it was. I'm so sorry," she mumbled. Discarding her notebook, quill, and the vial, she made for what Seamus assumed was the kitchen. "Have a seat, and I'll be out in a minute."

Seamus gave a curt nod, pulling out one of the stools. Upon sitting, he realized this nook hadn't been constructed for someone his size. He felt like a giant, balancing precariously on the tiny, periwinkle seat.

He sat there for a while, his cheeks red, absentmindedly fiddling with the end of the tablecloth, wrapping the frayed ends around his fingers. His mind wandered, yet again drifting back to that horrid nightmare. What did it mean? Those who worshipped the Stars tend to believe your dreams and nightmares have meaning. They could be warnings or premonitions. Anyone could have them. Not only that, but anyone could find a way to interpret them. That didn't mean the interpretation was right. The same went for 'constellations.' The Stars hadn't placed themselves in patterns. Earthly beings had looked up and decided certain clusters or lonesome stars had meaning. Earthly beings were *always* trying to find meaning in nothing. That's why people like Tiril and Helgi were so obsessed with religion—why they thought him to be some Celestial savior. They'd drawn the short end of the stick in life, but instead of succumbing to their problems like Seamus, they filled their heads with nonsense, hoping it'd ease the pain of it all. Seamus both pitied and envied them. Pitied because he knew if there were beings in the sky watching over them, they didn't seem to care. The day they realized this was not one he wanted to see. Yet he envied them because he wished he could go through life with stars in his eyes as they did. Like Ophelia. Like Ingrid. Like Syrena, who paraded around in Salvia's colors and floral motifs.

He also envied how sure they were in their beliefs, no matter how unorthodox. Half the time, Seamus didn't know *what* he believed. Part of him, his guilty conscience maybe, thought something else was out there. Spirits, or life amongst the Stars, whatever it may be. He'd almost bought into the whole thing. Then those around him who believed in the Stars had died, their deities unable or unwilling to protect them. Of course, being followers of the Celestial Pantheon, they believed in fate. To them, everything was written in the stars, and as such, all events and outcomes couldn't change. The Terrestrial Pantheon taught otherwise. Maybe that's why Ophelia and Syrena preferred those teachings. Seamus felt the Stars were awfully defeatist.

He scoffed. In that way, he guessed he agreed with them. Look at him, sitting there. Hungry, battered, and bruised, consumed by questions he hated entertaining. How was he meant to embody North Star if he couldn't find it in himself to believe in the other Spirits?

For most of his life, Seamus had questioned authority. From preachers and commanding officers to his alpha, none of them had made sense. They'd all spun half-truths out of honey-sweet lies. Now, even a supposed Celestial being was toying with him.

Scowling, he shook his head.

This wasn't what he wanted.

The door to the kitchen opened, breaking his train of thought, his worries and careful contemplation floating away to join the clouds. Syrena smiled down at him, holding a tray of pastries and all the fixings for tea. She nodded toward the fireplace, stifling a laugh.

"You look rather uncomfortable, wolfie," she laughed.

Seamus's cheeks were burning. He cleared his throat, struggling to unwrap his finger from the frayed end of the tablecloth. There was a joke he could make about the threads of fate and the Stars punishing him for having such blasphemous thoughts, but he decided he'd toyed with religion enough for one day.

Finally free of the lacy constraints, he hurried across the room—all two centimeters of it—settling in on a sun-bleached lounge across from the fire. A scuffed coffee table sat before him, the tea tray and a porcelain vase of salvia its only adornments. Syrena placed a steaming cup of tea in his hands as she sat in an empty armchair near him. She stared into the fire for quite some time, frowning. Somehow, the bitter smell that seemed to follow her intensified.

"Where did you find her?" she asked, her voice hushed.

"Ophelia?" Seamus said, shifting uncomfortably as he sipped his tea. He winced, burning his tongue. He thought for a moment, ultimately deciding honesty was the best policy with this woman. "An evil alchemist hid her in a town in Snøbolig. Why?"

Syrena chewed her bottom lip, the steam from her tea curling around her cheeks like dragons' breath. "And was she born there? Was the alchemist a relative? Was she—"

"What's with the questions, gingersnap?"

"I just—" Her eyes flickered in frustration. She sighed heavily, taking a long draught of tea. "I just need to know."

Seamus leaned forward, tapping his fingers on his cup. He studied her—every auburn strand of hair, every freckle, every petal making up her flower crown. She ignored his scrutinizing gaze, perfectly poised in her seat, staring in such a melancholic way at the flickering fireplace. From their previous conversations, her voice seemed to be her weapon. There were sharp edges to this floral healer. However, those edges seemed dull when she sat in silence.

"What would it matter?" Seamus asked carefully.

Syrena glanced at him, finally returning his analyzing

gaze. What was she looking for? "How long have you known her? How long ago did you find her?"

Seamus shrugged. "We've been together for a little under. . . three months? I think that's right."

"The alchemist wasn't a relative? Has she talked about her parents at all?"

"No, and no. She's never brought them up." Now that she mentioned it, Seamus thought that was odd. Weren't orphans supposed to obsess over finding their long-lost family members?

Syrena set down her teacup, turning to him. "Do you know where the alchemist was from originally? Was he from that town, or did he move there when he found her?"

Seamus narrowed his eyes at her. "What do you know, gingersnap?"

She sighed heavily, bringing her knees to her chest. "I grew up on the coast of Snøbolig, near Port Fantastisk. My mother was a healer, too. Greatest there ever was," she said, holding her head high. "I took over her practice when she'd grown too old and arthritic."

"And this is pertinent information because. . . ?" Seamus asked, circling his hand through the air in hopes she'd hurry this along—whatever 'this' was.

She glared at him, blowing hot air out her nose. Again, the steam of her tea looked like dragon's breath. "I was getting to that, mutt," she snapped. She readjusted herself in her seat, looking back at the fire. "There'd been a group of Skogens Søstre living in the woods near our town. They'd decided to settle, which was unusual. Come to find out, one of the younger women was pregnant. Most Søstre choose the religion. They normally aren't born into it. However, while a rarity among the Søstre, relationships aren't looked down upon."

"Syrena," Seamus grumbled.

"I'm telling a story!" she snapped. "Blessed Amaranth, how does she put up with you?"

Seamus inhaled sharply, sitting back in his seat. Seems they'd be here a while.

"Like I was saying—you know, before I was so *rudely* interrupted—the woman was pregnant," Syrena spat. Seamus didn't know how he knew, but he was certain she'd reserved this attitude solely for him. "Her caravan had been passing through, heading toward the ports, keen on fleeing Alle Årstider altogether. But Snøbolig is harsh; I'm sure you know this. Since the girl was with child, it wasn't safe to travel until she'd given birth."

"So, what happened? What are you saying?" Seamus asked. He had a theory but didn't dare speak it.

"For the first few months of her pregnancy, the woman was fine. She was an incredibly worrisome young lady, coming to my practice more than necessary. I always chalked her paranoia up to being a first-time mother, but one day, she came to me in the dead of night looking frantic. I'd asked what happened, but she refused to say. She just wanted to make sure the child was all right. I did all the routine things my mother had taught me. Everything was normal except for the burn marks all over her body. These burns seemed to be coming from inside. It was the strangest thing. I couldn't explain it, neither could she. Neither could my mother. But that young lady, she had this feeling. Something was wrong with the baby. I kept telling her the child was fine, but she'd hear none of it."

Seamus glanced at the stairs, thinking he'd seen a shadow coming down them. He listened for dainty footsteps and sniffed for mint but found nothing.

"As the months went on, more strange things started happening. Constant thunderstorms. Hail the size of chicken eggs. Sleet and snow. Waves off the coast so high that they threatened to destroy the port.

"At the center of it was the Skogens Søstre camp. It was the one untouched space. The eye of the storm." The way Syrena spoke sent shivers up Seamus's spine. "When that woman would come to town, the horrible weather would stop. She was rumored to be a Witch. Who could tell with the mask? It was either that or. . ."

"The baby would be," Seamus finished. His chest tightened.

Syrena nodded, tipping her cup to him. "I knew you were smart," she whispered. "Here's a puzzle for you, Mr. Norland. What do you think happens when the Ulvemordere hear about unnatural phenomena?"

Seamus's hands clenched so tightly around his cup he swore he heard it crack. "They'd send a scouting party."

"And what do you think happens when they find a woman covered in frostbite and burns that seemed to be coming from the womb? What happens when they catch wind of Witches?"

They sat in silence for a moment. Syrena stared him down, her face set in a look of disgust so deep that Seamus was sure it would stay like that forever.

"You asked me why I wouldn't turn the two of you in, and this is why," Syrena said, her voice barely a whisper. The tears in her eyes mixed with unbridled fury. The bitter smell wafting off her was twinged with sourness, shriveling Seamus's nose. "That woman came to me battered, bloodied, and bruised. The baby? I'll spare you the details, Mr. Norland, but—I—The baby was—" her voice cracked. She had to turn away, her shoulders shaking from a silent sob.

"Stillborn," Seamus mumbled.

She nodded, tears dripping into her tea. "I did everything I could, but. . ." She shivered, shutting her eyes.

"What happened to the woman?" Seamus asked, cringing at the sudden desperation in his voice.

"The Ulvemordere," Syrena scoffed. "They raided our town looking for her and the child. She'd run before they found her. I don't know what happened to her after that. She vanished without a trace, taking the stillborn child with her."

Seamus glanced at the stairs again. Syrena turned, following his gaze, a look of fear on her face. Finding the stairs empty, her expression softened.

Eyes still on the steps, she leaned as close to him as she could, her voice barely a whisper. "I don't know if you're the religious type, Seamus, but I am. I prayed my Spirits would heal that woman's mind and body, hoping it'd ease her pain. Seems the Spirits were happy to oblige, seeing as that girl of yours looks *exactly* like her mother. She's even wearing her mask. I hear a celebration of polar bears is a rarity."

Seamus slumped in his seat, unsure what to do with this information. There were two explanations for what'd happened—one logical, one steeped in superstition. Either the Skogens Søstre had a second child, and the Spirits saw fit she bring another Witch into the world. Or—and dare Seamus say it, this was what he believed—the Spirits brought her baby back from the dead. Whether that was the case or not, one thing was certain: Ophelia was special. Special beyond her Witch Marks. Special beyond her title. Special beyond her powers. As far as he knew, there weren't many stories of the Spirits—hers or his—favoring mortals.

Of course, there was more to it than that. How had Lochlan found Ophelia as a baby? What series of events led up to and then followed her hypothetical resurrection? What had happened to her mother? Her father? Were either of them looking for her? Were they alive?

And what of Ophelia? Did she know? His mind was reeling, thinking of when Tiril and Helgi had brought up the connections between both Pantheons. He'd bet money on her wisdom, whether it'd come from books or lived experiences. He wanted—*needed*—to know. But asking seemed impossible. It was like he was dealing with a scared or injured animal who refused help.

As he sat quietly beside Syrena, these questions troubled him greatly. Yet, on top of it all was the thing that bothered Seamus the most.

Ranking so high, he'd heard much of what happened within the Ulvemordere. Both on the island where their compound was hidden and on the main continent of Alle Årstider. He'd known about this. At least partially. Jette and him, alongside their comrades, had been sent off to investigate. If it hadn't been for the band of rebels they encountered along the way, he may have been the villain in this story.

What scared him the most was that he didn't know if he'd have spared the unborn child. Eighteen years ago had been a trivial time in Seamus's life. He'd just begun questioning his superiors' orders, unsure of his place in the world and what the Ulvemordere stood for. Had he found that woman and seen the mounting destruction her child had caused, Seamus wasn't sure his younger self would've had mercy. In fact, if he were honest with himself, he was certain he would've done something unforgivable.

The thought sickened him, but it was the truth.

Stars, he wanted to go back in time and beat some sense into himself. How could he have been so blind? How could they have brainwashed him to think any of this was right?

The past haunted him, a phantasm so deadly it threatened to snuff out his metaphorical light with just a touch. He tried to remind himself he wasn't that person anymore, and he hadn't been the one to hurt an unborn child, but it did little to ease his mind. Flickers of the good he'd done came to mind, but that phantom quickly scared them away.

Seamus looked down at his hands, unsure when he'd begun rubbing them on his trousers. His bare palms were red, nearly raw. In his mind's eye, he swore they were covered with soot made from the ashes of the lives he'd burned to the ground. Every ounce of his being told him to run as fast and as far as he could. Run from everything and everyone. Run to a dark hole in the ground where no one could find him and be sullied by his filth.

But he'd made a promise.

Instead of running away, he was supposed to run toward something worth believing in.

"D—Did you hear that?" Syrena asked.

Seamus looked up, realizing he *had* heard something.

It'd been a great thud from upstairs.

VALKNUT

Ophelia was stuck between sleep and consciousness. No matter how hard she tried, she couldn't force her eyes fully open. The blankets she lay curled under felt laden with iron, weighing her down and stealing her ability to move. If she didn't know otherwise, she would have figured Syrena had drugged her. Late yesterday morning, she'd returned to Buntry and had been stuck in a tearful daze ever since. How Syrena had coaxed her into bed was beyond her.

Through one half-open eye, she looked to Seamus, hoping he was—

All traces of sleepiness vanished. The blankets fought to keep her as she kicked and thrashed to free herself from their binds. With a yelp, she slipped off the bed and crashed hard onto the floor. Somehow, the fall had freed her. She stood, staring at the empty bed where Seamus should have been.

A thousand thoughts swirled in her mind. Where was he? Was he okay? Was he—Blessed Amaranth—was he *dead*? No, no, no. Syrena would've woken her if something like that had happened. At least, she hoped so. She wouldn't have just carted off his body without telling her, right?

But wait, what if someone had taken him in the night? Would any of the Spirits be that foolish? She'd tried her best to stay awake and protect him. . . Curses!

Ophelia grappled for her mask, her shaking hands struggling to tie it around her face. Just as she was about to throw caution to the wind and run off without it, the curtains parted, and—

"Seamus!" she screeched.

Relief flooded his face. "Are you okay? We heard—"

Ophelia tossed aside her mask, launching herself into his outstretched arms, wrapping her own around him as tight as she could. He picked her up and spun her, burying his face in her neck.

It was then she realized she'd been crying.

"Don't do that to me!" she sobbed. After watching the pelt overtake Saoirse, she couldn't handle seeing anyone else get hurt.

Seamus only laughed, setting her gently on the ground. He wiped her tears with his sandpaper thumbs. There was a strange light in his eyes that she couldn't explain. "You cry over nothin', pup," he said.

"I thought. . ." Her words trailed off, hanging heavily in the air between them.

Seamus's face filled with remorse. With a heavy sigh, he pulled her back into a hug, rocking side to side to soothe her.

"Are you okay?" she asked. She placed her ear over his heart, listening to the *thump-thump-thump* of its worrisome beat.

He nodded, then rested his cheek atop her head. "You?"

"Better now," she whispered, reveling in this moment.

Everyone else, she recoiled from. But with Seamus, she knew there was no place safer than next to him. She looked up at him, smiling her biggest, brightest, most childish smile.

"How did you sleep, love?" Syrena asked. She'd slipped past them and was remaking Ophelia's bed.

"All right," Ophelia shrugged. Seamus slowly released her from his bear hug but wrapped one arm around her shoulders. "Syrena, is there anything—"

"Let me guess: breakfast?" she asked, sighing contently. "Come on then, join us in the den."

She and Seamus slipped back downstairs, leaving Ophelia to freshen up and tidy her corner of the infirmary. Dressed and ready for the day, she skipped down the stairs to find Seamus lazing on the lounge, Syrena in an armchair beside him.

"Would you like some tea, Ophelia, dear?" Syrena asked as she reached for a cup.

Ophelia didn't have the heart to tell her she didn't care much for tea. "Oh, uh, yes, please, thank you."

Seamus gave her a knowing look before taking the cup from Syrena. He put four cubes of sugar in the tea, poured in a hefty amount of cream, and then stuck a biscotti in it before handing it off as she sat down beside him.

"Thank you," she whispered.

"You two are quite the pair," Syrena said thoughtfully. "Seamus was just filling me in on all your grand adventures."

"Was he?" Ophelia asked, her heart dropping. Even for just a moment, she'd rather forget the whole ordeal. "Quite a harrowing journey so far, I'd say."

"Her favorite parts have been the unnecessary detours she deems 'side quests,'" Seamus laughed. He buttered a biscuit, smothered it in jam, then pushed it in Ophelia's direction. "I was just getting to the dragon-rescuing incident. Would you like to take over?"

"Oh! Yes!" Ophelia exclaimed through a mouthful of jam and biscuit. Per Seamus's preference, more jam than anything. Now *that* she'd gladly talk about. "Have you ever heard of Dødbyen? It's this big city built inside a ravine. There are lifts down to the main level for those who can't fly, but they used to be powered by the labor of dragons. After I freed them and spoke with the local government, it's safe to say no dragon will ever be used for such things again. At least not in Dødbyen."

Syrena smiled into her teacup, glancing at Seamus, who was smiling drunkenly, as he always did whenever Ophelia was excited about something.

"I'm sure the dragons are very thankful you were there to stand up to such injustice," Syrena said, tipping her cup toward her.

"I think so too. One of them s—" Ophelia reddened, clearing her throat. Perhaps she shouldn't let slip that she'd heard one of their voices in her head. "One of them seemed more grateful than the other, though," she finished awkwardly.

Leaving them with that, she turned her attention to her tea and biscuit. Syrena looked slightly confused but didn't seem to catch on to what she'd meant to say. Seamus had. Seamus always did.

"You'll find Phee gets along well with all animals," he

said quickly.

Syrena nodded. "Skogens Søstre usually do," she said with a wink. "Speaking of, Ophelia, dear, I've been meaning to ask. . ." She wore a calculating pout, looking back and forth between her and Seamus, who had gone incredibly stiff. "Why do you wear the Polar Bear?"

"Ahh, well. . ." Ophelia began, filling her voice with wistful mystery. "I've come to resonate with what it represents. Hope above all things, yes?"

"She didn't always wear the Polar Bear," Seamus said rather quickly.

Syrena's eyes flicked toward him. "I see. And what ideals had you embodied before?"

"That of the fox," Ophelia said, shrinking in on herself. "Not by choice."

"But what was it you'd said?" Seamus asked, shifting uncomfortably beside her. "That 'when you spend so long parading around as one thing, people rarely expect you to be another.'"

Syrena's eyes lit up in surprise, but she nodded. "Oh, she's a clever one, isn't she, Seamus?"

"Too clever, if you ask me," he sighed, "I wouldn't have it any other way, though. She's gotten us out of some tricky situations," Seamus smiled. "One time, she flew us into a tree to hide from the Ulvemordere."

"I think I'm still bruised from that little accident," Ophelia grimaced. "Did I ever apologize for that?"

"No."

"S—"

"You're fine."

Syrena buttered herself a biscuit, obviously amused. "So, globetrotters, where will you be heading once I've decided you're free to go?"

Seamus paused mid-sip, eyes narrowing. Distrust was seeping off him, coiling around Ophelia's head, burying itself in the pit of her stomach. She suddenly had the sense they'd astronomically overshared.

"Why do you want to know?" he asked, his voice gruff.

Syrena shrugged, either unaware of or ignoring the

sudden change in atmosphere. "Someone should know where you're going."

Seamus's face and posture softened, and Ophelia knew why. She'd said roughly the same thing not long ago. Slowly, the knots of distrust in their stomachs unraveled.

"We're on our way to a very important party," Seamus said simply.

Syrena nodded to herself, tapping an unsteady rhythm on her cup. She looked toward the fire, chewing her bottom lip until she finally asked, "You think the hosts have room for one more?"

Seamus's eyebrows knit deep over his hazel eyes. "Why?"

"Well," Syrena began, setting down her cup, turning back to them. No, not *them*. Him. Just *him*. "The Lindwyrm alone proves you two get into more trouble than you should. Had you been stuck in the wilderness, either one of you could have died. I'm not keen to let that happen." The intensity in her eyes and her solemn nod made Ophelia think she'd missed something very important.

Seamus glanced at Ophelia, then at his hands. They shook slightly. He inhaled sharply, quickly setting down his cup and crossing his arms tight. "Are you offering your services, then?"

"In a sense."

"What do you think, kid? I'm only here because of you. It's your call," Seamus said, nudging her foot with his.

Ophelia felt her face flush red beneath her mask. "If you want to tag along, who am I to stop you?"

After Syrena made arrangements for the infirmary in her absence, she went off to pack whatever she may need. Several hours later, she stumbled downstairs with enough bags to suffocate a troll. If trolls had lungs, of course.

"Absolutely not," Seamus said, hands on his hips.

Ophelia stepped out of the way before Syrena could accidentally drop a bag on her toe. "What is all that?"

"Just the necessities," she smiled, rather pleased with herself.

Seamus pinched the bridge of his nose, grumbling to himself.

"Play nice, Seamus," Ophelia laughed.

"Listen, Phee and I have made do with far less than that," Seamus said. "Besides, our horses aren't equipped to carry all that."

Syrena rolled her eyes. "First off, you're barely scraping by. Second off, we're borrowing a cart. I sent word to the stables. You've not a thing to worry about it. Ophelia, dear, might you help me carry some of these?"

Seamus made to grab a bag, but Syrena flicked his shoulder before he could. "What the—"

"You're not supposed to carry anything heavy," Syrena spat. "How many times will I have to tell you?"

Most of the day had gone like this. Syrena would tell him all the things he couldn't do while injured, and Seamus would defiantly prove her wrong. Ophelia had the sneaking suspicion that the ride to the Frog & Lantern Inn would be a very long, annoying trek. Was this what she'd been reduced to? A babysitter for two grumpy adults keen on acting like children?

"I'll help you if I want to help you, Syrena," Seamus spat, yanking a bag off the floor. Though he tried to hide it, he winced.

"My hero," Syrena grumbled, giving Ophelia a knowing look.

"Do not drag me into it," Ophelia sighed, taking what she could carry and heading toward the stables.

They had bigger things to worry about than Syrena's bags and who would carry them. Tomorrow morning, they'd be off, and the penultimate battle would be closer. With that came unimaginable danger and burden Ophelia intended to carry alone.

CHAPTER NINETY-TWO

COME ONE, BE TRUTHFUL

If Seamus was uncomfortable with this situation, Rain and Frykt had to be exasperated. Frykt, especially, was not happy dragging along a rickety cart with uneven wheels. Rain kept giving Ophelia disapproving looks but—being the faithful companion he was—muddled through. They'd been on the road since sunrise, not stopping for breakfast or even lunch. With the sun starting to set, there was no use stopping now.

Everything ached, namely Seamus's arm, which was wrapped far too tight for his liking. Syrena had loosened his bandages twice now. Either she'd lied, or his arm was swelling. Neither outcome was preferable. Other than tending to his wounds, Syrena was quiet, staring out at the trees. So was Ophelia, who was stuffed into the cart between all their bags. She'd said she wanted to read, but Seamus was sure she hadn't turned a page for a concerning amount of time. He had half a mind to wonder if she'd fallen asleep with her eyes open.

Something was up with her; that much was certain. Poor kid. She'd probably had her fair share of nightmares the last few days. He hoped she'd get a good night's rest now that he was up and at 'em.

"We'll have to keep going until we get to the next town," Syrena said thoughtfully, snapping him out of his thoughts.

". . . why?" Ophelia asked, looking up from her book for the first time.

"So we may find someplace to sleep. I'm not tucking in beside you two on this shoddy old cart," she laughed. "We're not terribly far from a village, I think. Have you a map? We can tend to the cart in rotation if you like. I'll take the first shift since I suggested it."

"Syrena," Seamus said pointedly, "do you travel often?"

"Not at all."

"Oh, this'll be fun," he sighed. "Inns and towns are nice and all, but we're better off in the woods. Easier escape, cheaper fare."

A look of grave concern lit up Syrena's face. "Holy Hemlock, no wonder you got bit by a Lindwyrm! You sleep *outside*?"

"It's not all bad," Ophelia said, grimacing at 'Holy Hemlock.' She bookmarked her page and then stowed her novel neatly in her satchel. "You'll have the stars and all the woodland critters to keep you company."

"Like bears?" Syrena frowned.

"I hope so!"

The concern on her face doubled. "Is she always like this?"

"Pretty much," Seamus laughed.

A few minutes later, he'd steered the horses off the road and into the trees. Ophelia helped Syrena learn how to set up camp for the evening and tended to Rain and Frykt while Seamus set off to find firewood. When he returned, Syrena was shivering in her boots, a pelt wrapped around her shoulders.

"You do this every night?" she asked, watching Ophelia out of the corner of her eye. She was still with the horses, whispering her goodnights and sweet dreams.

"More or less," Seamus shrugged. "How are you fairing?"

"Well, Ophelia's given me an old bed roll and a pelt, so here's to hoping I won't freeze," she sighed. If only she knew. These 'cold' Høstlunden nights were nothing compared to those of Snøbolig.

"Chin up, gingersnap, I'm working on the fire," he replied, smiling to himself.

"Be quick about it, wolf," she grumbled.

"If you so desire, copper top," Seamus said with a wink over his shoulder. Was it his imagination, or did Syrena just *blush*?

Suddenly, a pit had formed in his stomach, but he didn't know why. It didn't feel like dread, not really. But that's what it was, wasn't it? Or maybe it was just the Lindwyrm venom leaving his system.

Thought preoccupied, he absent-mindedly began work on the campfire. Campfires in Høstlunden were always a breeze. The copious amounts of fallen leaves and peeling birchwood bark made for great tinder. It wasn't long before he and Syrena were warming their hands against a flickering blaze. Seamus took it upon himself to tend to dinner as well, but come tomorrow, there'd have to be a new chore distribution system. He'd been content to take most of the burden when it was just the two of them, but now that Syrena was around, it was time to delegate. If she didn't fancy cooking, she could be on firewood duty or in charge of setting up camp.

Handing off a sizzling cut of venison, he followed Syrena's gaze to where Ophelia was sitting on a branch, talking Rain and Frykt's ears off. Here and there, she gestured loosely to them as if telling the horses about their new companion.

"It's almost as if they're responding. . . See! Look there! The gray one just nodded," Syrena said, eyes wide. "Can she. . . Can she *talk* to them?"

Seamus bobbed his head side to side, thinking. "I'm going to be honest with you, Syrena, I'm not sure. She won't give me a straight answer."

Syrena shook her head playfully, tearing off tiny bits of venison. "She's a strange one, isn't she?" she said between bites.

"Exceptionally," Seamus nodded.

"But you wouldn't have it any other way, would you?"

"Not one bit."

She yawned again, eyes all droopy. Slowly, she turned to him. "She referred to you as her dad." Seamus felt his cheeks redden. Syrena studied his face for a long while, a sad but content smile tugging at her lips. "She loves you very much, wolfie."

"I love her very much, too," he replied softly, rubbing at his glowing cheeks.

"I hope you do," Syrena said, her expression suddenly serious. "Because I'm not losing that girl again," she whispered.

They glanced at Ophelia, who'd finally said her last goodnight to the horses. Seamus shared the same sentiment.

It was nice to know someone else was in her corner. He didn't know why, but he had complete and utter trust in Syrena. She could be lying through her teeth, of course. Yet, even if she was, Seamus felt he'd still trust her. She'd had to have had a good reason. Everyone had secrets. What they were and why they kept them were entirely different stories.

"Well, I'm heading off to bed, if that's all right with you," she yawned, shooing him off her bedroll, a mischievous light in her eyes. Seamus rolled his eyes playfully.

Not long after Syrena had wrapped herself up in pelts and settled in for the night, Ophelia came to join them around the fire. She and Seamus sat on the opposite side of the fire, finishing off dinner. Syrena was already out cold. It seemed she was a heavy sleeper, what with how loudly she snored. Seamus had to laugh. Passersby would mistake her snores for rumbling thunder. Or perhaps a growling bear. Either way, she may prove to be a great asset, her snores warding off all danger.

"How are the horses?" Seamus whispered.

"Restless. Still spooked from the Lindwyrms," Ophelia said. "Didn't like the stable much, either."

Seamus laughed to himself, looking over his shoulder to find Rain and Frykt huddling together for warmth. "What about you? Are you still spooked by those damn snakes?"

Ophelia did that odd little thing where she got incredibly quiet and curled in on herself. Her eyes slid across him, lingering on the bumps beneath his shirt, alluding to the bandages. "I'm okay," she mumbled.

As if Seamus believed that. "Do you want to talk—"

"No, thank you."

They sat staring into the fire for a while, shoulder to shoulder. The pit in his stomach was back, but this time, it showed its true face as guilt. Worrying over someone you loved wasn't fun. He could only imagine what Ophelia had felt seeing him like that. The bite mark on his arm itched. He hoped it would heal quickly so he could lose the bandages. Maybe then they could forget about all this.

Through the flames, he watched Syrena sleep.

There was something else he *couldn't* forget, however. No matter how badly he wanted to.

"Hey, can we talk for a minute?" he asked, tugging on

his earlobe nervously. Ophelia nodded. His hands searched for something to fidget with, finding his pocketknife. He twirled it between two fingers, lips set in a deep scowl. "Syrena told me something I think you should know. It's about your par—"

Ophelia blurted out, "I don't want to know." Her tone was harsh, almost angry.

Seamus furrowed his eyebrows, looking up. "Why?"

Her eyes darted back and forth between his. For the first time since they'd met, she traced the long scars on his face. Eventually, she said, "You're all I need."

"But don't you want to know? I think you should know."

"Is Syrena my mother? Or my aunt? A relative of any sort?"

"No, but—"

"Then it doesn't matter to me," Ophelia said simply. "You're all I need, Seamus. Sometimes, a family is a surly old wolf and a finicky Witch. Sometimes, a family is you and me. I don't need anything more than that."

"Pup," he sighed. He stabbed his pocketknife into the ground, turning to face her. "I know that, but I think it would—"

"If I know, then I'll pity them," Ophelia began sharply, "It'll only make me sad. I have a story in my head of what happened and why I was abandoned, and I'd like to believe it as the truth. Because if they were good people, and they loved and wanted me, then that means I was ripped from a life every child deserves. But if I keep on believing they were cowards who discarded a daughter born with Witch Marks, then I don't pity them. *I don't want to pity them.*"

Seamus traced her Marks as she had his scars before nodding to himself. "If that's what you want, then forget I said anything."

"Thank you," Ophelia mumbled.

He nodded but didn't exactly agree with her logic. Still, it wasn't his call to make. If she didn't want to know, then she didn't need to. He wasn't going to force that kind of knowledge upon her. Maybe some things were better off kept quiet.

"We should get some rest. Long few days ahead," Ophelia said, her voice flat.

Again, Seamus nodded. He stoked the embers one last

time, then unfurled his bedroll, settling in next to the dying fire. He'd made it small on purpose, knowing they'd all be asleep soon enough.

Ophelia stood, discarding her pack next to his. She made for a tree, presumably calculating which branch could hold her weight. Once she'd chosen a worthy home for the night, she began to climb. One hand over the other. A slow and steady climb. She got a few feet up, then stopped, hanging there momentarily before dropping down and turning back to Seamus and the fire. She came to hover at the edge of the light, swathed in shadows as she stood staring at the top of her boots.

Seamus furrowed his eyebrows. The buzzing was loud, louder than it should be. With a clenched jaw, Ophelia spread out her bedroll next to him so their heads would be level. Together, they lay staring up at the twinkling stars and gleaming waning gibbous moon, feet facing opposite directions. Maybe Ophelia was rubbing off on him, but Seamus found it oddly poetic. Sometimes, he felt they were working toward drastically different goals.

He watched her out of the corner of his eye, noting the stiffness of her expression. She'd been quieter than usual, which was saying something for a girl who rarely said anything to anyone. A shooting star passed overhead. It struck him as odd that she didn't point it out.

"Ophelia?" he asked softly, his voice barely a whisper.

That look in her eyes told him she was miles away, probably somewhere amongst the stars, staring down at everything and nothing at all. Sometimes, he wondered if her feet had ever touched solid ground to begin with.

He spoke again, louder, yet his words were still soft as falling snow. "Hey, pup?"

There was hesitation as she turned her head, her eyes flicking back to the sky before settling on his face. "Yes, Seamus?" she replied, a thin smile on her lips, all trace of melancholy gone.

Floating in the air was the stench of mint.

"You're distant," he said, searching her face for clues as she stared unblinking at him.

"I'm just tired."

The tiniest hint of sadness crept back into her eyes—he could see it clawing at the corners, fighting to consume her. With the softest sigh, she turned her attention back to the stars.

Seamus thought for a moment, following her gaze. She'd been off for a while now, but he hadn't worked up the nerve to ask why until now. "Is something wrong? Did I say or do something?"

"No," she whispered. "I'm just tired."

Another shooting star tore through the sky, its edges a brilliant green. The kind of green, she'd say, was hard to come by—the kind of green she'd want in her paint set.

"Sky's pretty tonight," Seamus said as quietly as he could.

"Goodnight, Seamus," Ophelia said curtly, rolling onto her side, away from him.

"Night, kid."

Seamus lay there for quite some time, just staring at the sky, finding no joy in the exquisite display the sky had put on just for them. To him, shooting stars were just a lucky anomaly. Sometimes these things happen. No one could explain why. He didn't think much about it. But Ophelia? She was so easily filled with wonderment. How many times had she seen shooting stars? Surely not so often that they'd lost their awe.

"Phee?"

Though there was no answer, he heard her heart skip a beat.

"You can talk to me. You know that, right? About anything."

She tensed, curling in on herself.

"Goodnight, Seamus," she said, her voice devoid of all emotion.

"If there's—"

"Goodnight."

CHAPTER NINETY-THREE

You're Here, Yet I Miss You

Three days later, they were almost at their destination. The traveling was fine. Seamus could stay on the road for ages, never tiring of the passing scenery, looking forward to sleeping under the stars. It was the moment his boots stood still, standing on even ground, a crowd of people laughing, smiling, living—that was the part that needled him. All those towns he'd seen, no matter how long he stayed, were the worst parts, one way or another. It didn't make any sense. Why was he like this? Why couldn't he be normal? Those smiling faces, those people living lives worthy of their laughter, why did it make his skin crawl?

Needless to say, he was dreading arriving at the Frog & Lantern Inn.

Syrena was asleep, snoring from the cart, using one of her bags as a pillow. She'd switched seats with Ophelia, yawning about needing a nap. From the volume of her snores, she really *had* needed the rest.

Ophelia seemed like she needed a nap, too. Seamus looked sidelong at her, thinking back to all the times she'd gotten hurt as of late, specifically the full moon. Flashes of their fight, Egill's betrayal, seeing Ophelia unmoving on the ground. . . it all flickered before his eyes. He doubted the guilt of that day would ever go away, but there was more to it than that. The full moon heightens emotions and feelings you've harbored your whole life. It doesn't toy with things that aren't already there. If there hadn't been a full moon, his nerves still would've gotten the best of him. Granted, he wouldn't have been so tremendously intolerable, but still.

Sensing his gaze, Ophelia turned to him. She was wearing her mask, but he knew she was giving him a questioning look.

Seamus cleared his throat, pulling his collar away from his neck. "We're nearly there," he began, "have you given any thought to how you will announce yourself to the rebels?"

Again, he could picture her expression. Furrowed eyebrows, most likely. "How do you mean?"

"Will you do some grand gesture? Some dramatic entrance?"

"Uh. . ." she laughed, "No. No, I don't think so."

"Yeah, you're right. That's probably for the best."

"Yup."

There it was again, that empty silence that became suffocatingly loud the longer it sat in the air. Ophelia sat stiff next to him. He wished he could see her eyes behind that blasted mask. They always spoke multitudes—he knew they *saw* multitudes too, the likes of which he could never comprehend, even if he spent a lifetime trying.

He leaned in close, his voice hushed. "You've been quiet again."

"I find silence comes when one has nothing to say," she replied briskly.

He nodded, ignoring her tone. Something was very wrong, and as long as she confided in him eventually, he was okay with her snapping at him now. That tricky little polar bear was meant to bare her teeth now and then. She seemed to forget that.

"Not when it has lingered for days," Seamus frowned.

He was sure she rolled her eyes.

"Phee—"

"Was there something you needed to say, Seamus?" she asked. It was a dismissive question, one she didn't want nor need answered. Her hands clenched tightly around the strap of her satchel in anticipation.

What would she say if roles were reversed? How would she handle his ever-changing moods and snarky remarks? With kindness, no doubt. She'd find just the right way to ease his mind. Somehow, she always knew what he needed. Maybe it was time he did the same for her.

He shifted uncomfortably in his seat, thinking long and hard about how to phrase the words tumbling out of his mouth.

Clearing his throat, he whispered, "I've never been one for the quieter things. . . But I'll gladly sit in silence if it means I get to sit with you."

The death grip she had on her satchel strap loosened. Without looking at him, she reached for his hand, interlocking her bandaged fingers between his. The movement had been rather fast and jerky, startling him. He could feel her heartbeat pounding against his palm.

She didn't say anything—didn't need to. He rubbed his thumb over hers reassuringly, a sudden realization piercing his heart like a well-aimed crossbow bolt.

"I'm still here, pup," he said solemnly. She squeezed his hand tightly, mustering up all the strength she could. "I'm not leaving anytime soon."

Ophelia swallowed hard, turning to him. "I went to see Arild," she blurted out.

Seamus could only stare at her in awe of her sudden stupidity. "You did *what*?" he asked as levelly as he could.

"Egill followed us to Buntry, and I—"

Seamus yanked on the horse's reins, jerking them to a stop. In a fit of anger, he stood, feeling as though he was going to burst. "Are you insane? You are, aren't you? Blessed be the Stars and all They shine upon. You're mental! You went to see Arild—Arild Melhus—*alone*? Are you *trying* to kill yourself?"

"N—No, I just figured—"

"I cannot believe you'd be so stupid!" Seamus spat, hopping off the cart, beginning to pace. "You—You—You—I can't even—Holy shit, Ophelia!"

Syrena snorted awake, looking dazed.

"We were supposed to meet him before the full moon! I understand you're mad, but I didn't know if or when you'd wake up! I couldn't just sit there and do nothing!" Ophelia said, gesturing wildly with her bandaged hands. The sight made Seamus sick to his stomach, imagining all the pent-up nervous energy causing physical damage.

"I'm not mad, I'm disappointed!" he yelled.

No, no, no. He didn't yell.

He just. . . 'raised his voice.'

Ophelia groaned, holding her head in her hands. "That's somehow worse."

"I don't give a shit!" Seamus snapped.

They were both quiet for a long moment, Ophelia with her shaking shoulders and Seamus with his hands on his hips.

Eventually, Seamus inhaled sharply, trying to soften his posture. "Are you okay? Did he hurt you? I swear on my life if he—"

Ophelia tore off her mask and threw it at him. Her face was drenched in tears and snot, and her Witch Marks were a deep, violent blue.

"He had Saoirse," she said, her voice clipped by what could only be described as grief. She stood, gesturing to her heart. "He had her, and he used her to make a point. He killed her Seamus; he used the pelt on her."

Seamus's wolf sprang to life inside his mind. He wanted nothing more than to rip into Arild's throat, to soak in his blood, cause him every ounce of pain he'd caused Ophelia, then double it.

"The Kirkeby's sentries couldn't find my people because they're dead. *They're all dead.* Åsmund, Saoirse—all of them. Because of *me*," Ophelia said, her words barely audible through her choked sobs. "I killed them. I killed her. Arild said that—that—that my people denied the Ulvemordere, choosing me over their *lives. I killed them.*"

Her Witch Marks were growing darker by the second. The long, icicle-like marks curving down her cheeks grew, slithering like Lindwyrms down her neck. The bandages on her fingertips were smoldering, filling the air with smoke and the smell of burning flesh.

"They're *dead*, Seamus. *Dead*," she cried.

Overhead, thunder rumbled.

Seamus had been murderous after losing his pack. If anyone knew how she was feeling, it was him. That feeling hadn't gone away, but with time, it'd dulled. He could commiserate with that, even have an open conversation with her about grief and anger. But the thing he couldn't understand was what it felt like for a Witch to lose control of their emotions like this. Especially one that could barely keep them under wraps on a good day.

Panicked, he rushed forward, pulling her off the cart. Sharp-shooting pain erupted up his arm, sparks dancing up his sleeve. Ophelia tried to wiggle away, tried to flee, tried to scream at him to let her go, but he wouldn't loosen his grip. Instead, he pulled her into a hug and held her like he wished someone would've held him all those years ago. Syrena crawled out of the cart, shakily reaching toward them. Seamus shook his head, gesturing for her to stay back. He rested his cheek atop Ophelia's head, trying his best to hold her broken pieces together.

The first few droplets of rain were soft as butterfly kisses, but in seconds, they stood in a torrential downpour the likes of which Høstlunden had probably never seen. Thunder rolled, spooking the horses. Lightning crashed, illuminating the clouds in a mix of silver and blue. All around, tree branches were tossed about by violent bursts of wind.

Seamus couldn't exactly make out Ophelia's words beneath the howling wind and pouring rain, but he did catch, 'I miss her.'

If he could take away her hurt, he would. It killed him knowing there was little he could say or do, knowing nothing would stop the storm in her heart or the one surrounding them.

Ever so slowly, he pushed her away just enough so she'd look at him. Wiping away her tears, he said, "You are not to blame."

"But Arild said—"

"Listen to me," he said, placing his forehead against hers. "You are not to blame for what you inspire—good or bad. It doesn't sound right or fair or just, but it is a truth you must accept as a leader. People will follow you of their own accord, not because you force them. *That* will be the difference between you and Arild. You will rule a Witchdom so full of love and light the darkness wouldn't dare come close. And those who stand by your side will be there because they believe in that light. We know the consequences of standing beside you, Ophelia, and we are prepared for them. That is not on you. You are not responsible for other's decisions."

She looked barely older than a child, with her lip quivering and her tired eyes full of self-hatred. Seamus kissed her forehead and gently coaxed her head to rest on his shoulder. How long they stayed like that, he didn't know. It could've been hours—could've been days. Truth be told, he really didn't care. However long she needed him, he'd be there. Come darkened clouds or clear skies.

CHAPTER NINETY-FOUR

WHO?

Ophelia's eyes were puffy, her nose dripping snot, her mouth dry. She sat in the back of their cart, a blanket wrapped around her shoulders, unable to stop crying. The pelting rain wouldn't stop no matter how loudly she pleaded. Seamus had been right. The world reacted to her whether she wanted it to or not. How she would be able to shut it all off, she didn't know. She didn't even know if she *wanted* to shut it off. The rain beating down on her was almost comforting.

Seamus and Syrena were drenched, both absolutely miserable. They tried their best to act as if nothing was out of the ordinary, but that only made Ophelia feel worse. Seamus's switching from yelling at her to trying to ease her anguish made her feel worse. Syrena giving her looks of pity made her feel worse. *Everything* made her feel worse.

I don't want this, she thought. All she wanted was to curl up in a ball and disappear.

For the very first time, Ophelia wondered what it would've been like had she not been born a Witch. What would it have been like to lead an inconspicuous life? Would she be happy?

Pulling her blanket tight around her body, she nestled herself between Syrena's bags, shutting her eyes as tightly as possible. In a few short hours, they'd arrive at their destination, and she'd be expected to pretend to be a stoic leader. But Ophelia wasn't stoic. She didn't know how to pretend to be and didn't want to lie to people she was meant to send to war.

If not us, then who?

Those words rattled around in her mind, piling onto

the guilt she was already drowning in. An eighteen-year-old shouldn't have the world on her shoulders, that much she knew. A young lady who only desired to paint and read and talk with her animal friends should not be going to war.

Ophelia Av'Skogen should not be here.

Ophelia Av'Skogen should be in Tø, hiding the things that made her special.

Ophelia Av'Skogen—Ophelia of The Forest—should be reduced to nothing more than a lonesome cultist.

But she wasn't Ophelia Av'Skogen, and she'd never been. That name had never belonged to her. Never once had she claimed it. She hated that name and what it stood for. She didn't hate the person she'd been, but she mourned that naïve, too-kind young lady. Never again would she be that girl. If she wasn't already dead, 'Ophelia Av'Skogen' was dying.

Yet, beneath the ash, beneath the rubble, someone else was coming alive.

Ophelia Norland *should* be here.

Ophelia Norland should *never* hide the things that made her special.

Ophelia Norland—Alle Årstider's one and only Winter Witch—should have an army behind her.

I don't want this, she thought, *but the path ahead is mine to walk.* For every soul in Tø, for every member of Seamus's pack, and for every being lost to fear, greed, and jealousy, she'd walk that path.

8. The Frog & Lantern Inn

One For All

The sight that greeted them at the Frog & Lantern Inn was indeed a sight for sore eyes. The inn—tavern, more like—itself was off the beaten path, hidden at the base of Juvel Hjem between birchwood and oaks. Hiding in the surrounding woods were scores of tents and caravans. Seamus couldn't believe his eyes. There had to be over one hundred beings here, ready to take up arms with people they barely knew. He spotted quite a few beings around Ophelia's age that wouldn't have been born the last time a fight like this had occurred.

"I didn't expect to see so many," Syrena whispered, awe-struck.

"Me either," Ophelia said, adjusting her mask.

Seamus had suggested riding in without it, but she'd politely refused. If wearing the mask one last time quelled her tears, he wouldn't press the subject. If a few more minutes of hiding behind it meant a lifetime of freedom, he didn't mind.

"This is it, pup," Seamus said, parking the cart and horses in one of the only empty patches of grass. "You ready?"

"No," Ophelia admitted, looking out over the many beings who'd turned their way. "Not at all."

Seamus gave a sympathetic smile, hopping out of the driver's seat to help Syrena down.

The Frog & Lantern was small, barely more than a two-story cottage. Ivy clung to the walls, snaking all the way around the abode. Had Seamus had bad eyesight, he may have mistaken the place for one giant bush. Boisterous laughter and jolly voices seeped through the windows, the building shaking with the patrons' glee.

Ophelia hesitated before climbing out of the cart, patting Rain's hindquarters as they walked to the open tavern door. Inside, every seat was occupied, every table piled high with plates, mugs, and half-eaten turkey legs. Somewhere, a familiar voice was singing over the ruckus.

Reija was the first to spot them. In all the years he'd known her, Seamus had never seen her so excited. He'd also never seen her in armor.

"Lady Ophelia!" she called, waving them over.

Ophelia waved sheepishly, quickening her pace. Reija met her with a hug, and to Seamus's surprise, Ophelia didn't flinch. Not even a little. At Reija's table, an array of familiar faces greeted them. Most of them were Dødbyen's guards and servants like Matei, but Seamus recognized a few wolves from across Snøbolig. They greeted him with solemn nods, thankfully stowing the awkward 'hellos.'

"Tiril is upstairs. She'll be looking for you," Reija said, wrapping her arm around Ophelia's shoulders. Her eyes drifted to Syrena, then Seamus. "Glad to see you're not dead, snake-killer."

"If only I believed you," Seamus sighed, giving her a friendly nod.

"Come, sit with us a moment," Matei said. That was the first kind word Seamus had ever heard from him.

Introductions were passed around, laughs were shared, and old friendships were rekindled. The same would've happened under the Hunter's Moon, but there was an underlying sense of mourning. The Hunter's Moon was usually an excuse for everyone to get drunk and complain about the Ulvemordere, but today could be the end of families and friendships. It was a last hurrah, so to speak. One last day to revel in frivolity. One last night of pleasure, no matter how you came about it.

Seamus found himself sitting in the corner, surrounded by folks he'd thought were long dead. Syrena was beside him, a little too close for Seamus's liking. It surprised him how easily she fit in—not only amongst this lot but with himself and Ophelia. They bickered as if they'd known each other since the beginning of time. Seamus barely knew the woman, yet he felt like she'd been there all his life.

Ophelia, however, looked rather out of place. Her mask

stood out like a sore thumb, though there were plenty of Skogens Søstre amongst them. It was the polar bear that was odd. Such a creature was rarely worshipped, or so Seamus had heard.

Helgi had appeared at some point and was spinning tall tales, obviously inebriated. Syrena hung on his every word, eyes aglow. One of these stories involved a masked child freeing dragons. It was only then that Syrena's smile began to falter.

"You know, I think I've heard that story somewhere before," she said, giving Ophelia a pointed look.

Ophelia smiled to herself but otherwise kept quiet. Beneath the overpowering stench of sweat and leather, Seamus caught a hint of mint mixed with pomegranate.

A great roar of applause echoed through the tavern, coming from the corner where Seamus had spotted a flash of yellow.

Seamus leaned over to her, pointing toward the uproar. "Is that your musician friend?"

"Zimri?" Ophelia asked, swiveling to see where he was pointing. The visible part of her face turned a little green. "Oh, you've got to be kidding me."

"He's quite the sight, isn't he?" Syrena asked, following their gaze.

Helgi, too, turned his attention to the young man in bright yellow attire. "Is he pretending to be Jonquil?"

Ophelia stiffened. "No," she said without turning back. She cleared her throat, waving maniacally. "Zimri!" she yelled.

The musician, who was bowing to his newfound fanbase, looked up at the sound of her voice. Zimri must've looked around the room ten times before spotting her. He threw his arms wide, his face full of relief and delight. He turned to his troupe, ditching his lute before squeezing through the sea of people to get to them.

"Darling girl!" he exclaimed, leaning lazily on Ophelia's side of the table. "Oh, how I missed you." Though he smiled ear to ear, his golden eyes had an air of sadness.

Speaking of his ears, Seamus suddenly realized they were pointed. He was also suddenly aware that the yellow-eyed fool had no wings. Was he a disgraced fairy like Egill? Seamus was still incredibly confused as to how these two knew each other.

"What are you doing here?" Ophelia asked.

Zimri tapped an excited rhythm on her arm with both his hands. "My band is playing tonight. I hear we're celebrating someone rather special."

The chances of Ophelia rolling her eyes beneath her mask were very high. "Really?"

"You know, you used to be fun," Zimri scowled.

Ophelia glanced over her shoulder at Seamus and Syrena, frowning. "Your *mother*," she began, stressing the word until it snapped, "won't be happy, *Zimri*."

Seamus furrowed his eyebrows.

"Oh, screw Nar—" He cleared his throat, looking wildly between Seamus and Syrena. "Ahem, I—uh—" Zimri laughed sheepishly. "Isn't this *some* party?" he asked Ophelia as he pushed away from the table.

A winged woman walked by with two glasses of wine. Zimri reached out and plucked one out of her hands, mumbling into it as he drank. Seamus caught something about a 'close call.' The woman scowled but inevitably turned back to the bar without a word.

"Why are you always so weird around each other?" Seamus asked.

Syrena stared at Zimri with wide eyes, her mouth hanging open slightly. "What was your mother's name?" she asked, leaning in close.

Zimri's eyes went as wide as hers. "Why?"

"You look familiar, that's all," she replied. Her eyes went to Zimri's face paint, then flicked to Ophelia. Beneath the noise, Seamus heard his Witch's heart skip a beat. "Say, jonquil flowers are quite pretty, aren't they?"

"They're daffodils," Ophelia and Zimri corrected.

"Yes, but 'Jonquil' is its other name, isn't it?" she said pointedly.

"Yes," Helgi said, looking dazed.

Zimri emptied his wine glass, expressionless. Ophelia's mouth was hanging open. Something unspoken passed between them, leaving Seamus in the dark, as per usual. After staring at Ophelia for a while, Zimri cleared his throat, pointing to where his band waited for him.

"Well," he said, nodding to himself. "That happened."

Without another word, he returned to his troupe.

Ophelia lingered a moment, then excused herself and went off to find Tiril. Seamus decided to let her go alone in fear the lovely hag would once again attack him with a pillow. Suffocated to death by an old crone was not how he intended to go out.

"That was weird, right?" Seamus asked, staring after her.

Syrena, in turn, was staring at him, awestruck yet obviously irritable. "You're so incredibly oblivious to the things happening around you, Seamus Norland."

CHAPTER NINETY-SIX

YOUR ARMOR, YOUR SHIELD

Ophelia had expected a crowd, but what she hadn't expected was Jonquil. Was he the only Spirit in the tavern? Why was he here? Ophelia could only hope that if something were wrong, he would've told her. Perhaps he'd been truthful. Maybe he was just here to celebrate her. Or better yet, to protect her. She'd ask, but he was back to playing his lute while dancing across a long, creaking table. Interrupting one of his songs after *that* exchange would be suspicious. Syrena—and possibly Helgi—had already put the puzzle pieces together. If Seamus had half a mind, he would too.

Reija had pointed her to the room Tiril had commandeered, then went on to pester the barmaids. Left to her own devices, Ophelia took the stairs two at a time, hugging herself tight. How Seamus was handling the cacophony caused by those hollering around them, Ophelia didn't know. It was all she could do not to cover her ears and run outside.

On the opposite side of the inn, lounging against the banister, was another familiar face. Thankfully, as far as she knew, this one was mortal.

It was the winged pirate. Beside him was a man, maybe a touch older. From the expression on that man's face, it wasn't Ophelia's place to interrupt, though she desperately wanted to. Had the pirate come here for *her*? No, no, no, that was silly! His captain probably dragged the crew here, right? The letters they'd sent out had been vague. There were no nods to Witches, just that there would be an announcement of sorts. Anyway, why would it matter? They didn't even know each other.

"There you are!" came Tiril.

Ophelia yelped, startled from her thoughts. "Yes, here I am," she laughed.

"I was coming down to—" Tiril's eyes went to where the winged pirate stood. "Oh. . . well, I never. Sight-seeing, are we?"

Ophelia tilted her head to the side in confusion, genuinely not understanding what that meant. "I suppose? Høstlunden is very beautiful, yes."

Tiril laughed to herself, opening the door to her room. Ophelia quickly stepped inside, though not without one last look over her shoulder. The pirate had disappeared, gone without a trace as though he'd never even been there. That was almost becoming a bad habit.

"How's Seamus? Is he all right?" Tiril asked, sitting on the edge of a dusty bed. She patted the empty space beside her, waving away the plume of dust that wafted into the air.

"He acts like he's fine, though I suspect otherwise," Ophelia sighed, settling in beside her.

"And you, my dear?"

To Ophelia, Tiril was defined by one sole characteristic: she was a secret keeper through and through. Whatever was said here today, she knew Tiril would never, in a million years, share—not even if it meant the fate of the universe.

"I find myself terrified," Ophelia said, untying her mask.

"Well, I believe that is to be expected."

Ophelia nodded, but the notion didn't make her feel any better. She imagined Holly had felt like this, too. Hundreds of times, probably. Fear was normal; it was one of the characteristics of having a soul. But the beings here today needed someone with courage, someone who would lead them without second guessing themself. In all honesty, they needed Seamus, not this frightened young Witch.

"Did you have a safe journey?" Ophelia asked, wanting to change the subject.

Tiril gave her a knowing look, taking hold of her hands. "You are very brave, Ophelia, darling. I'm not sure I would be here had I been in your shoes."

"I'm not sure *how* I ended up here, Tiril," Ophelia whispered. It was the strangest feeling, but she was glad someone was holding her hand at that moment. Part of her—a very large part—didn't want to let go.

"If I'm to be honest, I've wondered the same now and again. One day, I'll have to tell you about my life in Vårretten. I was a seamstress, you know," she said, holding her head high.

"Is that where all the dresses came from?" Ophelia asked.

Tiril nodded, gently letting go of her hands. She slipped off the bed, kneeling. From beneath the bedframe, she pulled out a long, thin box tied shut with a pale blue ribbon.

"Give me a day or two, a bolt of fabric and a pair of scissors, and I'll show you some real magic," she said with a wink, carefully placing the box on the bed. "Go ahead."

Ophelia fingered the massive bow at the center of the box, feeling somewhat guilty. Whatever was in this box, she knew it had to be incredibly special. Why did she, of all people, deserve it? Taking a calming breath, she tugged at the ribbon, carefully folding it up once it slipped off the box. There was a moment's hesitation before she lifted the lid, afraid to look.

Inside was a coat similar in style to the one she wore now. Comparing the two, however, was like comparing night and day. Her tattered, muddy, ragged coat was sun-bleached, bound together by threads threatening to snap at any moment. This coat was pristine, a stark, cobalt blue with silver piping and buttons shaped like polar bear faces. Ophelia was gobsmacked, to say the least. Ever so carefully, she lifted the coat, surprised at its weight. It was lined with some kind of dense, spotted fur. Around the collar and sleeves, barely noticeable, were swirling snowflakes.

"Reija and Noomi helped with the embroidery," Tiril said, audibly and visibly choked up. "Do you like it?"

An overwhelming rush of sadness swept through Ophelia's body. It was the sort of sadness you felt when you realized you'd been mourning something for a very, very long time. Yet, at the same time, there was a sliver of hope. A single ray of sunlight on a rainy day, the kind that caused the most magnificent rainbows one had ever seen.

Every sock, every pair of bloomers, every dress—they'd all been secondhand. Every clothing item ever given to her had come stained, torn, or mismatched. Not once had she owned something new, and she'd surely never had something tailor-made just for her. To say she 'liked' this coat would be a massive understatement.

A single tear dropped onto the coat, and Ophelia realized she'd been crying. Again.

"Tiril, I love it," she said, her voice barely a whisper.

Tear stricken herself, Tiril reached up and wiped away her tears, tucking a strand of hair behind her ear. "Count your blessings as you do up the buttons, knowing we're forever on your side. Pick at the loose threads, and know we will listen to your worries, big and small. Wear this, Ophelia, and know you are surrounded by people who love you. Let this be your armor, knowing we are your shield."

Something clicked in Ophelia's mind as Tiril kissed her forehead. She didn't like to be touched, not because people had hurt her, but because she'd been made to feel unworthy of such things. In fact, for the longest time, she hadn't felt worthy of any of this. But she *was* worthy, and she always had been. Now that she knew it, she wouldn't let anyone ever try to prove her wrong. She was a being capable of love, compassion, and kindness, things she gave so freely despite never receiving them herself. But now she had. Her cosmic karma had finally come, appearing in the form of a surly wolf, two washed-up librarians, a handmaiden, and a healer. This coat was more than armor, more than proof that someone cared. It was everything she'd ever wished for wrapped up in a neat little package.

Ophelia would not flinch from the people who loved her, though getting used to their touch may still take time. Further still, she would not waver in believing that a good deed and kind heart could and would change the world.

"Thank you," Ophelia said, leaning into Tiril's hand as she used her thumb to wipe another tear. "From the bottom of my heart, thank you."

"You're so very welcome, my dear."

CHAPTER NINETY-SEVEN

BEST BUDS

"What do you suppose is taking her so long?" Syrena asked, gazing around thoughtfully at the beings filling the tavern.

'Partygoers' was a more accurate term. The strange preemptive wake was in full swing. About seventy percent of those surrounding them were drunk; the other thirty percent were desperately trying not to be.

"Tiril, probably," Seamus laughed, wincing as another round of rowdy laughter erupted behind them.

"Tiril was one of the zealots, right?"

Seamus nodded, smiling to himself. He'd had filled her in on every little detail, unsurprised to see their plight fill her with determined fury. Syrena had admitted she wasn't much of a fighter, but if a healer were needed, she'd be at their beck and call.

"And we trust her?"

"Yes," he laughed. "Very much so."

"So I shouldn't be worrying?"

"Take it from me, you're always going to worry about her," Seamus sighed. "I believe it's part of her charm."

"Yes, I agree. She has this sort of. . . this sort of 'wounded animal' quality to her."

Seamus turned to her, eyes wide. "That's *exactly* what it is! It's like finding an injured puppy. No matter how stoic you pretend to be, your immediate reaction is to help."

Syrena laughed, patting his arm. "I doubt she'd appreciate us saying that."

Seamus smirked to himself, wholeheartedly agreeing.

They sat in awkward silence for a moment, both watching the stairs. Syrena leaned against him, sighing contently. It was startling how touchy-feely she was. Still, Seamus made no move to push her away.

"I wish we could stop time," she said. "Can't we stay here forever?"

"Now, wouldn't that be something?"

Syrena turned to him, green eyes full of life and wonderment. "You smell," she said.

Seamus, feeling as though he'd gotten drunk off Helgi's breath, hadn't really processed what she said. "What?" he asked wistfully.

"I said you smell," she laughed. "We should probably get cleaned up before the festivities begin, hmm?"

That immediately sobered him up. A nervous laugh escaped him, his cheeks burning. Now that she mentioned it, he really did stink. The last time this tunic had been washed was weeks ago. How he'd not caught a sniff of himself before was beyond him.

Syrena stood, giving a slight bow. "Seriously, Seamus. Soap. Ever heard of it?"

Before he could devise a witty remark, she'd vanished into the crowd, leaving Seamus laughing. He turned to Helgi, finding the old fool had fallen asleep, his head resting in a bowl of soup. Seamus shook him, grinning ear to ear.

"Helgi! Helgi, wake up," he said.

Helgi swatted his hands away, looking up dazed. "Hmm? What? What's going on?"

"Where's the washroom?"

"Why?"

"I stink."

"And?" Helgi blinked, wiping a piece of carrot off his face.

"Soap. Ever heard of it?"

After saying a quick hello to the horses and grabbing a change of clothes, Seamus quickly washed up. Now, he stood near the makeshift stage Zimri had created from two tables pushed together. Upon the stage, the flowery musician and a rather drab-looking flute player were trying to upstage each other. Needless to say, Zimri was definitely the crowd favorite.

Seamus tugged nervously at the collar of his high-necked tunic. It was the black and blue one he'd stolen from the Kirkeby manor, the one that matched Ophelia. He'd made the laces too tight and couldn't undo the knot with his fumbling fingers. He'd have to have Syrena help.

Halfway asphyxiated, he set off to find her, nearly plowing over a stunning woman dressed in sage green. Her copper hair shone like polished metal, cascading down her shoulders like—

"Syrena?" he gasped, unable to hide the shock in his voice or gaze. His hands were on her bare shoulders to steady her, the warmth of her skin seeping into his fingers. ". . . You look. . . nice." He cleared his throat, slowly lifting his hands. "I guess," he added quickly.

He took a few awkward steps back, running a hand through his hair, which was still wet from a quick attempt at washing it.

"Thank you, Seamus. You've such a way with words," Syrena teased, her voice clipped as she smoothed her dress.

Seamus swore on Rabbit's name he'd never seen a woman so beautiful as Syrena Skora in that dress. Such a lovely pale green, matching her eyes. Seamus had always loved the color green, hadn't he? Wasn't it his favorite color? If it hadn't been before, it was now. Next to blue, of course. The dress itself was simple: oversized, poofy sleeves and carefully placed pleats. There was less of a bodice and more of a sort of. . . swoop? Seamus's knowledge of fashion was limited. Whatever you called it, it was pretty. Apparently, that was all that mattered at that moment. Over the dress, she wore a tight-fitting vest made of brown velvet. It pinched her waist and accentuated. . .

Seamus felt his face redden, glad she could not read his mind. He tugged at his collar again, soaking her in. This morning, he hadn't thought much about her appearance or presence—beyond how she toyed with him, of course. But now? Seamus had many, many thoughts. A bright, blinding light was resonating off her, and damn, oh, damn, did Seamus want to drink in that light for as long as he lived. Too long had he hid in the darkness.

He felt his mouth go dry, realizing he'd been staring open-mouthed the whole time. Meanwhile, Syrena was red from the top of her head to her fingertips. She was glowing. Wholly and purely glowing. Radiant. Luminous. Ophelia would've come up with a thousand other synonyms. Still, none of them could properly express the woman before him. Seamus's thoughts were fuzzy, that strange pit in his stomach she gave him returning full force. The sight of her was almost enough to knock him out.

"Do you really think so?" Syrena asked, her voice cracking with some sort of emotion Seamus wasn't socially adept enough to place. "That I look all right, I mean. I—I feel a wee bit awkward, truthfully. Not sure why I dressed up."

Of course, he'd heard what she'd said, but to put it simply, he really hadn't.

"I mean, it's awfully low cut," she laughed.

Before Seamus could catch himself, he said, "It's perfect."

Syrena's cheeks were the color of wine. If he stared too long, he'd surely get drunk off the glow as if he'd drained an entire cellar.

"I mean—That is to say—I just think—" he began, his voice squeaky.

"Well, of course—" Syrena cut in.

"Yeah," he finished.

Whether on instinct or out of embarrassment, they shimmied away from each other, trying ever so hard not to glance back. Seamus found this far more difficult than Syrena. He had to physically turn his back to her, or else he'd not have been able to tear his eyes away.

"Quite the turnout," Syrena said, clearing her throat.

"Lots of people," Seamus nodded.

Appearing out of nowhere, Zimri poked his head between them, still plucking away at his lute. "No one will mind the two of you dancing," he winked before twirling away.

Syrena rocked back and forth on her heels, brushing against Seamus's shoulder. "Everyone else is certainly steeped in merriment."

"It'd just be rude not to join them," Seamus said, holding out his hand.

Syrena took it, pulling him into the throng of folks dancing in the tavern's center. Toes were stepped on, and beings were pushed and shoved into one another, but for a second, all was right in the world. Seamus's heart was beating so fast he figured it would explode. What in the ever-darkening night sky was wrong with him? Never once had he felt like this.

Laughing, he spun her into him, her skirts floating around her ankles. Zimri's music wrapped them in a warm embrace as he led a waltz through an inebriated crowd. His hand found the small of her waist, his thumb stroking the ruffle at the base of her vest. Syrena put her hand on his shoulder, smiling to herself.

"And here I thought you'd have two left feet," she laughed.

"I'll try not to take offense at that," he smiled, spinning her.

"My apologies, my good sir, I only—Oh." Syrena did a double take, staring over his shoulder. She went still so abruptly that Seamus nearly tripped over her feet.

The music faded, and the crowd settled, falling quiet. A cool breeze ruffled their hair, sending shivers down Seamus's spine. He turned, following the collective gaze to the stairs.

There, standing on the landing, was his Witch.

Yes, it was her, his Ophelia, his Witch, his daughter. . . But she didn't *look* like the pup he knew. *This* was the young Queen he'd glimpsed in Dødbyen.

Oh, Tiril had had her fun; that much was apparent. She'd done Ophelia up like a princess, dressing her in all that glittered and gleamed. She wore a stark blue jacket and dark gray boots trimmed with fur, both of which he knew Tiril had procured especially for her. Seamus smiled, spotting the hilt of the dagger he'd given her. Even her ebony hair shimmered as she walked down the steps, stopping midway.

All of this was fine and dandy, but the crowning jewel was her Witch Marks. They seemed to cast a faint blue glow on her surroundings, making her look rather ethereal.

The surrounding onlookers began to murmur, unable to

look away.

CHAPTER NINETY-EIGHT

OPHELIA, THE HOPEFUL

Expectant faces turned to her, each full of shock and awe. In their eyes, Ophelia saw a glimmer of belief, of hope. If they left here with one thing, it'd be that spark ignited tenfold.

"Hello," she said, trying to keep her voice level. "Thank you all for coming."

In the crowd, she spotted Seamus, who gave her a discreet thumbs-up and a reassuring nod.

Taking a steadying breath, she glanced over her shoulder at Tiril, who stood at the top of the stairs. She smiled, gesturing to the crowd. *Remember to project*, she'd said. *Make sure every ear can hear you.* She'd been given a crash course in addressing a kingdom, something Tiril seemed oddly adept at. Once again facing the crowd, Ophelia crossed her hands before her, hoping she gave off a regal air.

"My name is Ophelia Norland," she said as loudly as possible without yelling. "I am the last of my kind, the first Winter Witch in a thousand years."

The quiet murmur ebbing through the onlookers grew louder. Ophelia only caught bits and pieces of clipped voices, but it was obvious the rebels were confused. As Tiril had instructed, Ophelia held up a hand in an attempt to quiet them. It took a moment, but soon, the tavern descended into silence.

"My predecessor, Sigfreður, The Peaceful, left our world in shambles. His death ushered in an era of hatred and fear for both humans and magickind. I will not pretend to understand how his fall affected any of you, but I can share how it has affected me," she began, not knowing where any of these words came from.

"I grew up in a small, impoverished town in The Wilds called Tø. There, I was forced to hide my Marks in fear of execution. I lived in shadow, confined within the borders of that town, knowing that what lay beyond was certain death."

As she spoke, Seamus sighed heavily, reaching for Syrena's hand.

"No one should have to live like that. We should not be punished for our existence. It is not up to us to choose how we are born into this world, but we *can* choose what we do with the mind, body, and soul we are given," she continued, placing her hand over her heart. "For too long, that choice has been taken from us. If you'll allow me, I'd like to help reclaim those decisions."

A tall, scaled being with long, twisting horns fought their way to the front of the crowd. "And how do you plan on doing that?" they asked, blowing smoke out their nose. Several of the beings around them repeated the question.

"Whether the rebellion is to join us or not, we will be waging war on the Ulvemordere," Ophelia explained. "We plan to storm Juvel Hjem and rescue those imprisoned within the mines."

A woman with moth-like wings nodded. "Tiril mentioned that in her letter."

The scaly being weighed this, stepping back.

"Why are they so afraid of us? Why do they feel it just to steal our magic? Our friends and family? Our lives?" Ophelia asked. "When does it end? Is this what we want? To attend executions, aiding in the destruction of the magical community? To live in fear? To be seen as nothing but an ingredient or a scourge?"

A few beings hung their heads low.

From the back, someone called, "What sort of protection do you offer us?"

Tiril had guessed someone would bring that up. She'd suggested talking of Dødbyen, of the resources she and Helgi had, but Ophelia didn't want to be deceitful. The crowd was silent and still, patiently waiting for her response. Their eyes might have hope, but there was fear, too. They were afraid. Afraid to believe someone could rival the opposition. There hadn't been a ruling Witch in a thousand years, but there'd been plenty of Ulvemordere and corrupt nobles. The lies ran deep, but the disgust and disdain of the people ran deeper. Was that enough?

"Truthfully, I have little to offer you," Ophelia said, crossing her arms behind her back. "I refuse to make false promises. I may only barter myself, knowing many of you will not find this acceptable. I will not stand before you and use my Marks as a gambit, but I implore you to think about what they mean to you. What you do with your life is your choice, no one else's. Should you decide this fight is not for you, do not hesitate to leave. I would not ask you to endanger yourself for something you don't believe in."

The crowd split into their respective groups, most of which arguing amongst themselves. From the makeshift stage, Ophelia saw Jonquil turn to his troupe, using his lute to point at her. The tone-deaf harper stood tall, nodding solemnly. Reija and Matei stood a few feet away, seemingly defending her honor. The unsuspecting beings surrounding them looked afraid even to speak. Syrena, too, had inserted herself into an argument, hands on her hips.

Seamus was squeezing through the crowd, making his way to the stairs, grimacing. "Permission to speak, Your Highness?" he asked.

Ophelia nodded, trying her best not to smile.

Seamus rounded on the crowd, putting his pinkies in his mouth and whistling as loud as he could. Those with supernatural hearing covered their ears, shooting him a glare. Again, the inn fell silent.

"If you've been in this fight for a good long while," he began, arms crossed tight over his chest, "then you know we've not done much. We've tried our best, but we lack firepower. We lack numbers. What we don't lack, however, is hope. When I defected from the Ulvemordere, I was surrounded by those whose only driving force was just that. Hope. Now, I realize logically, this is a shit plan, but if we don't do something now, we never will. Our hope is a thousand years in the making. What are we going to do with it?"

"That's the problem, Norland," said one of the guards from Dødbyen. "This has been going on for a millennium. So many have tried to take them down, and it's only made things worse."

"They didn't have a Winter Witch," Seamus shrugged,

"and they weren't us."

"I, for one, am tired of hiding in the shadows." said a woman in a heavy woolen cloak. She had a thick accent and furry, pointed ears. "The Ulvemordere took everything from me. If I can protect even one person from that same fate, then I'm fulfilled. That's why we're rebels, isn't it? We've all got our stories and lost something or someone. I wouldn't wish that upon anyone."

The man beside her nodded, resting his arm on her shoulder. "If you take up the fight but can't rally behind the Witch, you're no better than the Ulve."

Ophelia held up a hand before anyone had a chance to argue. "I see the distrust in your eyes, and I understand. Believe me, I know how easy it is to hide. But what has hiding done for us? Where there is one, there will be many. If we reveal ourselves to the whole of Alle Årstider, you know our numbers will grow. *That* is why I stand before you, because I, too, am tired of hiding."

"The fact of the matter is, we are the 'one percenters.' It's a heavy burden, but we have to carry it," Seamus said, standing beside her. "Run toward something worth believing in."

No one moved.

No one spoke.

"The Ulvemordere have never served the people. They swept in all those years ago with promises of order, but our world has turned to chaos under their usurped dictatorship." Ophelia's voice was stronger than she felt. It echoed through the inn, rattling the walls as thunder boomed and lightning crashed outside. "Is this what you want?"

For a while, the crowd stood in stunned silence. Ophelia's heart pounded in her chest, terrified that each one would turn and leave.

Syrena pushed her way to the front of the crowd, kneeling. Those able to see what she'd done looked to one another, then they, too, knelt.

One by one, the crowd dropped to their knees, their heads bowed.

Seamus found Ophelia's hand, raising it high above their heads. "*Ære være Vinterheksen,*" he chanted, looking at her with such pride and love Ophelia couldn't help but feel the same. "*Ære være Vinterheksen.*"

Glory to the Winter Witch, he'd said.

"*Ære være Vinterheksen*," said a hundred voices. "*Ære være Vinterheksen.*"

CHAPTER NINETY-NINE

FIGHT, FLIGHT, FREEZE

Ophelia had slipped into the role of benevolent ruler quite easily. Seamus was so incredibly proud of her. The second he got her alone, he'd tell her just that. Unfortunately, that might not happen anytime soon.

Zimri's stage had been turned into a map table. It now stood beneath the mezzanine, this darkened inn corner acting as a war room. Here, Ophelia, Seamus, Tiril, Helgi, and a handful of skilled warriors stood devising a plan. Ophelia had delegated the tactical planning to Seamus. He knew how the Ulvemordere worked, but more importantly, he knew how *Arild* worked. Cathal, too. Syrena had been appointed as head medic. She was whisked off to prepare the rooms upstairs so they'd be ready to receive the injured. Those unable to fight went with her, taking a crash course in herbal healing. A few elderly folks were even tasked with caring for the children strewn across their makeshift camp. For the most part, the rebellion was happy to take up arms, but there would always be the hesitant few. Despite their trepidation, anyone on the fence was told to join in the preparations. If they decided to join the militia in the morning, they'd be prepared. If not, then they'd still done their part.

The plan was simple enough. They'd work in waves, mirroring the Ulvemordere's tactics. Seamus had been taught at a very young age that to win, you had to exhaust your enemy. The Ulvemordere would throw everything they had at them, never relenting. In turn, they'd do the same. Be it melee or ranged, they had ample weaponry. Armor was scarce, but a good portion of their army was malnourished, to put it lightly. They'd be but bugs beside a fully transformed Ulvemordere.

Agile little bugs, that is. Not the kind that are easily squashed.

Come tomorrow, Juvel Hjem wouldn't know what had hit it.

"Okay, answer me this," said Karran, a dark-skinned human in a sand-colored tunic. Seamus didn't know where he'd come from, but so far, he'd offered several helpful insights. "If we all head to Veil, what happens to the people here? Shouldn't a few of us stay behind?"

Across the table, a being wrapped in dark cloth shook their head. Their entire face was covered, not even their eyes visible. Their voice was nondescript and vaguely gravelly. Not once had they offered a name or any identifying information. Seamus had begun referring to them as 'the shadow.' They hadn't protested, so the others followed suit.

"We are already few. You mean to lessen our numbers further?" they asked. For whatever reason, they'd countered nearly every one of Karran's points.

Karran frowned, gesturing to the staircase. "There are children here, children who deserve our protection."

"Are you volunteering, then?" the shadow asked.

"We can offer it as an option to those undecided," Tiril said, gesturing for them to settle. "Even if only a few decide to stay back, they'll be protected."

Karran looked rather self-righteous, nodding his agreement.

The shadow scoffed.

"If you've problems, you're free to speak your mind, but I won't have feeble arguments jeopardizing the rest of us," Ophelia said, hands on her hips. "We've enough brains between us to resolve any problem that may arise."

Seamus gave the shadow a smug smile, daring them to try and debate her point.

"Apologies, Your Highness. I did not mean to cause trouble," they said, standing stiff. Seamus, accustomed to people hiding behind masks, knew they'd averted their eyes from Ophelia's piercing glare.

"I've a question!" came a tiny, squeaky voice. Sat atop a stack of cups was an elf, her pointy cap ever so slightly too big for her head. It kept falling to the side, covering one of her eyes. "What if we have to scatter? Where should we rendezvous?"

"Dødbyen," Helgi said quickly, pointing to the location on the map.

Tiril's eyes flickered with concern, but she nodded. "Our doors are always open to each and every one of you."

"What about the Witch's castle?" asked the elf. "Wouldn't it be safer there?"

Ophelia's cheeks went purple and red. "I. . . I don't have a castle."

The elf about fell off her stack of cups in shock. "But what about 'The Wild Thawed Palace?' Or was it 'The Wild Thawed *Place?*'"

"Ahh, I think you misheard. Tø was just a village in the Villeste Skog," Ophelia replied sheepishly.

"Oh," the elf said, her ears drooping. "I was rather looking forward to seeing a castle."

Tiril had a far-off look in her eyes as if she, too, had been hoping to visit a castle.

"What if one isn't welcome in Dødbyen?" Karran asked.

Helgi furrowed his eyebrows, giving him the death stare. "Are you not welcome in Dødbyen, Mr. Yamit?"

"My wife isn't," he said, grimacing.

Tiril sighed heavily, patting Helgi's arm before he could inquire further. "Consider whatever she's done forgiven. At least temporarily."

"Buzzing! I'll pass that along."

Change the words around, switch the speakers, and you'd have the next three hours. As Ophelia stated, they had enough mental prowess to solve almost anything. It was almost pleasant to be back in such a setting. Seamus hadn't planned something like this since before he lost Ingrid and his pack.

Ingrid.

His heart dropped to his toes. He hadn't thought about her in ages. Was that wrong of him? Was he. . . was he *moving on?* Somehow, that didn't sit right with him. Shouldn't he still be mourning the life the Ulvemordere had taken away? Glancing at Ophelia, he thought otherwise. Had Ingrid been alive, the two of them might never have met. He was almost—almost— thankful things had turned out this way. How crazy was that?

"Lady Ophelia!" came a frantic voice. Matei was weaving through the busy crowd around them, shaking something in the air. "Lady Ophelia, you've a letter!"

The crowd parted, letting him through. The young servant bowed, shakily handing over the letter. Another threat from Arild, surely. Frowning, Ophelia tore it open, scanning it quickly.

Whatever Arild had written made her go pale.

"What? What does it say?" Seamus asked.

"He looks forward to seeing us," Ophelia said, folding the letter and shoving it in her pocket. "He's just being an ass, it's nothing."

Seamus wasn't convinced, but he dropped the subject. Whatever it was, it wasn't for the others to hear; that much was certain.

"That screams of imminent doom, doesn't it?" the shadow asked. "That doesn't give us much time to prepare."

"We'll manage," Helgi said, "I know we will."

"So, does that about cover it?" Karran asked, turning to Ophelia.

"If there's nothing else. . . ?" she said, looking expectantly at each of them. When no one spoke, she nodded. "Well then, you know your places. Please take to your duties."

The shadow placed a hand over their heart and bowed. Along with Karran, they went off to spread the good word. Tiril and Helgi lingered a moment, talking amongst themselves before dispersing with the others. The elf, grinning ear to pointy ear, tipped her cap to Ophelia and then vanished.

"That bad of a letter?" Seamus asked once they were alone. He leaned against the table, studying his Witch.

Ophelia shrugged, absentmindedly straightening one of the maps.

"I'm proud of you, you know. More than words can express," he whispered.

"I'm proud of you, too," she sighed, refusing to look at him. "I know you don't want to be here. Not really. I. . . I don't really want to be either."

"Ehh, it's not all bad," Seamus laughed.

If she'd cracked a joke or bantered with him, it would've

made things so much easier. Instead, she kept quiet, fiddling with one of the buttons on her jacket.

"Whatever it is, you can tell me," Seamus said softly, searching her eyes for the problem so he could solve it. "You know you can."

She looked at him with such misery that Seamus wondered how she hadn't melted into a puddle of tears. "Promise me you'll stay out of harm's way," she said simply.

"Beg your pardon?" he asked.

"I don't want you going anywhere near Arild. I forbid it."

"Pup—"

"Seamus Norland," Ophelia snapped, sparks dancing across her fingers. She'd removed her bandages, revealing blistered, blackened skin. "You will stay here and keep the tavern safe."

"Ophelia, you can't—"

"So help me, I will shock you into a coma," she spat, stamping her foot. "I do not want you going after Arild. Do you understand me?"

Seamus was taken aback. He hadn't seen this kind of anger in her in a very long time. "Is—Is this about the pelt?" he asked, unsure of what else could be troubling her so much. "Did Arild mention it in his letter? Let me see it."

He reached toward her, but she turned away, shaking her head. "We don't know what it will do to you, and I don't want to find out."

Seamus wanted to argue that the chances of Arild bringing that moldy old pelt to Juvel Hjem were low, but the words died on his tongue. Instead, he stood, placing his hands on Ophelia's shoulders, looking deep into her eyes.

"Ophelia," he said sternly. "I go where you go."

She shrugged him away, turning for the stairs.

"Pup, I don't want to fight with you. Not now, all right? Not when both our lives are on the line," he said, stopping her in her tracks. "I don't want what might be our last words to be spoken in anger."

Without replying, she walked away, leaving Seamus feeling empty.

The plan was simple. Ophelia would lead them to Juvel

Hjem, and they'd do what they could to Arild's army and Cathal's trolls. The only problem was that Seamus didn't trust his Witch to uphold her part of the bargain. If he knew her—and boy, did he—he knew she'd have some grand idea and act on it without consulting them. How he'd remedy that, he didn't know. Were all teenagers like this, or was this a trait specific to Witches? Time muddled one's memories, but he didn't remember being so defiant. The defiance came later when the world had shown its nasty face. Up until then, Seamus had been perfectly content.

Grumbling to himself, he set out to find Syrena.

After looking for a good long while, he found her folding sheets in an empty room, humming to herself.

"Hey, gingersnap," he sighed, leaning on the doorframe. "You got a minute?"

"For you, Seamus? Rarely," she said with a wink. "What's up?"

Seamus stood silently for a minute, watching her bustle about her makeshift infirmary. She fluffed pillows, adjusted blankets, straightened a line of jars and vials—the place had changed, but her practice hadn't.

"Did Phee say anything odd while I was out?" he asked.

"About what?"

Seamus shrugged. "Anything, really."

Syrena gave him a sidelong look. "Is this about whatever it is she's been hiding from you?"

"You picked up on that too, huh?"

"Let's just say I'm accustomed to kids keeping secrets," Syrena laughed. "You'd be surprised how many children—teenagers especially—came in with broken bones, begging me not to tell their parents."

"Ahh, I see."

"You've never raised a child before, have you?" Syrena asked, gazing over her shoulder at him.

"Am I that bad at it?"

Syrena sighed heavily, fluffing one last pillow before coming to stand before him. "It is my experience that the ones who worry they're doing a terrible job are the parents and guardians who genuinely care for their children. Caring for a newborn is hard enough, but you've got a full-blown person to watch out for. This is new to you, but it's new to her, too. You're both learning as you go."

"I suppose you're right," Seamus sighed, forcing himself to smile. "Thank you, Syrena."

She blushed, waving away his thanks. "Aww, well, you know me. Always happy to help."

They stared at each other for quite some time, ignoring the other beings walking in and out of the room, busy with the tasks she'd given them. That pit in Seamus's stomach was back, growing wider by the second.

"Can I ask you something?" he whispered.

"Anything."

"I know you've got a life to return to, but I could use your expertise. If we all make it out of this, you're more than welcome to stay with us," he said, averting his eyes.

"That was more of a statement rather than a question," Syrena pointed out.

He smirked. "I didn't finish."

"Well, darling, we're not getting any younger here."

Rolling his eyes, he said, "My question is, would you want to?"

Syrena stepped back, hands on her hips. It was apparent she was thinking long and hard about that. He really hoped she'd say yes. Keeping her around was more than just good business. Seamus wanted to know her better, to figure out how she ticked. Not only was she a valuable asset, but she was intriguing, too. He only felt that way about a handful of people.

"When would you need an answer by?" she asked, avoiding his gaze.

Seamus shrugged. "Whenever you give me one."

She nodded, sighing. "You know, there's another question beneath that."

"You a mind reader now?"

She gave him a bored look, crossing her arms. "If it comes to it, I'll stay with her. I promise," she said, looking back and forth between his eyes.

The world outside had gone dark. Distant thunder rumbled every now and then, accentuated by a drizzle. Ophelia sat on the floor, looking out the window. Counting the seconds between booms, the thunder seemed to be getting closer. She could feel it tugging on her consciousness.

Tiril, a very busy bee indeed, had left her room to her. Ophelia was alone with her thoughts, Arild's letter weighing heavily in her pocket.

Hello again, Galanthus, it read. *While your efforts are admirable, I'd hoped you'd have enough sense not to drag anyone else into this. I could have sworn chess was a two-person game. No matter; we both know who will win. I look forward to receiving my prize. All my best, Sir Arild Melhus, Acting Ulvemordere General.*

The ending to this story was fast approaching, and truthfully, Ophelia didn't know what to do. Her mind kept circling back to how he'd called her Galanthus. The prospect that the Abyss had told him made her skin crawl.

The Ulvemordere worshipped The Abyss, after all. The Ulvemordere had many secrets, but everyone knew what recruits swore when they joined. For the glory of The Abyss, kill or be killed. That tagline was even stitched onto their flags. *'Til avgrunnens ære, drep eller bli drept.'* Even thinking it made Ophelia's skin crawl. How could one devote themselves to undying evil?

Once upon a time, all there was, was darkness—pure, all-consuming darkness. It pulsed with unknown emotions. There were no words for what it felt. For centuries, it stood alone, lonely in the vast emptiness. Then, one day, it awoke with a sense of purpose. What if there were another? What if it had a companion?

From the darkness bloomed a pinprick of light.

A single star.

This star, this *North Star*, was The Abyss's first creation. It was no longer lonely in the void, but The Abyss craved more. With council from its creation, it decided to make something else, this time, something bigger, something brighter. Thus, the

Sun was born. To create balance, soon came the Moon. Then earth, and millions of other stars.

Still, this wasn't enough.

The Abyss was never satisfied with its creations, always dreaming of its next amazing feat until, one day, there was nothing else to make.

The other Celestial bodies, seeing their creator's frustration, went to North Star for guidance. On that day, many moons ago, the others realized they, too, had the ability to create. In an attempt to appease their creator, they banded together, filling the earth with all manner of flora and fauna. This caused great jealousy in The Abyss. Whereas it had exhausted its imagination, its creations' had constructed a wild and wonderful world. Earth was their sandbox, the limits to what they could create knowing no bounds.

The Sun had even created something called a 'human.' These beings, these loud, smelly, irritating beings, adored the Sun, going so far as to worship her.

Why had they chosen *her* over the thing that had created the very fabric of the universe?

Unhappy with how the world had turned out, The Abyss forbade the others to create anything else, inevitably prohibiting them from visiting the mortal realm. Of course, there were loopholes to this rule, but there were punishments, too. Those caught meddling in mortal affairs would swiftly be dealt with. Its creations, known to the mortals as Spirits, found this very unfair. Despite numerous warnings, they refused to leave the mortals without guidance, returning to the mortal realm.

One by one, those who disobeyed vanished, the light of their corresponding stars fading. In The Abyss's jealousy, they'd created an ever-darkening night sky. North Star, especially, saw this as wrong. Try as she might, she couldn't convince The Abyss to rethink these rules. Once, she'd been The Abyss's favorite creation. Now, she was nothing more than a defiant child.

Soon, even the great North Star began to dim.

The Abyss was on a warpath, destroying anything and everything.

Ophelia didn't know how exactly it'd happened, but the Sun, Moon, and the remaining Celestial bodies banded together to confine The Abyss and its abilities.

Now, all it was, was a black expanse beyond the stars.

A handful of mortals were visited by their Spirits, told to recount this tale. With heavy hearts, the Spirits left the mortal realm. To keep the Abyss at bay, they must divert their magic elsewhere. Only those explicitly praying to them would be granted their heart's desires.

Obviously, there was more to this story than what had been written in the old religious texts. Ophelia had tried many, many times to learn the truth of it all, but none of the Spirits were willing to tell her. Now, however, she knew there were fallen stars and mortal Spirits, and she wondered where they fit in on the grand celestial timeline. How long had The Abyss been gone before Sigfreður and Ljot were killed by those who worshipped it? *Why* did the Ulvemordere worship it? And if The Abyss felt so betrayed by and jealous of its creations, why had it suddenly created Seamus? Furthermore, *how* had it done that?

It wasn't likely Jonquil had the answers, but at the very least, she could ask.

Ophelia slipped into the hall, careful to make sure Seamus, Syrena, or any of the others weren't watching. Outside, the thunder was right overhead, and the light drizzle was now a downpour. Shielding her eyes from the rain, she scanned the tents and caravans for Jonquil's troupe. Beneath their caravan's awning, illuminated by a flickering campfire, he and his musicians sat tuning their instruments. Jonquil spotted her immediately, a look of concern marring his sharp features. He pointed to his caravan, beckoning her inside.

Jonquil's caravan was an explosion of gold and cream fabrics. It was like a tiny, mobile prince's bedroom. So this was what he spent his wealth on?

"What's wrong?" he asked, shutting the door.

Immediately, the outside noise disappeared. It was like they were standing in some pocket of the universe far, far away from mortal troubles.

Ophelia dug into her pocket, handing him Arild's letter. Jonquil's expression went dark as he read it. Ophelia told him everything Arild had said without thinking, emphasizing how The Abyss had promised the General something. For a moment, they stood in silence, just staring at each other. If anyone could understand her thoughts, it'd be Jonquil. From the look in his eyes, he'd come to the same conclusion.

"What are you going to do?" Jonquil asked, shaking his head as he returned the letter to her.

"I don't know," Ophelia sighed.

He chewed his bottom lip, staring off into space. "I cannot imagine a mortal finding a way to communicate with The Abyss. That had to come from someone in the Garden. Someone that's been around for a while."

Ophelia nodded. "Hemlock."

Jonquil nodded, fiddling with his ruffled cuffs. "Shall I come with you?"

"No. No, if Hemlock is there, he could sense you. I have a feeling that'll only make things worse."

"I don't like this, Ophelia."

"Me either," she sighed, running a shaking hand through her hair. "I've enough sense to protect myself, though; I know it. I can deal with both of them. They don't scare me, not really."

"It isn't Hemlock or—or this Arild character that I'm worried about," Jonquil said, hugging himself tight. "Its—"

"The Abyss," Ophelia finished.

"Yeah," he whispered. "It has been quiet for centuries, and now it has created another North Star. I really, I really, don't like this."

"I know," she smiled, "but I'll be okay."

She knew Jonquil wanted to talk her out of it, but it wouldn't do any good. Ophelia had made up her mind. Plus, if something did happen to her tonight, she had a feeling that would only spur the rebels onward.

"Listen, if something happens to me—"

"Phee," he said, putting up his hands.

"Quill," she sighed. It'd been a while since she had used that nickname. Usually, he scowled. Now, he just looked empty. "Take care of Seamus, okay? That's all I ask."

Jonquil exhaled sharply, shaking away his sadness. He dawned his showman smile, hands on his hips. "Just promise me this, Snowdrop; if you need a troubadour, you'll call. Believe me, I'll come running."

Ophelia took his face in her hands, staring deep into his eyes. "You always have."

He placed his forehead against hers, smirking. "Yeah, well. I wouldn't leave my best mate high and dry, now would I?"

Begrudgingly, Ophelia dropped her hands and turned to the door. Jonquil stepped aside, giving her a dramatic bow. She returned it with a curtsey and then went out into the wild and scary world.

"I'm not gonna say goodbye, y'know," he called after her. "That means you *have* to come back!"

She blew him a kiss and was about to turn back toward the inn when a deafening boom cut through laughter and music.

CHAPTER ONE HUNDRED

A STEP UP FROM NOTHING

Seamus had felt the explosion more than he'd heard it. He'd been asleep, sprawled out on a mattress far too small for his broad frame. The entire tavern shook, knocking mirrors and picture frames from the walls. At first, the only reaction was a few panicked voices from the hall. Quick as he could, Seamus grabbed his axes from the bedside table and rushed into the hall. Syrena was beside him in an instant, dark circles under her eyes.

When the second explosion came, there was a surge of screams—hundreds and hundreds of screams, all mixing into one horrifying crescendo. Helgi shrieked incoherently, stumbling down the hall, obviously woken from a deep slumber. He and Tiril yelled over each other, trying to make sense of what was happening.

"Shut up, both of you!" Seamus screamed, waving wildly to get their attention. "Where's Ophelia?"

"She's not with you?" Tiril asked, eyes wild.

"She was supposed to be in *your* room!" Seamus snapped.

"Well, she wasn't!"

"Do you think she's all right?" Helgi asked.

"We'll focus on that later," Syrena said, putting up a hand before Seamus could add to their worries. "Right now, we need to help—"

When the third explosion hit, Seamus smelt it. Faint as can be, so light he almost doubted himself. But then he looked to Tiril, and he knew.

Wolfsbane.

Seamus swore, sliding down the railing instead of taking the stairs. He and Syrena rushed to the door, beckoning anyone close inside. Outside the inn, thick purple smoke hung heavy in the air, obscuring Seamus's vision. Every breath was pure fire, burning him from the inside out. Creatures of all kinds ran aimlessly through the trees, seeking shelter and weapons. The only ones finding safety were those with wings. Even they were being shot down by harpoons or caught up by nets. A pair of bat-winged goblins close by were screaming bloody murder, attempting to free themselves from a spiky net.

Tiril bolted past, clutching a high heel in either hand, using them to take out an Ulvemordere's eye. Helgi ran in the opposite direction, making for an elderly woman pointlessly throwing brightly colored potions.

Another explosion sent a shockwave through the frantic civilians.

Seamus grimaced, slipping into the shadows with Syrena, attempting to use the collar of his shirt to protect his lungs from the wolfsbane. Already, he could feel himself getting light-headed. They had to be smart about this, or else they'd end up with their heads in a basket within minutes.

Where in the ever-darkening night sky had his Witch disappeared to now? His one and only concern was her. There may be flaming tree branches falling on his head and an army of black-clad soldiers fighting off unsuspecting civilians, but all he could think about was finding Ophelia.

From the look on Syrena's face, she was thinking the same.

Ahead, a being with the head of a wolf and the twisted body of a man came running at him. Oh, he hated it when they transformed. Shoving Syrena aside, he pressed himself against the caravan behind him, trying to dodge the soldier running at him. They narrowly missed his throat, their claws just grazing him. A rather large chunk of hair drifted onto the steps as Seamus ducked under another swipe of claws. He reached for his axes, panic setting in.

The towering Ulvemordere soldier before him seemed to read his mind. Their snout pulled into a smile as they licked their chops.

"Well, shit," Seamus croaked, realizing his lovely, sharp,

yet tiny axes were going to do little in that moment.

A gravelly voice responded, "Shit, indeed," as the lycanthrope leaned down to his eye level.

"Hey!" came another voice just as the abomination opened its enormous jowls.

The soldier whipped its head to the left, gazing down at—

"Reija!" Seamus laughed.

The servant—or whatever she was—came barreling out of the woods, a flaming flagon of ale at the ready. Seamus had just enough time to wrap his arms around Syrena and duck before she threw the explosive. Bright orange light seeped through his eyelids as the bottle exploded onto the soldier's side. They wailed and screeched as the smell of scorched fur and the sound of sizzling filled the air. Opening his eyes, Seamus watched as the beast ran off, ablaze. He stowed his axes, ready to—

A hand on his shoulder.

Seamus spun, fist at the ready, when he came face to face with—

"Reija!" he exclaimed for the second time, coughing on the wolfsbane-laden air. "Where's Ophelia?"

Reija's eyes went wide with terror. "W—What do you mean?"

"You haven't seen her?"

"No!"

Syrena, who'd been hiding behind Seamus, poked her head around his shoulder. "You're sure you haven't seen her?"

"She's Seamus's charge, not mine!" Reija snapped.

Seamus felt as though he'd burst. "Oh, that's rich!"

"She was supposed to be with Tiril!"

"We know!" Seamus and Syrena yelled.

Thankfully, another explosion cut off Reija's clipped voice. On instinct, Seamus grabbed hold of her and Syrena, shielding them from a sudden spray of shrapnel. Seamus's skin itched. Glancing at his hand, he found red splotches.

"That doesn't look good," Syrena said, taking his hand in hers.

"I'll be fine," Seamus choked out.

"Where are Tiril and Helgi? Helgi especially can't handle this amount of wolfsbane," Reija said, eyes full of fright.

Syrena placed a gentle hand on her shoulder, trying her best to smile. "We saw them just moments ago; we'll find them again."

"Tiril was using her heels as shivs," Seamus sighed, looking out at the chaos.

For now, they were hidden in the shadow of a caravan, the world none the wiser to their existence. Around them, wolf-like beasts stalked through the shadows, their hands and mouths drenched in blood, their eyes glowing red. Syrena covered her mouth, trying to keep quiet. Thunder rumbled as bombs went off, and screams echoed through the forest.

Another set of hands took Seamus's arm. Panicked, Seamus shoved Syrena and Reija back. Just in time, too, for the air around him grew unimaginably hot. The world shifted, the colors so bright they blinded him.

One second, he was hiding behind a caravan.

The next, he was being thrown against a wall.

Before he had time to react, someone's knee found his sternum, causing him to double over in pain. Just as he found the strength to breathe again, someone grabbed his throat, pinning him to the wall behind him. An opalescent dagger flicked into view, inches from his face. Behind it was the smiling face of one Egill Daae.

"Hello, old friend," he said.

"You again? We've *got* to stop meeting like this," Seamus sighed, more irritated than alarmed.

Egill made a *tsk-tsk-tsk*ing noise, angling his dagger toward Seamus's eye. "Care to match your good ol' buddy Helgi?"

"Returning favors, are we?" Seamus grunted. "Sounds fun."

With that, he kneed Egill in a place no man is ever prepared to be kneed. Egill screeched, dropping his dagger and loosening his grip on Seamus's neck. Seamus took hold of his arm, twisting it until the finicky fairy screamed in pain.

"Where's my kid?" he snarled, kicking out one of Egill's knees.

"Ha—Haven't found her y—yet—!" Egill quivered, eyes filling with tears.

Seamus bent the fairy's arm back as far as it would go without snapping it, smiling toothily as Egill's eyes and mouth widened with fear.

"I'll—I'll give her your best if I f—find her," he choked out, gritting his teeth against the pain as he shook Seamus away and then disappeared.

Seamus shut his eyes, waiting for Egill to make his move. Again, the air began to shift. Pulsing energy to his left. Seamus spun, clipping Egill's ear as he materialized beside him. Bright yellow eyes so wide you'd mistake them for twin suns consumed Seamus's vision. Egill blew hot steam out his nose, lunging at him. Seamus tried his best to swat him away, but instead, the world once again shifted, and he found himself lying on his back, pinned beneath Egill's knee.

"Listen to me," he hissed, his voice just loud enough beneath the chaos. Daring a look over his shoulder, Egill mumbled curses upon curses. "Arild wants to siphon the pelt."

"W—What?" Seamus asked, rolling to the side so the stupid, stupid fairy would get off of him.

Egill sat heavily on the ground, pointing his dagger at him. "He can't siphon its energy alone, nor while it consumes someone. He thinks if it bonds to you, he can siphon it that way."

Seamus stood, tightening his grip on his axes. "Need I explain how stupid that sounds?"

"If I've learned one thing as of late, it's that anything is possible. Your only limit is your imagination," Egill said, glaring up at him.

"Why are you telling me this?"

"I'm a flippant ass," he shrugged, standing. "Plus, I'm meant to be distracting you. Do you think your healer and the serving girl have found the Witch yet? They better hurry up if not."

With no mercy, grace, or anything even remotely resembling such ideals, Seamus balled his fist and hit Egill so hard his nose twisted up and to the right. The fairy stared dazed for a minute, licked blood off his upper lip, then slumped backward, unconscious.

Seamus stood over him, hands on his hips, shaking his head. "Check and mate, pin-wing," he sighed, then bent down and stripped him of his weapons. He shoved the opalescent daggers into his belt loops, stuffed a few smoke bombs in his pockets, and then took off to find his Witch.

CHAPTER ONE HUNDRED AND ONE

ALL'S WELL THAT ENDS WELL

How she'd gotten here, Ophelia couldn't exactly remember. Everything was a blur of explosions and frenzied creatures screaming for help. She'd been running, trying to find someone to blame for the chaos, when three guards from Dødbyen had called out to her. Now, the four of them were attempting to fend off a handful of Ulvemordere soldiers. To say Ophelia was confused was an understatement.

The snarky guard who'd picked on Seamus stood before her, locked in hand-to-hand combat with an armored woman thrice his size, her black armor absorbing the moonlight. Ophelia had fashioned herself an axe out of ice, stumbling through the movements Seamus had taught her. Somehow, she'd been paired with an Ulvemordere without a pelt. She'd forever be thankful for that. Still, this soldier was faster, stronger, and a lot more bloodthirsty than she was. She was tiring, unable to do more than swing her makeshift weapon around wildly.

"Duck!" came one of the guard's voices.

Ophelia immediately dropped to a crouch, covering her head with her arms. What happened next would haunt her forever. One of the guards swung their broadsword, chopping the head of the Ulvemordere she'd been fighting clean off. Seeing the young Witch was frozen in fear, the guard took her by the collar, dragging her away from the headless body.

"Sorry about that," one of the guards said, grimacing.

"Did what we had to do and nothing more. I swear it," said another.

"Yeah, yeah, whatever," Ophelia said, waving their words away. "Did you see—"

The third guard's eyes shifted, her gaze directed over Ophelia's shoulder.

Where the command had come from, Ophelia didn't know, but someone shouted, "Seize them!" which, in hindsight, felt very cliché.

The first guard jumped into action, brandishing their bloodied broadsword. Ophelia twisted, watching in horror as shining silver canisters collided with the ground, filling the forest with dense and hazy purple smoke that blocked her vision. Startled and angry voices sounded off all around, their words unintelligible. One of the guards tried screaming their own orders, but the ruckus drowned them out.

Ophelia thrust her hands forward, calling on the wind to clear the wolfsbane from the air, but the heavy smog was just too much. All she did was cause glittering purple swirls in the air. Smoke like this burned even *her* lungs. Any wolf breathing this in was a goner. Seamus, too.

"Get back!" Ophelia screamed, encasing herself and the others in an ice sphere as a transformed Ulvemordere emerged from the smoke. Their head collided with the ice, cracking it. Slowly, they fell to their knees, tipping backward.

"Nice," the female guard mumbled.

"Get her out of here," the snarky guard said. "Pleasure fighting alongside you, Vinterheks."

Ophelia gave him a reassuring nod, then took off with the other two.

Caravans and tents were ablaze.

Horses and other mounts ran wild. Ophelia spotted Rain and Frykt a few feet away, dragging behind them a cart full of screaming children. One of the guards at her side followed her gaze, rushing forward to help.

Stomping footsteps from behind startled Ophelia so badly that she nearly fainted out of fright. She spun, throwing up another shield of ice just as a mace came crashing down upon her.

A troll.

It just had to be a troll.

They swung their mace again, trying to crack Ophelia's shield.

"Go! Go, run!" the remaining guard called from behind,

guiding a few stray patrons toward some semblance of safety.

Every spell sent dizzying waves of pain up her arms. Given recent events, she really shouldn't be fighting like this.

"Help!" Ophelia screeched.

The guard turned, eyes wide. Without taking even a second to think, he grabbed Ophelia by the waist, pulling her out of harm's way. The troll's mace shattered her protective dome, narrowly missing her foot.

Out of nowhere, two winged beings swooped down from the sky, showering everyone in a plume of feathers. Everything happened in slow motion. The troll momentarily forgot about Ophelia, blindly swinging at the winged beings, who took hold of its mace and arms and lifted with all their might. The flap of their wings was nearly as loud as the rumbling thunder above. Ophelia reached toward them, once again calling upon the wind, pooling the breeze under their wings. Ever so slowly, they began to rise, the beat of their wings softening. Higher and higher, they rose until suddenly, they let go, and the troll went plummeting.

Ophelia and the guard took a few steps back, wincing as the poor troll shattered on the ground. The winged beings saluted her, then flew off in opposite directions.

"Impressive," the guard beside her said.

Ophelia shrugged, breathless. "Not the first time I've killed a troll. I assume it won't be the last."

He laughed, beckoning her to follow.

Someone was yelling her name. Ophelia looked up, spotting Jonquil a few feet away. He was swinging his golden lute at an iron-clad woman, trying his best to escape her. The most impressive part of the whole ordeal was how his lute hadn't taken any damage.

"You've got to be kidding me," the guard groaned, racing to his aid.

Running full speed, he tackled the woman. In seconds, he had her head in his hands, twisting with all his might.

"Oh, my—" Jonquil gagged, turning away. "What is *wrong* with you?"

The guard stood, wiping his hands on his pants, scanning the woman's body for weapons. "Many, many things."

"What?" Jonquil asked.

He looked up, shaking his head. "Talking to myself," he grumbled.

Jonquil rolled his eyes, a hand out to keep himself from seeing the body. "Did you have to snap her neck like that, you brute?"

"Have you seen Seamus?" Ophelia asked. She, too, ignored the body.

Jonquil frowned at them as though they were stupid. "I saw him and that healer take off when the first explosion hit."

"T—Take off?" the guard asked. "Took off to where?"

Jonquil plucked a sad little tune on his lute, shaking his head. "Mighty protectors, watch as they fall. Lost sight of the one who shelters them all," he sang. If Seamus were here, he'd want nothing more than to smash his lute over his head.

The guard turned to Ophelia. "Can I kill him? I want to kill him."

Ophelia rolled her eyes, hands on her hips. "I asked you to watch over him!"

"Yes, well, my troupe got attacked," he said rather matter-of-factly. "Some blond bloke appeared, and he vanished," he added, shrugging.

"Egill?"

"You know, I didn't catch his name, seeing as I was *running for my life*!" Jonquil screeched.

"You don't have a life to run for, Quill!" Ophelia snapped.

"Okay, enough of this," the guard said, violently shaking his head. "You, Witch, need to get to the mutt before he does something stupid."

"I second that," Jonquil said, beginning to strum. "Oh, daring wolf—"

"So help me, bard, I will shove that lute where the sun don't shine," the guard snapped.

"Are all werewolves so rude?" was Jonquil's only response.

CHAPTER ONE HUNDRED AND TWO

WOLFSBANE & WITCH BELLS

In an attempt to find the other's, Seamus had stumbled into all kinds of trouble. One of his arms hung loosely in its socket, and the other brandished one of Egill's daggers in a poor attempt to scare off whoever dared come near. He'd stayed in the shadows, hobbling along on unsteady feet, taking tiny, shallow breaths. The noise around him had muffled, mixing into an irksome rumbling.

The wolfsbane was getting to him. Which way was up? Which way was down? Left? Right? He didn't know. Every movement was sluggish. Every shifting shadow was a threat he couldn't fight.

Seamus's wolf was howling in agony, both from the wolfsbane and the fact he'd lost sight of not only Ophelia but Syrena and Reija, too. Seamus glanced down at his hands, finding his claws had broken through. He hadn't even felt it. A sudden wave of pain ran through him. He reached up to touch his face, feeling jagged cheekbones and fur.

Let me help, his wolf whispered. *I can help.*

"No," Seamus whispered. "You'll kill everything in sight."

We will, his wolf corrected. We *will kill everyone in sight.*

One of those shifting shadows moved toward him, and he realized he hadn't been walking for quite some time. He'd just been standing there, clinging to the wheel of an overturned cart. A muffled voice filled his ears, but he couldn't make out the words. Without looking, he swung his dagger, taking a cheap shot at his would-be attacker. Whoever it was grabbed his arm, squeezing it tight.

Seamus turned to look into his attacker's face, squinting

through bleary eyes to make out their features. All he saw was blue. Just blue and. . . was that a snowflake?

"Pup?" he asked, nearly losing his footing. As soon as it saw her, his wolf calmed, retreating to its cave, buried in the depths of his mind.

"What happened to you?!" Ophelia shrieked, struggling to support his weight as he pulled her into a bear hug with the arm that could still move freely. "Are you all right?"

Gasping for air, he pushed her back ever so slightly. "*Wolfsbane*," he choked out.

Ophelia grimaced, placing a hand on his chest. His lungs filled with air, swelling so much it hurt. His legs suddenly stopped wobbling, his mind clearing. He winced, covering his good ear as the rumbling battling cranked up in volume. He could hear every clash of metal, every scream, every pin being pulled from every smoke bomb. On his tongue, he tasted metal and sweat. All he could smell was blood. All he felt was the pain of his muscles constricting, his body caught between human and wolf.

"Better?" Ophelia asked.

"I'll get back to you on that one," Seamus frowned, gently moving her hand away so as not to nick her with his claws. "Are you hurt?"

"Surprisingly, I'm actually perfectly fine. You?"

"Yeah, yeah. . ." He winced, trying for the fifth time to pop his arm back into place. Apparently, five was the magic number. "Yeah, no. That's a no from me."

"Seamus!"

After coughing violently and rolling his shoulder a few times to fend off a wave of pain, Seamus said, "Hey, don't lecture me, missy! You were the one who ran off!"

"I didn't run off! I was protecting my people!"

Seamus shook his head accusingly but dropped the subject. There was no use arguing now.

"Where are Tiril and Helgi?"

"Don't know, trying not to care," Seamus grumbled. He could see the electric-green light from his eyes illuminating his face, and in her eyes was his reflection. Oh, he looked horrid. How could she stand to look at him like this? "I lost track of Syrena and Reija, too. Egill whizzed me off just so he could gloat."

"I heard," Ophelia sighed.

"Listen, we need to get to the horses—"

"I'm not leaving without our family," Ophelia said, taking a step back.

There was a split second there where Seamus wondered if he was hallucinating this whole thing. Still coughing, he looked up to see a crossbow peeking around the corner of a blazing stack of crates. He locked eyes with the shooter, barely able to wrench Ophelia out of the line of fire before they let their bolt loose. The bolt went through the hem of her dress, pinning her to the ground. Seamus tugged her away, making for cover.

"Watch out!" she screamed.

Something exploded at his feet, sending a plume of purple smoke into the air. The powered wolfsbane wafted up into his nose, choking him once again. Ophelia clapped her hands together, letting rip a bright white lightning bolt. Someone screamed in pain as they lit up with sparks, illuminating the smoke. Ophelia didn't seem to want to stick around and watch, for she shoved him through the smoke, steering him toward safety.

"Can't—breathe!" Seamus gagged as they hid behind a stack of crates.

Somewhere close by, more smoke bombs went off. By now, Seamus would've thought the panic had died down. Yet with every explosion, another round of horrified screams rang through the air.

"We're surrounded!" Ophelia cried. "They're everywhere!"

Eyes still blurry, Seamus peeked beyond the crates to see wave after wave of Ulvemordere soldiers spilling through the trees opposite them. The ground shook with armored footsteps. They were coming from every possible direction.

"We need to get out of here," Seamus croaked, rubbing his chest, wishing he could miraculously become immune to wolfsbane.

"Oh no!" Ophelia screeched.

Seamus whipped his head around to see where she was pointing. Several yards away was Tiril. An Ulvemordere had their claws in her scalp, attempting to drag her Stars-knew where. She kicked and thrashed with all her might, but nothing seemed to faze the abomination. Ophelia was already out of arm's reach before Seamus could jumpstart his body into action. Reacting as fast as he could, he rushed after her.

As if by an invisible force, the Ulvemordere manhandling Tiril was pulled backward, crashing hard into the muddy ground. Shocked, they loosened their grip on her long enough for Tiril to wriggle free. Ophelia covered her eyes and turned away as Tiril removed the soldier's helm and slashed their throat with her long, perfectly manicured claws.

"Perfect timing, my lady," Tiril said proudly, using her dress to dry her hands of blood.

"Mmm. . . yes, well, you're welcome," Ophelia mumbled.

"Where's Helgi?" Seamus asked, patting Ophelia's shoulder. She peeked at him through her fingers, grimacing.

Tiril shrugged, reaching up to wipe her brow rather daintily. "I've not a clue. We'll find him, I'm sure. Let's stick together, all right?"

Seamus was about to agree when two soldiers came barreling toward them. Ophelia stomped her foot, sending thick ice pillars to greet them. They ran straight into them, then slumped to the ground, dazed. For such deadly creatures, they were awfully stupid.

"I quite like having a Witch on our side," Tiril said thoughtfully.

"You get used to it, don't you?" Seamus nodded, clearing his throat.

Somewhere nearby, a child screamed for help. Seamus didn't even try to stop the blur of blue as it bolted past him. Trying to prevent Ophelia from doing what she thought was right would never work. It was high time he accepted that. So, instead of screaming at her to come back, he and Tiril just raced after her.

Two young fairy folk were hiding inside a collapsed tent. They were wailing and screaming, begging for someone to help, as four Ulvemordere soldiers poked and prodded at them, laughing and hollering to frighten them further.

Ophelia skidded to a stop. As her hands shot forward, the tent sprang to life. "Tiril!" she screamed.

Out of the three of them, Tiril was the fastest. Quick

as she could, she raced to the tent. Narrowly dodging a sword being swung at her head, she yanked the children out from the heavy canvas death trap.

"I've got a grand idea!" Seamus screamed, tugging on Ophelia's sleeve.

She turned, looking to where he was pointing. There, a well sat untouched despite the many fights, fires, and explosions going on around it. Ophelia arced her arms through the air, and the ground began to rumble. The well blew like a geyser, bending as Ophelia struggled to control it. A massive wave rushed forward, greeting the Ulvemordere like a riptide. The wave—which, if you looked closely, vaguely resembled a polar bear—crashed down upon them, sucked them up, then dragged them, screaming and gurgling back toward the well.

Meanwhile, Tiril and the children were untouched.

Seamus rushed forward, taking one of the fairy children into his arms. He was just a tiny thing with broken wings and tear-stained cheeks. Tiril had the other child on her hip, trying to soothe the squealing thing.

"My wing!" she cried, hugging Tiril tight. One of her beautiful, bright pink wings hung limp. A tear nearly split it in half. "I can't fly!"

"It's all right, we'll protect you," Tiril whispered, flicking a tear off the girl's cheek.

How could someone do such heinous things to a child?

Seamus turned to Ophelia, his heart doing somersaults as she staggered to the side. Catching his eye, she gave a slight shake of her head. He almost heard her think, 'Blessed Amaranth, lecture me later.'

Clearing her throat, she said, "Tiril, one of your guards is with Rain and Frykt, they'll—"

Seamus turned back to Ophelia a second too late. "PUP, MOVE!" he screamed.

The empty air behind her shimmered with fairy dust. Ophelia spun, coming face to face with the two people Seamus wanted dead more than anyone else: Egill Daae and the General, Sir Arild Melhus.

Ophelia swept her hands through the air, showering them with little shards of ice. Egill ducked, and Arild spun, his cloak absorbing the blast. Slowly, he turned back to her, picking a shard of ice out of his cheek. He was huffing and puffing, taking small, calculated steps forward.

"That. . . was a mistake," he growled. "Be smart, you little brat. A fast death or an agonizing one. Your choice."

"Actually, I choose the secret third option where I live! Thanks, though!" Ophelia smiled, giving a little bow. Seamus grimaced as she struggled to find her footing.

Eyes full of greed, Arild took his bejeweled baton out from under his patchwork cloak. He swung it, aiming for her head. Panicked, Ophelia threw her hands up, encasing her arms in ice. The baton collided with her forearms, cracking her frozen armor. The iron burned and sizzled, melting her mystical vambraces. Before the baton could touch her skin, she ducked to the side, then kicked Arild in the shin as hard as she could. He cried out in pain, stumbling for a second before rounding on her yet again.

"Seamus, give him here!" Tiril barked. "Seamus!"

Seamus looked down, remembering he held a wailing fairy child in his arms. Quickly, he passed the boy over to Tiril, giving her a reassuring nod.

Just as he turned back to help Ophelia, she stumbled into him, wiping blood from her upper lip. Arild flexed his off-hand, his iron gauntlet flecked with silver. Frowning, Seamus pushed his Witch back onto steady feet.

Egill made to follow Tiril, but Arild put his hand out. "The crone isn't worth our time."

"But—"

"Egill," Arild snapped, "are you being defiant again?"

"No, sir," he mumbled.

Arild snapped his fingers, then pointed at Seamus's belt. "Then take back your daggers, will you?"

Seamus's hands went instinctively to the stolen weapons. Egill's form dissolved into fairy dust as the air beside Seamus began to boil. Without thinking, he shoved Ophelia aside.

9. PENULTIMATE

CHAPTER ONE HUNDRED AND THREE

ACONITE BY ANY OTHER NAME

Egill's fist connected with Seamus's jaw the very second Arild reached forward and grabbed Ophelia by the collar, spinning her until he had her pinned between the crook of his arm and chest. Seamus stumbled to the side, stunned, haphazardly attempting to fend off the flippant fairy. Ophelia took hold of Arild's wrist, fighting to break free of his grip, eyes darting back and forth between his baton and Seamus.

"I figured I'd save you the trouble of storming Juvel Hjem," Arild said, his tone so full of arrogance it made Ophelia's stomach churn. "After all, there's nothing for you there. Saoirse and Åsmund are gone, remember?"

"Let go of me," she spat.

"Shh. . ." Arild whispered, his breath hot against Ophelia's cheek. "Let's talk for a moment, shall we?"

"Let's not and say we did," Ophelia said through gritted teeth.

Arild grabbed her face with his clawed gauntlet, forcing her to look at him. The iron burned her cheeks, the claws drawing blood. "You know, we never really discussed our deal, Vinterheks."

Ophelia's grip on Arild's wrist tightened. A thin layer of ice was trying to spread across his armor, but the potency of the iron burned it away almost instantly.

"Or—Or was it Galanthus?" Ophelia's heart did somersaults. "Oh, no, no, no, I'm sorry. You preferred 'Snowdrop,' didn't you?" Arild laughed. "Or, perhaps 'the Polar Bear?' But, of course, you haven't really earned those titles yet, have you?"

"I will *never* make a deal with *you*," Ophelia hissed.

"Oh, I know. But there's someone else who's been *dying* to meet you. My purpose is simply to bring you to them," Arild whispered. "Believe me, they've a deal you'll want to consider."

"Let me guess? The Abyss wants Seamus, and in return, it'll offer me my heart's greatest desire. That's a shit deal if you ask me," Ophelia laughed.

"You've no idea what it can offer," Arild said, unfazed.

"And *you* have no idea what you're messing with."

Arild scoffed. "Does Seamus know about your little secret, or have you been lying to him this whole time?"

Egill cried out in pain, startling them both. Arild's eyes darted to where Egill stood staggering, clutching the side of his face. Thin streams of blood seeped out from between his fingers. Seamus looked murderous, which wasn't anything new, but given Egill was around, Ophelia knew he'd follow through on those feelings.

"He doesn't know, does he?" Arild asked. "You know his cosmic secret—one he doesn't want to admit, I might add—but he doesn't know yours? *Tsk, tsk*, Ophelia. That doesn't seem very fair, does it?"

"Shut up," Ophelia spat, trying to wriggle free from his grip.

Arild only laughed, pushing against her arm, the baton tip dangerously close to her face. "I would revel in killing you, little Witch, but it isn't my destiny," he whispered. Rather aggressively, he tugged her head to the side, jerking his other arm free from her grip. "Then again, who is to say our 'destiny' even matters? What do *you* make of fate?"

Ophelia went completely stiff. The air around them had gone so cold she could barely breathe.

Arild's eyebrows twitched in mock surprise. "I've had eyes and ears everywhere, my dear."

"The Garden knows The Abyss has returned," Ophelia spat. "Amaranth and the others sealed it away once before. They can do it again."

"You think I'm afraid of a few flowers?" Arild laughed. "If they're so powerful, how did it break free to begin with?"

"I think you're more afraid than I am," Ophelia laughed. "No courageous man parades around their 'power' the way you do."

"Egill," he snapped.

Egill—who had Seamus in a headlock—looked over his shoulder, eyes wide with. . . was that *hatred*? Realizing he'd been caught off guard, Seamus headbutted him, attempting to run away.

"Seamus. . ." Arild sang.

Her wolf spun, the color draining from his face. His fists were balled so tight his claws punctured his palms. Arild inched the baton closer to her throat—so close she could feel something being tugged deep, deep inside her. Seamus swore, avoiding Ophelia's eyes as he dropped to his knees, hands behind his head.

"No!" Ophelia cried, trying once again to wriggle free from Arild's grip. "Seamus, no!"

No, no, no, no, *no*! This wasn't supposed to happen! Why had he given up this easily?

"You're going to be a good little Witch, or I'll pick off all your lovely friends one by one," Arild whispered. "We don't want that, do we?"

He whistled, and two towering beings with wolf-like heads and furry, muscular bodies came and dragged Ophelia away. Clawed hands wrapped in hammered iron held her as tight as they could. The heat of the iron seeped through her clothes and into her skin as she tried to fight against them. Neither of the Ulvemordere moved. Neither flinched. All she was to them was a toddler throwing a tantrum.

That may be true, but they didn't know just how powerful she was. She'd beaten iron once; she could do it again.

Arild looked to Egill, giving him a knowing smile. Egill rolled his eyes, digging into his jacket. From a hidden pocket, he procured a pair of iron shackles. Grumbling to himself, he yanked on Seamus's arms until the surly old wolf let him place the shackles on his wrists.

"All of this, over some kid," Arild laughed, "How pa—"

"She's not 'some kid,' she's *my* kid!" Seamus spat, shaking away Egill's grip on his shoulder. "Let. Her. Go."

"Oh, I will," Arild said, using his baton to point at him. "The Witch was never my concern, you see. She's just a happy accident. Two for the price of one, I suppose, aye Egill?"

Egill chewed the inside of his cheek, looking Ophelia up and down. "Good business," he grumbled.

"Witch," Arild began, "I've been told you like stories. Would you like to hear one?"

"The pelt, Sir," Egill spat.

Arild shot him a rather nasty look, a low, rumbling growl escaping his throat. Slowly, he swiveled on his heels, turning to Ophelia. "That day you watched Mawde Carre die, do you remember what my weapon did? Oh, yes, I knew you were there. I never forget a face," Arild laughed. "Anywho, if you need a refresher, this lovely little baton siphons magic. Did you ask the trolls where they found the gems to make it?"

Ophelia's heart was *thump-thump-thumping* in her chest, each beat filling her body with crackling electricity. Seamus's eyes were filled with a darkness she'd never seen in him, not even when he'd told her about Ingrid and his pack.

"A very, very long time ago, Seamus was tasked with retrieving the heartstones of trolls, though no one told us why. It was so strange at the time," Arild began, waving the baton like a wand. "You see, every magical being is a resource to exploit. You're all useful in one way or another. Trolls, especially. Heartstones contain life-sustaining magic. They pull energy from the cosmos, turning inanimate materials into something just shy of sentience. If you grind up the stones, you can use them as a drug, but our superiors found another use for them. When those heartstones encounter a *real* energy source. . . Well. . . you saw what happened."

Ophelia kicked and thrashed against the Ulvemordere holding her, crying out in anguish. "You're—"

"A monster, yes, we've established that," Arild sighed. "Have you no other vocabulary words?"

Seamus sagged, shutting his eyes tight. Ophelia could just about imagine what was going through his mind. His actions had brought a terrible, terrible weapon into the world. No wonder Cathal and his trolls hated him. In their eyes, he was the catalyst for their destruction.

"And would you like to know something else?" Arild asked, scarlet eyes gleaming with delight. "Those trolls you killed? The ones that shattered at your fingertips? I'm having *their* heartstones fashioned into a sword. My, oh, my. . . Can you imagine the destruction that'll cause?"

Ophelia stopped fighting against her captors, letting her limbs go limp. Seems they'd both brought terrible, terrible weapons into the world. Sigfreður and Ljot had done the same. History seemed to be repeating itself.

"See, we thought to siphon the pelt, but the damned thing consumed any and all that tried. We lost prisoners, we lost comrades—it's all been very messy." Arild shook his head, stroking the jeweled tip of his baton lovingly. "But then I had a rather grand idea. What if, when the pelt bonds to its *mortal* master, it can wither and die like a mortal, too? You should count yourself lucky, Ophelia, for we're the first to find out if I'm right."

He whistled again, and Egill disappeared.

One of the soldiers holding her took a long, expectant breath.

"Heads or tails," Arild mumbled. "The toss of a coin, a game for fools. Who wins? Who loses?"

CHAPTER ONE HUNDRED AND FOUR

CAN'T IMAGINE A WORLD WITH YOU GONE

Seamus's mouth and throat were dry, leaving a bitter taste on his tongue. Gritting his teeth, he glared at the soldiers holding Ophelia. Never once had he hated wolfsbane more than he did now. It messed up his abilities, causing him to get stuck between forms. He couldn't even hear his wolf's voice at this point. Oh, if he could transform right now, they'd be in for a world of hurt. . . Fortunately for them, it seemed the wolfsbane had done wonders. And fortunately for Arild, he wasn't keen on risking his Witch being executed right in front of him.

Ophelia had tried her best to stay stoic, but as soon as Egill had vanished, she'd broken down in tears.

Oh, she was livid. The stinging smell of flaming hot curry wafted off her, mixing with the sweet scent of mint. Stars, Seamus hoped Arild hated curry and mint. Ophelia's Marks were growing, too, turning navy blue. She must hate him for turning himself over so quickly. But why play Arild's little game any longer? Why prolong the thing he'd be running from all his life if it meant Ophelia's life hung in the balance? She could hate him all she wanted. One day, she'd thank him for sparing her life. She may cry now, but she'd laugh about this long after he was gone. She'd look back and smile, knowing someone had loved her enough to give up their very life.

"Shut her up, will you?" Arild snapped.

One of the soldiers yanked her arm with all their might; the other shook her. Cruelty was not a strong enough word to describe the actions of these monsters. Arild watched Seamus's reaction with the broadest grin, reveling in how he couldn't hide the fury from his face.

Ophelia went quiet.

"Thank you," Arild said, nodding to his soldiers.

Beside him, empty air began to spark and gleam until the flippant fairy returned. Egill stumbled to the side, gripping Arild's shoulder tightly to steady himself. A pained expression flitted across his face, gone the second he realized Seamus had spotted it.

Beside him was a trembling chest.

"It all boils down to this, huh?" Arild laughed, shrugging away Egill's hand.

The fairy took a step back, wincing. Inhaling deeply, he stood to his full height, shutting his eyes. After taking a minute to collect himself, he knelt to the chest, beginning to unlock its many, many padlocks.

Arild smiled to himself, catching Ophelia's eye. "His devotion knows no bounds. He knows his limits and is willing to push them for a cause he believes in. It's admirable, really."

"You're hurting him," Ophelia spat.

Those Ulvemordere had a tight grip on his Witch, but they couldn't hold her forever. Not when she let loose the storm she'd been harboring all her life.

"He's hurting himself," Arild scoffed, waving her words away. "Now, hush."

Egill hesitated before unlocking the last padlock. The chest shook violently, its lid bouncing up and down. Swallowing hard, he threw open the lid and reached inside. Seamus had seen the pelt once before, its image ingrained in his mind ever since. It was silky smooth, the color of the sky just before heavy rain. Grimacing, Egill came to stand behind him, holding tight to the thrashing thing.

Fear was rising in Seamus's chest. There was a pull on the edge of his consciousness, a voice whispering inaudibly in his ear. The battle around him had grown deafening, but the voice persisted.

Arild leaned in close, a wicked smile on his lips. "As always, you lose. Once again, it's my job to prove how pathetic you are. Honestly, Seamus? I'd assumed we would've grown up by now."

Seamus ignored him, ignored the heat at his back, ignored the shadow of the pelt held above his shoulders.

"Close your eyes," he said, staring into the piercing silver depths burning holes in his skull. "Close your eyes."

"Seamus!" Ophelia screamed. Her skin sparkled with electricity, the tiny bolts of lightning snuffed out by her captors' iron armor.

"It's okay," Seamus said, forcing himself to smile for her sake. "I'm okay. Just look away, all right? Promise me you'll look away."

Arild tilted his head toward Egill. Ophelia screamed, shutting her eyes as tight as she could, sinking to her knees.

The white-hot pressure at Seamus's back exploded. He couldn't breathe, couldn't think. All there was, was pressure on his back and pain radiating throughout his body. Seamus was screaming. That he knew for sure, but everything else was growing foggy.

Oh, the pain was unbearable. It came from everywhere. No part of him wasn't burning. It was as if his very soul was on fire. The pelt around his shoulders was growing ever heavier, too.

How could someone scream this long without coming up for air?

Where had the world gone? The darkness was consuming him.

That voice. . . that voice ringing in his ears. . . whose was it? He couldn't make out the words.

Something burst in his chest, stealing away the searing pain. All of a sudden, there was nothing but a frigid, empty expanse of black.

I'm cold, was his last thought.

You're Gonna Go Far, Kid

The screaming had been dreadful, but the silence was so much worse. Silence meant it was over. It meant. . .

Ophelia slowly opened her eyes, blinking away tears.

Seamus lay unmoving on the ground, the pelt gone as if it had never existed. Unlike Saoirse, he wasn't covered in constellation-like scars. Despite his claws and exaggerated features, he looked completely normal, as if he were just sleeping.

Arild scoffed a few times, descending into manic laughter. He spun in a circle, nearly tripping on his patchwork cloak. Muttering and mumbling to himself, he knelt, observing the lifeless body before him.

Ophelia was panting heavily, fists clenched tight, feeling millions of teeny tiny lightning bolts bouncing back and forth through her body. Above, the sky mirrored her feelings. Thunder clouds were split in two by great arcs of silver-blue light.

Arild twirled his baton, then placed the tip against Seamus's neck. Glowing red marks shot out across his skin, slithering like snakes. As they moved beneath his skin, they slowly faded to white. Slowly, his claws began to shrink, and his features softened. Seamus's skin was ashen, his face gaunt, almost skeletal.

A small crowd of Ulvemordere had amassed around them, each awestruck.   Arild stood, holding the baton up for everyone to see. The tip had changed from a stark red to a bright, pulsing white. The flickering light reflected Arild's eyes, snuffing out the scarlet glow. In his hands, he held the essence of a fallen star, the likes of which contained unimaginable power.

"For once, Seamus, you did something right," Arild whispered.

A sharp breeze ruffled Ophelia's hair. With it came pleading whispers. Every raindrop was screaming at her, begging her to do something, anything.

Beneath petrichor, she smelled smoke and burning flesh.

"I will make the world anew," Arild said, "And I will make it in your image." Smiling like the utter psychopath he was, he pointed the baton to the sky, then made to place the tip against his *own* neck.

Egill, who'd been looking on in horror, jolted to life. In the second it took Ophelia's heart to skip a beat, he'd twisted, his heel connecting with Arild's jaw. Ophelia wasn't aware Arild could be caught off guard like that, shocked to see him drop the baton and crumble to the ground.

Egill himself was shocked, too. He stared at his foot as if it had acted on its own accord.

Arild reached for the baton, trying to pop his jaw back into place.

"Grab it!" Ophelia screamed, struggling to her feet, pulling against the Ulvemordere with all her might.

The ground was shaking, though only Ophelia seemed to notice.

Egill lunged forward, trying to get a grasp on the baton. Just before he could, Arild grabbed hold of his legs. He stumbled and fell, inadvertently rolling the baton farther away. Arild dug his claws into Egill's back, attempting to crawl over him to get it.

Ophelia's blood went cold, her heart dropping to her feet.

All of a sudden, she was screaming. Lightning erupted from her hands, the sparks crawling across the Ulvemordere's armor. Each lick of electricity froze their armor until they were nothing but two frosty statues. Ophelia spread her fingers wide, feeling all the air leave her lungs as the Ulvemordere soldiers exploded into hundreds of shards of ice.

Free of her captors, she reached toward the baton, imagining the wind swirling around it, lifting it from the ground. As always, the wind was happy to comply. The baton lifted off the ground, whizzing toward her.

Just before she could catch it, Egill appeared before her, snatching it out of the air.

Once again, he vanished, appearing a few feet away, eyes darting back and forth between her and Arild.

Arild struggled to his feet, his jaw popping back into place with a sickening crunch. "YOU INSOLENT FOOL!" he screamed, flicking out his claws, his muscles twisting beneath his patchwork cloak.

Eyes wide, Egill looked to Seamus, then back at Ophelia. For a second, Ophelia thought he would try to transfer the magic to himself. Instead, obviously panicked, he began pulling on the baton's heartstone tip with all his might.

"I'LL KILL YOU!" Arild cried, his face elongating, his skin sprouting thick, multi-colored fur. Taking to all fours, he ran at Egill. Drool seeped out of his mouth; hot steam blew out his pointy nose. "I'LL KILL YOU!"

In a fit of rage, Egill slammed the baton into the ground.

On impact, the heartstone shattered.

A bright white wave of energy burst from the jewel, sending each of them flying backward. Ophelia went sliding through the mud, only stopping when she collided with a tree. There'd been no sound, but her ears rang, the world around her suddenly muffled. Blinking away bright spots of color, she looked to Seamus.

Laying in a puddle, pelted by rain, was his lifeless body.

Regaining her footing, Ophelia stumbled toward him, feeling something break inside her. Halfway to him, she collapsed to her knees, overcome by sobs.

What had she expected? That the heartstone breaking would miraculously heal him? She couldn't get so lucky.

Exhaustion immediately took over. Little by little, her strength drained away, the edges of her vision blurry.

"You stupid, stupid fairy!" Arild screamed.

Smoke drifted up from Ophelia's fingertips. Boils and bubbles spread across her hands and arms, instantly turning black. Every heartbeat was like a stab wound.

Could someone die from a broken heart? If they could, would it feel like this? Like the whole world was fracturing?

Behind her, the faintest hint of heat cut through the cold. Metal clashed against metal. Enraged insults were passed back and forth. Ophelia glanced over her shoulder to see Arild huffing and puffing, holding a broadsword before him as Egill stalked his prey. Arild's scarlet eyes pulsed as he rushed forward. Egill stepped to the side, dodging his blade, smiling to himself. He was winded but was far too agile for Arild's lumbering form.

Ophelia couldn't bring herself to watch any longer.

Her wolf, her Seamus, her *dad*, was *dead*.

As she stared at her shaking hands, she realized the rain was washing away her blackened flesh. In its place was vibrant blue skin, the same color as her Marks.

Tiny cracks spread out around her, the ground rumbling along with the thunder.

She could feel it all—every crack, every raindrop, every subtle change in the breeze. It was as though she were one with the elements. The distant din of the battle beyond the trees began to fade, replaced with whistling wind and crackling lightning.

Ophelia stood, turning to Egill and Arild, knowing damn well she would wind up killing them both alongside herself. So what? What did it matter? Did she even care? Without Seamus, no one was there to stop her. There wasn't much fight left in her, but if this was her final stand, she intended to go out with a bang.

Arild glanced at her, his lip curling in disgust, revealing incredibly sharp canines. His wolf-like face was an amalgamation of all the pelts he'd stolen, making him look like a haphazardly sewn stuffed animal.

Egill went pale, tightening his grip on his daggers.

"*I'm* going to kill *you*," Ophelia said, her voice shaking the ground and trees around them. "*Both* of you."

With a flick of her wrist, she caused a pillar of ice to shoot up from the ground. Arild rolled to the side, struggling to his feet. Egill stumbled back, nearly losing his footing. Both recovered quickly, forgetting about each other long enough to rush her. Ophelia clapped her hands together, causing two cracks in the ground to shoot toward them. Egill stumbled to the side, unscathed. Arild swore, his foot being sucked into the earth. Panicked, he dropped his sword, attempting to free himself. Egill lunged forward, grabbing his sword as he faded into glitter.

"If anyone will make the world anew—" Ophelia began, extending her hand toward him, feeling for the air in his lungs. As she spoke, she slowly clenched her bright blue hand into a fist. "—it will be *me.*"

Arild tried to scream, but all that came out was a tiny squeak as he clawed at his throat. Ophelia squeezed her fist as tight as she could, imagining his lungs collapsing.

Arild's eyes rolled back into his head, his body going limp.

"This is my world, Arild, and you don't belong in it," Ophelia whispered, sending a strong gust to knock him over.

There he lay unmoving, his muscles shrinking, his wolf-like features melting back to human.

Hundreds of pounds of pressure seemed to fall on Ophelia's shoulders. She swayed, nearly toppling forward, but someone caught her.

Bright light.

Melting colors.

Heat.

But not the fuzzy, cozy kind of heat. You know, the heat that makes you think of warm, far-off places. No, this was different. This heat was all-consuming, erupting at her side, pulsing like a flickering flame.

The bright light vanished, and Ophelia stood face to face with Egill. Egill shoved her back, searing pain tearing through her left side. There was a tree behind her, its jagged bark tearing into her back; before her was a fairy with murderous glee in his eyes.

And in her side was Arild's sword.

Egill smiled toothily, twisting the sword farther into her side. She opened her mouth to speak, but all that came out was a pathetic squeak. Her back was alight with tingling pain as Egill mustered up enough strength to skewer her through, pinning her to the tree. Ophelia grabbed his forearms, focusing all her power on him, but there wasn't much left. She saw her eyes reflect blue in his, their otherworldly light flickering. Egill's arms turned cold under her grip, a thin layer of ice crawling over the sleeves of his muddy tunic.

"No hard feelings, little Witch. It's just business," he whispered. He shook one of her hands away, reaching down to touch her stomach, his hand coming back drenched in silver. He leaned forward and whispered in her ear, sending shivers down her spine. "Such a messy thing, death."

When he leaned back, she saw the light from her eyes had faded just as quickly as her strength. Her legs shook like branches in a strong wind, her arms hanging in their sockets, heavier than cannonballs.

Ever so slowly, Egill stepped back, staggering a bit. "I'm sorry. Truly, I am." Bowing, he began to dematerialize until he was gone completely.

Ophelia was frozen. How ironic. All she could do was look down. He must have punctured a vital organ. Her silver blood was already tinged red. It shouldn't have shifted color so suddenly.

She wanted to scream. To cry. To rip Arild's cumbersome weapon from her side and chase after him. Try as she might, all she could do was slam her head back against the tree, trying to steady her shaking legs.

"H—Help!" she screamed as loud as she could, her abdomen burning in pain with the effort.

Tears slipped down her face.

Blessed Amaranth, how had this happened?

Taking a shaking breath to calm herself, her arms began to listen to her. Taking hold of the sword's hilt, she tried to pull it out, but it wouldn't budge. Every movement sent a wave of excruciating pain through her.

It was then she realized the rain and thunder had finally stopped. She couldn't feel her magic—couldn't feel the elements.

Her arms sagged as she realized this was where she died.

Not in glory.

Not as a hero.

As an idiot.

Her head swam.

Something wasn't right. She felt heavy and floaty all at the same time. Groggy, yet every sound and thought were clear. She could feel everything and nothing at all. Every breath was slower than the last, every wave of pain softer.

"Ophelia!" came a voice.

She hadn't realized her eyes were closed, but they shot open at the sound of her name. Footsteps came rushing toward her. Gold teeth and two-toned eyes—one teal, one brown—filled Ophelia's swimming vision.

"Blessed Amaranth! Oh shit—Help!" screamed the pirate, rushing to Ophelia's side, not daring to touch her or the blade holding her upright. "Karran, help!"

Staggering through the trees was the gentleman who'd been at their makeshift war room meeting. He paused a few feet away, ashen. Ophelia tried to call for him, but all that came out was a groan of pain. The pirate gave a great flap of his wings. For whatever reason, this made Karran snap back to reality. He ran to them, skidding to a stop, taking Ophelia's face in his hands, eyes on the blood—the *red* blood—seeping out of her, trickling down her leg, dripping on the tops of her boots.

"Th—That's a lot of blood," the pirate breathed, his voice choked with tears.

Ophelia's eyes closed against her will, her head lulling to the side, resting in Karran's hand. "Everythin' hurts," she groaned.

The pirate inhaled sharply, setting her head straight, patting her cheeks rather roughly. "Hey! Stay with me, Witch, all right? You're gonna be okay. We're—We're gonna fix this, right Karran?"

Ophelia sighed heavily, forcing her eyes open to look at him. She'd never seen someone so afraid, not even once. That wasn't a good sign.

"I'm s—so s—sorry," she choked out, panicked. "If—If it w—weren't for—I never should've—"

"You've got nothing to be sorry for, okay?" the pirate said, trying to smile. "We're going to get you patched up, okay? Karran will—" He turned to look at him. Ophelia didn't have to turn to know the look on his face screamed that they *wouldn't* be able to fix this. Not this time. Ophelia's luck had finally run out. "Karran's going to patch you up, ya hear?" he said anyway, running his hand through her hair over and over again as if that would help.

"Deucalion," Karran said softly.

Ophelia felt her heart do somersaults in her chest. Breathing felt like it would rip her in half.

Deucalion—what a pretty name—reached for the sword's hilt just as she had.

"Duke, don't! She'll bleed out!" Karran screeched.

"She's already bleeding out!" Deucalion's eyes were like stars in her darkening sight. Two mismatched orbs, keeping her here, keeping her alive. Those stars would go out eventually, but it was a nice sight while it lasted. "I'm not letting her di—Do something!" he screamed.

Karran grabbed Ophelia's arm, searching her eyes. She wondered what he saw. Did he see a corpse or a sliver of hope?

"You with us?" he asked, voice trembling.

Ophelia could barely nod.

Karran grabbed her hand and placed it near the wound. "When Duke removes the sword, you'll have to burn the wound, or we'll lose you. Use as much lightning as you can."

Deucalion's grip on both the sword and her face tightened.

"I—I can't!" she cried, eyes widening with the thought, hot tears streaming down her face and neck.

"Yes, you can," they said. They were so sure of it. Ophelia almost believed them.

"I can't feel my magic anymore," Ophelia whispered, shutting her eyes tightly and resting her head against the rough bark behind her. She took a staggering breath, squeezing Karran's hand so tightly she thought she would break his fingers.

"Use the pain of it," Karran blurted out. "Turn the pain into electricity." He seemed to know an awful lot about Witches.

"I don't—I don't know if—"

Searing pain screamed through her side as Deucalion ripped the sword from her body.

The world went dark.

She felt sparks dance across her fingertips as Deucalion's rough hands wrapped around her waist. He was screaming at her, but she couldn't make out the words. All she could hear was a sickening crackling accompanied by the stench of burning flesh, a smell far too familiar.

As quickly as the pain had come, it was gone.

One by one, her senses faded until all that was left was darkness.

She was falling now.

F a l l i n g . . .

F a l l i n g . . .

REQUIEM

O phelia was cold.

Unnaturally cold.

That was the only coherent thought her brain could form. Everything else was an amalgamation of fright and confusion.

Cold.

Just cold.

She was also very tired, but that somehow didn't seem as important.

Around her, the darkness had somehow. . . darkened? There had to be a better word, but Ophelia was too overcome by numbing confusion to dwell on such things. Whether her eyes were closed or something had snuffed out the sun, she didn't know. She did, however, know she lay on something, somewhere.

Her body was useless.

Try as she might, she couldn't move, her arms and legs either unwilling or unable. All around her, the cold seemed to pulse like soft waves lapping over her body. Was she floating somewhere? Down a stream, perhaps? Where was she?

A flicker of pain—the second coherent feeling—shot through her side. She groaned, finally managing to turn her head. A sliver of light cut the darkness. Her eyes *had* been closed.

All around her were stars. Hundreds—no, *millions*—of stars. They twinkled and danced, showing her shapes and patterns in the night. At the center of it all was the moon. So bright, so full.

"*Wake up,*" it whispered.

"*Wake up,*" said another voice, this time coming from behind.

Warmth bloomed across Ophelia's chest. Her fingers and limbs twitched, feeling coming back to her. Slowly, she sat up, looking down to see a silver sun shining below her.

Ophelia tried to speak, but her words were stolen, whisked away by a pulse of starlight.

What was happening? Everything before this moment was nothing but blurry images and fragments of sentences she couldn't make out. In an attempt to make sense of it all, she looked around again.

In the darkness, she saw another form.

Someone else lay a few feet away, their back to her.

Ophelia had the strangest feeling she knew who they were but couldn't quite form their name in her mind. Whoever it was, they were important. Everything in her told her to run to them, to wake them up so they could figure out a way out of here. Though she tried, she couldn't stand. Again, she attempted to speak, but not even a squeak came out.

"*Wake up,*" said the Sun, drawing her attention.

"*Wake up,*" said the Moon.

"*Hush,*" said another voice.

As soon as they spoke, the figure vanished. Each and every star shuttered. Their fear was palpable. Ophelia could almost taste it.

"*No,*" said the Moon.

"*Hush,*" said the voice.

Ophelia's head was pounding. All she wanted to do was curl up in a ball, shut her eyes, and wait out whatever this was. Was she dreaming? What was happening?

"*Listen,*" the voice whispered. It was masculine, and though its words were very soft, Ophelia could tell the speaker was angry. "*Let me help you, little Witch.*"

"*No!*" cried the Sun.

Wispy tendrils of silver sunlight reached forward, wrapping around Ophelia protectively. They hugged her tight and culminated in her lap, folding in on themselves and twisting into odd shapes.

Two ears.

A round, fluffy tail.

In her lap sat a rabbit made of glistening starlight.

Above her, the moon began to melt. Chunks of it dripped down, stacking atop one another, forming a shimmering bat.

Panic seized Ophelia's chest as she realized where she was and what was happening. This was the Celestial Realm. Had she been here before? Something deep inside her, something almost ancient, told her she had.

All queasy sleepiness disappeared. Again, she tried to speak, but nothing came out.

There was a flash of light, and the stars began to swirl before her like a whirlpool. They culminated in one spot, twisting in spirals until a throbbing void of starlight and darkness took form.

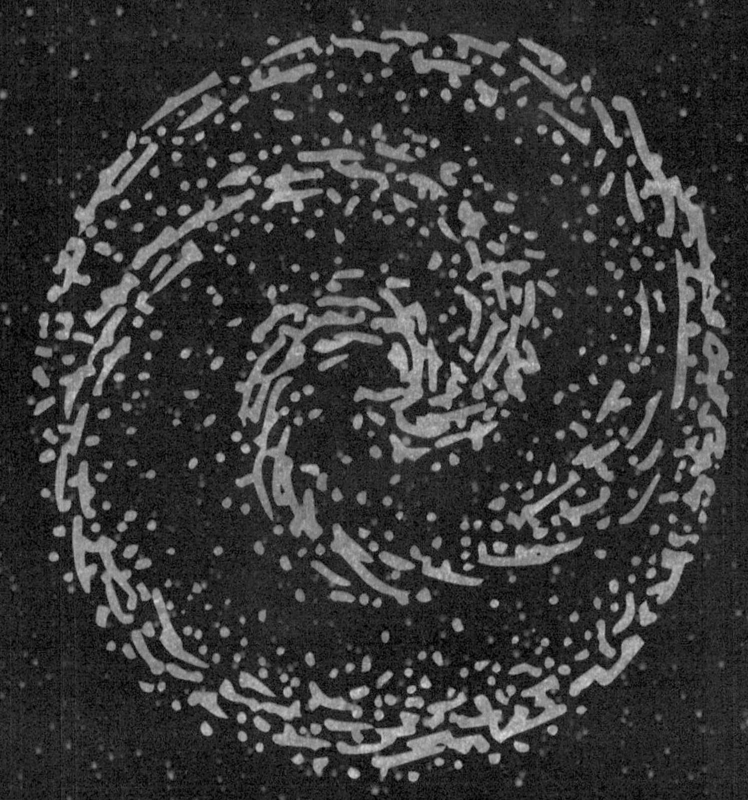

"*Let me help you*," the void—no, The *Abyss*—
said. "*I can help you.*"

The Bat chittered, flying into Ophelia's arms. The Rabbit's ears went up in fright, its pale pink eyes wide. Sprigs of amaranth and clusters of nightshade sprung up around her, forming a protective circle.

The Rabbit turned to her, its floppy ears now hanging low. "*Wake up*," it pleaded.

"*Snowdrop, wake up!*" said the Bat.

Ophelia wanted to; she really did. But wasn't she already awake? If not, how was she meant to 'wake up' from this? She tried to call for her magic, for her old friend, the wind, but felt nothing except emptiness and a sharp shooting pain in her back.

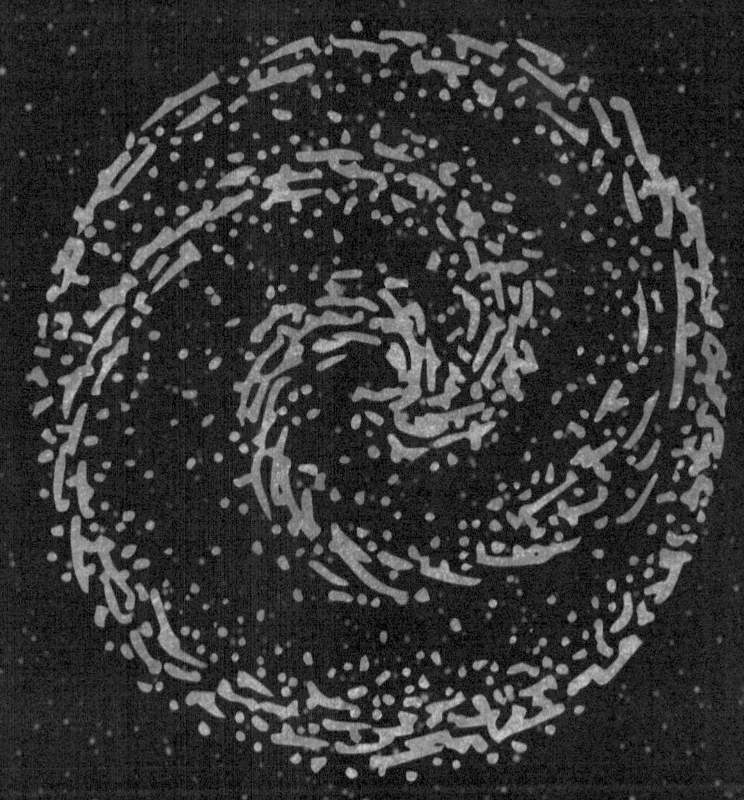

The Abyss laughed, a sound one could only describe as evil. *"You have no power here, little Witch. This is my realm."*

Ophelia hugged Rabbit and Bat to her chest, curling in on herself.

"*She is one of us,*" Bat said, her voice shaking with anger. "*Whether this is your realm or not, she* does *have power here!*"

The Abyss's swirling turned choppy.

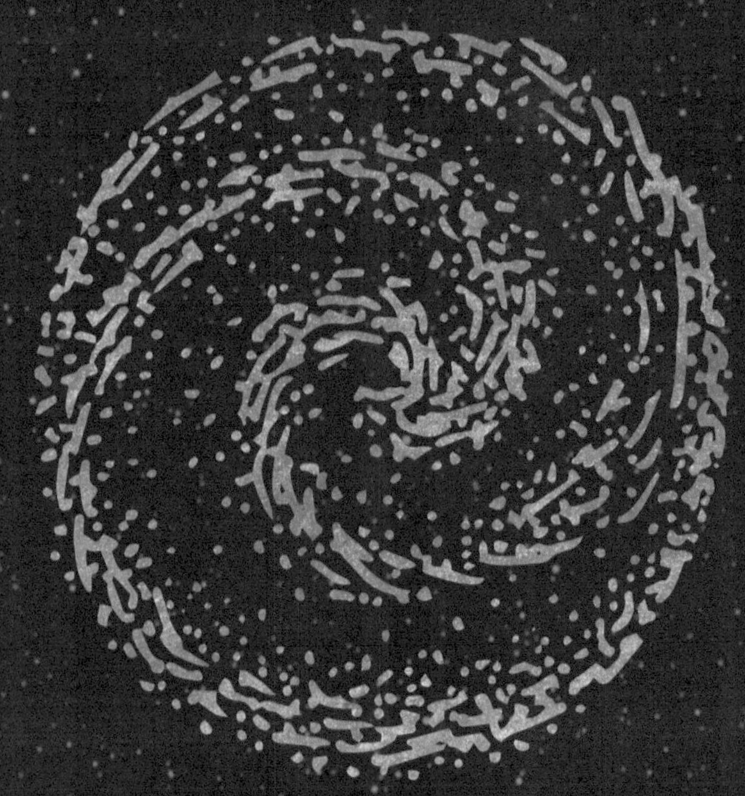

"*A Spirit in a mortal body, hmm? My, my. How frightening.*"

A fourth voice echoed through the darkness. "*She is not as we were.*" A sparkling deer edged around her, leaving holly bushes in its wake. "*It is you, old friend, whose power is obsolete.*"

"*You might be able to protect her, but the Wolf is, and always will be,* mine," Abyss whispered.

One by one, every swirling star blinked out. The only light came from the three celestial animals before her, each looking as terrified as Ophelia felt.

Rabbit stood, placing a paw on Ophelia's forehead. "*Wake up!*"

CADAVER DOG

"North Star. . . . Can you hear me? Yes, you. Have you fulfilled your duties?"

The cold surrounding Seamus began to feel less like a cage and more like a comfort. If he could feel something, anything, it meant he was alive. The voice. . . What had it called him? North Star? Where was it coming from?

"Open your eyes, North Star. Shh. . . it's all right. You're safe here."

Slowly, he opened his eyes. Before him was a swirling void of silver and black. It pulsed like starlight, reacting to even the tiniest movement. Seamus turned in a circle, finding the darkness stretched farther than the eye could see. The all-consuming dark was velvety soft, yet there was something sinister to it.

That single thought drowned out everything else. Everything in him was screaming that he needed to run, to find a way out of here—wherever 'here' was. He tried to move his feet, but they wouldn't budge. Looking down, he realized that was because he had no feet. Or legs. Or a body. Panicked, he reached toward the darkness but saw no hands. Was he dead?

"Clever. . . ."

There was that voice again.
Who was speaking? Where was he?

*"You are everywhere and nowhere all at once. I
am everything and nothing just as well."*

With every word, the void pulsed.
Was the voice coming from it?

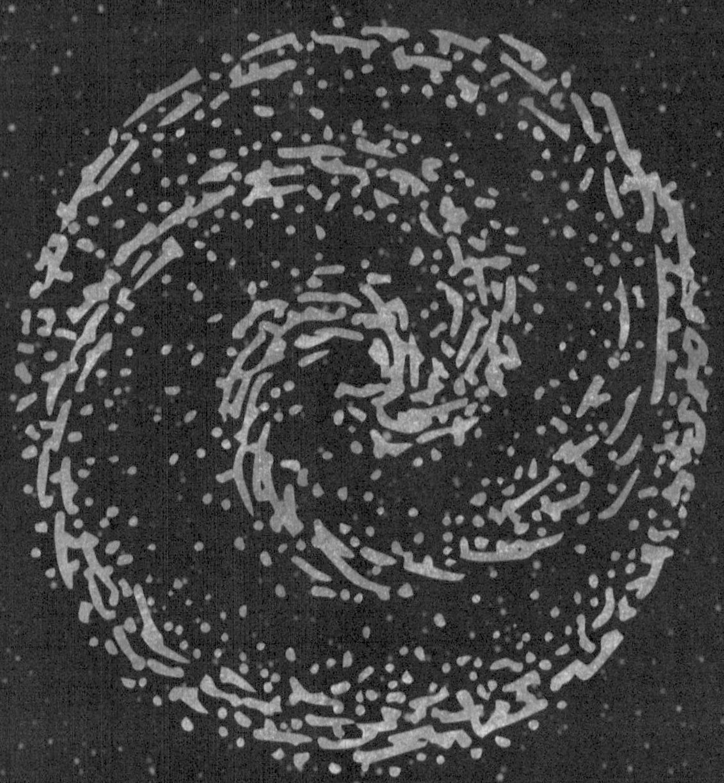

“Yes.”

Why was he here?

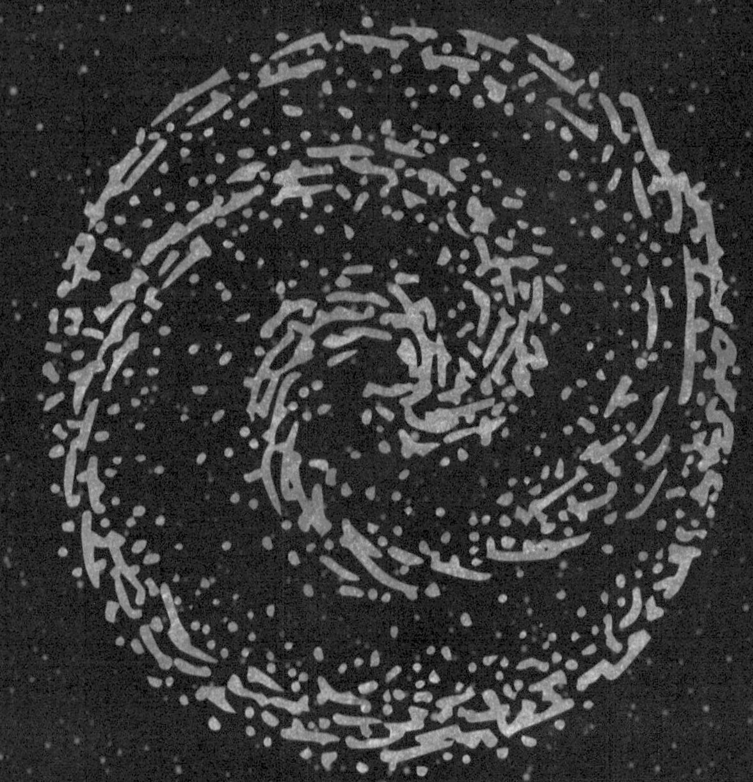

“Did you enjoy your time amongst the mortals, North Star?”

There was a flicker of a memory fighting to take center stage, but it was too hazy for him to make out. All he saw were colors, namely blue and silver. Those were important to him somehow. Deeply, deeply important. More important than life. More important than whatever *this* was.

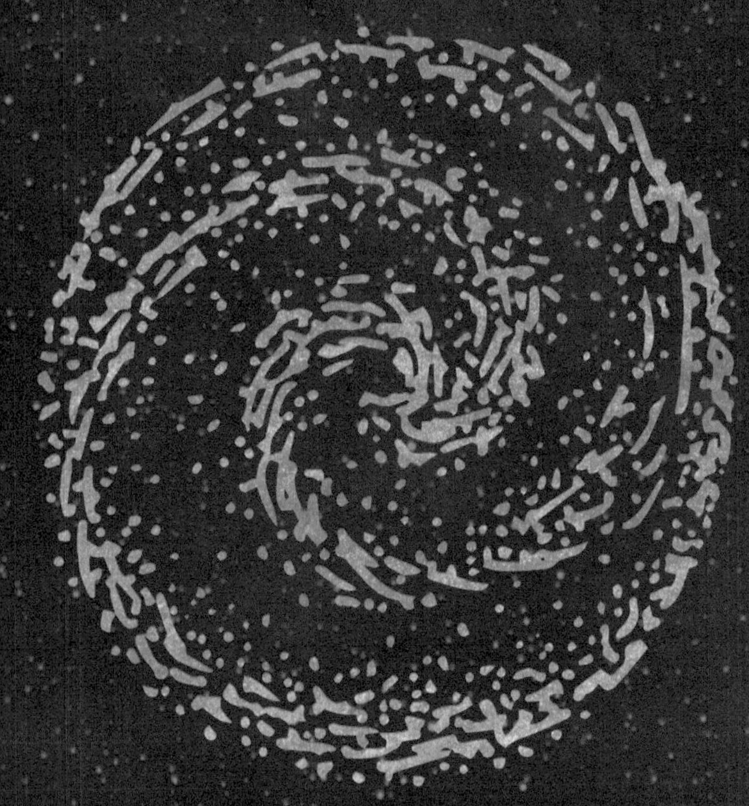

"*North Star,*" said the void, a hint of impatience to its tone.

Why did it keep calling him that?

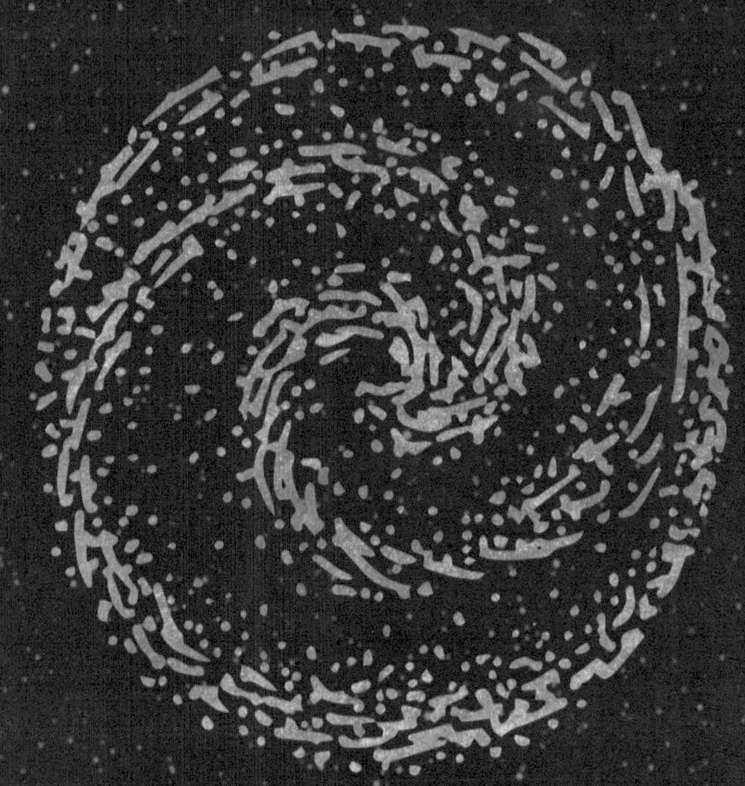

"It is your name. The name I gave you at the beginning. You do not remember, but I do."

The beginning?

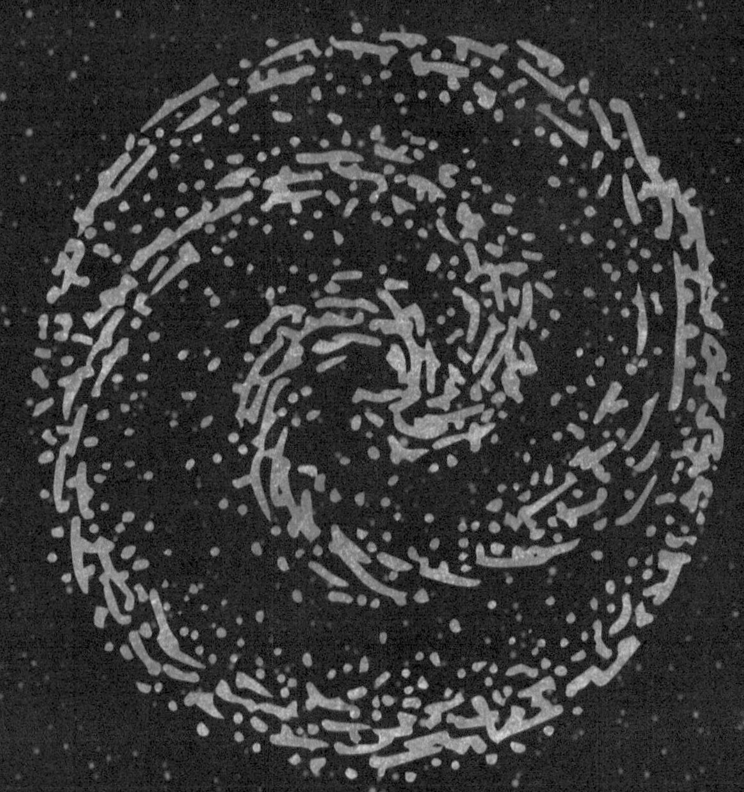

"Yes. Before the Stars. Before the Spirits. When there was nothing but darkness. You were the first. You were the guiding light."

Seamus was beyond confused. It was important to note he was still cold, too.

"Cold? Yes. You always liked the cold. In this
life and the last."

Blue. The color blue. Blue meant cold. Was that why he liked the color blue? Was it his favorite color?

There was a name on the edge of his consciousness. The longer he stared at the void, the foggier it got. If he had eyes, he shut them. For a second, the stars vanished, and all he saw was blue.

Blue.

Cold.

Snowflakes.

O. . . . ?

What was that blasted name?

Ph. . . ?

Ophe. . . . ?

Ophelia. . . . ?

Yes! Ophelia! That was it! That was the name!

Wait. . . .

Why was that name important? And what did it have to do with colors and weather?

"You need not trouble yourself with her. Not now, at least. When you find your way back to her, you can worry then."

His way back? What did that mean?

"You are dead, North Star. But you need not
remain that way."

Flickers of sizzling pain danced across his. . . fingers? Hands? Something. . . Something was stinging with warmth. It felt like a warning. The warmth was bad. He was safer in the cold with. . . what was her name again? Oh, right, Ophelia. Yes, he had to stay in the cold. The cold would always protect him.

Always.

"Do you know what I am?" The impatience
was back in the void's voice.

It pulsed, slowly morphing into an eye-like shape. If Seamus
had a face, he would've grimaced. A thought came to mind,
but he didn't quite understand it. Was he speaking with The
Abyss?

"... perceptive."

He tried to be.

"Do you know why you're here?"

Seamus took a moment to think, something he usually tried not to do. Beneath memories of the color blue and a young lady with moon-bright eyes, there was something. Suddenly, he felt an overwhelming sense of fear, triggered by visions of beings in iron armor and stolen pelts.

Those beings had been evil, and they worshipped this place, this Abyss. If he was dead, why was he here? Wasn't this the birthplace of evil? Had he been an evil man? Was this place his punishment?

"I am not a place, but I am punishment," said Abyss. If sentient voids could smile, Seamus figured it would have. *"Your Ulvemordere have used my name for heinous acts. We share the same hatred for them, you and I."*

A pause.

Yes, yes, Seamus knew that name.

Ulvemordere.

Oh, he hated that name. What it meant, he didn't know. Were those the beings in the armor?

"Would you like to do something about that ha-tred you feel?"

Yes.

That word popped into Seamus's brain before he could think through anything.

Again, there was white-hot pain somewhere on his invisible body.

Suddenly, there was another voice, one screaming in the distance. He could barely distinguish the words, but he knew someone—or some*thing*—was trying to warn him. He shouldn't trust this entity, this Abyss. He knew he shouldn't. . . . But he had to, didn't he?

There was that name again. Ophelia.

And another!

T. . . Tiril?

Ophelia and Tiril. They were his. . . his family? Yes, yes, his family! He had to get back to them. Seamus couldn't die, not now. Not when they needed him most.

"Yes," Seamus said. It was the first spoken word he'd said in this strange place. It echoed around him, rattling in his head, filling him with searing pain.

"Then I return to you your stolen power," Abyss said, its excitement palpable. *"We shall speak again. Ha det bra, North Star. Til avgrunnens ære, drep eller bli drept."*

For the glory of The Abyss, kill or be killed.

He'd heard that phrase before, but it hadn't held any meaning before this moment.

Suddenly, there was light all around him. Seamus looked down at his hands—he had hands again! Feet too!—realizing the pale silver light was emanating from him. His fingertips and toes were made of stardust. He looked up, about to ask what this meant, but The Abyss had disappeared. In its place was a wolf—the same wolf from his nightmares.

Its glowing silver eyes were two stars in the darkness. It stalked him like prey, inching ever closer.

"Do not forsake yourself." That was the voice of The Abyss, this time but a whisper.

"I won't," Seamus whispered.

He held out his hand, allowing the wolf to nuzzle his palm. Memories were flooding his mind. Ophelia had shown him how to treat all beings with kindness. This wolf deserved that, even if he didn't believe he was capable of such things. Gently, he stroked the wolf's long, dark fur, just as he'd done to the dying fox many moons ago. As he stroked the strange celestial creature, its fur became flecked with stardust, the stark black coat turning silvery-gray.

"Hello, old friend," he whispered. The wolf pulled away, circling him. "Let's get to our pup, aye?"

His wolf—*his wolf*—lunged at him. Bright white light engulfed him. Feeling was returning to his body. He'd be lying if he said he understood anything that just happened, but he knew he'd done the right thing.

Still, in the darkest corners of his mind, something whispered, *"You've just sided with the enemy."*

To Be Continued...

EXTRAS

Acknowledgments

How can one express just how much someone means to them? How much someone has helped them? Sometimes, 'thank you' isn't enough. In Norwegian, we say 'Tusen takk,' which translates to 'a thousand thanks.' While I still feel we need a better word in our lexicon, here are some folks I'd like to give a thousand thanks to!

Tusen takk, mamma og papa.

I'll dote on you guys forever and always! I truly have the best parents in the world, and I'm so thankful I've been blessed with such an awesome mom and dad. Thank you for allowing me to follow my dreams. Thanks for supporting me. Thanks for being good parents. Not a day goes by that I don't know how much you love Owen and me. Thanks for filling my head with stories and teaching me how to be brave enough to tell my own.

Tusen takk, Emily, my fantastic illustrator, for creating such beautiful art for my book and allowing me to include Seamus's wanted poster and the drawing of him and Phee. I've said it before, but I want you to know I mean it when I say you're a Godsend. I prayed so hard about finding the right artist, and I definitely did.

Tusen takk to Liz, my best friend in the whole dang universe, who has been incredibly patient regarding this story. She's been living off crumbs for months, and I'm so glad she finally gets to read this book. (And I can't wait to read hers!) Love you oh so much my moonflower, moonbeam, raccoon.

Tusen takk to my aunt, Erica, for delevoping an awesome

recipe I get to share with all of you.

Tusen takk to all the friends I've made through my Vinterheksen account. I'm so thankful to have you in my life. I hope you've enjoyed this story and that I've done justice to the characters you've come to know.

So yes, I'd like to offer a thousand thanks indeed to every one of you. I couldn't have done this without you!

With love,
Amelia
Your Winter Witch

RECIPE

Ophelia's Kringle
by Erica Brown of Sugar Struck Cookies

Ingredients:

Base:
- 1 cup Flour
- 1 Tbs Sugar
- 1/2 cup Butter
- 1 Tbs Water

Pastry:
- 1 Cup Water
- 1/2 Cup Butter
- 1 Cup Flour
- 1 Tbs Sugar
- 1/2 Tbs Almond Extract
- 3 Eggs

Glaze:
- 1Cup Powdered Sugar
- 2 Tbs Half and Half (or milk)
- 2 Tsp Almond Extract
- 1/2 cup chopped Pistachos

- Preheat oven to 375 °F (190 °C)

BASE

- In a medium bowl, mix together the flour and butter. Using a fork, work the butter into the flour until the butter is the size of peas. Sprinkle the mixture with water. It will be crumbly, but should form together when pressed with your hands.
- Line a cookie sheet with parchment paper and press the dough into a large log. Set aside.
- Make the pastry.
- Spread the pastry over the base.
- Bake for 30 minutes.

PASTRY

- In a medium saucepan heat the water and butter to a boil.
- Once boiling, remove from heat and add flour. Mix until smooth. Then add the sugar and almond extract. Next add eggs one at a time. Mix well after each egg.

GLAZE

- Mix all glaze ingredients together in a small bowl, pour over pastry once its cooled slightly. *Sprinkle with chopped pistachios.

*This recipe is versatile and you can use what's on hand. Get creative with it! You can use almonds, lemon, chocolate, and or fruit.

Playlists

HEI ELSKER!

If you know me, you know how important music is to my writing process. Creating carefully curated playlists is just as crucial as researching what foods Vikings would have eaten (At least to me!).

To help you better understand these characters, here are a few songs I feel best represent them. I highly suggest giving these songs a listen!

You might learn something new about our Witch and her surly old wolf. . .

(You can find full character playlists on Spotify under Amelia_Rikstad)

SONGS FOR SEAMUS *AND* PHEE:

Let Me Follow--Son Lux
In The Wind--Lord Huron
House A Habit--We Are the Guests
Close Behind--Noah Kahan
Partner In Crime--Madilyn Mei

OPHELIA:

Winter Is Coming--Radical Face
Oh Ms Believer--Twenty One Pilots
Frozen Pines--Lord Huron
Lonesome Dreams--Lord Huron
The Wishing Well--The Oh Hellos
my tears ricochet--Taylor Swift
Allies Or Enemies--The Crane Wives
Cinnamon Girl--Lana Del Rey
The Archer--Taylor Swift
Treehouse--Alex G

SEAMUS:

Hell's Comin' With Me--Poor Man's Poison
The World Ender--Lord Huron
Take Me To War (Live)--The Crane Wives
Bad Moon Rising--Creedence Clearwater Revival
Wolf Song--Caamp
Northern Attitude--Noah Kahan
The Balancer's Eye--Lord Huron
Lonely Day--System Of A Down
I'll Be Good--Jaymes Young
The View Between Villages--Noah Kahan

EGILL:
Problem--COIN
Allies or Enemies--The Crane Wives
What Do It Mean--Lord Huron
Cry--Benson Boone
Paul Revere--Noah Kahan

SYRENA:
Penny, Heads Up--Caamp
Homesick--Noah Kahan, Sam Fender
Leave The City--Twenty One Pilots
Willow--Taylor Swift
Almost (Sweet Music)--Hozier

DEUCALION:
Juliet--Cavetown
Air Catcher--Twenty One Pilots
Would That I--Hozier
You're Gonna Go Far--Noah Kahan
Dress Like A Pirate--Madilyn Mei

JONQUIL:
Rebel Sodville--Marcy Playground
Lake Missoula--Richy Mitch & The Coal Miners
Ut i Huttiheita--Resirkulert
Mirrorball--Taylor Swift
False Confidence--Noah Kahan

Pronunciations
AND DEFINITIONS

WORDS/SAYINGS:

The "Saga of The Winter Witch" series uses Norwegian/Bok-mål as our "super cool fantasy language." If I've forgotten something here, you may use your favorite translation tool to help!

Varulv
(var-oolv) Werewolf

Heks
(hex) Witch

Vinterheksen
(vin-tur-hex-en) Directly translates to "The Winter Witch"

Skitten Hex
(skit-en // hex) Filthy witch

Ulvemordere
(ool-vuh-mor-der-uh) Directly translates to "Wolf Killers"

Ulve
(ool-vuh) Directly translates to "Wolves," but in this world, it is the nickname for the Ulvemordere.

Skogens Søstre
(skog-ens // sos-truh) Directly translates to "Sisters of The Forest"

Til avgrunnens ære, drep eller bli drept

(til // awv-groo-nens // ar-uh // drep // eller // blee // drept)
For the glory of The Abyss, kill or be killed

Død mann

(duh // mon) Dead man

Dømte en

(dempt // n) This one is tricky. "Dømte" or dømt" can mean
several words. So can "en." In this world, it simply means
"Condemed one."

Hellige En

(helly // n) Holy One. (Could also be written as "Den
Hellige")

Ære være Vinterheksen

(ar-uh // var-uh // vin-tur-hex-en) Glory to The Winter
Witch

Så det begynner

(so // dey // be-inner) Directly translates to "So it begins" or
"So it starts"

Mange velsignelser

(mong-ay // vel-seena-el-sur) Many blessings

Jeg elsker deg

(yei // el-skur // dye) I love you

Takk
(tok) Thanks/Thank you

Tusen Takk
(two-sen // tok) Directly translates to a "A thousand thanks."
Used as "Thank you very much."

God morgen
(goo // mor-gan) Norwegian for "Good morning"

God natt
(goo // nat) Norwegian for "Good night"

God kveld
(goo // k-vel-d) Norwegian for "Good evening"

Ha det bra
(ha // dey // bra) Norwegian for "Goodbye"

PLACES:

Alle Årstider
(all-ay // ars-tee-dur) All Seasons

Snøbolig
(snow-bol-lih) Snow dwelling (or housing)

Den Villeste Skogen
(den // vil-es-teh // skog-en) The Wildest Woods (commonly refered to as The Wilds)

Tø
(tuh) Directly translates to "Thaw"

Dødbyen
(duh-be-en) Directly translates to "The Dead City" (though everyone just calls it City of The Dead)

Geiravör
(guy-raw-ver) Geiravör is a valkyrie from Norse Mythology. Valkyries choose who live or die in battle, which was a fitting analogy for what happens in this town.

Juvel Hjem
(yuvel // h-yem) Jewel Home

Høstlunden
(hust-lun-dun) Autumn Grove

Vårretten
(vor-ret-ten) The Spring Court

Dagslys Hul
(dogs-lis // hool) Daylight Hollow

Mørklagt Øy
(murk-loct // oi) Darkened Island

Port Fantastisk
(port // fan-tas-tisk) Port Fantastic (Wow, so different. You never would've guessed that, huh?)

NAMES:

Ophelia
(oh-phee-lia) Greek. Means "Help."

Seamus
(shay-mus) Irish. Means "Supplanter." (to 'take the place of' or 'usurp' etc)

Syrena
(suh-rena) Greek. "Enchanter."

Deucalion
(due-cal-e-un) Greek. Means "Sweet"

Saoirse
(ser-shuh) Irish. Means "Freedom."

Åsmund
(oz-mund) Norse. Means "God is protector."

Egill
(eg-ill) Old Norse. Means "Terror."

Sigfreður
(sig-freth-er) Icelandic/Old Norse. Equivalent to modern day "Sigfried." Means "Victory."

Ljot
(luh-jot) Icelandic. Means "Light."

Zimri
(zim-ree) Hebrew. Means "My Music." (Jonquil's alias)

Helgi
(hel-gee) Norse. Means "Holy."

Tiril
(ti-ril) Norwegian. Supposedly means "Fight" or "Battle"

Reija
(ray-yuh) Finnish. Means "Vigilant" or "Watchful."

Noomi
(noo-me) Hebrew. Means "Pleasantness."

Matei
(ma-tie) Romanian. Means "Gift of Yaweh."

Ingrid
(ing-rid) Old Norse. Means "Beautiful goddess of fertility)

Cathal
(ka-hal) Irish. Means "Battle" or "Mighty."

Arild
(ar-uld) Norwegian. Means "Battle commander."

Jette
(jet) Dutch/Danish. Means "Home ruler."

Lochlan
(lok-lun) Scottish Gaelic. Means "From the land of lakes."

Glossary of Spirits

The Abyss
(Aconite or Jackal)
Spirit of Chaos

North Star
(Wolf)
Spirit of Guidance

The Sun
(Amaranth or Rabbit)
Spirit of Life

The Moon
(Nightshade or Bat)
Spirit of Death

Fern or Cat
Spirit of Magic and the Supernatural

Holly or Deer
Spirit of Peace

Galanthus or Polar Bear
Spirit of Hope

Narcissus or Albatross
Spirit of Love and Devotion

Jonquil or Peacock
Spirit of Passion and Creativity

Salvia or Horse
Spirit of Healing

Celosia or Owl
Spirit of Knowledge

Lotus or Tortoise
Spirit of Enlightenment

Spruce or Badger
Spirit of Determination

Birch or Cricket
Spirit of Good Luck

Peony or Mouse
Spirit of Wealth

Foxglove or Fox
Spirit of Trickery and Illusions

Hemlock or Snake
Spirit of Fear

Orchid or Butterfly
Spirit of Beauty

Moonflower or Raccoon
Spirit of Mystery

Gladiolus or Tiger
Spirit of Courage

Higanbana or Scorpion
Spirit of Ruin

There will be more Spirits visiting throughout the series, so keep an eye out!